Val McDermid

Val McDermid grew up in a Scottish mining community then read English at Oxford. She was a journalist for sixteen years, spending the last three years as Northern Bureau Chief of a national Sunday tabloid. She is now a full-time writer and lives in South Manchester.

The Mermaids Singing won the 1995 CWA Gold Dagger Award for Best Crime Novel of the Year. *A Place of Execution*, her complex and disturbing stand-alone thriller, was published to great acclaim and is now available in paperback.

She has written six crime novels featuring Manchester PI Kate Brannigan, and the latest in this much-praised series, *Star Struck*, won the Grand Prix des Romans d'Aventure in France.

A further five novels feature journalist-sleuth Lindsay Gordon.

VAL McDERMID

THE MERMAIDS
SINGING

THE WIRE IN
THE BLOOD

HarperCollins*Publishers*

This omnibus edition published in 2001 by
HarperCollins*Publishers*

HarperCollins*Publishers*
77-85 Fulham Palace Road,
Hammersmith, London W6 8JB

ISBN 0 00 764576 7

Printed and bound in Great Britain by
Mackays of Chatham plc, Chatham, Kent

THE MERMAIDS SINGING

Acknowledgements

It's always disturbing when life seems to imitate art. I started planning this book in the spring of 1992, long before the killings that shook the gay community in London. I sincerely hope that there is nothing in these pages that will cause grief or offence to anyone.

As ever, I have picked brains galore and thoroughly exploited my friends while researching and writing *The Mermaids Singing*. I'd particularly like to thank senior clinical psychologist and offender profiler Mike Berry of Ashworth Top Security Psychiatric Hospital in Liverpool for giving so generously of his time and expertise in the preparation of this book. The insights and information I gleaned from him have been invaluable, as well as stopping the conversation at dinner parties dead in its tracks.

Thanks too to Peter Byram of the Responsive College Unit in Blackburn, who gave me advice on the finer points of computer technology. Alison Scott and Frankie Hegarty provided helpful information on matters medical. Detective Superintendent Mike Benison of the Sussex Police generously made time in his busy schedule to fill me in on the handling of major murder enquiries. Jai Penna, Diana Cooper and Paula Tyler demonstrated yet again that some lawyers are generous with their time and knowledge.

For their support, patience and advice throughout, I'd particularly like to thank Brigid Baillie and Lisanne Radice. It can't be easy putting up with someone who spends her days inside the head of a serial killer . . .

The northern city of Bradfield is entirely a creature of my imagination. In particular, the attitudes and behaviour attributed to assorted professionals, including police officers, were chosen for reasons of fictional necessity rather than verisimilitude. In Britain, we are fortunate to have few serial killers; that's because most of them are caught after their first murder. Let's hope the profilers and the police can keep it that way.

For Tookie Flystock, my beloved serial insect killer.

I have heard the mermaids singing, each to each.
I do not think that they will sing to me.

> 'THE LOVE SONG OF J. ALFRED PRUFROCK'
> T. S. ELIOT

The soul of torture is male

> COMMENT ON EXHIBIT CARD
> THE MUSEUM OF CRIMINOLOGY AND TORTURE,
> SAN GIMIGNANO, ITALY.

All chapter epigraphs are taken from
'On Murder considered as one of the fine arts'
by Thomas De Quincey (1827)

You always remember the first time. Isn't that what they say about sex? How much more true it is of murder. I will never forget a single delicious moment of that strange and exotic drama. Even though now, with the benefit of experience and hindsight, I can see it was an amateurish performance, it still has the power to thrill, though not any longer to satisfy.

Although I didn't realize it before the decision to act was forced upon me, I had been paving the way for murder well in advance. Picture an August day in Tuscany. An air-conditioned coach whisking us from city to city. A busload of Northern culture vultures, desperate to fill every moment of our precious fortnight's package with something memorable to set against Castle Howard and Chatsworth.

I'd enjoyed Florence, the churches and art galleries filled with strangely contradictory images of martyrdom and Madonnas. I had scaled the dizzy heights of Brunelleschi's dome surmounting the immense cathedral, entranced by the winding stairway that leads up from the gallery to the tiny cupola, the worn stone steps tightly sandwiched between the ceiling of the dome and the roof itself. It was like being inside my computer, a real role-playing adventure, working my way through the maze to daylight. All it lacked were monsters to slay on the way. And then, to emerge into bright day and amazement that up here, at

1

the end of this cramped ascent, there was a postcard and souvenir seller, a small, dark, smiling man stooped from years of lugging his wares aloft. If it had really been a game, I would have been able to purchase some magic from him. As it was, I bought more postcards than I had people to send them to.

After Florence, San Gimignano. The town rose up from the green Tuscan plain, its ruined towers thrusting into the sky like fingers clawing upwards from a grave. The guide burbled on about 'a medieval Manhattan', another crass comparison to add to the list we'd been force-fed since Calais.

As we neared the town, my excitement grew. All over Florence, I'd seen the advertisements for the one tourist attraction I really wanted to see. Hanging splendidly from lampposts, gorgeous in rich red and gold, the banners insisted that I visit the Museo Criminologico di San Gimignano. Consulting my phrasebook, I'd confirmed what I'd thought the small print said. A museum of criminology and torture. Needless to say, it wasn't on our cultural itinerary.

I didn't have to search for my target; a leaflet about the museum, complete with street plan, was thrust upon me less than a dozen yards inside the massive stone gateway set in the medieval walls. Savouring the pleasure of anticipation, I wandered around for a while, marvelling at the monuments to civic disharmony that the towers represented. Each powerful family had had its own fortified tower which they defended against their neighbours with everything from boiling lead to cannons. At the peak of the city's prosperity, there were supposedly a couple of hundred towers. Compared to medieval San Gimignano, Saturday night down the docks after closing time seems like kindergarten, the seamen mere amateurs in mayhem.

When I could no longer resist the pull of the museum, I crossed the central piazza, tossing a bicoloured 200-lire coin in the well for luck, and walked a few yards down a side street, where the now familiar red and gold hangings adorned ancient stone walls. Excitement buzzing in me like a blood-crazed mosquito, I walked into the cool foyer and calmly bought my entrance ticket and a copy of the glossy, illustrated museum guide.

How can I begin to describe the experience? The physical reality was so much more overwhelming than photographs or videos or books had ever prepared me for. The first exhibit was a ladder rack, the accompanying card describing its function in loving detail in Italian and English. Shoulders would pop out of their sockets, hips and knees separate to the sound of rending cartilage and ligament, spines stretch out of alignment till vertebrae fell apart like beads from a broken string. 'Victims,' the card said laconically, 'often measured between six and nine inches taller after the rack.' Extraordinary minds the inquisitors had. Not satisfied with interrogating their heretics while they were alive and suffering, they had to seek further answers from their violated bodies.

The exhibition was a monument to the ingenuity of man. How could anyone not admire the minds that examined the human body so intimately that they could engineer such exquisite and finely calibrated suffering? With their relatively unsophisticated technology, those medieval brains devised systems of torture so refined that they are still in use today. It seems that the only improvement our modern post-industrial society has been able to come up with is the additional frisson provided by the application of electricity.

I moved through the rooms, savouring each and every toy, from the gross spikes of the Iron Maiden to the more subtle and elegant machinery of pears, those slender, segmented ovoids which were inserted into vagina or anus. Then, when the ratchet was turned, the segments separated and extended till the pear had metamorphosed into a strange flower, petals fringed with razor-sharp metal teeth. Then it was removed. Sometimes the victims survived, which was probably a crueller fate.

I noticed unease and horror on the faces and in the voices of some of my fellow visitors, but recognized it for the hypocrisy it was. Secretly, they were loving every minute of their pilgrimage, but respectability forbade any public display of their excitement. Only the children were honest in their ardent fascination. I would have happily bet that I was far from the only person in those cool, pastel rooms who felt the surge of sexual desire between their legs as we drank in the exhibits. I have often wondered how many holiday sexual encounters have been spiced and salted by the secret recollection of the torture museum.

Outside, in a sun-drenched courtyard, a skeleton crouched in a cage, bones clean as if stripped by vultures. Back in the days when the towers stood tall, these cages would have hung on the outer walls of San Gimignano, a message to inhabitants and strangers alike that this was a city where the law exacted a harsh penalty if it was not respected. I felt a strange kinship with those burghers. I too respect the need for punishment after betrayal.

Near the skeleton, an enormous metal-shod spoked wheel leaned against the wall. It would have looked perfectly at home in an agricultural museum. But the card fixed to the wall behind it explained a more imaginative function. Criminals were bound to the wheel. First, they were flayed with scourges that ripped the flesh from their bones, exposing their entrails to the eager crowd. Then, with iron bars, their bones were broken on the wheel. I found myself thinking of the tarot card, the wheel of fortune.

When I realized I was going to have to become a killer, the memory of the torture museum rose before me like a muse. I've always been good with my hands.

After that first time, part of me hoped I wouldn't be

4

forced to do it again. But I knew that if I had to, the next time it would be better. We learn from our mistakes the imperfections of our actions. And luckily, practice makes perfect.

1

Gentlemen, I have had the honour to be appointed by your committee to the trying task of reading the Williams' Lecture on Murder, considered as one of the Fine Arts; a task which might be easy enough three or four centuries ago, when the art was little understood, and few great models had been exhibited; but in this age, when masterpieces of excellence have been executed by professional men, it must be evident, that in the style of criticism applied to them, the public will look for something of a corresponding improvement.

Tony Hill tucked his hands behind his head and stared up at the ceiling. There was a fine web of cracks around the elaborate plaster rose which surrounded the light fitting, but he was oblivious to it. The faint light of dawn tinged with the orange of sodium streetlamps filtered in through a triangular gap at the top of his curtains, but he had no interest in that either. Subconsciously, he registered the central-heating boiler kicking in, readying itself to take the edge off the damp winter chill that seeped in round door and window frames. His nose was cold, his eyes gritty. He couldn't remember the last time he'd had a straight night's sleep. His concerns about what he had to get through that day was part of the reason for the night's interrupted dreams, but there was more than that. Much more.

As if today wasn't more than enough to worry about. He knew what was expected of him, but delivering it was another story. Other people managed these things with nothing more than a short-lived flutter in the stomach, but not Tony. It required all his resources to maintain the façade he'd need to get through the day. In circumstances like these, he understood how much it took out of method actors to produce the fraught, driven performances that captivated their audiences. By tonight, he'd be good for nothing except another vain attempt at eight hours' sleep.

He shifted in bed, pulling one hand out and running it through his short dark hair. He scratched the stubble on his chin and sighed. He knew what he wanted to do today, but equally, he was well aware it would be professional suicide if he did. It didn't matter that he knew there was a serial killer loose in Bradfield. He couldn't afford to be the one to say it first. His stomach clenched on emptiness and he winced. With a sigh, he pushed the duvet back and got out of bed, shaking his legs to unfurl the concertina folds of his baggy pyjamas.

Tony trudged off to the bathroom and snapped on the light. As he emptied his bladder, he reached out with his free hand and switched on the radio. Bradfield Sound's traffic announcer was revealing the morning's projected bottlenecks with a cheerfulness that no motorist could have equalled without large doses of Prozac. Thankful that he wouldn't be driving that morning, Tony turned to the sink.

He gazed into his deep-set blue eyes, still bleary with sleep. Whoever said the eyes were mirrors of the soul was a true bullshit merchant, he thought ironically. Probably just as well, or he wouldn't have an intact mirror in the house. He undid the top button of his pyjama jacket and opened the bathroom cabinet, reaching out for the shaving foam. The tremor he spotted in his hand stopped him short. Angrily, he slid the door shut with a loud crack and reached up for his electric razor. He hated the shave it produced, never leaving him with the fresh, clean feeling that came

7

from a wet shave. But better to feel vaguely scruffy than to turn up looking like a walking illustration of the death of a thousand cuts.

The other disadvantage of the electric razor was that he didn't have to concentrate so hard on what he was doing, leaving his mind free to range over the day ahead. Sometimes it was tempting to imagine that everybody was like him, getting up each morning and selecting a persona for the day. But he had learned over years of exploring other people's minds that it wasn't so. For most people, the available selection was severely limited. Some people would doubtless be grateful for the choices that knowledge, skill and necessity had brought Tony. He wasn't one of them.

As he switched off the razor, he heard the frantic chords that preceded every news summary on Bradfield Sound. With a sense of foreboding, he turned to face the radio, tense and alert as a middle-distance runner waiting for the starting pistol. At the end of the five-minute bulletin, he sighed with relief and pushed open the shower curtain. He'd expected a revelation that would have been impossible for him to ignore. But so far, the body count was still three.

On the other side of the city, John Brandon, Bradfield Metropolitan Police's Assistant Chief Constable (Crime) stooped over the washbasin and stared glumly into the bathroom mirror. Not even the shaving soap covering his face like a Santa Claus beard could give him an air of benevolence. If he hadn't chosen the police, he'd have been an ideal candidate for a career as a funeral director. He was two inches over six feet, slim to the point of skinny, with deep-set dark eyes and prematurely steel-grey hair. Even when he smiled, his long face managed to sustain an air of melancholy. Today, he thought, he looked like a bloodhound with a head cold. At least there was good reason for his misery. He was about to pursue a course of action that would be as popular with his Chief Constable as a priest in an Orange Lodge.

Brandon sighed deeply, spattering the mirror with foam. Derek Armthwaite, his Chief, had the burning blue eyes of a visionary, but there was nothing revolutionary in what they saw. He was a man who thought the Old Testament a more appropriate handbook for police officers than the Police And Criminal Evidence Act. He believed most modern police methods were not only ineffective but also heretical. In Derek Armthwaite's frequently aired opinion, bringing back the birch and the cat-o'-nine-tails would be far more effective in reducing crime figures than any number of social workers, sociologists and psychologists. If he'd had any idea of what Brandon had planned for that morning, he'd have had him transferred to Traffic, the present-day equivalent of Jonah being swallowed by a whale.

Before his depression could overwhelm his resolve, Brandon was startled by a banging on the bathroom door. 'Dad?' his elder daughter shouted. 'You going to be much longer?'

Brandon snatched up his razor, dunked it in the basin and scraped it down one cheek before replying. 'Five minutes, Karen,' he called. 'Sorry, love.' In a house with three teenagers and only one bathroom, there was seldom much opportunity for brooding.

Carol Jordan dumped her half-drunk coffee on the side of the washbasin and stumbled into the shower, nearly tripping headlong over the black cat that wound himself round her ankles. 'In a minute, Nelson,' she muttered as she closed the door on his interrogative miaow. 'And don't waken Michael.'

Carol had imagined that promotion to detective inspector and the concomitant departure from the shift rota would have granted her the regular eight hours' sleep a night that had been her constant craving since the first week she joined the force. Just her luck that the promotion had coincided with what her team were privately calling the Queer Killings. However much Superintendent Tom Cross might bluster to the press and in the squad room that there were no forensic connections between the killings, and nothing to suggest the presence of a serial killer in Bradfield, the murder teams thought differently.

As the hot water cascaded over Carol, turning her blonde hair mouse, she thought, not for the first time, that Cross's attitude, like that of the Chief Constable, served his prejudices rather than the community. The longer he denied that there was a serial killer attacking men whose respectable façade hid a secret gay life, the more gay men would die. If you couldn't get them off the streets any longer by arresting them, let a killer remove them. It didn't much matter whether he did it by murder or by fear.

It was a policy that made a nonsense of all the hours she and her colleagues were putting in on the investigation. Not to mention the hundreds of thousands of pounds of taxpayers' money that these enquiries were costing, particularly since Cross insisted each killing be treated as an entirely separate entity. Every time one of the three teams came up with some detail that seemed to link the killings, Tom Cross dismissed it with five points of dissimilarity. It didn't matter that each time the links were different and the dissimilarities the same tired quintet. Cross was the boss. And the DCI had opted out of the strife completely, taking sick leave with his opportunistic bad back.

Carol rubbed the shampoo to a rich lather and felt herself gradually wake under the warm spray. Well, her corner of the investigation wasn't going to run aground on the rock of Popeye Cross's bigoted prejudice. Even if some of her junior officers were inclined to grasp at the boss's tunnel vision as an excuse for their own uninspired investigations, she wasn't going to stand for anything less than one hundred per cent committed action, and in the right direction. She'd worked her socks off for the best part of nine years, first to get a good degree and then to justify her place on the promotion fast track. She didn't intend her career to hit the buffers just because she'd made the mistake of opting for a force run by Neanderthals.

Her mind made up, Carol stepped out of the shower, shoulders straight, a defiant glint in her green eyes. 'Come on, Nelson,' she said, shrugging into her dressing gown and scooping up the muscular bundle of black fur. 'Let's hit the red meat, boy.'

Tony studied the overhead projection on the screen behind him for a final five seconds. Since the majority of his audience had expressed their lack of commitment to his lecture by pointedly not taking notes, he wanted at least to give their subconscious minds the maximum opportunity to absorb his flow chart of the criminal profile generating process.

He turned back to his audience. 'I don't have to tell you what you already know. Profilers don't catch criminals. It's bobbies that do that.' He smiled at his audience of senior police officers and Home Office officials, inviting them to share his self-deprecation. A few did, though most remained stony faced, heads on one side.

However he dressed it up, Tony knew he couldn't convince the bulk of the senior police officers that he wasn't some out-of-touch university boffin there to tell them how to do their jobs. Stifling a sigh, he glanced at his notes and continued, aiming for as much eye contact as he could achieve, copying the casual body language of the successful stand-up comics he'd studied working the northern clubs. 'But sometimes we profilers see things differently,' he said. 'And that fresh perspective can make all the difference. Dead men do tell tales, and the ones they tell profilers are not the same as the ones they tell police officers.

'An example. A body is found in bushes ten feet away from the road. A police officer will note that fact. He'll check the ground all around for clues. Are there footprints? Has anything been discarded by the killer? Have any fibres been snagged on the bushes? But for me, that single fact is only the starting point for speculations that, taken in conjunction with all the other information at my disposal, may well lead me to useful conclusions about the killer. I'll ask myself, was the body deliberately placed there? Or was the killer too knackered to carry it further? Was he hiding it or dumping it? Did he want it to be found? How long did he expect or want it to stay hidden? What is the significance of this site for him?' Tony lifted his shoulders and held out his hands in an open, questioning gesture. The audience looked on, unmoved. God, how many tricks of the trade was he going to have to pull out of the hat before he got a response? The prickle of sweat along the back of his neck was becoming a trickle, sliding down between his skin and his shirt collar. It was an uncomfortable sensation that reminded him of who he really was behind the mask he'd assumed for his public appearance.

Tony cleared his throat, focused on what he was projecting rather than what he was feeling, and continued. 'Profiling is just another tool that can help investigating officers to narrow the focus of their investigation. Our job is to make sense of the bizarre. We can't give you an offender's name, address and phone number. But what we *can* do is point you in the direction of the kind of person who has committed a crime with particular characteristics. Sometimes we can indicate the area where he might live, the kind of work we'd expect him to do.

'I know that some of you have questioned the necessity for setting up a National Criminal Profiling Task Force. You're not alone. The civil libertarians are screaming about it too.' At last, Tony thought with profound relief. Smiles and nods from the audience. It had taken him forty minutes to get there, but he'd finally cracked their composure. It didn't mean he could relax, but it eased his discomfort. 'After all,' he went on, 'we're not like the Americans. We don't have serial killers lurking round every corner. We still have a society where more than ninety per cent of murders are committed by family members or people known to the victims.' He was really taking them with him now. Several pairs of legs and arms uncrossed, neat as a practised drill-hall routine.

'But profiling isn't just about nailing the next Hannibal the Cannibal. It can be used in a wide variety of crimes. We've already had notable success in airport anti-hijacking measures, in catching drug couriers, poison-pen writers, blackmailers, serial rapists and arsonists. And just as importantly, profiling has been used very effectively to advise police officers on interview techniques for dealing with suspects in major crime enquiries. It's not that your officers lack interviewing skills; it's just that our clinical background means we have developed different approaches that can often be more productive than familiar techniques.'

Tony took a deep breath and leaned forward, gripping the edge of the lectern. His final paragraph had sounded good in front of the bathroom mirror. He prayed it would hit the right spot rather than stamp on people's corns. 'My team and I are now one year into a two-year feasibility study on setting up the National Criminal Profiling Task Force. I've already delivered an interim report to the Home Office, who confirmed to me yesterday that they are committed to forming this task force as soon as my final report is delivered. Ladies and gentlemen, this revolution in crime fighting is going to happen. You've got a year to make sure it happens in a form that you feel comfortable with. My team and I have all got open minds. We're all on the same side. We want to know what you think, because we want it to work. We want violent, serial offenders behind bars, just like you do. I believe you could use our help. I know we can use yours.'

Tony took a step backwards and savoured the applause, not because it was particularly enthusiastic, but because it signalled the end of the forty-five minutes he'd been dreading for weeks. Public speaking had always been firmly outside the boundaries of his comfort zone, so much so that he'd turned his back on an academic career after achieving his doctorate because he couldn't face the constant spectre of the lecture theatre. The ability to perform was not a reason in itself for doing so. Somehow, spending his days poking around in the distorted recesses of the minds of the criminally insane was far less threatening.

As the short-lived clapping died away, Tony's Home Office minder bounced to his feet from his front-row chair. While Tony provoked a wary distrust in the police section of his audience, George Rasmussen generated more universal irritation than a flea bite. His eager smile revealed too many teeth and a disturbing resemblance to George Formby that was at odds with the seniority of his Civil Service post, the elegant cut of his grey pinstripe suit and the yammering bray of a public-school accent so exaggerated that Tony was convinced Rasmussen had really been educated in some inner-city comprehensive. Tony half listened as he shuffled his notes together and replaced his acetates in their folder. Grateful for fascinating insight, blah, blah . . . coffee and those absolutely delicious biscuits, blah, blah . . . opportunity for informal questions, blah, blah . . . remind you all submissions to Dr Hill due by . . .

The sound of shuffling feet drowned out the rest of Rasmussen's spiel. When it came to a choice between a civil servant's vote of thanks and a cup of coffee, it was no contest. Not even for the civil servants. Tony took a deep breath. Time to abandon the lecturer. Now he had to be the charming, well-informed colleague, eager to listen, to assimilate and to make his new contacts feel he was really on their side.

John Brandon stood up and stepped aside to allow the other people in his row to move out of their seats. Watching Tony Hill's performance hadn't been as informative as he'd hoped. It had told him a lot about psychological profiling, but almost nothing about the man, except that he seemed self-assured without being arrogant. The last three quarters of an hour hadn't made him any more certain that what he was planning was the right course of action. But he couldn't see any alternative. Staying close to the wall, Brandon moved forward against the flow until he was level with Rasmussen. Seeing his audience vote with its feet, the civil servant had sharply wound up his speech and switched off his smile. As Rasmussen gathered up the papers he'd dumped on his seat, Brandon slipped past him and crossed the floor towards Tony, who was fastening the clasps on his battered Gladstone bag.

Brandon cleared his throat and said, 'Dr Hill?' Tony looked up, polite enquiry on his face. Brandon swallowed his qualms and continued. 'We haven't met before, but you've been working on my patch. I'm John Brandon . . .'

'The ACC Crime?' Tony interrupted, a smile reaching his eyes. He'd heard enough about John Brandon to know he was a man he wanted on his side. 'I'm delighted to meet you, Mr Brandon,' he said, injecting warmth into his voice.

'John. It's John,' Brandon said, more abruptly than he'd intended. He realized with a spurt of surprise that he was nervous. There was something about Tony Hill's calm assurance that unsettled him. 'I wonder if we can have a word?'

Before Tony could reply, Rasmussen was between them. 'If you'd excuse me,' he interjected without any note of humility, the smile back in place. 'Tony, if you'd just come through now to the coffee lounge, I know our friends in the police will be eager to chat to you on a more intimate basis. Mr Brandon, if you'd like to follow us.'

Brandon could feel his hackles rising. He felt awkward enough about the situation without having to fight to keep their conversation confidential in a room full of coffee-swilling coppers and nosy Home Office mandarins. 'If I could just have a word with Dr Hill in private?'

Tony glanced at Rasmussen, noting the slight deepening of the parallel lines between his eyebrows. Normally, it would have tickled him to wind up Rasmussen by continuing his conversation with Brandon. He always enjoyed pricking pomposity, reducing the self-important to impotent. But too much hung on the success of his encounters with other police officers today, so he decided to forego the pleasure. Instead, he turned pointedly away from Rasmussen and said, 'John, are you driving back to Bradfield after lunch?'

Brandon nodded.

'Perhaps you could give me a lift, then? I came on the train, but if you don't mind, I'd rather not wrestle with British Rail on the way back. You can always drop me at the city limits if you don't want to be seen fraternizing with the Trendy Wendies.'

Brandon smiled, his long face creasing into simian wrinkles. 'I don't think that'll be necessary. I'll be just as happy to drop you at force headquarters.' He stood back and watched Rasmussen steer Tony to the doors, fussing all the way. He couldn't shake off the slightly disconcerted feeling that the psychologist had given him. Maybe it was simply that he'd grown so accustomed to being in control of everything in his world that asking for help had become an alien experience that automatically made him feel uncomfortable. There was no other obvious explanation. Shrugging, Brandon followed the crowd through to the coffee lounge.

*　　*　　*

Tony snapped the seat belt closed and savoured the comfort of the unmarked Range Rover. He said nothing as Brandon manoeuvred out of the Manchester force headquarters' car park and headed for the motorway network, unwilling to interfere with the concentration necessary to avoid missing the way in an unfamiliar city. As they cruised down the slip road and joined the fast-flowing traffic, Tony broke the silence. 'If it helps, I think I already know what it is you wanted to talk to me about.'

Brandon's hands tensed on the wheel. 'I thought you were a psychologist, not a psychic,' he joked. He surprised himself. Humour wasn't his natural mode; he normally resorted to it only under pressure. Brandon couldn't get used to how nervous he felt asking this favour.

'Some of your colleagues would take more notice of me if I was,' Tony said wryly. 'So, do you want me to have a guess and run the risk of making a complete fool of myself?'

Brandon snatched a quick look at Tony. The psychologist looked relaxed, hands palm down on his thighs, feet crossed at the ankles. He looked as though he'd be more at home in jeans and a sweater than in the suit which even Brandon recognized as well past its fashionable sell-by date. He could relate to that, remembering the scathing comments his daughters routinely passed on his own plain clothes. Brandon said abruptly, 'I think we've got a serial killer operating in Bradfield.'

Tony released a small, satisfied sigh. 'I was beginning to wonder if you'd noticed,' he said ironically.

'It's by no means a unanimous opinion,' Brandon said, feeling the need to warn Tony before he'd even asked for his help.

'I'd gathered as much from the press coverage,' Tony said. 'If it's any comfort to you, I'm as certain as I can be from what I've read that your analysis is right.'

'That's not entirely the impression you gave in those

quotes of yours I saw in the *Sentinel Times* after the last one,' Brandon said.

'It's my job to cooperate with the police, not to undermine them. I assumed you had your own operational reasons for not going public with the serial-killer angle. I did stress to them that what I was saying was no more than an informed guess based on the information that was in the public domain,' Tony added, his genial tone contradicting the sudden tensing of his fingers that ruched the material of his trousers into loose pleats.

Brandon smiled, aware only of the voice. 'Touché. So, are you interested in giving us a hand?'

Tony felt a warm rush of satisfaction. This was what he had craved for weeks now. 'There's a service area a few miles down the road. D'you fancy a cup of tea?'

Detective Inspector Carol Jordan stared at the broken chaos of flesh that had once been a man, determinedly forcing her eyes to remain out of focus. She wished she hadn't bothered to snatch that stale cheese sandwich from the canteen. Somehow, it was acceptable for young male officers to throw up when they were confronted with victims of violent death. They even got sympathy. But in spite of the fact that women were supposed to lack bottle anyway, when female officers chucked up on the margins of crime scenes they instantly lost any respect they'd ever won and became objects of contempt, the butts of locker-room jokes from the canteen cowboys. Pick the logic out of that, Carol thought bitterly as she clamped her jaws tighter together. She thrust her hands deep into the pockets of her trench coat and clenched her fists, the nails pressing into her palms.

Carol felt a hand on her arm, just above the elbow. Grateful for the chance to look away, she turned to find her sergeant looming above her. Don Merrick towered a good eight inches over his boss, and had developed a strange hunchbacked stoop when he spoke to her. At first, she'd found it amusing enough to regale friends with over drinks or the occasional dinner party when she managed to squeeze a night off. Now, she didn't even notice. 'Area's all cordoned off now, ma'am,' he said in his soft Geordie accent. 'Pathologist's on his way. What d'you think? Are we looking at number four?'

'Don't let the Super hear you say that, Don,' she said, only half joking. 'I'd say so, though.' Carol looked around. They were in the Temple Fields district, in the rear yard of a pub which catered primarily to the gay trade, with an upstairs bar that was lesbian three nights a week. Contrary to the jibes of the macho men she'd overtaken in the promotion stakes, it wasn't a bar Carol had ever had reason to enter. 'What about the gate?'

'Crowbar,' Merrick said laconically. 'It's not wired into the alarm system.'

Carol surveyed the tall rubbish dumpsters and the stacked crates of empties. 'No reason why it should be,' she said. 'What's the landlord got to say?'

'Whalley's talking to him now, ma'am. Seems he locked up last night about half past eleven. They've got bins on wheels behind the bars for the empties, and at closing time they just wheel them into the yard back there.' Merrick waved over towards the back door of the pub, where three blue plastic bins stood, each the size of a supermarket trolley. 'They don't sort them out till the afternoon.'

'And that's when they found this?' Carol asked, gesturing over her shoulder with her thumb.

'Just lying there. Open to the elements, you might say.'

Carol nodded. A shudder ran through her that was nothing to do with the sharp north-eastern wind. She took a step towards the gate. 'OK. Let's leave this to the SOCOs for now. We're only in the way here.' Merrick followed her into the narrow alley behind the pub. It was barely wide enough for a single vehicle to squeeze down. Carol looked up and down the alley, now closed off by police tapes and guarded at either end by a pair of uniformed constables. 'He knows his turf,' she mused softly. She walked backwards along the alley, keeping the gate of the pub in constant view. Merrick followed her, waiting for the next set of orders.

At the end of the alley, Carol stopped and swung round to check out the street. Opposite the alley was a tall building, a former warehouse that had been converted into craft workshops. At night, it would be deserted, but in mid-afternoon, almost every window framed eager faces, staring out from the warmth within at the drama below. 'Not much chance of anyone looking out of a window at the crucial time, I suppose,' she remarked.

'Even if they had, they wouldn't have taken any notice,' Merrick said cynically. 'After closing time, the streets round here are jumping. Every doorway, every alley, half the parked cars have got a pair of poofs in them, shagging the arse off each other. It's no wonder the Chief calls Temple Fields Sodom and Gomorrah.'

'You know, I've often wondered. It's pretty clear what they were up to in Sodom, but what do you suppose the sin of Gomorrah was?' Carol asked.

Merrick looked bewildered. It increased his resemblance to a sad-eyed Labrador to a disturbing degree. 'I'm not with you, ma'am,' he said.

'Never mind. I'm surprised Mr Armthwaite hasn't got Vice pulling them all in on indecency charges,' Carol said.

'He did try it a few years back,' Merrick confided. 'But the police committee had his bollocks barbecued for it. He fought them, but they threatened him with the Home Office. And after the Holmwood Three business, he knew he was already on thin ice with the politicians, so he backed down. Doesn't stop him slagging them off every chance he gets, though.'

'Yeah, well, I hope this time our friendly neighbourhood killer has left us a bit more to go on, or our beloved leader might just pick another target for his next slagging off.' Carol straightened her shoulders. 'Right, Don. I want a door-to-door of the businesses, now. And tonight, we're all going to be out on the streets, talking to the trade.'

Before Carol could complete her instructions, a voice from beyond the tapes interrupted. 'Inspector Jordan? Penny Burgess, *Sentinel Times*. Inspector? What have you got?'

Carol closed her eyes for a brief moment. Dealing with the recalcitrant bigots in the chain of command was one thing. Dealing with the press was infinitely worse. Wishing she'd stayed in the yard with the grisly corpse, Carol took a deep breath and walked towards the cordon.

'Let me get this straight. You want me to come on board for the duration of this murder enquiry, but you don't want me to tell anyone?' The look of amusement in Tony's eyes masked his anger at the reluctance of influential policemen to accept the value of what he could do.

Brandon sighed. Tony wasn't making it easy for him, but then, why should he? 'I want to avoid any suggestions in the press that you are helping us. The only chance I have of getting you formally involved with the investigation is to persuade the Chief Constable that you're not going to be stealing the limelight from him and his coppers.'

'And that it won't become public knowledge that Derek Armthwaite, the Hand Of God, is turning to the mumbo-jumbo men for help,' Tony said, an edge in his voice betraying more than he wanted to.

Brandon's face twisted in a cynical smile. It was good to see that it was possible to ruffle that smooth surface. 'If you say so, Tony. Technically, it's an operational matter, and he's not really supposed to interfere unless I'm doing something that's counter to force and Home Office policy.

And it is the policy of BMP to use expert assistance whenever it is appropriate.'

Tony snorted with laughter. 'And you think he'll accept me as "appropriate"?'

'I think he doesn't want another confrontation with the Home Office or the police committee. He's due to retire in eighteen months, and he's desperate for the knighthood.' Brandon couldn't believe what he was saying. He didn't even voice this kind of disloyalty to his wife, never mind to a virtual stranger. What was it about Tony Hill that had made him open up so swiftly? There must be something in this psychology lark after all. Brandon comforted himself that at least he had harnessed that something in the service of justice. 'So what do you say?'

'When do I start?'

Even that first time, I planned the event more carefully than a theatre director plans the first production of a new play. In my mind, I crafted the experience, till it was like a bright and shining dream, there every time I closed my eyes. I checked and rechecked every choreographed move, making sure I hadn't missed some vital detail that would endanger my freedom. Looking back on it now, the mental movie I created was almost as pleasurable as the act itself.

The first step was to find a place where I could safely take him, a place we could be private together. I immediately dismissed my home. I can hear my neighbours' squalid arguments, the barking of their hysterical German shepherd and the irritating thud of their stereo's bass; I had no desire to share my apotheosis with them. Besides, in my terraced street, there are too many curtain twitchers. I wanted no witnesses to Adam's arrival or his departure.

I considered renting a lock up garage, but rejected that for the same reasons. Besides, it seemed too seedy, too much of a cliché from the world of television and film. I wanted something in keeping with what was going to happen. Then I remembered my mother's Auntie Doris. Doris and her husband Henry used to farm sheep on the moors high above Bradfield. Then, about four years ago, Henry died. Doris tried to keep things going for a while, but when her son Ken invited her out last year for an extended holiday with his family in New Zealand, she sold the sheep and packed her bags. Ken had written to me at Christmas, saying his mother had suffered a mild heart attack and wouldn't be coming back for the foreseeable future.

That night, I took advantage of a lull in work to call Ken. At first, he sounded surprised to hear from me, then muttered, 'I suppose you're using the phones at work.'

'I've been meaning to ring for ages,' I said. 'I wanted to know how Auntie Doris was doing.' It's much easier to appear solicitous via satellite. I made the appropriate noises while Ken bored on about his mother's health, his wife, their three kids and their sheep.

After ten minutes, I decided I'd had enough. 'The other thing is, Ken, I was worried about the house,' I lied. 'It's so isolated up there, someone should keep an eye on the place.'

'You're not wrong,' he said. 'Her solicitor's supposed to be doing that, but I don't reckon he's been near it.'

'Do you want me to pop out and check it over? Now I'm back living in Bradfield, it would be no bother.'

'Would you? That'd be a hell of a load off, I don't mind telling you. Between ourselves, I'm not sure Mum's ever going to be well enough to go back home again, but I'd hate to think of anything happening to the family home,' Ken said eagerly.

Hate to think of anything happening to his inheritance, more like. I knew Ken. Ten days later, I had the keys. On my next day off, I drove out there to check the accuracy of my recollection. The rutted track leading to Start Hill Farm was much more overgrown than the last time I'd been there, and my four-wheel drive jeep struggled to climb the three miles from the nearest single-track lane. I cut the engine a dozen yards from the grim little cottage and sat listening for five minutes. The biting wind from the high moors rustled the overgrown hedges, occasional birds sang. But there were no human sounds. Not even the distant thrum of traffic.

I got out of the jeep and had a look round. One end of the sheep shed had collapsed into a random pile of millstone grit, but what pleased me was that there was no sign of casual human visitations; no picnic remains, no corroding beer cans, no crumpled newspapers, no cigarette butts, no used condoms. I walked back to the house and let myself in.

It was little more than a two-up, two-down. Inside, it was very different from the cosy farmhouse I remembered. All the personal touches – photographs, ornaments, horse brasses, antiques – were gone, packed up in crates in storage, a very Yorkshire precaution. In a way, I was relieved; there was nothing here that could trigger off memories that would interfere with what I had to do. It was a blank tablet, with all humiliations, embarrassments and pain erased. Nothing of my past lurked to surprise me. The person I had been was absent.

I walked through the kitchen towards the pantry. The shelves were empty. God knows what Doris had done with her serried ranks of jams, pickles and home-made wines. Maybe she'd shipped them to New Zealand as a hedge against being fed alien food. I stood in the doorway, and stared at the floor. I could feel a foolish grin of relief spread across my face. My memory hadn't let me down. There was a trapdoor in the floor. I squatted down and pulled the rusty iron ring. After a few seconds, the door swung back on creaking hinges. As I sniffed the air from the cellar, I grew more convinced that the gods were with me. I had feared it would be damp, fetid and stale. But instead, it was cool and fresh, slightly sweet.

I lit my camping gas lamp and carefully descended the flight of stone stairs. The lamp revealed a sizeable room, about twenty feet by thirty. The floor was flagged with stone slabs, and a broad stone bench ran the length of one wall. I held the lamp high and saw the solid beams of the roof. The lath and plaster ceiling was the only part of the cellar that showed any signs of disrepair. I could easily fix that with plasterboard, which would serve the double purpose of preventing any light escaping through the bare floorboards above. At right angles to the stone bench was a slop sink. I remembered the farm was served by its own spring. The tap was stiff, but when I finally managed to turn it, the water ran out pure and clear.

Near the stairs stood a scarred wooden workbench, complete with vices and G-clamps, Henry's tools hanging in neat rows above. I sat on the stone bench and hugged myself. A few hours' work was all that was needed to turn this into a dungeon far superior to anything the games programmers had ever come up with. For a start, I didn't have to think about creating an in-built weakness so my adventurers could escape.

By the end of the week, coming out to the farm in my time off, I had completed the job. Nothing sophisticated; I'd fixed padlock and internal bolts to the trapdoor, I'd repaired the ceiling, and covered the walls in a couple of coats of whitewash. I wanted the place as light as possible to improve the quality of the video. I'd even run a spur off the ring main to provide me with electricity.

I'd thought long and hard before I'd decided how to punish Adam. Finally, I'd fixed on what the French call the chevalet, the Spanish escalero, the Germans the ladder, the Italians veglia and the poetic English 'The Duke of Exeter's Daughter'. The rack got its euphemistic name from the resourceful John Holland, Duke of Exeter and Earl of Huntingdon. After a successful career as a soldier, the duke became Constable of the Tower of London and somewhere around 1420 he introduced that splendid instrument of persuasion to these shores.

The earliest version consisted of an open rectangular frame raised on legs. The prisoner was laid underneath it, fastened by ropes round his wrists and ankles. At each corner, the ropes were attached to a windlass operated by *a warder pulling on levers. This inelegant and labour-intensive device became more sophisticated over the years, ending up more like a table or a horizontal ladder, often incorporating a spiked roller in the middle so that, as the prisoner's body moved, his back was shredded on the spikes. Pulley systems had also been designed which linked all four ropes together, making it possible for the machine to be used by one person alone.*

Fortunately, those who have applied punishment through the ages have been thorough in their descriptions and drawing. I also had the photographs in the museum handbook to refer to, and with the assistance of a CAD program, I'd designed my very own rack. For the mechanism, I'd cannibalized an old-fashioned clothes wringer that I picked up in an antique shop. I'd also bought an old mahogany dining table in an auction. I took it straight up to the farm and dismembered it in the kitchen, admiring the craftsmanship that had gone into the solid timber. It took a couple of days to build the rack. All that remained was to test it.

2

Let the reader then figure to himself the pure frenzy of horror when in this hush of expectation, looking, and indeed, waiting for the unknown arm to strike once more, but not believing that any audacity could be equal to such an attempt as yet, whilst all eyes were watching . . . a second case of the same mysterious nature, a murder on the same exterminating plan, was perpetrated in the very same neighbourhood.

As soon as Brandon started the engine, the mobile phone mounted on the dashboard trilled. He grabbed the handset and barked, 'Brandon.' Tony could hear the computerized voice say, 'You have messages. Please call 121. You have messages . . .'

Brandon took the phone from his ear, hit the keys and jammed it back again. This time, Tony couldn't hear what was said. After a moment, Brandon dialled another number. 'My secretary,' he explained briefly. 'Sorry about this . . . Hello, Martina? John. You were looking for me?'

A few seconds into the answer, Brandon squeezed his eyes shut, as if in pain. 'Where?' he asked, his voice dull. 'OK, got it. I'll be there within the half-hour. Who's dealing? . . . Fine, thanks, Martina.' Brandon opened his eyes and ended the call. He carefully replaced the handset and twisted in his seat to face Tony. 'You wanted to know when you could start? How about now?'

'Another body?' Tony asked.

'Another body,' Brandon agreed grimly, turning back

and slamming the car into gear. 'How do you feel about scenes of crime?'

Tony shrugged. 'I'll probably lose my lunch, but it's a bonus for me if I get to see them in a fairly pristine state.'

'There's nothing pristine about the way this sick bastard leaves them,' Brandon growled as he shot on to the motorway and made straight for the outside lane. The speedo read ninety-five before he eased back on the accelerator.

'Has he gone back to Temple Fields?' Tony asked.

Taken aback, Brandon shot him a quick look. Tony was staring straight ahead, his dark eyebrows corrugated in a frown. 'How did you know?'

That was a question Tony wasn't prepared to answer. 'Call it a hunch,' he stalled. 'I think last time out he was scared that Temple Fields might be getting a bit too hot. Dumping the third body in Carlton Park shifted the focus, maybe stopped the police concentrating on one area, probably relaxed people's vigilance a bit. But he likes Temple Fields. Either because he knows the patch really well, or else it's important to his fantasy. Or maybe it makes some kind of statement for him,' Tony mused aloud.

'Do you always come up with half a dozen different hypotheses every time someone tosses you a fact?' Brandon asked, flashing his lights at a BMW that was reluctant to give up possession of the fast lane. 'Shift, you bastard, before I get Traffic out to you,' he snarled.

'I try,' Tony said. 'That's how I do the job. Gradually, the evidence makes me eliminate some of my initial thoughts. Eventually, some sort of pattern begins to form.' He fell silent, already fantasizing about what he would find at the scene of the crime. His stomach felt hollow, muscles fluttering like a musician before a concert. Normally, all he ever got to see were the second-hand, sanitized versions of crime scenes. No matter how good the photographer and the other forensic officers, it was always someone else's vision he had to translate. This time, he was going to be as close to a killer as he'd ever been. For a man who lived his life behind the shield of learned behaviours, penetrating a killer's façade was the only game in town.

Carol said, 'No comment,' for the eleventh time. Penny Burgess's mouth tightened and her eyes flicked round the scene, desperate for someone who would be less of a stone wall than Carol. Popeye Cross might be a male chauvinist pig, but in between the patronizing comments he always salted a few memorable quotes. Drawing a blank, she focused on Carol again.

'What happened to sisterhood, Carol?' she complained. 'Come on, give us a break. Surely there must be something you can tell me apart from "No comment".'

'I'm sorry, Ms Burgess. The last thing your readers need to hear is ill-informed off-the-cuff speculation. As soon as I've got anything concrete to say, I promise you'll be the first to know.' Carol softened her words with a smile.

She turned to walk away, but Penny grabbed the sleeve of her mac. 'Off the record?' she pleaded. 'Just for my guidance? So I don't end up writing something that makes me look a pillock? Carol, I don't have to tell you what it's like. I work in an office full of guys that are running a book on when I'll make my next cock-up.'

Carol sighed. It was hard to resist. Only the thought of what Tom Cross would make of it in the squad room kept her mouth closed. 'I can't,' she said. 'Anyway, as far as I'm concerned, you've been doing just fine so far.' As she spoke, a familiar Range Rover turned the corner. 'Oh shit,' she muttered, pulling her arm away from the reporter. All she needed was John Brandon deciding she was the police source behind the *Sentinel Times*'s serial-killer hysteria. Briskly, Carol walked towards Brandon's car as it jerked to a halt, waiting for someone to shift the tapes keeping the crowd at bay. She stopped and waited while the constables rushed to impress the ACC with their efficiency. The Range

Rover nosed forward, giving Carol the opportunity to spot the stranger in Brandon's passenger seat. As the two men climbed down, she scanned Tony, committing the details to the memory bank she'd trained herself to develop. You never knew when you'd need to come up with a photofit. Around five-eight, slim, good shoulders, narrow hips, legs and trunk in proportion, short dark hair, side parting, dark eyes, probably blue, shadows under the eyes, fair skin, average nose, wide mouth, lower lip fuller than upper. Shame about the dress sense, though. The suit was even more out of fashion than Brandon's. It didn't look worn, however. Deduction: this was a man who didn't spend his working life in a suit. Equally, he didn't like throwing money away, so the suit was going to be worn till it fell to bits. Second deduction: he probably wasn't married or in a permanent relationship. Any woman whose partner needed a suit occasionally would have pitched him into buying a timelessly classic style that wouldn't look so absurd five years after its purchase.

By the time she'd reached this conclusion, Brandon was by her side, gesturing to his companion to join them. 'Carol,' he said.

'Mr Brandon,' she acknowledged.

'Tony, I'd like you to meet Detective Inspector Carol Jordan. Carol, this is Dr Tony Hill from the Home Office.'

Tony smiled and held out his hand. Attractive smile, Carol added to her list of particulars as she shook the hand. Good handshake, too. Dry, firm without the macho need to crush the bones that so many senior officers exhibited. 'Pleased to meet you,' he said.

A surprisingly deep voice, faintly northern. Carol kept her own smile tight. You never knew with the Home Office. 'Likewise,' she said.

'Carol's heading up one of the murder teams we've got on these killings. Number two, is it, Carol?' Brandon asked, already knowing the answer.

'That's right, sir. Paul Gibbs.'

'Tony's in charge of the Home Office National Crime Profiling Task Force feasibility study. I've asked him to take a look at these murders, to see if his experience can give us any pointers.' Brandon's eyes bored into Carol's, making sure she realized there were lines to be read between.

'I'd appreciate any help Dr Hill can give us, sir. From the brief look I've had at the scene of the crime, I don't think we've got any more to go on than in the previous similar cases.' Carol signalled that she understood what Brandon was saying. They were both walking the same tightrope, but from different ends. Brandon could not be seen to undermine Tom Cross's operational authority, and if Carol wanted a tolerable existence in the Bradfield force, she couldn't openly contradict her immediate superior, even if the ACC agreed with her. 'Would Dr Hill like to see the crime scene?'

'We'll all have a look,' Brandon said. 'You can fill me in as we go. What have we got here?'

Carol led the way. 'It's in the back yard of the pub here. The scene of crime is obviously not the scene of death. No blood at all. We have a white male, late twenties, naked. ID unknown. He appears to have been tortured before death. Both shoulders seem to have been dislocated, and possibly his hips and knees. Some tufts of hair are missing from the scalp. He's lying on his front, so we've not had a chance to see the full extent of his injuries. I'd guess the cause of death is a deep wound to the throat. It also looks like the body had been washed before it was dumped.' Carol ended her flat recitation at the yard gate. She glanced back at Tony. The only difference her words had made was a tightening of his lips. 'Ready?' she asked him.

He nodded and took a deep breath. 'As I'll ever be,' he said.

'Stay outside the tapes please, Tony,' Brandon said. 'The

SOCOs will still have a lot to do, and they don't need us dumping forensic traces all over their murder scene.'

Carol opened the gate and waved the two of them through. If Tony had thought her words had prepared him for the sight inside, one look told him otherwise. It was grotesque, made all the more so by the unnatural absence of blood. Logic screamed that a body so broken should be an island in a lake of gore, like an ice cube in a Bloody Mary. He had never seen a corpse so clean outside a funeral parlour. But instead of being laid out calm as a marble statue, this body was twisted into a loose-limbed parody of the human frame, a disjointed puppet left lying where it fell when the strings were cut.

When the two men entered the yard, the police photographer stopped snapping and gave John Brandon a nod of recognition. 'All right, Harry,' Brandon said, seemingly undaunted by the sight before him. No one could see the hands clenched into tight fists in the pockets of his waxed jacket.

'I've done all the long- and medium-range stuff, Mr Brandon. I've just got the close-ups to go,' the photographer said. 'There's a lot of wounds and bruising; I want to make sure I've got it all.'

'Good lad,' Brandon said.

From behind them, Carol added, 'Harry, when you've done that, can you snap all the cars parked up in the immediate area?'

The photographer raised his eyebrows. 'The lot?'

'The lot,' Carol confirmed.

'Good thinking, Carol,' Brandon chipped in before the scowling photographer could say anything more. 'There's always the outside chance that me laddo left the scene on foot or in the victim's car. He might have left his here to collect later. And photographs are that much harder for the defence brief to argue with than a bobby's notebook.'

With a sharp snort of breath, the photographer turned

back to the corpse. The brief exchange had given Tony time to get a grip on his churning stomach. He took a step closer to the body, trying to glean some primitive understanding of the mind that had reduced a man to this. 'What's your game?' he said inside his head. 'What does this mean to you? What translations are going on between this broken flesh and your desire? I thought I was the expert in keeping things battened down, but you're something else, aren't you? You are truly special. You're the control freak's control freak. You are going to be one of the ones they write books about. Welcome to the big time.'

Recognizing that he was dangerously close to admiration for a mind so disturbingly complex, Tony forced himself to focus on the realities of what lay before him. The deep slash to the throat had virtually decapitated the man, leaving the head tilted as if hinged at the back of the neck. Tony took a deep breath and said, 'The *Sentinel Times* said they all died from having their throats cut. Is that right?'

'Yes,' Carol said. 'They were all tortured while they were still alive, but it's the throat wounds that have been fatal in each case.'

'And have they all been as deep as this?'

Carol shook her head dubiously. 'I'm only completely familiar with the second case, and that was nowhere near as violent a gash as this. But I have seen the photographs of the other two, and the last one was nearly this bad.'

Thank God for something recognizably textbook, Tony thought. He took a couple of steps back and scanned the area. The body aside, there was nothing to distinguish it from the back yard of any other pub. Crates of empties were stacked against the walls, the lids on the big industrial wheelie bins were firmly closed. Nothing obvious taken away, nothing obvious left behind except for the corpse itself.

Brandon cleared his throat. 'Well, everything seems to

be under control here, Carol. I'd better go and have a word with the press. I saw Penny Burgess trying to rip the sleeve out of your coat when I got here. No doubt the rest of the pack are baying at her heels by now. I'll see you back at HQ later. Drop by my office. I want to have a chat with you about Dr Hill's involvement. Tony, I'll leave you in Carol's capable hands. When you're finished here, maybe you can arrange a session with Carol so she can go through the case files.'

Tony nodded. 'Sounds good. Thanks, John.'

'I'll be in touch. And thanks again.' With that, Brandon was gone, closing the gate behind him.

'You do profiling, then,' Carol said.

'I try,' he said cautiously.

'Thank God the powers that be have finally seen sense,' she said drily. 'I was beginning to think they'd never get round to admitting we've got a serial killer on our hands.'

'You and me both,' Tony said. 'I was worried after the first one, but I've been convinced since the second one.'

'And I suppose it's not your place to tell them that,' Carol said wearily. 'Bloody bureaucracy.'

'It's a sensitive point. Even when we have a national task force set up, I suspect we're still going to have to wait for the individual police forces to come to us.'

Carol's reply was cut off by the banging of the yard gate as it was thrown open. They both swung round. Framed in the doorway was one of the biggest men Tony had ever seen. He had the solid brawn of a prop forward run to seed, his beer gut preceding his massive shoulders by a good half-dozen inches. His eyes protruded like boiled gooseberries from a fleshy face, the source of Detective Superintendent Tom Cross's nickname. His mouth, like that of his cartoon namesake, was an incongruously small cupid's bow. Mousey hair fringed a bald spot like a monk's tonsure. 'Sir,' Carol greeted the apparition.

Pale eyebrows furled in a discontented scowl. Judging by the deep lines between his brows, it was a familiar expression. 'Who the bloody hell are you?' he demanded, waving a stubby finger at Tony. Automatically, Tony noted the bitten nail. Before he could respond, Carol spoke smartly. 'Sir, this is Dr Tony Hill from the Home Office. He's responsible for the National Crime Profiling Task Force feasibility study. Dr Hill, this is Detective Superintendent Tom Cross. He's in overall charge of our murder enquiries.'

The second half of Carol's introduction was drowned out by Cross's booming response. 'What the hell are you up to, woman? This is a murder scene. You don't let any old Tom, Dick or Home Office penpusher walk all over it.'

Carol closed her eyes fractionally longer than a blink. Then she said in a voice whose cheerful tone astonished Tony, 'Sir, Mr Brandon brought Dr Hill with him. The ACC thinks Dr Hill can help us profile our killer.'

'What d'you mean, killer? How many times do I have to tell you? We've not got a serial killer loose in Bradfield. We've just got a nasty bunch of copycat queers. You know what the trouble is with you fast-track graduates?' Cross demanded, aggressively leaning towards Carol.

'I'm sure you'll tell me, sir,' Carol said sweetly.

Cross stopped momentarily, with the slightly baffled air of a dog who can hear the fly but can't see it. Then he said, 'You're all desperate for glory. You want glamour and headlines. You don't want the bother of proper coppering. You can't be arsed grafting on three murder enquiries so you try to knock 'em all into one to minimize the effort and maximize the press coverage. And you,' he added, wheeling round towards Tony. 'You can remove yourself from my crime scene right now. The last thing we need is bleeding-heart liberals telling us we're looking for some poor sod who wasn't allowed to have a teddy bear when

36

he were a lad. It's not mumbo jumbo that catches villains, it's police work.'

Tony smiled. 'I couldn't agree more, Superintendent. But your Assistant Chief Constable seems to think that I can help you target your police work more effectively.'

Cross was too old a hand to fall for civility. 'I run the most effective team in this force,' he retorted. 'And I don't need some bloody doctor telling me how to catch a bunch of homicidal poofters.' He turned back to Carol. 'Escort *Doctor* Hill off the premises, Inspector.' He managed to make her rank sound like an insult. 'And when you've done that, you can come back here and fill me in on what you've managed to find out about our last killer.'

'Very good, sir. Oh, by the way, you might like to join the ACC. He's giving an impromptu press conference round the front.' This time, the sweetness was tinged with acerbity.

Cross gave a perfunctory glance at the body lying exposed in the yard. 'Well, *he*'s not going any place, is he?' he remarked. 'Right, Inspector, I'll expect a report just as soon as I've finished with the ACC and the press.' He turned on his heel and stormed out as noisily as he'd arrived.

Carol put a hand on Tony's elbow and steered him out of the gate. 'This is going to be worth seeing,' she muttered in his ear as she ushered him down the alley in Cross's wake.

Half a dozen reporters had joined Penny Burgess behind the yellow plastic tapes. John Brandon faced them. As they grew closer, they could hear the cacophony of questions the press were hurling at the ACC. Carol and Tony hung back as Cross pushed past a constable standing at Brandon's shoulder and shouted, 'One at a time, ladies and gentlemen. You'll all get heard.'

Brandon half turned towards Cross, his face expressionless. 'Thank you, Superintendent Cross.'

'Have we got a serial killer loose in Bradfield?' Penny Burgess demanded, her voice cutting through the momentary quiet like the cry of some bird of ill omen.

'There's no reason to suppose . . .' Cross started.

Brandon cut across him icily. 'Leave this to me, Tom,' he said. 'As I said a moment ago, this afternoon we have found the body of a white male in his late twenties or early thirties. It's too soon to be one hundred per cent certain, but there are indications that this killing may be connected to three previous homicides that have taken place in Bradfield over the last nine months.'

'Does that mean you're treating these murders as the work of one serial killer?' asked a young man with a tape recorder thrust forward like a cattle prod.

'We are examining the possibility that one perpetrator is responsible for all four crimes, yes.'

Cross looked as if he wanted to hit someone. His hands were bunched into fists at his sides, his brows so low they must have cut his vision to a slit. 'Though it's only a possibility at this stage,' he said mutinously.

Penny chipped in ahead of the opposition again. 'How will this affect your approach to the investigation, Mr Brandon?'

'As of today, we will be amalgamating the three previous murder enquiries with this latest one into a single major incident task force. We will be making full use of the Home Office Large Major Enquiry System computer to analyse the available data, and we are confident that this will enable us to develop new leads,' Brandon said, his lugubrious face belying the optimism in his voice.

'Yo, go for it,' Carol muttered under her breath.

'Haven't you left it a bit late? Hasn't the murderer had a head start because you wouldn't acknowledge he was a serial killer?' a voice from the rear of the pack shouted angrily.

Brandon squared his shoulders and looked stern. 'We're

policemen, not clairvoyants. We don't theorize ahead of the evidence. Rest assured, we will be doing everything within our power to bring this killer to justice as swiftly as is humanly possible.'

'Will you be using a psychological profiler?' It was Penny Burgess again. Tom Cross shot Tony a look of pure hatred.

Brandon smiled. 'That's all for now, ladies and gentlemen. There will be a statement later from the force press office. Now, if you'll excuse us, we've got a lot of work to do.' He nodded benevolently towards the press, then he turned away, taking Cross firmly by the elbow. They walked back towards the alley, Cross's back rigid with fury. Carol and Tony followed a few paces behind. As they went, Penny Burgess's voice rang out behind them. 'Inspector Jordan? Who's the new boy?'

'God, that woman doesn't miss a trick,' Carol muttered.

'I'd better keep out of her way, then,' Tony remarked. 'Me ending up front-page news could be a serious health hazard.'

Carol stopped in her tracks. 'You mean the killer could target you?'

Tony grinned. 'No. I mean your Chief Constable would have an apoplexy.'

The irresistible urge to mirror his smile hit Carol. This man was unlike any Home Office Jobsworth she'd ever encountered. Not only did he have a sense of humour, he didn't mind being indiscreet. And close up, he definitely fell into the category her friend Lucy described as 'a bit chewy'. He was showing signs of being the first interesting man she'd met in the Job for a very long time. 'You could be right,' was all she said, managing to sound noncommittal enough for her words not to be held against her.

They reached the corner of the alley in time to see Tom Cross round on Brandon. 'With respect, sir, you just contradicted everything I've been telling them buggers since this sideshow started.'

'It's time for a different approach, Tom,' Brandon said coolly.

'So why not discuss it with me instead of making me look a dickhead in front of that mob? Not to mention my own men.' Cross leaned forward belligerently. His hand strayed upwards, index finger pointed, as if he were going to stab Brandon in the chest with it. But common sense careerism prevailed, and the hand dropped back by his side.

'You think if I'd had you in my office and suggested a different approach I'd have got one?' There was steel beneath the mildness in Brandon's voice, and Cross recognized it.

His lower jaw jutted. 'At the end of the day, operational decisions are down to me,' he said. Beneath the belligerence, Tony pictured a small boy, an aggressive bully resenting the adults who still had the power to sort him out.

'But I'm the ACC Crime and the buck stops with me. I make the policy decisions, and I've just made one that happens to impact on your sphere of operations. From now on, this is one single major incident enquiry. Is that clear, Tom? Or do you want to take it further?' For the first time, Carol saw for herself how John Brandon had climbed so far up the greasy pole. The threat in his voice was no empty posturing. He was clearly prepared to do whatever it took to achieve his ends, and he acted with all the assurance of a man used to winning. There was nowhere left for Tom Cross to go.

Cross rounded on Carol. 'Have you got nothing better to do, Inspector?'

'I'm waiting to make my report, sir,' she said. 'You told me to wait for you after the press conference.'

'Before you get into that . . . Tom, let me introduce you to Dr Tony Hill,' Brandon said, motioning Tony to come forward.

'We've met,' Cross said, sullen as a schoolboy.

'Dr Hill has agreed to work closely with us in this investigation. He's got more experience in profiling serial offenders than just about anybody else in the country. He's also agreed to keep his involvement under wraps.'

Tony gave a self-deprecating, diplomatic smile. 'That's right. The last thing I want is to turn your enquiry into a sideshow. If there's any credit going when we nail this bastard, I want it to go to your team. They'll be the ones doing the work, after all.'

'You're not wrong there,' Cross muttered. 'I don't want you under our feet, getting in the road.'

'None of us want that, Tom,' Brandon said. 'That's why I've asked Carol to act as liaison officer between Tony and us.'

'I can't afford to lose a senior officer at a time like this,' Cross protested.

'You're not losing her,' Brandon said. 'You're gaining an officer with a unique overview of all the cases. Could prove invaluable, Tom.' He glanced at his watch. 'I better be off. The Chief's going to want a briefing on this one. Keep me posted, Tom.' Brandon sketched a wave and stepped back into the street and out of sight.

Cross pulled a packet of cigarettes out of his pocket and lit up. 'You know your trouble, Inspector?' he said. 'You're not as smart as you like to think you are. One step out of line, lady, and I'll have your guts for a jock strap.' He took a deep drag of his cigarette and leaned forward to blow smoke in Carol's direction. The gesture was ruined by the gust of wind that snatched the smoke away before it reached her. Looking disgusted, Cross turned on his heel and marched back to the scene of the crime.

'You meet a nice class of person in this job,' Carol said.

'At least I know now which way the wind blows,' Tony replied. As he spoke, he felt a drop of rain on his face.

'Oh shit,' Carol said. 'That's all we need. Look, can we meet tomorrow? I can grab the files tonight and skim them beforehand. Then you can get stuck in.'

'Fine. My office, ten o'clock?'

'Perfect. How do I find you?'

Tony gave Carol directions, then watched as she hurried back down the alley. An interesting woman. And attractive too, most men would agree to that. There were times when he almost wished he could find an uncomplicated response in himself. But he'd long since gone beyond the point where he would allow himself to be attracted to a woman like Carol Jordan.

It was after seven when Carol finally made it back to headquarters. When she rang John Brandon's extension, she was pleasantly surprised to find him still at his desk. 'Come on up,' he told her.

She was even more surprised when she walked through his secretary's door and found him pouring two steaming mugs from the coffee maker. 'Milk and sugar?' he asked her.

'Neither,' she said. 'This is an unexpected pleasure.'

'I gave up smoking five years ago,' Brandon confided. 'Now it's only the caffeine that holds me together. Come through.'

Carol walked into his office, fired with curiosity. She'd never been across the threshold before. The decor was regulation cream paint, the furniture identical to Cross's office, except that here the wood was gleaming, free from scuffs, scratches, cigarette burns and the telltale rings left by hot cups. Unlike most senior officers, Brandon hadn't decorated his walls with police photographs and his framed commendations. Instead, he'd chosen half a dozen reproductions of turn-of-the-century paintings of Bradfield street scenes. Colourful yet moody, often rain-soaked, they mirrored the spectacular view from the seventh-floor window.

The only item in the room that ran true to expectation was the photograph of his wife and children on the desk. Even that was no posed, studio shot, but an enlargement of a holiday snap on board a sailboat. Deduction: in spite of the impression Brandon strove to give as a bluff, straight-forward, conventional copper, he was actually far more complex and thoughtful under the surface.

He waved Carol to a pair of chairs in front of his desk, then sat down in the other one. 'One thing I want to be clear about,' Brandon said without preliminary. 'You report to Superintendent Cross. He's in charge of this oper-ation. However, I want to see copies of your reports and Dr Hill's, and I want to know any theories the pair of you come up with that you're not ready to commit to paper. Think you can handle that balancing act?'

Carol's eyebrows rose. 'There's only one way to find out, sir,' she said.

Brandon's lips twitched in a half smile. He'd always preferred honesty to bullshit. 'OK. I want you to make sure you are given access to everybody's files. Any problems with that, any sense that anyone's trying to stall you and Dr Hill, and I want to know about it, no matter who's responsible. I'll talk to the squad myself in the morning, make sure nobody's in any doubt about what the new rules of the game are. Anything you need from me?'

Another twelve hours in the day would be a start, Carol thought wearily. Loving a challenge was all very well. But this time, it looked like love was going to be an uphill struggle.

Tony closed his front door behind him. He dropped his briefcase where he stood and leaned against the wall. He'd got what he wanted. It was a battle of wits now, his insight against the killer's stockade. Somewhere in the pattern of these crimes there lay a labyrinthine path straight to a murderer's heart. Somehow, Tony had to tread that path,

43

wary of misleading shadows, careful to avoid straying into treacherous undergrowth.

He shrugged away from the wall, feeling suddenly exhausted, and headed for the kitchen, pulling off his tie and unbuttoning his shirt on the way. A cold beer, and then he could go through his scanty collection of press clippings on the three previous murders. He had just opened the fridge to grab a can of Boddingtons when the phone rang. He slammed the door shut and snatched up the extension, juggling with the cold can. 'Hello?' he said.

'Anthony,' the voice said.

Tony swallowed hard. 'This isn't a good time,' he said, cutting coldly across the husky contralto coming down the line. He dumped the can on the worktop and popped the ring pull with one hand.

'Playing hard to get? Oh, well, that's part of the fun, isn't it? I thought I'd cured you of trying to avoid me. I thought we'd left all that behind us. Don't say you're going to regress and hang up on me again, that's all I ask.' The voice was teasing, laughter bubbling just beneath the surface.

'I'm not playing hard to get,' he said. 'It really isn't a good time.' He could feel the slow burn of anger rising from the pit of his stomach.

'That's up to you. You're the man. You're the boss. Unless, of course, you want things different for a change. If you catch my drift.' The voice was almost a sigh, teasing him with its elusive quality. 'After all, this is strictly between you and me. Consenting adults, as they say.'

'So don't I have the right to say no, not right now? Or is it only women who have that right?' he said, hearing the tension in his voice as the anger rose like bile in his throat.

'God, Anthony, your voice gets so sexy when you're angry,' the voice purred.

Nonplussed, Tony held the phone away from his ear, staring at it as if it were an artefact from another planet. Sometimes he wondered if what came out of his mouth were the same words that arrived in his listeners' ears. With a clinical detachment he couldn't bring to his caller, he noted that his grip on the phone was so tight his fingers were white. After a moment, he put the receiver back to his ear. 'Just listening to your voice makes me wet, Anthony,' she was saying. 'Don't you want to know what I'm wearing, what I'm doing right now?' The voice was seductive, the breathing more audible than it had been at first.

'Look, I've had a hard day, I've got a load of work to do and much as I enjoy our little games, I'm not in the mood tonight.' Agitated, Tony looked desperately round his kitchen as if searching for the nearest exit.

'You sound so tense, my darling. Let me soothe all that pressure away. Let's play. Think of me as a relaxation technique. You know you'll work better afterwards. You know I give you the best time you've ever had. With a stud like you and a sex queen like me, there's nothing we can't do. And for starters, I'm going to give you the dirtiest, sexiest, horniest phone call we've ever shared.'

Suddenly, his anger found a weakness in the dam and burst free. 'Not tonight!' Tony yelled, slamming the phone down so hard the can of beer jumped. Creamy froth swelled up through the triangular hole in the top. Tony stared at it in disgust. He picked up the can and threw it in the sink. The can clattered against the stainless steel, then rolled from side to side. Beer and foam spurted out in brown and cream gouts as Tony dropped into a crouch, head down, hands over his face. Tonight, faced with staring into the depths of someone else's nightmares, he absolutely did not want the inevitable confrontation with his own deficiencies that the phone calls always brought in their wake. The phone rang again, but he remained motionless, eyes squeezed shut. When the answering machine picked up, the caller disconnected the line. 'Bitch,' he said viciously. 'Bitch.'

When my neighbours go out to work in the morning, they leave their German shepherd loose in the back yard. All day long, he lopes restlessly up and down the yard, quartering the poured concrete with the diligence of a prison officer who really loves the work. He's heavy-set, black and brindle, with a shaggy coat. Whenever anyone enters the yards on either side of his, he barks, a long, deep-throated cacophony that lasts far longer than any intrusion. When the bin men come down the back alley to trundle our wheelie bins to their truck, the dog becomes hysterical, standing on his hind legs, forepaws scrabbling uselessly against the heavy wooden gate. I've watched him from the vantage point of my back-bedroom window. He's nearly as tall as the gate itself. Perfect, really.

Next Monday morning, I bought a couple of pounds of steak and cut it into one-inch cubes, like all the best recipes say. Then I made a small incision in each cube and inserted one of the tranquillizers my doctor insists on prescribing for me. I never wanted them, and certainly never use them, but I'd had the feeling they might come in useful one day.

I came out of my back door and listened cheerfully to the dog's salvo of barks. I could afford to be cheerful; it would be the last time I'd have to endure it. I plunged my hand into the bowl of moist meat, enjoying its cool, slippery feel. Then I tossed it over the wall in handfuls. I

47

returned indoors, washed up and went upstairs to my vantage point by the computer. I chose the atmospheric world of Darkseed, calming my excitement with the gothic and macabre underworld I had come to know so well. In spite of my absorption in the game, though, I couldn't help glancing out of the window every few minutes. After a while, he slumped to the ground, tongue lolling out of his mouth. I exited from my game and picked up my binoculars. He seemed to be breathing, but wasn't moving.

I ran downstairs, picking up the holdall I'd prepared earlier, and got into the jeep. I reversed it down the alley till the tailgate was level with next-door's yard gate. I turned off the engine. Silence. I couldn't resist a certain smug satisfaction as I picked up my crowbar and jumped down. It took moments to force next-door's gate. As it swung open, I could see the dog hadn't stirred. I opened the holdall and crouched down beside him. I shoved his tongue back into his mouth and taped his muzzle shut with a roll of surgical tape. I bound his legs together, front and back, and dragged him to the jeep. He was heavy, but I keep myself in shape, and it wasn't too hard to manhandle him into the back.

His breath was coming in soft snores when we got to the farmhouse, but there was no flicker of consciousness, even when I thumbed back his eyelids. I tipped him into the wheelbarrow I'd left out there, wheeled him through the cottage and emptied him down the flight of steps. I switched on the lights and hauled the dog on to the rack like a sack of potatoes, then turned to study my knives. I'd fitted a magnetic strip to the wall, and there they hung suspended, each sharpened to a professional edge; cleaver, filleting knife, carving knife, paring knife and craft knife. I chose the craft knife, cut away the tape from the dog's legs and spread him out on his stomach. I fastened the strap round his middle to hold him tightly against the rack. That's when I realized I had a problem.

Sometime in the past few minutes, the dog had stopped breathing. I thrust my head against the rough hairs of his chest, searching for a heartbeat, but it was too late. I'd obviously miscalculated the drug dosage, and given him too much. I was furious, I have to admit. The dog's death wouldn't affect the practicalities of scientifically testing my apparatus, but I had been looking forward to his suffering; a small revenge for the dozens of times his demented barking had woken me up, especially when I'd come off a hard night shift. But he'd died without a moment's suffering. The last thing he'd known was a couple of pounds of steak. It didn't please me that he'd died happy.

That wasn't all; I soon discovered a second problem. The straps I'd fitted were fine for human ankles and wrists. But the dog didn't have hands or feet to stop his limbs slipping free.

I didn't puzzle for long. It was a far from elegant solution, but it served my purpose. I still had some six-inch nails left over from the repairs and modifications I'd made to the cellar. I carefully placed his left front paw so it straddled a gap in the timbers. I felt for the space between the bones and, with one blow of my club hammer, I drove the nail through at right angles to the paw, just above the last joint. I fixed the strap below the nail, and tugged at it. I reckoned it would hold for long enough.

I'd fixed the other legs within five minutes. Once he was securely strapped down, I was finally able to get started on the business of the day. Even with the bare prospect of a purely scientific experiment, I could feel the excitement rising in me till it was like a hard lump in my throat. Almost, it seemed, without conscious thought, my hand strayed to the handle of the rack. I watched it, detached, as if it were the hand of a stranger. It caressed the cogs, ran lightly over the wheel, and finally came to rest on the handle. The aroma of lubricating oil still hung lightly on the air, melding with the faint smell of paint and the stale, *doggy smell of my assistant in the experiment. I took a deep breath, shivered in anticipation, and slowly began to turn the handle.*

3

I do not stick to assert, that any man who deals in murder must have very incorrect ways of thinking, and truly inaccurate principles.

Don Merrick unzipped his flies. With a sigh of relief, he relaxed his muscles and let his bursting bladder empty. Behind him, the cubicle door opened. His pleasure was abruptly shattered when a heavy hand descended on his shoulder. 'Sergeant Merrick. Just the man I wanted to see,' Tom Cross boomed. Inexplicably, Merrick discovered he couldn't finish what he'd started.

''Morning, sir,' he said cautiously, shaking himself and quickly tucking his manhood out of Cross's sight.

'Told you about her new assignment, has she, your guv'nor?' Cross asked, all lads-together bonhomie.

'She mentioned it, yes, sir.' Merrick looked longingly at the door. But there was no escape. Not with Cross's hand still clamped on his shoulder.

'I hear you're planning on taking your inspector's exams,' Cross remarked.

Merrick's stomach clenched. 'That's right, sir.'

'So you'll be needing all the friends in high places you can find, eh, lad?'

Merrick forced his lips apart in what he hoped was a smile to match Cross's. 'If you say so, sir.'

'You've got the makings of a good officer, Merrick. As long as you remember where your loyalties lie. I know Inspector Jordan's going to be a very busy lady over the next few weeks. She might not always have time to keep me fully *abreast* of things.' Cross leered suggestively. 'I'll be relying on you to keep me informed of all developments. You understand, lad?'

Merrick nodded. 'Aye, sir.'

Cross dropped his hand and made for the door. Opening it, he turned back to Merrick and said, 'Especially if she starts shagging our doctor friend.'

The door sighed shut behind Cross. 'Fuck and bollocks,' Merrick said softly to himself as he moved to the washbasin and started scrubbing his hands vigorously under the hot tap.

Tony had been at his desk since eight. So far, all he'd done was make some photocopies of the Crime Analysis Report form he'd devised for the projected task force. Heavily based on the FBI's Violent Criminal Apprehension Program questionnaire, it aimed to produce a standard classification of every aspect of the crime, from the victim through to the forensic evidence. He shuffled the forms absently, then rearranged his newspaper cuttings into a neat pile. He justified his lack of activity by telling himself that until Carol arrived with the police files, there was little he could do. But that was merely an excuse.

The truth was, there was good reason why concentration was eluding him. She was in his head again. The mystery woman. At the start, he'd felt vulnerable, unwilling to take part in her games. Just like his patients, he thought ironically. How many times had he uttered the maxim that everybody was reluctant to cooperate with therapy at some level? He'd lost count of the number of times he'd slammed the phone down in the early days. But she had persisted, patiently continuing to administer her soothing persuasions till he had started to relax, even to join in.

She had completely thrown him off balance. She had seemed from the first to have an instinct for his Achilles heel, yet she never attacked it. She was everything anyone could desire in a fantasy lover, from gentle to raunchy. The key question for Tony was whether he was pathetic because he managed to relate to pornographic phone calls from a stranger, or whether he should congratulate himself on being so well adjusted that he understood what he needed and what worked for him. But he could not escape the fear that, if not yet dependent on the phone calls, he was at risk of succumbing to that danger. Already incapable of sustaining a normal sexual relationship, was he colluding in the worsening of his condition, or was he moving towards recovery? The only way to test which was correct was to attempt the shift from fantasy to reality. But he was still too wary of fresh humiliation for that. For now, it seemed he'd have to settle for the mysterious stranger who managed to make him feel like a man for long enough to drive the demons underground.

Tony sighed and picked up his mug. The coffee was cold, but he drank it anyway. In spite of himself, he began replaying past conversations in his mind. As if he hadn't run through it enough during the early hours of the morning when sleep had been as elusive as the Bradfield serial killer. The woman's voice buzzed in his ears, inescapable as someone else's Walkman in a train carriage. He tried to close off his emotions and treat the calls with the intellectual objectivity he brought to his work. All he had to do was shut himself off, the way he did when he was examining the perverse fantasies of his patients. He'd certainly had enough experience of refusing to recognize echoes in himself.

Stop the voice. Analyse. Who was she? What drove her? Maybe, like him, she simply enjoyed digging around in messy heads. That at least would explain how she'd wormed her way through his barricades. She was certainly a different animal from the women who worked for the sleazy telephone sex chatlines. Before he'd started this study for the Home Office, he'd been engaged in a piece of research into those chatlines. A significant number of the recently convicted offenders he had dealt with had admitted they were regular callers to the premium-rate phone lines where they could pour their sexual fantasies, however bizarre, obscene or perverse, into the ears of dismally paid women who were encouraged by their bosses to indulge the callers for as long as they were prepared to pay. He'd actually phoned some of the lines himself, just to sample what was on offer, and to discover, using the transcripts of some of his interviews, just how far it was possible to go before disgust overcame the profit motive or the desperate need to earn a living.

Finally, he'd interviewed a selection of the women who worked the phones. The one thing they all held in common was a sense of being violated and degraded, however some of them dressed it up in the contempt they voiced for their clients. He'd come to several conclusions, but the paper he'd subsequently written hadn't included all of them. Some he'd left out because they were too off the wall, others because he feared they might reveal too much about his own psyche. That included his conviction that the response of a man who had previously called a chatline to a dirty phone call from a member of the opposite sex would be radically different to that of a woman in the same situation. Instead of slamming down the receiver, or reporting it to Telecom, most of these men would be either amused or aroused. Either way, they'd want to hear more.

All he had to work out now was why, unlike the chatline workers, this woman found telephone sex with a stranger so appealing. What he needed was to satisfy the intellectual curiosity that was at least as strong as his urge to explore the sexual playground she had opened up for him. Maybe he should consider suggesting a meeting. Before he could go any further, the phone rang. Tony started, his hand stopping halfway in its automatic journey to the receiver. 'Oh, for God's sake,' he muttered impatiently, shaking his head like a high-diver surfacing. He picked up the phone and said, 'Tony Hill.'

'Dr Hill, it's Carol Jordan here.'

Tony said nothing, relieved that his thoughts had failed to conjure up the mystery woman.

'Inspector Jordan? Bradfield Police?' Carol continued into the silence.

'Hello, yes, sorry, I was just trying to . . . clear a space on my desk,' Tony stumbled, his left leg starting to jitter like a cup of tea on a train.

'I'm really sorry about this, but I'm not going to be able to make it for ten. Mr Brandon's called all the squad together for a briefing, and I don't think it would be politic to miss it.'

'No, I can see that,' Tony said, his free hand picking up a pen and unconsciously doodling a daffodil. 'It's going to be hard enough for you to act as go-between without making it look like you're not part of the team. Don't worry about it.'

'Thanks. Look, I don't think this briefing is going to last that long. I'll be with you as soon as I can. Probably around eleven, if that doesn't interfere with your schedule.'

'That's fine,' he said, relieved he wouldn't have too long to brood before they could get down to work. 'I've no meetings in the diary for today, so take your time. You're not putting me out.'

'OK. See you then.'

Carol replaced the phone. So far, so good. At least Tony Hill didn't seem a prisoner of his professional ego, unlike several of the experts she'd had dealings with. And, unlike most men, he'd perceived her potential difficulty, sympathized without patronizing her, and had happily gone along with a course of action that would minimize her problems.

Impatiently, she pushed away the memory of the attraction she'd felt for him. These days, she had neither the time nor the inclination for emotional involvement. Sharing a flat with her brother and finding the time to sustain a few close friendships took as much of her energy as she could spare. Besides, the ending of her last relationship had dealt her self-esteem too serious a blow for her to enter on another one lightly.

The affair with a casualty surgeon in London hadn't survived her move from the Met to Bradfield three years before. As far as Rob was concerned, it was Carol's decision to move to the frozen north. So travelling up and down motorways to spend time together was down to her. He had no intention of wasting any of his valuable off-duty time putting unnecessary mileage on his BMW just to go to a city whose only redeeming feature was Carol. Besides, nurses were a lot less stroppy and critical, and they understood long hours and shift work just as well as a copper if not better. His brutal self-interest had shaken Carol, who felt cheated of the emotion and energy she'd invested in loving Rob. Tony Hill might be attractive, charming, and if his reputation was correct, intelligent and intuitive, but Carol wasn't about to risk her heart again. Especially not with a professional colleague. If she was finding it hard to get him out of her mind, it was because she was fascinated by what she could learn from him about the case, not because she fancied him.

Carol ran a hand through her hair and yawned. She'd been home for precisely fifty-seven minutes in the previous twenty-four hours. Twenty of those had been spent in the shower in a futile attempt to inoculate herself against the effects of no sleep. She'd spent a large chunk of the evening out on the knocker with her CID team, pursuing fruitless enquiries among the nervous inhabitants, workers and regular customers of Temple Fields and its gay businesses. The men's reactions had ranged from total noncooperation o abuse. Carol felt no surprise. The area was seething with a mass of contradictory feelings.

On the one hand, the gay businesses didn't want the area swarming with police because it was bad for cash flow. On the other hand, the gay activists were angrily demanding proper protection now the police had belatedly decided that there was a gay serial killer on the loose. One group of customers were horrified to be questioned, since their gay life was a deep secret from wives, friends, colleagues and parents. Another group were happily playing macho men, boasting that they'd never get into a situation where they were slaughtered by some glassy-eyed maniac. Yet another group were eager for details, obscurely and, in Carol's eyes, obscenely excited by what could happen when one man went out of control. And there was a handful of hardline lesbian separatists who made no secret of their glee that this time, men were the targets. 'Maybe now they'll understand why we were so outraged during the Yorkshire Ripper hunt when men suggested single women should have a curfew,' one had sneered at Carol.

Exhausted by the turmoil, Carol had driven back to headquarters to begin her trawl of the files of the existing inquiries. The murder room was strangely quiet, since most of the detectives were out in Temple Fields, pursuing different lines of enquiry or taking advantage of a few hours off to catch up on their drinking, their sex lives or their sleep. She'd already had a quick word with her opposite numbers in the other two murder investigations, and they had reluctantly agreed to give her access to their files provided she had the material back on their desks first thing in the morning. It was exactly the response she'd expected; superficially cooperative, but, in real terms, calculated to cause her even more problems.

When she'd walked through her office door, she'd been appalled by the sheer volume of paper. Stacks of interview statements, forensic and pathology reports, files of photographs virtually buried her office. Why, in God's name, hadn't Tom Cross decided to use the HOLMES computer system for the earlier murders? At least then all the material would be accessible in the computer, indexed and cross-referenced. All she'd have had to do then was to persuade one of the HOLMES indexers to print out the relevant stuff for Tony. With a groan, she closed her door on the mess and walked through the empty corridors to the uniform sergeant's office. The time had come to test the ACC's instruction to all ranks to cooperate with her. Without another pair of hands, she'd never get through the night's work.

Even with the grudgingly granted help of a PC, it had been a struggle to get through the material. Carol had skimmed the investigation reports, extracting everything that seemed to hold the possibility of significance and passing it on to the constable for copying. Even so, there was a daunting pile of material for Tony and her to work through. When her assistant knocked off at six, Carol wearily loaded the photocopies into a couple of cardboard cartons and staggered down to her car with them. She helped herself to full sets of photographs of all the victims and scenes of crime, filling in a form to requisition fresh copies for the investigating teams to replace the ones she'd taken.

Only then had she headed home. Even there, she had no respite. Nelson waited behind the door, miaowing crossly as he wove his sinuous body round her ankles, forcing her to head straight for the kitchen and the tin opener. When she dumped the bowl of food in front of him, he stared suspiciously at it, frowning. Then hunger overcame his desire to punish her and he wolfed down the whole bowl without pause. 'Nice to see you missed me,' Carol said drily as she made for the shower. By the time she emerged, Nelson had clearly decided to forgive her. He followed her around, purring like a dialling tone, sitting down on every garment she selected from the wardrobe and placed on the bed.

'You really are the pits,' Carol grumbled, pulling her black jeans out from under him. Nelson carried on adoring her, his purr not disrupted in the slightest. She pulled on the jeans, admiring the cut in her wardrobe mirror. They were Katharine Hammett, but she'd only paid £20 for them in a seconds shop in Kensington Church Street, where she went on a twice-annual trawl for the designer clothes she loved but couldn't afford, even on an inspector's wages. The cream linen shirt was French Connection, the ribbed grey cardigan from a chain store men's department. Carol picked a few black cat hairs from the cardigan and caught Nelson's reproachful stare. 'You know I love you. I just don't need to wear you,' she said.

'You'd get a shock if he answered you,' a man's voice said from the doorway.

Carol turned to face her brother, who leaned against the doorjamb in his boxer shorts, blond hair tousled, eyes bleary with sleep. His face had a strange congruence with Carol's, as if someone had scanned her photograph into a computer and subtly altered the features away from the feminine and towards the masculine. 'I didn't wake you, did I?' she asked anxiously.

'Nope. I've got to go to London today. The money man cometh.' He yawned.

'The Americans?' Carol asked, crouching down and scratching the cat behind the ears. Nelson promptly rolled over on to his back, displaying his full stomach to be stroked.

'Correct. They want a full demo of what we've done so far. I've been telling Carl that nothing looks very impressive right now, but he says they want some reassurance that they're not just pouring their development money into a black hole.'

'The joys of software development,' Carol said, rumpling Nelson's fur.

'Leading-edge software development, please,' Michael

said, self-mockingly. 'How about you? What's happening down the murder factory? I heard on the news last night that you'd copped for another one.'

'Looks like it. At least the powers that be have finally admitted that we've got a serial killer on the loose. And they've brought in a psychological profiler to work with us.'

Michael whistled. 'Fuck me, Bradfield police enter the twentieth century. How's Popeye taking it?'

Carol pulled a face. 'He likes it about as much as a poke in the eye with a sharp stick. He thinks it's a total waste of bloody time,' Carol said, dropping her voice and affecting Tom Cross's Bradfield accent. 'Then when I was appointed liaison officer with the profiler, he perked up.'

Michael nodded, a cynical expression on his face. 'Two birds with one stone.'

Carol grinned. 'Yeah, well, it'll need to be over my dead body.' She stood up. Nelson gave a small miaow of protest. Carol sighed and headed for the door. 'Back to work, Nelson. Thanks for taking my mind off the bodies,' she said.

Michael swung out of the doorway to let her pass and gave her a hug. 'Take no prisoners, sis,' he said.

Carol snorted. 'I don't think you've quite grasped the principle of policing, bro.'

By the time she was behind the wheel, the cat and Michael were forgotten. She was back with the killer.

Now, a couple of hours and a stack of overnight murder team reports later, home seemed a memory as distant as her summer holiday in Ithaca. Carol forced herself out of her chair, picked up the paperwork and walked into the main CID office.

It was standing room only by the time she arrived, detectives normally based in other stations jockeying for position in the crowd. A couple of her detective constables shifted to make room for her, one offering his chair.

'Fucking brown nose,' a voice said audibly from the other side of the room. Carol couldn't see who had spoken, but recognized it wasn't one of her own team. She smiled and shook her head at her junior officer, choosing instead to perch on the edge of his desk beside Don Merrick, who nodded a morose greeting. The clock read nine-twenty-nine. The room smelled of cheap cigars, coffee and damp coats.

One of the other inspectors caught Carol's eye and started to move towards her. But before they could speak, the door opened and Tom Cross barrelled in, followed by John Brandon. The superintendent looked disturbingly benign as he marched in. The troops parted automatically before him, leaving a clear path for him and Brandon to walk to the whiteboard at the far end of the room.

''Morning, lads,' Cross said genially. 'And lasses,' he added as an obvious afterthought. 'There's nobody here that doesn't know we've got four unsolved murders on our hands. We've got IDs for the first three bodies – Adam Scott, Paul Gibbs and Gareth Finnegan. So far, we've not made any progress on the fourth victim. The lads down the path lab are working on him now, trying to come up with a face that won't frighten the horses when we release the picture to the press.'

Cross took a deep breath. If anything, his expression became even more benevolent. 'As you all know, I'm not a man given to theorizing ahead of the evidence. And I've been reluctant officially to connect these killings because of the media hysteria that would bring down about us. Judging by this morning's papers, I was right about that.' He pointed to several of the newspapers the detectives held.

'However, in the light of this latest killing, we're going to have to revise our strategy. As of yesterday afternoon, I have amalgamated the four murder enquiries into one major investigation.'

There was a murmur of support. Don Merrick leaned

forward and murmured in Carol's ear, 'Changes his tune more often than a juke box.'

She nodded. 'I wish he changed his socks as often.'

Cross glared in their direction. He couldn't have heard the remarks, but seeing Carol's lips move was enough of an excuse. 'Settle down,' he said sternly. 'I'm not finished yet. Now, it doesn't take much in the way of detective abilities to see that this place is too small for us *and* the normal activities of the station, so as soon as we're finished here this morning, we'll be moving this operation to the former station in Scargill Street, which some of you will remember was mothballed six months ago. Overnight, there's been a team of maintenance workers, computer whizz kids and British Telecom engineers getting it back to temporary operational status.'

A groan went up. No one had shed a tear when the old Victorian building in Scargill Street had been closed down. Draughty, inconvenient, short of parking spaces, ladies' toilets – everything except cells – the building had been earmarked for demolition and redevelopment. Typically, there hadn't been enough money in the budget to push ahead with the project. 'I know, I know,' Cross said, cutting across their complaints. 'But we'll all be under one roof, so I'll be able to keep an eye on you. I will be in overall charge of the enquiry. You'll have two inspectors to report to – Bob Stansfield and Kevin Matthews. They'll be sorting out your assignments in a minute. Inspector Jordan will be otherwise engaged on an initiative of Mr Brandon's.' Cross paused. 'Which I'm sure you'll all want to cooperate with.'

Carol kept her head high and looked around. The faces she could see mostly showed open cynicism. Several heads turned towards her. There was no warmth in their stares. Even those who might support the profiling initiative were brassed off that the prime job had gone to a woman rather than one of the lads.

'So Bob will take over Inspector Jordan's operational responsibilities for Paul Gibbs and Adam Scott, and Kevin will handle yesterday's body as well as Gareth Finnegan. The HOLMES team have been called in, and they'll be starting to input their data just as soon as the boffins have got the wires in place. Inspector Dave Woolcott, who some of you will remember from when he was a sergeant here, will be the enquiry manager in charge of the HOLMES team. Over to you, Mr Brandon.' Cross stepped back and waved the ACC forward. His gesture was only just on the right side of the border between insolence and politeness.

Brandon took a moment to look around the room. He'd never had to make a more important pitch. Most of the detectives in the room were jaded and frustrated. Many of them had been working on one of the previous murders for months now, with precious little to show for it. Tom Cross's powers of motivation were legendary, but even he was facing an uphill struggle, not least because of his pig-headed refusal to admit before now that the crimes were connected. It was time to beat Tom Cross at his own game. Bluntness had never been Brandon's strong suit, but he'd been practising all morning. In the shower, in front of the shaving mirror, in his head while he ate his egg on toast, in the car on the way to the station. Brandon thrust one hand in his trouser pocket and crossed his fingers.

'This is probably the toughest task of any of our careers. As far as we're aware, this guy is only operating in Bradfield. In a way, I'm glad about that, because I've never seen a better bunch of detectives than we've got here. If anyone can nail this bastard, it's you lot. You've got a hundred and ten per cent support from your senior officers, and all the resources you need are going to be made available, whether the politicians like it or not.' Brandon's note of belligerence won a murmur of agreement from the room.

'We're going to be blazing a trail here in more ways than one. You all know about the Home Office plans for a national task force for profiling repeat offenders. Well, we're going to be the guinea pigs. Dr Tony Hill, the man who's going to be telling the Home Office what to think, has agreed to work with us. Now, I know there are some amongst you who think that profiling is a load of crap. But like it or not, it's part of our future. If we cooperate and work with this guy, we're a lot more likely to see this task force end up something like we want it to be. If we piss him off, we're liable to be lumbered with a bloody great millstone round our neck. Is that clear to everyone here?'

Brandon looked sternly round the room, not missing out Tom Cross. The nods varied from enthusiastic to barely perceptible. 'I'm glad we all understand one another. Dr Hill's job is to assess the evidence we provide him with and to come up with a profile of the killer to help us focus our enquiries. I've appointed Inspector Carol Jordan as the liaison officer between the murder squad and Dr Hill. Inspector Jordan, can you just stand up a minute?'

Startled, Carol scrambled to her feet, dropping her files on the way. Don Merrick immediately got down on his knees and grabbed the spilling papers. 'For those of you from other divisions who don't know Inspector Jordan, there she is.' Nice one, Brandon, thought Carol. As if there were squads of female detectives to choose from.

'Inspector Jordan is to have access to each and every piece of paper on this enquiry. I want her kept fully informed of any developments. Anyone who is pursuing a promising lead should discuss it with her as well as with their own inspector, or Superintendent Cross. And any requests from Inspector Jordan must be treated as urgent enquiries. If I hear that anybody's being a smartarse, trying to freeze Inspector Jordan or Dr Hill out of the investigation, I won't be taking prisoners. The same goes for anybody who leaks anything about this aspect of the investigation to the media. So think on. Unless you've got a burning ambition to climb back into uniform and walk the streets of Bradfield in the rain for the rest of your career, you'll do everything in your power to help her. This isn't a competition. We're all on the same side. Dr Hill isn't here to catch the killer. That's your –'

Brandon stopped in mid-sentence. No one had noticed the door opening, but the words of the communications room sergeant captured everyone's attention faster than a gunshot. 'Sorry to interrupt, sir,' he said, his voice tight with suppressed emotion. 'We've got an ID on yesterday's victim. Sir, he's one of ours.'

It was an American journalist who said, 'I have seen the future and it works.' I know just what he meant. After the dog, I knew Adam wouldn't be any problem.

I spent the rest of the week in a state of nervous tension. I was even tempted to try one of the tranquillizers myself, but I resisted. This wasn't the time to give in to weakness. Besides, I couldn't afford to be anything less than completely in control of myself. My years of self-discipline paid off; I doubt if any of my colleagues noticed anything unusual in my behaviour at work, except that I couldn't bring myself to do the weekend overtime I usually volunteer for.

By Monday morning, I was at a peak of readiness. I was primed and polished, the perfect killer-in-waiting. Even the weather was on my side. It was a crisp, clear autumnal morning, the kind of day that brings a smile even to the lips of commuters. Just before eight, I drove past Adam's home, a new terraced three-storey town house with integral garage on the ground floor. His bedroom curtains were closed, the milk bottle still sitting on his doorstep, half a Daily Mail protruding from his letter box. I parked a couple of streets away outside a row of shops and retraced my journey. I walked down his street, satisfied that so far I was right on time. His bedroom curtains were drawn back, the milk and newspaper gone. At the end of the street, I crossed to the little park opposite and sat on a bench.

I opened my own **Daily Mail** *and imagined Adam reading the same stories that I was staring at unseeingly. I shifted my position so I could see his front door without craning round the paper, and put my peripheral vision on alert. Right on schedule, the door opened at eight-twenty, and Adam appeared. Casually, I folded up my paper, dumped it in the litter bin by the bench and strolled off down the street in his wake.*

The tram station was less than ten minutes' walk away, and I was right behind him as he strode on to the crowded platform. The tram glided into the station moments later and he moved forward with the flow of passengers. I hung back slightly and let a couple of people come between us; I was taking no chances.

He was craning his head as he entered the carriage. I knew exactly why. When their eyes met, Adam waved and squirmed through the crowd so they could chatter mindlessly all the way into town. I watched him as he leaned forward. I knew every expression on his face, every angle and gesture of his lean, muscular body. His hair; the little curls in the nape of his neck still damp, his skin pink and glowing from his shave, the scent of his Aramis cologne. He laughed aloud at something in their conversation, and I felt the sour taste of bile rise in my mouth. The taste of betrayal. How could he? It should have been me talking to him, making his face light up, bringing that beautiful smile to his warm lips. If my fixity of purpose had ever wavered, the sight of the pair of them enjoying their Monday-morning encounter would have turned my resolve to granite.

As usual, he left the tram in Woolmarket Square. I was less than a dozen yards behind him. He turned back to wave to his soon-to-be bereaved lover. I swiftly turned away, pretending to read the tram timetable. The last thing I wanted right then was for him to notice me, to realize I was dogging his steps. I gave it a few seconds, then took up the pursuit. Left into Bellwether Street. I could see his dark hair bobbing among the shop and office workers crowding the pavements. Adam cut down an alley to his right, and I emerged in Crown Plaza just in time to see him enter the Inland Revenue building where he worked. Satisfied that this was just another Monday, I carried on through the plaza, past the squat glass and metal office block, and into the newly restored Victorian shopping arcades.

I had time to kill. The thought brought a smile to my lips.

I went off to do some studying in the Central Library. They had nothing new in, so I settled for an old favourite, Killing for Company. Dennis Nilsen's case never ceases both to fascinate and repel me. He murdered fifteen young men without anyone even missing them. No one had the faintest idea that there was a gay serial killer stalking the homeless and rootless. He befriended them, took them home, gave them drink, but he could only cope with them once they had been perfected in death. Then, and only then, could he hold them, have sex with them, cherish them. Now that is sick. They'd done nothing to deserve their fate; they had committed no betrayal, no act of treachery.

The only mistake Nilsen made was in the disposal of the bodies. It's almost as if subconsciously he wanted to be caught. Chopping them up and cooking them was fine, but flushing them down the toilet? It must have been obvious to a man as intelligent as he was that the drains wouldn't be able to handle that volume of solids. I've never understood why he didn't just feed the meat to his dog.

However, it's never too late to learn from the mistakes of others. The blunders of killers never cease to amaze me. It doesn't take much intelligence to understand how the police and forensic scientists operate and to take appropriate precautions, especially since the men who earn their living trying to catch the killers have obligingly written detailed textbooks about the precise nature of their work. On the other hand, we only ever hear about the failures. I knew I was never going to appear in those catalogues of incompetence. I had planned too well, every risk minimized and balanced against the benefits it would bring. The only account of my work will be this journal, which will not see printer's ink until my last breath is a distant memory. My only regret is that I won't be around to read the reviews.

I was back at my post by four, even though I'd never known Adam leave work before a quarter to five. I sat in the window of Burger King on Woolmarket Square, perfectly placed to watch the mouth of the alley leading to his office. Right on cue, he emerged at 4.47 and headed for the tram stop. I joined the knot of people waiting on the raised platform, smiling quietly to myself as I heard the tram hoot in the distance. Enjoy your tram ride, Adam. It's going to be your last.

4

The fact was, I 'fancied' him, and resolved to commence
business upon his throat.

When Damien Connolly failed to turn up at the start of
his shift as local information officer in F Division's station
on the south side of the city, the duty sergeant hadn't been
unduly worried. Although PC Connolly was one of the
best collators in the force, and a trained HOLMES officer,
he was a notoriously bad timekeeper. At least twice a week,
he came hurtling through the doors of the station a good
ten minutes after his shift was due to start. But when he
still hadn't shown up half an hour after he was due on
duty, Sergeant Claire Bonner felt a twinge of irritation.
Even Connolly had enough sense to realize that if he was
going to be more than fifteen minutes late, he had to phone
in. Today of all days as well, when headquarters were
demanding a full turnout of HOLMES officers on the
serial-killer investigation.

Sighing, Sgt Bonner checked Connolly's home number
in her files and dialled it. The phone rang and rang, till
finally it was automatically disconnected. She felt a prickle
of concern. Connolly·was something of a loner outside the
job. He was quieter and maybe more thoughtful than most
of the officers on Sgt Bonner's relief, always keeping his
distance when he joined in the social life of the station. As
far as she was aware, there was no girlfriend in whose bed
Connolly might have overslept. His family were all up in
Glasgow, so there were no relatives to try locally. Sgt

Bonner cast her mind back. Yesterday had been a day off for the relief. When they'd knocked off from the previous night shift, Connolly had come for breakfast with her and half a dozen of the other lads. He'd not said anything about having plans for his time off other than catching up on his kip and working on his car, an elderly Austin Healey roadster.

Sgt Bonner went through to the control room and had a word with her opposite number, asking him to have one of the patrol cars swing round by Connolly's house to check he wasn't ill or injured. 'See if they can check the garage, make sure that bloody car of his hasn't come off the jack with him underneath,' she added as she went back to her desk.

It was after eight when the control room sergeant appeared in her office. 'The lads have checked Connolly's house. No answer to the door. They had a good scout round, and all the curtains were open. Milk on the doorstep. No sign of life as far as they could make out. There was only one thing a bit odd that they could see. His car was parked on the street, which isn't like him. I don't have to tell you, he treats that motor like the crown jewels.'

Sgt Bonner frowned. 'Maybe he's got somebody stopping with him? A relative, or a girlfriend? Maybe he's let them stick their car in the garage?'

The control room sergeant shook his head. 'Nope. The lads had a look in the garage window, and it was empty. And don't forget the milk.'

Sgt Bonner shrugged. 'Not a lot more we can do, then, is there?'

'Well, he's over twenty-one. I'd have thought he'd have more sense than to go on the missing list, but you know what they say about the quiet ones.'

Sgt Bonner sighed. 'I'll have his guts for garters when he shows his face. By the way, I've asked Joey Smith to stand in for him in the collator's office for this shift.'

The control room sergeant cast his eyes upwards. 'You really know how to make a man's day, don't you? Couldn' you have got one of the others? Smith can barely manag the alphabet.'

Before Sgt Bonner could argue the toss, there was knock at the door. 'Yeah?' she called. 'Come in.'

A PC from the control room entered hesitantly. Sh looked faintly sick. 'Skip,' she said, the worry in her voic obvious from the single word. 'I think you'd better have look at this.' She held out a fax, the bottom edge ragge where it had been torn hastily off the roll.

Being nearer, the control room sergeant took the flims sheet and glanced at it. He drew in his breath sharply, the closed his eyes for a moment. Wordlessly, he handed th fax to Sgt Bonner.

At first, all she saw was the stark black and white c the photograph. For a moment, her mind automaticall protecting her from horror, she wondered why someon had gone over her head and reported Connolly missin Then her eyes translated the marks on the paper int words. '*Urgent fax to all stations. This is the unidentifie murder victim discovered yesterday afternoon in the bac yard of the Queen of Hearts public house, Temple Field Bradfield. Photograph to follow later this a.m. Please circu late and display. Any information to DI Kevin Matthew at Scargill Street Incident Room, ext. 2456.*'

Sgt Bonner looked bleakly at the other two officer 'There isn't any doubt about it, is there?'

The PC looked at the floor, her skin pale and clammy 'I don't think so, skip,' she said. 'That's Connolly. I mea it's not what you'd call a good likeness, but it's definitel him.'

The control room sergeant picked up the fax. 'I'll get o to DI Matthews right away,' he said.

Sgt Bonner pushed her chair back and stood up. 'I'

etter go round to the morgue. They're going to need a
ormal identification as soon as possible so they can get
weaving.'

This makes it a whole new ball game,' Tony said, his face
ombre.

'It certainly ups the stakes,' Carol said.

'The question I'm asking myself is whether or not Handy
ndy knew he was giving us a bobby,' Tony said softly,
winging round in his chair to stare out of the window at
e city rooftops.

'Sorry?'

He gave a twisted smile and said, 'No, it's me who should
pologize. I always give them a name. It makes it personal.'
le swung back to face Carol. 'Does that bother you?'

Carol shook her head. 'It's better than the station
ckname.'

'Which is?' Tony asked, eyebrows raised.

'The Queer Killer,' Carol said, her distaste clear.

'That begs a lot of questions,' Tony said noncommittally.
ut if it helps them deal with their fear and anger, it's
robably no bad thing.'

'I don't like it. It doesn't feel personal to me, calling him
e Queer Killer.'

'What does make it personal to you? The fact that he's
ken one of yours now?'

'I felt like that already. As soon as we got the second
urder, the one I was handling, I was convinced we were
ealing with a serial offender. That was when it got per-
nal for me. I want to nail this bastard. I need to. Pro-
ssionally, personally, whatever.' The cold vehemence in
arol's voice gave Tony confidence. This was a woman
ho was going to pull out all the stops to make sure he
d what he needed to do his job. Her tone of voice and
e words she'd chosen were also a calculated challenge,
owing him she didn't give a damn what he made of her

desire. She was just what he needed. Professionally, at any rate.

'You and me both,' Tony said. 'And together, we can make it happen. But only together. You know, the first time I got directly involved in profiling, it was a serial arsonist. After half a dozen major fires, I knew how he was doing it, why he was doing it, what was in it for him. I knew exactly the kind of mad bastard he was, yet couldn't put a name or a face to him. It drove me crazy with frustration for a while. Then I realized it wasn't my job to do that. That's your job. All I can do is to point you in the right direction.'

Carol smiled grimly. 'Just point, and I'll be off like a gun dog,' she said. 'What did you mean when you said you wondered whether he knew Damien Connolly was a bobby?'

Tony ran a hand through his hair, leaving it spiky as a punk's. 'OK. We've got two scenarios here. Handy Andy may not have known Damien Connolly was a bobby. It may be nothing more than a coincidence, a particularly unpleasant coincidence for his colleagues, but a coincidence nevertheless. That's not a scenario I'm happy with, however, because my reading, based on the little I know so far, is that these aren't random victims snatched by chance. I think he chooses his victims with care, and plans thoroughly. Would you agree with that?'

'He doesn't leave things to chance, that's obvious,' Carol said.

'Right. The alternative is that Handy Andy knows full well that his fourth victim is a policeman. That in itself leads to two further possibilities. One: Handy Andy knew he'd killed a copper, but that fact is supremely irrelevant to the meaning of the killing for him. In other words, Damien Connolly fulfilled all the other criteria that Andy needs from his victims, and he would have died at that point whether he was a bobby or a bus driver.

74

'The other scenario is the one I like best, though. The fact that Damien was a copper is a crucial part of the reason why Handy Andy *chose* him as his fourth victim.'

'You mean he's thumbing his nose at us?' Carol asked.

Thank God she was quick. That was going to make the job so much simpler. She'd done well to get as far up the ladder as she had, given she had looks as well as brains. Either attribute without the other would have made promotion easier. 'That's certainly a possibility,' Tony acknowledged. 'But I think it's more likely to be about vanity. I think he'd started to get pissed off with Detective Superintendent Cross's refusal to acknowledge his existence. In his own eyes, he's very successful at what he does. He's the best. And he deserves recognition. And that desire for recognition has been thwarted by the police's refusal to admit there's only one offender behind these killings. OK, so the *Sentinel Times* has been speculating about a serial killer since the second victim, but that's not the same as being given the official accolade by the police themselves. And I may have unwittingly added fuel to the fire after the third killing.'

'You mean, the interview you did with the *Sentinel Times*?'

'Yeah. My suggestion that it was possible there were two killers at work will have made him angry that he wasn't being acknowledged as the master of his craft.'

'Dear God,' Carol said, torn between revulsion and fascination. 'So he went out and stalked a police officer so we'd take him seriously?'

'It's a possibility. Of course, it can't have been just any police officer. Even though making his point to the powers that be is important to Handy Andy, the prime directive is still to go for victims who fulfil his very personal criteria.'

Carol frowned. 'So what you're saying is that there's something about Connolly that makes him different from most other coppers?'

'Looks like it.'

'Maybe it's the sexuality thing,' Carol mused. 'I mean, there aren't many gays in the force. And those that there are tend to be so deep in the closet you could mistake them for a clothes hanger.'

'Whoa,' Tony laughed, holding up his hands as if to fend her off. 'No theorizing without data. We don't know yet whether Damien was gay. What might be useful, though, is to find out what shifts Damien worked recently. Say, the last two months. That'll give us some idea of the times he was at home, which might help the officers who'll be questioning his neighbours. Also, we should be asking around the other officers on his relief, to check out whether he always left alone, or if he ever gave anyone a lift home. We need to find out everything there is to know about Damien Connolly both as a man and as a bobby.'

Carol pulled out her notebook and scribbled a reminder to herself. 'Shifts,' she muttered.

'There's something else this tells us about Handy Andy,' Tony said slowly, reaching for the idea that had just swum into his consciousness.

Carol looked up, her eyes alert. 'Go on,' she said.

'He's very, very good at what he does,' Tony said flatly. 'Think about it. A police officer is a trained observer. Even the thickest plod is a lot more alert to what's going on around them than the average member of the public. Now, from what you've told me, Damien Connolly was a bright lad. He was a collator, which means he was even more on the ball than most officers. As I understand it, a collator's job is to act like the station's walking encyclopaedia. It's all very well having all the local information about known villains and MOs on file cards, but if the collator isn't sharp, then the system's worthless, am I right?'

'Spot on. A good collator is worth half a dozen bodies on the ground,' Carol said. 'And by all accounts, Connolly was one of the best.'

Tony leaned back in his chair. 'So if Handy Andy stalked Damien without setting any alarm bells ringing, he must be bloody good. Face it, Carol, if somebody was tailing you on a regular basis, you'd pick them up, wouldn't you?'

'I bloody hope so,' Carol said drily. 'But I'm a woman. Maybe we're just a bit more on our guard than the blokes.'

Tony shook his head. 'I think a copper as smart as Damien would have noticed anything other than a very professional tail.'

'You mean we might be looking for someone who's in the Job?' Carol demanded, her voice rising as she spoke the unthinkable.

'It's a possibility. I can't pitch it more strongly than that till I've seen all the evidence. Is that it?' Tony asked, nodding towards the cardboard box Carol had deposited by the door of his office.

'That's some of it. There's another box and some folders of photographs still in the car. And that's after some serious editing.'

Tony pulled a face. 'Rather you than me. Shall we go and fetch it, then?'

Carol stood up. 'Why don't you get started while I go and get the rest?'

'It's the photographs I want to look at first, so I might as well come and help,' he said.

'Thanks,' Carol said.

In the lift, they stood on opposite sides, both conscious of the other's physical presence. 'That's not a Bradfield accent,' Tony remarked as the doors slid shut. If he was going to work successfully with Carol Jordan, he needed to know what made her tick, personally as well as professionally. The more he could find out about her, the better.

'I thought you said you left the detective work to us?'

'We're good at stating the obvious, us psychologists. Isn't that what our critics on the force say?'

'Touché. I'm from Warwick, originally. Then university at Manchester and into the Met on the fast track. And you? I'm not great on accents, but I can spot you're a Northerner, though you don't sound like Bradfield either,' Carol replied.

'Born and bred in Halifax. London University, followed by a DPhil at Oxford. Eight years in special hospitals. Eighteen months ago, the Home Office head-hunted me to run this feasibility study.' Give a little to get a lot, Tony thought wryly. Who exactly was probing whom?

'So we're both outsiders,' Carol said.

'Maybe that's why John Brandon chose you to liaise with me.'

The lift doors slid open and they walked through the underground car park to the visitors' parking area where Carol had left her car. Tony hefted the cardboard box out of the boot. 'You must be stronger than you look,' he gasped.

Carol picked up the folders of photographs and grinned. 'And I'm a black belt in Cluedo,' she said. 'Listen, Tony, if this maniac is in the Job, what sort of stuff would you expect to find?'

'I shouldn't have said that. I was theorizing ahead of data, and I don't want you to place any weight on it, OK? Strike it from the record,' Tony panted.

'OK, but what would the signs be?' she persisted.

They were back in the lift before Tony answered her. 'Behaviour that exhibits a familiarity with police and forensic procedure,' he said. 'But in itself, that proves nothing. There are so many true-crime books and TV detectives around these days that anyone could know that sort of stuff. Look, Carol, please put it out of your head. We need to keep an open mind. Otherwise the work we do is valueless.'

Carol stifled a sigh. 'OK. But will you tell me if you still think that way after you've seen the evidence? Because if it's more than a slim possibility, we might need to rethink the way we're dealing with the enquiry.'

'I promise,' he said. The lift doors slid open, as if placing their own full stop on the conversation.

Back in the office, Tony slid the first set of photographs out of their folders. 'Before you start, could you fill me in on how you want to pursue this?' Carol asked, notebook at the ready.

'I'll go through all the pictures first, then I'll ask you to take me through the investigation so far. When we've done that, I'll work through the paperwork myself. After that, what I usually do is draw up a profile of each of the victims. Then we have another session with these,' he said, brandishing his forms. 'And then I walk out on the high wire and do a profile of the offender. Does that sound reasonable to you?'

'Sounds fine. How long is all that likely to take?'

Tony frowned. 'It's hard to say. A few days, certainly. However, Handy Andy seems to work on an eight-week cycle, and there's no sign that he's accelerating. That's unusual in itself, by the way. Once I've studied the material I'll have a better idea of how in control he is, but I think we've probably got a bit of time to spare before he kills again. Having said that, he may well have already selected his next victim, so we've got to make sure that we keep any progress we make well away from the press. The last thing we want is to be the catalyst for him speeding up the process.'

Carol groaned. 'Are you always this optimistic?'

'It goes with the territory. Oh, and one more thing? If you develop any suspects, I'd prefer not to know anything about them at this stage – there's a danger that my subconscious will alter the profile accordingly.'

Carol snorted. 'We should be so lucky.'

'That bad, is it?'

'Oh, we've pulled in anybody who's got form for

indecent assault or violent offences against gay men, but none of them looks even a remote possibility.'

Tony pulled a sympathetic face then picked up the photographs of Adam Scott's corpse and slowly started going through them. He picked up a pen and moved his A4 pad nearer to him. He glanced up at Carol. 'Coffee?' he asked. 'I meant to ask earlier, but I was too interested in what we were talking about.'

Carol felt like a co-conspirator. She had been enjoying their conversation too, in spite of a twinge of guilt that multiple murders shouldn't be a source of pleasure. Talking with Tony was like talking to an equal who had no axe to grind, whose primary concern was finding a path to the truth rather than a way to boost the ego. It was something she'd missed on this case so far. 'Me too,' she admitted. 'I'm probably approaching the point where coffee is a necessity. Do you want me to go and fetch some?'

'Good God, no!' Tony laughed. 'That's not what you're here for. Wait there, I'll be right back. How do you take yours?'

'Black, no sugar. In an intravenous drip, preferably.'

Tony took a large Thermos jug out of his filing cabinet and disappeared. He was back inside five minutes with two steaming mugs and the jug. He handed Carol a mug and gestured towards the Thermos. 'I filled it up. I figured we might be some time. Help yourself as and when.'

Carol took a grateful sip. 'Will you marry me?' she asked, mock romantic.

Tony laughed again, to cover the lurch of apprehension that shifted his stomach, a familiar response to even the most idle of flirtations. 'You won't be saying that in a few days' time,' he said evasively, turning his attention back to the photographs.

'Victim number one. Adam Scott,' he said softly, making a note on his pad. He went through the photographs one by one, then went back to the beginning. The first picture showed a city square, tall Georgian houses on one side, a modern office block on a second and a row of shops, bars and restaurants on the third. In the centre of the square was a public garden, crossed by two diagonal paths. In the middle was an ornate Victorian drinking fountain. The park was surrounded by a three feet high brick wall. Along two sides of the garden was deep shrubbery. The ambience was slightly seedy, the stucco of the houses peeling in places. He imagined himself standing on the corner, taking in the view, smelling the fumid city air mixed with the stink of stale alcohol and fast food, hearing the night sounds. The rev of engines, the sound of high heels on pavements, occasional laughs and cries borne on the wind, the twitter of starlings, conned out of sleep by the sodium light of streetlamps. Where did you stand, Andy? Where did you watch your ground from? What did you see? What did you hear? What did you *feel*? Why here?

The second photograph showed a section of the wall and the shrubbery from the street side. The photograph was clear enough for Tony to make out the little iron squares on the top of the wall, which were all that remained of railings that had presumably been removed during the war to make guns and shells. A section of the bushes showed broken branches and crumpled leaves. The third shot showed the body of a man, face down on the earth, his limbs splayed at strange angles. Tony let himself be drawn into the picture, trying to put himself in Handy Andy's shoes. How did it feel, Andy? Were you proud? Were you scared? Were you exultant? Did you feel a spasm of regret at abandoning the object of your desire? How long did you allow yourself to drink in this sight, this strange tableau that you created? Did the sound of footsteps move you on? Or did you not care?

Tony looked up. Carol was watching him. To his surprise, for once he didn't feel uncomfortable to have a woman's eyes on him. Perhaps because their relationship had so firm a professional base, but without direct competition. The tension in him relaxed a notch. 'The place where the body was found. Tell me about it.'

'Crompton Gardens. It's at the heart of Temple Fields, where the gay village and the red-light district overlap. It's poorly lit at night, mostly because the streetlights are always being vandalized by the sex vendors who want a bit of darkness to cover their activities. There's a lot of sex goes on in Crompton Gardens, in the bushes and on the park benches under the trees, in the office doorways, in the basement areas of the houses. Rent, prostitution and casual pick-ups. There are people around throughout the night, but they're not the sort who are going to come forward about anything unusual they might have seen, even if they noticed it,' Carol explained while Tony took notes.

'The weather?' he asked.

'Dry night, though the ground was pretty damp.'

Tony returned to the photographs. The body was shot from various angles. Then, following the removal of the body, the dumping ground was pictured in close-up sections. There were no visible footprints, but some scraps of black plastic were lying under the body. He pointed at them with the tip of his pen. 'Do we know what these are?'

'Bradfield Metropolitan Council bin bags. Standard issue to businesses, blocks of flats . . . anywhere wheelie bins are inappropriate. That grade of bag has been in use now for the last two years. There's apparently nothing to indicate whether they were already there or if they were dumped at the same time as the body,' Carol said.

Tony raised his eyebrows. 'You seem to have assimilated a helluva lot of detail since yesterday afternoon.'

Carol grinned. 'It's tempting to pretend I'm Superwoman, but I have to confess that I'd already made a point of finding out what I could about the other two enquiries. I was convinced they were linked, even if my boss wasn't. And in fairness to my colleagues, the inspectors leading the other two enquiries had an open mind. They didn't object to me making the occasional trawl through their stuff. Ploughing through it all overnight just refreshed my memory, that's all.'

'You've been up all night?'

'Like you said, it goes with the territory. I'll be fine till about four this afternoon. Then it'll hit me like a sledge-hammer,' Carol admitted.

'Message received and understood,' Tony replied, turning back to the photographs. He moved on to the series of shots from the postmortem. The body lay on its back on the white slab, the hideous wounds visible for the first time. Tony went slowly through the whole sequence of pictures, sometimes flicking back to previous shots. When he closed his eyes, he could picture Adam Scott's intact body, slowly breaking out in wounds and bruises like alien blooms. He could almost conjure up the slo-mo vision of the hands that brought flesh to such a pass. After a few moments, he opened his eyes and spoke again. 'These bruises on the neck and chest – what did the pathologist say?'

'Suck marks. Like love bites.'

A head descending, predatory, a bizarre parody of love. 'And these sections of the neck and chest. Three places where the flesh has been cut away?' Tony asked distantly.

'They were removed postmortem. Maybe he likes to eat them?'

'Maybe,' Tony said doubtfully. 'Was there any trace of bruising in the remaining tissues, can you remember?'

'I think there was.' Carol's surprise showed in her voice.

Tony nodded. 'I'll check the pathologist's report. He's a clever lad, our Handy Andy. My first reaction is that these aren't souvenirs, or indications of cannibalism. I think they might have been bite marks. But Handy Andy knows enough about forensic dentistry to realize that identifiable bite marks would be enough to put him away. So once the frenzy's spent, he's cooled down and removed the evidence. These cuts to the genitals – pre or postmortem?'

'Post. The pathologist remarked that they seemed quite tentative.'

Tony gave a small smile of satisfaction. 'Did the pathologist say what has caused the trauma to the limbs? The shots at the site look like a rag doll.'

Carol sighed. 'He didn't want to be pushed to an official conclusion. All four limbs were dislocated, and some of his vertebrae were out of alignment. He said . . .' She paused and imitated the pathologist's portentous delivery, '"Don't quote me, but I'd expect to see injuries like this after the Spanish Inquisition had put someone on the rack."'

'The rack? Shit, we're really dealing with a messy mind here. OK. Next set. Paul Gibbs. This one's yours, I think?' Tony asked as he replaced Adam Scott's photographs and took out the contents of the second folder. He repeated the process he'd gone through before. 'So where is this scene in relation to the first one?' Tony asked.

'Hang on a minute. I'll show you.' Carol opened one of the boxes and picked out the large-scale map she'd thought to bring with her. She unfolded it and spread it out on the floor. Tony got up from his desk and crouched down beside her. She was instantly aware of the smell of him, a mixture of shampoo and his own faint, animal scent. No macho aftershave, no cologne. She watched his pale, square hands on the map, the short, almost stubby fingers, with their neatly trimmed nails and a sparse scattering of fine black hairs on the bottom section of each finger. Appalled, she felt a stirring of desire. You're pathetic as an adolescent, she savagely chided herself. Like a teenager who fancies the first teacher who says anything nice about your work. Grow up, Jordan!

Under the guise of pointing out the sites on the map, Carol inched away. 'Crompton Gardens is here,' she said.

'Canal Street is about half a mile away, over here. And the Queen of Hearts pub is just along here, about midway between the two.'

'Is it safe to assume he knows the area well?' Tony asked, making his own mental map of the murder sites.

'I think so. Crompton Gardens is a pretty obvious dumping ground, but the other two imply quite a high degree of familiarity with Temple Fields.' Carol sat back on her haunches, trying to work out if the pattern of sites implied an approach from one specific direction.

'I need to take a look at the scenes. Preferably around the time the bodies were dumped. Do we know when that was?' Tony said.

'We don't know about Adam. Estimated time of death is an hour either side of midnight, so not before then. With Paul, we know the doorway was clear just after three a.m. Gareth's time of death is estimated at between seven and ten p.m. the evening before his body was found. And with Damien, the yard was clear at half past eleven,' Carol recited, closing her eyes to recall the information.

Tony found himself staring at her face, glad of the freedom her shuttered eyelids gave him. Even without the animation of her blue eyes, he could see that she'd be classified beautiful. Oval face, broad forehead, clear pale skin, and that thick blonde hair, cut slightly shaggy. A strong, determined mouth. A furrow that appeared between her brows when she concentrated. And his appreciation was as clinical as if she were a photograph in a casebook. Why was it that, faced with a woman any normal man would regard as attractive, something in him closed down? Was it because he refused to allow himself to feel the first stirrings that might lead him to a place where he was no longer in control, where humiliation lurked? Carol's eyes opened, registering surprise when she saw him watching her.

He felt his ears tingle with a blush and turned back to the map. 'So he's a night owl,' he said abruptly. 'I'd like to take a look at the area tonight, if I can. Maybe you can get someone else to show me round so you can catch up on your sleep.'

Carol shook her head. 'No. If we can get through here by five, I'll go home and grab a few hours' shut-eye. I'll pick you up around midnight and we can go then. Is that OK?' she asked, belatedly.

'Perfect,' Tony said, getting to his feet and retreating behind his desk. 'As long as you don't mind.' He picked up the photographs and forced himself back behind Handy Andy's eyes. 'He's made a real mess of this one, hasn't he?'

'Paul's the only one who's been beaten up like this. Gareth has cuts to his face, but nothing as extreme. Paul's face has been smashed to a pulp – broken nose, broken teeth, broken cheekbone, dislocated jaw. The anal injuries are horrendous as well; he's been partially disembowelled. The degree of violence is one of the reasons why the Super felt we were looking at a different perpetrator. Also, none of his limbs are dislocated, unlike the other three.'

'This is the one the papers said was covered up with bin bags?'

Carol nodded. 'Same variety as the scraps found under Adam's body.'

They moved on to Gareth Finnegan. 'I'm going to have to give some serious thought to this one,' he said. 'He's changed his pattern in at least two significant ways. First, the dumping ground moves from Temple Fields to Carlton Park. It's still a gay cruising area, but it's an aberration.' He stopped himself short and gave a hollow laugh. 'Listen to me. As if his whole behaviour isn't wildly aberrant. The second thing is his letter and video to the *Sentinel Times*. Why did he decide to announce this body and none of the others?'

'I've been thinking about that,' Carol said. 'And I wondered if it had something to do with the fact that it could have lain there for days, even weeks, otherwise.'

Tony made a note on his pad and gave her the thumbs-up sign with the other hand. 'These wounds to the hands and feet. I know it sounds off the wall, but it almost looks like he was crucified.'

'The pathologist wasn't crazy about going on the record with that one either. But the hand wounds, coupled with the dislocation of both shoulders, makes crucifixion a conclusion that's hard to resist, especially when you remember this probably happened on Christmas Day.' Carol got to her feet, rubbing the sleep out of her eyes. She couldn't manage to stifle a jaw-cracking yawn. She paced round the small office, shrugging her shoulders to loosen the taut muscles. 'Sick bastard,' she muttered.

'The genital mutilations are getting more severe,' Toby observed. 'He's virtually castrated this one. And the fatal wounds, the cutting of the throat. That's getting deeper too.'

'Does that tell us anything?' Carol asked, almost unintelligible through another yawn.

'Like your pathologist, I'm reluctant to speculate just yet,' Tony said. He moved on to the final set of pictures. For the first time, Carol saw his professional mask slip. Horror swept across Tony's face, widening his eyes, drawing his lips back in a hissed intake of breath. She wasn't surprised. When they'd turned Damien Connolly over, a six-foot rugby-playing detective had keeled over in a dead faint. Even the experienced police pathologist had turned away momentarily, visibly struggling not to be sick.

Rigor mortis had frozen Damien Connolly's limbs in a parody of human gesture. The dislocated joints stuck out at crazy angles. But there was more, and worse. His penis had been severed and thrust into his mouth. His torso was branded from chest to groin in a bizarre, random pattering of starburst burns, none more than half an inch across.

'Dear God,' Tony breathed.

'He's really getting the hang of this, isn't he?' Carol said bitterly. 'Takes a pride in his work, doesn't he?'

Tony said nothing, forcing himself to study the appalling photographs as closely as he'd done with the previous sets. 'Carol,' he eventually said. 'Has anybody come up with any theories as to what he's used to make these burn marks?'

'Not a one,' she said.

'They're odd,' he said. 'The patterns vary. It's not like he's used some random object and kept on using it. There are at least five different shapes. Have you got anybody who can do computer pattern analysis? To see if there's any hidden message here? There must be dozens of these bloody burns!'

Carol rubbed her eyes again. 'I don't know. Me and computers are about as compatible as the Prince and Princess of Wales. I'll ask when I go back to the office. And if we don't have someone, I'll ask my brother.'

'Your brother?'

'Michael's a computer genius. He works in games software development. You want a pattern analysed, manipulated, turned into a shoot-'em-up arcade game, he's your man.'

'And he can keep his mouth shut?'

'If he couldn't, he wouldn't be doing the job he does. Millions of pounds depend on his company getting on the next rung of the ladder before anybody else. Believe me, he knows when to button his lip.'

Tony smiled. 'I didn't mean to sound offensive.'

'You didn't.'

Tony sighed. 'I wish to God I'd been brought in sooner on this. Handy Andy's not going to stop here. He's too much in love with his work. Look at these pictures. This bastard's going to carry on capturing and torturing and killing until you catch him. Carol, this guy's a career killer.'

I walked boldly up the path and pressed Adam's doorbell.
In the seconds before he answered the chime, I composed
my face into what I believed was an apologetic smile. I
could see the fuzzy outline of his head and shoulders as he
walked down the hall. Then the door opened and we were
face to face. He half smiled quizzically. As if he'd never
noticed me before in his life.

'I'm sorry to bother you,' I said. 'Only my car's broken
down, and I don't know where there's a pay phone, so I
wondered if I might use your phone to call the AA? I'll
pay for the call, of course . . .' I let my voice trail away.

His smile broadened and relaxed, his dark eyes crinkling
at the corners. 'No problem. Come in.' He stepped back
and I moved inside the door. He gestured down the hall.
'There's a phone in the study. Just on the right there.'

I moved slowly down the hall, ears alert for the sound
of the front door closing behind me. As the lock snapped
back into place, he added, 'There's nothing worse, is there?'

'I'll just look up the number,' I said, pausing in the
doorway to reach in my backpack. Adam kept on walking,
so that when I pulled out the Mace spray, he was only a
couple of feet away from me. It couldn't have been more
perfect. I let him have it full in the face.

He roared in pain and stumbled back against the wall,
hands clawing at his face. I moved in swiftly. One foot
between his ankles, hands on his shoulders, a quick twist

and down he went, face crushed into the carpet, gasping for breath. I was down on top of him in seconds, gripping one wrist and twisting his arm up his back while I snapped the handcuff over it. He was struggling against me by now, tears streaming down his face, but I managed to grab his other flailing arm and snap the other half of the cuffs on it.

His legs were thrashing under me, but my weight was enough to keep him pinned to the floor while I took a ziplock plastic bag from my backpack. I opened it, extracted a pad soaked in chloroform and clamped it over his nose and mouth. The sickly odour drifted upwards into my nostrils, making me feel slightly light-headed and queasy. I hoped the chloroform hadn't gone off; I'd had the bottle for a couple of years, ever since I'd stolen it from the dispensary on a Soviet ship where I'd spent the night with the first officer.

Adam struggled even harder when he felt the cold compress cut off his access to the air, but within minutes his legs stopped their pointless thrashing. I waited a little longer, just to be on the safe side, then I rolled off and fastened his legs together with surgical tape. I returned the chloroform pad to its secure bag, then I taped Adam's mouth shut.

I stood up and took a deep breath. So far, so good. Next, I pulled on a pair of latex gloves and took stock. I am familiar with the theory of the French forensic scientist Edmond Locard, first demonstrated in a murder trial in 1912, that every contact leaves a trace; a criminal will always take something away from the scene of his crime and leave something behind. With this in mind, I had carefully chosen my wardrobe for today. I was wearing Levi 501s, the same brand I'd seen Adam wear often. I'd topped it with a baggy V-necked cricket sweater, the exact double of one I'd watched him buy in Marks and Spencer a couple of weeks before. Any stray fibres I left behind would inevi-

tably be ascribed to the contents of Adam's own wardrobe.

I took a quick look round the study, pausing by his answering machine. It was one of the old-fashioned ones, with a single cassette tape. I opened the machine and helped myself to the tape. It would be nice to have a memory of his voice sounding normal; I knew that the soundtrack on the video wouldn't have that same relaxed quality.

The door to the garage was locked. I headed off up the stairs, where I found the jacket of his suit tossed over the back of a chair in the kitchen diner. The bunch of keys was in the left-hand pocket. Back downstairs, I opened the garage door and unlocked the hatchback of his two-year-old Ford Escort. Then I went back for Adam. He had, of course, come round. His eyes were filled with panic, muffled grunts came from behind the gag. I smiled down at him as I pressed the chloroform pad over his nose again. This time, of course, he couldn't struggle effectively at all.

I pulled him into a sitting position, then brought a chair through from the study. I managed to get him on to the chair, and from there I was able to sling him over my shoulder and stagger through into the garage. I dumped him in the luggage space, and slammed the tailgate shut. Not a trace of his body was visible.

I checked my watch. Just after six. It would be another hour till it was dark enough to be certain none of the neighbours passing casually would notice a stranger driving out of Adam's garage. I filled the time by browsing through his life. Packets of photographs revealed friends, a family Christmas dinner. I would have fitted into this life perfectly. We could have had it all, if he hadn't been such a fool.

I was startled out of my reverie by the phone. I let it ring, and went through to the kitchen. I helped myself to a bottle of creme cleanser and a cloth and carefully washed down all the paintwork in the hall. I put the used cloth in my backpack, then fetched the vacuum cleaner. I went over the entire hall slowly and carefully, erasing all traces of the struggle from the hard-wearing Berber carpet. I trailed the vac behind me, right into the garage, where I left it in a corner, looking as if it had always lived there. Satisfied I'd removed all traces of me, I climbed into Adam's car, pressed the remote-control button on his key-ring and started the engine as the garage door rose smoothly before me.

I shut the door behind me, and drove off. I could hear muffled noises from the back of the car. I raked around in the glove box till I found a Wet, Wet, Wet cassette. I shoved it into the player and turned the volume up high. I sang along with the music as I drove out of the city and on to the moors.

I'd been worried that Adam's car might not make it all the way up the track, and I'd been right. About half a mile from home, the road became too overgrown and rutted. With a sigh, I got out and walked up to collect the wheel-barrow. When I opened the tailgate to tip him into the barrow, his eyes were wide and staring. His muffled calls were wasted on me, however. I dragged him unceremoniously out of the car and into the barrow. It was a hard half-mile up the track, since his constant struggling made steering more difficult. Luckily, Auntie Doris had had the foresight to buy a proper builder's barrow, one with two wheels in front.

When we reached the farmhouse, I opened the trapdoor. The cellar below looked dark and welcoming. Adam's eyes widened in terror. I stroked his soft hair and said, 'Welcome to the pleasure dome.'

5

As to ... the mob of newspaper readers, they are pleased
with anything, provided it is bloody enough. But the mind
of sensibility requires something more.

After he'd seen Carol to her car, Tony walked across the
campus to the general stores and bought a copy of the
evening paper. If publicity was what Handy Andy craved,
he'd finally achieved it. Fear and loathing stalked the pages
of the *Bradfield Evening Sentinel Times*. Five of them, to
be precise. Pages 1, 2, 3, 24 and 25, plus an editorial, were
devoted to the Queer Killer. If the nickname was anything
to judge by, the police were already leaking like a Cabinet
committee.

'You're not going to like being called the Queer Killer,
are you, Andy?' Tony said softly to himself as he walked
back to his office. Back behind his desk, he studied the
paper. Penny Burgess had had a field day. The front page
screamed, QUEER KILLER STRIKES AGAIN! in banner headlines. In smaller headline type, readers were told, POLICE
ADMIT SERIAL KILLER STALKS CITY. Beneath was a lurid
account of the discovery of Damien Connolly's body, and
a photograph of him at his passing-out parade. The turnover on pages two and three was a sensationalist summary
of the three previous cases, complete with sketch map.
'Bricks without straw, right enough,' Tony said to himself
as he flicked through to the centre spread. GAYS TERRIFIED
BY QUEER KILLER MONSTER left the reader in no doubt who
the *Sentinel Times* had decided were at risk. The copy

focused on the supposed hysteria gripping Bradfield's gay community, complete with interior shots of cafés, bars and clubs that made the scene look seedy enough to pander to the readers' prejudices.

'Oh boy,' Tony said. 'You're really going to hate this, Andy.' He turned back to the editorial.

'At last,' he read, 'police have admitted what many of us have believed for some time. There is a serial killer on the loose in Bradfield, his target the young, single men who frequent the city's sordid gay bars.

'It's a disgrace that the police have not warned the city's homosexuals to be on their guard before now. In the twilight world of anonymous pick-ups and casual sex, it cannot be difficult for this predatory monster to find willing victims. The police's silence can only have made it easier for the killer.

'Their reluctance to speak out has probably increased the gay community's existing suspicion of the police, making them fear that the authorities value the lives of gay men less than those of other members of the community.

'Just as it took the murders of "innocent" women rather than prostitutes to make the police pay full attention to the Yorkshire Ripper, it is wrong that a police officer has had to be murdered before Bradfield Metropolitan Police takes this Queer Killer seriously.

'In spite of this, we urge the gay community to cooperate fully with the police. And we demand that the police investigate these horrific killings diligently and with compassion for the concerns of Bradfield's homosexuals. The sooner this vicious killer is caught, the safer we all will be.'

'The usual mixture of self-righteousness, indignation and unrealistic demands,' Tony said to the Devil's Ivy on his windowsill. He clipped the articles and spread them across the desk. He switched on his micro-cassette recorder and spoke.

'*Bradfield Evening Sentinel Times*, February 27th. At last, Handy Andy has made the big time. I'm wondering how important that is to him. One of the tenets of profiling serial offenders is that they crave the oxygen of publicity. But this time, I'm not so sure he's too bothered about that. There were no messages after the first two killings, neither of which received that much publicity after the initial discovery of the bodies. And although there was a message directing the police to the third body via a newspaper, that note made no claims about the earlier killings. I had puzzled over that until Inspector Carol Jordan offered an alternative explanation for the note and accompanying video, namely that without direction, the body may have lain undiscovered for some time. So, while Handy Andy may not be obsessive about creating headlines and panic, it's clear he wants the bodies found while they are still recognizably his work.' He switched off the cassette with a sigh. Although he'd turned his back on the academic circus years before, he couldn't escape his training; every stage of the process had to be on record. The prospect of this investigation providing the raw material for articles or even a book was something Tony found hard to resist.

'I'm a cannibal,' he said to the plant. 'Sometimes I disgust myself.' He shovelled the clippings together and tucked them into his press-cuttings folder. He opened the boxes and took out the stacks of document wallets they contained. Carol had labelled them all neatly. Fluent capitals, Tony noted. A woman comfortable with the written word.

Each victim had a pathology report and a preliminary forensic report. The witness statements were divided into three groups: Background (victim), Witness (scene of crime) and Miscellaneous. Selecting the Background (victim) files, he walked his wheeled chair across to the table where his personal computer stood. When he'd arrived at Bradfield, the university had offered him a terminal linked into their network. He'd declined, not wanting to waste time learning a new set of protocols when he was perfectly at home with his own PC. Now, he was glad he didn't have to add data security to the list of worries that kept him awake at nights.

Tony called up the customized software that would allow him to make comparisons between the victims, and started the long slog of inputting the data.

Five minutes in the Scargill Street station was enough to make Carol wish she'd gone straight home. To get to the office she'd been allocated for the duration of the investigation, she had to walk the length of the main squad room. Copies of the evening paper were strewn over half the desks, mocking her with their thick black headlines. Bob Stansfield was standing with a couple of DCs halfway down the room and he called to her as she passed. 'The good doctor knocked off already, has he?'

'From what I've seen of the good doctor, Bob, he could give some of our bosses a few lessons in working overtime,' Carol said, wishing she could think of some sharper put-down. Doubtless it would come to her hours later in the shower. On the other hand, maybe it was as well she hadn't come up with something too devastating. Better not alienate the lads any more than her assignment had already done. She stopped and smiled. 'Anything new?' she asked.

Stansfield detached himself from his juniors, saying, 'Right, lads, get on with it.' He moved over to Carol's side and said, 'Not as such. The HOLMES team are working flat out, smacking all we've got so far into the computer, see what correlations they can come up with. Cross has ordered us to pull in all the nonces again. He's convinced one of them's our best bet.'

Carol shook her head. 'Waste of time.'

'You said it. This bastard's not got form, I'd put money on it. Kevin's got a team going out tonight to try something a bit different, though,' he added, taking out and lighting his last cigarette. He tossed the packet in a nearby bin, an expression of disgust on his face. 'If we don't get a fucking break soon, I'm going to have to put in for a raise to cover my bloody nicotine consumption.'

'Me, I'm drinking so much coffee I've got a permanent case of the jitterbug boogies,' Carol said ruefully. 'So what's this idea of Kevin's?' Gently does it. First the rapport, then the question. Funny how getting information out of colleagues followed the same rules as interrogating suspects.

'He's got an undercover team going out on the gay scene, concentrating on the clubs and pubs with a reputation for S&M.' Stansfield snorted. 'They've all been down Traffic this avvy, scrounging leather trousers off the bike boys.'

'It's worth a try,' Carol said.

'Yeah, well let's hope Kevin's not sending in a bunch of closet pansies like Damien Connolly turned out to be,' Stansfield said. 'Last thing we want is a bunch of CID fairies ending up wearing their own handcuffs.'

Carol refused to dignify the comment with a reply and moved off towards her office. She'd got her hand on the door when Cross's voice boomed down the room. 'Inspector Jordan? Get your body in here.'

Carol closed her eyes and counted to three. 'Coming, sir,' she said cheerfully, turning back and walking the length of the room to Cross's temporary office. He'd only been in there a day, but already he'd marked it like a tomcat spraying his territory. The room reeked of cigarette smoke. Half-drunk polystyrene cups of coffee strategically placed on window ledge and desk top had butts floating in them. There was even a girlie calendar on the wall, proof that sexism was alive and well and working in the advertising industry. Hadn't they realized *yet* that it was the women who stood in the supermarkets deciding which brand of vodka to buy?

Leaving the door open in a bid for air, Carol walked into Cross's office and said, 'Sir?'

'What's Wonder Boy come up with then?'

'It's a bit early for conclusions, sir,' she said brightly. 'He's got to read through all the reports I copied for him.'

Cross grunted. 'Oh aye, I forgot he's a bloody professor.' He spat the word out sarcastically. 'Everything in writing, eh? Kevin's got some more stuff on the Connolly business; you'll have to catch up with him. Was there anything else, Inspector?' he asked belligerently, as if she were the one who had imposed herself on him.

'Dr Hill has a suggestion, sir. About the burn marks on PC Connolly's body. He wondered if there was anyone on the HOLMES team who could do statistical pattern analysis.'

'What the bloody hell is statistical pattern analysis?' Cross said, dumping the end of his cigarette into a coffee cup.

'I think it means –'

'Never mind, never mind,' Cross interrupted. 'Go and see if anybody down there knows what the hell you're on about.'

'Yes, sir. Oh, and sir? If we can't do it here, my brother works in computers. I'm sure he could do it for us.'

Cross stared at her, his expression unreadable for once. When he spoke, he was all affability. 'Fine. Go ahead. Mr Brandon gave you carte blanche, after all.'

So that's what a passing buck sounds like, Carol thought as she headed downstairs to the HOLMES room. A five-minute conversation with a harassed Inspector Dave Woolcott confirmed what she'd already suspected. The HOLMES team had neither the software nor the expertise to carry out the analysis Tony wanted. As Carol walked down to the canteen in search of Kevin Matthews, she hoped Michael could deliver in complete confidence. Keeping quiet about technological developments was very different from resisting the urge to gossip about a high-profile murder enquiry. If he let her down, she could kiss goodbye to a future outside Personnel.

Kevin was hunched alone over a cup of coffee, a plate with the remains of a fry-up next to him. Carol pulled out the chair opposite him. 'Mind if I join you?'

'Be my guest,' Kevin said. He looked up and gave her the ghost of a grin, pushing his unruly ginger curls back from his forehead. 'How's it going?'

'Probably a lot easier than it is for you and Bob.'

'What's this Home Office boffin like, then?'

Carol considered for a moment. 'He's cautious. He's quick, he's sharp, but he's not a know-all, and he doesn't seem to want to tell us how to do our job. It's really interesting watching him work. He looks at things from a different perspective.'

'How do you mean?' Kevin asked, looking genuinely interested.

'When we look at a crime, we look for physical clues, leads, things that point us to who we might want to talk to or where we might want to look. When *he* looks at a crime, he's not interested in all that stuff. He wants to know why the physical clues happened the way they did so he can work out who did it. It's as if we use information to move us forward and he uses it to move him backwards. Does that make sense?'

Kevin frowned. 'I think so. You think he's got what it takes?'

Carol shrugged. 'It's early days yet. But yeah, on first impressions, I'd say he's got something to offer.'

Kevin grinned. 'Something to offer the investigation or something to offer you?'

'Piss off, Kevin,' Carol said, tired of the innuendo that

followed her round the job. 'Unlike some, I never shit on my own doorstep.'

Kevin looked momentarily uneasy. 'Only joking, Carol, honest.'

'Jokes are supposed to be funny.'

'OK, OK, sorry. What's he like to work with, though? Nice bloke, or what?'

Carol spoke slowly, measuring her words. 'Considering he spends his working life getting inside the minds of psychopaths, he seems pretty normal. There's something quite ... closed off about him. He keeps his distance. Doesn't give much away. But he treats me like an equal, not like some thick plod. He's on our side, Kevin, and that's the main thing. I'd guess he's one of those workaholics who's more interested in getting the job done than anything else. And speaking of getting the job done, Popeye says you've turned something up on PC Connolly?'

Kevin sighed. 'For what it's worth. One of the neighbours came home from work at ten to six. She knows the time because the shipping forecast had just started on the car radio. Connolly was on his drive, closing the bonnet of his car. He had overalls on. The neighbour says he must have been working on the car, he was always at it. By the time the neighbour got out of her car and into the house, Damien was reversing his car into the garage. The same neighbour came out about an hour later on her way to a game of squash, and she noticed Connolly's car parked on the street. She was a bit surprised, because he never left the car sitting out, especially after dark. She also noticed that the light was on in Connolly's garage. And that's about the size of it.'

'Is it an integral garage?' Carol asked.

'No, but it's attached to the house, and there's a door from the garage leads into the kitchen.'

'So it looks like he was snatched from the house?'

Kevin shrugged. 'Who knows? There's no sign of a

struggle. I spoke to one of the SOCOs who turned the place over, and he said not to hold our breath.'

'Sounds just like the first two.'

'That's what Bob says.' Kevin pushed his chair back. 'I better get weaving. We're going out on the town tonight.'

'I might bump into you later,' Carol said. 'Dr Hill wants a tour of the crime scenes at the sort of time when the bodies were dumped.'

Kevin got to his feet. 'Just don't let him talk to any strange men.'

Tony took the plastic container of lasagne out of the microwave and sat down at the breakfast bar in his kitchen. He'd input all the data that he could find on the four victims, then he'd transferred the files to a floppy disk so he could work on it at home while he waited for Carol to arrive. As soon as he'd reached the tram stop, he'd realized he was ravenous. Then he remembered he'd eaten nothing since his breakfast cereal. He'd been working with such concentration, he hadn't even noticed. He found the hunger curiously satisfactory. It meant he was too involved in what he was doing to be conscious of himself. He knew from long experience that his best work came when he lost self-consciousness, when he could immerse himself in the patterns of another human being, locked into that other's idiosyncratic logic, in tune with a different set of emotions.

He attacked the food with gusto, shovelling it down as quickly as possible so he could get to his computer and carry on with his victim profiles. There were still a couple of forkfuls left in the dish when the phone rang. With no pause for thought, Tony snatched up the phone. 'Hello?' he said cheerfully.

'Anthony,' the voice said. Tony dropped the fork, tipping the pasta out on the worktop.

'Angelica,' he said. He was back in his own world, anchored within his own head at the sound of her voice.

'Feeling more sociable today?' the sweet huskiness asked.

'I wasn't feeling anti-social yesterday. I just had things to do I couldn't ignore. And you distract me,' Tony said, wondering why he bothered to justify himself to her.

'That's the general plan,' she said. 'But I missed you, Anthony. I was so horny for you, and when you discarded me like an old sock, all my pleasure in the day was over.'

'Why do you do this with me?' he demanded. It was a question he'd asked before, but she had always deflected him.

'Because you deserve me,' the voice said. 'Because I want you more than anyone in the world. And because you don't have anyone else in your life to make you happy.'

It was the same old story. Cut off the question with some flannel. But tonight, Tony wanted answers, not flattery. 'What makes you think that?' he asked.

The voice chuckled softly. 'I know more about you than you can possibly dream. Anthony, you don't have to be alone any more.'

'What if I like being alone? Isn't it fair to assume that I'm alone because I want to be?'

'You don't look like a happy boy to me. Some days, you look like you need a hug more than anything in the world. Some days, you look like you haven't slept for more than a couple of hours. Anthony, I can bring you peace. Women have hurt you before, we both know that. But I won't. I can stop it hurting. I can make you sleep like a baby, you know that. All I want is to make you happy.' The voice was soothing, gentle.

Tony sighed. If only . . . 'I find that hard to believe,' he stalled. Right from the start of these conversations, part of him had wanted to slam the phone down on this exquisite torture. But the scientist in him wanted to hear what she had to say. And the damaged man inside had enough self-awareness to know he needed to be cured, and that this might just be the way. He reminded himself of his earlier resolve not to let her get under his skin, so that when the time came, he could walk away without pain.

'But you let me try.' The voice was so self-assured. She was confident of her power over him.

'I listen, don't I? I join in. I haven't put the phone down yet,' he said, forcing artificial warmth into his voice.

'Why don't you do just that? Why don't you put down this phone and go upstairs to your bedroom and pick up the extension there? So we can be comfortable?'

A cold stab of fear hit Tony in the chest. He struggled to frame the question professionally. Not, 'How do you know that?', but, 'What makes you think I've got a phone in the bedroom?'

There was a pause, so brief that Tony couldn't be certain he wasn't imagining it. 'Just guessing,' she said. 'I've got you sussed. You're the kind of man who has a phone by the bed.'

'Well guessed,' Tony said. 'OK. I'm going to put the phone down and I'll pick up in the bedroom.' He replaced the receiver and hurried through to his study, where he switched the answering machine over to 'record' mode. Then he picked up the phone again. 'Hello? I'm back,' he said.

'Are we sitting comfortably? Then I'll begin.' Again that low, sexy chuckle. 'We are going to have some real fun tonight. Wait till you hear what I've got lined up for you tonight. Oh, Anthony,' she said, her voice dropping almost to a whisper. 'I've been dreaming about you. Imagining your hands on my body, running your fingers over my skin.'

'What are you wearing?' Tony asked. It was, he knew, the standard question.

'What would you like me to be wearing? I have an extensive wardrobe.'

Tony bit back the crazy urge to say, 'Fishermen's waders,

a tutu and a rainmate.' He swallowed hard and said, 'Silk. You know how I like the feel of silk.'

'That's why you love my skin. I take a lot of trouble to keep myself in perfect condition. But just for you, I've covered some of my skin with silk. I'm wearing a pair of black silk French knickers and a sheer black silk camisole. Oh, I love the feeling of silk against my body. Oh, Anthony,' she groaned. 'The silk's rubbing against my nipples, gently, like your fingers would. Oh, my nipples are hard as rocks, sticking up, inflamed with you.'

In spite of himself, Tony began to feel the stirrings of interest. She was good, no two ways about it. Most of the women he'd heard on the chatlines had sounded stale and bored, their responses predictable and stereotypical. Nothing in their conversations had aroused anything other than scientific interest in him. But Angelica was different. For one thing, she sounded like she meant it.

She moaned softly. 'God, I'm wet,' she breathed. 'But you can't touch me yet, you've got to wait. Just lie back, that's a good boy. Oh, I love to undress you. I've got my hands under your shirt, my fingers are running over your chest, stroking you, touching you, feeling your nipples under my fingers. God, you're wonderful,' she sighed.

'That's nice,' Tony said, enjoying the caress of her voice.

'That's just the beginning. Now I'm straddling you, unbuttoning your shirt. I'm leaning over you, my nipples inside the silk brushing against your chest. Oh, Anthony!' her voice exclaimed in pleasure. 'You really are pleased to see me, aren't you? You're hard as a rock underneath me. Oh, I can't wait to get you inside me.'

Her words froze Tony. The erection he'd felt hardening inside his trousers died like a snowflake in a puddle. They were there again. 'I think I'm going to disappoint you,' he said, his voice cracking.

That sexy chuckle again. 'No way. You're already more

than I dreamed. Oh, Anthony, touch me. Tell me what you want to do to me.'

Tony could find no words.

'Don't be shy, Anthony. There are no secrets between us, nowhere we can't go. Close your eyes, let the feelings flow. Touch my breasts, go on, suck my nipples, eat me, let me feel your hot wet mouth all over me.'

Tony groaned. This was almost more than he could bear, even in the interests of science.

Angelica's voice was more breathy now, as if her words were arousing her as much as they should have been arousing him. 'That's right, oh God, Anthony, that's wonderful. Oh-oh-oh,' she said in a shuddering moan. 'See, I told you I was wet. That's right, plunge your fingers deep into my cunt. Oh God, you're the best ... Let me ... let me, oh God, let me get at you.'

Tony heard the sound of a zipper down the phone line. 'Angelica ...' he started to say. It was falling apart again, just as it always did, spiralling out of control like a wounded bird.

'Oh, Anthony, you're beautiful. That's the most beautiful cock I've ever seen. Oh, let me taste you ...' Her voice tailed off with the sound of sucking.

The blood rushed to Tony's face in a sudden wave of shame and anger. He slammed the phone down and immediately took it off the hook again. Jesus, what kind of a man couldn't even get it up over the phone? And what kind of scientist couldn't divorce his own pathetic failings from the exercise of objective data collection?

The worst of it was, he recognized his own behaviour. How many times had he sat across the table from a multiple rapist, arsonist or killer and watched them reach the point in their reliving of events where they could no longer face themselves. Just like him, they closed down. They couldn't disconnect a phone, but they closed down just the same. Eventually, of course, with the right therapy, they breached the walls and managed to confront what had brought them there. That was the first step towards recovery. Part of Tony prayed that Angelica knew enough about the theory and practice of psychology to stick with him till he too could break down the barriers and stare into the face of whatever it was that had bred this sexual and emotional cripple.

But the other part of him hoped she'd never call again. Never mind 'no pain, no gain'. He just wanted no pain.

John Brandon scrupulously wiped his plate with the last piece of nan bread and smiled at his wife. 'That was great, Maggie,' he said.

'Mmm,' his son Andy agreed through a mouthful of lamb and aubergine curry.

Brandon shifted awkwardly in his chair. 'If it's all right with you, I think I'll pop back down to Scargill Street for an hour. Just to see how things are going.'

'I thought ranking officers like you didn't have to work evenings,' Maggie said good-humouredly. 'I thought you said the troops didn't need you breathing down their necks?'

Brandon looked sheepish. 'I know. But I just want to see how the lads are going on.'

Maggie shook her head, a resigned smile on her face. 'I'd rather you went down and got it out of your system than you sat all night fidgeting in front of the telly.'

Karen perked up. 'Dad, if you're going back into town, can you drop me at Laura's? So we can work on our history project?'

Andy snorted. 'Work on how you're going to get off with Craig McDonald, more like.'

'You know nothing,' Karen huffed. 'Will you, Dad?'

Brandon got up from the table. 'Only if you're ready now. And I'll pick you up on my way back.'

'Oh, Dad,' Karen complained. 'You said you were only

going to be gone an hour. That's not nearly long enough for us to do all we want to.'

It was Maggie Brandon's turn to snort with laughter. 'If your father's back before half past nine, I'll make Scotch pancakes for supper.'

Karen looked at each parent in turn, the anguish of choice written on her fourteen-year-old face. 'Dad?' she said. 'Can you pick me up by nine o'clock?'

Brandon grinned. 'Why do I feel like I've been stitched up?'

It was just after half past seven when Brandon arrived in the HOLMES room. Even that late, every terminal was occupied. The sound of fingers hitting keyboards clicked away under the quiet conversations taking place at a few of the desks. Inspector Dave Woolcott sat beside one of the collators, who was pointing out some detail on the screen. No one looked up when Brandon entered.

He walked over behind Woolcott and waited till he had finished talking to the constable on the terminal. Brandon suppressed a sigh. It was definitely time he started thinking about retirement. It wasn't just the bobbies that looked young to him now; even the inspectors didn't look old enough to be out of probationer's cap bands. 'Keep trying for a match, Harry, cross-ref with the CROs,' he heard Woolcott say. The lad on the keyboard nodded and stared into his screen.

''Evening, Dave,' Brandon said.

Woolcott swung round in his chair. Registering who the newcomer was, he got to his feet. ''Evening, sir.'

'I was on my way home, and I thought I'd swing by and see how you were doing,' Brandon lied smoothly.

'Well, sir, it's early days. We'll have teams working round the clock for the next couple of days, feeding in all the statement details from the earlier cases as well as PC Connolly's. I'm also liaising with the team manning the hot-line phones. Most of it's the usual spite, vengeance and paranoia, but Sergeant Lascelles is doing a good job of prioritizing the messages.'

'Anything coming out yet?'

Woolcott rubbed his bald spot in the reflex gesture which his second wife claimed had caused the problem in the first place. 'Bits and pieces. We've got a few names of blokes who were out and about in Temple Fields on at least two of the nights in question, and those are being actioned. We've also been hammering the PNC with car index numbers that have shown up regularly around the times of the killings. Luckily, ever since the second killing, Inspector Jordan's had somebody clocking car numbers round the gay village. It's a long job, sir, but we'll get there.'

If he's in there, Brandon thought. It was he who had been adamant that this was a case for the HOLMES team. But this killer was unlike any he'd seen or read about. This killer was careful.

Brandon didn't know much about computers. But one adage had stuck: garbage in, garbage out. He hoped fervently that he hadn't given his men a job that should have gone to the Cleansing Department.

Carol's eyes snapped open, heart pounding. In her dream, a heavy cell door had slammed shut, leaving her a prisoner of cold, sweating windowless walls. Still groggy from sleep, it took her a moment to realize that the familiar weight of Nelson's body wasn't lying across her feet. She heard footsteps, the rattle of keys being thrown on a table. A narrow sliver of light spilled through the few inches of open door Nelson required for his comings and goings. She rolled over with a groan and grabbed the clock. Ten past ten. Robbed of twenty minutes' precious sleep by Michael's noisy return.

Carol stumbled out of bed and pulled on her heavy towelling bathrobe. She opened her bedroom door and walked into the enormous room that made up most of the third-floor flat she shared with her brother. Half a dozen floor-mounted up-lights of different heights cast a warm and elegant glow on the room. Nelson appeared from the kitchen doorway, bouncing lightly on the stripped-wood flooring. Then he crouched and, in a leap that seemed to defy gravity, bounded into the air, touching briefly on a tall thin speaker before landing delicately on top of a blond wood bookcase. From there, he stared superciliously across the room at Carol, as if to say, 'I bet you can't do that.'

The room was about forty feet by twenty-five. At one end, a group of three two-seater sofas covered with quilted throws surrounded a low coffee table. At the opposite end stood a dining table with six chairs in the style of Rennie Mackintosh. Near the sofas was a TV and video on a black trolley. About half of the back wall was occupied by shelves crammed with books, videos and CDs.

The walls were painted a cool dove-grey, except for the far wall, which was exposed brickwork, with five high arched windows looking out over the city. Carol walked across the room till she could just see the edge of the black ribbon of the Duke of Waterford canal below. The city lights glittered like a cheap jeweller's window. 'Michael?' she called.

Her brother stuck his head out of the narrow galley kitchen, looking surprised. 'I didn't realize you were home,' he said. 'Did I wake you?'

'I was getting up soon anyway. I've got to go back to work. I was just grabbing a few hours,' she said resignedly. 'Is the kettle on?' She walked across to the kitchen and perched on a high stool while Michael made tea and carried on building himself a sandwich with ciabatta, beef tomatoes, black olives, spring onions and tuna.

'Eat?' he asked.

'I could handle one of those,' Carol admitted. 'How was London?'

Michael shrugged. 'You know. They like what we're doing, but could we have it finished yesterday.'

Carol pulled a face. 'Sounds just like the *Sentinel Times*'s editorials about the serial killer. What exactly is it you're doing at the moment anyway? Is it explainable in words of one syllable to a techno-illiterate?'

Michael grinned. 'The next big thing is going to be computer adventure games with the same quality as videos. You film real stuff and digitize it and manipulate it to produce gameplay that's as real as a movie. So we're on to the next, next big thing. Imagine you're playing a computer adventure, but all the characters are people you know. You're the hero, but not just in your imagination.'

'You've lost me now,' Carol said.

'OK. When you install the game on your computer, you'll plug in a scanner and scan photographs of yourself and anybody else you want in your game. The computer reads that information, and translates it into screen images. So instead of Conan the Barbarian leading the quest, it's Carol Jordan. You can import pics of your best friends or your lust objects to be your companions in the game. Anybody you don't like, you turn into the baddies. So, you could have an adventure with Mel Gibson, Dennis Quaid and Martin Amis, and fight enemies like Saddam Hussein, Margaret Thatcher and Popeye,' Michael explained enthusiastically as he stuffed the ingredients into the bread. He dumped the sandwiches on plates and together they walked back into the living room and sat staring out over the canal as they ate.

'Clear?' he asked.

'As it needs to be,' Carol said. 'So once you've got this software up and running, presumably you could use it to put people in compromising positions? Like blue movies?'

Michael frowned. 'Theoretically. Your average computer nerd wouldn't even know where to begin. You'd need to know what you were doing and you'd also need seriously expensive hardware to get decent quality stills or videos off your computer.'

'Thank God for that,' Carol said, with feeling. 'I was beginning to think you were creating a Frankenstein's monster for blackmailers and tabloid journalists.'

'No chance,' he said. 'Anyway, close analysis would show it up. So what about you? How's your quest coming along?'

Carol shrugged. 'I could do with a few superheroes to help out, to be honest.'

'What's this profiler like? He going to shake things up a bit?'

'Tony Hill? He already has. Popeye's going around with a face like a melted wellie. But I'm hopeful we might get something constructive out of him. I've had one session with him already, and he's bursting with ideas. He's a nice guy as well, no hassle to work with.'

Michael grinned. 'That must be a refreshing change.'

'You're not kidding.'

'And is he your type?'

Carol pulled a piece of crust off her bread and threw it at Michael. 'God, you're as bad as the sexist pigs I work with. I haven't got a type, and even if I did and Tony Hill was it, you know I won't mix work with pleasure.'

'Given the fact that you work all hours and spend all your spare time asleep, I guess you're looking at a lifetime of celibacy,' Michael replied drily. 'So is he gorgeous, or what?'

'I hadn't noticed,' Carol said stiffly. 'And I doubt whether he's even noticed I'm female. The man's a workaholic. In fact, he's the reason I'm working again tonight. He wants to see the scenes of crime at around the time the bodies were dumped so he can get a feel for it.'

'Shame you've got to go out again,' Michael said. 'It's ages since we've had a night in with the telly and a few bottles of wine. We see so little of each other just now, we might as well be married.'

Carol smiled ruefully. 'The price of success, eh, bro?'

'I guess so.' Michael got up. 'Oh well, if you're going to work, I might as well do a couple of hours before I sack out.'

'Before you go . . . I need a favour.'

Michael sat down again. 'As long as it doesn't involve doing your ironing.'

'What do you know about statistical pattern analysis?'

Michael frowned. 'Not a lot. I did a little bit when I was doing part-time jobbing work while I was doing my PhD, but I don't know what's state of the art right now. Why? You want something looking at?'

Carol nodded. 'It's a bit grisly, I'm afraid.' She outlined the sadistic injuries to Damien Connolly. 'Tony Hill has an idea they might yield some kind of a message.'

'Sure, I'll have a look for you. I know a bloke who's almost certainly got the latest software in the field. I'm sure he'd let me have some time on his machine to fiddle about with this,' Michael said.

'Not a word to anybody what it's about,' Carol said.

Michael looked offended. 'Of course not. What do you take me for? Listen, I'd rather get on the wrong side of a serial killer than you. I'll keep my mouth shut. Just get the stuff to me tomorrow, and I'll do my best, OK?'

Carol leaned over and rumpled her brother's blond hair. 'Thank you. I appreciate it.'

Michael grabbed her in a quick hug. 'This is seriously weird territory, little sis. Be careful out there, huh? You know I can't afford the mortgage on this place alone.'

'I'm always careful,' Carol said, ignoring the small voice inside her warning not to tempt fate. 'I'm a survivor.'

'I wanted you the first time I saw you,' I said softly. 'I've wanted you for so long.'

Adam's lolling head straightened slightly. I pressed the remote record button on the tripod-mounted video camera. I didn't want to miss a thing. Adam's eyelids, heavy from all that chloroform, struggled open to a slit, then suddenly snapped wide as memory kicked in. His head thrashed from side to side as he tried to see where he was, how he was restrained. As he took in his nakedness, spotted the details of the soft leather wrist and ankle cuffs, and realized that he was fastened to my rack, a moan of what sounded like panic escaped from behind the tape over his mouth.

I stepped out of the shadows behind him and moved into his line of vision, my body oiled and shining in the bright lights. I had stripped down to my underwear, carefully chosen to show off my superb body to its best advantage. When he saw me, his eyes opened even wider. He attempted to speak, but all that came out was a strained mumble.

'But you decided you couldn't allow yourself to want me, didn't you?' I said, my voice hard and accusing. 'You betrayed my love. You didn't have the courage to choose a love that would have exalted us both. No, you ignored your real self and went for a stupid little bimbo, that trashy tart. Don't you realize? I'm the only one in the world who understands, really understands, what you need. I could have given you ecstasy, but you chose the safe, pathetic option. You didn't have the nerve for a marriage of true minds and bodies, did you?'

Drops of sweat were trickling down his temples, in spite of the coolness of the cellar. I moved forward and stroked his body, running my hand over his pale, muscular chest, fluttering my fingers over his groin. He flinched convulsively, his dark-blue eyes pleading. 'How could you betray what I know is in your heart?' I hissed, digging my nails into the soft flesh above the wiry curls of his dark pubic hair. He tensed against me. I thrilled to the sensation. I took my hand away and admired the scarlet half-moons my nails had left in his skin. 'You know you belong to me. You told me. You wanted me, we both know you did.'

Another groan from behind the gag. Now the sweat had spread to his chest, droplets matting the thick dark hair that tapered down his abdomen into a thin line pointing to his cock lying curled and useless as a slug between his legs. Even though it was obvious that he didn't want me, the very sight of his vulnerable nakedness aroused me. He was beautiful. I could feel the blood flowing faster, feel my flesh expanding, ready to take him, ready to explode. I hated myself for that weakness, and I turned away before he could see the effect he was having.

'All I wanted was to love you,' I said quietly. 'I didn't want it to be like this.' My hand strayed to the handle of the rack and caressed the smooth wood. I turned my head and gazed at Adam's beautiful face. Slowly, infinitely slowly, I started to turn the handle. His body, already taut, tightened against the pull of the straps. His effort was wasted. The gears on the winding mechanism multiplied my small exertion till it equalled the strength of several men. Adam was no match for my machine. I could see the muscles of his arms and legs bulge, his chest heaving as he struggled for breath.

'It's not too late,' I said. 'We could still be lovers. Would you like that?'

Desperately, he moved his head. There was no mistaking it, it was a nod. I smiled. 'That's more like it,' I said. 'Now all you have to do is show me you mean it.'

I ran one hand over his damp chest, then rubbed my face against the fine dark hairs. I could smell his fear, taste it in his sweat. I buried my head in his neck, sucking and biting, nibbling his ears. His body stayed rigid, but I felt no trace of an erection beneath me. Frustrated, I pulled away. I leaned over him and, in one swift agonizing movement, I yanked the tape away from his mouth.

'Aagh!' he yelled as the adhesive ripped his skin, rasping on the faint stubble. He licked dry lips. 'Please, let me go,' he whispered.

I shook my head. 'I can't do that, Adam. Maybe if we were really lovers . . .'

'I won't tell anyone,' he croaked. 'I promise.'

'You betrayed me once,' I said sadly. 'How can I trust you now?'

'I'm sorry,' he said. 'I didn't realize . . . I'm sorry.' But there was no penitence in his eyes, only desperation and fear. I'd played this scene so many times in my head. Part of me exulted that I'd predicted the shape of it so well, that the dialogue was almost identical to the scenario I'd conjured up. Part of me felt an inexpressible sadness that he was exactly as weak and faithless as I'd feared. And yet another part of me was almost uncontrollably excited by what lay ahead, whether love or death, or both.

'It's too late for words,' I said. 'It's time for actions. You said you wanted us to be lovers, but that's not what your body's saying. Maybe you're scared. But there's no need to be. I'm a generous person, a loving person. You could find that out for yourself. I'm going to give you one last chance to atone for your betrayal. I'm going to leave you now for a while. When I come back, I expect you to be able to control your fear and show me how you really feel about me.'

I let him go and walked over to the camcorder. I took out the tape that had been recording our encounter and replaced it with a fresh one. At the top of the stairs, I turned back. 'Otherwise, I'll be forced to administer punishment for your treachery.'

'Wait!' he howled desperately as I disappeared from sight. 'Come back,' I heard as I dropped the trapdoor into place. I expect he carried on yelling. But I couldn't hear him. I went upstairs to Auntie Doris and Uncle Henry's bedroom. I slotted the video into the player I'd set up on the chest at the end of the bed, switched on the TV and climbed between the cold cotton sheets. Even if Adam didn't want me, I couldn't escape my desire for him. I watched him on his rack, my hand stroking me, touching myself with all the skill and ingenuity I wanted from him, imagining his beautiful cock swelling in my mouth. Every time I reached the point of orgasm, I stopped, gripping myself tight, forcing myself not to come, to save myself for what lay ahead. After I'd gone through the video for the fourth time, I decided he'd had long enough.

I slipped out of bed and went back downstairs. I looked at him spread-eagled on the rack. 'Please,' he said. 'Let me go. I'll do anything you want, but let me go. I'm begging you.'

I smiled and gently shook my head. 'I will take you back to Bradfield, Adam. But first, it's time to party.'

6

People begin to see that something more goes to the composition of a fine murder than two blockheads to kill and be killed – a knife – a purse – and a dark lane. Design, gentlemen, grouping, light and shade, poetry, sentiment, are now deemed to be indispensable to attempts of this nature.

Work might not solve anything, but it was a great diversionary tactic. Tony stared into the screen, scrolling down through the tabulated information he'd gleaned from the police reports. Satisfied that he'd incorporated everything useful, he switched on the printer. While it chattered and stuttered its way through the print-out, Tony opened another file and started to sketch out the conclusions he had drawn from the raw data. Anything, anything to keep her at bay.

He was so absorbed in his work he barely registered the doorbell's first peal. When it rang out a second time, he looked up, startled, at the clock. Five past eleven. If it was Carol, she was earlier than he'd anticipated. They'd already agreed that there was little point in beginning their trip before midnight. Tony got to his feet, uncertain. Since she knew his phone number, it wouldn't be too hard for Angelica to discover his address too. He arrived at the front door just as the bell rang for the third time. Wishing he'd installed a peephole, Tony cautiously inched the door open.

Carol grinned. 'You look like you're expecting Handy Andy,' she said. When Tony said nothing, she added, 'Sorry

I'm a bit early. I did try ringing, but you were engaged.'

'Sorry,' Tony mumbled. 'I must have accidentally left it off the hook from earlier. Come on in, it's no problem.' He found a smile from somewhere and led Carol into his study. As he reached his desk, he slid the phone back on the hook.

Carol registered that the phone's engaged signal had been no accident. Deduction: he didn't want to be disturbed, not even by the answering machine. Probably, like her, he couldn't resist a ringing phone. She glanced at the sheets of paper sitting on the printer table. 'You've obviously been busy,' she said. 'And there was me thinking you were taking your time answering the door because you'd gone for a quick zizz.'

'Did you get some sleep?' Tony asked, noting that she looked more clear-eyed than she had done earlier.

'Four hours. Which is about ten too few. I've got a couple of bits of information for you, by the way.' She filled him in succinctly on the results of her visit to Scargill Street, leaving out Cross's hostility.

Tony listened carefully, making a couple of notes on his pad. 'Interesting,' he said. 'I don't think there's a lot of point in pulling in the sex offenders again, though. If Handy Andy's got form, it's more likely to be juvenile offences, petty burglary, minor violence, that sort of thing. Still, I've been wrong before.'

'Haven't we all? By the way, I checked with the HOLMES room, and there's no one there who knows anything about statistical pattern analysis, so I've asked my brother to see what he can do for us. Should I just give him a set of the photographs, or is there some other way of presenting the raw data?'

'I suppose there's less chance of a mistake if he works directly from the photographs,' Tony said. 'Thanks for sorting that out for me.'

'No sweat,' Carol said. 'Secretly, I think he's quite

chuffed to be asked. He thinks I don't take him seriously. You know, he writes games software, I do the real thing.'

'And do you?' Tony asked.

'What? Take him seriously? You bet I do. I respect anybody that understands something as far beyond my grasp as computers. Besides, he earns about twice what I do. That has to be serious.'

'I don't know about that. Andrew Lloyd Webber probably earns more in a day than I do in a month, but I still don't take him seriously.' Toby stood up. 'Carol, do you mind if I abandon you for ten minutes? I need a quick shower to wake me up.'

'Fine, feel free. It's me that's early.'

'Thanks. D'you want a brew while you're waiting?'

Carol shook her head. 'I'll pass, thanks. It's cold out there, and there aren't many places a woman can have a pee in Temple Fields in the early hours.'

Almost shyly, Tony picked up the sheaf of a print-out and proffered it to Carol. 'I've started the work on the victims. Maybe you'd like to take a look while I'm gone?'

Eagerly, Carol took the paper. 'I'd love to. I'm fascinated by this whole process.'

'This is just very preliminary,' Tony stressed, backing towards the door. 'I mean, I've not drawn any conclusions yet. I'm working on that.'

'Relax, Tony, I'm on your side,' Carol said as he left the room. She stared after him momentarily, wondering what it was that had unsettled him. By the time they parted in the afternoon, they had built up an easy camaraderie, she'd thought. But now, he was edgy, abstracted. Was it that he was tired, or was it that he was uncomfortable to have her sitting in his home? 'God, does it matter?' she muttered to herself. 'Concentrate, Jordan. Pick the man's brains.' She focused on the first sheet and studied the data.

	Adam S.	Paul G.	Gareth F.	Damien C.
Victim No.	1	2	3	4
Date of crime	6/7.9.93	1/2.11.93	25/26.12.93	20/21.2.94
Bradfield resident?	Yes	Yes	Yes	Yes
Sex	M	M	M	M
Ethnic origin	Caucasian	Caucasian	Caucasian	Caucasian
Nationality	British	British	British	British
Age	28	31	30	27
Star sign	Gemini	Cancer	Scorpio	Capricorn
Height	5'10"	5'11"	5'11"	6'
Weight	147lb	136lb	151lb	160lb
Build	Medium	Slim	Medium	Medium
Musculature	Good	Average	Average	Excellent
Hair length	Abv collar	Collar	Abv collar	Abv collar
Hair colour	Brown	Dark brown	Brown	Reddish brown
Hair type	Wavy	Straight	Straight	Curly
Tattoos	No	No	No	No
Clothing	None	None	None	None
Occupation	Civil servant	University lecturer	Solicitor	Police officer
Place of work	City centre	South of city centre	City centre	Southern suburbs
Car owned	Ford Escort	Citroën AX	Ford Escort	Classic Austin Healey
Hobbies	Working out, angling	Walking	Working out, theatre, cinema	Car restoration
Residence	Modern terraced town house; integral garage	Edwardian terraced house; no garage	Thirties semi; no garage	Modern detached estate house; attached garage
Relationship status	Divorced Lived alone NCP RP	Single Lived alone NCP NRP	Single Lived alone CP NRP	Single Lived alone NCP NRP
Personal items missing?	Wedding ring, watch	Watch	Signet ring, watch	Watch
Items missing from home?	Answering-machine tape	Answering-machine tape	None known	None known

	Hetero	Hetero	Hetero	Not known
Known sexual history	Hetero	Hetero	Hetero	Not known
Last seen by previous acquaintance	Tram home from work, 6 p.m. approx.	Leaving work, 5.30 p.m. approx.	Home, 7.15 p.m.	Home, 6 p.m.
Criminal record	None	None	None	None
Connection to scene of crime	None known	None known	None known	None known
Status of body-recovery site	Urban	Urban	Suburban/rural	Urban
Site of first contact with killer	Unknown	Unknown	Unknown	Unknown
Site of death	Unknown	Unknown	Unknown	Unknown
Disposition of body	Semi-hidden to cause short delay before discovery	Semi-hidden to cause short delay before discovery	Hidden; note to police via newspaper required	Openly displayed but in area unattended until specific time
Body posed?	No	No	No	No
*Has the body been washed?	Yes	Yes	Yes	Yes
Cause of death	Throat cut	Throat cut	Throat cut	Throat cut
**Ligatures?	Wrists Ankles Adhesive gag	Wrists Ankles Adhesive gag	Wrists Ankles Adhesive gag	Wrists Ankles Adhesive gag
Bite marks	No	No	No	No
Putative bite marks (i.e., flesh removed)	Yes	Yes	Yes	Yes
Location of marks	Neck (2) Chest (1)	Neck (2)	Neck (3) Abdomen (4)	Neck (3) Chest (2) Groin (4)

Signs of torture or unusual assault?	Yes (see A)	Yes (see B)	Yes (see C)	Yes (see D)

*BODY WASHING: No fragranced materials appear to have been used, suggesting that the offender is not using the washing process as a means of denial; rather, in line with the rest of his cautious behaviour, I suggest that this washing is intended to obliterate forensic clues, especially since the killer appears to have taken particular care with the fingernails. Scrapings on all four victims showed nothing except traces of unperfumed soap.

**LIGATURES: None were found on bodies, but postmortems reveal bruising consistent with handcuffs on wrists, slight traces of adhesive, missing hairs and bruising round ankles consonant both with parcel tape and with separate ligatures, and traces of adhesive on face around mouth. No traces of blindfolds.

A: *Adam Scott.* Dislocation of ankles, knees, hips, shoulders, elbows and several vertebrae. Consistent with being stretched on a rack. Tentative postmortem cuts to penis and testicles.

B: *Paul Gibbs.* Severe lacerations to rectum, virtual destruction of anal sphincter and partial disembowelment. Suggestive of spiked object repeatedly inserted via anus. Also some burnt tissue internally, suggesting the possibility of heat or electric shock. Face badly beaten before death; bruising, broken facial bones and teeth. Postmortem cuts to genitals, more pronounced than in A.

C: *Gareth Finnegan.* Irregular pierce wounds to hands and feet, ½" diameter approx. Lacerations to left cheek and nose, suggestive of glass or bottle being broken across face by right-handed assailant. Shoulders dislocated. ?Possible crucifixion? Postmortem wounds to genitals, virtually castrated.

D: *Damien Connolly.* Dislocations similar to A, but no major spinal trauma, ruling out the idea of a rack. Large number of small, star-shaped burns to torso. Penis severed postmortem and inserted in victim's mouth.
Query: Were Damien Connolly's handcuffs still in his home or police locker?

Query: Why are the bodies always dumped Monday night/ Tuesday morning? What happens on Monday that allows him to be free? Does he work nights and have Monday off? Is he perhaps a married man who has Monday free because his wife does things with friends, e.g., girls' night out? Or is it that Monday isn't a traditional 'going out' night and he can be more sure of finding his victims at home?

Carol was aware that Tony had returned, but she carried on reading, simply raising one hand and waving her fingers to indicate she knew he was there. When she reached the end of the report, she took a deep breath and said, 'Well, Dr Hill, you *have* been busy.'

Tony smiled and shrugged himself away from the door-jamb he'd been leaning against. 'I can't believe there's anything in there that you didn't already have filed neatly away in your head.'

'No, but seeing it laid out like that somehow makes it clearer.'

Tony nodded. 'He has a very specific type.'

'Do you want to talk about it now?'

Tony looked down at the floor. 'I'd rather leave most of it for now. I need to let it sink in, and I need to go through all the rest of the witness statements before I can think about a profile.'

Carol couldn't help feeling disappointed. 'I understand,' was all she said.

Tony smiled. 'Were you expecting more?'

'Not really.'

His smile broadened. 'Not even a smidgen?'

The smile was infectious. Carol grinned back. 'Hoping, maybe. Expecting, no. By the way, there was one thing I didn't understand. NCP? CP? NRP? I mean, we're not talking National Car Parks and the Communist Party here, are we?'

'No current partner. Current partner. No recent partner. Acronymitis. It's the disease that afflicts all of us in the soft sciences like psychology, sociology. We have to mystify the uninitiated. Sorry about that. I try to keep things as jargon-free as possible.'

'So you don't confuse us thick plods, eh?' Carol teased.

'It's more about self-preservation. The last thing I want is to give the sceptics another big stick to hit me with. It's hard enough getting people to accept that my reports are even worth reading without alienating them with all that unnecessary pseudo-scientific mumbo jumbo.'

'I believe you,' Carol said ironically. 'Shall we go?'

'Sure. There is one thing I would like to bounce off you now,' Tony said, suddenly serious again. 'The victims. Everybody's assuming this killer is targeting gay men. Now, there are hundreds, probably thousands of openly gay men in Bradfield. We've got the biggest gay scene in the country outside London. Yet every one of those victims has no known history of homosexuality. What does that say to you?'

'He's in the closet himself and he only goes for men who are closeted too?' Carol hazarded.

'Maybe. But if they're all busily passing as straight, how does he meet them?'

Carol straightened the edges of the papers to give herself a moment. 'Contact magazines? Small ads? Multi-user phone chatlines? The Internet?'

'OK, all possibilities. But there was no evidence of any of those interests, according to the reports of the officers who searched their houses. Not in one single case.'

'So what are you trying to say here?'

'I don't think Handy Andy gets turned on by gay men. I think he likes them straight.'

Sergeant Don Merrick decided he'd never felt more fed up. As if it wasn't bad enough that he had Popeye on his back over the guv'nor's new assignment, he was now a servant of three masters. He was supposed to make sure that Inspector

Jordan's orders were carried out when she wasn't around, and he was also supposed to be working for Kevin Matthews on the Damien Connolly case as well as liaising with Bob Stansfield on the work that he and Inspector Jordan had already completed on the Paul Gibbs case. To top it all, he was spending his evening in the Hell Hole.

Never, in his opinion, was a club more aptly named. The Hell Hole advertised itself in the gay press as 'The club that dominates Bradfield. One visit and you'll be enslaved. You're *bound* to have the time of your life in the Hell Hole!' All of which was a coy way of saying that the Hell Hole was the place to go to pick up partners if sado-masochism and bondage was how you got your rocks off.

Merrick felt like Snow White at an orgy. He didn't have a clue how he was supposed to behave. He wasn't even sure if he looked right. He'd opted for an old, ripped pair of Levis that normally only saw the light of day when he was doing odd jobs around the house, a plain white T-shirt and the battered leather jacket he used to wear on his motorbike in the days before the kids came along. In his back pocket were his official handcuffs, there in the hope they'd lend some verisimilitude to his pose. Looking round the dimly lit bar, Merrick spotted so much distressed denim and leather that he expected to see an SOS flare rising above the dance floor. Superficially, at least, he thought he might just look the part. Which was worrying in itself. As his eyes grew accustomed to the low lighting, he caught sight of a few of his colleagues. Mostly, they looked as uncomfortable as he felt.

The club had been virtually empty when he'd first arrived just after nine. Feeling incredibly conspicuous, Merrick had asked for a pass-out and gone back on to the streets. He'd wandered round Temple Fields for the best part of an hour, stopping in a café-bar for a cappuccino. He'd wondered why some of the gay clientele had been giving him strange looks until he realized that he was the only customer wearing leather and denim. Clearly he'd transgressed some unwritten dress code. Uncomfortable, Merrick had swallowed the scalding coffee as quickly as he could and got back out on to the streets.

He felt seriously vulnerable, alone on the pavements and walkways of Temple Fields. The men who passed him, either singly, in couples or in groups, all eyed him up and down speculatively as he passed, most glances pausing at his crotch. He squirmed inside, wishing he'd picked a pair of jeans that didn't hug his body quite so tightly. As a couple of black youths walked past, arms entwined, he heard one say loudly to the other, 'Great ass for a white guy, huh?' Merrick felt the blood rise to his cheeks, unsure whether it was anger or embarrassment. In a moment of dreadful clarity, he realized what women meant when they complained of being treated as objects by men.

He returned to the Hell Hole, relieved that the place had filled up now. Loud disco music throbbed, the beat so strong Merrick seemed to feel it inside his chest. On the dance floor, men in leather adorned with chains, zips and peaked caps moved energetically, showing off their Nautilus-hardened muscles, thrusting their groins into empty air in bizarre parodies of sex. Stifling a sigh, Merrick pushed his way through the crowd to the bar. He ordered a bottle of American beer that tasted unbelievably insipid to a palate trained to expect the nutty sweetness of Newcastle Brown.

Turning round to face the dance floor again, Merrick leaned against the bar and surveyed the room, desperately trying to avoid eye contact with anyone in particular. He'd been standing like that for about ten minutes when he became aware that the man standing next to him wasn't actually trying to be served. Merrick glanced round to discover the man's eyes fixed on him. He was almost as tall as the detective, but with a broader, more muscular build. He wore tight black leather trousers and a white vest. His blond hair was cut short at the sides, longer on top, and his body was as tanned and smooth as a Chippendale. He raised his eyebrows and said, 'Hi. I'm Ian.'

Merrick grinned weakly. 'Don,' he replied, raising his voice to combat the music.

'I've not seen you in here before, Don,' Ian said, moving closer so that his naked arm pressed against the worn leather of Merrick's sleeve.

'It's my first time,' Merrick said.

'You new in town, then? You don't sound local.'

'I'm from the North East,' Merrick said carefully.

'That explains it. A bonny laddie from Geordieland,' Ian said, with a bad imitation of Merrick's accent.

Merrick felt his smile grow sick and die. 'You a regular here, then?' he asked.

'Never miss it. Best bar in town for the kind of guy I like.' Ian winked. 'Can I buy you a drink, Don?'

The sweat trickling down Merrick's back had nothing to do with the warmth of the bar. 'I'll have another one of these,' he said.

Ian nodded and turned round to the bar, using the crowd around him as an excuse to thrust himself against Merrick. Merrick stared across the room, his jaw set. He noticed one of the other murder squad detectives watching him. His colleague gave a grotesque wink and mimed one finger pumping into the closed fist of his other hand. Merrick turned away, coming face to face with Ian, who had been served. 'There you go, bonny laddie,' Ian said. 'So, you looking for a bit of fun tonight, Geordie?'

'Just checking out the scene,' Merrick said.

'What's the scene like up in Newcastle, then?' Ian asked. 'Bit lively? Cater for all tastes, does it?'

Merrick shrugged. 'I don't know. I'm not from Newcastle. I come from a little village up on the coast. It's not the kind of place where you can be yourself.'

'I get you,' Ian said, laying a hand on Merrick's arm.

'Well, Don, if you want to be yourself, you've come to the right place. And you've found the right guy.'

Merrick prayed he didn't look as terrified as he felt. 'It's certainly busy enough,' he tried.

'We could go somewhere quieter, if you like. There's another room through the back there, where the music isn't so loud.'

'No, I'm fine here,' Merrick said quickly. 'I like the music, if I'm honest.'

Ian moved forward so his torso leaned against Merrick's. 'What is it you're into, Don? Top or bottom?'

Merrick choked on his beer. 'I'm sorry?' he gasped.

Ian laughed and rumpled Merrick's hair. His light-blue eyes glinted wickedly, holding Merrick's stare. 'You really are an innocent abroad, aren't you? What I'm saying is, what do you like best? Handing it out or taking it?' His hand strayed down to Merrick's trousers. Just when the detective thought he was going to be groped in a way that no one apart from his wife had ever done, Ian's hand slid to one side and moved round to stroke Merrick's buttock.

'That depends,' Merrick croaked.

'On what?' Ian asked suggestively, moving so close that Merrick could feel the other man's erection against his leg.

'On how much I trust the person I'm with,' Merrick replied, trying not to let his revulsion show in voice or expression.

'Oh, I'm very trustworthy, me. And you look like the reliable kind too.'

'Are yez not a bit worried, like, about strangers? With this serial killer doing the rounds?' Merrick asked, using the opportunity of putting his empty bottle back on the bar to move away slightly from Ian's insistent body.

Ian's smile was cocky. 'Why should I be? These guys that are getting topped don't hang out in places like this. Stands to reason that this isn't where this mad bastard's picking them up.'

'How do you know that?'

'I've seen the pictures in the papers, and I've never spotted a single one of them out on the scene. And believe me, I know the scene. That's how I knew you were the new kid in town.' Ian moved closer again and thrust a hand in Merrick's back pocket. He ran his fingers over the hard outline of the handcuffs. 'Hey, that feels interesting. I'm starting to get a picture of what you and me could be like.'

Merrick forced a laugh. 'For all you know, I could be the killer.'

'So what if you are?' Ian said, all self-assurance. 'I'm not the type this fucking nutter goes for. He likes closet queens, not macho men. If he picked me up, he'd want to fuck, not commit murder. Besides, a good-looking guy like you doesn't need to kill somebody to get a fuck.'

'Yeah, well, maybe so, but how do I know you're not the killer?'

'Tell you what, just to prove I'm not, I'll let you top tonight. You'll be in charge. I'll be the one with handcuffs on.'

Carry on like this and you won't be wrong, Merrick thought to himself. He reached down and gripped Ian's wrist hard, removing his hand from the pocket. 'I don't think so,' he said. 'Not tonight. Like you said, I'm the new kid in town. I'm not going home with anybody till I know a bit more about them.' He released Ian's wrist and stepped back. 'Nice talking to you, Ian. Thanks for the drink.'

Ian's face altered in an instant. His eyes narrowed and the smile changed to a snarl. 'Wait a minute, Geordie. I don't know what sort of poxy Watch With Mother clubs you're used to, but in this city, you don't get into a clinch with somebody and take drinks off him if you're not prepared to come across.'

Merrick tried to get away, but the press of bodies round the bar made any movement difficult. 'I'm sorry if there's been a misunderstanding,' he said.

Ian's arm shot out and gripped Merrick firmly just below his bicep. The pain was excruciating. Merrick found a moment to wonder what sort of person actively sought out pain like this as part of their sexual pleasure. Ian thrust his face so close that Merrick could smell the bad breath he'd learned to associate with amphetamine abuse. 'It's not a misunderstanding,' Ian said. 'You came here tonight for sex. There's no other reason to be here. So sex is what we're going to do.'

Merrick swivelled on the balls of his feet and jabbed his elbow sharply underneath Ian's ribcage. His breath burst out of him in a sudden 'whoosh', and he doubled over, letting go of Merrick's arm in the reflex of clutching at his solar plexus. 'No, we're not,' Merrick said mildly, moving away through the space that had cleared around him as if by magic.

On his way across the room, one of the other undercover officers fell into step beside him. 'Nice one, Sarge,' he said out of the corner of his mouth. 'You did what we've all been wanting to do ever since we got in here.'

Merrick stopped and smiled at the constable. 'You're supposed to be doing an undercover. Either fucking dance with me or fuck off and let one of these poofters chat you up.'

Leaving the constable open mouthed, Merrick walked over to the far side of the dance floor and leaned against the wall. The commotion he'd left at the bar had died down. Ian pushed his way through the crowd, still holding his stomach, and left the club, shooting venomous glares at Merrick.

Before long, Merrick had company again. This time, he recognized his companion as a detective constable from one of the other divisions who had only joined the murder squad that day. He was sweating under the weight of heavy leather jacket and trousers that looked suspiciously like standard police motorcycle issue. He leaned close to

Merrick, so he wouldn't be overheard in the crowd round the dance floor and said urgently, 'Skip, there's a guy I think we should take a look at.'

'Why?'

'I overheard him mouthing off to a couple of blokes that he knew the dead guys. He was boasting about it. Reckoned there weren't many that could say that. And I heard him say that the killer must be a body-builder like him, on account of lugging bodies around. He was saying he bet there were people here tonight who didn't know they knew a murderer. Boasting, like, all the way.'

'Why don't you bring him in yourself?' Merrick asked, his interest quickened by what he'd heard, but reluctant to deprive the constable of the credit of pulling in a suspect.

'I tried to strike up conversation with him, but he gave me the brush-off.' The constable gave a wry smile. 'Maybe I'm not his type, skip.'

'And what makes you think I am?' Merrick demanded, not sure whether he was being subtly insulted here.

'He's wearing the same kind of gear as you.'

Merrick sighed. 'You better point him out to me.'

'Don't look now, sir, but he's standing over by the disco speakers. IC1 male, five foot six, short dark hair, blue eyes, clean shaven, heavy Scottish accent. Dressed like you. Drinking a pint of lager.'

Merrick leaned back against the wall and slowly scanned the room. He got the suspect on the first pass. 'Got him, I think,' he said. 'OK, son, thanks. Look fucked off when I go.'

He shrugged away from the wall and left the constable practising his depressed look. Slowly, Merrick moved round the room until he found himself next to the man who'd been pointed out to him. He had the bulky build of a weightlifter and the face of a boxer. His outfit was almost identical to Merrick's, save that his jacket had more buckles and zips. 'Busy in here tonight,' Merrick said.

'Aye. Lots of new faces. Half of them probably polis,' the man said. 'See that jerk you were just talking to? He might as well have come in his Panda car. Did you ever see a more obvious busy in all your born days?'

'That's why I fucked him off sharpish,' Merrick replied.

'I'm Stevie, by the way,' the man said. 'Busy night you're having with the unwanted solicitations. I saw you sort that toerag out earlier. Nicely done, pal.'

'Thanks. I'm Don.'

'Nice to meet you, Don. You new about here, then? Accent like that, you're obviously not a local.'

'Does everybody know everybody else here?' Merrick asked with a wry smile.

'Pretty much. It's a real village, Temple Fields. 'Specially the S&M scene. Let's face it, if you're gonnae let somebody tie you up, you want to know what you're getting into.'

'You're not wrong, Stevie,' Merrick said with feeling. 'Even more so when there's a killer on the loose.'

'My point exactly. I mean, I don't suppose these guys that got themselves killed thought they were up for anything more than a bit of rough. I knew them, you know. Adam Scott, Paul Gibbs, Gareth Finnegan and Damien Connolly. Every last one of them, and let me tell you, I wouldn't have had them pegged for that sort of scene. Just shows you, doesn't it? You can never tell what goes on in people's heads.'

'How come you knew them, then? I thought the paper said they weren't known on the scene,' Merrick said.

'I run a gym,' Stevie said proudly. 'Adam and Gareth, they were members. We used to go out for a drink now and again. That Paul Gibbs, I knew him through a mate of mine, used to have a pint with him and all. And that copper, Connolly, he came round the gym after we had a burglary.'

'I bet there's not many around here that can say they knew all the poor sods,' Merrick said.

'You're right there, pal. Mind you, I don't suppose the killer had anything more in mind than a wee bit of fun.'

Merrick's eyebrows rose. 'You think it's fun to murder folk?'

Stevie shook his head. 'Naw, you're no' following me. See, I don't think he sets out to kill these guys. Naw, it's kind of an accident, if you get my meaning. They're playing their games, and your man just gets carried away, and it all gets out of hand. He's obviously strong, he carts these bodies about and dumps them in the middle of the city, for God's sake. He's not going to be a seven-stone weakling, now is he? If he's a real body-builder like me, he maybe doesn't know his own strength. Could happen to anybody,' he added after a moment's pause.

'Four times?' Merrick demanded incredulously.

Stevie shrugged. 'Maybe they asked for it. Know what I mean? Prick teases and that? Promising what they didnae want to deliver when push came to shove? I've been there, Don, and let me tell you, there've been times when I've wanted to strangle the wee bastards.'

The detective in Merrick was straining at the leash. Carol Jordan wasn't the only Bradfield copper who'd been reading up on the psychology of the serial killer. Merrick had read cases where killers got off on this kind of justification, swaggering in front of a third party. The Yorkshire Ripper, he knew, had boasted to his male cronies about 'doing' prostitutes. He wanted Stevie in an interview room. The only problem was how to get him there.

Merrick cleared his throat. 'I suppose the only way to avoid that is to get to know the people you go to bed with before you get there.'

'My point exactly. You fancy getting out of here? Maybe going for a cup of coffee down the diner? Getting to know each other a wee bit better?'

Merrick nodded. 'Sure,' he said, dumping the remains of his beer on a nearby table. 'Let's go.' Soon as they got outside, he could switch his radio to 'transmit only' and one of the back-up teams would pick them up. Then they could test Stevie's bravado in Scargill Street.

Although it was after midnight, the street outside the Hell Hole was far from deserted. 'This way,' Stevie said, pointing to his left. Merrick slid his hand into his jacket and adjusted the radio switch.

'Where is it we're going?' he asked.

'There's an all-night diner in Crompton Gardens.'

'Great. I could murder a bacon butty,' Merrick said.

'Very bad for your health, all that grease,' Stevie said seriously.

As they rounded the corner into the alley leading into the square, Merrick sensed someone stepping out of a darkened doorway behind him. He started to turn towards the sound of footsteps.

Just like Bonfire Night, was his last conscious thought as a starburst of light erupted behind his eyes.

It didn't last as long as I'd expected. Surprisingly, Adam
proved more fragile than the German shepherd. Once he'd
lapsed into unconsciousness following the dislocation of
his limbs, he proved impossible to rouse. I waited for hours,
but nothing seemed to bring him round; not pain, not cold
water, not warmth. I was disappointed, I admit it. His
pain had been a mere shadow of mine, his punishment not
enough for the betrayal that occasioned it.

I finished what I had to do, neatly and swiftly, just after
midnight. Then I took him off the rack and folded him
into a heavy-duty garden rubbish sack. I put that inside a
black Bradfield Metropolitan Council bin bag. It was a
struggle to get the dead weight back up the cellar steps
and into the wheelbarrow, but my hours pumping iron
paid off.

I couldn't wait to get home to my computer, to transform
the evening into something transcendent. But I still had
work to do before I could relax and indulge myself. I drove
into the city centre just above the legal speed limit – not
so fast I'd get pulled for speeding, and not so slow that
I'd be stopped on suspicion of being a careful drunk driver.
I made for the gay cruising area behind the university.
Temple Fields used to be a student area, filled with small
cafés, restaurants, shops and bars with low prices and
standards. Then, about ten years ago, a couple of the bars
became gay. Our left-wing city council responded to

pressure and funded a gay and lesbian centre, which moved into the basement of an Indian restaurant. That seemed to trigger a domino effect, and within a year or two, Temple Fields had become Cruising City and the straight students had moved over to Greenholm on the far side of campus. Now, Temple Fields was home to gay bars, clubs, chichi bistros, shops selling leather and bondage gear, and a nightly rent rack right along the canal.

By half past one on a Tuesday morning, there were still quite a few men out on the streets. I drove around a couple of times, concentrating on the area round Crompton Gardens. The square was dark; most of the streetlights had been vandalized for reasons of sexual privacy, and the council was too strapped for cash to repair them. Besides, none of the local businesses was complaining; the darker the square, the more desirable the area, the bigger their profits.

I looked around cautiously. Nothing stirred. I wrestled the bag to the lip of the boot, then half rolled, half carried it on to the low wall. I tipped it over the edge with a rustling thud and closed the tailgate as quietly as I could. I took a penknife out of my pocket, leaned over the wall and slit the bags open. I pulled them free of the body and crumpled them into a ball.

Just after two, I parked Adam's car a couple of streets away from his house then walked back to my jeep, stuffing the bags in a litter bin on the way. I was in bed by three. In spite of my burning desire to carry on with my work, I was overwhelmed with exhaustion. Not surprising, considering the effort I'd expended. I was asleep as soon as I switched off the light.

When I woke, I rolled over and looked at the clock. Then I checked with my watch. I had to accept its corroboration. I'd been asleep for thirteen and a half hours. I don't think I've ever slept for that length of time, not even after general anaesthetic. I was furious with myself. I'd been looking forward to sitting down at my computer to relive and rebuild my encounter with Adam till it more closely resembled my deepest fantasies. But now I barely had enough time to shower and eat.

On my way into work, I picked up a late city final edition of the Bradfield Evening Sentinel Times. I'd made page two of the paper:

NAKED BODY FOUND

The mutilated body of a naked man was found in Bradfield's gay village early this morning.

Council worker Robbie Greaves made the grisly discovery as he made a routine rubbish collection in the Crompton Gardens area of Temple Fields.

Now the city's gay community fears this may be the first act of a gay serial killer like the man who recently terrorized London's homosexuals.

The body was found among shrubs behind a wall in the park, a notorious night-time meeting place for gay men looking for casual sex.

The man, said to be in his late twenties, has not yet been identified. Police describe him as white, 5ft 10ins, muscular build, with short dark wavy hair and blue eyes. He has no distinguishing marks or tattoos.

A police spokesman said, 'The man's throat had been cut and his body mutilated. Whoever committed this callous crime is a violent and dangerous man. The nature of the victim's injuries mean the killer must have been covered in blood.

'We believe the man was killed elsewhere and the body dumped in the park sometime during the night.

'We would urge anyone who was in the Crompton Gardens area of Temple Fields last night to come forward for the purposes of elimination. All information will be treated in the strictest confidence.'

Robbie Greaves, 28, the council worker who discovered the body, said, 'I'd only just started work. It was just after half past eight. I was using my grab to pick up litter. When it touched the body, I thought at first it was a dead cat or dog. Then I lifted up the bushes and saw the body.

'It was horrible. I threw up, then I ran to the nearest phone box. I've never seen anything like it in my life and I hope I never do again.'

Well, at least they'd got one thing correct. The body was killed somewhere else and dumped in Crompton Gardens. As for the rest of it ... If this was any indication of the police's skills, I didn't think I'd have too much to worry about. That was fine by me. The last thing I wanted was to be arrested, since I'd already chosen Adam's successor. Paul, I knew, was going to be different. This time, it wouldn't have to end in death.

7

All his acquaintances afterwards described his dissimulation as so ready and so perfect, that if, in making his way through the streets . . . he had accidentally jostled any person, he would . . . have stopped to offer the most gentlemanly apologies: with his devilish heart brooding over the most hellish of purposes, he would yet have paused to express a benign hope that the huge mallet, buttoned up under his elegant surtout, with a view to the little business that awaited him about ninety minutes further on, had not inflicted any pain on the stranger with whom he had come into collision.

Carol turned off the main drag and cut through the back doubles to emerge in Crompton Gardens. 'Adam Scott was found just there,' she said, pointing to a spot halfway down one side of the shrubbery.

Tony nodded. 'Can you drive slowly round the square, then park up against the wall where the body was found, please?'

Carol did as he asked. As they cruised round the square, Tony gazed out intently, swinging round in his seat a couple of times to snatch a second look. When the car stopped, he got out. Without waiting for Carol, he crossed to the pavement and prowled round the edge of the square. Carol got out of the car and followed in his wake, trying to see what Tony saw.

Neither the murders nor the freezing weather had changed the habits of those who frequented Temple Fields.

Doorways and basement areas still held grunting couples, heterosexual and homosexual alike. A few froze momentarily at the sound of Carol's heels on the pavement, but most ignored it. A great place to hang out if you were into voyeurism, Carol thought cynically.

Tony reached the end of the houses and crossed the street to the shop and bar fronts. Here, there were no copulating couples. The city's crime rate dictated heavy shutters and grilles for windows and doors. Ignoring them, Tony looked over towards the gardens in the centre of the square, matching what he'd seen on the photographs with the reality. There were no bushes on this side, only the low wall. He barely noticed two men walking past, wrapped round each other like competitors in a three-legged race. He wasn't interested in anyone else but Handy Andy.

'You've been here,' he said to himself. 'This isn't a place you just happened on, is it? You've walked this pavement, watched these parodies of love and affection that people pay for. But that's not what you were after, was it? You wanted something different, something a lot more intimate, something you didn't have to pay for.' How had they felt, those voyeuristic adventures of Handy Andy? Tony concentrated.

'You've never had a normal relationship with another person,' he thought. 'The prostitutes don't bother you, though. Or the rent boys. You're not killing them. You're not interested in what you can do with them. It's the couples that get to you, isn't it? I know, you see, I know that for myself. Am I projecting? I don't think so. I think you're looking for coupledom, the perfect relationship, the one where you can be yourself, the one that will value you as highly as you think you should be valued. And then it will be all right. The past won't matter. But it does matter, Andy. The past is what matters most of all.'

He was suddenly aware of Carol standing by his side, looking at him curiously. Probably his lips were moving.

He'd better be careful, or she'd be consigning him to the bin marked 'nutter' too. He couldn't afford that, not if he was to keep her on his side long enough to achieve the result he needed.

The last building on that side was an all-night diner, its windows opaque with condensation. In the bright light inside, shapes moved like creatures of the deep. Tony moved forward and pushed open the door. A handful of customers glanced up at him before returning to their fry-ups and chat-ups. Tony stepped back on to the street and let the door sigh shut behind him. 'I don't think you go in there,' he decided. 'I don't think you want to be seen to be alone in a place that's meant for companionship.'

The third side of the square consisted of a couple of modern office blocks. In the doorways, a clutch of homeless teenagers slept, bundled in clothes, newspapers and cardboard boxes. By now, Carol had caught up with him. 'Have they been interviewed?' Tony asked.

Carol pulled a face. 'We tried. My dad used to do a bit of folk singing. When I was a kid, he used to sing me a song with the chorus, "Oh, but I may as well try and catch the wind." Now I know what it means.'

'That good, eh?'

They crossed to the houses on the fourth side of the square, passing a pair of hookers on the corner. 'Hey, gorgeous!' one of them shouted. 'I could give you a better time than that tight-arsed bitch.'

Carol snorted with laughter. 'Now there's a triumph of hope over experience,' she said wryly.

Tony said nothing. The words had barely penetrated his reverie. He continued slowly down the pavement, pausing every few steps to drink in the atmosphere. Conflicting music filtered out faintly into the night from the flats and bedsits. The smell of curry wafted on the breeze that rustled the litter and sent polystyrene fast-food trays tumbling along the gutters. The square was never entirely empty, he noted. 'You despise their messy lives, don't you?' he said to himself. 'You like things clean and neat and orderly. That's partly why you wash the bodies. That's at least as important to you as erasing the forensic traces.' He turned the final corner and walked across to the rear of Carol's car, feeling the first stirrings of confidence that he was capable of mapping this complex and fatally skewed mind.

'He probably had to sit here for a few minutes to make sure he wasn't being watched,' Tony said. 'Depending on what kind of vehicle he's using, it could have taken as little as a minute to get the body out and over the wall. But he'd want to be sure no one was watching.'

'We did a full door-to-door across the street, but nobody admitted to seeing anything out of the ordinary,' Carol replied.

'Let's face it, Carol, when you look at what's ordinary round here, it leaves plenty of scope for a serial killer. OK, I've seen enough. Shall we go?'

Cross bounded into the squad room, surprisingly light on his feet as fat people often are, as if somehow moving lightly negates the bulk of their body. 'All right, then, where is the scumbag?' he bellowed. Then he caught sight of the thin figure leaning against the wall, his conversation with Kevin Matthews interrupted by Cross's entrance.

'Sir?' Cross said, stopping in his tracks. 'I wasn't expecting you in.' He threw a look of pure venom at Kevin Matthews.

Brandon straightened up. 'No, Superintendent, I don't suppose you were.' He took a couple of steps towards Cross. 'I left instructions with the control room that if any arrests were made in connection with the serial killings I was to be informed at once. This is going to be a high-profile case when it comes to court, Tom. I want us to be seen to be squeaky clean.'

'Yes, sir,' Cross said mutinously. However Brandon

dressed it up, what he was saying was that he didn't believe Cross was the man to make sure that over-zealous detectives didn't go too far. With Brandon pacing the corridors, no serial-killer suspects were going to have unfortunate accidents in custody. Cross turned to Kevin Matthews. 'What exactly happened?'

Kevin, so pale with tiredness and stress that his freckles stood out on milk-white skin like some vicious pox, said, 'As far as we can make out, Don Merrick came out of the Hell Hole with some bloke. One of the back-up teams saw them. Don switched his radio on to transmit, so we're assuming he wanted this bloke picked up for questioning. They were heading for the all-night diner in Crompton Gardens, according to the back-up boys. There's an alley that's a short cut through to the gardens, and they went down there. Next thing the back-up hear is a scuffle going on. They leg it round there and find Don on the floor and two blokes slugging it out. They arrested the pair of them and they're kicking their heels in the cells.'

'What about Merrick?' Cross demanded. For all his faults, Cross was a copper's copper. His men were almost as important to him as his own career.

'He's down Casualty getting stitches in a sore head. He came round in the ambulance. I've got one of my lads down there with him taking a statement.' Kevin glanced at his watch. 'He should be back any time now.'

'So what are we looking at here?' Cross demanded. 'Have we got a suspect, or what?'

Brandon cleared his throat. 'I think we can assume that Merrick thought the man he was with was worth a chat. As for the man who attacked them, I suspect we'll need to wait for Merrick's statement. I suggest Inspector Matthews and one of his team talk to the attacker while you and I have a preliminary chat with Merrick's target. That OK with you, Tom?'

Cross nodded, disgruntled. 'Yes, sir. And as soon as your

143

lad gets back from Casualty, Kevin, I want to see him.' He moved towards the door, looking over his shoulder expectantly at Brandon.

Brandon said, 'Before we go, Tom, I think we need Inspector Jordan and Dr Hill in here.'

'With respect, sir, it's the middle of the night. Do we really need to bugger up the man's sleep?'

'I don't want to get into questioning anyone about the murders until I've had the chance to take Dr Hill's advice about how the interview should proceed. Besides, the two of them are probably still out working. DI Jordan was planning to show Dr Hill the crime scenes tonight. Can you fix that, Inspector?'

Kevin glanced at Cross, who nodded slightly. 'No problem, sir. I'll page Inspector Jordan right away. I'm sure she'll be delighted to lend a hand.'

Brandon smiled and walked past Cross into the corridor. 'Just shows what happens to your bottle when you get behind a desk,' Cross muttered, shaking his head in mock-sorrow. 'You get so's you need a bloody psychologist to tell you how to interview some scumbag off the streets.'

Canal Street was still busy. People came in and out of clubs, taxis dropped off and picked up, couples shared their kebabs and chips on street corners, rent boys and hookers watched the slow-moving traffic, pouncing on the least opportunity. 'Interesting, isn't it, how areas become defined?' Tony said to Carol as they walked briskly along the street.

'You mean this is the zone for public encounters, while Crompton Gardens is for the dark side?'

'And ne'er the twain shall cross over,' Tony said. 'It's really quite lively for the time of night, isn't it? Are Monday nights quieter?'

'A bit,' Carol said. 'A couple of the clubs shut on Mondays. And one of the others has a women-only night.'

'So there's probably not as much street traffic,' Tony mused. As they'd driven round the streets, speculating on Handy Andy's approach route, Tony had been struck by how very public an area he'd chosen for his first two victims. Almost as if he were setting himself challenges. Now, at the corner of the alley leading to the side door of Shadowlands, he looked along the street and mused. 'He's desperate to be the best,' he said softly.

'Sorry?'

'Handy Andy. He just doesn't go for the easy options. His victims are all in the high-risk category. His dumping grounds aren't obscure, deserted hiding places. The bodies are cleaned of forensic clues. He's smarter than us, he thinks, and he has to keep proving it to himself. I'd hazard a guess that the next body's going to be dumped somewhere very, very public.'

Carol felt a shiver run through her that was nothing to do with the cold. 'Don't talk about the next body as if we're not going to find him before then,' she pleaded. 'It's just too depressing to think about.'

Carol led the way into the short dark cul-de-sac. 'Now, the second body, Paul Gibbs, was found just down here. All there is down here is the fire exit for the Shadowlands club.'

'It's dark enough,' Tony complained, stumbling over the edge of a disintegrating cardboard carton.

'We did suggest to the manager that a security light would be a good idea, if only to prevent him being mugged when he's locking up at night, but you can see how seriously he's taken the idea,' Carol replied, raking through her handbag to find her mini-torch. She snapped it on and the narrow beam revealed Tony silhouetted against a hooker in a red rubber dress giving a blow-job to a bleary-eyed businessman in the fire-exit doorway.

'Hoy!' the outraged man shouted. 'Bugger off, Peeping Tom!'

Carol sighed. 'Police. Zip your dick or you're nicked.' Before she'd even finished the sentence, the hooker was on her feet and heading for the mouth of the alley as fast as her stilettoes would let her. Realizing it wasn't worth arguing now the whore had gone, the man quickly fastened his trousers and pushed past Tony. As he turned the corner, he shouted, 'Frigid cunt!' back at her.

'You all right?' Tony asked, his genuine concern obvious.

Carol shrugged. 'When I started in the job, it really shook me when punters abused me like that. Then I realized it was them that had the problem, not me.'

'The theory's sound. How does it work in practice?'

Carol pulled a face. 'Some nights I go home and stand in the shower for twenty minutes and I still don't feel clean.'

'I know exactly what you mean. Some of the messy heads I have to poke about inside leave me feeling like I'll never have a normal relationship with another human being again.' Tony turned away, not wanting his face to betray him. 'So this is where you found Paul?'

Carol moved forward to stand beside him. She shone her torch into the doorway. 'He was lying there, with a couple of bin bags tucked around him so he wasn't immediately obvious. Judging by the condoms lying around, the working girls had been screwing the night away smack bang next to a corpse.'

'I take it you've talked to the girls?'

'Yes, we've had them all in. The one that scuttled out of here like a cockroach when the light goes on uses this spot most nights. She says she had a punter some time around four in the morning. She knows it was then because this bloke is a regular who comes off his shift at the newspaper-printing plant about then. Anyway, she was going to bring him down here, but there was a car in the way.' Carol sighed. 'We thought we'd cracked it, because she could remember the make, model and the numbers on the licence plate, because it was the same as the number of her house. Two-four-nine.'

'Don't tell me. Let me guess. It was Paul Gibbs's car.'

'Got it in one.'

The insistent bleep of Carol's pager cut into the conversation, demanding as a baby's cry. 'I have to find a phone,' Carol said.

'What is it?'

'One thing you can always say for sure,' Carol said, hurrying back out of the alley. 'It's never good news.'

'Look, I've told youse all I know. I'd just met this guy Don in the Hole, we was going for a cup of tea and suddenly there's footsteps and Don hits the ground like Vinny Jones just tackled him and I turn round and there's this bampot with a brick. So I give him the citizen's arrest with the left hook, and that's when your boys turn up mob-handed, and here I am.' Stevie McConnell spread his hands out in front of him. 'Youse should be giving me a commendation, no' the third degree.'

'And you expect us to believe this . . .' Cross consulted his notes. 'This Ian attacked this Don just because he'd turned him down earlier in the evening?'

'That's about the size of it. Look, this Ian, he's known about the town. He's a heidbanger. He gets out of his brain on speed and thinks he's God Almighty. This Don gave him a right showing up, you know, made him look like a big jessie instead of macho man, so your man was for getting his own back. Look, you gonnae let me go, or what?'

Cross was spared from replying by a knock on the door. Brandon shrugged away from the wall he'd been leaning against and opened the door. He exchanged a few murmured words with the constable outside then came back in. 'Interview suspended at 1.47 a.m.,' he said, leaning past

Cross to turn off the tape recorder. 'We'll be back shortly, Mr McConnell,' Brandon promised.

Outside the interview room, Brandon said, 'Inspector Jordan and Dr Hill are upstairs. And DS Merrick has come back from Casualty. Apparently, he says he's well enough to run through the evening's events himself.'

'Right. Well, we'd better hear what he's got to say, and then we can have a proper go at Jock.' Cross marched upstairs to the squad room, where a concerned Carol was hovering over Merrick. Tony sat a few feet away, feet propped up on the rim of a wastepaper bin.

'Bloody hell, Merrick!' Cross roared, seeing the dramatic bandage that turbanned his head. 'You've not turned into one of them bloody Sikhs, have you? Christ, I knew it was a risk sending a team into poofterville undercover, but I wasn't expecting religious mania.'

Merrick smiled weakly. 'I figured that way you couldn't send me back into uniform for cocking up, sir.'

Cross gave a grudging smile in return. 'Let's be hearing it, then. Why have I got a bolshie little sporran-sucker in my nick?'

Brandon, standing a couple of feet behind Cross, interrupted. 'Before DS Merrick runs through the evening's events for us, I just want to explain to Dr Hill why we've dragged him in here at this time of night.' Tony straightened up in his chair and pulled a sheet of paper towards him. 'When you were giving your lecture the other day,' Brandon continued, moving past Cross and sitting on the edge of a desk, 'you mentioned that psychologists can often give pointers to detectives about interview approaches. I wondered if you could apply that to this situation.'

'I'll do my best,' Tony said, uncapping his pen.

'How do you mean, interview approaches?' Cross said suspiciously.

Tony smiled. 'A recent example from my own experience. A force I'd been advising had arrested a suspect in two rape cases. He was the macho type, all bluster and muscle. I suggested that they send in a woman CID officer to interview him, preferably a small, very feminine woman. That made him angry right from the start, because he held women in contempt and thought he wasn't being treated with the appropriate respect. I'd briefed her in advance to suggest in her line of questioning that he couldn't possibly be the rapist since, frankly, she didn't think he had it in him. The result was, he blew his stack and coughed to the two rapes they had him in the frame for, as well as three other offences they didn't even know about.'

Cross said nothing. 'DS Merrick?' Brandon asked.

Merrick took them through his experiences in the bar with frequent pauses for thought. At the end of his recital, Brandon and Carol looked expectantly towards Tony. 'What do you think, Tony? Are either of them a possible?' Brandon asked.

'I don't think Ian Thomson is a starter. This killer is far too careful to get involved in something as ridiculously high profile as a street brawl. Even if Don hadn't been a police officer, the chances are that Thomson would have ended up in trouble for going after someone with a half-brick. Even in a city where attacks on gays are not noted for their high priority in policing terms,' he added drily.

Cross scowled. 'Gays get treated same as everybody else by the lads,' he blustered.

Tony wished he'd kept his mouth shut. The last thing he wanted was to get into a head-to-head with Tom Cross on Bradfield police's 'gays and blacks don't count' policy. He decided to ignore the comment and forged on. 'Also, there's nothing in what we know about the killer's behaviour to suggest that he's an upfront S&M gay man. It's clearly not from the gay scene that he's selecting victims. However, McConnell sounds more interesting from your point of view. Do we know what he does for a living?'

'He's the manager of a gym in the city centre. The same gym that Gareth Finnegan used,' Cross said.

'Hasn't he been questioned before?' Brandon asked. Cross shrugged.

'One of Inspector Matthews's team has spoken to him,' Carol butted in. 'I noticed the report when I was preparing the material for Dr Hill,' she added hastily, when she saw the beginnings of a scowl on Cross's face. God forbid he should think she was trying to undermine him. 'My dustbin memory,' she continued, trying to make a joke of it. 'As far as I can remember, it was simply a routine enquiry, checking up on whether Gareth had had any particular buddies or contacts at the gym.'

'Do we know McConnell's domestic arrangements?' Tony asked.

'He shares a house with another couple of shirt-lifters,' Cross said. 'He says they're both in the body-building game too. So, is he in the frame or not?'

Tony doodled in the margin of his notes. 'It's possible,' he said. 'What are the chances of getting a search warrant?'

'On what we've got at the moment? Not good. And we've no grounds for a search without one. Not even in our wildest dreams can we claim that a street assault gives us grounds to search McConnell's house for evidence relating to serial killings,' Brandon said. 'What would we be looking for in particular?'

'A camcorder. Any indication that he has access to somewhere isolated and deserted like an old warehouse, factory, derelict house, lock-up garage.' Tony ran a hand through his hair. 'Polaroid photographs. Sado-masochistic pornography. Souvenirs of his victims. The jewellery missing from the bodies.' He looked up and met Tom Cross's sneer. 'And you should check the deep freeze just on the off chance that he's kept the pieces of flesh he removed from the bodies.' He felt a moment's gratification when Cross's expression changed to disgust.

'Charming. But first we have to get something more to go on. Any suggestions?' Brandon asked.

'Send DS Merrick and Inspector Jordan in to interview him. The realization that the man he tried to pick up is a police officer will unsettle him, make him feel that his instincts can't be trusted. There's a chance too that he has problems with women –'

'Of course he's got problems with women,' Cross interjected. 'He's a bloody arse bandit.'

'Not all gay men dislike women,' Tony said mildly. 'But a lot do, and McConnell may be one of them. At the very least, Carol will make him feel threatened. All-male situations offer him the opportunity for camaraderie, so we take that off him.'

'Let's try it, then,' Brandon said. 'If DS Merrick is up to it.'

'I'm game, sir,' Merrick said.

Cross looked as if he couldn't decide whether to hit Brandon or Tony. 'I might as well bugger off home, then,' he blustered.

'Good idea, Tom. You've had more than your fair share of all-nighters lately. I'll hang on here, see what comes out of McConnell's interview.'

Cross stomped out of the squad room, passing Kevin Matthews on the way. The atmosphere visibly lightened in Cross's absence. 'Sir?' Kevin said. 'Ian Thomson – it looks like he's out of the frame on the murders.'

Brandon frowned. 'I thought I told you not to bring the murders up? At this stage, all we want to front Thomson with is the assault.'

'I didn't bring up the murders, sir,' Kevin said defensively. 'But it emerged during the interview that Thomson works three nights a week as a DJ in Hot Rocks. That's a gay club in Liverpool. He does Monday, Tuesday and Thursday. It should be easy enough to check whether he was working on the nights of the murders.'

'OK, get someone on it,' Brandon said.

'Which leaves McConnell,' Carol said thoughtfully.

'Let's do it,' Brandon said.

'Any tips?' Carol asked Tony.

'Don't be afraid to patronize him. Stay sweetness and light, but make it clear that you're the ranking officer. And DS Merrick – you can afford to play the gratitude card a bit.'

'Thanks,' Carol said. 'OK, Don?'

They left Brandon and Tony together. 'How is it going?' Brandon asked, getting up and stretching.

Tony shrugged. 'I'm starting to get a feel for his victims. There's a definite pattern there. He's a stalker, I'm sure of it. I should have a rough profile in a day or two. It's just bad timing that you've pulled in a suspect now.'

'How do you mean, bad timing?'

'I understand why you wanted my input. But I don't like knowing about suspects before I draw up my profile. The danger is that I skew the profile subconsciously so that it's a better fit for the suspect.'

Brandon sighed. He'd always found it hard to be optimistic in the small hours. 'We'll cross that bridge when we come to it. By this time tomorrow, our suspect might just be a distant memory.'

Getting to know Paul was somehow more exciting than Adam had been. Partly, I suppose, because I knew now I could handle it if things didn't work out the way I wanted. Even if Paul didn't have the insight to see that I could give him more than anyone else, even if he rejected my love, even if he went as far as Adam and actually betrayed the inevitability of our partnership with someone else, I knew that there was an alternative scenario that could give me almost as much satisfaction as the achievement of what I deserved.

But this time, I felt sure that I would get what I wanted. Adam, I now saw, had been immature and weak. Paul was neither of those, I could tell at once. For a start, he hadn't chosen to live in the yuppie part of town like Adam. Paul lived on the south side of the city in Aston Hey, a leafy suburb beloved of university lecturers and alternative therapists. Paul's house was in one of the more inexpensive streets. Like mine, it was terraced, though his two-up and two-down rooms were obviously far bigger. Unlike mine, he had a small garden at the front, and his back yard was twice the size, scattered with terracotta planters and tubs filled with flowers and dwarf shrubs. The perfect place to sit together for a preprandial drink after work on summer evenings.

Now with Paul, I'd have the chance to live in Aston Hey, to enjoy those quiet streets, to walk in the park together, to *be just like other couples. He had an interesting job, too – lecturer at Bradfield Institute of Science and Technology, specializing in CAD programs. We already had so much in common. It was a shame I'd never be able to show him what I'd achieved with Adam.*

One of the major advantages of having no mortgage is that I have virtually all of my salary to play with. It's a substantial disposable income for someone of my age and with my lack of dependants. That means I can afford a state-of-the-art computer system, with regular upgrades to keep me out there at the leading edge. Given that one software program alone cost me nearly three thousand pounds, it's just as well I don't have anyone leeching off me. With my new CD-ROM system, video digitizer and special-effects software, it took me less than a day to import the videos into my computer. Once they were digitized and installed there, I could manipulate and morph the images to tell any story I wanted to see. Thanks to other video erotica I'd already installed on my system, I was even able to give Adam the erection he'd failed to achieve in life. Finally, I could fuck him, suck him, fist him, and watch him do the same to me. But the knowledge that I would be able to do that still hadn't been enough to save him. Not even my computer and my imagination could give me the joy and satisfaction he could have done if he'd only been honest with himself about his desire for me. And so, every day he had to die all over again. The ultimate fantasy, constantly changing, shaped to fit my every mood and whim. At last, Adam was performing everything he could ever have fantasized about. It was a shame he couldn't share in my pleasure.

It wasn't perfect, but at least I was having more fun than the police. From what I read, it was clear they were getting nowhere. Adam's death barely merited a mention in the national media, and even the Bradfield Evening Sentinel Times gave up after five days. Adam's body was identified after four days, when anxious colleagues reported him missing after failing to get any reply from his phone or his doorbell. I was interested in their tributes (popular, hard-working, well liked, etc.) and I felt a moment's regret that his stupidity had deprived me of their friendship. The *Sentinel Times's* crime reporter had even managed to track down Adam's ex-wife, a mistake he'd made at twenty-one which he'd extricated himself from by his twenty-fifth birthday. Her comments made me laugh out loud.

Adam Scott's ex-wife Lisa Arnold, 27, fought back the tears as she said, 'I can't believe this could have happened to Adam.

'He was a friendly man, really sociable. But he wasn't a big drinker. I can't imagine how this weirdo managed to get hold of him.'

Lisa, a primary-school teacher who has since remarried, went on, 'I've no idea what he was doing in Crompton Gardens. He never showed any gay tendencies when we were married. Our sex life was quite normal. If anything, it was a bit boring.

'We married too young. Adam's mother had brought him up to expect a wife who waited on him hand and foot, and that just wasn't me.

'Then I met someone else and I told Adam I wanted a divorce. He was really upset, but I think it was more that his pride was hurt.

'I haven't seen him since the divorce, but I heard he was living on his own. I know he's had a few affairs over the last three years, but nothing serious as far as I know.

'I just can't get used to the idea that he's dead. I know we hurt each other, but I'm still devastated that he's been murdered like this.'

I didn't rate the chances of Lisa's second marriage lasting the course if she still had as little insight into the workings of the male mind. Boring? Lisa was the only reason sex with Adam could be boring.

And as for calling me a weirdo! She was the one who had turned her back on a charming, handsome man who loved her so much that he was still talking about her to complete strangers three years after she'd rejected him. I knew all about it; I'd listened to him. If anyone was a weirdo, it was Lisa.

8

No unpractised artist could have conceived so bold an idea as that of a noon-day murder in the heart of a great city. It was no obscure baker, gentlemen, or anonymous chimney-sweeper, be assured, that executed this work. I know who it was.

Stevie McConnell ran both hands through his hair in a gesture of desperation. 'Look, how many times do I have to tell you? I was telling porkies. I was trying to make myself sound the big man. I wanted to cop off, I was trying to make myself interesting. I never knew Paul Gibbs or Damien Connolly. I never saw either of them in my life.'

'We can prove you knew Gareth Finnegan,' Carol said coldly.

'OK, I admit I knew Gareth. He was a member down the gym, I can't pretend I'd never met him before. But Christ, woman, the man was a lawyer. He must have known thousands of people in the city,' McConnell said, thumping the table with a solid fist.

Carol didn't even flinch. 'And Adam Scott,' she went on relentlessly.

'Yeah, yeah,' he said wearily. 'Adam Scott had a trial one-month membership down the gym about two years ago. He never joined up. I bumped into him a couple of times in my local pub, we had a jar together, that's all there was to it. I have a drink with a lot of people, you know. I'm not a bloody hermit. Christ, if I killed everybody

I've ever stood at a bar with, youse bastards would be busy from now till the next century.'

'We will prove you knew Paul Gibbs and Damien Connolly. You know that, don't you?' Merrick chimed in.

McConnell sighed. His hands clenched, forcing the muscles in his powerful forearms into sharp relief. 'If you do, you'll have to make it up, because you can't prove what isn't true. You're not going to do a Birmingham Six on me, you know. Look, if I was really this mad bastard, do you think I'd have hung around to help you? First sign of trouble, I'd have legged it. Stands to reason.'

Sounding bored, Carol said, 'But you didn't know then that Sergeant Merrick was a police officer, did you? So give us your alibi for Monday night.'

McConnell leaned back in the chair and stared at the ceiling. 'Mondays is my day off,' he recited. 'Like I said, the guys that share my house are on their holidays, so I was on my tod. I got up late, went down the supermarket for my messages, then I went for a swim. About six o'clock, I drove out to the multi-screen off the motorway, and I went to see the new Clint Eastwood film.'

Abruptly, he lurched forward in the chair. 'They'll be able to confirm it. I paid by credit card, and their system's all computerized. They can prove I was at the pictures,' he said triumphantly.

'They can prove you bought a ticket,' Carol said laconically. From the cinema to Damien Connolly's house would take no more than half an hour round the motorway, even allowing for rush-hour traffic.

'I can tell you the whole plot, for fuck's sake,' McConnell said angrily.

'You could have seen it any time, Stevie,' Merrick said gently. 'What did you do after the pictures?'

'I went home. Cooked myself a steak and some vegetables.' McConnell paused and stared at the table. 'Then

I went into town for the last hour. Just for a quick drink with a few mates.'

Carol leaned forward, sensing McConnell's reluctance. 'Where in town?' she demanded.

McConnell said nothing.

Carol leaned further forward, the tip of her nose an inch from his. Her voice was quiet but icy cold. 'If I have to stick your face on the front page of the *Sentinel Times* and send a team into every pub in the city, I'll do it, Mr McConnell. Where in town?'

McConnell breathed in heavily through his nose. 'The Queen of Hearts,' he spat.

Carol leaned back, satisfied. She stood up. 'Interview terminated at 3.17 a.m.,' she said, leaning over to switch off the tape recorder. She looked down at McConnell. 'We'll be back, Mr McConnell.'

'Wait a minute,' he protested as Merrick got up and the two of them made for the door. 'When am I going to get out of here? You've got no right to keep me!'

Carol turned back in the doorway, smiled sweetly and said, 'Oh, I have every right, Mr McConnell. You've been arrested for assault, let's not forget. I have twenty-four hours to make your life a misery before I even have to think about charging you.'

Merrick gave an apologetic smile as he backed out of the room in Carol's wake. 'Sorry, Stevie,' he said. 'The lady's not wrong.'

He caught up with Carol as she was asking the custody sergeant to return McConnell to the cells. 'What do you think, ma'am?' Merrick asked as they walked off together.

Carol stopped and eyed Merrick critically. His skin was pale and clammy, his eyes feverishly bright. 'I think you need to go home and get some sleep, Don. You look like shit on a stick.'

'Never mind me. What about McConnell, ma'am?'

'We'll see what Mr Brandon has to say.' Carol set off for the stairs, Merrick trailing behind her.

'But what do *you* think, ma'am?'

'On the face of it, he could be our man. He's got nothing approaching an alibi for Monday night, he runs the gym where Gareth Finnegan worked out, he knew Adam Scott and by his own admission he was in the Queen of Hearts on Monday night for the last hour. He's certainly strong enough to have carted the bodies in and out of a car. He's got form, even if it is only a couple of breaches of the peace and a Section 18 wounding. And he's into S&M. But that's all circumstantial. And I still don't think we've got grounds for a search warrant,' Carol rattled off. 'What about you, Don? Got a feeling in your water about this one?'

They turned down the corridor towards the murder squad room. 'I kind of like him,' Merrick said grudgingly. 'I can't imagine that I'd take a liking to the bastard that's been doing these murders. But then, I suppose that's a pretty daft reaction. I mean, he's not the two-headed man, is he? He's got to have something about him that lets him get close enough to his victims to do the business. So maybe it *is* Stevie McConnell.'

Carol opened the door to the squad room, expecting to find Brandon and Tony still sitting there, fuelled by coffee and canteen sandwiches. The room was empty. 'Where's the ACC got to now?' Carol said, tiredness lending her voice a note of exasperation.

'Maybe he's left a message at the front desk,' Merrick suggested.

'And maybe he's done the sensible thing and buggered off home to bed. Well, that's us for tonight, Don. McConnell can stew for a bit. See what the bosses have to say in the morning. Maybe we can try for a search warrant now we know McConnell was in the Queen of Hearts. Now, get out of my sight and go home to bed before your Jean accuses me of leading you off the straight and narrow. Get some sleep. I don't want to see you before noon, and if your head's hurting, stay in bed. That's an order, Detective Sergeant.'

Merrick grinned. 'Yes, ma'am. See you.'

Carol watched Merrick walk back down the corridor, worried at the slow deliberation of his movements. 'Don?' she called. Merrick turned enquiringly back to her. 'Get a taxi. My authorization. I don't want you wrapped round a lamppost on my conscience. And that's an order, too.' Merrick grinned, nodded and disappeared down the stairs.

With a sigh, Carol walked down the squad room to her temporary office. There was no message on her desk. Bloody Brandon, she thought. And bloody Tony Hill. Brandon at least should have waited till she'd finished her interrogation of McConnell. And Tony might have left some indication of when he expected them to meet to discuss his profile. Muttering under her breath, Carol followed Merrick out of the building. As she reached the foyer, the officer minding the front desk called, 'Inspector Jordan?'

Carol turned back. 'I'm what's left of her.'

'The ACC left a message for you, ma'am.'

Carol approached the desk and took the envelope the constable handed her. She ripped it open and pulled out a single sheet of paper. 'Carol,' she read. 'I have taken Tony off on a little mission. I'll drop him at home afterwards. Please be in my office for ten this morning. Thanks for your hard work. John Brandon.'

'Great,' Carol said bitterly. She gave the constable a tired smile. 'I don't suppose you know where Mr Brandon and Dr Hill were headed?'

He shook his head. 'Sorry, ma'am. They didn't say.'

'Wonderful,' she muttered sarcastically. Turn your back for a minute and they were off playing their boys' games. Little mission, indeed. Bollocks to that, Carol thought as she marched back to her car. 'Three can play at that game,' she said as she turned the ignition key.

Tony flicked through the last of the magazines and returned it to the box file in the bedside storage cube. 'S&M always leaves me feeling faintly queasy,' he remarked. 'And this lot's particularly nasty.'

Brandon agreed. McConnell's collection of hard-core pornography consisted mostly of magazines crammed with glossy colour pictures of well-muscled young men torturing each other and masturbating. A few were even more disturbing, with their graphic shots of male couples indulging in full sex with an array of sado-masochistic trappings. Brandon couldn't remember seeing nastier examples, even when he'd done a six-month attachment with Vice.

They were sitting on the bed in Stevie McConnell's room. As soon as Carol and Merrick had left for their interrogation, Brandon had said, 'Would it be helpful to you to see where McConnell lives?'

Tony picked up his pen again and started to doodle on the sheet of paper. 'It might give me some insight into the man. And if he is the killer, there could be evidence that ties him into the crimes. I don't mean murder weapons, or anything like that. I'm thinking more of the souvenirs. Photographs, newspaper clippings, as well as the stuff I was talking about before. But it's academic, isn't it? You said there was no chance of getting a search warrant.'

Brandon's melancholy face lit up in a strange smile, almost a leer. 'When you've got a suspect in custody, there are things you can do to circumvent the rules. You game?'

Tony grinned. 'I'm fascinated.' He followed Brandon downstairs to the cells. The custody sergeant hastily dropped the Stephen King novel he'd been reading and jumped to his feet.

'It's all right, Sergeant,' Brandon said. 'If I only had a couple of prisoners to think about, I'd be enjoying a good read, too. I'd like to have a look at McConnell's property.'

The sergeant unlocked the property cupboard and handed the transparent plastic bag to Brandon. There was a wallet, a handkerchief and a bunch of keys inside. Brandon opened it and removed the keys. 'You haven't seen me, have you, Sergeant? And you won't see me when I come back in a couple of hours, will you?'

The sergeant grinned. 'You couldn't possibly have been here, sir. I'd have been bound to notice.'

Twenty minutes later, Brandon was parking the Range Rover outside McConnell's terraced house. 'Lucky for us McConnell happened to mention that the two blokes he shares the house with are away on holiday.' He took a cardboard box out of the glove compartment and gave Tony a pair of latex gloves. 'You'll need these,' he said, slipping a pair over his own hands. 'If we do get a search warrant, it would be a bit embarrassing when the finger-print team turn up you and me as prime suspects.'

'There's one thing I'm curious about,' Tony said as Brandon inserted the key in the mortice lock.

'What's that?'

'This is an illegal search, right?'

'Right,' Brandon said, opening the door and stepping into the hall. He groped for the light switch, but didn't turn it on when he found it.

Tony followed him, closing the door behind him. Only then did Brandon snap the light on, revealing a carpeted hall and stairs. There were a couple of framed posters of body-builders on the walls. 'So if we find any evidence, presumably it's inadmissible?'

'Also right,' said Brandon. 'But there are ways round that. For example, if we find a bloodstained cut-throat razor under McConnell's bed, it will mysteriously find its way on to the kitchen table. Then we go to the magistrate, explain that we went to McConnell's house to check he was telling the truth when he said his house-mates were on holiday, and we happened to look through the windows and we spotted what we have reason to believe is the weapon used to kill Adam Scott, Paul Gibbs, Gareth Finnegan and Damien Connolly.'

Tony shook his head in amusement. 'Bent? Us? Never, your honour!'

'There's bent and there's bent,' Brandon said grimly. 'Sometimes you need to give things a shove in the right direction.'

Tony and Brandon moved through the house, room by room. Brandon was intrigued by Tony's method. He would walk into a room, stand in the middle of the floor and slowly scan the walls, the furniture, the floor coverings, the shelves. He almost sniffed the air. Then, meticulously, he opened cupboards and drawers, lifted cushions, examined magazines, checked titles of books, CDs, cassettes and videos, handling everything he touched with the care and precision of an archaeologist. Within seconds, his mind was busy, analysing everything he saw and touched, slowly building a picture in his mind of the men who lived here, constantly matching it against the embryonic picture of Handy Andy that was developing in his mind like a photographic print in developer fluid.

'Have you been here, Andy?' he asked himself. 'Does this feel like you, smell like you? Would you watch these videos? Are these your CDs? Judy Garland and Liza Minnelli? The Pet Shop Boys? I don't think so. You're not camp, I know that much about you. And there's nothing camp or chichi about the house. This place is so aggressively masculine. A living room furnished in eighties chrome and black. But it's not a straight man's house, is it? No girlie magazines, not even car magazines. Just body-building periodicals stacked under the coffee table. Look at the walls. Men's bodies, oiled and shining, muscles like carved wood. The men who live here know who they are, they know what they like. I don't think this is you,

Andy. You're controlled, Andy, but not this controlled. It's one thing to keep yourself buttoned up, it's another thing altogether to be strong enough to project so coherent an image. I should know, I'm the expert. If you were as firmly rooted in your identity as the guys who live here, you wouldn't have to do what you do, would you?

'Look at the books. Stephen King, Dean R. Koontz, Stephen Gallagher, Iain Banks. Arnold Schwarzenegger's biography. A couple of paperbacks about the Mafia. Nothing soft, nothing gentle, but nothing off the wall either. Would you read these books? Maybe. I think you'd like to read about serial killers, though, and there's none of that here.'

Tony turned slowly towards the door. It was a small shock to see Brandon standing there. He'd become so absorbed in his scrutiny that he'd lost all sense of being in company. Watch yourself, Tony, he warned himself. Stay inside your head.

In silence, they trooped through to the kitchen. It was spartan, but well equipped. In the sink there was a dirty soup bowl and a mug half full of cold tea. A small shelf of cookery books testified to the occupants' obsession with healthy eating. 'Fart city,' Tony observed wryly, opening a cupboard filled with jars of pulses. He opened the drawers, noting the kitchen knives. There was a small vegetable knife with a blade worn thin from sharpening, a bread knife whose blade was pitted with age, and a cheap carving knife, the handle bleached from the dishwasher. 'These are not your tools, Andy,' Tony said to himself. 'You like knives that do their work properly.'

Without consulting Brandon, he walked out of the kitchen and up the stairs. Brandon watched him stick his head round the first bedroom door and reject it. As he passed, he saw that it was obviously the couple's room. He followed Tony through the door across the landing. In McConnell's bedroom, Tony seemed to drift away altogether into a world of his own. The room was simply furnished with modern pine bed, chest of drawers and wardrobe. An array of weightlifting trophies sat on the deep windowsill. A tall bookcase was crammed with pulp science fiction and a handful of gay novels. On a small table, there was a games computer and a television monitor. On a shelf above was a collection of games. Tony browsed through Mortal Kombat, Streetfighter II, Terminator 2, Doom and a dozen other games whose keynote was violent action.

'This is more like it,' he murmured. He stood by the chest of drawers, hand poised to open one. 'Maybe it's you after all,' he thought. 'Maybe you leave the living room to the other two. What if this is your only domain? What would I expect to find here? I'd want your souvenirs, Andy. You need to keep something by you, otherwise the memory disintegrates too fast. We all need something tangible. The discarded perfume spray that holds her fragrance and summons her before my eyes like a hologram; the theatre programme from the night we first made love and it was all right. Keep the good memories, throw away the bad. What have you got for me?'

The first three drawers were disappointingly innocuous: underwear, T-shirts, socks, jogging suits and shorts. When Tony opened the bottom drawer, he sighed in satisfaction. The drawer contained McConnell's S&M gear – handcuffs, leather restraint straps, cock rings, whips, and a clutch of items that looked to Brandon as if they ought to be in some kind of laboratory or mental institution. As Tony calmly took them out and examined them, Brandon shuddered.

Tony sat down on the bed and looked around. Slowly, cautiously, he tried to construct a picture of the man who lived in this room. 'You like to exercise power through violence,' he thought. 'You enjoy the flow of pain in your sexual experience. But there's no subtlety here. No sign that you're a man who plans things with care and detail.

You worship your body. It's a temple to you. You've achieved things, and you're proud of that. You're not socially inadequate. You manage to share a house with two other men, and you're not obsessive about your privacy, since there's no lock on the door. You don't have a problem with your sexuality, and you're comfortable with the idea of picking up a man in a club, provided you have the chance to get to know him a bit first.'

His picture-building was interrupted by Brandon. 'Look at this, Tony!' he said excitedly. The ACC had been painstakingly going through a shoebox full of papers, mostly receipts, electrical guarantees, bank and credit-card statements. The box was almost empty, but now, he held out a flimsy slip of paper.

Tony took it. It was some kind of official police form. He frowned. 'What's this?'

'It's the form you get when an officer stops you in a car and you haven't got your documents with you. You have to take them to a police station within a fixed period, so they can check everything's in order. Look at the name of the officer,' Brandon urged.

Tony looked again. The name that had at first seemed a scrawled jumble suddenly resolved itself into 'Connolly'.

'I recognized his number,' Brandon said. 'You can hardly make out the name.'

'Shit,' Tony breathed.

'Damien Connolly must have stopped him for some minor traffic offence, or just on a spot check, and asked him to produce his documents,' Brandon said.

Tony frowned. 'I thought Connolly was a local information officer? What was he doing dishing out a traffic ticket?'

Brandon looked over Tony's shoulder at the slip of paper. 'It was nearly two years ago. Connolly obviously wasn't a collator then. Either he was doing a stint with Traffic or he was on duty in the area car when he saw

McConnell doing something he shouldn't have been.'

'Can you check that out discreetly?'

'No problem,' Brandon said.

'You've cracked it, then, haven't you?'

Brandon looked astonished. 'You mean ... you think that clinches it? McConnell's the man?'

'No, no,' Tony said hastily. 'Not at all. All I meant was that if you can track that back from the other end, you should be able to get a magistrate to grant you an official search warrant on the basis that McConnell knew three of the four victims, which goes beyond mere coincidence.'

'Right,' Brandon said, sighing. 'So you're still not convinced McConnell's the killer?'

Tony stood up and paced to and fro across the carpet, its jagged geometric pattern of grey, red, black and white reminding him of the one and only migraine he'd ever had. 'Before you found this, I'd come to the conclusion you'd got the wrong man,' he said after a few moments. 'I know I've not had time to sit down and write out a full profile yet, but I felt like I was beginning to get a sense of what this killer's like. And there are too many things here that don't fit that picture. But this is a hell of a coincidence. This is a big city. We've established that Stevie McConnell knew or at least had met three out of the four victims. How many people are going to be in that position?'

'Not many,' Brandon said grimly.

'I still don't like McConnell for the killer, but it's possible that the killer is someone he knows, someone who's met Adam Scott and Gareth Finnegan through him,' Tony said. 'Maybe even somebody who was with him when he got that traffic ticket, or someone that he pointed Damien out to. You know the kind of thing: "That's the bastard who nicked me for speeding."'

'You really don't think it's him, do you?' Brandon said flatly, disappointment in his voice. 'I suppose it's thin. After all, there's no evidence as such to connect the house to the killings,' he said cautiously. 'But you said yourself, he's more likely to be doing his killing somewhere else. That might be where he keeps his souvenirs.'

'It's not just the absence of souvenirs,' Tony said. 'Putting it crudely, John, serial murderers kill to turn their fantasies into reality. Typically, they have fantasies developed to the point where they are more real to them than the world around them. There's nothing here to suggest McConnell is that type of personality. Sure, he's got a stack of porn mags. But so have most single men of his age, regardless of sexual orientation. He's got violent computer games, but so have thousands of teenagers and grown men too. What there is is plenty of evidence to suggest that Stevie McConnell isn't a sociopath. Look around you, John. This whole house reeks of normality. The kitchen calendar has dates for people coming round for dinner. Look at that pile of Christmas cards on his bookshelf. There must be fifty there. Look at his holiday snaps. He was obviously with the same partner for four or five years, judging by the locations and hairstyle changes. Stevie McConnell doesn't seem to have problems forming relationships with people. OK, so there doesn't seem to be anything relating to his family, but a lot of gay people get cut off by their families when they come out. It doesn't mean that his family were dysfunctional in the ways that typically lead to the development of a serial killer. I'm sorry, John. I wasn't sure at first, but the more I've seen, the more this guy just doesn't smell right to me.'

Brandon got to his feet and carefully replaced the slip of paper exactly where he'd found it. 'It grieves me to say so, but I think you're right. When I interviewed him earlier, I thought he was way too calm to be our man.'

Tony shook his head. 'Don't let that mislead you. Chances are when you do pull the right guy, he'll be calm too. Don't forget, this is something he's planned carefully. Although he thinks he's the best, he'll still have made contingency plans. He'll expect to be brought in for questioning sooner or later. He'll be ready for you. He'll be reasonable, pleasant. He won't look like a con. He'll be bland, helpful, and he won't ring alarm bells with your detectives. His alibi will be no alibi. He'll probably say he's been with a tart, or been to an away football match on his own. He'll end up being eliminated from your enquiries because other suspects will be superficially far more appealing.'

Brandon managed to look even more depressed than normal. 'Thanks, Tony. You've really cheered me up now. So what do you suggest?'

Tony shrugged. 'Like I said, it's a possibility that he knows the killer. He may even have his own suspicions. I'd hang on to him for a bit longer, sweat him for what and who he does know. But I wouldn't call off the team. Get a warrant. Do a proper search, under the floorboards, in the loft. You never know what you might turn up. Don't forget, I could be completely wrong.'

Brandon glanced at his watch. 'Right. I'd better get these keys back before the end of the custody sergeant's shift. I'll drop you off on the way.'

With a last look to check they'd left nothing out of place, Brandon and Tony left McConnell's house. As they approached the Range Rover, a voice from the shadows said, 'Good morning, gentlemen. You're nicked.' Carol stepped forward into the light of the streetlamp. 'Dr Anthony Hill, and Assistant Chief Constable John Brandon, I am arresting you on suspicion of breaking and entering. You do not have to say anything . . .' At that point, the giggles took over.

Brandon's heart had thudded into his throat at her first words. 'Hellfire, Carol,' he protested. 'I'm too old for tricks like that.'

'But not for ones like this, I see,' Carol said drily, gesturing with her thumb towards McConnell's house.

'Unauthorized search, and with a civilian? Just as well for you I'm off duty, sir.'

Brandon gave a weary smile. 'So why are you loitering with intent around the suspect's house?'

'I'm a detective, sir. I thought I might find you and Dr Hill here. Any joy?'

'Dr Hill thinks not. What about your interview?' Brandon asked.

'Your suggestions worked really well, Tony. McConnell's got no alibi to speak of for Damien Connolly's murder, apart from one hour late on in the evening, by which time Damien could have been dead already. The significant thing is where he was for that hour. Sir, he was drinking in the pub where the body was dumped.'

Tony's eyebrows climbed and he sucked his breath in sharply. Brandon turned to him. 'Well?'

'It's exactly the cheeky sort of thing Handy Andy could pull. You might want to get someone to check if he's a regular in there. If he isn't, it makes it significant,' Tony said slowly. Before he could say more, he was overwhelmed by a huge yawn. 'Sorry,' he yawned. 'I'm not a night bird.'

'I'll drive you home,' Carol said. 'I think the ACC has something to drop off at the station.'

Brandon looked at his watch. 'Fine. Make it eleven, not ten, Carol.'

'Thank you, sir,' Carol said with feeling as she unlocked her car for Tony. He slumped into the passenger seat, unable to stop the wave of yawns that had engulfed him.

'I'm really sorry,' she made out through a jaw-cracker. 'I can't stop yawning.'

'Did you find anything to make it worthwhile?' Carol said, her tone more sympathetic than her words.

'Damien Connolly nicked him a couple of years ago for a traffic offence,' Tony said heavily.

Carol whistled. 'Gotcha! We've caught him in a double lie, Tony! McConnell originally told Don Merrick he'd met

Connolly after a burglary at the gym. Then in the interview he denied ever having seen him. He said he'd been lying to make himself seem interesting. But now it turns out he really had met him! What a break!'

'Only if you believe he's the killer,' he said. 'I'm sorry to disappoint you, Carol, but I don't think he's the one. I'm too tired to go through it all now, but once I've drawn up my profile and we go through it, you'll see why I can't get excited about Stevie McConnell.' He yawned again and leaned his head on his hand.

'When can we do that?' Carol asked, fighting the urge to shake his thoughts out of him.

'Listen, give me the rest of today to myself, and by tomorrow morning I'll have a draft profile for you. How's that?'

'Fine. Anything else you need in the meantime?'

Tony said nothing. Carol gave him a quick sidelong glance and realized he had dozed off. All right for some, she thought. Forcing herself to concentrate, she drove across town to Tony's house, a turn-of-the-century brick-built semi in a quiet street a couple of tram stops away from the university. Carol pulled up outside. The car's slow glide to immobility did nothing to disturb Tony, whose breathing had become audible.

Carol undid her seat belt and leaned over to shake him gently. Tony's head came up in a startled gesture, his eyes wide and frantic. He stared uncomprehendingly at Carol. 'It's all right,' she said. 'You're home. You fell asleep.'

Tony rubbed his eyes with his fists, muttering something unintelligible. He looked blearily at Carol and gave a sleepy, lopsided smile. 'Thanks for bringing me home.'

'No problem,' Carol said, still twisted round in her seat, fiercely aware of his closeness. 'I'll give you a ring this afternoon, we can fix up a time to meet tomorrow.'

Tony, awake now, felt claustrophobic. 'Thanks again,' he said, retreating hastily, opening the car door and almost tumbling on to the pavement, thanks to the combination of haste and sleepiness.

'I can't believe I wanted him to kiss me,' Carol said to herself as she watched Tony open his gate and walk up the short path. 'Dear God, what is happening to me? First I treat Don like a mother hen, then I start fancying the expert witnesses.' She saw the front door open, stuffed a cassette in the stereo and drove off. 'What I need,' she told Elvis Costello, 'is a holiday.'

'You tease, and you flirt, and you shine all the buttons on your green shirt,' he sang back.

'Last night, we were practically sticking the champagne on ice. Now you're telling me you want to let McConnell go?' Cross shook his head in a gesture of exasperation so ancient it probably appeared on a Greek vase. 'What's happened to change everything? Come up with a cast-iron alibi, has he? Out on the razz with Prince Edward and his body-guards, was he?'

'I'm not saying let him go this minute. We need to question him closely about his associates, check if he introduced anyone to both Gareth Finnegan and Adam Scott. And after that, we have to let him walk. There's no real evidence, Tom,' Brandon said wearily. Lack of sleep had transformed his face into a grey mask that wouldn't have looked out of place in a Hammer Horror film. Cross, on the other hand, looked and sounded as fresh as a toddler who's just had a nap.

'He was in the Queen of Hearts that night. For all we know, he had Damien Connolly's body in the boot of his car, just waiting for closing time. It's got to be grounds for searching his gaff.'

'As soon as we've got enough evidence to get a search warrant, we'll do it,' Brandon said, reluctant to admit that he'd already taken that unorthodox step. Earlier, he'd asked Sergeant Claire Bonner to check all Damien

Connolly's arrests and traffic tickets, supposedly on the off chance of a connection to McConnell, but so far, she hadn't unearthed the crucial information that he knew was lurking there.

'I suppose this is all down to Boy Wonder,' Cross said bitterly. 'I suppose the shrink says McConnell's childhood wasn't unhappy enough.'

Carol bit her tongue. It was bad enough being the fly on the wall in this clash of the titans without reminding either of her bosses she was witnessing their conflict.

Brandon frowned. 'I have consulted with Dr Hill, and yes, he does feel that on the basis of what we've got so far, McConnell probably isn't our man. But that's not the main reason why I think we should let him loose. The lack of evidence is a hell of a lot more important to me.'

'And to me. That's why we need time to collect some more. We need to interview these poofters he was drinking with on Monday night, to see what kind of state he was in. And we need to take a look at what McConnell's got under his mattress,' Cross said forcefully. 'We've had him in custody for less than twelve hours, sir. We're entitled to keep him till gone midnight. Then we can charge him with the assault for now, and ask the magistrates for a lie-down in police custody, which gives us another three days. That's all I'm asking for. I'll have nailed him by then. You can't say no to that, sir. You'll have the lads up in arms.'

Wrong, Carol thought. You were doing fine up till then, but the emotional blackmail just scuppered you.

Brandon's ears flushed scarlet. 'I hope no one thinks that because we are questioning someone the work stops,' he said, a dangerous edge in his voice.

'They're dedicated, sir, but they've been working on this a long time without a break in the case.'

Brandon turned away, staring out of the window at the city below. His instincts said to let McConnell go after they'd had one last attempt at digging his contacts out of him, but he had known without Cross's clumsy comments that having a suspect had given the murder squad a new lease of energy. Before he could make a decision, there was a knock at the door. 'Come in,' Brandon called, swinging round and dropping heavily into his chair.

Kevin Matthews's carrot curls appeared round the door. He looked like a kid who's been promised a trip to Disneyland. 'Sir,' he said. 'Sorry to interrupt, sir, but we've just had a report from Forensic on the Damien Connolly killing.'

'Come in and tell us, then,' Cross invited genially.

Kevin gave an apologetic smile and slid his slim frame round the door. 'One of the SOCOs found a scrap of torn leather caught on a nail on the gate,' he said. 'It's a secure area, the public can't just walk in, so we thought it might be significant. Obviously, we had to eliminate the people who work at the pub, and the draymen who deliver there. Anyway, it turns out that the yard was whitewashed and the gates were painted only a month ago, so we didn't have to chase too many bodies. Bottom line is, no one admitted owning anything made from leather like this, so we sent it off to Forensic and asked them to look at it double urgent. The report's just come back.' He proffered the report to Brandon, eager as a Boy Scout.

The relevant passage had been highlighted in yellow. It leapt off the page at Brandon. 'The fragment of dark-brown leather is extremely unusual. For a start, it appears to be deerskin of some sort. More significantly, analysis indicates that it has been cured in sea water rather than a specialist chemical-curing medium. I know of only one source of such leather: the former Soviet Union. Because regular supplies of the correct chemicals are difficult to come by, many tanners there still use the old method of curing with sea water. I would guess that the fragment has come from a leather jacket that originated in Russia. Leather like this is not available commercially elsewhere, since it does not meet the quality levels required by Western retail outlets.' Brandon read it, then tossed it across the desk towards Cross.

'Bloody hell!' Cross said. 'You mean we're looking for an Ivan?'

At the top of the page, partially visible faded text from the preceding page:

for several further attempts to persuade Paul too gave me unalloyed pleasure. By W——— ——— his Sexton ——— to them as—— attitude that he ——— those ——— ——— is one of those attitudes ———— ——— then the ——— — which men and animals ———— ————— by ——— as a mistake the ——— ——— ——— ———— as ——— a—————.

I read somewhere that murder enquiries cost a million pounds a month. When Paul demonstrated he was every bit as stupid and treacherous as Adam, I began to realize the actions I'd been forced to take might start to have a significant impact on local taxes. Not that I minded a few extra pence a year on my council-tax bills; it was a small price to pay for the satisfaction I gained from dealing with their perfidy.

I was devastated by Paul's defection. Just as I'd set the scene for the triumphant celebration of our love, he turned his back on me and chose another. The night he made his first approach, I don't know how I got home. I can't remember a single detail of the journey. I sat in my jeep outside the farm, raging against his shallowness, his failure to recognize that I was the one he truly loved. My anger was so strong I'd lost all physical coordination. I virtually fell out of the driver's seat and staggered like a drunk towards the haven of my dungeon.

I climbed on to the stone bench and hugged my knees to my chest while the unfamiliar tears rolled down my cheeks and splashed on the raw stone, staining it dark as Adam's blood. What was wrong with them? Why couldn't they let themselves have what I knew they wanted?

I wiped my eyes. I owed it to both of us to make the experience as rich and as perfect as possible. It was time for new toys. Adam had been the dress rehearsal. Paul was going to be the first night.

The ploy of the car that wouldn't start had served me well with Adam, so I used it on Paul. It worked like a dream. Before I was three steps down the hall, he'd even invited me to have a drink while I was waiting for the AA man. But I didn't fall for his blandishments; he'd had his chance, and it was too late now for me to abort my plans for our union on my terms.

When he came round, he was strapped into a Judas chair. It had taken me a few days to construct it, since I'd had to start from scratch. The Judas chair was one of my San Gimignano discoveries. I'd only ever seen a couple of references to it in my books, none of which made it at all clear how exactly it was constructed. But there in the museum, they had their very own working model. I had taken a couple of photographs to augment the one in the museum catalogue, and equipped with those, I had worked out a practicable design on my computer.

It's not a machine that inquisitors have used much, though I can't quite see why. The San Gimignano museum puts forward a theory which frankly seems absurd to me. Coupled with some of the other descriptions on the cards, this daft theory convinces me that the cards have been written by some blinkered, obsessive feminist. The theory goes thus: it was OK to use implements of torture on women such as vaginal pears that shredded the cervix and vagina, so-called 'Chastity' belts which ripped their labia to a bloody pulp, implements that chopped nipples as efficiently as a cigar cutter, because women were a separate species from the inquisitors, and indeed were often creatures of the devil. On the other hand, so this demented theory goes, torture instruments used on men tend not to be directed against their sexual organs, in spite of the

tenderness of those areas, because – wait for it – the torturers felt subconsciously connected to their victims and
therefore any mutilation inflicted on their cocks and balls
were unthinkable. Clearly, the caption writer in San Gimignano is far from au fait with the refinements of the Third
Reich.

My Judas chair, even if I say so myself, is a masterpiece
of the type. It consists of a square frame with a leg at each
corner, with arm supports for the forearms and a thick
plank up the back. Much like a primitive carving chair,
except that there is no seat. Instead, below the gap where
the seat should be, there is a sharply barbed conical spike,
attached to the chair legs at its base by a cross-brace of
strong wooden struts. For the spike, I'd used one of the
large cones that cotton yarn used to be wound round on
industrial looms. You can pick them up in the souvenir
shop of any outpost of the heritage industry. I'd covered
it with a thin, flexible sheet of copper, and fastened thin
strands of razor wire in a spiral round the outside. I'd
added my own refinement to the example in the torture
museum; my spike was wired up to the electrical supply
via a rheostat, allowing me to apply electric shocks of
varying intensity. The whole thing is bolted to the floor to
prevent accidents.

While he'd still been unconscious, Paul had been held
above the spike by a strong leather strap under his armpits,
binding him to the back of the chair. I'd also strapped each
ankle to one of the front legs of the chair. As soon as I
unfastened the strap, he'd be thrown on his own resources,
relying on the muscles in his calves and his shoulders to
keep him from the savage spike, carefully sited immediately
below his anus. Since the chair was so high that only his
toes could reach the floor, I didn't expect him to hold out
too long.

His eyes registered the same panic I'd already seen in
Adam. But his situation was entirely of his own making.

I told him so before I ripped the tape away from his mouth.

'I had no idea, no idea,' he gabbled. 'I'm sorry, I'm so sorry. You've got to let me make it up to you. Just let me out of this thing, and I promise we can make a fresh start.'

I shook my head. 'Robert Maxwell got one thing right. He said trust is like virginity; you can only lose it once. You have a treacherous soul, Paul. How can I believe in you?'

His teeth began chattering, though not, I suspect, from cold. 'I made a mistake,' he forced out. 'I know that. Everybody makes mistakes. Please, all I ask is the chance to make it right. I can make it right, I promise.'

'Show me, then,' I said. 'Show me you mean it. Show me you want me.' I stared at his shrivelled cock, dangling with his balls in the space where the seat should have been. I had looked forward to beauty, but he had failed me there, too.

'N-not here, not like this. I can't!' His voice rose in a pathetic wail.

'It's this or nothing. Here or nowhere,' I told him. 'By the way, in case you're wondering, you're strapped into a Judas chair.' Carefully, I explained how the chair worked. I wanted him to make an informed choice. As I talked, his skin turned grey and clammy with fear. When I explained about the electricity, he lost it completely. Piss dribbled from his cock, splashing on the floor beneath him. The stink of warm urine rose and choked me.

I slapped him so hard his head cracked against the back board of the Judas chair. He cried out, and tears sprang into his eyes. 'You dirty, filthy baby,' I shouted at him. 'You don't deserve my love. Look at you, pissing and crying like some little girl. You're not a man.'

Hearing my mother's words coming from my mouth shattered my self-control as nothing else could have done. I kept hitting him, revelling in the crunch of cartilage as his nose collapsed under my fist. I was beside myself with anger. He'd fooled me into thinking he was something he wasn't. I'd thought Paul was strong and brave, intelligent and sensitive. But he was just a stupid, cowardly, lecherous pig, a pathetic excuse for a man. How had I ever let myself imagine he could be a worthy partner? He wasn't even resisting, just sitting there mewing like a kitten, letting me hit him.

Panting with exertion and anger, I finally stopped. I stepped back and stared contemptuously at him, watching his tears wash lines through the blood on his face. 'You brought this on yourself,' I hissed. All my careful plans had gone up in smoke.

But now, I didn't want to give him the second chance I'd given Adam. I didn't want Paul's love, not under any circumstances. He didn't deserve me. I stepped round to the back of the chair and grasped the tongue of the strap. 'No,' he whimpered. 'Please, no.'

'You had your chance,' I said angrily. 'You had your chance and you blew it. You've no one to blame but yourself, coming here and pissing on the floor like a baby who can't control itself.' I pulled the strap, tightening it enough to let me slip it free of the buckle. Then I let it slide free.

Paul's muscles instantly clenched, holding him rigidly in place, a scant half-inch above the spike. I moved round into his line of vision and slowly stripped off, caressing my body, imagining what his hands would have felt like. His eyes bulged with effort as he tried to keep himself in place. I sat down and slowly, deliciously began to rub myself, irresistibly turned on by his fight to stay away from the agonizing spike.

'You could have been doing this,' I sneered, aroused still further by the quivering of his thighs and calves. 'You could have been making love instead of fighting to keep your arse in working order.'

If he'd worked out like Adam had, the pleasure would have lasted longer. As it was, his screams of agony mingled with my groans of pleasure. I came like a Guy Fawkes rocket, fire flashing through me and erupting in an orgasm that had me buckling at the knees.

He tried to pull free, but the barbs just cut deeper into his tender flesh. I lay back in the chair, savouring the waves of pleasure that flowed through me after my orgasm, Paul's moans and screams an extravagant counterpoint to my sexual satisfaction.

As time passed, he sank lower on the spike, and his screams moderated to whimpering groans. To my surprise, I felt sexual desire rise in me again. After the exquisite pleasure of my first orgasm, I wanted my excitement matched again. I reached for the control box for the electrical current to the spike, and pressed the button that completed the circuit. Even with a relatively low current, Paul's body convulsed in an arc that wrenched him almost clear of the spike, a fine spray of blood spattering the floor for a couple of feet around.

I matched the rhythms of our two bodies, the speed and intensity of our mutual excitement keeping perfect pace. I felt my muscles quiver like his as I thrust against my hand. As I came, my body arched in sync with his, my gasps echoed by his last agonized cries before unconsciousness came.

I have to confess I was surprised by how much I enjoyed Paul's punishment. Perhaps because he had deserved so much more than Adam, perhaps because I had had higher expectations of him in the first place, or perhaps simply because I was getting better at what I had to do. Whatever the reason, my second excursion into murder left me feeling as if I'd found my true vocation at last.

9

We dry up our tears, and ... discover that a transaction which, morally considered, was shocking, and without a leg to stand upon, when tried by principles of Taste, turns out to be a very meritorious performance.

'OK, Andy, it's showtime,' Tony said to the blank screen of his computer. After Carol had dropped him off, he'd stumbled upstairs, kicking off his shoes and letting his quilted baseball jacket lie where it fell on the landing. Pausing only to empty his bladder, he'd burrowed under the duvet and fallen into the deepest sleep he'd known for months. When he'd woken, it had been after noon. But for once, he felt no guilt about the work he should have been doing. He felt refreshed, excited, elated even. Searching Stevie McConnell's house had given him a new certainty that he really did understand what he was doing. He had known, with absolute clarity, that Handy Andy did not live like that. And although it wasn't something he could admit to anyone outside the tight circle of fellow profilers, there was a real rush in realizing that he could probably find his way into Handy Andy's head and map a path through the tortured labyrinth of his unique logic. All he had to do now was find the key to the door.

In the office, Tony powered his way through the remaining piles of documents, making notes as he went along. Then he closed the blinds and told his secretary to hold all his calls. He moved his own chair round the desk so that it faced the visitor's chair. On the desk to one side, he placed his tape recorder, still switched off. He walked over to the door and stood with his back to it, contemplating the room. Some poem he'd once read echoed in his mind. Something about a road that divided in a wood, and the importance of choosing the branch less travelled by. For as long as he could recall, his fascinations had led him down the road less travelled by. It was the road that his patients walked, the dark path that led into the undergrowth, away from the dappled sunshine of the broad path. 'I need to understand why you chose that road, Andy,' Tony murmured. 'This is what I do best, Andy. You see, I know what draws me to that road. But I'm not like you. I can go back when I want to. I can choose the sunny path. I don't have to be here. All I'm doing is studying your footsteps. Or at least, that's what I tell the world.

'But we know the truth, don't we? You can't hide from me, Andy,' he said softly. 'I'm just like you, you see. I'm your mirror image. I'm the poacher turned gamekeeper. It's only hunting you that keeps me from being you. I'm here, waiting for you. Journey's end.' He stood for a moment longer, savouring the admission he'd made to himself.

Finally, he sat down in his chair and leaned forward, elbows on knees, hands loosely linked. 'OK, Andy,' he said. 'It's just you and me. We're going to skip the preliminaries; all that stuff where we do the verbal arm wrestling and you eventually decide to talk to me. We're going straight for it. First off, I want to say how impressed I am. I've never seen a cleaner job. I don't just mean the bodies, I mean the whole thing. Sweet as a nut, you did it. Never a witness. Let me rephrase that. Never anybody seeing any significance in what they saw or heard, because there must have been people who saw or heard something, but they didn't make the connection. How did you manage to be so invisible?' He pressed 'record' on the cassette recorder then stood up and stepped across to the other chair.

Tony took a deep breath and deliberately relaxed his body. He used breathing techniques to put himself into a light state of trance. He instructed his conscious mind to let go, to allow his higher self to access directly all he knew about Handy Andy and to answer for him. When he spoke, even his voice was different. The timbre was rougher, the tones deeper. 'I blended in. I took care. I watched and I learned.'

Tony swapped chairs again. 'You obviously did a good job of it,' he said. 'How did you choose them?'

Back into Andy's chair. 'I liked them. I knew it would be special with them. I wanted to be like them. They all had good jobs, a nice life. I'm good at learning things, I could have learned to be like them. I could have fitted into their lives.'

'So why kill them?'

'People are stupid. They don't understand me. I was the one they always laughed at, then they learned to be afraid of me. I don't like being laughed at, and I'm tired of people being wary of me, like I'm some animal that's going to go for them. I gave them a chance, but they didn't give me any choice. I had to kill them.'

Tony sank back in his own chair. 'And after you'd done it once, you realized that was the best thing in the world.'

'I felt good. I felt in control. I knew what was going to happen. I'd planned it all out, and it worked!' Tony surprised himself by the degree of enthusiasm that came out. He waited, but nothing more seemed to emerge.

He returned to his own chair. 'Didn't last for long, did it? The pleasure? The sense of power?'

In Andy's chair, he felt at a loss for the first time. Usually, he found role play loosened up his ideas, let his thoughts flow free. But something was clogging this up. That something was clearly at the heart of the issue. Tony moved back to his own seat and thought about it. 'Serial killers act out their fantasies in their crimes. The crime itself never lives up to the fantasy, so it has limited power. Its details are incorporated into the fantasies, which are then realized in a second, often more ritualistic killing. And so on. But as time goes by, the fantasies have less and less staying power. The killings have to get closer and closer together to keep the fantasies fuelled. But your killings don't get closer together, Andy. Why is that?'

He moved across, not hopeful. He allowed his mind to blank, letting his consciousness drift off, hoping it would come up with an answer that might satisfy his idea of Andy. After a few moments, Tony felt himself slipping away from consciousness. All at once, from what felt like a long way away, a deep chuckle rumbled through him. 'That's for me to know and you to find out,' his own voice mocked him.

Tony shook his head like a diver coming to the surface. Dazed, he got to his feet and snapped the blinds open. So much for alternative techniques. What was interesting, however, was the point at which his brain had snagged. This was one of the factors about Handy Andy that was unique. The gaps stayed constant. Even allowing for his use of a camcorder, it was still remarkable.

The line of thought restored Tony's earlier vigour and he decided to take a side trip to the university library's media-studies section where he went through the back numbers of the *Bradfield Evening Sentinel Times* for the appropriate dates. A careful scrutiny of the entertainments pages revealed little in common between the four evenings in question, unless he was prepared to consider that the local art cinema always showed classic British black-and-white comedies on Mondays. Somehow, he couldn't imagine *Passport to Pimlico* fuelling homicidal sexual fantasies. Finally, just after seven, he was ready to start on the profile.

He started with the usual caveat.

The following offender profile is for guidance only and shouldn't be regarded as an identikit portrait. The offender is unlikely to match the profile in every detail, though I would expect there to be a high degree of congruence between the characteristics outlined below and the reality. All of the statements in the profile express probabilities and possibilities, not hard facts.

A serial killer produces signals and indicators in the commission of his crimes. Everything he does is intended, consciously or not, as part of a pattern. Uncovering the underlying pattern reveals the killer's logic. It may not appear logical to us, but to him it is crucial. Because his logic is so idiosyncratic, straightforward traps will not capture him. As he is unique, so must be the means of catching him, interviewing him and reconstructing his acts.

Tony continued the profile with a detailed account of the four victims. He included everything he'd gleaned from the police reports about their domestic circumstances, employment history, reputation among friends and colleagues, habits, physical condition, personality, family relationships, hobbies and social behaviour. Next, he wrote a short résumé of the pathologist's report on each man, the nature of their injuries and a description of the crime scenes. Then he began the crucial process of organizing and arranging his information into meaningful patterns so he could start to draw his conclusions.

None of the four victims had any history of homosexual relationships, as far as can be ascertained. (We cannot exclude a secret homosexual/bisexual orientation, but there is no evidence in any of the four cases to suggest this.) Yet each body was dumped in an area known primarily for its use by the gay community. In particular, the bodies were dumped in spots which are notorious for the consummation of casual sexual encounters. What does this say about the killer?

1. He is a man who is not comfortable with his own sexuality. He deliberately chooses men who are not openly gay-identified. It may well be that he has made a sexual approach to his victims in the past and has been rebuffed. The killer is almost certainly not an out gay; he probably represses his own sexuality at some personal cost. He probably grew up in an environment where masculinity was highly prized and praised and homosexuality condemned, possibly on religious grounds. If he is in a sexual/domestic relationship, it will be with a woman. And he will almost certainly have sexual problems within that relationship, probably ones of potency.

Tony stared bleakly at the screen. Sometimes he hated the way his job constantly forced him to confront his own problems. Did his own sexual failings mean he was really stuck on the road less travelled by? Was there going to be a night when some woman went too far, when her determination to translate his problem into a comment on her womanhood tipped him over the edge? For Tony, it was a scenario that was all too vivid. That's why Angelica was safe. When she drove him to distraction, he could slam the phone down, rather than slap her face. Or worse. Best stay out of risk, he thought. Don't even think about thinking about Carol Jordan. You've seen it in her eyes, she's interested in more than your mind. Don't even think about it, fuck-up. Get back to work.

2. He despises those who express their homosexuality openly. At least part of his motivation in using these dumping grounds is to show his contempt for them, as well as to frighten them. He's also demonstrating his superiority; 'Look at me, I can come and

go among you and none of you know me. I can desecrate your places, and you can't stop me.'

3. He is nevertheless familiar with areas where gay men go to socialize and to pick up sexual partners. It may be that his job takes him into the Temple Fields area from time to time, perhaps to make deliveries or to provide some service to businesses. He is fascinated with the gay culture, to the extent that he has scouted out the specific area in Carlton Park where gay cruising goes on.

4. He has a high degree of self-control. He is driving into a populous area and dumping bodies without behaving in a way that draws attention to himself.

'Tell me about it,' Tony said bitterly. He got up and stalked a path from the window to the door. 'I could have written the manual.' Ever since the bullies had started to pick on him, the smallest boy in the street and in his class, he'd learned the harsh lessons of self-control. 'Never show you're hurt, it only encourages them. Never show they've hit the mark, it only reveals your weak points. Learn to be one of the lads. Learn the vocabulary, learn the body language, acquire the attitude. Mix it all together and what do you get? You get a man who hasn't got the remotest idea of who he is. You have a consummate actor, a human impostor who can take on local colour like a chameleon.' The miracle was that it fooled so many people. Brandon clearly thought he was a good bloke. Carol Jordan obviously fancied him. Claire, his secretary, thought he was the best boss she'd ever had. He was passing for human, all right. The only one he couldn't fool was his mother, who still treated him with the thinly disguised contempt which was all he'd ever known from her. His fault his father had left them, and no wonder, according to her. She'd have dumped him in some children's home if it hadn't been for her need to keep in with her parents, the ones who held the purse strings. As it was, she'd dived head first into a career as soon as she'd been able to persuade her mother to mind little Tony. He'd done his best to be good, as Granny had instructed him, but it wasn't always easy. She wasn't a bad woman, just constrained by her own upbringing into the belief that children should be seen and not heard. His grandfather's response to domestic tyranny was to escape to the betting shop, the bowling green and the Legion. Tony had swiftly learned self-control the hard way. Was that what had happened to Andy, too? Rubbing his hand across eyes surprisingly damp, Tony threw himself back into his chair and started typing frantically.

5. His domestic and work situation allows him to be free on Monday evenings, and he does not expect to be spotted in Temple Fields by anyone who knows him. This throws up several possibilities: he may have chosen Monday nights specifically because it's his night off work or because his wife/girlfriend is away from home on Monday nights; he may have decided to kill on Mondays because the first time was a Monday and it worked out for him and now has superstitious power; or he may have decided to keep on killing on Mondays in the hope that it will skew the investigation. He is obviously intelligent, and such careful planning should not be presumed to be beyond him.

Tony paused for thought, flicking through the pages of notes he'd made. He wasn't thinking like Handy Andy yet, but the elusive mind was getting closer and closer. He wondered again if his involvement in the twisted logic of killers was a surrogacy, the only thing that prevented him from joining their number. God knows, there were times when the inevitable drive that surged through their heads seemed attractive. And there were times enough when he'd felt murderous rage, though it was usually turned against himself rather than the person he was in bed with. 'Enough, already,' Tony said aloud, and returned to the glowing screen.

The offender is an organized serial killer, who is managing to maintain a constant eight-week gap between killings. This consistency is unusual in itself, since the normal pattern is that the space between murders decreases as they lose their power to satisfy the killer's fantasies. One reason for the maintenance of this gap may be that he spends so long stalking his victim before the kill. Thus the delights of anticipation, coupled with the savour of his previous kills, acts as a brake. I also believe that the killer is using his camcorder to record his activities and that this is also fuelling his fantasies between kills.

Tony stopped to consider what he had written. The stumbling block. His analysis probably looked good enough to convince the lay person, but he was far from satisfied with it. But no amount of dredging of his mind or his data could come up with a better explanation. With a sigh, he continued.

What is the primary intent of his killings? We can rule out killing in the course of criminal activity, such as armed robbery or burglary. We can also rule out emotional, selfish or cause-specific killings, such as self-defence, compassion, assassination or domestic disputes. This places the killings in the category of sexual homicides.
The chosen victims all fall into the low-risk category. In other words, they all had occupations and lifestyles that didn't make them vulnerable targets. The

flip side of this is that the killer has to take high-level risks to capture and kill them. What does this tell us about the killer?

1. He is operating under extremely high stress levels.

2. He plans his kills very carefully. He cannot afford to make mistakes, because if he does, his victims will escape and put him at risk, both physically and legally. He is almost certainly a stalker. He chooses his victims carefully, and studies their lives in detail. Interestingly, so far he has not been thwarted in his choice of evening. Is this a result of careful planning, prearrangement or just luck? We know that the third victim, Gareth Finnegan, told his girlfriend he was going on a lads' night out, but none of his male friends or colleagues seemed to know anything about it, and it is not clear whether he was abducted from his home or if the contact took place at a prearranged point. It may be that the killer has had prior arrangements to meet each of his victims, either at their homes or elsewhere. He may even be posing as an insurance salesman or something similar, though I feel it's unlikely that he would have the people skills to do such a job successfully for a living.

3. He likes the extra excitement that walking out on the high wire gives him. He needs that buzz.

4. He must have some areas of emotional maturity in his make-up that allow him to hold himself under control in these highly stressful situations. This may also allow him to buck the poor work-history pattern so common among serial offenders. (See below.)

Most serial offences demonstrate a degree of escalation, indicating the killer's need for more thrills, better execution of his fantasies. Like a roller coaster, each high needs to be bigger to compensate for the inevitable low that has preceded . . .

Tony looked up, startled. What was that noise? It had sounded like the door to the open-plan outer office, but at this time of night, there shouldn't be anyone on this floor. Nervously, he pushed himself away from the computer desk, steering his chair across the carpet on silent castors till he was behind his desk and out of the pool of light shed by the lamp beside the computer. He held his breath and listened. Silence. The tension gradually began to ooze away. Then, abruptly, a line of light appeared under his office door.

The metallic taste of fear gripped Tony. The nearest thing to an offensive weapon on his desk was a chunk of agate he used as a paperweight. He snatched it up and moved stealthily out of his chair.

When Carol opened the door, she was taken aback to find Tony halfway across the room, hefting a rock in his hand. 'It's me,' she yelped.

Tony's arms dropped to his side. 'Oh shit,' he said.

Carol grinned. 'Who were you expecting? Burglars? Journalists? The bogeyman?'

Tony relaxed. 'I'm sorry,' he said. 'You spend all day trying to get inside some nutter's head and you end up as paranoid as he is.'

'Nutter,' Carol mused. 'Now would that be some technical term you psychologists use?'

'Only inside these four walls,' Tony said, walking back to his desk and putting the agate back where it belonged. 'To what do I owe the pleasure?'

'Since British Telecom don't seem to be able to connect us, I thought I'd better come round personally,' Carol replied, pulling up a chair. 'I left a message on your machine at home this morning. I assumed you'd already left for work, but you weren't here either. I tried again around four, but there was no reply from your extension. At least, I assume that's why the switchboard operator said, "I'm putting you through now," and I ended up in a black hole.

And, of course, now the switchboard have all gone home and I never thought to ask for your direct line.'

'And you a detective,' Tony teased.

'That's my excuse, anyway. Actually, I couldn't face another minute in Scargill Street.'

'Want to talk about it?'

'Only if I can talk with my mouth full,' Carol said. 'I'm starving. Could you go a quick curry?'

Tony glanced at his computer screen, then back at Carol's drawn face and tired eyes. He liked her, even though he didn't want to get close, and he needed her on his side. 'Just let me save this file, and I'm out of here. I can come back later and finish this.'

Twenty minutes later they were attacking onion bhajis and chicken pakora in an Asian café in Greenholm. The other customers were students and those of the terminally right-on tendency who hadn't quite adjusted to the fact they were no longer studying anything except political correctness. 'It's not exactly Good Food Guide, but it's cheap and cheerful, and the service is quick,' Tony apologized.

'Fine by me. I'm more egg on toast than Egon Ronay. My brother got the gourmet genes in our family,' Carol said. She glanced quickly around her. Their table for two was less than a foot away from the next. 'Did you bring me here deliberately so we couldn't talk about work? Some psychologist's ploy to refresh my mind?'

Tony's eyes widened. 'I didn't even think of that. You're right, of course, we can't talk about it in here.'

Carol's smile lit up her eyes. 'You can have no idea how much pleasure that gives me.'

They ate in silence for a few minutes. Tony broke the silence. That way, he stayed in control of the subject. 'What made you decide to be a copper?'

Carol raised her eyebrows. 'Because I like oppressing the underprivileged and hassling racial minorities?' she tried.

Tony smiled. 'I don't think so.'

She pushed her plate to one side and sighed. 'Youthful idealism,' she said. 'I had this crazy idea that the police should be there to serve and protect society from lawlessness and anarchy.'

'It's not such a crazy idea. Believe me, if you dealt with the people I used to handle, you'd feel relieved that they weren't on the streets.'

'Oh, the theory's fine. It's just the practice that's such a bummer. It all started when I read sociology at Manchester. I specialized in the sociology of organizations, and all my contemporaries despised the police force as a corrupt, racist, sexist organization whose sole role was to preserve the illusory comfort of the middle classes. To some extent, I agreed with them. The difference was that they wanted to attack institutions from the outside, whereas I've always believed that if you want fundamental change, it has to come from inside.'

Tony grinned. 'You little subversive, you!'

'Yeah, well, I guess I didn't realize what I was getting into. David knocking out Goliath was a piece of piss compared with trying to change things in the police.'

'Tell me about it,' Tony said with feeling. 'This national task force could revolutionize the clear-up rate on serious crimes, but the way some senior officers carry on, you'd think I was setting up a scheme to allow paedophiles to retrain as child minders.'

Carol giggled. 'You mean, you'd rather be back in the locked ward with your nutters?'

'Carol, sometimes I feel like I've never left. You've no idea what a refreshing change it is to work with people like you and John Brandon.'

Before Carol could reply, the waiter arrived with their main courses. As she spooned out lamb and spinach, chicken karahi and pilau rice, Carol said, 'Does your job create the same problems with having a private life as the police service does?'

Instantly defensive, Tony answered with a question. 'How do you mean?'

'Like you said earlier, you get obsessed with the job. You spend your time dealing with shitheads and animals –'

'And that's just your colleagues,' Tony butted in.

'Yeah, right. And you come home at night after dealing with broken bodies and fractured lives and you're expected to sit down and watch the soaps and act like normal people do.'

'And you can't because your head's still plugged into the horrors of the day,' Tony finished. 'And with *your* job, you have the added complication of shift work.'

'Exactly. So, do you get the same problems?'

Was she asking out of idle curiosity or was this an oblique way of finding out about his private life? Sometimes Tony wished he could just switch off the part of his head that had to analyse every statement, every gesture, every intricate piece of body language and just revel in the pleasure of eating dinner with someone who seemed to enjoy his company. Suddenly aware that he had left too long a pause between the question and the answer, Tony said, 'I'm probably even worse at switching off than you. Men generally seem to get much more obsessive than women. I mean, how many female train spotters, stamp collectors or football fanatics do you know?'

'And that interferes in your personal relationships?' Carol persisted.

'Well, none of them have ever gone the distance,' Tony said, struggling to keep his voice light. 'I don't know if that's down to the job, or to me. Mostly, the last thing they've screamed at me as they walked out the door hasn't been, "you and your bloody nutters", so I guess it must be me. How about you? How do you handle the problems of the job?'

Carol's fork continued its journey to her mouth and she chewed and swallowed her mouthful of curry before she answered. 'I've found that men aren't very sympathetic towards shifts unless they do them too. You know, you're never there with the tea on the table when they've got to rush out to that vital squash match. Add to that the difficulty of getting them to understand why the job drives you inside your head and what are you left with? Junior doctors, other coppers, fire fighters, ambulance drivers. And in my experience, there aren't many of them who want a relationship with an equal. I guess the job takes too much out of us for us to have much left over. The last guy I was involved with was a doctor, and all he wanted to do when he wasn't working was sleep, fuck and party.'

'And you wanted more?'

'I wanted the occasional conversation, maybe even a movie or a night out at the theatre. But I put up with it because I loved him.'

'So what made you end it?'

Carol stared down at her plate. 'Thanks for the compliment, but I didn't. When I moved up here, he decided that driving up and down the motorway was a waste of good shagging time, so he dumped me for a nurse. Now it's just me and the cat. He doesn't seem to mind the irregular hours.'

'Ah,' Tony said. He had heard the real pain under the surface, but for once, all his professional skills didn't seem adequate to the response.

'How about you? You involved with anyone?' Carol asked.

Tony shook his head and carried on eating.

'Nice bloke like you, I'd have thought you'd have been snapped up ages ago,' Carol said, the tease in her tone covering something Tony wished he was imagining.

'Ah, but you've only seen the charming side. When the moon's full, I sprout hair on the palms of my hands and bay at the moon.' Tony leered melodramatically at Carol. 'I am not what I appear to be, young woman,' he growled.

'Oh, Grandmamma, what big teeth you've got!' Carol said in falsetto.

'All the better to eat my curry with,' Tony laughed. He knew this was the point where he could have moved the relationship forward, but he had spent too long constructing his defences against precisely these moments of weakness to let them down that easily. Besides, he told himself, he had no need of a relationship with her. He had Angelica and bitter experience had taught him that was all he could handle and still function.

'So how did you get into this soul-destroying line of work?' Carol asked.

'I discovered while I was working on my DPhil that I hated getting up on my hind legs and talking to an audience, which kind of ruled out academic work. So I went into clinical practice,' Tony said, slipping easily into a flow of anecdotes about his work. He felt himself relax, like a man walking on a frozen lake who realizes he's back on dry land.

They spent the rest of the meal on the safer ground of their careers, and Carol asked the waiter for the bill when he came to clear off the table. 'I'm picking up the tab, OK? Nothing to do with feminism; you're a legitimate business expense,' Carol said.

As they walked back to Tony's office, he said, 'So, back to work. Tell me about your day.'

The swift switch away from the personal back to the case confirmed to Carol the need to play it cool with Tony. She'd never seen anyone back off so fast at gentle flirtation. It was puzzling, all the more since she sensed he liked her. And she had no doubts about her capacity to attract men. At least tracking Handy Andy with him gave her space and time to build a bridge between them. 'We got a break this morning. At least, that's what we're all hoping.'

Tony stopped abruptly and turned to face Carol. 'What kind of a break?' he demanded.

'Don't worry, you're not being ignored,' Carol said. 'It's something that would be a minor detail in most investigations, but because we've got so little to go on here, it's got everybody excited. There was a torn fragment of leather on a nail by the gate in the Queen of Hearts's yard. Forensic did a rush job on it, and it turns out that it's very unusual. It's deerskin, and it comes from Russia.'

'Oh, my good God,' Tony said softly. He turned away and took a couple of steps. 'Don't tell me, let me guess. You can't get it in this country, and you'd probably need to send someone to Russia to source it, it's so obscure. Am I right?'

'How the hell did you know that?' Carol asked, catching him up and grabbing his sleeve.

'I've been expecting something like this,' he said simply.

'Like what?'

'An outrageous red herring that'll have the entire police force running around like headless chickens.'

'You think this is a red herring?' Carol almost shouted. 'Why?'

Tony rubbed his hands over his face and ran them through his hair. 'Carol, this guy has been so careful. He's been almost clinical in his obsession with leaving no clues. Serial killers have typically got high IQs, and Handy Andy is certainly one of the cleverest I've ever come across, either personally or in the whole literature. Yet suddenly, out of nowhere we get not just any old clue, but a clue so obscure that it could only possibly be left by a tiny segment of the population. And you're standing here telling me you think this is for real? That's exactly what he's trying to achieve. I bet the lot of you have been running around like blue-tailed flies all day trying to suss out where this obscure piece of Russian leather came from, haven't you? Oh, and don't tell me, let me guess. I bet there's now a whole squad tracking back through Stevie McConnell's life trying to establish where the hell he got it from.'

Carol stared at him. It seemed so blindingly obvious when he explained it like that. Yet not one of them had questioned the validity of the leather scrap.

'Am I right?' Tony asked, more gently this time.

Carol pulled a face. 'Not a whole squad. Just me and Don Merrick and a couple of DCs. I've spent most of the day on the phone talking to governing bodies in weightlifting and body-building, trying to establish if McConnell's ever been on a national or regional team that either competed in Russia or competed against Russians. And Don and the lads have been grilling travel agencies trying to check if he's ever been on holiday there.'

'Oh, Christ,' Tony groaned. 'And?'

'Five years ago, he was one of a team of weightlifters from the North West who competed in an event in what was then Leningrad.'

Tony took a deep breath. 'The poor unlucky bastard,' he said. 'I don't expect the idea that this was deliberately planted to have occurred to any of you,' he added. 'I don't mean that patronizingly. I realize how much closer you are to all of this and how desperately you want to catch this bastard. I just wish someone had told me earlier, before it assumed this major significance for everyone.'

'I did *try* to phone you this morning,' Carol said. 'You still haven't said where you were.'

Tony held his hands up. 'I'm sorry. I'm overreacting. I was in bed, asleep, with the phones turned off. I was exhausted after last night, and I knew I couldn't concentrate on writing the profile unless I had some sleep. I should have checked my answering machine when I got up. Sorry, I shouldn't have had a go.'

Carol grinned. 'I'll let you off this time. Just save the fearsome bit for when we catch Handy Andy, huh?'

Tony pulled a face. 'Shouldn't that be "if"?'

He looked so vulnerable and fallible, his shoulders slumped, his head down, that Carol's impulses overrode the decision she'd taken only minutes before to play it cool. She stepped forward and pulled Tony into a tight hug. 'If anyone can do it, you can,' she whispered, rubbing the side of her head against his chin like a cat marking its territory.

Brandon stared at Tom Cross, his face a mask of horror. 'You did *what*?' he demanded.

'I searched McConnell's house,' Cross said belligerently.

'I thought I said categorically that we had no right to do that? No judge in the land is going to accept that arrest for common assault in the street gives sufficient grounds for suspicion of murder.'

Cross smiled. It was a rictus that would have raised a Rottweiler's hackles. 'With respect, sir, that was then. Once Inspector Jordan had established that McConnell had been to Russia, the picture changed. Not a lot of people have had access to obscure Russian leather jackets, after all. It puts him in the frame. And there's more than one JP around that owes me one.'

'You should have cleared it with me,' Brandon said. 'The last order I gave on the subject was no search.'

'I tried, sir, but you were in a meeting with the Chief,' Cross said sweetly. 'I thought I'd better strike while the iron was hot, being as how we don't have him banged up indefinitely.'

'So you wasted more time searching McConnell's house,' Brandon said bitterly. 'Don't you think you and your men could have been better employed?'

'I haven't told you yet what we found,' Cross said.

Brandon felt his chest constrict. He wasn't a man given to premonitions, but the sinking foreboding that gripped him now was as palpable as any solid fact he'd ever examined. 'Think very carefully about what you say next, Superintendent,' he said cautiously.

A momentary frown of puzzlement flashed over Cross's features, but he was too full of the message he bore to worry about the ACC's words. 'We've got him, sir,' he said. 'Bang to rights. We found one of Gareth Finnegan's firm's Christmas cards in McConnell's bedroom, and a sweater that's a dead ringer for the one Adam Scott's bird says was missing from his house. Plus a traffic ticket with Damien Connolly's badge number on it. Add that to the Russian connection, and I think it's time to charge the little arse bandit.'

Of course, the discovery that one has a natural bent for something does not necessarily mean one should pursue it blindly. While I was disposing of Paul's body, this time in a dark doorway in an alley in Temple Fields, I had already decided who my next target would be. But even after so magnificent an experience as the one I'd just shared with Paul, I had no intention of repeating it with Gareth.

It was going to be third time lucky. Gareth, I already knew, was a man of rich and fertile sexual imagination. Even as I was digitizing Paul's pathetic performance into the computer, I was mourning the fact that, thanks to Gareth, I would never have the opportunity to perfect the extraordinary talent I had discovered in myself. With the resources at my command, I've been making movies like I've never seen. The ultimate snuff stuff. If I could have marketed them, I would have made a fortune. I know there's a market out there. Plenty of people would pay a lot of money to watch Paul fuck me in his death spasms on the Judas chair. And as for what I've done with Adam . . . Let's just say that no one's ever seen sixty-nine like it.

As a treat, I went to the cemetery where Adam had been buried a few weeks before. The funeral had featured on the local television news, which I'd video-taped and studied so I could be fairly sure where the grave was. After dark, I made my way through the graves, and found Adam's within twenty minutes. I opened the can of red spray paint

I'd brought with me and sprayed 'WANKER' on one side of the grey granite, and 'POOFTER' on the other side. That should give the police something to occupy their minds.

The following evening, while I was waiting for Gareth to emerge from the firm of solicitors where he was a salaried partner, I whiled away the time with the hyperbole of the Bradfield Evening Sentinel Times. This time, I'd made the front page.

GAY KILLER STRIKES AGAIN?

The mutilated body of a naked man was found this morning in Bradfield's gay village.

The murder victim had been dumped in the fire-exit doorway of the gay club Shadowlands in an alley off Canal Street in the notorious Temple Fields district.

This is the second time in two months that the body of a naked man has been discovered in the gay cruising area.

Now locals fear a perverted serial killer is stalking the city's large homosexual community.

Today's gruesome discovery was made by nightclub owner Danny Surtees, 37, as he arrived for a meeting with his accountant.

He said, 'I always go into the club through the fire door at the side. I park my car in the alley. This morning, the door was blocked by something covered by a couple of black bin bags.

'When I grabbed hold of the bags to try and pull them away from the door, they just came away in my hands and I saw there was a body under them.

'He was horribly injured. There was no way he was still alive. I'm going to have nightmares about this for the rest of my life.'

Mr Surtees said the doorway had been clear when

he locked up his club just after three this morning.

The victim, said to be in his early thirties, has not yet been identified. Police describe him as white, 5ft 11ins, slightly built, with dark-brown collar-length hair and hazel eyes. He has an old scar from an appendicectomy.

A police spokesman said, 'We believe the man was killed elsewhere and the body dumped in the alley between three and eight a.m.

'We would urge anyone who was in the Temple Fields area last night to come forward for the purpose of elimination. All information will be treated in the strictest confidence.

'At this stage of our enquiry, there is no evidence to connect this killing with the murder two months ago of Adam Scott.'

Carl Fellowes, the full-time worker at the Bradfield Gay and Lesbian Centre, said today, 'The police say that they don't think there's a connection between these two murders.

'I don't know what makes me more worried on behalf of the city's gay community – the thought that there's one nutter out there killing gay men, or the thought that there are two of them.'

I didn't know whether to laugh or cry. One thing was clear, though. PC Plod was a long way from covering himself in glory over this case. I'd obviously done a good job covering my tracks.

I folded up my newspaper, finished my cappuccino and signalled for my bill. Any minute now, Gareth would emerge from his office and walk through the rush-hour streets to the tram. I wanted to be ready for him. I had something really special planned for him tonight, and I wanted to make sure he was home alone to enjoy it.

10

The world in general, gentlemen, are very bloody-minded; and all they want in a murder is a copious effusion of blood; gaudy display in this point is enough for them. But the enlightened connoisseur is more refined in his taste.

Penny Burgess topped up her glass of Californian Chardonnay from the bottle in the fridge and walked back through to her living room in time to hear the headlines on the BBC local news. Nothing fresh to worry about, she thought with relief. An armed robbery she could catch up with first thing in the morning. The police were still questioning a man in connection with the gay serial killings, but no charges had been laid yet. Penny sipped her wine and lit a cigarette.

They were going to have to move soon, she thought. By morning, they'd either have had to charge him with something or let him go. So far, no one had got a sniff of the suspect's identity, which was pretty remarkable. The whole pack had been leaning heavily on their personal police contacts, but for once, the reservoir of information had resolutely refused to leak. Penny decided she'd better take a look at the magistrates' court lists in the morning. There was an outside chance that the cops had something fairly innocuous to charge their suspect with so they could hang on to him while they dug around for the evidence they needed to make the serial killing charges stick.

As the news cut away to the weather forecast, the phone

rang. Penny reached over to the occasional table by the sofa and grabbed the receiver. 'Hello?' she said.

'Penny? It's Kevin.'

Hallelujah, Penny thought, sitting up and grinding out her cigarette. All she said, however, was, 'Kevin, my man. How's it hanging?' She raked in her handbag for a pencil and her notebook.

'Something's come up you might be interested in,' the police inspector said cautiously.

'It wouldn't be the first time,' Penny said suggestively. Her occasional sexual encounters with the very married Kevin Matthews had provided her with more than an inside track on Bradfield Metropolitan Police. He'd turned out to be one of the best lovers she'd ever had. She just wished he could overcome his Catholic guilt more often.

'This is serious,' Kevin protested.

'So was I, superstud.'

'Listen, do you want this info or not?'

'Definitely. Especially if it's the name of the guy you've got in custody for the Queer Killings.'

She heard the sharp intake of breath. 'You know I can't tell you that. There are limits.'

Penny sighed. It was the story of their relationship. 'OK, so what can you tell me?'

'Popeye's been suspended.'

'He's off the case?' Penny asked, her mind racing. Tom Cross? Suspended?

'He's off the *job*, Pen. He's been sent home pending disciplinary action.'

'Who by?' Jesus, this was a story and a half. Just what had Popeye Cross been up to this time? She felt a momentary panic. What if he'd been caught out giving the suspect's name to one of her rivals? She almost missed Kevin's reply.

'John Brandon.'

'What the hell for?'

'Nobody's saying,' Kevin said. 'But the last thing he did before he saw Brandon was to carry out a search of our suspect's house.'

'A legal search?' Penny probed.

'Far as I know he had grounds under PACE,' Kevin said cautiously.

'So what's going on, Kevin? Has Popeye been planting evidence, or what?'

'I don't know, Pen,' Kevin said plaintively. 'Look, I've got to go. If I hear anything else, I'll call you, OK?'

'OK. Thanks, Kev. You're a star, you know.'

'Yeah, well. I'll speak to you soon.'

The line went dead. Penny dumped the phone back on the base unit and jumped to her feet. She hurried through to her bedroom, pulling off her dressing gown on the way. Five minutes later, she was running down the two flights of stairs from her flat to the underground garage. In the car, she checked the address in her A–Z, then set off, mentally rehearsing what she was going to say on the doorstep.

It was Tony who had pulled away from the clinch first. His body withdrew from hers in a gesture that rendered four inches forty.

Trying to keep it light, to cover the awkwardness that had sprung up between them, Carol said, 'Sorry, you just looked like you needed a hug.'

'Nothing wrong with that,' Tony said stiffly. 'We use it all the time in group therapy.'

They stood for a moment, eyes not quite meeting. Then Carol moved to Tony's side, slipped a hand through his unyielding arm and steered him forwards across the university courtyard. 'So when do I get to look at this profile?'

The conversation was on safe ground again, but Carol was still too close for comfort. Tony could feel the tension inside him, like a cold hand squeezing his chest. He forced himself to speak in a calm, normal voice. 'I want to do another couple of hours' work now, and I'll get stuck into it again first thing in the morning. I should have a draft ready for you by early afternoon. How does three o'clock sound to you?'

'Fine. Look, do you mind if I stick around now while you're working? I could do with rereading some of those statements, and I'll get no peace if I go back to Scargill Street.'

Tony looked doubtful. 'I suppose.'

'I promise not to molest you, Dr Hill,' Carol teased.

'Damn,' Tony said, snapping his fingers in mock-disappointment. Look at you, he thought cynically. Passing for human, sure of all the moves. 'Actually, it's not that. I'm only hesitating because I'm not used to working with someone else in the room.'

'You won't know I'm there.'

'I doubt that very much,' Tony said. She might read that as a compliment, but he knew the truth.

Penny pressed the doorbell of the mock-Tudor detached house in one of south Bradfield's more select streets. Even on a superintendent's salary, it should have been beyond Tom Cross's reach. But Popeye's reputation for being lucky had been enhanced a few years back when he'd won a high five-figure sum on the pools. The subsequent party had passed into police mythology. Now, it looked like he'd dropped his lucky pixie somewhere along the road.

A light snapped on in the hallway and someone lumbered towards the door, turned into an amorphous lump by the stained glass. '*Friday the Thirteenth* meets *Hallowe'en*,' Penny muttered under her breath as she heard the lock turn. The door cracked open a suspicious few inches. Penny angled her head round to smile at the shape behind the door.

'Superintendent Cross,' she said, the white cloud of her

breath meeting the swirl of smoke issuing from the door. 'Penny Burgess, *Sentinel Times*.'

'I know who you are,' Cross snarled, the slur of drink evident in those few words. 'What the hell do you want, coming round here this time of night?'

'I hear you've had a bit of a problem at work,' Penny tried.

'You hear wrong then, madam. Now, bugger off.'

'Look, it'll be all over the media tomorrow. You're going to be under siege. The *Sentinel Times* has always supported you, Mr Cross. We've been on your side all through this investigation. I'm not some visiting fireman from London, up here to put the boot in. If you've been sidelined, our readers have got a right to hear your side of the story.' The door was still open. If she'd managed to say that much without him slamming it shut in her face, the chances were that she was going to get something usable out of him.

'What makes you think I'm off the case?' Cross asked defiantly.

'I heard you've been suspended. I don't know why, and that's the reason I wanted to hear your side of it, before we get fed the official line.'

Cross scowled, his gooseberry eyes seeming to pop even further out. 'I've got nothing to say,' he told her, grudging every syllable.

'Not even off the record? You're willing to stand by and let them trash your reputation after all you've done for the force?'

Cross opened the door wider and looked down his drive towards the street. 'You on your own?' he asked.

'Not even my newsdesk know I'm here. I only just heard.'

'You'd better come in a minute.'

Penny stepped across the threshold into a hall that looked like a Laura Ashley sample book. At the far end of the hall, a door was half open, the television voices distinct even at that distance. Cross steered her in the opposite direction, into a long sitting room. When he switched the lights on, Penny's eyes were assaulted by more patterns than a knitting shop. The only thing the curtains, carpets, rugs, wallpaper, frieze and scatter cushions had in common was that they were all shades of green and cream. 'What a lovely room,' she stammered.

'You think so? I reckon it's bloody hideous. The wife says it's the best money can buy, which is the only argument I've heard for staying potless,' Cross grumbled, heading for a cocktail cabinet. He poured himself a stiff drink from a decanter, then, as an afterthought, said, 'You'll not be wanting one, with you having the car.'

'That's right,' Penny said, forcing the warmth into her voice. 'Can't take chances with your lads out on the roads.'

'You want to know why them gutless bastards have suspended me?' he demanded belligerently, thrusting his head forward like a hungry tortoise.

Penny nodded, not daring to take out her notebook.

'Because they'd rather listen to some poncey bloody doctor than a proper copper, that's why.'

If Penny had been a dog, her ears would have been standing to attention. As it was, she settled for a polite raise of the eyebrows. 'A doctor?' she said.

'They've brought this wanker of a shrink in to do our job. And he says the arse bandit we've got banged up is innocent, so it's bollocks to the evidence. Now, I've been a copper for twenty-odd years, and I trust my instincts. We've got the bastard, I can feel it in my water. All I did was try to make sure he stayed behind bars till we nail down all the bloody loose ends.' Cross downed his drink and banged his empty tumbler on the cabinet. 'And they've got the fucking nerve to suspend *me*!'

Manufacturing evidence, then. Although she was desperate to know more about the mysterious doctor, Penny sensed that she'd better let Cross air his grievances first. 'What did they say you'd done?' she asked.

'I've done nothing wrong,' he said, pouring another massive slug from the decanter. 'Trouble with bloody Brandon is he's been flying a desk for so long, he's forgotten what the job's about. Instinct, that's what it's about. Instinct and hard bloody work. Not some fucking trick cyclist with a head full of daft bloody notions like a fucking social worker.'

'Who is this guy, then?' Penny asked.

'Dr Tony bloody Hill. From the fucking Home Office. Sits in his ivory tower and tells us how to catch villains. He's got no more idea of coppering than I have of nuclear bloody physics. But the good doctor says, let the poofter go, so Brandon says yes, sir, no, sir, three bags full, sir. And just because I don't agree, I'm out on my arse.' Cross swallowed more whisky, his face flushed with anger and drink. 'Anybody'd think we were dealing with bloody Mastermind here, not some fucking dumbshit arse bandit who's had a bit of luck so far. You don't need smartarses with bloody "doctor" in front of their name to catch scum like this. All you do is give the homicidal little fairy ideas above his station.'

'It's fair to say, then, that you don't agree with the line the investigation's taking?' Penny asked.

Cross snorted. 'That's one way of putting it. You mark my words, if they let this little fucker back on the streets, we'll be looking at another body.'

To Tony's surprise, Carol proved to be true to her word. She sat at his desk, working her way through the pile of statements while he carried on working at his computer. Far from distracting him, he found her presence curiously soothing. He had no trouble picking up the profile where he'd left off earlier.

Like a roller coaster, each high needs to be bigger to compensate for the inevitable low that has preceded it. In this instance, there are three principal signs of escalation. The wounds to the throat have become increasingly deep and assured. The sexual mutilation has developed from a few tentative cuts in the genital region to full-scale amputation. And the bites he inflicts then cuts away have increased in number and in depth. Yet he has managed to stay sufficiently in control to cover his tracks.

It is difficult to assess whether or not the level of torture he is administering is escalating, since he seems to be using different torture methods in each case. The fact that he needs the stimulus of these different methods is, however, in itself a form of escalation.

Judging by the pathologist's report, the sequence of events would seem to be:

1. Capture, using handcuffs and ligatures round the ankles.

2. Torture, including sexually motivated acts such as biting and sucking.

3. The fatal blow to the throat.

4. Postmortem genital mutilation.

What does this tell us about the killer?

1. He has sophisticated and highly developed fantasies, which he is exploring through his torture methods.

2. He has a killing place. The amounts of blood and other bodily fluids generated by his activities could not be readily cleaned away from a normal domestic environment; it would be taking far more of a chance than his other cautious behaviour indicates. It will almost certainly have facilities for him to clean himself up after his killings, and power so he can run lights and a camcorder. We should be looking for something like a lock-up garage, a building that is secure but probably has running water and electricity. It may also be in an isolated location, thus avoiding the possibility

of his victims' screams being overheard. (He will almost certainly remove any gags while he is torturing them; he will want to hear them scream and plead for mercy.)

3. He is obsessed with torture, and obviously has enough manual skills to construct his own engines of torture. He does not appear to have either medical or butchery skills, judging by the clumsy and tentative nature of the early throat-cutting and genital mutilation.

Tony turned away from the screen and glanced across at Carol. She was totally absorbed in her reading, the familiar frown line between her eyes. Was he being crazy to back off from what she appeared to be offering? More than anyone he'd ever been involved with she would understand the pressures of his job, the highs and lows that accompanied getting inside the head of a sociopath. She was intelligent and sensitive, and if she committed herself as thoroughly to a relationship as she did to her career, she might just be strong enough to work through his problems with him rather than use them as a stick to beat him with.

Suddenly aware of his eyes on her, Carol looked up and flashed him a tired smile. In that instant, Tony made his mind up. No way. He had enough problems dealing with the crap in his head without allowing anyone else to make it a hostage to fortune. Carol was just too sharp to let her any nearer. 'Going OK?' she asked.

'I'm starting to get a feel for him,' Tony admitted.

'That can't be a very pleasant place to be,' Carol said.

'No, but it's what I'm paid for.'

Carol nodded. 'And I guess it's satisfying. And exciting?'

Tony smiled wryly. 'You could say that. I sometimes wonder if that makes me as twisted as them.'

Carol laughed. 'You and me both. They say the best thief-takers are the ones who get inside the heads of the villains. So if I'm going to be the best at what I do, I have to think like a villain. That doesn't mean I want to do what they do, though.'

Strangely comforted by her words, Tony turned back to his screen.

The time the killer spends with his victims can also provide pointers. In three of the four cases, the killer appears to have made contact in the early evening and to have dumped the bodies in the early hours of the following morning. Interestingly, in the third case, he spent far longer with his victim, apparently keeping him alive for the greater part of two days. This was the killing that took place over Christmas.

It may be that he is normally unable to spend long with his victims because of the other demands of his life, demands which altered over the Christmas period. These are more likely to be work-related demands than domestic ones, though it is possible that he is in a relationship with someone who returned alone to their family at Christmas, thus giving him time to spend with his victim. Another possibility is that the extended time he spent with Gareth Finnegan was a bizarre Christmas present to himself, a reward for the good performance of his previous 'work'.

The short space of time that elapses between the killings and the dumping of the bodies suggests that he does not use drink or drugs to any significant degree during the torture and murders. He would not risk being stopped by the police for erratic driving while he has a body in the boot, whether alive or dead. Also, although he appears to have used his victims' cars on occasion, it is clear that he also has a vehicle of his own. The chances are that this is a reasonably new vehicle in good condition, since he can't afford to take the chance of being stopped in a routine police check.

Tony hit the 'save' key on his computer and sat back with a satisfied smile. This was as good a place to stop as any. Tomorrow morning, he'd complete the detailed checklist of characteristics he'd expect to find in Handy Andy, and outline proposals for potential courses of action by the police officers on the case.

'You done?' Carol asked.

He turned to see her leaning back in the chair, her pile of folders closed. 'I didn't realize you'd finished,' he said.

'Ten minutes ago. I didn't want to disturb the flying fingers.'

Tony hated others studying him the way he studied them. The idea of being a patient on the receiving end of his own probing was one of those nightmares that he woke from in a sweat. 'I've had it for tonight,' he said, making a copy of his file on a floppy disc which he then pocketed.

'I'll give you a lift home,' Carol said.

'Thanks,' Tony said, getting to his feet. 'I can never be bothered bringing the car into town. To tell you the truth, I don't much like driving.'

'Can't say I blame you. The city traffic's hell on wheels.'

When Carol pulled up outside Tony's house, she said, 'Any chance of a cup of tea? Not to mention a pee?'

While Tony put the kettle on, Carol slipped upstairs to the bathroom. She came downstairs to the sound of her own voice issuing from his answering machine. She paused at the foot of the stairs, spying on him as he leaned against his desk, pen and paper in hand, listening to his messages. She enjoyed her growing sense of familiarity with his face and the lines of his body. Her voice ended and the machine beeped. 'Hi Tony, it's Pete,' the next voice announced. 'I've got to be in Bradfield next Thursday. Any chance of a bed and a beer Wednesday night? Congratulations on getting on board the Queer Killer investigation, by the way. Hope you catch the bastard.' Beep. 'Anthony, my darling.

Wherever can you be? I'm lying here, longing for you. We've got some unfinished business, lover boy.'

At the sound of the voice, Tony straightened up and he turned to stare at the machine. The voice was husky, sexy, intimate. 'Don't think you can –' Tony's hand shot out and cut the voice off abruptly.

So much for not being involved with anyone, Carol thought bitterly. She stepped forward through the doorway. 'Let's just forget the tea. I'll see you tomorrow,' she said, her voice cold and brittle as ice on a winter puddle.

Tony whirled round, panic in his eyes. 'It's not what it seems,' he blurted out without thought. 'I've never even met the woman!'

Carol turned out of the doorway and walked down the hall. As she fumbled with the lock, Tony spoke coldly. 'I'm telling you the truth, Carol. Even though it's actually none of your business.'

She half turned, found a smile from somewhere and said, 'You're quite right. It *is* none of my business. Till tomorrow, Tony.'

The closing of the door reverberated through Tony's head like a jackhammer. 'Thank God you're a psychologist,' he said bitterly as he slumped against the wall. 'A layman might have really buggered that one up. You really believe in making the job a piece of piss, don't you, Hill?'

When Gareth half smiled at me on the tram, I was convinced that my dreams were on the point of fulfilment.
Because of an unexpected crisis at work, and all the extra
overtime that entailed, I hadn't been able to follow him
for more than a week.

His image had lulled me to sleep when I came home at
all hours from work, and his voice throbbed hungrily in
my ears, but I needed to see him in the flesh. I'd set my
alarm clock to give me plenty of time to be outside his
house before he left for work, but I was so exhausted I
slept right through it. When I started into wakefulness, I
realized my only chance was to catch up with his tram a
couple of stops further down the line.

The tram was pulling in as I ran on to the platform. I
eagerly scanned the first section, but couldn't see him.
Anxiety rose in my throat like bile. Then I saw his gleaming
head, sitting right by the door of the second carriage. I
pushed through the crowd and managed to stand right
next to him, my knees brushing his. At the physical contact,
he looked up. His grey eyes crinkled at the corners and
a smile flickered on his mouth. I smiled back and said,
'Sorry.'

'No problem,' he said. 'This tram gets busier by the day.'

I wanted to continue the conversation, but for once I
could think of nothing to say. He returned to the Guardian
and I had to settle for watching him out of the corner of

my peripheral vision while I pretended to stare out at the passing cityscape. It wasn't much, I know, but it was a start. He had acknowledged me; he knew I existed. Now, it could be only a matter of time.

Shakespeare got it right when he said, 'The first thing we do, let's kill all the lawyers.' That way at least there would be fewer liars at large. Even the words sound the same; lawyer, liar. I should have expected nothing else from a man who speaks one day for the plaintiff, the next for the defendant.

I'd parked just round the corner from Gareth's house, where I could watch him come home without being seen, thanks to the tinted windows of my jeep. His house had no hedge, so I could see right into his living room from my vantage point.

I knew his habits by now. He arrived home just after six, went through to the kitchen for a can of Grolsch, and returned to the living room where he drank his beer and watched TV. After about twenty minutes, he'd fetch some food from the kitchen – pizza, TV dinner, baked potato. Cooking clearly wasn't his forte. When we were together, I'd have to take over responsibility for that side of our life.

After the news, he'd leave the room, presumably to do some work in another room of the house. I imagined law books arrayed on pine shelves. Then, he'd either return to the TV later in the evening, or walk down to the pub on the corner for a couple of lagers.

Gareth needed someone to share his life, I thought as I waited for him to come home. I was just the person to do that. Gareth was going to be my Christmas present to me.

At a quarter past five, a white Volkswagen Golf slipped into a parking place just beyond Gareth's house and a woman got out. She leaned back into the car and picked up a briefcase bulging with files and a shoulder bag. I thought she looked vaguely familiar as she walked down the pavement. Petite, light-brown hair pulled back in a heavy plait, big tortoiseshell glasses, black suit, white blouse with a froth of lace at the throat.

When she turned in at Gareth's gate, I couldn't quite believe it. For the few seconds it took her to get to the door, I told myself she was his estate agent, his insurance agent, a colleague dropping off some papers. Anything. Anything.

Then she opened the flap of her bag and took out a key. My mind screamed 'No!' as she inserted the key into the lock and let herself in. The living-room door opened and she dumped her briefcase by the settee. Then she was gone again. Ten minutes later, she was back, wrapped in Gareth's big white towelling dressing gown.

Frankly, I was with Shakespeare all the way.

'Twas the season to be jolly, so I forced myself not to let my disappointment colour my mood. Instead, I concentrated on researching my next project. I wanted something appropriate to the season, some good old barbaric Christian symbolism. There's not really a lot you can do with a manger and swaddling clothes, so I allowed myself some artistic licence and went for the other end of the life.

Crucifixion as a form of punishment was probably borrowed by the Romans from the Carthaginians. (Interesting, isn't it, how the Romans referred to everyone else as the barbarians . . .) The Romans adopted it round about the time of the Punic Wars, and initially, it was a punishment reserved for slaves only. Which seems appropriate enough, since that was the only role I expected Gareth to be fit for now. Later in the days of empire, it became a more general punishment, meted out to any locals who had the temerity to misbehave after the Romans had kindly come along and conquered – sorry, civilized – them.

Traditionally, the felon was flagellated, then forced to carry the crossbeam through the streets to the place where *a tall stake had been driven into the ground. Then he was nailed to the crossbeam and hauled up by a system of pulleys. His feet were sometimes nailed, sometimes tied to the stake. On occasion, death by exhaustion was given a helping hand by the soldiers, who broke the legs of the victim, which must have allowed him a merciful lapse into unconsciousness. For my purposes, however, I decided to opt for the more decorative St Andrew's Cross. For one thing, it would place more interesting stresses on Gareth's muscles. For another, should he rise to the occasion, it would make access a lot easier.*

Interestingly, crucifixion was never used as a punishment for soldiers except for the crime of desertion. Maybe the Romans had the right idea after all.

11

But who meantime was the victim, to whose abode he was hurrying? For surely he could never be so indiscreet as to be sailing about on a roving cruise in search of some chance person to murder? Oh, no: he had suited himself with a victim some time before, viz., an old and very intimate friend.

Brandon stared bleakly at the sheet of paper in the type-writer. Tom Cross might have been a long way from the ACC's idea of the perfect copper, but he'd always appeared to be a good thief-taker. Antics like tonight's served only to raise a question mark over his whole career. Just how many other people had Cross fitted up over the years without anyone being any the wiser? If Brandon hadn't himself bent the rules and taken Tony on their illicit search, no one would have doubted the 'evidence' Tom Cross had turned up. No one except Stevie McConnell would have known that two of Cross's three 'finds' had arrived with him. The mere thought of the consequences of that was enough to send a prickle of cold sweat down Brandon's back.

Cross had left Brandon with no option but to suspend him. The disciplinary hearing that would inevitably follow would be painful for all concerned, but that was the least of Brandon's worries. He was far more troubled about the effect on the murder squad's morale. The only way to combat it was to take direct responsibility for the enquiry himself. Now, all he had to do was convince the Chief that he was right. With a sigh, Brandon pulled the last sheet of paper out of the machine and inserted another page.

His memo to the Chief Constable was brief and to the point. That only left one task before he could crawl home to bed. Sighing, Brandon glanced at the clock. Thirty minutes to midnight. He pushed the typewriter away from him and started writing on a sheet of his personal memo paper. 'To Detective Inspector Kevin Matthews. From John Brandon, ACC (Crime). Re: Steven McConnell. Following the suspension of Superintendent Cross, I will assume direct command of the murder squad. There are no grounds for charging McConnell with anything other than assault. McConnell should be released on bail pending a court date for the assault charge, and on separate bail to return to Scargill Street in a week so that we can question him further if more evidence arises. In view of his refusal to give us any information about his contacts, or any names of people he might have introduced to Gareth Finnegan and Adam Scott, we should pursue any contacts he does make. A warrant for a tap on his phone should also be obtained, on the basis of his connection to Scott and Finnegan, and the contact we now know he had with Damien Connolly in a professional capacity. Our enquiries into the four related murders should continue on a broad front, though I suggest that, following his release on bail, we maintain close surveillance of McConnell. There will be a case conference of senior officers tomorrow at noon.' He signed the memo and sealed it in an envelope. How to make friends and influence people, he thought as he walked downstairs to the desk sergeant. Brandon prayed that Tony Hill was right about Stevie McConnell. If Tom Cross had been right to follow his instinct, it would be more than the morale of the CID that would be at risk.

Carol slumped over the dining table, chin resting on her folded forearms, one hand tickling Nelson's belly. 'What do you think, boy? Is he just another lying bastard, or what?'

'Prrrt,' the cat said on a rising intonation, his eyes closed to slits.

'I thought you'd say that. I agree, I know how to pick them,' Carol sighed. 'You're right, I should have kept my distance. That's what happens when you make the running. You get the knockbacks. They don't usually come from that far out of left field, though. At least now I know why he kept backing off. Better off without him, cat. Life's tough enough without playing second fiddle.'

'Mrrr,' Nelson agreed.

'He must think I'm brain dead, expecting me to believe that a total stranger leaves messages like that on his answering machine.'

'Rowrr,' Nelson complained, rolling over on to his back, batting her fingers with his paws.

'All right, so you think it's ridiculous too. But the man's a psychologist. If he was going to make something up to explain the fact that he'd lied to me, he'd make it a damn sight more plausible than funny phone calls. All he had to say was that it was somebody he'd finished with who wouldn't take the message.' Carol rubbed the sleep out of her eyes, yawned and stood up in one languid movement.

The door to the boxroom Michael used as a study opened and he stood framed in the doorway. 'I thought I heard voices. You could talk to me, you know. At least I answer you.'

Carol gave a tired smile. 'So does Nelson. It's not his fault we don't speak cat. I didn't want to disturb you; I could see you were working.'

Michael walked over to the drinks cabinet and poured himself a small Scotch. 'I was only play-testing, trying to spot the glitches in what we've done so far. No big deal. How's your day been?'

'Don't ask. They've moved us over to Scargill Street. It's

a hellhole. Imagine going back to doing your calculations on an abacus, and you get the picture of my current working environment. The atmosphere's shit, and Tony Hill's spoken for. Apart from that, everything's magic.' Carol followed Michael's example and poured herself a drink.

'Want to talk about it?' he asked, perching on the arm of one of the sofas.

'Thanks, but no thanks.' Carol swallowed her drink in one, shuddered at the kick of the spirit and said, 'I've brought you a set of pictures, by the way. How soon can you take a look at them?'

'I've scrounged some computer time with the software tomorrow evening. That do you?'

Carol put her arms round Michael and gave him a hug. 'Thank you, bro,' she said.

'My pleasure,' he said, returning the embrace. 'You know how I love a challenge.'

'I'm going to bed,' she said. 'It's been a long one.'

No sooner had Carol turned out the light than she felt the familiar thud of Nelson landing on the foot of the bed. It was reassuring to feel his warmth against her legs, though it was no substitute for the body she'd hoped for earlier in the evening. Of course, as soon as her head hit the pillow, her sleepiness vanished. The exhaustion was still there, but her mind was racing. Please God, by tomorrow afternoon, the awkwardness between her and Tony would have evaporated. The sting of humiliation would still be there for her, but she was a grown-up and a professional. Now she knew he was off limits, she wouldn't place him in a difficult position again, and now he knew she knew, maybe he'd be able to relax. Either way, the profile should provide more than enough neutral ground between them. She could hardly wait to see what he'd come up with.

On the other side of the sleeping city, Tony too lay in bed, staring at the ceiling, tracing imaginary road maps in the cracks round the plaster rose. He knew there was no point in switching out his bedside lamp. Sleep would elude him, and in the darkness, he'd start to feel the slow choke of claustrophobia closing in on him. Counting sheep had never appealed; the slow watches of the night were when Tony Hill became his own therapist. 'Why did you have to ring tonight?' he murmured. 'I *like* Carol Jordan. I know I don't want her in my life, but I didn't want to hurt her either. Hearing your blandishments on the answering machine must have felt like a smack in the face, after me saying there wasn't anybody in my life.

'An outsider would say we hardly know each other, everything that happened tonight was an overreaction. But outsiders don't understand the bonding, the intimacy that springs out of nowhere when you're working closely together on a manhunt, when the clock's ticking the next victim's life away.'

He sighed. At least he hadn't blurted out the one thing that might have convinced Carol he wasn't lying, the truth he'd so carefully kept locked inside himself. What was it he told his patients? 'Let it out. It doesn't matter what it is, speaking it is the first step in taking away the pain.'

'What a load of crap that is,' he said bitterly. 'It's just another one of the tricks in my magic bag, designed to legitimize my prurient curiosity, tailored to unleash the twisted minds of the fuck-ups who are driven to act out their fantasies in a way society can't accommodate. If I'd told Carol the truth, said the i-word, it wouldn't have taken my pain away. It would only have made me feel even more of a worthless piece of shit. It's all very well for old men to be impotent. Men my age who can't get it up are a joke.'

The phone rang, startling him. He rolled over, scrambling for the receiver. 'Hello?' he said, his voice tentative.

'Anthony, at last. Oh, how I've missed you!'

His surge of anger at the languid, husky voice died as soon as it flared. What was the point in raging at her? She wasn't the problem. He was. 'I got your message,' he said, resigning himself. She hadn't caused the awkwardness with Carol; there would have been no grounds for awkwardness at all if he hadn't been such a pathetic excuse for a man. No point in even thinking about relationships with nice, normal women. He would have blown it with Carol, just as he'd always blown it with women as soon as they got close. The best he could hope for was telephone sex. At least it generated a kind of equality; it allowed men to fake not just orgasm but erection too.

Angelica chuckled. 'I thought I'd leave you something nice to come home to. I hope you're not too tired for some recreation.'

'I'm never too tired for your kind of recreation,' Tony said, swallowing the self-disgust that threatened to overwhelm him. Think of it as therapy, he told himself. Tony lay back and let the voice flow over him, his hand straying down his chest towards his groin.

The cleaners were gossiping by the lift as Penny Burgess emerged on the third floor of the *Bradfield Evening Sentinel Times* office. She walked down the newsroom, snapping on lights as she passed, humming tunelessly under her breath. She tossed her bag on the desk by her computer terminal and logged on. She executed the commands that took her into the library database, and pressed the key for 'search'. Five options were offered: 1. Subject; 2. Name; 3. By-line; 4. Date; and 5. Pictures. Penny hit 2. At the 'surname' prompt, she typed 'Hill'. At the 'forename' prompt, she keyed in 'Tony', and at the 'title' prompt, she entered, 'Dr'. Then she sat back and waited while the computer sorted through the gigabytes of information stored in its huge memory. Penny flipped open her cigarette packet and pulled out her first cigarette of the day. She was only a couple of drags into it when the screen flashed 'Found (6)'.

Penny retrieved the six items and called them up on her screen. They appeared in reverse order of date. The first was a two-month-old cutting from the *Sentinel Times*. It had been written by one of the news reporters. Although she'd read it at the time, she'd completely forgotten about it. As she read it, Penny whistled softly.

INSIDE THE MIND OF A KILLER

The man the Home Office have chosen to spearhead the hunt for serial killers spoke today about the latest slaying that has terrified the city's gay community.

Forensic psychologist Tony Hill is one year into a major study funded by the government which will lead to the setting up of a criminal profiling task force similar to the FBI unit featured in *The Silence of the Lambs*.

Dr Hill, 34, was formerly the chief clinical psychologist at Blamires Hospital, the maximum-security mental unit which houses Britain's most dangerous criminally insane offenders, including mass murderer David Harney and serial killer Keith Pond, the Motorway Madman.

Giving his verdict, Dr Hill said, 'I have not been called in by the police to consult on any of these cases, so I know no more than your readers do about them.'

Either Dr Hill had been lying to her colleague, or his formal involvement with the case came after the interview. If that was the case, Penny could see how to exploit it in a way that would appeal to her editor. She could picture the headline now. 'POLICE FOLLOW *BEST*'S LEAD IN MURDER HUNT.' She quickly flicked through the rest of the piece. It didn't tell her anything she didn't already know, although she was interested that Dr Hill had speculated that the discrepancies in the third killing might mean there were two killers out on the streets. That was an idea that seemed to have sunk without trace. It was something to ask Kevin about next time she managed to get him on the end of a phone.

The next cutting was from the *Guardian*, and announced the setting up of the Home Office programme for developing a national task force to deal with serial offenders. The project was to be based at Bradfield University. The article gave her more background on Dr Hill, and she jotted down his career details in her notebook. No dummy, this guy. She'd have to handle him carefully. She tapped her teeth with her pen and wondered why the *Sentinel Times* hadn't run a feature on the study, with a profile of Dr Hill. Maybe they tried and had been knocked back. She'd have to check with her colleagues on Features.

The next two cuttings were from a national tabloid, a two-part series on serial killers that had been timed to coincide with the general release of *The Silence of the Lambs*. Dr Hill was quoted in both articles, talking in general terms about the work of psychological profilers.

The last two cuttings dealt with one of his most prominent patients, Keith Pond, the so-called Motorway Madman. Pond had abducted five women from motorway service areas, then savagely raped and murdered them. At the time of his trial, only two of the bodies had been found. But after extensive therapy with Dr Hill, Pond had revealed the whereabouts of the other three bodies. Dr Hill had been hailed as a worker of miracles by the bereaved family of one of the victims. One of the two pieces had attempted a profile of Dr Hill, but they had scant information to go on. As usual, the journalist hadn't let that stand in the way of a good story.

Tony Hill, who has never married, is devoted to his work. A former colleague said, 'Tony's a workaholic. He's married to the job.

'He's totally driven by the desire to understand what makes his patients tick. There's probably not another psychologist in the country who has his knack of getting inside their twisted minds and working out what makes them do what they do.

'I sometimes thought he related better to mass murderers than he did to normal punters.'

The reclusive Dr Hill lives alone and is notorious for not mixing socially with colleagues. Apart from studying the minds of serial killers, the only hobby he apparently indulges in is hill-walking. On weekends off, he regularly drives to the Lakes or the Yorkshire Dales and tramps the fells.

'Sounds like a real barrel of laughs,' Penny said aloud, scribbling more notes on her pad. She returned to the main menu, where she selected the fifth option. Again, she entered Tony's name for a picture search. The data banks revealed there was one stock picture on file. Penny called it up and stared at the face that appeared on her screen. 'Gotcha!' she exclaimed. She had only seen him once before, but now she knew who Carol Jordan's new sidekick was.

Penny leaned back in her seat, savouring her third cigarette, and registered that the newsroom was starting to fill up. One quick phone call, then she could afford the time to treat herself to a fry-up in the canteen. Reaching for the phone, she dialled Kevin Matthews's home number. He picked up on the second ring. 'DI Matthews,' came the sleepy mumble.

'Hi, Kev, it's Penny,' she said, savouring the stunned silence that greeted her announcement. 'Sorry to bother you at home, but I thought you'd rather answer my questions there than in the office.'

'Wh-what?' he stuttered. Then, muffled, 'Yeah, it's work. Go back to sleep, love.'

'How long has Dr Tony Hill been on the team?'

'How did you hear about that? Shit, that's supposed to be top secret!' he exploded, his nervousness transforming itself into anger.

'Tut, tut. Kev, she'll never get back to sleep if you yell like that. Never mind how I know, just be grateful you can put your hand on your heart and deny it came from you. How long, Kev?'

He cleared his throat. 'Just a couple of days.'

'Was it Brandon's idea?'

'That's right. Look, I really can't talk about this. It's supposed to be kept under wraps.'

'He's doing a profile, right?'

'What do *you* think?'

'Working with Carol Jordan? Brandon's blue-eyed girl on this one, is she?'

'She's the liaison officer. Look, I've got to go. I'll talk to you about this later on, OK?' Kevin tried to sound menacing, but failed.

Penny smiled and slowly exhaled a mouthful of smoke. 'Thanks, Kev. I owe you a very special one.' She replaced the handset, cleared her screen and opened a story file.

'Exclusive. By Penny Jordan,' she typed. Never mind breakfast. She had far more interesting stuff to do.

Tony was back in front of his screen by half past eight. Instead of the guilt he'd expected to feel about his erotic encounter, he felt refreshed. Giving himself permission to indulge himself with Angelica had somehow released and relaxed him. Surprising though he found it under the circumstances, he'd actually become aroused as she'd talked him through an outrageous, imaginative sexual encounter. He hadn't actually managed to sustain his erection as far as orgasm, but because there was no one there to share his failure, it hadn't seemed to matter. Maybe a few more calls from Angelica would be all he needed to contemplate the reality with something less than abject panic.

But not at work. What he needed now was complete peace. He'd already instructed his secretary to hold all his calls, and he turned off the ringer on his direct line. Nothing and nobody was going to interrupt the flow of his thoughts. His feeling of satisfaction continued as he read through the work he'd done the day before. He was ready now to put himself on the line and commit his conclusions about Handy Andy to paper. Tony poured himself a cup of coffee from his Thermos and took a deep breath.

We are dealing with a serial killer who will certainly kill again unless he is caught. The next killing will take place on the eighth Monday following the death of Damien Connolly unless some trigger accelerates this. What might push him over the edge into extreme escalation could be some catastrophic event that causes him to lose whatever it is he is using to keep the fantasy alive. Since, for example, he is using videos, loss of or damage to his tapes could lead to loss of control. Another possible scenario is that an innocent person is charged with the killings. That would be such an affront to his sense of himself that he might commit his next murder ahead of schedule.

I believe it is likely that he has already selected his next victim and is familiarizing himself with that victim's movements and lifestyle. The chances are that the chosen victim is a man not known to the gay community. He will be, to all intents and purposes, a straight man living a heterosexual lifestyle.

The fact that his last victim was a police officer is disturbing. It is highly probable that this was choice, not accident or coincidence. The killer is sending a message to the investigation. He is demanding that we take notice of him, that we take him seriously. He is also telling us that he is the best; he can catch us but we can't catch him. There is a theory that such behaviour is a way of inviting capture, but I do not believe that is what is going on in this case.

It is possible that his next target may also be a police officer, perhaps even one who is working on the investigation. This alone will not be sufficient motive for the killer to choose them; they must also fit the victim criteria that he has drawn up in his own mind in order for the killing to assume its full meaning for him. I would strongly recommend that any officers who fit the victim profile employ extra vigilance at all times, noting any suspicious vehicles parked near their homes, and checking to see whether they are being followed to and from work and social events.

The stalking and preparation serves two main purposes for the killer: it cuts down on the potential surprise elements when he comes to carry out the killing, and it also fuels the fantasy that is the all-important area of the killer's life.

Our killer is probably a white male, aged between 25 and 35. He is likely to be at least 5ft 10ins tall, well muscled, with considerable upper-body strength. In spite of this, he probably has a poor body image. He may work out in a gym, but if he can afford it, he would prefer to use his own equipment in the privacy of his home. He is right-handed.

He won't look like a con. He'll look deeply, deeply average. He will have a demeanour that doesn't provoke suspicion. He's the sort of bloke you wouldn't look at twice, and certainly wouldn't suspect of being a multiple murderer. He may have tattoos and/or self-inflicted scars, but these are likely to be fairly discreet.

He is familiar with Bradfield, and his knowledge of Temple Fields is clearly current. This implies someone who lives and probably works in the city. I don't think he's a casual visitor, nor a former resident who simply comes back here to kill. There is no obvious geographical pattern to the homes or workplaces of his victims, except that they all lived in reasonably close proximity to a tram line. The first victim's home is most likely to be geographically closest to where the killer lives or works. Looking at the general background and style of the victims, and working on the principle that he's sticking to the kind of environment he knows and understands, I would suspect that the killer lives in privately owned property rather than rented, a house rather than a flat, in a suburban area of similar properties to those of the victims. The victims' houses are probably worth more than the killer's; these are men that in some way he aspires towards.

He is probably of above average intelligence, though I would not expect him to have a university degree. His school record is probably quite patchy, with poor attendance and highly variable marks. He will never have lived up to his potential or to other people's expectations of him. Most serial killers have a bad employment record, flitting from job to job, being sacked more often than resigning. But this man exhibits an extraordinary level of control in the commission of his murders, so I would expect him to be capable of holding down a steady job, possibly even one with some degree of responsibility and forward planning. However, I don't think his job will involve much contact with his fellow human beings, since his relationships with others will be characterized by their dysfunctional nature. His victims are all white-collar workers, with the marginal exception of Damien Connolly, which indicates to me that he probably operates in a similar working environment. I wouldn't be surprised to find him working in a technology-related area, possibly computers. This is an employment area where people can hold down good jobs without having significant people skills. People who don't fit in are accepted and acceptable in the weird world of software engineers; indeed, they are often highly prized since they are hard to replace. I doubt if our killer is a leading-edge creative person in the software world, but I wouldn't be surprised to find him as a systems manager or a program tester. He probably doesn't get on well with his bosses, being inclined to be insubordinate and argumentative.

He will be middle class in terms of his job, his aspirations, his clothes and his home, although he may be working class in background. He is good with his hands, but I am inclined to think he is not in a manual occupation, if only because of the high degree of planning involved in these murders.

Socially, he feels isolated. He may not necessarily be a loner, but he does not connect with people. He feels like an outsider. He probably has developed superficial social skills, but somehow his behaviour always strikes the wrong note. He's the one who laughs too loudly, the one who thinks he's making jokes when he's actually being deeply offensive, the one who sometimes seems to have drifted off in a daydream all of his own. He's the one who doesn't really have any friends, who will join in with the group but never pair off with one buddy in particular. He has little insight into his social failings. He prefers to be alone with his fantasies, because when others are involved socially, he can't fully control what's happening around him.

It's entirely possible that he does not live alone. If he lives with someone, it will be a woman rather than a man. Because he is sexually attracted to men and cannot accept that, he will not under any circumstances be living with a man, not even in a platonic relationship. His relationships with women may well be sexual, but he will not be an enthusiastic or successful lover. His performance will be barely adequate, and he may regularly experience problems in achieving and/or sustaining an erection. However, he will not be impotent during the commission of his crime, and will almost certainly be able to complete a full sexual act of some sort with his victims.

Tony paused and stared out of the window. Sometimes it felt like the chicken and the egg. Did he empathize with his patients because he too knew the frustrations and anger of impotence, or had his sexual problems increased precisely so that he could do his job better? 'Does it matter?' he said impatiently. He ran a hand through his hair and concentrated once again on the screen.

If he is living with someone, she will almost certainly have no suspicion whatsoever that her partner is the killer. It's therefore quite likely that her first instinct will be to alibi him, since in her heart, she knows it couldn't possibly be him. Any suspects solely alibied by girlfriends or wives should therefore not be eliminated on those grounds alone.

He is mobile, with his own car, which is in good condition (see above). And on Monday nights, he's free to roam without hindrance or obligation to be somewhere.

He is a highly structured personality, a control freak. The sort who has a tantrum because his girlfriend has forgotten to buy his favourite cereal. He believes he's absolutely justified; he thinks that in his crimes, all he is doing is actually committing the actions that everybody else wants to but lacks the bottle for. He has a big chip on his shoulder and feels that the world has conspired against him; how come, since he's so bright and talented, he's not running the company instead of doing this poxy job? How come, since he's so charming, he's not going out with some supermodel? The answer is, the world is out to do him down. He has the egocentric world view of the spoiled child, and has no insight into the impact of his behaviour on others. All he sees is the way events affect him.

He is a persistent fantasist and daydreamer. His fantasies are elaborately constructed and seem more significant to him than reality. His fantasy world is where he retreats both from choice and also whenever he faces any kind of setback or obstacle in his day-to-day life. The fantasies are likely to involve violence as well as sex and may also be fetishistic. These fantasies don't remain static; they lose their power and have to be developed further.

He is certain that he can act out his violent fantasies without anyone being able to stop him. He has supreme confidence that he is smarter than the police. He is not planning for the day he will be caught. He thinks he's too clever for that. He has been very careful to erase forensic traces, which is why, as I have already outlined to Inspector Jordan, I am convinced that the fragment of Russian deerskin left at the scene of the fourth killing is a red herring of the grossest kind. He is almost certainly keeping a close eye on the investigation, and will doubtless be laughing his socks off as we run round trying to source the leather. Even if the police do trace it, I suspect that when we find the killer there will be nothing among his possessions that will remotely connect to it.

If he has any criminal record at all, it is likely to be a juvenile one. Possible offences include: vandalism, minor arson, stealing, cruelty to younger children or animals, assault on teachers. However, somewhere along the line, our killer has learned enormous self-control, and he's unlikely to have an adult record.

He will keep abreast of the investigation as much as possible, and will thrive on publicity as long as it appears to accord him the glamour and respect he craves. It is interesting that Adam Scott's grave was desecrated shortly after the second murder. This may have been an attempt to raise the profile of his crimes. He is possibly someone who has contacts with police officers, and if he does, he will endeavour to use this to gain information about the progress of the investigation. Any officer who feels they are being pumped in this way should be encouraged to report it to senior officers in the murder squad.

Tony saved his file and read the whole thing through again. Some of the psychologists he'd worked with incorporated great slabs of background about the likely childhood background of the killer, as well as a checklist of behaviours that the killer would possibly have exhibited when he was growing up. Not Tony. There was time enough for that sort of information once there was a suspect ripe for interrogation. Tony never forgot that he was dealing with coppers who were out there at the sharp end. Men like Tom Cross, who didn't give a toss what kind of hideous childhood their suspect had endured.

Thinking of Tom Cross sharpened Tony's critical eye. Convincing him of the value of the profile was going to be a nightmare.

The first edition of the *Bradfield Evening Sentinel Times* hit the street just before noon. The eager searchers after flats, jobs and bargains snatched the first copies from the street vendors without even looking at the front page. They turned straight to the section of small ads that they hoped would meet their needs, holding the front and back pages up to the advantage of passers-by. Anyone curious enough to glance at the banner headlines on the front page would have discovered 'MURDER HUNT BOSS DUMPED. Exclusive, by our Crime Correspondent, Penny Burgess.' Further down the page, the bottom right-hand quarter was taken up with a photograph of Tony, saying, 'MURDER COPS FOLLOW *BEST* LEAD. Exclusive by Penny Burgess.' If they'd been intrigued enough to buy their own copy, they could have read a sub-headline saying, 'Top shrink we chose joins Queer Killer hunt, see story p. 3.'

In an office high above the bustling streets of Bradfield, a murderer stared at the paper, excitement churning inside. Things were working out beautifully. It was as if the police were acting out the killer's own fantasies, proving that wishes do come true.

The world was out in the city streets, buying Christmas presents they'd still be paying for at Easter, the fools. I was in my dungeon, making sure I would have a Christmas I'd never forget. Even though it was to be Gareth's last on this earth, I was sure every detail of it would be as clearly etched on his memory as it was going to be on my video tape.

I'd arranged our meeting with all the care and precision I could. The advent of the bitch meant I couldn't take the chance of capturing him at home as I'd done with Adam and Paul. I'd had to make alternative plans.

I sent him an invitation. I reasoned that Christmas Eve would be spoken for, either by family or by the bitch, so I chose December 23rd. I couched it in terms I knew he wouldn't be able to resist and that he'd never dare show the bitch. The final sentence read, 'Admission by invitation only.' A clever touch, that. It meant he'd have to bring with him the only evidence of contact between us.

The directions on the back led, if he cared to check it out in advance, to an isolated holiday cottage high up on the moors between Bradfield and the Yorkshire Dales; the opposite side of the city to Start Hill Farm and my dungeon. I anticipated that the cottage would be let over Christmas. But I had no intention of allowing Gareth to get that far.

*   *   *

It was a Christmas-cliché sort of night; bone-white crescent moon, stars twinkling like diamond chips on a cocktail watch, grass and hedgerows heavy with rime. I pulled over on to the verge of the single-track moorland road that led up to the holiday cottage and a couple of farms. In the distance, I could see the dual carriageway leading into Bradfield like a ribbon of fairy lights strung across the Pennines.

I turned on my hazard lights, got out of the jeep and opened the bonnet. I placed what I needed near at hand, then I leaned against the front wing and waited. It was freezing, but I didn't care. I'd calculated well. I'd only been waiting for about five minutes when I heard the sound of an engine straining up the steep incline. The lights swung round the bend below me and I stepped out, waving furiously, looking frozen and worried.

Gareth's elderly Escort stopped abruptly in front of the jeep. I took a couple of hesitant steps towards him as he opened the door and got out. 'Some kind of a problem?' he asked. 'I'm afraid I know next to nothing about cars, but if I can maybe give you a lift . . . ?'

I smiled. 'Thanks for stopping,' I said. There was no flicker of recognition in his face as he drew nearer. I hated him for that.

I stepped back towards the jeep, gesturing under the bonnet. 'It's not a big problem,' I said. 'Only, I need three hands. If you can just hold this part in place so I can get a spanner on this nut . . .' I pointed into the engine. Gareth leaned over the bonnet. I picked up the spanner and let him have it.

Within five minutes, he was trussed tighter than a turkey in the boot of his own car. I had his car keys, his wallet and the invitation I'd sent him. I drove back down through the city to the farm, where I dumped the unconscious body unceremoniously down the cellar steps. I didn't have time to do any more then, not if I was going to get back to the jeep.

I drove Gareth's car into the centre of Bradfield, leaving it in Temple Fields in a back alley off Crompton Gardens. Nobody noticed me; they were all too busy partying. It was a mere ten minutes' walk across town to the railway station.

A twenty-minute train ride and a brisk fifteen-minute walk brought me back to the jeep. Cautiously, I approached. There was no sign of life, no suggestion that anyone had been poking around. I drove back to Start Hill Farm whistling 'Hark The Herald Angels Sing'.

When I switched the cellar light on, Gareth's dark-grey eyes flashed angry fire at me. I liked that. After the pathetic terror of Adam and Paul, it was refreshing to see a man who had some guts. The muffled sound that came from behind the tape on his mouth was more like an angry grunt than a plea.

I stooped over him and stroked his hair back from his forehead. At first, he jerked away from me, then he became calm and still, calculation in his eyes. 'That's more like it,' I said. 'No need to fight, no need to resist.'

He nodded, then grunted, signalling down towards his gag with his eyes. I kneeled beside him and picked at one corner of the surgical tape. Once I had a good grip, I ripped it free in one swift movement. It's kinder than doing it gradually.

Gareth worked his jaw, licking his dry lips. He glared at me. 'Some fucking party,' he snarled, his voice a little shaky.

'It's exactly what you deserve,' I said.

'How the fuck do you work that out?' he demanded.

'You were meant for me. But you took up with that slag. And you tried to keep it a secret.'

Light dawned in his eyes. 'You're . . .' he started.

'That's right,' I interrupted. 'So now you know why

you're here.' My voice was as cold as the stone floor. I stood up abruptly and walked over to the bench where I'd laid out my equipment.

Gareth was talking again, but I shut out the sound of his voice. I know how persuasive lawyers can be, and I wasn't about to be deflected from my course by any amount of sweet talking. I opened the ziplock bag and took out the chloroform pad. I turned back to Gareth and kneeled beside him. With one hand, I gripped his hair and with the other I applied the pad to his mouth and nose. He struggled so convulsively that I ended up with a clump of hair in my hand before he subsided into unconsciousness. Just as well I was wearing my latex gloves, otherwise his hair would have cut me. The last thing I needed was my blood mingling with his.

When he was out cold, I cut his clothes off. I took the strap from the Judas chair and fastened it round his chest, under the armpits. I'd fixed a rudimentary pulley and hoist to one of the ceiling beams, and I attached the hook to the strap. I raised Gareth's body with the hoist till he swung like mistletoe in a draught. Once he was up in the air, it was the work of moments to undo the handcuffs and fasten him to my Christmas tree.

I'd bolted two planks to the wall in the shape of a St Andrew's Cross, and covered them thickly with prickly boughs of blue Norwegian spruce. To each arm of the cross, I'd attached leather straps, which I fastened around his wrists and ankles. I opened up Gareth's curled fists and taped his hands open to the cross. Finally, I removed the hook and let the wrist straps take the strain. His body slumped alarmingly, and for a moment I was concerned that I hadn't fitted strong enough straps. There was a brief creaking of leather on wood, then silence. He hung like a martyred apostle on the dungeon wall.

I laid out my club hammer and the sharpened cold chisels

I'd chosen for the job. We'd be together now till Christmas night. I intended to savour every minute of our forty-eight hours.

12

Very few men commit murder upon philanthropic or patri-
otic principles ... As to the majority of murderers, they
are very incorrect characters.

The four detective inspectors sat stony-faced in what had
been Tom Cross's office as John Brandon gave them the
official version of the superintendent's suspension. Sometimes, Brandon wished he was one of the lads again, able
to explain his reasons without appearing to undermine his
own position by doing so. 'What we've got to do is put
this behind us and move this enquiry forward,' he said
briskly. 'Now, what's the score with McConnell?'

Kevin leaned forward in his seat. 'I did as you instructed,
sir. He left our custody just before midnight, and I've had
a team on him ever since. He hasn't put so much as a toe
out of line so far. He went straight home, seemed to go to
bed, judging by the lights. He was up at eight this morning,
and he's gone off to work. I've got one lad in the gym,
posing as a new member, and another one out on the
street.'

'Stick with it, Kevin. Anything else? Dave, anything
interesting coming out of the computer yet?'

'We're following up a lot of car numbers and blokes
with previous for any gay-related offences, both on the
gay-bashing and the gross indecency side. We're also about
to cross-check those lists with the ones Don Merrick's been
getting from travel agents of people who have booked
holidays in Russia. Once we get the profile, we might be

able to develop some suspects, but it's uphill at the moment, sir.'

Carol chipped in. 'Some of the weightlifting associations said they'd supply us with lists of their members who'd either been to Russia or competed against Russian teams.'

Dave pulled a face. 'Oh goody, more bloody lists,' he said.

'I've got a contact in the leather business,' Stansfield said. 'Biggest importer in the UK. I asked him about the leather scrap and he said that with it being deerskin, it's probably not your common-or-garden labourer's jacket. He said it was likely to be someone with a bit of clout but not real power. You know. Somebody like a DI,' he grinned. 'Or a town-hall official halfway up the greasy pole. A deputy stationmaster. The second mate on a ship. That sort of thing.'

Dave grinned. 'I'll tell HOLMES to keep an eye out for ex-KGB men.'

Brandon started to say something, but he was cut off by the peal of the telephone. He grabbed it and said, 'Brandon here . . .' His face lost all expression, turning as wooden as the coffins he looked as if he should be carrying. 'Yes, sir. I'll be there right away.' He put the phone down gently and stood up. 'The Chief Constable is interested in hearing how this evening's paper came to look the way it does.' He crossed the room and paused by the door, one hand on the handle. 'I'm sure the person who washed our dirty linen in Ms Burgess's sink will be hoping I can persuade him not to make an example of him.' He gave Carol a frosty smile. 'Or her, come to that.'

Tony locked his office door behind him and gave the project secretary a happy wave and smile. 'I'm going out for a bite of lunch, Claire. I'll probably go to Café Genet in Temple Fields. Inspector Jordan's due at three, but I'll be back by then. OK?'

'You're sure you don't want to return one of these calls from the journalists?' Claire called after him.

Tony swung round, continuing to walk backwards across the office. 'What journalists?' he asked.

'First off, that Penny Burgess from the *Sentinel Times*. She's been trying every half-hour since I came in. Then, in the last hour, they've been on from all the national newspapers, and Radio Bradfield.'

Tony frowned, baffled. 'Why?' he asked. 'Did they say what they wanted?'

Claire held up the copy of the *Sentinel Times* she'd nipped out to buy from the campus newsagent. 'I'm no psychologist, Tony, but I think it might have something to do with this.'

Tony stopped in his tracks. Even across the office he could read the headlines and make out his own photograph splashed across the front page of the paper. Like an iron filing pulled by a magnet, Tony moved closer to the paper till he could read Penny Burgess's name on both stories. 'May I?' he said hoarsely, reaching out for the paper.

Claire relinquished it and watched his reaction. She liked her boss, but she was human enough to relish his discomfort at being exposed in the evening paper. Tony hastily flicked the front page over, hunting for the full story about himself. With a mounting sense of horror, he read:

Dr Hill is well equipped to enter the twisted mind of the Queer Killer. As well as his two university degrees and a wealth of experience in dealing directly with the criminal perverts who have terrorized society, he has a reputation for dogged determination.

A colleague said, 'He's married to the job. It's all he lives for. If anyone can catch the Queer Killer, it's Tony Hill.

'It's only a matter of time now, I'm convinced. Tony

is relentless. He won't give up till this bastard is nailed down tight.

'Let's face it, Tony's got a top-class brain. These serial killers might have high IQs, but they're never very smart when it comes to staying out of custody.'

'Dear Christ,' Tony groaned. Apart from the fact that no self-respecting colleague would ever have given quotes like that, the article was tantamount to throwing down the gauntlet to Handy Andy. It read like a challenge. He felt sure Handy Andy would find a way to respond to that. Tony threw the paper down on the desk and scowled at it.

'It is a bit over the top,' his secretary said sympathetically.

'It's bloody irresponsible, never mind over the top,' Tony raged. 'Oh, bollocks to it. I'm going for lunch. If the Chief Constable rings, tell him I've left for the day.' He walked off again towards the door.

'What about Inspector Jordan? What if she rings?'

'You can tell her I've left the country.' With the door open, he paused. 'No, only joking. Tell her I'll be here for our meeting.'

As he stood waiting for the lift, Tony realized nothing in his experience had prepared him for a direct confrontational challenge with a killer. This was one he'd have to fly by the seat of his pants.

Kevin Matthews drained his pint glass and waved it at the barmaid. 'Even if it is a red herring, he's still got to have had access to this bloody obscure bit of leather in the first place, hasn't he?' he demanded stubbornly of Carol and Merrick. 'Same again?'

Merrick nodded. 'I'll have a coffee this time, Kevin,' Carol said. 'And chuck us a menu, would you? I've got a feeling I'm in for a long session with the doc, and he's got a nasty habit of forgetting about food.'

Kevin ordered the drinks then turned back to Carol. With the persistence that had won him promotion, he said, 'I'm right though, aren't I? To plant the leather like that, not only has he had access to it, he also knows how unusual it is.'

'Agreed,' Carol said.

'So it's not a waste of time trying to source it, is it?'

'I never said it was,' Carol said patiently. 'Now, are you going to fill me in on what happened with Tom Cross, or do I have to copy our murderer and bring out the torture gear?'

While Kevin explained what had happened, Merrick's attention drifted. He'd already heard the tale more times than enough. He leaned against the bar and surveyed the clientele. The Sackville Arms wasn't the nearest pub to the Scargill Street station, but it sold draught Tetleys from Yorkshire and Boddingtons from Manchester, which inevitably made it the police local. The pub was on the outer fringes of Temple Fields, which had given it an added attraction for the local officers when Scargill Street had still been open. The location had meant that hookers or petty villains who wanted to drop a word in the ear of their personal contact on the force could manage it unobtrusively. However, in the few months that Scargill Street had been mothballed, the pub had subtly changed. The regulars had got used to having the place to themselves, and there was a clearly discernible distance between the coppers and the rest of the customers. The officers who'd been using the pub in an attempt to recruit new sources from the community's underbelly had met with a chilly reception. Even with a serial killer on the loose, no one wanted to get back into the habit of informing now they'd kicked it.

With his policeman's eyes, Merrick slowly scanned the room, classifying the drinkers. Hooker, dealer, rent boy, pimp, rich man, poor man, beggar man, wimp. He was jolted out of his scrutiny by Carol's voice. 'What do you think, Don?' he caught.

'Sorry, ma'am, miles away. What do I think about what?'

'That it's about time we developed some of our own snouts among the toms, instead of having to rely on the Vice Squad's girls. They've been round the houses so many times, I'd go outside to check if they told me it was raining.'

'Never mind the hookers,' Merrick said. 'We need to know a damn sight more about how the gay community works. I don't mean the lads that are out of the closet and down the Hell Hole. I mean the secretive ones. The ones that don't flaunt it. They're the ones who might have come across this guy before. I mean, from all I've ever read about serial killers, sometimes they don't actually kill the first time, they just have a go. Like the Yorkshire Ripper did. So maybe there's some frightened little guy in the closet who's been on the receiving end of a bit of violence that got out of hand. That might be the road to a break.'

'And God knows we need a break,' Kevin said. 'But if we don't know how the connections are made, how do we connect?'

Carol said thoughtfully, 'When in doubt, ask a policeman.'

'Do what?' Kevin asked.

'There are gay officers in the Job. More than most, they must know about keeping a low profile. They'd be able to tell us.'

'That doesn't answer the question,' Kevin protested doggedly. 'If they're so busy keeping it quiet, how do we know who they are?'

'The Met has an association of gay and lesbian police officers. Why don't we get in touch with them, in confidence, and ask for their help? Somebody must have some contacts in Bradfield.'

Merrick stared at Carol with admiration, Kevin with

frustration, both wondering silently how it was that Inspector Jordan always had an answer.

Tom Cross glanced down at the front page of the *Sentinel Times*, a smirk of satisfaction twitching his cigarette up and down. Ms Burgess might have thought she was in control of their little encounter the night before, but Tom Cross knew different. He'd played the spider to her fly, and she'd done exactly what he expected of her. No, credit where it's due. She'd done better than he'd expected. That line about the police staggering lamely in the wake of the *Sentinel Times* when it came to seeking out Dr bloody Hill was a corker.

There were going to be a lot of angry men in Bradfield police today. That was the revenge element of Tom Cross's game with Penny Burgess. But someone else was going to be angry too. When he read tonight's paper, the killer was going to be more than a little put out.

Tom Cross stubbed out his cigarette and slurped from his mug of tea. He folded his paper and placed it on the table in front of him and stared out of the café window. He lit another cigarette. He'd set out to provoke the Queer Killer. Provoked, he'd start to get careless, to make mistakes. And when Stevie McConnell did that, Tom Cross would be ready and waiting. He'd show those sorry bastards in command how to catch a killer.

Tony was back in the office by ten to three. Even so, he wasn't early enough to beat Carol. 'Inspector Jordan's here,' Claire said as soon as he opened the outer office door. She gestured with her head towards his office. 'She's in there waiting. I told her you'd be back.'

Tony's responding smile was strained. As he gripped the door handle, he clenched his eyes tightly and took a deep breath. Nailing what he hoped was a welcoming smile on his face, Tony opened the door and stepped into his office.

At the sound of the door, Carol turned away from the window she'd been staring out of and gave him a cool, appraising look. Tony closed the door behind him and leaned against it.

'You look like a man who's just stepped in a puddle that's deeper than his shoe,' Carol remarked.

'That's an improvement, then,' Tony said with more than a trace of irony. 'Usually I feel like I've stepped in a puddle that's deeper than my head.'

Carol took a step towards him. She'd rehearsed what she was going to say. 'There's no need to feel like that with me. Last night ... well, you were less than candid and I misread the signals. So can we please forget the whole thing and concentrate on what's important between us?'

'Which is?' Tony sounded impersonal as a therapist, his question conversational rather than challenging.

'Working together to nail this killer.'

Tony pushed himself away from the door and made for the safety of his seat, careful to keep the desk between them at all times. 'That's fine by me.' He gave a crooked smile. 'Believe me, I'm far better at professional relationships than the other kind. Think of it as a lucky escape.'

Carol walked round to the opposite side of the desk and pulled up a chair. She crossed her trouser-clad legs and folded her hands in her lap. 'So let's have a look at this profile.'

'We don't have to behave as if we're strangers,' Tony said quietly. 'I respect you, and I admire the way you're so open to learning new aspects of the job. Look, before ... before what happened last night, we seemed to be moving towards a friendship that went beyond work. Was that such a bad thing? Couldn't we settle for that?'

Carol shrugged. 'It's not easy making friends after you've exposed your weaknesses.'

'I don't think showing someone you're attracted to them is necessarily a weakness.'

'I feel foolish,' Carol said, not quite sure why she was opening up like this. 'I had no right to expect anything from you. Now, I'm angry with myself.'

'And with me too, I expect,' Tony said. This was proving less traumatic than he had imagined. His counselling techniques hadn't rusted over from lack of use, he thought with relief.

'Mostly with myself,' Carol said. 'But I can deal with that. The important thing for me is that we get the job done.'

'Me too. It's pretty rare for me to find a police officer who seems to have a grasp of what I'm trying to do.' He picked up the papers on his desk. 'Carol ... This isn't about you, you know. It's about me. I have problems of my own that I need to deal with.'

Carol stared at him long and hard. He felt a quick twitch of panic as he realized he could not read her eyes. He had no idea what she was feeling. 'I hear what you're saying,' she replied, her voice cold. 'Speaking of problems,' she added, 'haven't we got some work to do?'

Carol sat alone in Tony's office with his profile of the serial killer. He had left her to read it while he worked next door with his secretary, catching up on the correspondence that had piled up since Brandon had hijacked him only a handful of days before. She couldn't remember ever having been so fascinated by a report in her entire career. If this was the future of policing, she desperately wanted to be part of it. At last, she came to the end of the main body of text and turned to a separate sheet.

Points to pursue:
1. Had any of the victims ever mentioned to a friend/relative that they had been the subject of an unwanted homosexual approach? If so, when, where and from whom?

2.   The killer is a stalker. His first encounter with his victims probably takes place quite a long time before he kills – weeks rather than days. Where is he encountering them? It may be something as banal as where they take their dry-cleaning, where they have their shoes heeled, where they buy sandwiches, where they have tyres or exhausts put on their cars. Given that they all lived close to the tram network, I think we should check whether the victims regularly used the trams to go to and from work, or to go out in the evenings. I suggest that in-depth background checks are done, going through bank accounts, credit-card statements and anecdotal evidence from colleagues, girlfriends and family members. This may help develop suspects.

3.   Is there any indication that the victims were keeping the night in question free for any particular purpose? Gareth Finnegan lied to his girlfriend about it – did any of the others?

4.   Where is he doing his killing? It's unlikely to be in his home, since he will have calculated the possibility of being arrested, and will have taken pains to avoid leaving forensic traces there. It's also got to be big enough for him to build and use the torture engines we are assuming in these cases. It may be an isolated lock-up garage, or a unit on an industrial estate which is deserted at night. Bearing in mind that he almost certainly lives in Bradfield, it's possible that there exists an isolated rural property that he has undisturbed access to.

5.   He must have found out about instruments of torture somewhere so that he could construct his own. It might be worth checking with bookshops and libraries to see if any of their customers has enquired about or ordered books on torture.

Carol flicked back a few pages, rereading a couple of paragraphs which had particularly struck her first time through. She found it hard to credit how quickly Tony had assimilated the stacks of files she'd delivered. Not only that, but he'd drawn out of them the key points that created for the first time in Carol's mind a picture, albeit shadowy, of the man she was hunting.

But the profile raised questions in her mind. At least one of those questions didn't seem to have occurred to Tony. She wondered if it wasn't referred to because he had dismissed it out of hand. Either way, she had to know. And she had to find a way of asking that didn't sound like an attack.

I hated to keep Gareth hanging on, but I had to leave him
for one little errand. In his car, I'd found a few of the
Christmas cards his company sent out to favoured clients,
already signed by all the partners. Inside one, with a fountain
pen, a stencil set and Gareth's blood, I'd written in block
capitals, 'A MERRY CHRISTMAS TO ALL YOUR
READERS; YOUR EXCLUSIVE CHRISTMAS GIFT IS
WAITING IN THE SHRUBBERY OF CARLTON PARK
BEHIND THE BANDSTAND. COMPLIMENTS OF THE
SEASON FROM SANTA CLAWS.' It wasn't easy to write
with the blood; it kept congealing on the nib, which I had to
clean every few letters. Luckily, there was no shortage of ink.

I addressed a Jiffy bag to the editor of the Bradfield
Evening Sentinel Times and put the card in it, along with
a video I'd made a couple of weeks before, when I'd started
to plan what to do with Gareth. I'd already decided to
change my modus operandi slightly. Temple Fields was
bound to be risky now; even if the queens were too drunk
or stoned to be vigilant, the police would be keeping an
eye open for more than the occasional cottaging poof. But
the nature trail through the shrubbery of Carlton Park is
almost as notorious a pick-up area.

Early on a rainy Sunday morning, when there was
nobody about, I'd driven out to Carlton Park with my
camcorder. I started off by the wrought-iron bandstand. I
walked around it, filming it from every angle. It wouldn't

take long before somebody in the BEST office recognized the landmark. After all, Carlton Park is the biggest park within the city boundaries, and there's a brass-band concert there every Sunday from April to September. I deliberately kept the camcorder at chest level rather than on my shoulder; I've read of instances where correct estimates of height have been made simply from the angle photographs have been taken from. If some forensic scientist was going to draw any conclusions from this video, I wanted to be sure they would be the wrong ones.

Leaving the bandstand behind, I walked down the nature trail towards the shrubbery. I panned across the general area where I thought I'd dump the body, then stopped filming. I passed nobody on my way back to the jeep. That was probably just as well, since I was grinning from ear to ear at the thought of the news editor puzzling over my Christmas message.

The message would also serve two other functions. It would minimize the time it took to identify Gareth's body, which meant the publicity machine would have plenty of fodder to keep it going through what was always a slack news period. Secondly, it would send the police on a wild goose chase, working out who could have had access to the Christmas cards.

The police might even decide that someone connected with Gareth through work had decided to bump him off and make it look like a, copycat killing by dumping the body in a gay cruising area. Just the sort of thing a deranged and disillusioned client would do. If I got really lucky, they might even give the bitch a hard time, too.

I drove into the city centre to post the packet at the main post office. There were enough last-minute panicking gift-givers for me to be unremarkable. I stopped at an off licence on the way back to buy a bottle of champagne. I don't normally drink when I'm working, but this was a special occasion.

When I got back, Gareth was semi-conscious, mumbling incomprehensibly. 'Santa's here,' I said cheerfully as I came down the stairs. I popped the cork on the champagne and poured two glasses. I took one over to Gareth and, standing on tiptoe, I gently lifted his lolling head. I held the glass to his lips and tilted it. 'You'll enjoy this,' I said. 'It's vintage Dom Perignon.'

His eyes snapped wide open. For a moment, he looked bewildered, then he remembered and he fixed me with a look of pure hatred. But he was parched, and couldn't resist the champagne. He swallowed it greedily, not savouring it at all. Then he belched in my face, a look of strange satisfaction in his eyes.

'Wasted on you,' I said angrily. 'Like all the fine things in life.' I stepped back and slashed the glass across his face. It shattered against his nose, cutting his cheek to ribbons. I was glad Auntie Doris wouldn't be coming back. She'd had that set of six fragile crystal glasses as a silver-wedding present, and she'd never used them, terrified that someone would break one. She'd been right to be concerned.

Gareth shook his head. 'You're evil,' he slurred. 'Pure evil.'

'No, I'm not,' I said softly. 'I'm justice. Remember justice? It's what you're supposed to stand for.'

'Twisted, evil bastard,' he replied.

I couldn't believe he still had the stamina for bravado. It was time to show him who was boss. I'd already pinned his hands to the cross with a couple of cold chisels. The blood had congealed around them, black and hard. Now it was the turn of his feet.

When he saw me pick up my tools from the workbench, he finally cracked. 'There's no need for this,' he said desperately. 'Please. You could still let me go. They'd never find you. I've no idea where we are. I don't know who you are, where you live, what you do for a living. You could move away from Bradfield and they'd never find you.'

I took a step closer. Tears welled up in his eyes and spilled over, trickling through the blood on his cheek. They must have stung, but he never flinched. 'Please,' he whispered. 'It's not too late. Even if you killed those other men. Was it you who killed them?'

He was smart, I had to give him that. Too smart for his own good. He'd just earned himself some more suffering. I turned away and dropped the chisel and club hammer on the workbench. Let him think I was having second thoughts. Let him spend the night convinced I was going to have mercy. That would make Christmas Day all the sweeter.

I shut the cellar door behind me and went upstairs to bed, armed with my videos and the best part of a bottle of vintage champagne. I was having the best Christmas I'd ever had. I remembered all those years of desperate hope, praying that this would be the year my mother would buy me presents like other children got. But all she'd ever done was let me down. Now I'd worked out that the only person who could give me what I craved was myself; I knew that for the first time in my life, I could look forward to the kind of Christmas other people have, filled with surprises, satisfaction and sex.

13

Reading his acts by the light of such mute traces as he left
behind him, the police became aware that latterly he must
have loitered. And the reason which governed him is striking; because at once it records – that murder was not pursued by him simply as a means to an end, but also as an
end for itself.

The Wunch of Bankers was one of the few city-centre
watering holes where Kevin Matthews felt safe meeting
Penny Burgess. A fun pub with blaring rap music and decor
modelled on soap operas – the Rover's Return Snug, the
Woolpack Eaterie, the Queen Vic Lounge, and the Cheers
Beer Bar – was the last place he was likely to see another
copper or Penny another journalist.

Kevin made a face as his taste buds clenched on the
strong bitter coffee that lurked under a swirl of foam that
looked more like industrial effluent than a cappuccino.
Where the hell was she? He glanced at his watch for the
twentieth time. She'd promised she'd be here by four at
the latest, and now it was ten past. He pushed the half-
empty cup away from him and grabbed his fashionable
raincoat from the banquette beside him. He was about to
stand up when the pub's revolving door hissed round and
disgorged Penny. She waved and headed straight over to
his table.

'You said four o'clock,' Kevin greeted her.

'God, Kevin, you're getting really anal in your old age,'
Penny complained, giving him a peck on the cheek as she

subsided on to the seat beside him. 'Get me one of those mineral waters with a hint of fruits of the forest, there's a love,' she said, her voice mocking the pretensions of her chosen drink.

When Kevin returned with a glass already sweating with condensation, Penny immediately put a proprietorial hand on the inside of his thigh. 'Mmm, thanks,' she said, sipping her drink. 'So what's new? Why the urgent meeting?'

'Today's paper,' he said tonelessly. 'The shit's really hit the fan.'

'Oh, good,' Penny said. 'Maybe we'll get some positive action. Like a suspect you've got some evidence against.'

'You're not understanding. They're hunting for the mole. The Chief had Brandon on the carpet this morning, and the upshot is that Internal Affairs have mounted a leak enquiry. Penny, you've got to cover my back,' Kevin said desperately. Penny took her time lighting a cigarette. 'Are you listening to me?' Kevin demanded.

'Of course I am, sweetheart,' Penny soothed automatically, her mind already planning her story for the morrow. 'I just don't understand why you're getting so worked up. You know a good journalist never reveals her sources. What's the problem? You think I'm not a good enough journalist?' With an effort, Penny forced herself to listen to Kevin's reply rather than the voice in her head reeling off headlines.

'It's not that I don't trust you,' Kevin said impatiently. 'It's inside the force I'm worried about. Everybody will be desperate to put themselves in the clear, so anybody that knows about us will be falling over themselves to tell Internal Affairs. And once they know that we're, well, you know? That'll be it. I'll have had it.'

'But nobody knows about us. Or not from me, they don't,' Penny said calmly.

'I thought nobody knew too. Then Carol Jordan said something that made me think she does.'

'And you think Carol's going to shop you to Internal Affairs?' Penny said, failing to hide the incredulity she felt. She hadn't had many dealings with the CID's most glamorous officer, but what she knew of the inspector didn't incline her to cast her in the role of grass.

'You don't know her. She's totally bloody ruthless. She wants to go all the way, that one, and she'd drop me in it soon as look at me if she thought it would take her a rung up the ladder.'

Penny shook her head in exasperation. 'You're over-reacting. Even if Carol Jordan has mysteriously discovered that we're seeing each other, I'm sure she's too busy covering herself with glory from her liaison with Dr Hill to be bothered with shopping you. Besides, if you think about it rationally, she's got nothing to gain from getting herself a reputation with the lads as a grass.'

Kevin shook his head dubiously. 'I don't know, Penny, you've no idea what it's like on this job. We're all working eighteen-hour days, and we're getting nowhere.'

Penny stroked the inside of his thigh. 'Sweetheart, you're under a lot of pressure. Look, tell you what. If it all comes on top and somebody fingers you, Internal Affairs are bound to come to us and front us up. They'll be looking for corroboration. If that happens, I'll make it look like Carol Jordan's my source, OK? That should muddy the waters.'

Kevin's smile was worth the flannel, she decided. That, and one or two other things about him. Reassured, he bounced to his feet. 'Thanks, Pen. Listen, I've got to be a place. I'll call you soon so we can get together, OK?' He leaned over and kissed her deep and hard.

'Keep me posted, lover boy,' Penny said softly to his retreating back. Before he even reached the doors, her intro was taking shape. Oh yes, she could see it now.

Bradfield police are devoting new resources to the hunt for the serial killer who has claimed four victims and placed men in jeopardy as never before.

But the extra officers will not be joining the search for the monstrous Queer Killer. Their job will be to police the police themselves.

Top brass in the force are so alarmed by the accuracy of the *Sentinel Times*'s stories on the killings that they have set up a full-scale mole hunt to uncover the source of our stories. Instead of catching the killer, the mole-catchers will be tracking down fellow officers who subscribe to the view that the terrified public have a right to know what's going on.

Carol opened the door to the outer office and said, 'I'm all done. Can we talk?'

Tony looked up from the computer screen absently, held up one finger and said, 'Yeah, sure, give me a minute,' and finished what he was doing.

Carol retreated and took a deep breath. No matter how professional she tried to be, she couldn't help the surge of attraction she felt for this man. Ignoring it was easier said than done. Moments later, Tony joined her. He perched on the edge of his desk, his hair standing on end like Dennis the Menace from thrusting his fingers through it while he concentrated. 'So,' he said. 'What's the verdict?'

'I'm impressed,' she said. 'It really pulls everything together. There were a couple of things, though.'

'Only a couple?' Tony asked, his voice close to a chuckle.

'You talk a lot about how he must be strong, to overpower his victims and move them around. Also, you speculate about how he gets them into a vulnerable position in the first place. I was wondering if maybe there were two of them.'

'Go on,' Tony said, no hint of frost in his voice.

'I don't mean two men. I mean a man and someone else

263

who appears vulnerable. Maybe an adolescent boy or, more likely, a woman. I don't know, maybe even a person in a wheelchair. A partner in crime. Like Ian Brady and Myra Hindley.' Carol shuffled the papers, putting them back in order. Still Tony said nothing. After a few moments watching his expressionless face, she added, 'I know you've probably thought about it already, I just wondered if it was a possibility we should still bear in mind.'

'Sorry, I didn't mean to look like I was ignoring you,' Tony said hurriedly. 'I was reviewing the thought, weighing it against what we know and against the profile. One of the first things I considered was whether or not it was a solo. On the balance of overwhelming probability, I decided it was. Cases like the Moors Murders where you have two people acting in tandem to carry out atrocities are incredibly rare, for a kick off. Also, I'd expect to find more variation in the methodology and the pathology if there were two people involved; it's hard to believe their fantasies would coincide so exactly. But it's interesting that you've come up with it. You're right in one respect. If he's working with a woman it does explain how he gets close to his victims without them putting up a fight.' Tony sat staring straight ahead, brows lowered in thought.

Carol stayed motionless in her seat. Eventually, Tony turned to face her and said, 'I'm going to stick with my soloist. Yours is an interesting idea, but I can't see evidence that convinces me I should shift from the most highly probable scenario.'

'OK, point taken,' Carol said calmly. 'Moving on from that, have you considered the possibility of a transvestite? Like you just said, a woman could get close without them putting up a fight. What about if the woman was a man in drag? Wouldn't that have the same effect?'

Tony looked startled for a moment. 'Maybe you should think about applying to join the national task force when it's set up,' he stalled.

Carol grinned. 'Flattery will get you nowhere.'

'I mean it. I think you've got what it takes to do this kind of work. You see, I'm not infallible. I hadn't actually considered a transvestite. Now, why did I ignore that possibility?' he mused, thinking aloud. 'There must be some subconscious reason why I rejected it before it even got to the front of my mind . . .' Carol opened her mouth to speak, but he said, 'No, wait a minute, please, let me work this out.' His hands ran through his hair again, rearranging the dark spikes.

She subsided, telling herself he was just as arrogant as all the rest, unable to accept he might just have missed something. Stop kidding yourself he's different, she told herself sternly.

'Right,' Tony said, his voice rich with satisfaction. 'We're dealing with a sexual sadist, agreed?'

'Agreed.'

'Sado-masochism is the power trip of sexual fetishes. But transvestism is the diametric opposite of that. TVs want to assume the supposedly weaker role that women have in society. What underpins transvestism is the belief that women have a subtle power, the power of their gender. It couldn't be further removed from the brute transaction of pain and power that sado-masochists crave. That's not part of a TV's fantasy at all. To convince the victims that they're dealing with a woman and not a man in drag, the killer would have to be an accomplished cross-dresser. But, uniquely in my experience of clinical psychology, he'd also have to be a sexual sadist. The two just don't go together,' Tony explained with an air of finality. 'The same goes for a transsexual. Probably more so, in fact, because of the counselling they have to go through before they're accepted for treatment.'

'So you're ruling it out, then,' Carol said, feeling unreasonably crushed.

'I never rule anything out. That's asking to make a fool

of yourself in this game. What I think is that it's so unlikely that I would be loath to include it in a profile because its very inclusion might push people in the wrong direction. But by all means keep it in mind. You're thinking along the right lines.' He smiled, unexpectedly, taking the sting of patronage out of his words. 'Like I said at the start, Carol, together we can crack it.'

'And you're absolutely convinced that it isn't a woman?' she asked.

'The psychology's all wrong. Taking the most obvious point, this killer's an obsessive, and that tends to be a male trait. How many women do you know who hang about station platforms in the rain in anoraks writing down train numbers?'

'But what about that syndrome, what's it called, where people get obsessed with someone else to the point where they make their lives a misery? I thought it was mainly women who suffer from that?'

'De Clerambault's Syndrome,' Tony said. 'And yes, it is principally women who suffer from it. But they only focus on one person, and the only person who's likely to get dead as a result is the sufferer, who sometimes commits suicide. The thing is that women's obsessions and compulsions are different from men's. Men's obsessions are about control; they collect stamps and catalogue them, they collect a pair of knickers from every woman they've slept with. They need trophies. Women's obsessions are about submission; in eating disorders, it's the obsession that takes them over and controls them rather than the other way about. A sufferer from de Clerambault's Syndrome who married the object of her desire would probably be the chauvinist's ideal of the perfect wife. That pattern doesn't fit our killer.'

'I see what you mean,' Carol said, loath to give up the one fresh idea she felt she'd contributed to the profiling process.

'Add to that the sheer physical strength involved here,' Tony continued, seeing her reluctance. 'You're fit. You're probably quite strong for your height. I'm only a couple of inches taller than you. But how far do you think you could carry me? How long would it take you to pick my body up from the boot of a car and dump it over a wall? Could you throw me over your shoulder and carry me through Carlton Park to the shrubbery? Now bear in mind that all the victims have been taller and heavier than me.'

Carol gave a rueful smile. 'OK, you win. I'm convinced. There was one other thing that occurred to me.'

'Let's hear it.'

'Reading your profile, it seems to me that the reason you advance for the maintenance of the gaps between the killings just isn't strong enough,' she started tentatively.

'You noticed that too,' he said wryly. 'It didn't convince me either. But I couldn't think of anything else to explain it. I've never encountered anything quite like it, either face to face or in the literature. All the serial offenders I know about go through escalation.'

'I've got a theory that might cover the problem,' Carol said.

Tony leaned forward, his expression absorbed. 'Speak to me, Carol,' he said.

Feeling like a goldfish in a bowl, Carol took a deep breath. She'd wanted his attention, but she wasn't quite sure if she liked it now she had it. 'I remember what you said to me a couple of days ago about the intervals.' She closed her eyes and recited, '"With most serial killers, the gap between the killings tends to decrease quite dramatically. It's their fantasies that trigger off the killings in the first place, and the reality never quite matches up to the fantasy, no matter how much they refine their killing procedures. But the more extreme they get, the more blunted their sensibilities become and the more stimulus they need to get the sexual buzz that killing provides. So the kills have to become more frequent. Shakespeare said it. 'As if increase of appetite had grown by what it fed on.'" Am I right?'

'Remarkable,' Tony breathed. 'Can you do that with visuals as well, or is it only auditory?'

Exasperated, Carol cast her eyes upwards. 'Auditory only, I'm afraid. Anyway, when I read the bit in the profile where you suggest he might work with computers, something clicked. The question you didn't actually put but is obviously bothering you is, why isn't he getting desensitized to the videos faster as time goes by?'

Tony nodded. The point she'd raised was powerful, and it was precisely what was troubling him. He searched to find an answer that would satisfy them both. Groping for the solution as he went along, he said, 'Suppose, for the sake of argument, that the first video had the potential to keep him stable for twelve weeks. But he'd already set in train the process of capturing his second victim, and the opportune moment came along before he was actually compelled to kill again. He just couldn't resist the chance when it presented itself so perfectly. Afterwards, he realizes he's left eight weeks between the killings and he decides that eight weeks is going to be his pattern. So far, the videos have allowed him to maintain that. Maybe that is going to change now.'

Carol shook her head. 'It's plausible, but I'm not convinced.'

Tony grinned. 'Thank God for that. Neither am I. There's got to be a better explanation, but I don't know what it is.'

'How much do you know about computers?' she asked.

'I know where the on/off switch is and I know how to use the software I need to work with. Other than that, I'm a moron.'

'Well, that makes two of us. My brother, however, is a computer whizz kid. He's a partner in a games software house. The stuff he works on is leading-edge technology. Right now, he and his partner are developing a low-cost system that will allow games players to put images of themselves in the games that they're playing. In other words, instead of it being Arnie kicking the shit out of the bad guys on the screen in *Terminator 2*, it would be Tony Hill. Or Carol Jordan. The point is that there's already the hardware and software around that allows you to scan video tape and import the images into a computer. I think they call it digitized images. Anyway, once you've got that into the computer, you can manipulate it exactly how you want to. You can incorporate still photographs, or bits from other videos. You can superimpose things. When they first got the original hardware about six months ago, Michael showed me this sequence he'd made up himself. He'd taped some of the Tory Party conference and he'd also imported a video sex guide. He'd selected all these government ministers' faces while they were giving their speeches and superimposed them on the sex video.' Carol snorted with laughter at the memory. 'It was a bit choppy, but believe me, you've never seen John Major and Margaret Thatcher getting on so well! It gave a whole new meaning to the word "gobbledegook"!'

Tony stared at Carol in stunned silence. 'You're kidding me,' he said.

'It's the perfect explanation of why the videos manage to keep him under control.'

'Wouldn't that mean he'd have to be a real boffin, like your brother?'

'I don't think so,' Carol said. 'From what I gathered, the actual techniques involved are fairly simple. But the software and the peripherals that you need to do it are incredibly expensive. You could be talking two or three grand just for one piece of software. So he's either working for a company where he has that sort of equipment on tap and the privacy to work on his own stuff, or else he's a computer hobbyist with a lot of disposable income.'

'Or a thief,' Tony added, only half joking.

'Or a thief,' Carol agreed.

'I don't know,' Tony said dubiously. 'It does answer the problem, but it's totally off the wall.'

'And Handy Andy isn't?' Carol said belligerently.

'Oh, he's off the wall, all right, but I'm not sure he's that together.'

'He builds torture machines. That would be a lot easier with a computer design program. Tony, something's keeping him stable on his eight-week cycle. Why not this?'

'It's a *possibility*, Carol, no more than that at this stage. Look, why don't you make some preliminary enquiries, see how feasible what you're suggesting would be in practice?'

'You don't want to include it in the profile?' Carol asked, bitterly disappointed.

'I don't want to undermine the things I feel are strongly probable by including something that's really only a bit of kite-flying at this stage. You said yourself, it was triggered off by one of the few bits in the profile that is little more than speculation. Don't get me wrong, I'm not knocking the idea. I think it's brilliant. But we're going to have to work bloody hard as it is to overcome the resistance in some quarters to the profile as a whole. Even people who are broadly in support of the idea aren't necessarily going to agree with some parts of it. So let's not give them any easy targets. Let's bottom it, present it to them gift-wrapped so the snipers can't just knock it straight off the perch. OK?'

'Fine,' she said, knowing in her heart he was right. She picked up a sheet of paper and a pen. 'Check out software manufacturers and consultancies in Bradfield area,' she muttered to herself as she wrote. 'Check with Michael about manufacturers of necessary hardware/software then check sales records. Check recent thefts.'

'Computer clubs,' Tony added.

'Thanks, yes,' Carol said, adding that to her list. 'And bulletin boards. Oh boy, I'm going to be really popular with the HOLMES team.' She got to her feet. 'It's going to be a long job. I'd better get cracking. I'll take this down to Scargill Street now and give it to Mr Brandon. We'll need you to come in and go through it.'

'No problem,' Tony said.

'I'm glad something isn't.'

Tony stared out of the window of the tram, watching the city lights pass in a blur of rain. There was something cocoon-like about the gleaming white interior of the tram. Graffiti-free, warm, clean; it felt like a safe place to be. As the driver approached traffic lights, he gave a blast on the breathy horn. It sounded like a noise from childhood, the sort of hooting that a cartoon train would produce, he decided.

He turned away from the window and covertly studied the half-dozen other passengers on the tram. Anything to take his mind off the curious emptiness he felt now he had delivered his profile. It wasn't as if this would be the end of his involvement with the case. Brandon had told Carol that she was to have a daily briefing with him.

He wished he could have been more encouraging about her computer theory, but years of training and practice had rendered the habit of caution ingrained. The idea itself was brilliant. Once she had done some research into the practicability of what she was suggesting, he'd be only too happy to endorse it with her fellow officers. But for the sake of his profile's credibility, he had to keep his distance from ideas that the average copper would dismiss as science fiction.

He wondered how the police were faring that evening. Carol had called him to say that teams were going out in Temple Fields, trawling the area's regulars, trying to see if the profile suggestions produced any recognition. With luck, they might get some names that would cross-reference to data already in HOLMES, either from previous criminal records or from the car index numbers whose registered keepers had been fed into the system.

'The next stop will be Bank Vale station. Bank Vale station next stop,' the electronic voice from the speakers announced. With a start, Tony realized they had left the city centre far behind and were emerging on the far side of Carlton Park, less than a mile from his home. Bank Vale came and went, and Tony swung round in his seat, ready to make for the exit doors when the next stop was announced.

He walked briskly through the neat suburban streets, past the school playing fields, skirting the small copse that was all that remained of the plantation that had given the Woodside area its name. Tony glanced at the trees as he hurried past, thinking wryly that the path cutting diagonally through the wood would almost certainly be completely deserted. First it was the women walking home alone who had abandoned it. Then it was the children, kept away by anxious parents. Now, in Bradfield, it was the men who were learning the bitter lessons of life in jeopardy.

Tony turned into his street, relishing the quiet of the cul-de-sac. He'd get through the evening somehow. Maybe drive down to the supermarket and buy the ingredients for a chicken biryani. Pick up a video. Catch up on his reading.

As he turned the key in the lock, the phone started ringing. Dropping his briefcase, Tony ran for the phone, kicking the door to behind him. He picked up the phone, but before he could say anything, her voice trickled into his ear like warm olive oil soothing an earache. 'Anthony, darling, you sound like you're panting for me.'

He'd managed to avoid thinking about it all the way home, but he knew this was what he'd been hoping for.

Brandon had turned out the bedside light less than a minute before the phone rang. 'You should have known better,'

Maggie murmured as he dragged himself away from her complaisant warmth and reached for the receiver.

'Brandon,' he growled.

'Sir, it's Inspector Matthews,' the tired voice said. 'We've just picked up Stevie McConnell. The lads have just lifted him at the ferry port in Seaford. He was about to get on a ship for Rotterdam.'

Brandon sat up in a tangle of duvet, ignoring Maggie's protests. 'What have they done?'

'Well, sir, they didn't think there was a lot they could do, being as how he's on police bail and there's no conditions for him to breach.'

'Are they holding him?' Brandon was out of bed and reaching for his underwear drawer.

'Yes, sir. They've got him in the Customs lads' office.'

'What on?'

'Assaulting a police officer.' Kevin's voice somehow summoned up the image of a smirk as disembodied as the Cheshire Cat's smile. 'They rang me to ask what they should do next, and since you've taken such a personal interest in the case, I thought I should ask you first.'

Don't push it, Brandon thought savagely. All he said, however, was, 'I'd have thought it was pretty obvious. Arrest him for attempting to pervert the course of justice and bring him back to Bradfield.' He wrestled into a pair of boxer shorts and leaned over to pick up his trousers from the back of a chair.

'I take it we show him to the magistrates this time and ask that they refuse bail?' Kevin's voice was so sweet it was on the border of costing him his teeth, and not from decay.

'That's what we normally do when we have grounds, Inspector. Thanks for keeping me informed.'

'One other thing, sir,' Kevin said unctuously.

'What?' Brandon growled.

'The lads have also had to make another arrest.'

'*Another* arrest? Who the hell else have they had to arrest.'

'Superintendent Cross, sir. Apparently, he was trying rather forcibly to prevent McConnell from boarding the ferry.'

Brandon closed his eyes and counted to ten. 'Is McConnell hurt?'

'Apparently not, sir, just a bit shaken up. The super has a black eye, though.'

'Fine. Tell them to let Cross go home. And tell them to ask him to call me tomorrow, OK, Inspector?' Brandon replaced the phone and leaned over to kiss his wife, who had reclaimed the duvet and was rolled up tight as a hibernating dormouse.

'Mmm,' Maggie murmured. 'Are you sure you have to go in?'

'It's not my idea of a good time, believe me, but I want to be there when they bring this prisoner in. He's just the sort of bloke who might fall downstairs.'

'A problem with his balance?'

Brandon shook his head grimly. 'Not *his* balance. Other people sometimes get a bit unbalanced, love. We've already had one maverick on the prowl tonight. I'm not taking any more chances. I'll see you when I see you.'

Fifteen minutes later, Brandon walked into the murder squad room. Kevin Matthews was slumped over a desk at the far end of the room, his head cradled in his arms. As Brandon approached, he heard the soft snore of Kevin's breathing. He wondered when any of the squad had last had a straight night's sleep. It was when officers got tired and edgy at the lack of results that the serious mistakes happened. Brandon desperately wanted to avoid his name in lights ten years down the road as the man who masterminded a sensational miscarriage of justice, and he'd go to any lengths to avoid it. There was only one problem with that, he wryly acknowledged to himself as he sat down opposite Kevin. In order to keep his finger on the pulse of the investigation, he had to work the same kind of ridiculous hours that led to the very misjudgements he wanted to avoid. *Catch 22*. He'd read that, a few years back now, when Maggie had decided to go to evening classes and take the A Levels she'd never got round to at school. She'd said it was a wonderful book, funny, savage, sharply satirical. He'd found it almost too painful. It reminded him too strongly of the Job. Especially on nights like tonight when previously sane men turned desperado.

The phone rang. Kevin stirred, but didn't wake. Pulling a sympathetic face, Brandon reached over and lifted it. 'CID. Brandon speaking.'

There was a momentary, confused silence. Then a strained voice said, 'Sir? Sergeant Merrick here. Sir, we've copped for another body.'

Getting Gareth to Carlton Park was less easy than I'd anticipated. I'd done my reconnaissance carefully, I thought, and I'd counted on being able to drive down the access road used by the gardeners. What I hadn't taken into account was the long Christmas break. The road was blocked off by two metal posts slotted into the asphalt and locked in place with heavy padlocks. I could probably have squeezed through on the verge, since the jeep would have had no problem flattening the small shrubs that lined the road. But I would inevitably have left tyre tracks and probably tiny traces of paint. I had no intention of allowing Gareth to deprive me of my liberty, so that option was closed to me.

I parked the jeep round the back of the storage shed where the park staff kept their equipment. At least there I was out of sight both from the road and the park. There weren't many people around at two o'clock on Boxing Day morning, but success is all about taking pains.

I got out of the jeep and scouted around. The shed was out; it had a burglar alarm. But the gods were smiling on me now. Around the side of the shed, there was a low wooden trolley, the kind that porters used to wheel along station platforms in the days when there were railway porters who didn't think shifting luggage was beneath them. The gardeners probably used it to transport plants round the park. I pushed it back to the jeep and tipped Gareth's naked body on to it. I tucked a couple of black plastic bin liners round the body and sprayed the axles with a quick blast of lubricating oil to cure a nasty squeak, then stealthily I set off towards the shrubbery.

Again, I was lucky. I saw no one. I steered the trolley round to the rear of the bandstand towards the shrubs that covered the steep slope behind. At the edge of the path, I pushed the trolley on to the grass verge and into the edge of the shrubs. Then, wary of leaving footprints on the soft ground, I clambered on to the trolley and rolled Gareth's body off the end and into the bushes. I stepped back and jumped down, pulling the trolley after me. The bushes looked a little battered, but there was no sign of Gareth. With luck, he'd remain undiscovered until the postman delivered my Christmas message to the BEST.

Ten minutes later, the trolley was back in place and I was nosing out of the park's rear entrance on to a quiet lane opposite the churchyard. Even though the chances of being spotted were slim, I waited until the main road was in sight before I turned my lights on. Unlike Temple Fields, this was exactly the sort of area where some nosy insomniac would notice a strange vehicle in the early hours.

I drove home and slept for twelve hours, waking up in time for an interesting couple of hours on my computer before I went in to work. Luckily, it was a busy night, so I had plenty of complex problems to take my mind off the anticipation of the following day's Sentinel Times.

They'd done me proud, in spite of the short time they'd had to deal with my message. They'd obviously got on to the plod right away, and managed to persuade them to take it seriously. They'd given me the front page, complete with a photograph of my message, though without anything that would identify who the card had come from.

KILLER ALERTS BEST!

The naked and mutilated victim of a twisted killer has been discovered in a city park following a bizarre message sent to the Sentinel Times.

The killer, who signed himself 'Santa Claws', revealed in a grisly Christmas message that he had dumped the body in Carlton Park.

The sick communiqué appeared to be written in blood. It was scrawled on the company Christmas card of one of the city's leading firms of solicitors.

It was accompanied by a home video of the body's location, which BEST staff immediately recognized from the distinctive bandstand on Park Hill.

Alerted by BEST reporters, police dispatched a squad of uniformed and plain-clothes officers to the area of the park mentioned in the Christmas card.

After a short search among bushes off the nature trail near the bandstand, as indicated in the video, a uniformed constable discovered the body of a man.

According to police sources, the body was naked. The man's throat had been cut and his body mutilated.

It is believed that he may have been tortured before his death.

Although this area of Carlton Park is known as a pick-up area for predatory homosexuals, police are not presently connecting this killing with the murders earlier this year of two young men whose bodies were dumped in the Temple Fields 'gay village' area of the city.

The body has not yet been identified, and police have not released a description of the victim, who is believed to be in his late twenties or early thirties.

The package, which had been posted on Christmas Eve in Bradfield, arrived at the offices of the Sentinel Times in this morning's post, addressed to the news editor, Matt Smethwick.

Mr Smethwick said, 'My first thought was that someone was playing a sick joke, especially since I know one of the solicitors in the firm concerned.

'Then I realized my friend was out of the country on a skiing holiday, so it couldn't have been him who posted the package.

'I rang the police right away, and luckily they took it seriously.'

I should think they did. I'd never been more serious in my life. In spite of what the police were saying, the thought that Gareth was the third in a series must have made the short journey across their minds. It had certainly not escaped the attention of the journalists, who used the latest discovery as an excuse to rehash the killings of Adam and Paul. By the time the City Final edition hit the streets, they'd even found a rent-a-quote academic to spout forth.

INSIDE THE MIND OF A KILLER

The man the Home Office have chosen to spearhead the hunt for serial killers spoke today about the latest slaying that has terrified the city's gay community.

Forensic psychologist Tony Hill is one year into a major study funded by the government which will lead to the setting up of a criminal profiling task force similar to the FBI unit featured in The Silence of the Lambs.

Dr Hill, 34, was formerly the chief clinical psychologist at Blamires Hospital, the maximum-security mental unit which houses Britain's most dangerous criminally insane offenders, including mass murderer David Harney and serial killer Keith Pond, the Motorway Madman.

Giving his verdict, Dr Hill said, 'I have not been called in by the police to consult on any of these cases, so I know no more than your readers do about them.

'I'm reluctant to make a snap judgement, but if pushed, I'd say it was certainly possible, and possibly likely that the murders of Adam Scott and Paul Gibbs were committed by the same person.

'On the surface, this latest killing looks similar, but there are certain crucial differences. For a start, the body has turned up in a very different sort of location. Even though Carlton Park is also known as a gay cruising area, it's got a very different ambience from the urbanized Temple Fields.

'Also, the sending of the message to the Sentinel Times is a significant variation. Nothing similar happened in the earlier cases, and the killer makes no reference to previous killings.

'That inclines me to think we may be dealing with at least two separate individuals here.'

And so on and so forth, all of it in much the same vein. All of it saying in neon lights, 'We haven't got the faintest idea where to start looking.' I didn't think that worrying about Dr Tony Hill was going to keep me awake at nights. I decided it was time to teach the powers that be a couple of lessons they wouldn't forget in a hurry.

14

A man is not bound to put his eyes, his ears, and understanding into his breeches pocket when he meets with a murder. If he is not in a downright comatose state, I suppose he must see that one murder is better or worse than another, in point of good taste. Murders have their little differences and shades of merit, as well as statues, pictures, oratorios, cameos, intaglios or what not.

Tony lay sprawled in his bath, a snifter of brandy close at hand. Languid, relaxed, spent, he couldn't remember the last time he'd felt this comfortable, this optimistic. His experiences on the phone with Angelica, coupled with his conviction that he'd done a good job on the profile, had given him fresh hope. Maybe he didn't have to be dysfunctional. Maybe he could join the rest of the world, the ones who handled things, who assimilated the past and shaped their world according to what they wanted to see. 'I can change my life,' he announced.

The cordless phone rang. In a slow, flowing movement, Tony reached for it. It held no terrors for him now. Strange how he had grown to welcome rather than fear Angelica's calls. 'Hello,' he said cheerfully.

'Tony, it's John Brandon. I'm sending a car round for you. We've got another one.'

Tony sat up, the water swilling up and down like an experiment in a marine laboratory. 'You're sure?'

'Carol Jordan and Don Merrick were at the scene within five minutes of the shout.'

Tony squeezed his eyes shut. 'Oh God,' he groaned. 'Where is it?'

'The public toilets in Clifton Street. Temple Fields.'

Tony stood up and stepped out of the bath. 'I'll see you there,' he said heavily.

'OK, Tony. The car should be with you in five minutes or thereabouts.'

'I'll be ready.' Tony cut off the connection and walked out of the bathroom, towelling himself dry as he went. His mind racing, he pulled on jeans, T-shirt, shirt, sweater and leather jacket, adding an extra pair of socks as he remembered how bitter the night had been earlier. The doorbell rang just as he was tying the laces of his boots.

In the squad car, the atmosphere of tension wrecked any possibility of constructive thought as they sped through the night streets, blue light strobing against the unearthly orange of the streetlights. His escort, a pair of macho traffic cops, maintained a taciturn pose of absolute control that didn't lend itself to conversation. Tyres squealing, they swept into Clifton Street, the driver slamming on the anti-lock brakes at the sight of the police tapes that cut off access to the central section of the street.

The tape was lifted for Tony, who headed for the middle of the street where a cluster of police vehicles and an ambulance were parked at seemingly random angles. As he drew closer, he could see the sign for the public toilets, lit up against the looming dark of the building. By the ambulance, he spotted the conspicuous figure of Don Merrick, unmistakable with his bandaged head. Ignored by the milling officers, Tony pushed his way through to Merrick, who was deep in conversation on a mobile phone. He gave Tony a quick wave to signal he'd spotted him, and wound up his phone conversation with, 'All right, thanks, sorry to have bothered you.'

'Sergeant,' Tony said. 'I'm looking for Mr Brandon. Or Inspector Jordan.'

Merrick nodded. 'They're both inside. You'll be wanting a look too, I suppose.'

'Who found the body?'

'One of the street girls. She claims all the ladies loos were full, and that's why she went into the disabled cubicle. Me, I'd lay money she was with a client. He'll have legged it at the first sight of trouble.'

Out of the corner of his eye, Tony saw Carol emerge from the toilets. She made straight for the pair of them. 'Thanks for turning out,' she said as Merrick moved away and continued making his phone calls.

'If I said I wouldn't have missed it for the world, someone would almost certainly take it the wrong way,' Tony replied wryly. 'What makes you think it's Handy Andy?'

'The victim's naked, and his throat's been cut. He'd obviously been brought there in a wheelchair, but he'd been tipped out on to the floor. And lying on top of him, there was a copy of last night's *Sentinel Times* front page,' Carol replied, her voice strained, her eyes haggard. 'We provoked him, didn't we?'

'We didn't. The newspaper might have, but we didn't,' Tony said bleakly. 'I didn't expect him to react this fast, though.'

Merrick approached again and said cheerfully, 'Looks like I've tracked down the wheelchair. One went walkabout from the maternity hospital reception earlier on tonight. With a bit of luck, somebody might have seen it.'

'Good work, Don,' Carol said. 'Shall we take a look, then?' she asked Tony. He nodded and followed her as she shouldered her way through the milling officers towards the toilet entrance. Tony slowly walked into the lavatories, making a mental inventory as he looked around him, conscious of the black rubber tiled floor with its raised circles, the apparently random pattern of the grey and black tiles on the wall, the defiant graffiti, the raw dank air, the smell of disinfectant barely masking the piss. Inside the entrance, the toilets split in two, men to the left, women to the right. The disabled toilet was to the right, just by the entrance to the women's toilets. Brandon and Kevin Matthews stood by the door, looking in through the wide doorway. Tony walked up and joined their glum and silent communion. A photographer was standing just inside the door, off to one side, recording a scene that would shake some jury to the core, provided Brandon's men could deliver Handy Andy to them. Every few seconds, the stark white light of the flash etched the scene on the retinas of the watching men.

Tony stared intently at the body lying sprawled on the floor. It was, as Carol had said, naked, but it was not clean. There were smears of some sort of dark, oily substance on knees, elbows and one ankle. And there were bloodstains on the body too. The cut to the throat was wide, but not, Tony suspected, deep enough to have caused death. As far as he could see, the sexual organs themselves were undamaged, but the man's rectum and anus and the soft flesh around there had been savagely removed with deep cuts from a sharp blade. A warm surge of relief flowed through him, forcing him to recognize what he'd been refusing to think about. Like Carol, he too had been afraid that somehow his activities had provoked Handy Andy to break his cycle and to strike again. Ever since Brandon's phone call, that horror had been sitting on his shoulder like a malevolent bird of prey.

Tony turned to Brandon and said bluntly, 'It's not him. You've got a copycat.'

From the shadows at the far end of Clifton Street, coat collar turned up, Tom Cross joined the ghouls who seemed to spring from under the pavement itself and watched the familiar ritual dance of a murder-scene investigation. His lips pursed in a tight smile and he moved further back into the shadows. He took his diary out of his inside pocket

284

and ripped out a page for notes. In the dim light from a streetlamp, he wrote, 'Dear Kevin; I bet you a bob to a gold clock that the Queer Killer didn't do this one. All the best, Tom.'

Seaford had been embarrassing as well as painful, but Tom Cross was not a man who allowed humiliation to stand in the way of his purpose. He folded the note in four and wrote, 'Detective Inspector Kevin Matthews. Personal', on it. He pushed his way through the crowd till he caught the eye of one of the constables behind the tape. 'You know who I am, don't you, lad?' Cross demanded.

The constable nodded hesitantly, casting a quick glance to either side, to see who was watching his encounter with the force's current leper.

Cross proffered the note. 'See that Inspector Matthews gets this, there's a good lad.'

'Yes, sir,' the constable said smartly, enclosing the note in his gloved fist, finding a moment to wonder who'd had the bottle to give Popeye Cross a shiner like that.

'I'll remember you when I'm back in harness,' Cross said over his shoulder as he pushed back through the spectators.

Cross cut back through an alley to the Volvo, parked in front of a nightclub's fire exit. The day had been far from satisfactory, and the morning held no promises of improvement. But the conviction that his message to Kevin Matthews was the truth made Tom Cross feel there had been some point to his activities.

'The postmortem will back me up,' Tony said stubbornly. 'Whoever killed this guy, it wasn't our serial killer.'

Bob Stansfield scowled. 'I don't see how you can be so sure, just because of a few oil stains.'

'It's not just that the body wasn't clean.' Tony ticked the points off on his fingers. 'He's the wrong age group. He's barely twenty, if that. Far from being in the closet, he was well known on the gay scene. You'd identified him by three this morning.'

Kevin Matthews nodded. 'Well known to Vice. Chaz Collins. An ex-rent boy who worked in a bar and liked rough sex.'

'Exactly,' Tony said. 'Also, there's not a mark on his penis or his testicles, whereas our killer has been progressively violent with those organs. All the press have been told so far is that the victims have been sexually mutilated. We haven't indicated how or where. This killer has interpreted that as a justification for getting rid of the whole anal area. I suspect he's done that because he buggered the victim before he killed him and he wanted to make sure Forensic didn't pick up any semen.' Tony paused to collect his thoughts, and to pour another cup of coffee from the pot that the canteen had sent up with the breakfast trolley John Brandon had ordered for their morning conference.

'The wheelchair,' Carol said. 'He took a big risk stealing that from the maternity hospital. I don't think that fits with the cautious behaviour the serial killer has always displayed so far.'

'And he's not been tortured,' Kevin added, through a mouthful of sausage-and-egg roll. 'Or not obviously, anyway.' He had a note in his pocket that would determine his view as much as anything that was said inside this room. Popeye might be off the job, but Kevin would back his instinct against anyone's.

But Bob Stansfield wasn't giving up. 'OK, what if he's doing it differently to make us think it's a copycat? What if he's deliberately trying to confuse us? After all, you can't ignore the newspaper lying there. And Dr Hill's profile warned us that the stress of inaccurate newspaper coverage might throw his pattern out.'

Tony carried on meticulously building a bacon-and-egg roll. He squirted an aureole of brown sauce round the yolk, closed the lid, squashed it so the yolk broke, then said,

'There's nothing wrong with that as a theory. It's perfectly feasible that he might kill just to flaunt his skills. It wouldn't be planned so far ahead as the others, so his choice of victim might well be very different. But the underlying pattern would be the same.'

'But it is,' Stansfield insisted. 'This kid had his throat cut, same as the other ones. And this bastard had made a right mess of him. How can you say he wasn't tortured when you look at the state of his arse?'

'If I was a betting man, I'd lay you a hundred to one that Chaz Collins didn't die from having his throat cut. I'd bet he was manually strangled and his throat cut afterwards to make it look like he's one of the serial-killer victims. I think what happened here is that some rough sex got a bit out of hand. Chaz was struggling while he was being sodomized, and his sex partner grabs him round the throat to get him to calm down. In the frenzy of orgasm, he squeezes too tight and he has a corpse on his hands. He figures his only chance of getting away with it is making it look like the serial killer's handiwork, and just in case we don't get the message, he dumps last night's paper on the body.'

'It's certainly plausible,' Brandon said, fastidiously wiping his greasy fingers on a paper tissue from a pack in his pocket.

'I think Tony's right,' Carol said decisively. 'My first reaction was that this was the fifth victim, but the more I think about it, the more I think I was wrong. You know what really clinches it for me?' Four pairs of eyes looked quizzically at her. She felt under as much pressure as she ever had in the witness box. 'Last night wasn't Monday.'

Tony grinned. Stansfield cast his eyes upwards. Kevin nodded reluctantly, and Brandon said, 'You think the night of the week's that important to him?'

Carol nodded. 'There's obviously some very strong reason why he goes for Monday, whether it's practical or superstitious. And whatever it is, it means a lot to him. I don't think he'd break it just to stick two fingers up to us.'

'I agree with Carol,' Kevin chipped in. 'Not just because of the night of the week. The other stuff, too.'

Stansfield looked surprised. 'Well, I'm obviously outvoted here,' he said good-naturedly. 'Separate job it is. Who's going to handle it, then?'

Brandon sighed. 'I'll have a word with Chief Superintendent Sharples at Central, pass the buck on to him. If it's not one of ours, it'll be down to their chief inspector.'

'He's off sick,' Kevin reminded him absently.

'So he is. Well, it'll be passed on to whichever inspector drops unlucky this morning. Now, I know the events of last night deprived us of the chance to give Dr Hill's profile the attention it demands, but I think we should –' Brandon was cut short by a knock at the door. 'Come in,' he said, trying to keep the irritation out of his voice.

The uniformed desk sergeant came in with a couple of envelopes. 'These have just come in, sir. One from Forensic, one from the path lab,' he said, laying them on the desk in front of Brandon. He was gone by the time Brandon had taken a sheaf of papers from each.

The others hid their impatience as Brandon skimmed through the pathologist's preliminary findings. ' "Dear John",' he read out, ' "I know you'll be screaming for something on this one, since on the face of it, it looks like your serial killer has finally left some forensic traces. The bad news is, I don't think this is your man's handiwork. The victim was already dead from asphyxiation before his throat was cut. He was probably strangled manually. Also, I don't think he was cut with the same blade as your four earlier victims. From the look of it, this was a longer and thicker blade, more like a chef's vegetable chopping knife. Whereas, as you know, I reckon the earlier ones were done with something more like a filleting knife. Time of death I'd put between eight and ten p.m. last night. I'll let you have a full report as soon as ..." blah, blah, blah. Well, looks like you were right, Tony.'

'Just as well I'd agreed to go along with you in time, otherwise I'd have looked a right prat,' Bob Stansfield said, extending a hand to Tony. 'Nice one, Doc.' Carol smiled secretly. Thank God the rest of the team were finally starting to accept Tony had something worth saying. It was amazing how different the atmosphere was now that Cross had gone.

Kevin shifted uncomfortably in his chair and said, 'What have Forensic got to say? Anything about our cases, or is it all preliminary stuff on Chaz Collins?'

Brandon flicked through the other papers. 'Prelims ... prelims ... prelims ...' He drew his breath in sharply. 'Jesus Christ,' he said, baffled disgust in his voice.

'What is it, sir?' Carol asked.

Brandon rubbed a hand over his long face and stared at the paper again, as if checking that he hadn't misread it. 'They've been looking at the burns on Damien Connolly's body. Trying to work out what caused them.'

Tony stopped moving, the last bite of his sandwich half-way to his mouth. 'So what's the verdict?' Bob Stansfield demanded bluntly.

'This is totally bloody mental,' Brandon said. 'The only thing the lads in Forensic can come up with is the attachments for a cake-icing kit.'

'Of course,' Tony breathed dreamily, a distant smile lighting up his eyes. 'All the different star shapes. It's obvious, once it's pointed out.' He was suddenly aware that the other four were staring at him. Carol alone looked concerned. On the other faces, he saw expressions he'd seen before. Wariness, repugnance, disgust, incomprehension.

'Twenty-four-carat head banger,' Stansfield said bitterly. No one was quite certain whether he meant the killer or Tony.

*   *   *

The day Penny Burgess took over the *Bradfield Evening Sentinel Times*'s crime beat, she resolved that she was going to have better contacts than any of her male predecessors had managed. She realized that the male rituals of the masonic lodge and the smoker were going to remain closed worlds to her, but she determined that nothing was going to happen of any significance even there without her knowledge.

It wasn't surprising, then, that her home phone had rung twice between six and seven that morning. Both calls were from police officers, telling her that the man who'd been questioned earlier in connection with the Queer Killings had been arrested trying to skip the country. No names, no pack drill, but the anonymous suspect would be up before the magistrates that morning to be remanded in custody on a charge of attempting to pervert the course of justice. Following on from the discovery of a fifth body that had kept Penny out of her bed till gone two that morning, the connection was obvious.

Penny smiled dreamily to herself over her second cup of strong Earl Grey. It would be another front page for her tonight. Provided the editor and the lawyer didn't lose their bottle. She dumped her cup and cereal bowl in the sink and picked up her coat. Either way, it was going to be an interesting day.

Carol had drawn the short straw when it came to going to court to make sure everything went according to plan before the magistrates. Stansfield and Kevin had a backlog of routine enquiries to pursue, and Tony had gone to Leeds to keep a long-standing appointment with a Canadian academic psychologist who was attending a conference in the city. They needed, said Tony, to discuss some esoteric aspect of his task-force study. 'Conceptual mapping,' he'd told her as they'd snatched a few moments together after the group briefing.

He might as well have said 'quantum mechanics,' she thought ironically as she ran up the steps of the court building, her collar turned up against an east wind that promised sleet before dinner. She was going to have to learn a lot if she was going to get anyone to consider her seriously for this task force, that much was clear.

Any thoughts of the task force vanished as soon as she cleared the security check and turned into the long corridor that housed half of the dozen magistrates' courts. Instead of the usual disgruntled and defiant knots of low-level law breakers and their depressed families, she came face to face with a milling mob of journalists. She'd never seen that kind of media turnout at a Saturday-morning court, normally the quietest of the week. At the heart of the crowd, she could see Don Merrick, his back to the courtroom door, looked harassed.

Carol immediately wheeled round on her heel. But she was too late. She'd not only been spotted but also recognized by one of the handful of journalists who weren't visiting firefighters sent up by the national media networks at the sniff of a good tale. As she rounded the corner, they shot after her. All except Penny Burgess, who leaned against the wall and gave Don Merrick a tired smile.

'You weren't the only one that got the early-morning phone call, then,' he said cynically.

'Unfortunately not, Sergeant. At least the lads seem more interested in your guv'nor than they do in you.'

'She's better looking,' Merrick said.

'Oh, I wouldn't say that.'

'So I've heard,' Merrick said drily.

Penny's eyebrows climbed. 'You must let me buy you a drink sometime, Don. Then you can find out for yourself if the gossip's true.'

Merrick shook his head. 'I don't think so, pet. The wife wouldn't like it.'

Penny grinned. 'Not to mention the guv'nor. Well, Don,

now the pack's gone off in full cry after Inspector Jordan, are you going to let me exercise my democratic right to report the proceedings of the magistrates?'

Don Merrick stood clear of the door and waved her in. 'Be my guest,' he said. 'Just remember, Ms Burgess, the facts, and nothing but the facts. We don't want innocent people put at risk, do we?'

'You mean, like the Queer Killer's been doing?' Penny asked sweetly as she slipped past him and into the court.

Brandon stared in disbelief at Tom Cross. His face was knit in an expression of deep complacency, his multi-coloured eye socket the only disruption to a picture of smug self-satisfaction. 'Just between ourselves, John,' he was saying, 'you have to admit I was bang on the button about McConnell. That stiff last night – it wasn't down to the Queer Killer at all, was it? Well, it couldn't have been, could it, on account of you had me laddo banged up downstairs.' Ignoring the absence of ashtrays in the ACC's office, Cross lit a cigarette and puffed a happy cloud of smoke into the air.

Brandon struggled, but he couldn't find the words. For once, he was speechless.

Cross looked around vaguely for somewhere to flick his ash, and settled for the floor, rubbing it into the carpet with the toe of his shoe. 'So when do you want me to start back on the job?' he asked.

Brandon leaned back in his chair and stared at the ceiling. 'If it was up to me, you'd never work in this town again,' he said pleasantly.

Cross choked on a mouthful of smoke. Brandon looked back down and savoured the moment. 'By heck, you like your joke, John,' Cross spluttered.

'I've never been more serious in my life,' Brandon said coldly. 'I called you here this morning to warn you off. What you did to Steven McConnell yesterday afternoon was assault. The file stays open, Superintendent. If you come anywhere near this investigation again, I'll have no hesitation in charging you. In fact, I'll enjoy it. I will not have this force brought into disrepute by any officer, serving or under suspension.' As Brandon's words sank in, Cross paled, then turned puce with anger and humiliation. Brandon stood up. 'Now get out of my office and my station.'

Cross got to his feet like a man concussed. 'You'll regret this, Brandon,' he stuttered furiously.

'Don't make me, Tom. For your own sake, don't make me.'

Thinking on her feet, Carol led the journalists round to the small lounge outside the lawyers' cafeteria. 'OK, OK,' she said, trying to damp down their baying with exaggerated hand movements. 'Look, if you'll just give me two minutes, I'll come right back and answer your questions, OK?'

They looked uncertain, one or two at the back showing a tendency to drift back towards the courts. 'Look, people,' she said, gently massaging her jaw, 'I'm in agony. I've got raging toothache, and if I don't ring my dentist before ten, I've got no chance of him fitting me in today. Please? Give me a break? Then I'm all yours, promise!' Carol forced a pained smile and slipped through to the cafeteria. There was a phone on the far wall, which she picked up. She made great play of taking out her diary and looking up a page, while dialling the familiar number of the court. 'Court one, please.' She waited for the connection, then said to the clerk, 'This is Inspector Jordan here. Can I speak to the CPS solicitor?'

Moments later, she was talking to the Crown Prosecution Service lawyer. 'Eddie? Carol Jordan. I've got about thirty hacks here waiting for Steven McConnell to come up. They're dying to jump to all the wrong conclusions, and I think you might prefer to get him on now while I've got them tied up at an impromptu press conference. Can you swing it with the clerk?' She waited while the solicitor muttered with the court clerk.

'Can do, Carol,' he said. 'Thanks.'

Keeping up the pretence, Carol put the phone down and scribbled something in her diary. Then she took a deep breath and headed back towards the pack.

Damien Connolly, the ultimate PC Plod. I couldn't have found a better person to teach the police a lesson if I'd searched for a year. But he was already there, on my list, one of my own personal Top Ten. He was harder to stalk than the others, because his shift pattern was often in conflict with the hours I work. But, as my grandmother always used to say, nothing worth having comes easy.

I trapped him in the usual way. 'I'm sorry to trouble you, but my car's broken down and I don't know where the nearest call box is. Can I use your phone to ring the AA?' It's almost laughably easy to get across the threshold of their homes. Three men dead, and still they fail to take the most elementary precautions. I almost felt sorry for Damien, since of all of them, he is the only one who had not betrayed me. But I needed to make an example of him, to show the police how pathetically useless they are. It was galling to find myself in agreement with the so-called 'gay community', but they were one hundred per cent correct when they said that while supposedly gay men were being killed, the police would do nothing. Killing one of their own would be the one thing that would make them sit up and notice. At last, they'd be forced to give me the recognition and respect I deserve.

To mark this, I had devised something a bit special for Damien. An unusual method of punishment, used occasionally to act as a terrible example pour décourager les autres. *It seems to have been most commonly used in cases of high treason, where men had plotted to kill the king. Appropriate,* I thought. *For what was Damien if not an integral part of the group that would bring me down if only they could?*

The earliest record of this treatment in England was in 1238, when some minor nobleman broke into the royal lodge at Woodstock intent on killing Henry III, there on a hunting trip. To demonstrate to any other potential traitors that the king was serious about attempts on his life, the man was sentenced to be torn limb from limb by horses then beheaded.

Another would-be royal assassin met the same fate in the mid eighteenth century. The aspiring assassin's name just had to be an omen. François Damiens stabbed King Louis XV at Versailles. His sentence read that 'his chest, arms, thighs and calves be burned with pincers; his right hand, holding the knife with which he committed the said attack, burned in sulphur; that boiling oil, melted lead, and rosin and wax mixed with sulphur be poured into his wounds; and after that his body be pulled and dismembered by four horses.'

According to reports of the execution, Damiens's dark-brown hair turned white during the torture. Casanova, that other great lover, reported in his memoirs, 'I watched the dreadful scene for four hours, but was several times obliged to turn my face away and to close my ears as I heard his piercing shrieks, half the body having been torn away from him.'

Obviously, I couldn't get a team of horses down into the cellar, so I'd had to come up with my own arrangement. I'd built a system of ropes and pulleys, attached to floor and ceiling and linked with one of those powered winches that are used on yachts. Each rope ended in a steel shackle that would fasten round wrist or ankle. By adjusting the lengths and tensions on the ropes, I had suspended Damien in midair, his limbs spread in a massive, human X, his pathetic genitals dangling in the middle like something in a butcher's shop.

The chloroform had a worse effect on him than it did on any of the others. As soon as he came round, he vomited violently, not an easy thing to achieve when you're hanging upright four feet above the floor. It was just as well I'd removed his gag, or he'd have choked on his own vomit, which would have cheated me out of my satisfaction in his punishment.

He was completely bewildered. He had no idea why he was there. 'Because I chose you,' I told him. 'You were just unlucky enough to choose the wrong job. Now I'm going to question you the way you question your suspects.'

While I'd been poking around in Auntie Doris's kitchen, vaguely looking to see if she had anything I might find useful, I'd come across her icing set. I remembered that icing set. Every year, her Christmas cakes were a miracle of artistry that any of Bradfield's bakers would have been hard pressed to equal. Once, she'd been called away by Uncle Henry while she was doing the big cake, and I'd picked up the icing bag, determined to help. I can't have been more than six.

When she came back from whatever disgusting farmyard task she'd been helping with and saw my efforts, she went berserk. She grabbed the weighted leather strop that Uncle Henry used to keep his cut-throat razors sharp and beat me so hard she tore my shirt. Then she locked me in my room without any supper, leaving me there for the best part of twenty-four hours with nothing but a bucket to piss in. I knew I had to find an appropriate use for her treasured icing set.

There was a blowlamp in the cellar which I used to heat up the icing attachments so I could leave my mark on Damien, just as the executioner had on his namesake Damiens two hundred and forty years before. There was something quite beautiful about the way his skin blossomed into scarlet starbursts as the red-hot piping rosettes came into contact with his pale flesh. It was also astonishingly effective. He told me everything I wanted to know and lots of rubbish I didn't give a damn about. I was just sorry he wasn't directly involved in the investigation into my previous work. I could have confirmed at first hand how hopelessly at sea the police are.

I decided to deposit the remains in Temple Fields again. I'd used the time since Gareth to find additional safe sites for the disposition of my handiwork. The back yard of the Queen of Hearts was perfect for my purpose; secluded and isolated at night. But it would come alive the next day, ensuring Damien wouldn't be left out in the cold for too long.

The time was ripe for a new game. In preparation for this, shortly after Adam, I went up into the loft and opened the trunk that contains those parts of my past I have retained. One of the things I'd kept as a souvenir was a leather jacket that was given to me by the engineer on a Soviet factory ship, in lieu of payment for a night he won't forget in a hurry. It looks and feels different from anything I've ever seen in this country. I ripped strips of leather from the sleeve until I was satisfied that I'd got something that could have been snagged on a nail or the sharp corner of a lock. I tucked the scrap in a drawer, then I chopped the rest of the jacket into shreds, stuck it in a plastic bag with eggshells and vegetable peelings, and drove into town until I found a skip to dump it in. By the time I needed to use the red herring, the remains of the jacket would be long buried in some anonymous landfill.

I couldn't help feeling a thrill at the thought of how many man-hours the police would waste trying to track down where this strange little piece of leather had come from, but they'd never tie it in to me. Apart from anything else, no one in Bradfield has ever seen me wear it.

This time, the publicity outshone everything I'd achieved so far. At last, the police admitted that one mind was behind all four killings. Finally, they had realized it was time to take me seriously.

With Damien off the planet and in my computer, I still had one more person to deal with before I could return to my original project. I couldn't settle to the task of finding a man worthy of me, a man to share my life as an equal and respectful partner, not until I had punished the man who had publicly treated me with such contempt.

Dr Tony Hill, the fool who hadn't even realized that Gareth Finnegan was one of my bodies, was the target. He had insulted me. He had poured scorn on me, refusing to acknowledge the extent of my achievements. He had no idea of the calibre of the mind he was up against. He was going to have to pay for his arrogance.

I couldn't help but see his disposal as a challenge. Wouldn't anyone?

15

Can they not keep to the old honest way of cutting throats, without introducing such abominable innovations . . . ?

The sound of a roaring crowd greeted Carol as she closed the door of the flat behind her. Michael, sprawled on one of the sofas, didn't even take his eyes off the rugby match on the television. 'Hi, sis,' he said. 'Needle match. Ten minutes, and I'm all yours.'

Carol glanced at the screen where muddy giants in England and Scotland's colours were sprawled across the turf in a collapsed scrum. 'Very hi-tech,' she muttered. 'I need a shower.'

Fifteen minutes later, brother and sister were sharing a celebratory bottle of cava. 'I have some print-out for you,' Michael said.

Carol perked up. 'Anything significant?'

Michael shrugged. 'I don't know what's significant to you. Your killer used five different-shaped objects to make the marks. I separated them out into five separate patterns. You've got what looks like a heart and some rudimentary letters. A, D, G and P. Mean anything to you?'

Carol shivered involuntarily. 'Oh, yes. Plenty. You got the print-out here?'

Michael nodded. 'It's in my briefcase.'

'I'll look at it in a bit. Meanwhile, can I pick your brains again?'

Michael drained his glass and refilled it. 'I don't know. Can you afford me?'

'Dinner, bed and breakfast at the country-house hotel of your choice, first weekend I have off,' Carol offered.

Michael pulled a face. 'At this rate, I could be collecting my pension before I collect on that one. How about you do my ironing for a month?'

'A fortnight.'

'Three weeks.'

'Consider it a done deal.' She offered her hand and Michael shook it.

'So, what do you want to know, sis?'

Carol outlined her theory about the computer manipulation of the killer's videos. 'What do you think?' she asked anxiously.

'It's a can-do,' he said. 'No question about that. The technology's available, and it's not difficult software to use. I could do it standing on my head. But you're talking serious money. Say three hundred for a video capture card, four hundred for a ReelMagic card, another three to five for a decent video digitizer, plus at least a grand for a state-of-the-art scanner. The real killer is the software, though. There's only one package that will do what you're talking about to any real quality. Vicom 3D Commander. We've got it, and it set us back nearly four grand, and that was six months ago. The last upgrade cost us another eight hundred. Manual thick as a house brick.'

'So it's not a piece of software that many people would have?'

Michael snorted. 'Damn right it isn't. It's a serious bit of kit, that. Professionals like us, video production studios and very serious hobbyists only.'

'How readily available is it? Could you buy it over the counter?' Carol asked.

'Not really. We dealt directly with Vicom, because we wanted them to run us a full demo before we committed ourselves to laying out that much dosh. Obviously, some specialist business suppliers sell it, but they wouldn't be shifting it in bulk. That would be mail order, anyway. Most computer stuff is.'

'The other stuff you mentioned – are they things that lots of people would have?' Carol asked.

'They're not uncommon. Off the top of my head, say two or three per cent market penetration on the video stuff, maybe fifteen per cent on the scanner. But if you're thinking of tracking down your man, I'd start with the Vicom end,' Michael advised.

'How do you think they'd be about letting us look at their sales records?'

Michael pulled a face. 'Your guess is as good as mine. You're not a competitor, and this is a murder investigation. You never know, they might be happy to cooperate. After all, if this guy is using their stuff, it'd be bad PR if they didn't. I can dig out the name of the guy we dealt with. He was their sales director. Scottish bloke. One of those names you can't tell which is the Christian name. You know, Grant Cameron, Campbell Elliott . . . It'll come to me . . .'

While Michael searched through his contacts book, Carol refilled her glass and savoured the prickle of bubbles against her palate. Lately, pleasure seemed to have been in short supply. But if she could come up with some leads on her theory, all of that might change.

'Got it!' Michael exclaimed. 'Fraser Duncan. Give him a ring Monday morning and mention my name. Time you got a break, sis.'

'You're not wrong,' Carol said with feeling. 'Believe me, I deserve it.'

Kevin Matthews lay sprawled across the rumpled king-sized bed, smiling up at the woman straddling him. 'Mmm,' he murmured. 'That was a bit nice.'

'Better than home cooking,' Penny Burgess said, running

her fingers through the dark auburn hair that curled across Kevin's chest.

Kevin chuckled. 'Just a bit.' He reached for the remains of the hefty vodka and coke Penny had poured for him earlier.

'I'm surprised you could get away tonight,' Penny said, moving forward languidly so her nipples brushed his.

'We've had so much overtime lately she's given up expecting me home for anything except for a bit of kip.'

Penny let her upper body fall heavily on Kevin, thrusting the breath out of his body. 'I didn't mean Lynn,' she said, 'I meant work.'

Kevin grabbed her wrists and wrestled her off him. When they subsided, lying side by side, giggling breathlessly, he finally said, 'There wasn't much to do, tell you the truth.'

Penny snorted incredulously. 'Oh yeah? Last night Carol Jordan finds body number five, the suspect is arrested trying to leave the country and you tell me there's nothing much doing? Come on, Kevin, this is me you're talking to.'

'You've got it all wrong, darling,' Kevin said magnanimously. 'You and all the rest of your media cronies.' It wasn't often he got the chance to put Penny right and he intended to make the most of it.

'What do you mean?' Penny propped herself up on one elbow, unconsciously covering her body with the duvet. This wasn't a bit of fun any more; this was work.

'Number one. The body Carol found last night wasn't one of the serial killer's victims. It was a copycat job. The postmortem proved that beyond reasonable doubt. It was just another seedy little sex murder. Central should clear it up in a few days with a bit of help from Vice,' Kevin said, the self-satisfaction obvious in his voice.

Penny bit on the bullet and said sweetly through clenched teeth, 'And?'

'And what, darling?'

'If that was number one, there must be a number two.'

Kevin smiled, so smug that Penny made the instant decision that he was on the out just as soon as she had an acceptable alternative lined up. 'Oh yes, number two. Stevie McConnell isn't the killer.'

For once, Penny ran out of words. The information was shocking in itself. But more shocking was the fact that, knowing this, Kevin had said nothing. He had remained silent and let her paper run a story that was eventually going to make her look an ill-informed pillock. 'Really?' she said, in the superior accent she hadn't used since the day she'd gratefully quit boarding school and made the decision to go vocally downmarket.

'That's right. We knew that before he legged it.' Kevin lay back on the pillows, blissfully unaware of the look of distilled hatred that Penny was beaming in his direction.

'So what exactly was that pantomime at court this morning in aid of?' she demanded in tones her elocution mistress would have been proud of.

Kevin smirked. 'Well, most of us had already decided that McConnell wasn't our man. But Brandon had put a tail on him, so when he tried to skip the country, we were more or less obliged to pull him in. By that time, it was starting to look definite that McConnell isn't the Queer Killer. Plus, he doesn't fit the profile that Tony Hill came up with.'

'I don't believe I'm hearing this,' Penny said sharply.

Kevin finally registered that all was not well. 'What? You got a problem, darling?'

'Just a fucking bit,' said Penny, enunciating each syllable crisply. 'You mean to tell me you've not only put an innocent man on remand, you've also let the world's press broadcast the assumption that this man is quite probably the Queer Killer?'

Kevin propped himself up and took another swig of his drink, reaching out to rumple Penny's hair with his other hand. She pulled away with a jerk. 'It's no big deal,' he said patronizingly. 'Nobody can get a lynch mob together and go round his house while he's inside. And we reckon that telling the world between the lines that we've got the killer banged up might just provoke the real killer into getting in touch with us to make sure we know he's still out there.'

'You mean you want to drive him to kill again?' Penny demanded, her voice rising.

'Of course not,' Kevin said indignantly. 'I mean, to get in touch. Like he did after he'd killed Gareth Finnegan.'

'My God,' Penny said wonderingly. 'Kevin, how can you sit there and tell me that nothing bad can happen to Stevie McConnell while he's locked up in prison?'

While Penny Burgess and Kevin Matthews were arguing the morality of Stevie McConnell's remand, in C Wing of Her Majesty's Prison Barleigh, three men were taking turns to show Stevie McConnell what happens to sex cases in prison. At the end of the landing, a warden stood impassively, appearing as oblivious to McConnell's screams and entreaties as a deaf man with his hearing aid switched off. And on the moors above Bradfield, a ruthless killer put the finishing touches to the torture instrument that would help show the world that the man in prison was not the person responsible for four perfectly executed serial punishments.

The HOLMES room was a quiet hum of activity, operators staring into screens and tapping keys. Carol found Dave Woolcott sitting in his office picking listlessly at fish and chips. He looked up when she entered and managed a wan smile. 'Thought you were having a night off,' he said.

'I'm still hoping to. My brother promised to buy me a bucket of popcorn all to myself if I make it to the multiscreen before the film begins. I just wanted to swing by and run something past you.' She dumped two plastic bags on Dave's desk. Glossy computer magazines spilled out.

'I've got this theory,' she said. 'Well, more of a hunch.'
For the third time, Carol outlined her idea about the killer
importing videos and transforming them into supports for
his fantasies.

Dave listened carefully, nodding as Carol's ideas sank
in. 'I like it,' he said simply. 'I've read that profile a couple
of times now, and I really can't accept what Dr Hill says
about keeping stable just by using videos of the killings. It
doesn't make sense. Your idea does. So what do you want
from me?'

'Michael reckons that tracing the buyers of Vicom 3D
Commander might lead us to him if we're right. I'm not
so sure. It's possible that the company the killer works for
has the software, and he does the manipulation work there.
To be on the safe side, though, he'd need to do all the
scanning and digitizing at home. So I thought it would
also be worthwhile doing a trawl of the suppliers of video
digitizers and video capture cards. We can find suppliers
via the ads in these magazines, since virtually all computer
stuff comes mail order. We should also contact local computer clubs too. If you've got any bodies to spare, that is.'

Dave sighed. 'Dream on, Carol.' He picked up a magazine and flicked through the pages. 'I suppose I could draw
up a list tonight and tomorrow, and first thing Monday
morning we could get a couple of DCs to do a ring-round.
When my operators will have time to input the data, I
don't know, but I will see that it gets done. OK?'

Carol grinned. 'You're a star, Dave.'

'I'm a bloody martyr, Carol. My youngest's cut two teeth
that I haven't even seen yet.'

'I could stay and help you go through the magazines,'
Carol said reluctantly.

'Oh, bugger off. Go and enjoy yourself. It's about time
one of us did. What are you going to see?'

Carol pulled a face. 'It's a Saturday Special double bill
– *Manhunter* and *The Silence of the Lambs*.'

Dave's laughter echoed in her ears all the way to the car.

The long howl seemed to come from the pit of his stomach. As his orgasm shuddered through him like a runaway train, Tony felt a glorious sense of release. 'Oh, God,' he groaned.

'Oh, yeah, yeah,' Angelica gasped. 'I'm coming again, again, oh, Tony, Tony . . .' Her voice faded in a gulping sob.

Tony lay back on his bed, chest heaving, the smell of sweat and sex heavy around him. He felt as if he'd been suddenly detached from a burden he had been carrying for so long he had ceased to notice its weight. Was this what being cured felt like, this sense of light and colour, this sensation of having dumped the past like sacks of coal in a bunker? Was this how his patients felt when they'd unloaded their mess on him?

In his ear, he could hear the ragged sound of her breathing. After a few moments, she said, 'Wow. Just wow. That was the best ever. I just love the way you love me.'

'It was good for me, too,' Tony said, meaning it for once. For the first time since they had started this strange combination of therapy and sexual gameplaying, he'd had no trouble with his erection. Right from the start, he'd been hard as a rock. No fading, no wilting, no shame. Just the first problem-free sex he'd had for years. OK, so Angelica wasn't actually in the room with him, but it was a giant step in the right direction.

'We make the sweetest music,' Angelica said. 'Nobody's ever turned me on like you do.'

'Do you do this often?' Tony asked languidly.

Angelica chuckled, a husky, sexy gurgle of laughter. 'You're not the first.'

'I could tell that. You're far too much of an expert,' Tony flattered, not entirely insincerely. She'd been the perfect therapist for him, that much was certainly true.

'I'm very choosy about the men I allow to share with me,' Angelica said. 'It's not everyone who appreciates what I have to offer,' she added.

'They'd have to be very strange not to enjoy it. I know I do.'

'I'm glad, Anthony. You'll never know how glad. I have to go now,' she said, her tone changing abruptly to the businesslike one Tony had come to associate with the end of their calls. 'Tonight has been really special. We'll talk soon.'

The line went dead. Tony switched off the phone and stretched out. Tonight, with Angelica, for the first time in his life, Tony had felt a protective care that succoured without smothering. His grandmother, he knew intellectually, had loved him and cared for him, but theirs had never been a demonstrative family, and her love had been brusque and practical, meeting her needs rather than his. The women he'd been involved with in the past had, he now realized, been her emotional doppelgangers. Thanks to Angelica, he dared hope the pattern had been broken. It had caused him enough pain over the years.

His sexual life had started later than most of his contemporaries, in part because his body had been reluctant to mature. Until his seventeenth year, he'd been by far the smallest boy in his class, condemned to dating the thirteen- and fourteen-year-olds who were even more scared of sex than he was. Then, suddenly, he'd shot up five inches in as many months. By the time he'd gone to university, he'd lost his virginity in a clumsy fumble on a single bed, the candlewick bedspread leaving him with uncomfortable friction burns for days afterwards. His girlfriend, relieved to be rid at last of the encumbrance of her virginity, had dumped him days later.

At university, he'd been too shy and hard-working to improve his experience by much. Then, when he'd started work on his doctorate, he'd fallen head over heels with a young philosophy tutor in his college. Because he was bright and interesting, he captured her interest. Patricia made no secret of the fact that she was a woman of the world, just as she made no secret of the fact that she had ended their relationship because of his lacklustre performance between the sheets. 'Face it, sweetheart,' she'd told him, 'your brain might be DPhil material, but your fucking wouldn't earn you an O level.'

It had been downhill from then. The last couple of women Tony had been involved with had thought he was a perfect gentleman, never pressurizing them into bed. Until they got him there and discovered how seldom he could actually deliver. He had long ago discovered how hard it was to convince a woman that the fact that he couldn't get it up had nothing whatsoever to do with her. 'They just got fed up with having their egos bashed,' he said aloud.

Maybe now he had finally found a way to confront the past and move forward. A few more nights like tonight with Angelica and maybe, just maybe, he'd be ready to try the real thing. He wondered if her services extended to that. Perhaps he should start thinking about dropping a few hints.

Brandon read the sheet of paper on his desk and rubbed the grit of sleep from his eyes. He and Dave Woolcott had spent the evening going through the dozens of reports that had flowed in from the actions Dave had ordered in response to the correlations thrown out by the HOLMES computer. In spite of their determined efforts to find some slender thread of evidence to unravel back to the killer, there was nothing that either of them could identify as a lead.

'Maybe this idea of Carol's will do the business for us,' Dave yawned.

'We've tried everything else,' Brandon said, his voice as depressed as his face. 'It can't hurt to run with it.'

'She's a smart operator, that one,' Dave remarked. 'She'll be running the shop one of these days.' There was no bitterness in his tone, only a tired admiration. Another yawn split his face.

'Go home, Dave. When was the last time you saw Marion awake?'

Dave groaned. 'Don't you start, sir. I was going to knock off anyway, there's not a lot doing. I'll be in tomorrow, finish off listing these computer suppliers.'

'OK, but not too early, you hear? Give your family a treat. Eat breakfast with them.' Before he took his own advice, Brandon wanted to go through the witness statements and officers' impressions once more, unable to believe that there wasn't something lurking in there that would give them their first serious break. By the time he was halfway through he was finding it almost impossible to motivate himself to get through the rest of the pile. The prospect of tucking himself round Maggie's warm body was overwhelmingly appealing.

Brandon sighed and focused on the next sheet of paper. His scrutiny was interrupted by the insistent trill of his telephone. 'Brandon,' he sighed.

'Sergeant Murray here, front desk. Sorry to interrupt you, sir, but none of the inspectors are in the station at the moment. Thing is, there's a gentleman down here I think you'll want to talk to. He's a neighbour of Damien Connolly's, sir.'

Brandon was already out of his chair. 'I'm on my way,' he said.

The man at the front desk was sitting on the wooden bench that ran along the wall, head down, the rough blur of stubble dark along his jaw. As Brandon came round from behind the counter, he looked up. Late twenties, Brandon estimated. Sun-bed tan, bruised circles under his eyes. Some sort of businessman, judging by the expensive but sombre suit and the silk tie hanging askew under the open top button of the shirt. He had the rumpled, red-eyed look of someone who's been travelling so long they've forgotten which day or which city it is. Seeing someone more tired than himself seemed to inject Brandon with fresh energy. 'Mr Harding?' he said cheerfully. 'I'm John Brandon, the Assistant Chief Constable in charge of the investigation into Damien Connolly's death.'

The man nodded. 'Terry Harding. I live a couple of doors down from Damien.'

'My sergeant tells me you might have some information for us.'

'That's right,' Terry Harding said, his voice thick with exhaustion. 'I saw a stranger driving out of Damien's garage the night he was killed.'

*I had already started work on Dr Tony Hill even before I
had dispatched Damien Connolly. It seemed poetic justice
to me that, like Damien, his name was already on my
list as a potential partner. If I had needed any kind of
reinforcement that I was doing the right thing by punishing
him, that was it.*

*So, I already knew where he lived, where he worked and
what he looked like. I knew what time he left the house
in the morning, what tram he caught to work, and how
long he stayed in his little office in the university.*

*I only realized how smoothly everything had gone up
till now when things started to move in directions I hadn't
predicted and didn't like. I suppose I'd made the mistake
of underestimating the stupidity of the forces opposed to
me. I'd never thought there was much brain power shared
out among the officers of Bradfield police, but the latest
developments shook even me. They arrested the wrong
man!*

*Their incredible lack of intelligence and perception was
matched only by the media, following uncritically like
sheep. I couldn't believe it when I picked up the Sentinel
Times to read that a man was in custody helping police
enquiries into my killings. The arrest came after a street
assault involving a police officer. How on earth could they
imagine that someone who had taken as much care as I
had would end up in some street brawl in Temple Fields?*

It was an insult to my intelligence. Did they really think I was some out-of-control street yob?

I read and reread the article, unable to credit the depths of their foolishness. Anger burned inside me. I could feel it in my guts like indigestion and wind cramps rolled into a spiky ball. I wanted to do something vicious and dramatic, something that would prove to them how wrong they were.

I worked out with my weights till my muscles were trembling from effort and my kit was saturated with sweat, but still the anger refused to abate. I stormed upstairs to my computer and worked on the videos of Damien that I'd imported into my system. By the time I'd finished, we'd performed sexual gymnastics that the Russian national team would have been proud of. But nothing satisfied me. Nothing took the anger away.

Luckily, unlike them I'm not stupid. I know how dangerous uncontrolled anger could be for me. I needed to harness my anger, to be creative with it and make it work for me. I forced myself to channel my rage into constructive pathways. I planned in meticulous detail how I would capture Dr Tony Hill, and what I would do with him when I got him. I'd be keeping him in suspense – literally.

Squassation and strappado. The Spanish Inquisition knew exactly how to make the most of what was available. They simply harnessed the most powerful force on the planet, the force of gravity. All you need is a winch, a pulley, a few ropes and a lump of stone. You fasten the victim's hands behind his back and run a rope from them through the pulley. Then you tie the stone to his feet.

In his book The Horrid Cruelties of the Inquisition, *published in 1770, John Marchant described this efficient torture most eloquently:*

He is then drawn up on high, till his head reaches the pulley. He is kept hanging in this manner for some time, that by the greatness of the weight hanging at his feet, all his joints and limbs may be dreadfully stretched, and on a sudden he is let down with a jerk, by the slacking of the rope, but is kept from coming quite to the ground, by which terrible shake, his arms and legs are disjointed, whereby he is put to the most exquisite pain; the shock which he receives by the sudden stop of his fall, and the weight at his feet stretching his whole body more intensely and cruelly.

The Germans added a refinement that attracted me. Behind the victim, they placed a spiked roller, so that as he descended, the rollers cut into and excoriated his back, leaving his body a bloody, dislocated mass. I considered reproducing this effect, but even after a lot of juggling with the layout, I couldn't come up with a design on the computer that I was satisfied would work smoothly, unless I cuffed his hands in front of him, which makes the squassation and strappado far less effective. Keep it simple, that's my motto.

While I was planning and constructing, I took steps to draw my web even tighter around Dr Hill. He might think he could climb inside my head, but he'd got things the wrong way round.

I couldn't wait to get started. I was counting the hours.

16

'Now, Miss R., supposing that I should appear at about midnight at your bedside, armed with a carving knife, what would you say?' To which the confiding girl had replied, 'Oh, Mr Williams, if it was anybody else, I should be frightened. But as soon as I heard your voice, I should be tranquil.' Poor girl; had this outline sketch of Mr Williams been filled in and realized, she would have seen something in the corpse-like face, and heard something in the sinister voice, that would have unsettled her tranquillity forever.

When the phone rang, Carol's first reaction was outrage. Ten past eight on a Sunday morning could only mean work. She stirred, a long, low growl of discontent making Nelson's ears prick. Carol's arm appeared from under the covers, groping around on the bedside table. She connected with the phone and grunted, 'Jordan,' into it.

'This is your early-morning alarm call.' The voice was far too cheerful, Carol decided, before the identity of her caller registered.

'Kevin,' she said. 'This better be good.'

'It's better than good. What would you say to a witness who saw the killer drive away from Damien Connolly's house?'

'Say again?' she mumbled. Kevin repeated his announcement. The second time round, his voice catapulted Carol into a sitting position, on the edge of the bed. 'When?' she demanded.

'The guy walked in late last night. He's been out of the

country on business. Brandon interviewed him. He's called a meeting for nine,' Kevin said, excited as a Christmas child.

'Kevin, you bastard, you might have called me before now . . .'

He chuckled. 'I thought you needed your beauty sleep.'

'Bollocks to beauty sleep . . .'

'No, I've only been in five minutes myself. Can you bring the doc in with you? I just tried calling him, but there was no reply.'

'OK, I'll swing round by his place and see if I can raise him. He seems to have a habit of switching the phones off. Fancy thinking he could get away with a decent night's sleep. You can tell he's not a copper,' she added. Carol replaced the phone abruptly and headed for the shower. The thought that Tony might have switched off his phone because he was with the woman on the answering machine crossed her mind. The idea made her stomach hurt. 'Silly bitch,' she muttered to herself as the water cascaded over her.

By twenty to nine, she was leaning on Tony's doorbell. After a couple of minutes, the door opened. Bleary eyed, struggling with the belt of his dressing gown, Tony peered out at her. 'Carol?'

'Sorry to wake you,' she said formally. 'You weren't answering your phone. Mr Brandon asked me to pick you up. There's a meeting at nine. We've got a witness.'

Tony rubbed his eyes, looking bemused. 'You better come in.' He walked down the hall, leaving Carol to close the door behind her. 'Sorry about the phones. I was late getting to sleep, so I switched them off.' He shook his head. 'Can you hang on while I have a shower and a shave? Otherwise, I'll make my own way in. I don't want you to be late on my account.'

'I'll wait,' Carol said. She picked the paper off the mat and flicked through it, leaning against the wall, alert for the telltale signs of a third person's presence. She felt unreasonably pleased when she heard none. Even though she knew her reaction was childish, it didn't mean these responses were going to stop overnight. She was just going to have to learn to disguise them until they died away, as she felt sure they would eventually, starved out of existence by Tony's lack of interest.

Ten minutes later, Tony reappeared in jeans and rugby shirt, hair damp and neatly brushed. 'Sorry about that,' he said. 'My brain doesn't work until I've had a shower. Now, what's all this about a witness?'

Carol told him the little she knew on the way to the car.

'That's great news,' Tony enthused. 'First big breakthrough, isn't it?'

Carol shrugged. 'It depends how much he can tell us. If the guy was driving a red Ford Escort, it doesn't take us a lot further forward. We'd need something solid to cross-match. Maybe something like the computer angle.'

'Oh yes, the computer theory. How goes that?'

'I discussed it with my brother. He reckons it's perfectly feasible,' Carol said coldly, feeling patronized.

'Great!' Tony enthused. 'I really hope that works out. I wasn't trying to pour cold water on it, you know. I have to work with the balance of probabilities, and your idea's way beyond my parameters. But it's the kind of investigative brainwave that we're going to need on the national task force. I really think you should seriously consider signing up when we get the show on the road.'

'I didn't think you'd be comfortable with the idea of working with me after this,' Carol said, eyes firmly fixed on the road.

Tony took a deep breath. 'I've never met a police officer I'd rather work with.'

'Even if I do trespass on your personal space?' she asked bitterly, hating herself for picking at the hurt like an old scab.

Tony sighed. 'I thought we'd agreed we could be friends? I know I . . .'

'Fine,' she interrupted, wishing she'd never opened up the conversation. 'I can do friends. What do you think of Bradfield Victoria's chances in the Cup?'

Startled, Tony twisted in his seat and stared at Carol. He saw a smile twitching at the corner of her mouth. Suddenly, they were both laughing.

The latest government threats to the prison service meant the officers at HM Prison Barleigh had started to work to rule. That in turn meant that prisoners were banged up for twenty-three hours in every twenty-four. Stevie McConnell lay on his side on his bunk bed in the cell he had to himself. Following the attack that had left him with two black eyes, a couple of cracked ribs, more bruises than he could count, and the kind of sexual damage that made sitting down an option too painful to contemplate readily, he had asked for and been granted solitary confinement.

It didn't matter how much he protested that he wasn't the Queer Killer. Nobody cared, neither cons nor screws. He'd realized that the warders held him in as much contempt as his fellow prisoners when he'd heard the sounds of slopping-out all along the wing. But no officer had unlocked his cell door to allow him to empty the stinking bucket of his sewage that sat in the corner, its smell insistent and somehow more disgusting than any of the dozens of public toilets where Stevie had picked up strangers for sex.

As far as he could see, his prospects were bleak. The very fact that he was behind bars was enough to condemn him in most people's eyes. Probably the whole world was convinced that the Queer Killer had taken his last victim now that Stevie McConnell was in jail. After he'd been released following his first stretch of questioning, he'd been painfully aware that everyone at work, staff and clients, were giving him a wide berth, refusing to meet his eyes.

One drink in a Temple Fields bar where he'd been a regular for years had been enough to show him that gay solidarity had mysteriously deserted him too. The police and the press clearly thought he was their psychopath. And until they caught the Queer Killer, Bradfield wasn't going to be a welcoming place for Stevie McConnell. The decision to move out to Amsterdam where an ex-lover ran a gym had seemed to make sense at the time. It hadn't occurred to him that they'd be tailing him.

The irony that this had all happened to him because he'd rushed to the defence of a police officer in the first place was not lost on Stevie. He gave a bitter bark of laughter. That big Geordie sergeant was probably counting his blessings that he'd been smacked with a half-brick, figuring that that was the only thing that had saved him from being the Queer Killer's next victim. The reality was that Stevie McConnell was the only victim around that night. And it wasn't going to get any better. Even his shocked family didn't want to know, according to his solicitor.

Lying there, examining his future dispassionately, he came to a decision. Grimacing with pain, Stevie rolled off the bunk and took off his shirt, wincing at the stab of pain from his ribs. With his teeth and nails, painstakingly he unpicked the seams that held the denim together. On the sharp end of a bed spring, he ripped the edges of the material so he could tear it into thin strips, which he plaited together for extra strength. He tied one end of the makeshift ligature round his neck in a tight noose, then climbed on to the top bunk. He fastened the other end of his short rope to the bottom rail of the upper berth.

Then, at seventeen minutes past nine on a sunny Sunday morning, he threw himself head first over the edge.

Like an ailing company which has won a life-saving tender against all odds, Scargill Street was buzzing with excited activity. At the heart of it all was the HOLMES room, where officers stared into screens, manipulating the new information, evaluating the new correspondences the system was throwing out.

In his office, Brandon held a council of war with his four inspectors and Tony, all of them clutching a photocopy of Brandon's notes on his interview with Terry Harding. The ACC had only had five hours' sleep, but the prospect of movement on the enquiry had given him a new energy, betrayed only by the heavy shadows around his deep-set eyes. 'To recap, then,' Brandon said. 'At about quarter past seven the night Damien Connolly was killed, a man drove out of his garage in some kind of big four-wheel drive jeep, dark in colour. He got out of the jeep to close the garage door, and that's when our witness got his best look at him. The description we've got is white, five ten to six feet, aged between twenty and forty-five, possibly with his hair tied back in a ponytail. Wearing white trainers, jeans and a long waxed coat. Overnight, the HOLMES team have been going through the vehicles clocked in Temple Fields that fit the description. Most of these drivers have already been interviewed, but they're all going to be followed up and questioned more thoroughly now we've got Terry Harding's evidence. Bob, I want you to take charge of that, and I want alibis checking too.'

'Right, boss,' Stansfield said, flicking the ash off his cigarette with a determined motion.

'Oh, and Bob? Can you get someone to check that Harding really has been in Japan all week on a business trip? I want to make sure we cover all the bases on this one.' Stansfield nodded.

'I'm sending a car round for Harding at eleven o'clock,' Brandon went on, checking the list he'd made in the kitchen at seven. 'Carol, I want you to do the interview. Check what taxi firm Harding used to take him to the airport; let's see if we can get that time narrowed down a bit more. Tony, I'd like you to sit in on it. Maybe you can help us with strategies to improve his recollection, see if we can get any firm description of what this character looks like.'

'I'll do my best,' he said. 'At least I can probably distinguish between what he really remembers and what he thinks he remembers.'

Brandon gave him an odd look, but carried on regardless. 'Kevin, I want you to organize a team to hit the car showrooms, get as many brochures and posters as you can of four-wheel drive jeeps, so we can show them to Mr Harding and see if he can give us a positive ID.'

'Will do, sir. Do you want us to go back to the neighbours in the earlier cases, see if anyone noticed the same vehicle there?' Kevin asked eagerly.

Brandon considered for a moment. 'Let's see how we go on today,' he said after a few moments. 'It'll take a lot of bodies and time to go over the old ground again, and we might not need it. It's probably worth having a word with the rest of the neighbours in Connolly's street, though. Now we've got something positive to hit them with. Good idea, Kevin. Now, Dave. What can you do for us?'

Woolcott outlined the actions the HOLMES team were already carrying out. 'With it being Sunday, I'm holding back on contacting Swansea until we've tried to get the vehicle narrowed down. The more information we can give them, the fewer possibilities we'll have to deal with. If this Harding bloke can give us make, model and year, or at least eliminate some models, we can ask DVLC to let us have a list of all the matches throughout the UK. Then we can start interviewing registered keepers, starting with Bradfield and moving out from there. It's a helluva big job, but we should get there in the end.'

Brandon nodded his acknowledgement. 'Anybody got anything else?'

Tony lifted a hand. 'If you're questioning neighbours anyway, it might be worth extending the enquiries slightly.'

All eyes were on him, but he was only aware of Carol's. What had happened between them had sharpened his desire to be instrumental in capturing Handy Andy. 'This guy is a stalker, I don't think anyone would dispute that now. I think he'd been watching Damien Connolly for a while. Given that we're in the middle of winter and it's not the ideal weather for standing around in the open, chances are he did the bulk of his spying from his car. He probably didn't park up in the close itself, since he'd be too noticeable in such a short street. I'd guess he parked on the street that runs along the bottom, somewhere that he had the house in his line of sight. Maybe someone there noticed an unfamiliar vehicle parked outside for long stretches.'

'Good thinking,' Brandon said. 'Kevin, can you cover that?'

'Will do, sir. I'll get the lads on to it.'

'And the lasses,' Carol said sweetly. 'And maybe we should ask them not to concentrate on the four-wheel drive motor. If this guy's as careful as we think he is, he might only use the jeep for the actual snatches and go for something different when he's doing the stalking, just in case a nosy neighbour has clocked him.'

'What do you think, Tony?' Brandon asked.

'It wouldn't surprise me,' he said. 'It's important we don't forget how competent this killer is. He might even be using hired cars.'

Dave Woolcott groaned. 'Oh God, don't do this to me.'

Bob Stansfield looked up from the pad where he'd been scribbling the names of his team. 'I take it that the other lines of enquiry that Dr Hill suggested are on the back burner for now?'

Brandon pursed his lips grimly. The euphoria had died somewhere during the briefing. The weight of the work ahead seemed unbearable, the idea of finding the killer almost as distant as it had before Terry Harding walked into the station. 'That's right. No disrespect, Tony, but your suggestions are hypotheses, and what we've got now is our first solid set of facts.'

'No problem,' Tony said. 'Hard evidence always comes first.'

'And Carol's idea about the computer stuff? Should we still pursue that?' Dave asked.

'Same thing applies,' Brandon said. 'It's a hunch, not a fact, so yes, it goes on the back burner.'

'With respect, sir,' Carol chipped in, determined not to be sidelined. 'Even if Terry Harding gives us a positive ID on the make and model of the vehicle, we might be no further forward. We need other elimination factors before we can narrow things down. If I'm right about the computer, we'd be looking at such a small segment of the population that it would be significant if we did get a cross-match.'

Brandon considered for a moment. Then he said, 'Point taken, Carol. OK, we can pursue it, Dave, but not as a priority. Only as and when we have bodies freed up from the main enquiry. Right, are we all clear what we've got to do?' He looked around expectantly, registering the series of nods. 'OK, team,' Brandon said, his voice stern. 'Let's go for it.'

'And may the force be with you,' Kevin said under his breath to Carol as they emerged from the office.

'I'd rather have the force than the gutter press,' she said drily, turning her back on him. 'Tony, can we find a quiet corner and plan our strategy for this interview?'

'The only way you're going to get more out of him is by hypnosis,' Tony told Carol as they talked in the corridor after an hour with Terry Harding.

'Can you do that?' Carol asked.

'I've got the basic technique. Judging by his eye movements and body language, he was telling the truth about what he saw, not making anything up or exaggerating, so he might come across with more detail under hypnosis, particularly if we have pictures to show him.'

Ten minutes later, Carol was back with a sheaf of car brochures that Kevin's team had scavenged from city dealerships. 'This what we need?'

Tony nodded. 'Perfect. You sure you want me to give this a go?'

'It's got to be worth a try,' Carol said.

They walked back into the interview room, where Terry Harding was finishing a mug of coffee. 'Can I go now?' he said plaintively. 'Only I'm due to fly out to Brussels tomorrow and I haven't even unpacked my bag.'

'Not much longer, sir,' Carol said, sitting down to one side of the table. 'Dr Hill would like to try something with you.'

Tony smiled reassuringly. 'We've got some pictures of the kind of jeep you saw leaving Damien's garage. What I'd like to do, if you're agreeable, is to put you in a light hypnotic trance and ask you to look at them.'

Harding frowned. 'Why can't I just look at them as I am?'

'The chances are better that you'd recognize the particular model,' Tony explained soothingly. 'Thing is, Mr Harding, you're obviously a very busy man. Since you saw the incident, you've travelled to the other side of the world, you've had a series of important business meetings, and you've probably not had enough sleep. All of that means your conscious mind has probably filed away the details of what you saw last Sunday. Using hypnosis, I can help you retrieve that information.'

Harding looked dubious. 'I don't know. Always supposing you could get me to go under, you could make me say anything.'

'Unfortunately, that's not the case. If it was, hypnotists would all be millionaires,' Tony joked. 'Like I said, all it does is free up the stuff you've buried because it's not important.'

'What do I have to do?' Harding said suspiciously.

'Just listen to my voice and follow what I tell you,' Tony said. 'You'll feel a little strange, a little spaced out, but you'll be in control at all times. I use a technique called neuro-linguistic programming. It's very relaxing, I promise you.'

'Do I have to lie down, or what?'

'Nothing like that. And I'm not going to wave a watch in front of you. Are you prepared to give it a try?'

Carol held her breath, watching Harding as an assortment of expressions chased each other across his face. Finally, he nodded. 'I doubt you'll be able to get me under,' he said. 'I'm a man who knows his own mind. But I'm willing to try.'

'OK,' said Tony. 'I want you to relax. Close your eyes if it feels more comfortable. Now, I want you to go deep down inside yourself . . .'

Elated with their success, Tony and Carol bounced into the murder squad room. Bob Stansfield was standing by the window, staring out at the rain-drenched street below, his shoulders slumped, a cigarette burning unheeded in his hand. He glanced round and Carol called, 'Cheer up, it might never happen.'

Stansfield swung round and said bitterly, 'You obviously haven't heard the news.'

'What news?' Carol asked, walking over to him.

'Stevie McConnell topped himself.'

Carol rocked on her heels and stumbled against a desk. Her ears were ringing and she thought she was going to faint. Instinctively, Tony moved forward and steered her into a chair. 'Deep breaths, Carol. Deep and slow,' he said softly, leaning over her, staring intently at her white face.

She closed her eyes, dug her nails into her palms and

obeyed. 'Sorry,' Stansfield said. 'It knocked me for six too.'

Carol looked up and pushed her hair away from a forehead suddenly clammy. 'What happened?'

'Apparently he took a beating yesterday. A sex-case special, by all accounts. So, this morning he tore up his shirt and hung himself. The fucking warders never noticed, on account of they're playing at work to rule,' he added savagely.

'The poor bastard,' Carol said.

'There's going to be hell to pay,' Stansfield predicted. 'I'm glad it was fuck all to do with me. At least it won't be my arse in the fire. I mean, Brandon's bombproof, so it's going to be some poor fucker of an inspector who's going to carry the can.'

Carol looked at him as if she'd like to hit him. 'Sometimes, Bob, you really fuck me off,' she said coldly. 'Where's Brandon?'

'Down in the HOLMES room. Probably hiding from the Chief.'

They found Brandon and Dave Woolcott closeted in the inspector's cubby hole off the main room. 'We've got a positive make, sir,' Carol said, her initial exuberance flattened by Stansfield's news. 'We know what car he was driving.'

Penny Burgess turned off the main road on to the Forestry Commission track that led deep into the heart of the woodland. She was aiming for a car park and picnic area in the middle of the woods. It was one of her favourite spots from which to strike off through the trees and up on to the bare gritstone edges where the wind could blow away all the accumulated dross of the week. She certainly needed it after the last few days of hard graft, big stories and not enough sleep.

The record on the radio finished and the announcer said,

'And now, over to the newsroom for the headlines on the hour.' The news ident followed, then a woman said in a voice altogether too bright for her subject matter, 'Northern Sound news on the hour. A man who was questioned by Bradfield police in connection with the serial killings that have terrorized the city was found dead this morning in his cell at Barleigh jail.'

In her shock, Penny took her foot off the accelerator and pitched forward as the car stalled. 'Shit!' she exclaimed, her hand shooting out to twist the volume higher.

'Steven McConnell is thought to have committed suicide by hanging himself with a noose made from his own clothes. McConnell, the manager of a body-building gym in the city, was arrested last week after a street brawl involving an undercover police officer in the city's gay village,' the newsreader continued, sounding for all the world as if she were announcing the results of the Eurovision Song Contest. 'He was released on bail, but rearrested after attempting to flee the country. A Home Office spokesman said there would be a full enquiry into the circumstances of his death.

'The economy has never been in a better position, the Prime Minister said today . . .' Penny turned the key in the ignition and did a perilous five-point turn in the narrow lane before stamping on the gas and shooting back towards the road. It was just as well, she thought, that she'd already decided to dump Kevin. After the story she was about to write, she couldn't imagine him ever wanting to see her again anyway.

Tony drummed his fingers on the back of the cab's seat, a curious restlessness possessing him. Leaving Scargill Street hadn't been easy, but he knew he had no role while the police worked on their one piece of solid evidence. The last thing they needed in that maelstrom of reproach and driven activity was for him to sit around reminding them of all the reasons why he'd never been convinced that Stevie McConnell was their man.

His consolation was that he felt certain that Angelica would phone tonight. As the taxi hissed through the wet and empty streets, Tony rehearsed the conversation. He felt a new confidence, a certainty that tonight he would have no problems, that he had finally wrestled his demon into submission thanks to her strange erotic therapy. He would tell her she had no idea how much her phone calls had meant to him. That she had helped him more than she could know. Satisfied that he had things under control, Tony sighed comfortably and cleared his mind of Handy Andy.

Penny Burgess popped the top on a can of Guinness, lit a cigarette and switched on her computer. After making a handful of phone calls to firm up the version of events she'd heard on the radio, she was fired with the self-righteous enthusiasm that only politicians, journalists and fundamentalist preachers seem capable of harnessing for professional advancement.

She inhaled a long stream of smoke, thought for a moment, then started to hammer the keys.

Bradfield's serial killer claimed his fifth victim yesterday (Sunday) when gay body-builder Stevie McConnell killed himself in a prison cell.

Police had implied that McConnell was himself the Queer Killer in a cynical bid to force the real killer's hand.

But their twisted exercise ended in tragedy when McConnell, 32, hung himself with a makeshift rope woven from his own torn shirt. He tied it to the top bunk in his solitary-confinement cell at Barleigh prison and threw himself off, strangling himself.

And last night, a police officer involved in the

Queer Killer investigation admitted, 'We've known for several days that Stevie McConnell wasn't the killer.'

McConnell had pleaded with prison staff to put him in solitary after a barbaric attack by fellow inmates the previous day.

A source inside Barleigh prison said, 'He took a real beating. The word on the grapevine when he arrived was that he was the Queer Killer, only the police didn't have enough evidence to charge him yet.

'Prisoners don't like sex killers, and they tend to make their feelings known. McConnell got a brutal hammering. He was badly beaten up, and sexually assaulted too.'

Warders are said to have turned a blind eye to McConnell's savage battering. Then yesterday (Sunday) because of a prison officers' work to rule, he was left unattended in his cell for long enough to end his life. A Home Office spokesman said there would be a full enquiry into the incident.

McConnell managed Bodies gym in the city centre, where the killer's third victim, solicitor Gareth Finnegan, was a member.

McConnell faced a minor assault charge after coming to the rescue of an undercover police sergeant who was attacked by a third man in the Temple Fields gay village.

He then tried to flee the country while he was out on bail. Police rearrested him as he was about to board a ferry for Holland, and persuaded magistrates to remand him in custody.

A police source revealed, 'What we did made people think that McConnell was the killer, and that's what we wanted.

'Serial killers are very vain, and we thought that the killer would be so outraged that we had pointed the finger at the wrong person that he would break cover and make contact.

'It's all gone horribly wrong.'

A friend of McConnell's said last night, 'Bradfield police are murderers. As far as I'm concerned, they killed Stevie.

'The police really grilled him about the serial killings. They put him under all kinds of pressure.

'Even though they let him go afterwards, mud like that sticks. He got the cold shoulder at work, and out in the gay bars.

'That's why he decided to leg it. It's a tragedy. Worse than that, it's a pointless tragedy.

'This hasn't taken the police an inch closer to finding the killer.'

Penny lit another cigarette and read through her copy. 'Pick the bones out of that, Kevin,' she said softly, hitting the keys that would save the file and transmit it via her modem to the office computer. Then, as an afterthought, she typed:

Memo to newsdesk.
From Penny Burgess, Crime Desk.
I am taking tomorrow (Monday) as time off in lieu of working extra hours last week and today. Hope this doesn't pose too many problems!

'A Land Rover Discovery, metallic grey or dark blue?' Dave Woolcott confirmed, making a note on a pad.

'That's what the man said,' Carol agreed.

'Right. With it being Sunday, I can't get a full run-down from Swansea on every vehicle like that on our patch,' Dave said.

'What we could do, though, is get a team going round

the main dealerships and the quality second-hand dealers asking for their records of anyone who's bought one,' Kevin suggested. Like all of them, he was fired with an excitement only slightly tempered by the tragic news from Barleigh.

'No,' Brandon said. 'That's a waste of time and personnel. There's no guarantee that the killer bought his vehicle locally. We wait until tomorrow morning. Then we go flat out.'

Everyone looked disappointed, even though they recognized the force of Brandon's argument. 'In that case, sir,' Carol said, 'I'd like to work with Dave compiling lists of computer hardware and software suppliers so we're ready to roll with that as soon as there are some spare bodies to hit the phones.'

Brandon nodded. 'Good thinking, Carol. Now, why don't the rest of us go home and rediscover what our houses look like?'

Tony was stretched out on the sofa, trying to persuade himself he was enjoying the luxury of watching TV when the doorbell rang. The hope of company come to rescue him from his restless boredom catapulted him to his feet and down the hall. He opened the door, a smile already spreading across his face.

The smile died halfway as he registered that he was out of luck. There was a woman on the doorstep, but she wasn't one of his friends or colleagues. She was tall, big-boned, with heavy, blunt features and a strong, square jaw. She pushed her long dark hair away from her face and said, 'I'm really sorry to trouble you, only my car's broken down and I don't know where there's a pay phone. I wondered if I might use your phone to call the AA? I'll pay for the call, of course . . .' Her voice trailed off and she smiled apologetically.

From 3½" *disc labelled:* Backup.007; *file* Love.017

When I clocked Sergeant Merrick in the Sackville Arms, I thought I was going to pass out. I'd only gone there because I knew the detectives from Scargill Street use it. I wanted to hear what the gossip was among the murder squad. I wanted to hear them talk about me and my accomplishments. The last thing I expected was to see so familiar a face staring out at me.

I was sitting unobtrusively in the corner when I saw Merrick come in. I debated whether to leave, but I decided that might make me noticeable. The last thing I wanted was for him to recognize me and follow me for whatever reasons of his own. Besides, why should I let a policeman drive me away from my lunch break?

But I couldn't stop the churning in my stomach in case he caught sight of me and moved across to speak to me. I wasn't afraid of him, but I just didn't want to draw attention to myself. Luckily, he was with two of his colleagues, and they were too busy discussing something – me, probably, had they but known it – to pay much attention to anybody else. I recognized the woman from the papers. Inspector Carol Jordan. She looks better in the flesh than in print, probably because her hair's a lovely shade of blonde. The other man I hadn't seen before, but I filed his face away for future reference. Carroty-red hair, pale skin, freckles, boyish features. And of course, Merrick, head and shoulders above the others, some kind of dressing on his head. I wondered how he'd come by that.

I'd never hated Merrick the way I hated some of the others, even though he'd taken me into custody a couple of times. He'd never treated me with the contempt they had. He'd never sneered at me when he arrested me. But I could see he still saw me as an object, someone not worthy of respect. He never understood that when I sold my body to sailors it was for a purpose. But whatever I did then is irrelevant now. I am different now, I am a changed person. What happened back in Seaford feels as irrelevant and remote as something I'd seen at the cinema.

In a strange way, being in the presence of the very officers who are trying to track me down was quite exciting. I got a real buzz out of being only feet away from my hunters, who didn't sense their prey. They didn't even have enough sixth sense to realize there was something extraordinary happening, not even Carol Jordan. So much for women's intuition. I see it as a sort of test, a measure of my ability to delude my pursuers. The notion that they can catch me is so absurd, it's unthinkable.

I felt so strong after that encounter that the next day's paper hit me like a blow with a sandbag. I was walking through the main computer room when I saw an early edition of the Sentinel Times lying on some junior engineer's desk. FIFTH BODY IN QUEER KILLER'S RAMPAGE screamed out at me.

I wanted to rage and shout, to throw things through windows. How dare they? My handiwork is so individual, how could they mistake some blundering copycat's body for one of mine?

I was trembling with suppressed fury when I made it back to my own office. I'd wanted to ask the engineer if I could have a look at his paper, but I didn't trust myself to speak. I wanted to rush out of the office to the nearest newsagent's and snatch a copy off the counter. But that would have been unforgivable weakness. The secret of success, I told myself, was to behave normally. To do nothing that would make my colleagues think there was something peculiar going on in my life.

'Patience,' I told myself, 'is the cardinal virtue.' So I sat at my desk, fiddling with the intricacies of a piece of software that needed rewriting. But my heart wasn't in it, and I know I wasn't justifying my salary that afternoon. By four o'clock, I could stand it no longer. I grabbed my phone and dialled the special number that broadcasts Bradfield Sound to callers.

The story was the lead item on the news bulletin, as it ought to have been. 'The body of a man found in the Temple Fields area in the early hours of the morning is not the fifth victim of the serial killer who has brought terror to Bradfield's gay community, police revealed this afternoon.' As the newsreader's words sank in, I felt my anger depart, the hollowness inside me whole once more.

Without waiting for more, I slammed the phone down. They'd got something right at last. But I'd gone through four hours of hell because of their mistake. Every hour I'd suffered would be an hour added on to the agonies of Dr Tony Hill, I vowed.

Because the Bradfield police have now committed the ultimate absurdity. Dr Tony Hill, the stupid man who hadn't even recognized that all my crimes belonged to me, has been appointed the official police consultant to the serial-killer enquiry. The poor, deluded fools. If that's their best hope, then they clearly have no hope.

17

In a murder of pure voluptuousness, entirely disinterested, where no hostile witness was to be removed, no extra booty to be gained and no revenge to be gratified, it is clear that to hurry would be altogether to ruin.

The agony was so extreme Tony wanted to believe he was in a nightmare. He had never understood before how many different kinds of pain there were. The dull throb in his head; the harsh rasp in his throat; the screaming, wrenching rip in his shoulders; and the knives of cramps in his thighs and calves. At first, the pain blocked all his other senses. His eyes screwed up tight, all he knew was suffering so stark it made the sweat pop out on his forehead.

Gradually, he learned to bear the extremes of his pain, realizing that if he took his weight on his feet, the cramps would slowly subside and the excruciating tearing in his shoulders grow less. As the torment became more tolerable, he grew aware that he felt nauseous, a deep queasiness that sat in his stomach and threatened to spill over at any moment. God alone knew how long he'd been hanging here.

Slowly, fearfully, he opened his eyes and raised his head, a movement which sent a spasm of agony through his neck and shoulders. Tony looked around. Instantly, he wished he hadn't. He knew immediately where he was. The room was brightly lit, spotlights mounted on the ceiling and walls revealing a whitewashed room, its rough stone floor marked with dark stains that he knew without examination were the visible remains of the blood that had pooled and splashed there. Facing him was the blind eye of a camcorder on a tripod, a red light on the side indicating that his scrutiny was not going unrecorded. Fixed to the far wall was a magnetic strip with a selection of knives hanging neatly on it. In one corner of the room, he saw the unmistakable implements of torture. A rack; a strange contraption like a chair which he recognized but could not name at first. Something religious? Something vaguely Christian? Something treacherous, not what it seemed? A Judas chair, that was it. And on the wall, a huge wooden saltire, like some hideously perverted holy relic. A soft moan escaped from his dry lips.

Now he knew the worst, he took stock of his own position. He was naked, his skin gooseflesh in the chill of the cellar. His hands were fastened behind his back; judging by the hard edges cutting into his wrists, by handcuffs, held taut in their turn by a rope or chain or something that was obviously fastened to the ceiling. This hawser was tight enough to force his upper body forward, leaving him doubled over at the waist. Tony managed to push himself on to the tips of his toes and twist his body sideways. Out of the corner of his eye, he could see a strong nylon rope leading from behind him, through a pulley, along the ceiling, through another pulley on to a winch.

'Jesus Christ,' he croaked. He was afraid to look at his feet, lest his worst fears should be confirmed, but he forced his eyes downwards nevertheless. As he had feared, each ankle was encased in a leather strap. The straps in their turn were attached to a rope cradle that held a heavy stone flag. An involuntary shudder of fear rippled through him, stressing his tortured muscles even further. He knew about torture; to treat his patients he'd had to study the history of sadism. Not even in his worst moments had he imagined he would face so inhuman a fate.

His mind was already racing ahead. He would be

winched up till he reached the ceiling. His muscles would wrench and tear, his joints strain to their utmost limit. Then the winch would be released, letting him drop a few feet before the brake was applied. The weight of the stone flag, still hurtling downwards accelerating at thirty-two feet per second, would finish the job, ripping his joints apart, leaving him dangling in a jumble of dislocated limbs. If he was lucky, the shock and pain would thrust him into unconsciousness. Strappado, brought to a fine art by the Spanish Inquisition. No need for high tech in torture.

In a bid to escape the blind panic his knowledge had brought him to, he forced himself to cast his mind back to what had happened. The woman at the door, that was where it had started. As he had let her into the house, Tony had felt a niggle of familiarity. He felt sure he'd seen her somewhere, but he couldn't imagine having seen someone so distinctively ugly and not remembering. He'd walked ahead of her down the hall and into his study. Then, the faintest whiff of a strangely medicinal, chemical smell, before a hand had sneaked round his neck and clamped a cold, disgusting pad on his face. A kick behind his knee to buckle his legs and bring him down. He'd struggled, but with her weight on top of him, it had only lasted for moment before he had lost consciousness.

Then he had drifted in and out of a half-world of light and dark, aware only of the pad that seemed constantly to send him out as soon as he struggled into consciousness. Until, finally, he had come round. In Handy Andy's torture chamber. Out of nowhere, a quotation sprang into his mind. 'Depend upon it, sir, when a man knows he is to be hanged in a fortnight, it concentrates his mind wonderfully.' Somewhere, he knew there was a clue in what had happened that might just allow him to escape what seemed inevitable. All he had to do was to find it.

Had he been completely wrong in his profile? Was the woman who had kidnapped him Handy Andy? Was she the one? Or was she just the decoy, the willing accomplice who got off on her master's vice? Again, he replayed what his memory would allow him to snatch back. He summoned up the woman's image again. Clothes first. Beige mac, cut continental style, just like Carol's, swinging open to reveal a white shirt, enough buttons undone to reveal the swell of full breasts and a deep cleavage. Jeans, trainers. Trainers. They were the same make and model as his own. But none of this was significant, Tony told himself. They were only outward symbols of the care Handy Andy took not to be caught. The woman's garb had been chosen so that if she did leave any stray fibres, they wouldn't show up as having any significance, being identifiable as having come from either Carol's clothes or his. And Carol had been in his house often enough now for her to have left stray fibres.

The woman's face didn't really ring any bells either. She was tall for a woman, at least five feet ten, with chunky bone structure to match. Not even her mother could have called her attractive, with her heavy jaw, slightly bulbous nose, wide mouth and eyes set curiously far apart. Even though she was skilfully, if heavily, made up, there wasn't a lot she could do with the basic building materials. He was sure they'd never been in a room together, though he couldn't rule out having passed her in the street, at the tram station or on campus.

The trainers. For some reason he kept coming back to the trainers. If only the pain would stop long enough for him to focus properly. Tony locked his legs straight, trying to relieve the agonizing strain on his shoulders. The fraction of an inch he gained wasn't nearly enough. Again, visceral fear gripped him and he blinked away a tear.

What was it about the trainers? Tony summoned every ounce of concentration he could master, and called up the image of the woman again. With a slow gasp of understanding, he realized what it was. The feet were too big.

Even for a woman of that height, the feet were too big. As soon as he grasped that, he remembered the hands too. First, black leather, later thin latex gloves covering big hands, fingers thick and strong. The person who had brought him here had not always been a woman.

Carol pressed the doorbell again. Where the hell was he? The lights were on, the curtains drawn. Maybe he'd nipped out to pick up a pizza, post a letter, buy a bottle of wine, rent a video? With a frustrated sigh, she turned away and walked down to the end of the street, turning into the ginnel that ran between Tony's street and the houses behind. She walked down to his back yard, where a previous owner had demolished the wall and concreted half the area to provide the hard standing where Tony had told her he always kept his car.

The car was in place, exactly where it should have been. 'Oh, bloody hell,' Carol complained. Edging past the car, she walked up to the house and peered through the kitchen window. The light from the open door into the hall cast a pale glow over the room. No sign of life. No dirty dishes, no empty bottles.

On the off chance, Carol tried the back door. No joy. 'Bloody men,' she grumbled as she strode back to her car. 'Five minutes, pal, then I'm off,' she said, throwing herself into the driver's seat. Ten minutes crawled by, but no one appeared.

Carol started the engine and drove off. At the end of the street, she glanced across at the pub on the other side of the main road. It was worth a try, she supposed. It took less than three minutes to check the smoky, crowded rooms and discover that wherever Tony Hill was, it wasn't in the Farewell to Arms.

Where else could he be within walking distance at nine o'clock on a Sunday night? 'Anywhere,' she told herself. 'You can't be his only friend in the world. He wasn't expecting you; you only called round to arrange a meeting for tomorrow.'

Giving up, Carol drove home. The flat was empty. Michael, she remembered, was out to dinner with some woman he'd met at a trade fair. She decided to give up on the world and go to bed. But first, she'd better leave a message on Tony's machine. If she turned up two mornings running without warning, he might start to get twitchy. The answering machine checked in after a couple of rings, but there was no outgoing message, just a series of clicks followed by the tone. 'Hi, Tony,' she said. 'I don't know if your machine's working properly, so I don't know if you'll get this message. It's twenty past nine, and I'm about to have an early night. I'll be in the office first thing, working on the computer supplies stuff. Mr Brandon's called a case conference for tomorrow at three. If you want to get together before then, give me a call. I'll be in the HOLMES room if I'm not in the squad room.'

Sitting down with Nelson on her lap and a stiff drink by her side, Carol thought about the job that lay ahead. The list of computer supplies companies who sold the peripherals and hardware Handy Andy would need to construct his own images was depressingly long. She had told Dave not to start work on it until she'd had a chance to check out the software company. Their list of customers would be shorter, and they would have the Discovery to cross-reference that list with. Only if that came up blank would she set Dave's team loose on the dozens of numbers she'd painstakingly compiled that evening. 'We'll get there, Nelson,' she told the cat. 'It just better be worth the trip.'

The clatter of high heels on stone cut through the delirium of pain like a wire through cheese. So everyday a sound, translated by its location into a threat. He had no idea whether it was day or night, or how long had passed since he had been snatched from his life. Tony forced himself into alertness as the sound approached him from behind. She was coming downstairs. At the foot of the stairs, the clicking ended. He heard a low chuckle. Slowly, one step at a time, the footsteps crossed behind him. He could sense the scrutiny he was under.

She took her time, skirting round his trussed body until she moved into his line of vision. Tony was momentarily taken aback by the magnificence of her body. From the neck down, she could have been a model for a soft-porn magazine. She stood with legs apart, arms akimbo. She wore a loose red silk kimono, which fell open to reveal an extraordinary red leather basque with peephole nipples and a split crotch. Black stockings sheathed shapely, muscular legs which ended in black stilettoes. Even under the kimono, he could see the clear outline of strong, well-muscled arms and shoulders. From where he was hanging, she was as erotic as a kaolin poultice.

'Worked it out yet, *Anthony*?' she drawled, the warmth of suppressed laughter evident in her voice.

The stressing of his full name was the last turn in the Rubik's cube of his memory. His mind racing, Tony said, 'I suppose a couple of paracetamol would be out of the question, Angelica?'

The low chuckle again. 'Glad to see you haven't lost your sense of humour.'

'No, only my dignity. I wasn't expecting this, Angelica. Nothing in our phone conversations led me to imagine this is what you had in mind for me.'

'You had no idea who I was, did you?' Angelica said, pride unmistakable in her tones.

'Yes and no. I didn't know you were the person who killed those men. But I did know you were the woman for me.'

Angelica frowned, as if uncertain how to respond. She turned away and checked the camcorder. 'You took long enough to get that far. Do you have any idea how many times you slammed the phone down on me?' Her voice was angry, not hurt.

Tony sensed the danger and tried to find emollient words. 'That was because I had a problem, not because of you.'

'You had a problem with me,' she said, moving over to the stone benches that ran along one wall. She picked up another cassette and walked back to the camera.

Tony tried again. 'Quite the opposite,' he said. 'I've always had trouble with relationships with women. That's why I didn't know how to treat you in the beginning. But it got so much better. You know it did. You know we were wonderful together. Thanks to you, I feel like all my problems are behind me.' He hoped she wasn't alive to the unintentional irony in his words.

But Angelica was no fool. 'I think you can safely say that, Anthony,' she said with a wry smile.

'You outsmarted me, you know. I was convinced the killer was a man. I should have known better.'

With her back to him, Angelica swapped the cassettes in the camcorder. Then she wheeled round and said, 'You'd never have caught me. And with you out of the way, no one else will either.'

Ignoring the threat, Tony continued to chat, straining to keep his voice warm and even. 'I should have realized you were a woman. The subtlety, the attention to detail, the care you took to clear up after yourself. It was stupid of me not to grasp that those were the hallmarks of a woman's mind, not a man's.'

Angelica smirked. 'You're all the same, you psychologists.' She spat the word out as though it were an obscenity. 'You've got no imagination.'

'But I'm not like them, Angelica. OK, I made that one crucial mistake, but I bet I know more about you than any of them ever did. Because you've shown me the inside of

342

your mind. And not just through the killings. You've shown me the real woman, the woman who comprehends love. But I guess they didn't understand you, did they? They didn't believe you when you told them you had a woman's spirit trapped in a man's body. Oh, I expect they pretended to, I expect they patronized you and talked down to you. But deep down, they wrote you off as a freak, didn't they? Believe me, I've never done that.' Tony's voice cracked as he reached the end of his speech, his mouth dry with a mixture of fear and chloroform. At least the adrenaline coursing through his veins seemed to be acting as an analgesic.

'What do you know about me?' she said roughly, the pain on her face a strange contrast with the coquettish pose she had adopted.

'I need a drink if we're going to talk,' Tony said, gambling that her narcissism would demand that she share her exploits, that she needed to hear his version of herself. If he was to have any chance of escaping with his life, he needed to build up a relationship with her. A drink would be the first brick in the wall. The more he could get her to see him as an individual, not as a cipher, the higher his chances rose.

Angelica scowled suspiciously. Then, with a toss of her head that sent her long hair swirling, she turned away and walked to a slop sink set against the wall. She turned on the tap and looked around vaguely for a drinking vessel of some kind. 'I'll get a glass,' she muttered, passing him and clattering up the steps again.

Tony felt a surge of relief at his small victory. Angelica was gone for less than thirty seconds, returning with a thick white mug. Kitchen above, Tony deduced as she walked back to the sink. She moved well in the heels, her stride measured and feminine. It was interesting, since she had obviously reverted to more masculine movements under the stress of kidnapping and killing. That was the only way to account for Terry Harding's conviction that he'd seen a man driving off from Damien Connolly's.

Angelica filled the mug and approached Tony cautiously. She gripped his hair, pulled his head back agonizingly and tipped freezing water into his mouth. As much went down his chin as his throat, but the relief was palpable. 'Thanks,' he gasped as she withdrew.

'One should always be hospitable to one's guests,' she said sardonically.

'I hope to remain one for some time,' Tony replied. 'You know, I admire you. You've got style.'

She frowned again. 'Don't bullshit me, Anthony. You won't get round me with stupid flattery.'

'It's not bullshit,' he protested. 'I've spent days and nights poring over the details of what you've achieved. I'm so deep inside your head, how could I not admire you? How could I not be impressed? The other ones you brought here, they didn't have a clue about who you are, what you can do.'

'That's true, I'll grant you that. They were like babies, frightened, stupid babies,' Angelica said contemptuously. 'They didn't appreciate what a woman like me could do for them. They were treacherous. lecherous fools.'

'That's because they didn't know you like I know you.'

'You keep saying that. Prove it. Prove you know anything about me.'

The gauntlet was well and truly down now, Tony thought. Never mind singing for your supper, talk for your life. This was the proving ground, the place where he would discover if his psychology was indeed a science or just bullshit.

'Fraser Duncan? Hello, this is Detective Inspector Carol Jordan of Bradfield police,' she said. Carol had never grown used to referring to herself by her full title. She felt as if, any moment, someone was going to jump out and shout,

'Oh no, you're not! We found you out at last.' Luckily, that didn't seem to be happening today.

'Yes?' The voice was cautious, the single syllable drawn out in a question.

'Actually, it was my brother, Michael Jordan, who suggested you might be able to help me with an enquiry we're pursuing.'

'Oh, yes?' The climate was getting warmer. 'How is Michael? Is he enjoying the software?'

'I think it's absolutely his favourite toy,' Carol replied.

Fraser Duncan laughed. 'An expensive toy, Inspector. Now, what can I do for you?'

'It's the Vicom 3D Commander I wanted to talk to you about. In strictest confidence, you understand. We're pursuing a major murder investigation, and one of the theories I'm looking at is that our killer might be using your software to edit his own videos, maybe even to import other material into them. That would be possible, wouldn't it?'

'More than possible. It would be perfectly straightforward.'

'So, do you keep records of all your customers?' Carol asked.

'We do. We don't sell all the packages direct, obviously, but anyone who buys the Commander should register their purchase with us since that gives them access to a free customer helpline and also means they get priority mailings when we develop upgrades.' Duncan was positively expansive now. 'Do I detect a request for access to our customer database, Inspector?'

'You do indeed, sir. This is a murder enquiry and the information could be crucial to us. Can I stress too that it would be completely confidential? I would personally undertake to ensure that your data is removed from our system as soon as we have finished with it,' Carol said, trying not to sound as if she was begging.

'I don't know,' Duncan said hesitantly. 'I'm not sure I like the idea of you and your colleagues hammering on the doors of my customers.'

'It wouldn't be like that, Mr Duncan. No way. What we would do is input the list into our Home Office Major Large Enquiry System and cross-match it against existing data. We would only act on any correlations that came up with people who are already in there.'

'Is this the serial killer you're after?' Duncan asked abruptly.

What did he want to hear, Carol wondered momentarily. 'Yes,' she said, taking a gamble.

'Let me call you back, Inspector. Just to make sure you are who you say you are.'

'No problem.' She gave him the main police switchboard number. 'Ask them to put you through to me in the HOLMES room at Scargill Street.'

The next five minutes passed in a fever of impatience. The phone barely chirruped before Carol had it to her ear. 'Inspector Jordan?'

'You owe me, sis.'

'Michael!'

'I've just been telling Fraser Duncan what an honourable little person you are and despite what he's heard about the police, he can trust you.'

'I love you, bro. Now get off the phone and let the man talk to me!'

Within the hour, Vicom's data was inside the HOLMES computer network, thanks to Dave Woolcott and the miracles of modern technology. Carol had passed Fraser Duncan on to him after they had agreed the ground rules for the data use, and Carol had listened uncomprehendingly to Dave's end of a conversation which consisted of alien expressions like 'baud rate' and 'ASCII files'.

Carol sat by Dave's side as he worked on one of the terminals. 'OK,' he said. 'We've got the list from Swansea of everyone within a twenty-mile radius of Bradfield who has one of these Discoveries. We've also got the list of names from Vicom of people who have bought their software. I hit this key, and go down this menu to this option, wild-card match, and now we sit back and let the machine talk to itself.'

For an agonizing minute, nothing happened. Then the screen cleared and a message flashed up. '[2] matches found. List matches?' Dave hit the 'y' key and two names and addresses appeared on the screen.

1: *Philip Crozier, 23 Broughton Crag, Sheffield Road, Bradfield BX4 6JB*
2: *Christopher Thorpe [sort criterion 1]/Angelica Thorpe [sort criterion 2], 14 Gregory Street, Moorside, Bradfield BX6 4LR*

'What does that mean?' Carol asked, pointing to the second option.

'The Discovery is registered to Christopher Thorpe and the software was bought by Angelica,' Dave explained. 'Using the wild-card option means that the machine sorted by address as well as by name. Well, Carol, you've got something. Whether it means anything or not, we'll have to see.'

Penny Burgess strode over the rough, fissured limestone of Malham Pavement. The sky was the bright blue of early spring, the rough moorland grasses starting to look more green than brown. From time to time, larks shot out into the air and poured their songs into her ears. There were two occasions when Penny really came alive. One was on the trail of a hot story. The other was up on the high moorlands of the Yorkshire Dales and the Derbyshire Peak District. Out in the open air, she felt free as the skylarks, all pressure gone. No newsdesk demanding copy by an hour ago, no contacts to be appeased, no looking over her shoulder to be sure of staying ahead of her rivals. Just the sky, the moors, the extraordinary limestone landscape, and her.

For no reason, Stevie McConnell burst into her thoughts. He'd never see the sky again, never walk a moor and watch the turning of the seasons. Thank God she had the power to make sure that someone would pay for that inhuman deprivation.

Philip Crozier's house was a narrow, terraced three-storey modern town house, the ground floor consisting mainly of an integral garage. Carol sat in the car, eyeing it up and down. 'We going in, ma'am?' the young detective constable in the driving seat asked.

Carol thought for a moment. Ideally, she'd wanted Tony to be with her when she interviewed the people whose names the computer had spat out. She'd tried ringing him at home. No reply. Claire said he hadn't come into the office yet, which surprised her since he'd had a nine-thirty appointment. Carol had swung round by the house, but it looked exactly the same as it had the night before. Off having fun with his lady friend, she'd decided. Serves him right if he misses out on the showdown with Handy Andy, she thought maliciously, then immediately regretted her childishness. Failing Tony, she'd have liked to have had Don Merrick with her. But he was out pursuing other lines of enquiry that had flowed from the identification of the Discovery. The only person she could find who wasn't urgently involved with something else was DC Morris, on the third month of his secondment to CID.

'We might as well see if he's in,' Carol said. 'Though he's probably at work.'

They walked up the path, Carol taking in the details of the neatly trimmed lawn and the smart paintwork. The house didn't really fit Tony's profile. It was more like the victims' houses in terms of value and status, rather than the home of someone who aspired to their lifestyles. Carol pressed the bell and stepped back. They were about to give up and return to the car when Carol heard feet pounding downstairs. The door swung open to reveal a stocky black man dressed in grey sweat pants and a scarlet T-shirt, his feet bare. He couldn't have looked more different from Terry Harding's description. Carol's heart sank momentarily, then she reminded herself that Crozier might not be the only person with access to his software and his Discovery. He was still worth interviewing. 'Yeah?' he said.

'Mr Crozier?'

''S right. Who wants to know?' His voice was relaxed, the Bradfield accent strong.

Carol produced her warrant card and introduced herself. 'I wonder if we could come in and have a word, sir?'

'What about?'

'Your name has cropped up in some routine enquiries and I'd like to ask you some questions for the purposes of elimination.'

Crozier's brows furrowed. 'What sort of enquiries?'

'If we could just come in, sir?'

'No, hang on, what's all this about? I'm trying to get some work done here.'

Morris stepped to Carol's side. 'There's no need to be difficult, sir, it's just routine.'

'Mr Crozier isn't being difficult, Constable,' Carol said coolly. 'I'd feel just the same in your shoes, sir. A car answering the description of yours has been involved in an incident, and we need to eliminate you from our investigation. We're speaking to several other people in connection with this enquiry, sir. It won't take long.'

'All right then,' Crozier sighed. 'You'd better come in.'

They followed him up stairs carpeted in functional cord carpet into an open-plan living room-cum-kitchen. It was furnished in expensive but minimalist style. He waved them to two leather and wood armchairs and dropped into a leather bean bag on the polished wood floor. Morris pulled out his notebook and ostentatiously opened it to a fresh page.

'You work from home, then?' Carol asked.

''S right. I'm a freelance animator.'

'Cartoons?' Carol said.

'I do mostly science animations. You want something for your Open University course that shows how atoms collide, I'm your man. So what's all this about?'

'You drive a Land Rover Discovery?'

''S right. It's in the garage.'

'Can you tell me if you were driving it last Monday night?' Carol asked. God, was it only a week ago?

'I can. I wasn't. I was in Boston, Massachusetts.'

She went through the routine questions that established precisely what Crozier had been doing, and who she could check the information with. Then she stood up. Time for the key question, but it was important to keep it looking casual. 'Thanks for you help, Mr Crozier. One more thing – is there anyone else who has access to your house while you're away? Someone who could have borrowed your car?'

Crozier shook his head. 'I live on my own. I don't even have a cat or plants, so nobody has to come in when I'm away. I'm the only one with keys.'

'You're sure of that? No cleaning lady, no colleague who drops in to use your system?'

'Sure, I'm sure. I do my own cleaning, I work alone. I split up with my girlfriend a couple of months back and I changed the locks, OK? Nobody's got keys except me.' Crozier was starting to sound tetchy.

Carol persisted. 'And no one could have borrowed your keys without your knowledge and had them copied?'

'I don't see how. I'm not in the habit of leaving them lying around. And the car's only insured for me, so nobody else has ever driven it,' Crozier said, his irritation clearly mounting. 'Look, if somebody did anything criminal in a car with my number on, they were using faked-up plates, OK?'

'I accept what you're saying, Mr Crozier. I can assure you that if the information you've given me checks out, you won't be hearing from us again. Thanks very much for your time.'

Back at the car, Carol said, 'Find me a phone. I want to try Dr Hill again. I can't believe he's gone AWOL the one time we really need him.'

It's laughable. They pick a man who can't even tell whether I've carried out a particular punishment or not and they employ him to help them catch me. They could at least have shown me the respect of employing someone who has some reputation, an opponent worthy of my skills, not some idiot who has never encountered someone of my calibre.

Instead, they insult me. Dr Tony Hill is supposed to be producing a profile of me, based on his analysis of my killings. When this account is published, years hence, after my death in my bed from natural causes, historians will be able to compare his profile with the reality and laugh at the gross inaccuracies of his pseudo-science.

He will never come close to the truth. For the record, I set down that truth.

I was born in the Yorkshire port of Seaford, one of the busiest fishing and commercial docks in the country. My father was a merchant seaman, the first officer on oil tankers. He went all over the world, then he would come home to us. But my mother was as bad a wife as she was a mother. I can see now that the house was always in chaos, the meals irregular and unappetizing. The only thing she was good at, the only thing they could share, was the drinking. If there was an Olympic pairs event for pissheads, they'd have walked off with the gold.

When I was seven, my father stopped coming home. Of

course, my mother blamed me for not being a good enough son. She said I'd driven him away. She told me I was the man of the house now. But I could never live up to her expectations. She always wanted more from me than I was capable of, and ruled me by blame rather than praise. I spent more time locked in the cupboard than most people's coats do.

Without my father's pay cheque, she was thrown on the resources of the welfare system, which was barely enough to live on, never mind get drunk on. When the building society repossessed the house, we went to live with relatives in Bradfield for a while, but she couldn't handle their disapproval, so we moved back to Seaford, when she turned to the town's other boom industry, prostitution. I grew accustomed to the procession of disgusting, drunken sailors traipsing through the succession of grubby flats and bedsits where we lived. We were always behind with the rent, usually doing a moonlight flit just before the bailiffs got really heavy.

I grew to hate the ugly, grunting copulation that I was a constant witness to, and stayed out of the house as much as I possibly could, often sleeping rough down by the docks. I used to pick on kids that were younger than me to get their money off them so I could afford to eat. I moved schools almost as often as we moved house, so I never did too well there, in spite of the fact that I knew I could run rings round most of the other kids, who were just stupid.

As soon as I was 16, I left Seaford. It wasn't a wrench; it wasn't as if I'd ever managed to make many friends, what with moving all the time. I'd seen enough of men to know that I didn't want to grow up like them, and I felt different inside. I thought if I moved back to a big city like Bradfield I'd find it easier to work out what I wanted. One of my mother's cousins got me a job at the electronics firm where he worked.

About that time, I discovered that dressing in women's

clothes made me feel good about myself. I got my own bedsit so I could do it whenever I wanted to, and that calmed me down a lot. I started studying computer science at evening classes, and eventually got some proper qualifications. About that time, my mother got left a house in Seaford in her brother's will.

I got the chance of a job back in Seaford, working in computer systems for the local private phone company. I didn't really want to go back there, but the job was too good to turn down. I never went near my mother. I don't think she even knew I was there.

One of the few good things about Seaford is that it's handy for the ferry to Holland. I used to go there every other weekend, because in Amsterdam I could go out dressed as a woman and nobody batted an eyelid. Over there, I met a lot of transsexuals as well as transvestites, and the more I talked to them, the more I realized that I was just like them. I was a woman trapped in a man's body. That explained why I'd never had much sexual interest in girls. And although I found men attractive, I knew I wasn't a poof. They disgust me, with their pretence at normal relationships when everybody knows that it's only men and women that can fit together properly.

I went to see the doctors at Jimmy's in Leeds, where they do all the sex-change operations in the north, and they turned me down. Their psychologists were as stupid and blinkered as all the rest of their brotherhood. But I managed to find a private doctor in London who prescribed the hormone treatment I needed. Of course, I couldn't go on working while this was going on, but I spoke to the boss and he said he'd give me a good reference for another job when I'd had the operation and I was a woman.

I had to go abroad for the operation, and it was all much more expensive than I expected. I went to my mother and asked her if she'd mortgage the house to lend me the money and she just laughed at me.

So I did what I'd learned from her. I sold myself on the docks. It's amazing how much money sailors will pay for a travesti. They get out of their heads with excitement at the thought of someone who has breasts and a cock. I wasn't like the other hookers either; I didn't blow it all on drink or drugs or a pimp. I stashed it all away till I could afford the operation.

When I came to Seaford, not even my own mother recognized me at first. I'd only been back a few days when she took that tragic accidental overdose of drink and pills. Nobody was surprised. Yes, Doctor, you can add her to the list.

With my qualifications, experience and reference, I had no trouble getting a job as a senior systems analyst with the phone company in Bradfield. The money I made from the sale of the house in Seaford bought me my home in Bradfield, and I started the task of finding a worthy man to share my life.

And Dr Tony Hill presumes to understand me, without knowing any of this? Well, in a very short time, I'll share it all with him. Such a shame he won't have the chance to write it down for himself.

18

The truth is, I am a very particular man in everything relating to murder; and perhaps I carry my delicacy too far.

Don Merrick walked into the HOLMES room munching a two-inch-thick double cheese and Bar-B-Q bacon burger. 'How do you do it?' Dave Woolcott asked. 'How do you get those slack Alices down the canteen to cook you edible food? They could burn a cup of tea, that lot, but you always manage to twist them round your little finger.'

Merrick winked. 'It's my natural Geordie charm,' he said. 'I just pick on the ugliest one and tell her she reminds me of my mother when she was in her prime.' He sat down and stretched his long legs. 'I've checked out the half-dozen Discoveries your sergeant gave me. They're all in the clear. Two of them are women, two of them have got rock-solid alibis for at least two of the nights in question, one's got multiple sclerosis, so he couldn't have done the jobs, and the sixth sold his to a dealership in the Midlands three weeks ago.'

'Great,' Dave said heavily. 'Give the list to one of the operators so we can update the file.'

'Where's the guv?'

'Carol or Kevin?'

Merrick shrugged. 'I still think of Inspector Jordan as my guv'nor.'

'She's off chasing wild geese,' Dave said.

'She got a result, then?' Merrick asked.

'Two cross-matches.'

'Let's have a look,' Merrick said.

Dave rummaged among his papers and found three sheets of paper stapled together. The first listed the two correlations. Merrick frowned and flicked over a page. The second was a print-out of the result of a criminal records search on Philip Crozier. Nothing known. Hurriedly, he turned to the third page, which listed two Christopher Thorpes. One had a last-known address in Devon and several convictions for burglary. The second had a last-known address in Seaford. There were a string of juvenile convictions; assaulting a football referee, breaking windows at a school, shoplifting. There were half a dozen adult convictions, all for soliciting prostitution. Merrick sucked in his breath sharply and turned back to the front page. 'Fuck,' he said.

'What is it?' Dave asked, suddenly alert.

'This here. Christopher Thorpe, the Seaford one?'

'Yeah? Carol reckoned it wasn't the same one as ours. I mean, he's got convictions for being a male prostitute, but this one in Bradfield looks to be married, because the woman at the same address has his surname. And let's face it, you don't get dockland rent boys driving around in serious motors like the Discovery.'

Merrick shook his head. 'No, you've got it all wrong. I know this Christopher Thorpe from Seaford. I worked on Vice in Seaford before I came here, remember? I was the arresting officer on two of these charges in soliciting. Christopher Thorpe was halfway to a sex change at the time. He had the tits and everything, he was trying to earn enough money to get the operation. Guess what his working name was? Dave, Christopher Thorpe isn't *married* to Angelica Thorpe, he *is* Angelica Thorpe.'

'Fuck,' Dave echoed.

'Dave, where the hell is Carol?'

* * *

Angelica stood in front of him, hands on hips, chewing one corner of her mouth. 'You can't, can you? You can't prove it because you know nothing about my life.'

'In one sense you're absolutely right, Angelica. I don't know the facts of your life,' Tony said carefully, 'but I think I know a bit about the shape of it. Your mother didn't do a very good job of loving you. Maybe she had a problem with drink or with drugs, or maybe she just didn't understand what a little kid needed. Either way, she didn't make you feel loved when you were little. Am I right?'

Angelica scowled. 'Go on. Dig yourself a hole.'

Tony felt a prickle of fear tingle at the base of his skull. What if he'd got it wrong? What if this woman was the exception to every statistical near certainty Tony had held at the front of his mind during the whole enquiry? What if she was the one serial killer who had come from a happy, loving family? Dismissing his doubts as a luxury he couldn't afford right now, Tony ploughed on. 'Your father wasn't around much when you were growing up, and he never showed you he was proud of his son, even though you did everything you knew how to make him feel that pride. Your mother expected too much of you, kept telling you you were the man of the house, and giving you a bad time when you behaved like the child you were instead of the man she wanted to pretend you were.' Angelica's face twitched in a spasm of recognition. Tony paused.

'Go on,' she grated between clenched teeth.

'It's not easy for me to talk, doubled over like this. Can't you slacken the rope a bit, let me stand upright?'

She shook her head, her mouth sulky as a child's.

'I can't look at you properly like this,' Tony tried. 'You've got a fabulous body, you must know that. If it's going to be the last thing I see, at least let me appreciate it.'

She cocked her head to one side, as if replaying his words to check them for truth or trickery. 'All right,' she conceded. 'It doesn't mean anything's changed, though,' she added as she moved to the winch and released it. She let out about a foot of slack.

Tony couldn't bite back· the scream of pain that shot through his shoulders as the muscles were released from the strain that had stretched them to their limit. 'It'll wear off,' Angelica said roughly as she returned to her station by the camcorder. 'Keep talking,' she instructed him. 'I've always enjoyed fantasy fiction.'

He eased himself upright, struggling against the pain. 'You were a bright kid,' he gasped. 'Brighter than the rest of them. It's never easy making friends when you're so much smarter than the other kids. And maybe you moved around a bit. Different neighbours, maybe even different schools.'

Angelica was back in control of herself, her face impassive as he continued. 'It wasn't easy to make friends. You knew you were different from everybody else, special, but you couldn't work out why at first. Then as you grew up, you realized what it was. You weren't the same as the other boys because you weren't a boy at all. You had no interest in girls sexually, but it wasn't because you were gay. No way. It was because you were really a girl yourself. What you discovered was that dressing up in women's clothes made you feel like you'd come home, like this was how you were meant to be.' He paused and gave her a crooked smile. 'How am I doing so far?'

'Very impressive, Doctor,' she said coldly. 'I'm fascinated. Carry on.'

Tony flexed his shoulder muscles, relieved to discover that the damage so far seemed to be only temporary. The pins and needles that raged across his back seemed no more than a minor irritation after what he'd been through. He took a deep breath and carried on. 'You decided to become the person you were inside, the woman you knew you really were. God, Angelica, I've got so much respect for you, putting yourself through that. I know how hard it is to get the medical profession to take the idea seriously. All the hormone therapy, the electrolysis, living as a half-man, half-woman while you waited for the operations, and then all the pain of the surgery.' He shook his head, wonderingly. 'I know I wouldn't have the courage to put myself through all that.'

'It wasn't easy.' The words escaped from Angelica's lips, almost against her will.

'I believe you,' Tony said sympathetically. 'And after all that, to find yourself wondering if it had been worth it after all, when you realized that the stupidity, the insensitivity, the lack of insight you'd identified in men didn't just disappear because you were a woman. They were still the same old bunch of bastards, incapable of recognizing an exceptional woman when they were offered her love and affection on a plate.' He paused, studying her face, deciding if the time was right for the big gamble. The coldness had left her eyes, replaced by a look almost of misery. He softened his voice and lowered the volume. Please God, let his training pay off.

'They rejected you, didn't they? Adam Scott, Paul Gibbs, Gareth Finnegan, Damien Connolly. They turned you down.'

Angelica shook her head violently, as if by activity she could deny the past. 'They *let* me down. They *let* me down, they didn't turn me down. They betrayed me.'

'Tell me about it,' Tony said softly, praying that his hard-earned techniques weren't going to fail him now. 'Tell me about it.'

'Why should I?' she shouted, stepping forward and slapping him so hard he tasted blood as his cheek impacted against his teeth. 'You're no better than them. What about that slag? That blonde bitch, that fucking plonk you've been giving one to?'

Tony swallowed the warm salty blood that filled his

mouth. 'You mean Carol Jordan?' he said, playing for time. How should he play this? Should he lie or tell the truth?

'You know full well who I mean. I know you've been with her, don't fucking try lying to me,' she hissed, raising her hand again. 'You treacherous, faithless bastard.' Her hand cracked him across the face again, so hard he heard his neck crick under the force of it.

Tears sprang to his eyes involuntarily. The truth wasn't going to work. It would only earn him more punishment. Praying he could lie with conviction, Tony pleaded, 'Angelica, she was just a fuck, just someone to scratch the itch. You'd got me so horny with your phone calls. I didn't know when you were going to call again, or even if you were.' He allowed anger to creep into his voice. 'I wanted you and you didn't tell me how I could get hold of you. Angelica, it's like you with the other ones. I was filling in time, waiting for my equal. You can't believe that a mere cop would answer my fantasies, do you? You should know, you've had one too.'

Angelica stepped back, shock on her face. Sensing he had made some kind of a breakthrough, Tony pursued her with his words. 'We were different, you and me. They weren't worthy of you. But we were special. You must know that, from our phone calls. Didn't you sense that we had something extraordinary? That this time it would be different? Isn't that what you really want? You don't want the killing. Not really. The killing only happened because they weren't worthy, because they let you down. What you really want is a worthy partner. What you want is love. Angelica, what you want is me.'

For a long moment she stared at him, eyes wide, mouth open. Then confusion took over, as obvious to Tony as a hooker's come-on. 'Don't use that word to me, you worthless scumbag,' she stuttered. 'Don't fucking say it!' Her voice was a low, throaty scream. Suddenly, she turned on her heel and ran from the room, her heels clattering up the stairs.

'I love you, Angelica,' Tony shouted desperately after her retreating footsteps. 'I love you.'

Carol and DC Morris stood on the doorstep of the small terraced house in Gregory Street. She didn't need to be a psychologist to read his body language. Morris was fed up at trailing round pursuing Carol's daft hunch. 'They must be out at work,' he remarked after their fourth assault on the doorbell.

'Looks that way,' Carol agreed.

'Shall we come back later?'

'Let's go on the knocker,' Carol suggested. 'See if any of the neighbours are around. Maybe they can tell us when the Thorpes get back from work.'

Morris looked as if he'd rather be on crowd control at a student demo. 'Yes, ma'am,' he said in a bored voice.

'You take across the street, I'll go for this side.' Carol watched him trudge across the street as wearily as a miner at the end of his shift, shook her head with a sigh and turned her attention to number twelve. This was much more the kind of territory Tony had suggested for their killer. Thinking of Tony just made Carol cross again. Where the hell was he? She really needed his input today, not to mention a bit of support for an idea that everybody else seemed to think was a complete waste of time. He couldn't have picked a worse moment to go on the missing list. It was unforgivable. At least he could have phoned his secretary and not left her having to field his calls and make excuses for him.

There was no bell on the door of number twelve, so Carol bruised her knuckles on the solid wood. The woman who opened it looked like a caricature from a soap opera. In her forties, her make-up would have been over the top for dinner in LA, never mind mid-afternoon in a Bradfield back street. Her dyed platinum blonde hair was piled high in a lopsided beehive. She wore a tight black sweater with a scoop neck revealing a cleavage the texture of crumpled tissue, shiny blue skin-tight leggings, white stilettoes and a thin gold ankle chain. A cigarette dangled from a corner of her mouth. 'What is it, love?' she said nasally.

'Sorry to trouble you,' Carol said, flashing her warrant card. 'Detective Inspector Carol Jordan, Bradfield police. I'm trying to get in touch with your next-door neighbours at number fourteen, the Thorpes, but there doesn't seem to be anybody home. I wonder if you happen to know what time they get in from work.'

The woman shrugged. 'Search me, love. That cow comes and goes at all hours.'

'What about Mr Thorpe?' Carol asked.

'What Mr Thorpe? There's no Mr Thorpe next door, love.' She gave a croak of laughter. 'It's easy seen you've never clapped eyes on her. Any man that married that ugly cow would have to be blind and bloody hard up. So what've you got her for?'

'It's just routine enquiries,' Carol said.

The woman snorted. 'Don't give me that fanny,' she said. 'I've watched enough episodes of *The Bill* to know they don't send inspectors out on routine enquiries. It's about time you put that cow behind bars, if you want my opinion.'

'Why is that, Mrs . . . ?'

'Goodison, Bette Goodison. As in Bette Davis. Because she's an ugly, anti-social cow, that's why.'

Carol smiled. 'I'm afraid that's not a crime, Mrs Goodison.'

'No, but murder is, isn't it?' Bette Goodison crowed triumphantly.

Carol swallowed, hoping the effect of the word wasn't as visible as it was palpable. 'That's a very serious accusation.'

Bette Goodison took a final drag of her cigarette and

expertly flipped the dog end across the narrow pavement and into the gutter. 'I'm glad you think so. It's more than your mates at Moorside nick did.'

'I'm sorry you feel you've not been well served by my colleagues,' Carol said in a concerned tone. 'Perhaps you could tell me what you're talking about?' Please God, let this not be a rerun of the Yorkshire Ripper case, where the killer's best friend told the police they suspected he was the Ripper and the police paid no attention.

'Prince, that's who we're talking about.'

For one wild moment, Carol had a vision of the diminutive American rock star buried in the back yard of a Bradfield terrace. Pulling herself together, she said, 'Prince?'

'Our German shepherd. Always complaining about him, that Angelica Thorpe was. And she had no grounds. That dog was doing her a service. Anybody so much as walked down our ginnel and that dog let you know about it. She'd have paid a fortune for a burglar alarm as efficient as that dog. Any road up, a few months back . . . August, it were, weekend before Bank Holiday, we come home from work, Col and me, and Prince is gone. Now, there's no way he could have got out of that yard, and he'd have gone for anybody that came in. There's only one way he could have disappeared, and that's if he was murdered,' Mrs Goodison said, stabbing Carol in the chest with her finger for emphasis. 'She poisoned him and then she got rid of the body so there would be no proof. She's a murderer!'

Normally, Carol would have walked a mile barefoot to avoid this conversation, but she was in pursuit of Handy Andy, and any oddity was something to be grasped eagerly. 'How can you be so sure it was Mrs Thorpe?' she asked.

'Stands to reason. She were the only one that ever complained about him. And the day he went missing, me and Col were out at work, but she were home all day. I know that for a fact, because she were on nights that week. And when we knocked on her door to ask did she know anything about him going missing, she just smiled all over that ugly gob of hers. I could have put her face in for her,' Mrs Goodison said emphatically. 'So what are you going to do about it?'

'I'm afraid that without evidence, there's not much we can do,' Carol said sympathetically. 'You're sure, are you, that Mrs Thorpe lives alone?'

'Nobody'd want to live with an ugly cow like that. She never even has visitors. Not surprising, mind, she looks like a brick shithouse in drag.'

'Do you happen to know what kind of car she drives?' Carol asked.

'One of them bloody yuppie jeep things. I ask you, who needs a bloody great jeep in the middle of Bradfield? It's not like we live up some farm track, is it?'

'And do you know where she works?'

'I don't know and I don't care.' She glanced at her watch. 'Now, if you don't mind, my serial's starting.'

Carol watched the door close behind Bette Goodison, an unpleasant suspicion starting to form in her mind. Before she could try number ten, her pager bleeped insistently. 'Phone Don at Scargill Street. Double urgent,' she read.

'Morris!' Carol shouted. 'Get me to a phone. Pronto monto.' Whatever was going on in Gregory Street could wait. Don clearly couldn't.

Exhausted, Tony had slipped into some nightmare delirium doze. A gout of freezing water thrown in his face smacked him straight to agonized attention, his head snapping back painfully. 'Augh,' he groaned.

'Wakey, wakey,' Angelica said roughly.

'I was right, wasn't I?' Tony said through swollen lips. 'You've had time to think about it, and you know I'm right. You want the killing to stop. They had to die, they deserved to die. They let you down, they betrayed you,

365

they didn't deserve you. But all that can change now. It can be different with me, because I love you.'

The rigid mask of her face crumpled before his eyes, becoming softer, more tender. She smiled at him. 'It's never been about sex, you know. I could always have sex. Men paid me for sex. They paid me a lot of money for sex. That's how I paid for the surgery, you know. They always wanted me.' Her voice was filled with a strange mixture of pride and anger.

'I can see why,' Tony lied, arranging his face in what he hoped was an expression of hunger and admiration. 'But what you really wanted was love, wasn't it? You wanted more than loveless sex on the streets or faceless sex down the phone. You deserve that. God, you deserve it. That's what I can give you, Angelica. Love isn't just physical attraction, though God knows you're attractive. But love's about respect, admiration, fascination, and I feel all of that for you. Angelica, you can have what you want. You can have it with me.'

Her warring emotions were written plainly on her face. He could see that part of her desperately wanted to believe him, wanted to escape into the normal world of relationships. But that part had to contend with a level of self-esteem that was so low she couldn't imagine anyone worth loving wanting to love her. And, underlying it all, suspicion that he was trying to entrap her. 'How can we?' she demanded harshly. 'You've been trying to hunt me down. You're with the police. You're on their side.'

Tony shook his head. 'That was before I realized you were the same woman I'd fallen in love with on the phone. Angelica, love is the one emotion that overrides duty. Yeah, I've worked with the police, but I'm not one of them.'

'You lie down with dogs, you get up with fleas,' she sneered. 'You've been trying to put me away, Anthony. You expect me to believe you? You must think I'm really stupid.'

'Quite the opposite. If you want to talk about stupid, talk about the police. Mostly, they're one-dimensional, boring bigots who couldn't keep a psychologist interested for more than five minutes. I don't have anything in common with them,' he argued desperately.

She shook her head, more in sorrow than in anger. 'You work for the Home Office. Your whole career, you've spent catching serial offenders and treating them. And you expect me to believe you'd suddenly change sides and stay loyal to me? Come on, Anthony, I'm not going to fall for crap like that.'

Tony felt his powers flagging. His brain just wasn't fast enough any longer to keep her at bay. Wretchedly, he said, 'I've not made a career of catching people, only treating them. I had to do that, don't you understand? Inside the places where I've worked is the only place where I can find minds that are complex enough to be interesting. It's like going to see animals at the zoo. You want to watch them in their natural habitat, but if the only way you are ever going to see them is at the zoo, you go. I've always had to wait till they were in captivity before I could study them. But you, you're still in the wild, still the way you want to be, perfected in your craft. And compared to them, you're the cream of the crop. You're exceptional. I want to spend the rest of my life being excited by your mind. I can't imagine ever finding you boring.' Terrifying, maybe, but never boring.

Her lower lip thrust out, bringing an expression of calculating petulance to her face. She nodded in the direction of his groin, where his penis hung limp. 'So if you find me that attractive, how come it doesn't show?'

It was the one question to which Tony had no answer at all.

'What have we actually got, Carol?' Brandon challenged.

Carol paced the floor of Brandon's office, ticking off

her points on her fingers. 'We've got a transsexual. Not a transsexual who went through the controlled, counselled National Health Service process, but one who, according to Don, was turned down for a sex change here and had to finance an operation abroad by selling sex. So right from the start, we know we've got someone who has been examined by psychiatrists and found to be unstable. We've got this transsexual driving a vehicle identical to the one driven by a suspect in Damien Connolly's murder. We've got a neighbour who's convinced that Angelica Thorpe offed her dog. The dog was killed a fortnight before the first murder. Angelica Thorpe bought software that would allow her to manipulate videos in her computer system, which fits a theory of the killer's behaviour developed by me and endorsed by our psychological profiler. She even lives in the kind of house Tony said she would,' Carol argued vehemently.

'When she was Christopher, she was definitely a few butties short of a picnic,' Don chipped in.

'I wish we could ask Tony about this,' Brandon said, stalling.

'So do I,' Carol said through her teeth. 'But he's obviously found something more important to do today.' A sudden thought hit Carol like a sandbag to the neck. Her knees started to buckle and she collapsed into the nearest chair. 'Oh, my God,' she gasped.

'What is it?' Brandon asked, concerned.

'Tony. He hasn't been in touch with anybody since he left here yesterday. He had two task-force meetings arranged for today, according to his secretary, but he hasn't shown up at work, and he hasn't phoned in. He wasn't home last night, and he's not there now.' Carol's words hung in the air like a cloud of poisonous smoke. A wave of nausea lurched up from her stomach, almost choking her. Somehow, she maintained her composure under Brandon's concentrated stare.

With fingers that trembled, Carol picked up Brandon's copy of the profile from his desk. Urgently, she flicked through the pages till she found what she was looking for. '"It is possible that his next target may also be a police officer, perhaps even one who is working on the investigation. This alone will not be sufficient motive for the killer to choose them; they must also fit the victim criteria that he has drawn up in his own mind in order for the killing to assume its full meaning for him. I would strongly recommend that any officers who fit the victim profile employ extra vigilance at all times, noting any suspicious vehicles parked near their homes, and checking to see whether they are being followed to and from work and social events." Think about it, sir. Think about the victim profile. Sir, Tony fits it perfectly.'

Not wanting to believe what Carol was suggesting, Brandon said, 'But it's not eight weeks. It's not time!'

'But it *is* a Monday. Don't forget, Tony also pointed out that his timetable could be accelerated if something happened to traumatize him. Stevie McConnell, sir. Think of all the publicity. Someone else was getting the credit for his crimes. Look, it's in here, sir: "Another possible scenario is that an innocent person is charged with the killings. That would be such an affront to his sense of himself that he might commit his next murder ahead of schedule." Sir, we've got to move on this now!'

Brandon's hand was on the phone before she'd even started her last sentence.

The front door opened directly into the house. Downstairs couldn't have looked more normal. The small living room was furnished inexpensively but comfortably with a two-seater sofa and matching chair upholstered in moss-green Dralon. There was a TV, video, mid-priced stereo system and a coffee table complete with a copy of *Elle*. A pair of framed posters of whales in the ocean hung on the walls.

The single bookshelf contained a selection of science-fiction classics, a couple of Stephen King novels and a trio of Jackie Collins bonkbusters. Carol, Merrick and Brandon moved cautiously through the room, past the stairs and into the kitchen diner. It was surgically neat as a show-room, work surfaces clean and uncluttered. On the drainer, one mug, one plate, one fork, one knife.

With Brandon leading the way, they climbed the narrow stairs built between the two downstairs rooms. The front bedroom was pink and frothy as a strawberry milkshake. Even the kidney-shaped dressing table, with its skirt of lace, was pink. 'Barbara Cartland, eat your heart out,' Merrick muttered. Brandon opened the wardrobe and flicked through the array of women's clothes. Carol headed for the drawers in a pink tallboy and worked her way down. They contained nothing more disturbing than a selection of tacky underwear, much of it in red satin.

It was Merrick who first broached the back bedroom. As soon as he opened the door, he knew no one was going to be screaming to the papers about magistrates granting warrants on non-existent evidence. 'Sir?' he shouted. 'I think we've cracked it.'

The room was arranged as an office. A large desk held a computer and assorted peripherals that none of them could identify. To one side was a telephone linked to a sophisticated tape recorder. A small video-editing desk was in one corner, next to a filing cabinet. A wheeled trolley carried a television and video, both state of the art and top of the range. Shelves lined two walls, filled with computer games, videos, cassettes and computer disks, each box labelled neatly in firm capitals. The only alien object in the room was a leather recliner, the material slung hammock-like on a steel frame.

'Bingo,' Brandon breathed. 'Well done, Carol.'

'Where the fuck do we start?' Merrick said.

'Do either of you know how to work the computer?' Brandon asked.

'I think we should leave that to the experts,' Carol said. 'It might be programmed to crash the data if someone else tries to log on.'

'OK. Don, you take the filing cabinet, I'll take the videos, and Carol, you take the cassettes.'

Carol moved across to the shelves of cassettes. The first couple of dozen seemed to be music tapes, ranging from Liza Minnelli to U2. Next were a dozen marked 'AS' and numbered from one to twelve. Fourteen marked 'PG' followed, then fifteen with 'GF', eight with 'DC' and six with 'AH'. The concatenation of initials was far beyond the boundaries of coincidence. Carol picked the first 'AH' tape and, heart heavy with misgivings, slotted it into the cassette player. She picked up the headphones plugged into the machine and gingerly pushed them into her ears. She heard the sound of a telephone ringing, then a voice so familiar she could have wept. 'Hello?' Tony said, his voice reduced by the telephone line.

'Hello, Anthony,' a voice not entirely strange to her said.

'Who is this?' Tony asked.

A chuckle, low and sexy. 'You'll never guess. Not in a million years.' Got it, thought Carol, grim foreboding gripping her. The voice on the answering machine.

'OK, so tell me,' Tony said, his voice curious, friendly, joining in the game.

'Who would you like me to be? If I could be anyone in the world?'

'Is this some kind of wind-up?' Tony demanded.

'I've never been more serious in my life. I'm here to make your dreams come true. I'm the woman of your fantasies, Anthony. I am your telephone lover.'

There was a moment's silence, then the phone slammed down at Tony's end. Over the dialling tone, Carol heard the strange woman say, '*Hasta la vista*, Anthony.'

She stabbed the stop button and violently pulled out the headphones. She turned round to see Brandon transfixed by the image of Adam Scott stretched out on a rack, naked and apparently unconscious. Part of her mind could not comprehend what she was seeing. Evil, she thought, should be drenched in blood, not prosaically displayed on a sub-urban television screen.

'Sir,' she forced out. 'The tapes. She's been stalking Tony.'

Tony tried a laugh. It came out more like a sob, but he carried on regardless. 'You expect me to get an erection? Trussed up like this? Angelica, you chloroformed me, kid-napped me and left me to come round alone in a torture chamber. I'm sorry to disappoint you, but I've got no experience of bondage. I'm too bloody scared to get a hard-on.'

'I'm not letting you go, you know. Not to run straight back to them.'

'I'm not asking you to let me go. Believe me, I'm happy to be your prisoner if that's the only way I can spend time with you. I want to get to know you, Angelica. I want to prove my feelings to you, I want to show you what love feels like. I want to show you whose side I'm really on here.' Tony tried to turn on the kind of smile he'd learned that women responded to.

'So show me,' Angelica challenged, letting one hand run caressingly down her body, lingering over her nipples and edging towards her crotch.

'I'm going to need your help. Just like I needed you on the phone. You made me feel so good, like a real man. Please, help me now,' Tony pleaded.

She took a step towards him, moving sinuously as a stripper. 'You want me to turn you on?' she drawled in a ghastly parody of seduction.

'I don't think I can do it like this,' Tony said. 'Not with my arms pinned behind me like this.'

Angelica stopped dead and scowled. 'I said, I'm not letting you go.'

'And I said I'm not asking you to. All I'm asking is that you cuff my hands in front of me. So I can touch you.' Again, he forced the gentle smile.

She looked at him consideringly. 'How do I know I can trust you? I'd have to set your hands free so I could cuff them in front of you. Maybe you're trying to double-cross me.'

'I won't. I give you my word. If it makes you feel safer, chloroform me again. Do it while I'm unconscious,' Tony said, gambling again. Her reaction would tell him all he needed to know about his chances.

Angelica moved behind him. An exultant voice in his head screamed 'Yes!' He felt the warmth of her hand between his as she gripped the cuffs and painfully jerked them up. 'Shit!' Tony yelled as new arrows of pain shot up his arms and through his shoulders. He heard a click of metal as the shackle connecting the rope to the handcuffs snapped free. Angelica released the handcuffs and Tony collapsed to his knees, his legs buckling under him. 'Jesus Christ!' he swore as he crashed forwards on to his face, feeling the rough stone graze his cheek.

Moving swiftly, Angelica unlocked one side of the handcuffs, seized the back of his hair and pulled him upwards. Still holding the arm with the handcuffs attached, she stepped in front of him and roughly gripped his other arm just below the bicep, dragging it across his body. Seconds later, his hands were cuffed again, this time in front of him. He knelt like a supplicant, his discomfort doubled by the tight leather straps round his ankles. 'You see?' he gasped. 'I told you I wouldn't try anything.'

Panting slightly, Angelica stood in front of him, legs apart. 'So show me,' she demanded.

'You'll have to help me up. I can't do it by myself,' he protested weakly.

She bent down and grabbed his hair again, hauling him up on to legs whose muscles trembled with the effort of staying upright. They stood, inches apart, the silk of her kimono brushing his hands. He could feel the warmth of her breath on the raw flesh of his grazed cheek. 'Kiss me,' he said softly. Whores never get to kiss, he told himself. This'll make it different.

Something flickered in Angelica's eyes, but she leaned over him, releasing his hair and pulling his face to hers. It took every ounce of his willpower not to flinch as her lips met his, her tongue invading his mouth, exploring his teeth and tongue. Your life depends on it, he told himself. You've got a plan. Tony forced himself to kiss her back, thrusting his tongue into her mouth, telling himself there were worse things in the world, and this woman had made her previous victims endure some of them.

After what felt like the longest kiss of his life, Angelica pulled away, looking critically down to his groin. 'I'm going to need some help here,' Tony said. 'It's not been an easy day.'

'What kind of help?' Angelica asked, panting slightly through parted lips. It was clear that she was having no difficulty with the sexual arousal that was beyond him.

'Give me head. That's the one thing that always works when I'm having trouble. I've felt your mouth now; I just know you'll be terrific. Please, I really want to make love to you.'

Almost before he'd finished speaking, she was on her knees, hands flickering over his balls. Tenderly, she lifted his flaccid penis and slipped it into her mouth, not taking her eyes from his face. Tony reached out and began to stroke her hair. Then, with what felt like infinite slowness, he pulled her head forward on to him, forcing her head down, her eyes away from him.

Then, summoning up what remained of his strength,

Tony raised his hands and brought the handcuffs crashing down on the back of Angelica's head.

The blow caught her completely off guard and she went crashing forward between his legs, her teeth snagging agonizingly on him. Tony let himself fall backwards, feeling a tearing in his ankles as they protested against a movement they were never designed to make. As he hit the ground, he doubled forwards and grabbed Angelica's head, banging it hard on the stone floor till her body stopped thrashing.

He dragged himself over her prone figure till his numb fingers could reach the ankle straps. With maddening clumsiness, he struggled to unfasten the sets of buckles that fixed him to the stone slab. After what felt like hours, he was finally free. As he tried to stand, his ankles refused the challenge, turning over and catapulting him to the floor again, sending excruciating daggers of pain up his legs. Moaning, he dragged himself across the floor towards the steps. He had barely travelled a couple of yards when the body on the floor groaned. Angelica lifted her head, blood and mucus turning her face into a grisly Hallowe'en mask. When she saw him, she roared like a wounded animal and started scrambling to her feet.

The search for a clue to Angelica's killing ground was growing more desperate as their fear and concern for Tony grew. They had emptied out the contents of the filing cabinet on to the floor. Every scrap of paper was scrutinized for any hint of the location of the cellar revealed in the video. Invoices, guarantees, bills and receipts all got the treatment. Carol was wading through a file of official correspondence, hoping to come across some lease or mortgage details, anything that related to another property. Merrick was ploughing through the files relating to Thorpe's sex change. Brandon had already had one false alarm, coming across a stack of solicitor's letters relating to a property in Seaford. It soon became clear, however, that they concerned the sale of Thorpe's late mother's home in the town.

It was Merrick who found the key. He'd finished with the sex-change files and started on a bundle of assorted letters, filed under 'Tax'. When he came across the letter, he had to read it twice to make sure wishful thinking wasn't making him imagine things.

'Sir,' he said cautiously. 'I think this might be what we're looking for.'

He handed the letter to Brandon, who read the letterhead of Pennant, Taylor, Bailey and Co., Solicitors. 'Dear Christopher Thorpe,' it said. 'We have received a letter from your aunt, Mrs Doris Makins, in New Zealand, authorizing us to pass on to you the keys for Start Hill Farm, Upper Tontine Moor, by Bradfield, W. Yorkshire. As her agents, we are empowered to allow you access to said property for the purposes of maintenance and security. Please make arrangements with this office to collect the keys at your convenience . . .'

'Access to an isolated rural property,' Carol said, looking over Brandon's shoulder. 'Tony said that's what the killer might have. And now she's got him there.' A wave of anger poured through her, displacing the slow burn of fear that had been eating through her from the moment they'd unlocked the macabre secrets of that superficially normal office.

Brandon closed his eyes momentarily then said tightly, 'We don't know that, Carol.'

'And even if she has got him, he's a clever bloke. If anyone can keep himself out of trouble with his gob, it's Tony Hill,' Don chipped in.

'Never mind whistling in the bloody dark,' Carol said sharply. 'Where the hell is Start Hill Farm? And how soon can we get there?'

Tony looked around in desperation. The rack of knives was over to his left, impossibly high up. As Angelica got to her knees, he clawed at the stone bench and hauled himself upright. His hand closed on the haft of the knife as she staggered to her feet and threw herself at him, still bellowing like a cow bereft of its calf.

Her weight and the momentum of her charge bent Tony backwards over the bench. Her hands scrabbled for his throat, gripping his windpipe so tightly that white lights started to dance in front of his eyes. Just when he thought he could hold on no longer, he felt the warm, sticky gush of blood against his stomach and Angelica's grasp became flabby as a wet newspaper.

Before he could take it all in, he heard footsteps crashing down the stone steps. Like a mad vision of paradise, Don Merrick crashed downstairs, rapidly followed by John Brandon, his jaw dropping at the tableau in front of him.

'Fucking hell,' Brandon breathed.

Carol pushed past the two men and stared uncomprehendingly at the carnage before her.

'You lot took your time,' Tony gasped. As he passed out, the last thing he heard was his own hysterical laughter.

Epilogue

Carol pushed open the door of the side ward. Tony was propped up on a pile of pillows, the left side of his face swollen and bruised.

'Hi,' Tony said, a wan half-smile the best he could manage without too much pain. 'Come on in.'

Carol closed the door behind her and sat down on a chair by the bed. 'I brought you some bits and pieces,' she said, dumping a plastic bag and a padded envelope on the coverlet.

Tony reached out for the bag. Carol winced inside as she saw the bracelet of bruises round his inflamed wrists. He took out a copy of *Esquire*, a can of Aqua Libra, a tin of pistachio nuts and a Dashiel Hammett omnibus. 'Thanks,' he said, surprised by how her choice touched him.

'I wasn't sure what you liked,' she said defensively.

'Then you're obviously a good guesser. The perfect task-force officer.'

'If a little slow on the uptake,' Carol said bitterly.

Tony shook his head. 'John Brandon was here earlier. He told me how you worked it all out. I don't see how you could have got there any quicker.'

'I should have realized sooner that you wouldn't have done a disappearing act at such a crucial time. Come to that, I should have realized as soon as I saw that profile that you could be a target and taken steps to protect you.'

'Bollocks, Carol. If anyone should have realized that, it was me. You did a bloody good job.'

'No. If I'd been on the ball, we'd have got there in time to save you having to . . . to do what you did.'

Tony sighed. 'You mean, you'd have saved Angelica's life? For what? Years in a secure mental hospital? Look on the bright side, Carol. You've saved the state a fortune. No expensive trial, no years of incarceration and treatment to pay for. Shit, they'll probably give you a medal.'

'That's not what I meant, Tony,' Carol said. 'I meant you wouldn't have to live with the knowledge that you've killed someone.'

'Yes, well, I can't pretend it was the perfect outcome, but I'll learn to live with it.' He forced a smile. 'Don't take this the wrong way, but the first thing I'm going to do when I can walk again is go out and buy you a new mac,' he said. 'Every time I look at that coat of yours, I get the urge to scream.'

'Why?' Carol frowned in puzzlement.

'Didn't you know? She was wearing the identical mac when she turned up on the doorstep. That way, if she left any fibres at the scene, Forensic would assume they'd come from you.'

'Terrific,' Carol said ironically. 'How are the ankles, by the way?'

Tony pulled a face. 'I don't think I'll ever play the violin again. I managed to make it to the loo on crutches, but I had to sit on the edge of the bath to pee. They're saying there probably won't be any permanent damage, but it'll take a while for the torn ligaments to heal. How was your day?'

Carol pulled a face. 'Grisly. I suspect you'd have been in your element. You were right about keeping the fantasy alive. She, he, it, had tapes of all the telephone-sex conversations she'd had with her victims, and she'd stolen the outgoing message tapes from the men who had answering machines.

'It took the boffins a little while to crack the computer stuff. We didn't have anybody who really knew what they were doing, but my brother Michael came in and sorted it out for us.'

Tony gave a twisted smile. 'I didn't want to say anything at the time, but for a wild moment, I actually wondered about your brother.'

'Michael? You're kidding!'

Embarrassed, Tony nodded. 'It was when you posited the idea of the computer manipulation of the videos. Michael had the expertise to do that, no question. He's in the right age group, he lives with a woman but not in a sexual relationship, he's got access to all the information the killer needed about the way the police and forensic scientists work, his job is in the general area where I'd expect the killer to work, and he was in a position to know exactly what the police were up to and be involved in the investigation. If we hadn't caught Angelica when we did, I'd have been scrounging an invitation to dinner to check him out.'

Carol shook her head. 'See what I mean about being slow on the uptake? I had access to all the same information as you, and Michael never even crossed my mind as a possibility.'

'Not so surprising. You know him well enough to know he's not a psychopath.'

Carol shrugged. 'Do I, though? It wouldn't be the first time a close family member, a wife even, has made the same mistake.'

'Usually, they're either deluding themselves or they're emotionally unstable and dependent on the killer in some way. Neither of which would have applied in this case.' He gave a tired smile. 'Anyway, tell me about what your Michael uncovered.'

'The computer was a total goldmine. She'd kept her own diary of the stalking and the murders. It even says that she wanted it published after her death. Can you beat that?'

'Easily,' Tony said. 'Remind me to show you some of the academic papers I've got on the subject of serial killers.'

Carol shivered. 'Thanks, but no thanks. I got a print-out

of the diary for you. I figured you'd be interested.' She gestured to the envelope. 'It's in there. Also, as you'd surmised, she had video-taped the killings, and as I suggested, she'd imported them into her computer and manipulated the images to keep the fantasy alive. It was absolutely gruesome, Tony. It went way beyond nightmare.'

Tony nodded. 'I won't say you get used to it, because you never do if you're going to be any use at this job. But you do get to the stage where you can lock it away, so it doesn't jump out and wreck your head unawares.'

'Oh, yeah?'

'That's the theory. Ask me again in a few weeks,' he said grimly. 'Was there anything in there about how she chose her victims?'

'Just a fucking bit,' Carol said bitterly. 'She'd been at this for months before she even picked out the first victim. She worked for the phone company, a computer systems manager. Apparently, she used to work for a small private phone company back in Seaford, which gave her the experience to get the job in Bradfield. She was what they call a super-user of the computer system, so she had access to every piece of data in there. She used the phone company's computer to extract all the residential numbers who had made regular calls to sex chatlines in the past year.' Carol paused, letting the obvious question hang in the air.

'It was research,' Tony said wearily. 'I published a paper on the role of chatlines in the development of fantasies among serial offenders. Someone should have told Angelica not to jump to conclusions.'

Reading his remark as a veiled reproach, Carol moved on. 'She cross-referenced that against the electoral roll and came up with men who lived alone. Then she just checked them out by watching their houses. She had a clear picture of the physical type she wanted, and she wanted one with his own house, a decent income and good career prospects. Can you believe it?'

'Only too well,' Tony said grimly. 'Her rationale was that she never wanted to kill them, she only wanted to love them. But they made her murder because they betrayed her. She kept telling herself that what she really wanted was a man who would love her and live with her.'

Don't we all, Carol thought but didn't say. 'Anyway, once she'd decided on the likely candidate, she paved the way with the dirty phone calls. She got them on the hook that way, on account of all you sleazy men can't resist anonymous sex.'

'Ouch,' Tony said, wincing. 'In my defence, I'd have to say that a large part of my interest was purely academic. I was interested in the psychology of a woman who would do what she did on the phone.'

Carol smiled tightly. 'At least I know now that you were telling the truth when you said you didn't know the woman who was leaving the sexy messages on your answering machine.'

Tony looked away. 'And the discovery that a man you were attracted to was getting his rocks off in kinky telephone sex with a stranger must have been delightful for you.'

Carol was silent, unsure what to say. 'I've heard the tapes now,' she admitted. 'Yours are very different from the others. You were clearly uncomfortable a lot of the time. Not that it's any of my business.'

Still unable to meet her eyes, Tony spoke, his voice clipped and clinical. 'I have a problem with sex. To be precise, I have problems with achieving and maintaining an erection. The honest truth is that only part of me was treating the calls with professional interest. The other part of me was trying to use them as a kind of therapy. I know that makes me sound like a pervert, but part of the trouble with doing the job I do is that it's virtually impossible to find a therapist I can respect and trust who isn't connected in some way to the world I work in. And however much they verbally espouse the principle of client confidentiality, I've always been reluctant to expose myself to the risk.'

Realizing the difficulty Tony had had in making his confession, Carol reached out for his hand and covered it lightly with hers. 'Thank you for telling me that. It won't go any further. And if it makes you feel any better, the only people who have heard the tapes in full are me and John Brandon. You don't have to worry about what people are saying about you behind your back within the force.'

'That's something, I suppose. So, go on. Tell me about Angelica's phone calls to the other victims.'

'It was obvious that the men thought this was sex without any commitment or comeback. Angelica's analysis was completely different. She'd convinced herself that their responses meant they were falling in love with her. Unfortunately for the guys, they decided otherwise. As soon as they showed any interest in another woman, they signed their death warrants. Apart from Damien, that is. She killed him to teach us a lesson. You were going to be the other lesson.'

Tony shuddered. 'No wonder she had to go abroad for the sex-change operation. The NHS psychologists she saw must have had a field day with her attitudes and aspirations.'

'Apparently, they decided she was not an appropriate candidate for a sex change because of her lack of insight into her sexuality. They concluded that she was a gay man who couldn't cope with his sexuality because of cultural and family conditioning. They recommended counselling with a sex therapist rather than a sex change. There was an ugly scene at the time. He threw one of the psychologists through a glass door,' Carol revealed.

'Pity they didn't press charges,' Tony said.

'Yes. And you'll be pleased to hear they're definitely not going to charge you.'

'I should think not! Like I said, think of the taxpayers'

money I've saved. Maybe we should have dinner to celebrate when I get out of here?' he asked tentatively.

'I'd like that. There is one other good thing that came out of all of this,' Carol said.

'What's that?'

'Penny Burgess took the day off yesterday to go walking in the dales. Apparently, her car broke down and she got stranded in the middle of a forest all night. She missed the whole shooting match. There's a dozen by-lines in the *Sentinel Times* tonight, and not a single one of them is hers!'

Tony lay back and stared at the ceiling. Papering over the cracks, that's what they were doing. He suspected Carol knew that as well as he did, and he wasn't sorry for the effort she was making. But he'd had enough for now. He closed his eyes and sighed.

'Oh God, I'm sorry,' Carol said, getting to her feet. 'I wasn't thinking. You must still be exhausted. Look, I'm out of here. I'll leave you this stuff to read when you feel up to it. I could drop in tomorrow if you like . . .'

'I think I'd like that,' Tony said wearily. 'It just comes over me in waves sometimes.'

He heard her feet cross the floor and the click of the door opening. 'Take care,' Carol said.

The door closed behind her and Tony pushed himself back up till he was leaning against the pillows. He reached for the padded envelope. While he couldn't cope with conversation, his curiosity wouldn't let him ignore Angelica's diary. He pulled out a thick wedge of A4 paper. 'Let's see what you were really made of,' he said softly. 'What's the story? How did you justify, what did you hide behind?' Hungrily, he began to read.

Wading through the outpourings of the psychologically damaged was normally a routine exploratory experience for Tony. But this was different, he realized after only a few paragraphs. At first, he couldn't pin down what it was.

The writing was more literate, more controlled and more immediate than most of their ramblings, but that didn't explain why his response was so different. He moved on a few pages, fascinated and repelled equally. It was no more or less self-obsessed than other things he'd read, but there was a chilling relish here that was unusual. Most killers whose writings he'd read had gloried far more in their own bloody role, reflecting less on what they'd done to their victims and its effect on them, but here was someone who identified herself as much in terms of them. But even that couldn't entirely explain why he felt so unsettled by what he was reading. Whatever it was, it was making him more reluctant to continue the more he read, the opposite to his normal response. He'd been so obsessively keen to get inside the head of the killer he'd dubbed Handy Andy, but now it was laid out before him, it was as if he didn't want to know.

As he forced himself to read on, mentally chalking up the correct assumptions he'd made in his profile, it eventually dawned on him that what he was feeling was personal. These words were touching him in ways he'd never experienced before because the life outlined in these pages had touched him with a directness he'd never known before. These were the footsteps of his own personal nemesis that he was tracing, and it was an uncomfortable journey.

He tossed the papers to one side, unable to keep going, seeing his own fate mirrored in the broken bodies Angelica had meticulously described. The trouble with being a psychologist was that he knew exactly what was happening to him. He knew he was still in shock, still deep in denial. Although he couldn't get the events in the cellar out of his mind, there was still a distance between him and the memory, as if he were watching them from a long way off. One day the horror of the previous night was going to come roaring back in stereo, splashed across his inner eye in Cinemascope. Knowing that, this numbness was a blessing.

Already, he knew, his answering machine would be crammed with lucrative offers for the story of how the hunter turned killer. One day, he was going to have to tell that story. He hoped he'd have the strength to save it for a psychiatrist.

It was no comfort to rationalize that having been the target of one serial killer, he was statistically unlikely ever to find himself in that position again. All he could think of was the hours in the cellar, dredging his experience and knowledge for the magic words that would give him a few minutes longer to try for the key to his freedom.

Then that kiss. The whore's kiss, the killer's kiss, the lover's kiss, the saviour's kiss, all rolled into one. A kiss from the mouth that had been seducing him for weeks, the mouth whose words had given him hope for his future, only to leave him finally stranded in this place. He had spent his working life worming his way into the heads of those who kill, only to end up one of them, thanks to a Judas kiss.

'You've won, haven't you, Angelica?' he said softly. 'You wanted me, and now you've got me.'

THE WIRE IN
THE BLOOD

ACKNOWLEDGEMENTS

It's hard to imagine how I could have written this book without a lot of help from several key people. For their specialist knowledge and willingness to give so freely of their expertise, I'd like to thank Sheila Radford, Dr Mike Berry, Jai Penna, Paula Tyler and Dr Sue Black. I owe an apology to Edwina and Lesley, who ran around like headless chickens researching something that was cut in the rewrites. Without Jim and Simon at Thornton Electronics, Mac and Manda, I would almost certainly have had a complete nervous breakdown when the hard disk crashed. But the perseverance and perspicacity of three women in particular got me through to the end. For that reason, this book is for:

Julia, Lisanne and Brigid
With love

The trilling wire in the blood
Sings below inveterate scars
Appeasing long forgotten wars.

Four Quartets,
Burnt Norton
T. S. Eliot

PROLOGUE

Murder was like magic, he thought. The quickness of his hand always deceived the eye, and that was how it was going to stay. He was like the postman delivering to a house where afterwards they would swear there had been no callers. This was the knowledge that was lodged in his being like a pacemaker in a heart patient. Without the power of his magic he'd be dead. Or as good as.

He knew just from looking at her that she would be the next. Even before the eye contact, he knew. There had always been a very particular combination that spelled perfection in his thesaurus of the senses. Innocence and ripeness, mink-dark hair, eyes that danced. He'd never been wrong yet. It was an instinct that kept him alive. Or as good as.

He watched her watching him, and under the urgent mutter of the crowd, he heard echoing in his head the music. '*Jack and Jill went up the hill to fetch a pail of water. Jack fell down and broke his crown . . .* ' The chiming tune swelled and burst then battered his brain like a spring tide against a breakwater. And Jill? What about Jill? Oh, he knew what happened to Jill. Over and over again, repetitious as the barbaric nursery rhyme. But it was never enough. He had never quite been satisfied that the punishment had fit the crime.

And so there had to be a next one. And there he was, watching her watching him sending her messages with his eyes. Messages that said, 'I've noticed you. Find your way to me and I'll notice you some more.' And she read him. She read him, loud and clear. She was so obvious; life hadn't scarred her expectations with static yet. A knowing smile quirked the corners of her mouth and she took the first step on the long and, for him, exciting journey of exploration and pain. The pain, as far as he was concerned, was not quite the only necessity but it was certainly one of them.

She worked her way towards him. Their routes varied, he'd noticed. Some direct, bold; some meandering, wary in case they'd misread what they thought his eyes were telling them. This one favoured the spiral path, circling ever inward as if her feet were tracing the inside of a giant nautilus shell, a miniature Guggenheim Gallery compacted into two dimensions. Her step was measured, determined, her eyes never wavering from him, as if there were no one else between, neither obstacle nor distraction. Even when she was behind his back, he could feel her stare, which was precisely how he thought it should be.

It was an approach that told him something about her. She wanted to savour this encounter. She wanted to see him from every possible angle, to imprint him on her memory forever, because she thought this would be her only chance for so detailed a scrutiny. If anyone had told her what the future truly held, she'd have fainted with the thrill of it.

At last, her decaying orbit brought her within his grasp. Only the immediate circle of admirers stood between them, one or two deep. He locked on to her eyes, injected charm into his gaze and, with a polite nod to those around him, he took a step towards her. The bodies parted obediently as he said, 'Delightful to have met you, do excuse me?'

Uncertainty flitted across her face. Was she supposed to move, like them, or should she stay in the ambit of his mesmerizing stare? It was no contest; it never was. She was captivated, the reality of this evening outstripping her every fantasy. 'Hello,' he said. 'And what's your name?'

She was momentarily speechless, never so close to fame, dazzled by that spectacular dental display all for her benefit. My, what big teeth you've got, he thought. All the better to eat her with.

'Donna,' she finally stuttered. 'Donna Doyle.'

'That's a beautiful name,' he said softly. The smile he won in response was as brilliant as his own. Sometimes, it all felt too easy. People heard what they wanted to hear, especially when what they were hearing sounded like their dream come true. Total suspension of disbelief, that's what he achieved every time. They came to these events expecting Jacko Vance and everyone connected to the great man to be exactly what was projected on TV. By association, anyone who was part of the celebrity's entourage was gilded with the same brush. People were so accustomed to Vance's open sincerity, so familiar with his very public probity, it never crossed their minds to look for the catch. Why should it, when Vance had a popular image that made Good King Wenceslas look like Scrooge? The punters listened to the words and they heard Jack and the Beanstalk – from the little seed Vance or his minions planted, they pictured the burgeoning flower of a life at the top of the tree right alongside his.

In that respect, Donna Doyle was just like all the others. She could have been working from a script he'd written for her. Having moved her strategically into a corner, he made as if to hand her a signed photograph of Vance the megastar. Then he did a double take so exquisitely natural it could have been part of De Niro's repertoire. 'My God,' he breathed. 'Of course. Of course!' The exclamation was the verbal equivalent of smiting himself on the forehead with the heel of his hand.

Caught with her fingers inches from his as she reached out to take what had been so nearly offered, she frowned, not understanding. 'What?'

He made a twisted little *moue* of self-disparagement. 'Ignore me. I'm sorry, I'm sure you've got much more interesting plans for your future than anything we superficial programme makers could come up with.' The first time he'd tried the line, hands sweating, blood thudding in his ears, he'd thought it was so corny it couldn't fool a drunk one sip from catatonia. But he had been right to go with his instincts, even when they had led him down the path of the criminally naff. That first one, just like this next one, had grasped instantly that something was being offered to her that hadn't been on the agenda for the insignificant others he'd been talking to earlier.

'What do you mean?' Breathless, tentative, not wanting to admit she already believed in case she'd misunderstood and left herself open to the hot shaming flush of her misapprehension.

He gave the faintest of shrugs, one that hardly disturbed the smooth fall of his immaculate suiting. 'Forget it,' he said with a slight, almost imperceptible shake of the head, disappointment in the sad cast of his eye, the absence of his gleaming smile.

'No, tell me.' Now there was an edge of desperation, because everybody wanted to be a star, no matter what they said. Was he really going to snatch away that half-glimpsed magic carpet ride that could lift her out of her despised life into his world?

A quick glance to either side, making sure he wasn't overheard, then his voice was both soft and intense. 'A new project we're working on. You've got the look. You'd be perfect. As soon as I looked at you properly, I knew you were the one.' A regretful smile. 'Now, at least I have your image to carry in my head while we interview the hundreds of hopefuls the agents send along to us. Maybe we'll get lucky . . .' His voice trailed off, his eyes liquid and bereft as the puppy left behind in the holiday kennels.

'Couldn't I . . . I mean, well . . .' Donna's face lit up with hope, then amazement at her forwardness, then disappointment as she talked herself out of it without saying another word.

His smile grew indulgent. An adult would have identified it as condescending, but she was too young to recognize when she was being patronized. 'I don't think so. It would be taking an enormous risk. A project like this, at so delicate a stage . . . Just a word in the wrong ear could wreck it commercially. And you've no professional experience, have you?'

That tantalizing peep at what could have been her possible future uncapped a volcano of turbulent hope, words tumbling over each other like rocks in the lava flow. Prizes for karaoke at the youth club, a great dancer according to everybody, the Nurse in her form's reading of *Romeo and Juliet*. He'd imagined schools would have had more sense than to stir the tumultuous waters of adolescent desire with inflammatory drama like that, but he'd been wrong. They'd never learned, teachers. Just like their charges. The kids might assimilate the causes of the First World War but they never grasped that clichés got that way because they reflected reality.

5

Better the devil you know. Don't take sweets from strangers.

Those warnings might never have set Donna Doyle's eardrum vibrating if her present expression of urgent eagerness was anything to go by. He grinned and said, 'All right! You've convinced me!' He lowered his head and held her gaze. Now his voice was conspiratorial. 'But can you keep a secret?'

She nodded as if her life depended on it. She couldn't have known that it did. 'Oh, yes,' Donna said, dark blue eyes sparkling, lips apart, little pink tongue flickering between them. He knew her mouth was growing dry. He also knew that she possessed other orifices where the opposite phenomenon was happening.

He gave her a considering, calculated stare, an obvious appraisal that she met with apprehension and desire mingling like Scotch and water. 'I wonder . . .' he said, his voice almost a sigh. 'Can you meet me tomorrow morning? Nine o'clock?'

A momentary frown, then her face cleared, determination in her eyes. 'Yes,' she said, school dismissed as irrelevant. 'Yes, I can. Whereabout?'

'Do you know the Plaza Hotel?' He had to hurry now. People were starting to move towards him, desperate to recruit his influence to their cause.

She nodded.

'They have an underground car park. You get into it from Beamish Street. I'll be waiting there on level two. And not a word to anyone, is that clear? Not your mum, not your dad, not your best friend, not even the family dog.' She giggled. 'Can you do that?' He gave her the curiously intimate look of the television professional, the one that convinces the mentally troubled that news-readers are in love with them.

'Level two? Nine o'clock?' Donna checked, determined not to screw up her one chance of escape from the humdrum. She could never have realized that by the end of the week she'd be weeping and screaming and begging for humdrum. She'd be willing to sell what remained of her immortal soul for humdrum. But even if someone had told her that then, she would not have comprehended. Right then, the dazzle and the dream of what he could offer was her complete universe. What could be a finer prospect?

'And not a word, promise?'

'I promise,' she said solemnly. 'Cross my heart and hope to die.'

PART ONE

PART ONE

Tony Hill lay in bed and watched a long strip of cloud slide across a sky the colour of duck eggs. If anything had sold him on this narrow back-to-back terraced house, it was the attic bedroom with its strange angles and the pair of skylights that gave him something to look at when sleep was elusive. A new house, a new city, a new start, but still it was hard to lose consciousness for eight hours at a stretch.

It wasn't surprising that he hadn't slept well. Today was the first day of the rest of his life, he reminded himself with a wry smile that scrunched the skin round his deep-set blue eyes into a nest of wrinkles that not even his best friend could call laughter lines. He'd never laughed enough for that. And making murder his business had made sure he never would.

Work was always the perfect excuse, of course. For two years, he'd been toiling on behalf of the Home Office on a feasibility study to see whether it would be useful or possible to create a national task force of trained psychological profilers, a hit squad capable of moving in on complex cases and working with the investigative teams to improve the rate and speed of clean-up. It had been a job that had required all the clinical and diplomatic skills he'd developed over years of working as a psychologist in secure mental hospitals.

It had kept him off the wards, but it had exposed him to other dangers. The danger of boredom, for example. Tired of being stuck behind a desk or in endless meetings, he'd allowed himself to be seduced away from the job in hand by the tantalizing offer of involvement in a case that even from a distance had appeared to be something very special. Not in his wildest nightmares could he have imagined just how exceptional it could be. Nor how destructive.

He clenched his eyes momentarily against the memories that always stalked on the edge of his consciousness, waiting for him to drop his guard and let them in. That was another reason why he slept badly. The thought of what his dreams could do to him was no enticement to drift away and hand control over to his subconscious.

The cloud slipped out of sight like a slow-moving fish and Tony rolled out of bed, padding downstairs to the kitchen. He poured water into the bottom section of the coffee pot, filled the mid-section with a darkly fragrant roast from the freezer, screwed on the empty top section and set it on the gas. He thought of Carol Jordan, as he did probably one morning in three when he made the coffee. She'd given him the heavy aluminium Italian pot when he'd come home from hospital after the case was over. 'You're not going to be walking to the café for a while,' she'd said. 'At least this way you can get a decent espresso at home.'

It had been months now since he'd seen Carol. They'd not even taken the opportunity to celebrate her promotion to detective chief inspector, which showed just how far apart they'd grown. Initially, after his release from hospital, she'd come to visit whenever the hectic pace of her job would allow. Gradually, they'd both come to realize that every time they were together, the spectre of the investigation rose between them, obscuring and overshadowing whatever else might be possible for them. He understood that Carol was better equipped than most to interpret what she saw in him. He simply couldn't face the risk of opening up to someone who might reject him when she realized how he had been infected by his work.

If that happened, he doubted his capacity to function. And if he couldn't function, he couldn't do his job. And that was too important to let go. What he did saved people's lives. He was good at it, probably one of the best there had ever been because he truly understood the dark side. To risk the work would be the most irresponsible thing he could ever do, especially now when the whole future of the newly created National Offender Profiling Task Force lay in his hands.

What some people perceived as sacrifices were really dividends, he told himself firmly as he poured out his coffee. He was permitted to do the one thing he did supremely well, and they paid him money for it. A tired smile crossed his face. God, but he was lucky.

Shaz Bowman understood perfectly why people commit murder. The revelation had nothing to do with the move to a new city or the job that had brought her there, but everything to do with the cowboy plumbers who had installed the water supply when the former Victorian mill-owner's mansion had been converted into self-contained apartments. The builders had done a thoughtful job, preserving original features and avoiding partitions that wrecked the fine proportions of the spacious rooms. To the naked eye, Shaz's flat had been perfect, right down to the French windows leading to the back garden that was her exclusive domain.

Years of shared student dives with sticky carpets and

scummy bathtubs, followed by a police section house and a preposterously expensive rented bedsit in West London had left Shaz desperate for the opportunity to check out whether house-proud was an adjective she could live with. The move north had provided her first affordable chance. But the idyll had shattered the first morning she had to rise early for work.

Bleary-eyed and semi-conscious, she'd run the shower long enough to get the temperature right. She stepped under the powerful stream of water, lifting her hands above her head in a strangely reverent gesture. Her groan of pleasure turned abruptly to a scream as the water switched from amniotic warmth to a scalding scatter of hypodermic stings. She hurled herself clear of the shower cubicle, twisting her knee as she slipped on the bathroom floor, cursing with a fluency she owed to her three years in the Met.

Speechless, she stared at the plume of steam in the corner of the bathroom where she had stood moments before. Then, as abruptly, the steam dissipated. Cautiously, she extended a hand under the water. The temperature was back where it should be. Inch by tentative inch, she moved under the stream of water. Letting out her unconsciously held breath, she reached for the shampoo. She'd got as far as the halo of white lather when the icy needles of winter rain cascaded on her bare shoulders. This time, her breath went inwards, taking enough shampoo with it to add a coughing retch to the morning's sound effects.

It didn't take much to work out that her ordeal was the result of someone else's synchronous ablutions. She was supposed to be a detective, after all. But understanding didn't make her any happier. The first day of the new job and instead of feeling calm and grounded after a long, soothing shower, she was furious and frustrated, her nerves jangling, the muscles in the nape of her neck tightening with the promise of a headache. 'Great,' she growled, fighting back tears that had more to do with emotion than the shampoo in them.

Shaz advanced on the shower once again and turned it off with a vicious twist of the wrist. Mouth compressed into a thin line, she started running a bath. Tranquillity was no longer an option for the day, but she still had to get the suds out of her hair so she wouldn't arrive in the squad room of the brand new task force looking like something no self-respecting cat would have bothered to drag in. It was going to be unnerving enough without having to worry about what she looked like.

As she crouched in the bath, dunking her head forward into the water, Shaz tried to restore her earlier mood of exhilarated anticipation. 'You're lucky to be here, girl,' she told herself. 'All those dickheads who applied and you didn't even have to fill in the form, you got chosen. Hand-picked, elite. All that shit work paid off, all that taking the crap with a smile. The canteen cowboys going nowhere fast, they're the ones having to swallow the shit now. Not like you, Detective Constable Shaz Bowman. National Offender Profiling Task Force Officer Bowman.' As if that wasn't enough, she'd be working alongside the acknowledged master of that arcane blend of instinct and experience. Dr Tony Hill, BSc (London), DPhil (Oxon), the profiler's profiler, author of the definitive British textbook on serial offenders. If Shaz had been a woman given to hero-worship, Tony Hill would have been right up there in the pantheon of her personal gods. As it was, the opportunity to pick his brains and learn his craft was one that she'd cheerfully have made sacrifices for. But she hadn't had to give up anything. It had been dropped right into her lap.

By the time she was towelling her cap of short dark hair, considering the chance of a lifetime that lay ahead of her had tamed her anger though not her nerves. Shaz forced herself to focus on the day ahead. Dropping the towel carelessly over the side of the bath, she stared into the mirror, ignoring the blurt of freckles across her cheekbones and the bridge of her small soft nose, passing over the straight line of lips too slim to promise much sensuality and focusing on the feature that everyone else noticed first about her.

Her eyes were extraordinary. Dark blue irises were shot through with striations of an intense, paler shade that seemed to catch the light like the facets of a sapphire. In interrogation, they were irresistible. The eyes had it. That intense blue stare fixed people like superglue. Shaz had a feeling that it had made her last boss so uncomfortable he'd been delighted at the prospect of shipping her out in spite of an arrest and conviction record that would have been remarkable in an experienced CID officer, never mind the rookie of the shift.

She'd only met her new boss once. Somehow, she didn't think Tony Hill was going to be quite so much of a pushover. And who knew what he'd see if he slid under those cold blue defences? With a shiver of anxiety, Shaz turned away from the remorseless stare of the mirror and chewed the skin on the side of her thumb.

Detective Chief Inspector Carol Jordan slipped the original out of the photocopier, picked up the copy from the tray and crossed the open-plan CID room to her office with nothing more revelatory than a genial, 'Morning, lads,' to the two early bird detectives already at their desks. She presumed they were only there at this hour because they were trying to make an impression on her. Sad boys.

She shut her door firmly behind her and crossed to her desk. The original crime report went back into the overnight file and onwards into her out tray. The photostat joined four similar previous overnight despatches in a folder that lived in her briefcase when it wasn't sitting on her desk. Five, she decided, was critical mass. Time for action. She glanced at her watch. But not quite yet.

The only other item that cluttered the desk now was a lengthy memo from the Home Office. In the dry civil service language that could render Tarantino dull, it announced the formal launch of the National Offender Profiling Task Force. 'Under the supervision of Commander Paul Bishop, the task force will be led by Home Office clinical psychologist and Senior Profiler Dr Tony Hill. Initially, the task force will consist of a further six experienced detectives seconded to work with Dr Hill and Commander Bishop under Home Office guidelines.'

Carol sighed. 'It could have been me. Oh yeah, it could have been me,' she sang softly. She hadn't been formally invited. But she knew all she'd have had to do was ask. Tony Hill had wanted her on the squad. He'd seen her work at close quarters and he'd told her more than once that she had the right cast of mind to help him make the new task force effective. But it wasn't that simple. The one case they'd worked together had been personally devastating as well as difficult for both of them. And her feelings for Tony Hill were still too complicated for her to relish the prospect of becoming his right-hand woman in other cases that might become as emotionally draining and intellectually challenging as their first encounter.

Nevertheless, she'd been tempted. Then this had come along. Early promotion in a newly created force wasn't an opportunity she felt she could afford to miss. The irony was that this chance had emerged from the same serial killer hunt. John Brandon had been the Assistant Chief Constable at Bradfield who'd had the nerve to bring in Tony Hill and to appoint Carol liaison officer. And when he was promoted to Chief Constable of the new force, he wanted her on board. His timing couldn't have been better, she thought, a faint pang of regret surfacing in spite of herself. She stood up and took the three steps that were all she needed to cross her office and stare down at the docks below where people moved around purposefully doing she knew not what.

Carol had learned the Job first with the Met in London and then with Bradfield Metropolitan Police, both leviathans fuelled by the perpetual adrenaline high of inner city crime. But now she was out on the edge of England with East Yorkshire Police where, as her brother Michael had wryly pointed out, the force's acronym was almost identical to the traditional Yorkshire yokel greeting of 'Ey-up'. Here, the DCI's job didn't involve juggling murder inquiries, drive-by shootings, gang wars, armed robberies and high-profile drug deals.

In the towns and villages of East Yorkshire, there wasn't any shortage of crime. But it was all low-level stuff. Her inspectors and sergeants were more than capable of dealing with it, even in the small cities of Holm and Traskham and the North Sea port of Seaford where she was based. Her junior officers didn't want her running around on their tails. After all, what did a city girl like her know about sheep rustling? Or counterfeit cargo lading bills? Besides which, they all knew perfectly well that when the new DCI turned up on the job, she wasn't so much interested in finding out what was going down as she was in sussing out who was up to scratch and who was busking it, who might be on the sauce and who might be on the take. And they were right. It was taking longer than she'd anticipated, but she was gradually assembling a picture of what her team was like and who was capable of what.

Carol sighed again, rumpling her shaggy blonde hair with the fingers of one hand. It was an uphill struggle, not least because most of the blunt Yorkshiremen she was working with were fighting a lifetime's conditioning to take a woman guv'nor seriously. Not for the first time, she wondered if ambition had shoved her into a drastic mistake and backed her flourishing career into a cul-de-sac.

She shrugged and turned away from the window, then pulled out the file from her briefcase again. She might have opted to turn her back on the profiling task force, but working with Tony Hill had already taught her a few tricks. She knew what a serial offender's signature looked like. She just hoped she didn't need a team of specialists to track one down.

One half of the double doors swung open momentarily ahead of the other. A woman with a face instantly recognizable in 78 per cent of UK homes (according to the latest audience survey) and high heels that shouted the praises of legs which could have modelled pantyhose strode into the make-up department, glancing over her shoulder and saying, '. . . which gives me nothing to work off, so tell Trevor to swap two and four on the running order, OK?'

Betsy Thorne followed her, nodding calmly. She looked far too wholesome to be anything in TV, dark hair with irregular strands of silver swept back in a blue velvet Alice band from a face that was somehow quintessentially English; the intelligent eyes of a sheepdog, the bones of a thoroughbred racehorse and the complexion of a Cox's Orange Pippin. 'No problem,' she said, her voice every degree as warm and caressing as her companion's. She made a note on the clipboard she was carrying.

Micky Morgan, presenter and only permissible star of *Midday with Morgan*, the flagship two-hour lunchtime news magazine programme of the independent networks, carried straight ahead to what was clearly her usual chair. She settled in, pushed her honey blonde hair back and gave her face a quick critical scrutiny in the glass as the make-up artist swathed her in a protective gown. 'Marla, you're back!' Micky exclaimed, delight in her voice and eyes in equal measure. 'Thank God. I'm praying you've been out of the country so you didn't have to look at what they do to me when you're not here. I absolutely forbid you to go on holiday again!'

Marla smiled. 'Still full of shit, Micky.'

'It's what they pay her for,' Betsy said, perching on the counter by the mirror.

'Can't get the staff these days,' Micky said through stiff lips as Marla started to smooth foundation over her skin. 'Zit coming up on the right temple,' she added.

'Premenstrual?' Marla asked.

'I thought I was the only one who could spot that a mile off,' Betsy drawled.

'It's the skin. The elasticity changes,' Marla said absently, completely absorbed in her task.

'*Talking Point*,' Micky said. 'Run it past me again, Bets.' She closed her eyes to concentrate and Marla seized the chance to work on her eyelids.

Betsy consulted her clipboard. 'In the wake of the latest revelations that yet another junior minister has been caught in the wrong bed by the tabloids, we ask, "What makes a woman want to be a mistress?"' She ran through the guests for the item while Micky listened attentively. Betsy came to the final interviewee and smiled. 'You'll enjoy this: Dorien Simmonds, your favourite novelist. The professional mistress, putting the case that actually being a mistress is not only marvellous fun but a positive social service to all those put-upon wives who have to endure marital sex long after he bores them senseless.'

Micky chuckled. 'Brilliant. Good old Dorien. Is there anything, do you suppose, that Dorien wouldn't do to sell a book?'

'She's just jealous,' Marla said. 'Lips, please, Micky.'

'Jealous?' Betsy asked mildly.

'If Dorien Simmonds had a husband like Micky's, she wouldn't be flying the flag for mistresses,' Marla said firmly. 'She's just pig sick that she'll never land a catch like Jacko. Mind you, who isn't?'

'Mmmm,' Micky purred.

'Mmmm,' Betsy agreed.

It had taken years for the publicity machine to carve the pairing of Micky Morgan and Jacko Vance as firmly into the nation's consciousness as fish and chips or Lennon and McCartney. The celebrity marriage made in ratings heaven, it could never be dissolved. Even the gossip columnists had given up trying.

The irony was that it had been fear of newspaper gossip that had brought them together in the first place. Meeting Betsy had turned Micky's life on its head at a time when her career had started curving towards the heights. To climb as far and as fast as Micky meant collecting an interesting selection of enemies ranging from the poisonously envious to the rivals who'd been edged out of the limelight they thought was theirs of right. Since there was little to fault Micky on professionally, they'd homed in on the personal. Back in the early eighties, lesbian chic hadn't been invented. For women even more than men, being gay was still one of the quickest routes to the P45. Within a few months of abandoning her formerly straight life by falling in love with Betsy, Micky understood what a hunted animal feels like.

Her solution had been radical and extremely successful. Micky had Jacko to thank for that. She had been and still was lucky to have him, she thought as she looked approvingly at her reflection in the make-up mirror.

Perfect.

Tony Hill looked around the room at the team he had hand-picked and felt a moment's pity. They thought they were walking into this grave new world with their eyes open. Coppers never thought of themselves as innocents abroad. They were too streetwise. They'd seen it all, done it all, got pissed and thrown up on the T-shirt. Tony was here to instruct half a dozen cops who already thought they knew it all that there were unimaginable horrors out there that would make them wake up screaming in the night and teach them to pray. Not for forgiveness, but for healing. He knew only too well that whatever they thought, none of them had made a genuinely informed choice when they'd opted for the National Offender Profiling Task Force.

None of them except, perhaps, Paul Bishop. When the Home Office had given the profiling project the green light, Tony had called in every favour he could claim and a few he couldn't to make sure the police figurehead was someone who knew the gravity of what he was taking on. He'd dangled Paul Bishop's name in front of the politicians like a carrot in front of a reluctant mule, reminding them of how well Paul performed in front of the cameras. Even then it had been touch and go till he'd pointed out that even London's cynical hacks showed a bit of respect for the man who'd headed the successful hunts for the predators they'd dubbed the Railcard Rapist and the Metroland Murderer. After those investigations, there was no question in Tony's mind that Paul knew exactly the kind of nightmares that lay ahead.

On the other hand, the rewards were extraordinary. When it worked, when their work actually put someone away, these police officers would know a high unlike any other they'd ever experienced. It was a powerful feeling, to know your endeavours had helped put a killer away. It was even more gratifying to realize how many lives you might have saved because you shone a light down the right path for your colleagues to go down. It was exhilarating, even though it was tempered with the knowledge of what the perpetrator had already done. Somehow, he had to convey that satisfaction to them as well.

Paul Bishop was talking now, welcoming them to the task force and outlining the training programme he and Tony had thrashed out between them. 'We're going to take you through the process of profiling, giving you the background information you need to start developing the skill for yourself,' he said. It was a crash course in psychology, inevitably superficial, but covering the basics. If they'd chosen wisely, their apprentices would go off in their own preferred directions, reading more widely, tracking down other specialists and building up their own expertise in particular areas of the profiling craft that interested them.

Tony looked around at his new colleagues. All CID-trained, all but one a graduate. A sergeant and five constables, two of them women. Eager eyes, notepads open, pens at the ready. They were smart, this lot. They knew that if they did well here and the unit prospered, they could go all the way to the top on the strength of it.

His steady gaze ranged over them. Part of him wished Carol Jordan was among them, sharing her sharp perceptions and shrewd analyses, tossing in the occasional grenade of humour to lighten the grimness. But his sensible head knew there would be more than enough problems ahead without that complication.

If he had to put money on any of them turning into the kind of star that would stop him missing Carol's abilities, he'd go for the one with the eyes that blazed cold fire. Sharon Bowman. Like all the best hunters, she'd kill if she had to.

Just like he'd done himself.

Tony pushed the thought away and concentrated on Paul's words, waiting for the signal. When Paul nodded, Tony took over smoothly. 'The FBI take two years to train their operatives in offender profiling,' he said, leaning back in his chair in a deliberate attitude of relaxed calm. 'We do things differently over here.' A note of acid in the voice. 'We'll be accepting our first cases in six weeks. In three months' time, the Home Office expects us to be running a full case-load. What you've got to do inside that time frame is assimilate a mountain of theory, learn a series of protocols as long as your arm, develop total familiarity with the computer software we've had specially written for the task force, and cultivate an instinctive understanding of those among us who are, as we clinicians put it, totally fucked up.' He grinned unexpectedly at their serious faces. 'Any questions?'

'Is it too late to resign?' Bowman's electric eyes sparkled humour that was missing from her deadpan tones.

'The only resignations they accept are the ones certified by the pathologist.' The wry response came from Simon McNeill. Psychology graduate from Glasgow, four years' service with Strathclyde Police, Tony reminded himself, reassuring himself that he could recall names and backgrounds without too much effort.

'Correct,' he said.

'What about insanity?' another voice from the group asked.

'Far too useful a tool for us to let you slip from our grasp,' Tony told him. 'I'm glad you brought that up, actually, Sharon. It gives me the perfect lead into what I want to talk about first today.' His eyes moved from face to face, waiting until his seriousness was mirrored in each of their faces. A man accustomed to assuming whatever personality and demeanour would be acceptable, he shouldn't have been surprised at how easy it was to manipulate them, but he was. If he did his job properly, it would be far harder to achieve in a couple of months' time.

Once they were settled and concentrating, he tossed his folder of notes on to the table attached to the arm of his chair and ignored them. 'Isolation,' he said. 'Alienation. The hardest things to deal with. Human beings are gregarious. We're herd animals. We hunt in packs, we celebrate in packs. Take away human contact from someone and their behaviour distorts. You're going to learn a lot about that over the coming months and years.' He had their attention now. Time for the killer blow.

'I'm not talking about serial offenders. I'm talking about you. You're all police officers with CID experience. You're successful cops, you've fitted in, you've made the system work for you. That's why you're here. You're used to the camaraderie of team work, you're accustomed to a support system that backs you up. When you get a result, you've always had a drinking squad to share the victory with. When it's all gone up in smoke, that same squad comes out and commiserates with you. It's a bit like a family, only it's a family without the big brother that picks on you and the auntie that asks when you're going to get married.' He noted the nods and twinges of facial expression that indicated agreement. As he'd expected, there were fewer from the women than the men.

He paused for a moment and leaned forward. 'You've just been collectively bereaved. Your families are dead and you can never, never go home any more. This is the only home you have, this is your only family.' He had them now, gripped tighter than any thriller had ever held them. The Bowman woman's right eyebrow twitched up into an astonished arc, but other than that, they were motionless.

'The best profilers have probably got more in common with serial killers than with the rest of the human race. Because killers have to be good profilers, too. A killer profiles his victims. He has to learn how to look at a shopping precinct full of people and pick out the one person who will work as a victim for him. He picks the wrong person and it's good night, Vienna. So he can't afford to make mistakes any more than we can. Like us, he kicks off consciously sorting by set criteria, but gradually, if he's good, it gets to be an instinct. And that's how good I want you all to be.'

For a moment, his perfect control slipped as images crowded unbidden to the front of his mind. He was the best, he knew that now. But he'd paid a high price to discover that. The idea that payment might come due again was something he managed to reject as long as he was sober. It was no accident that Tony had scarcely had a drink for the best part of a year.

Collecting himself, Tony cleared his throat and straightened in his seat. 'Very soon, your lives are going to change. Your priorities will shift like Los Angeles in an earthquake. Believe me, when you spend your days and nights projecting yourself inside a mind that's programmed to kill until death or incarceration prevents it, you suddenly find a lot of things that used to seem important are completely irrelevant. It's hard to get worked up about the unemployment figures when you've been contemplating the activities of somebody who's taken more people off the register in the last six months than the government has.' His cynical smile gave them the cue to relax the muscles that had been taut for the past few minutes.

'People who have not done this kind of work have no notion of what it is like. Every day, you review the evidence, raking through it for that elusive clue you missed the last forty-seven times. You watch helplessly as your hot leads turn out colder than a junkie's heart. You want to shake the witnesses who saw the killer but don't remember anything about him because nobody told them in advance that one of the people who would fill up with petrol in their service station one night three months ago was a multiple murderer. Some detective who thinks what you're doing is a bag of crap sees no reason why your life shouldn't be as fucking miserable as his, so he gives out your phone number to husbands, wives, lovers, children, parents, siblings, all of them people who want a crumb of hope from you.

'And as if that isn't enough, the media gets on your back. And then the killer does it again.'

Leon Jackson, who'd made it out of Liverpool's black ghetto to the Met via an Oxford scholarship, lit a cigarette. The snap of his lighter had the other two smokers reaching for their own. 'Sounds cool,' he said, dropping one arm over the back of his chair. Tony couldn't help the pang of pity. Harder they come, the bigger the fall.

'Arctic,' Tony said. 'So, that's how people outside the Job see you. What about your former colleagues? When you come up against the ones you left behind, believe me, they're going to start noticing you've gone a bit weird. You're not one of the gang any more, and they'll start avoiding you because you smell wrong. Then when you're working a case, you're going to be transplanted into an alien environment and there will be people there who don't want you on the case. Inevitably.' He leaned forward again, hunched against the chill wind of memory. 'And they won't be afraid to let you know it.'

Tony read superiority in Leon's sneer. Being black, he reasoned, Leon probably figured he'd had a taste of that already and rejection could therefore hold no fears for him. What he almost certainly didn't realize was that his bosses had needed a black success story. They'd have made that clear to the officers who controlled the culture, so the chances were that no one had really pushed Leon half as hard as he thought they had. 'And don't think the brass will back you when the shit comes down,' Tony continued. 'They won't. They'll love you for about two days, then when you haven't solved their headaches, they'll start to hate you. The longer it takes to resolve the serial offences, the worse it becomes. And the other detectives avoid you because you've got a contagious disease called failure. The truth might be out there, but you haven't got it, and until you do, you're a leper.

'Oh, and by the way,' he added, almost as an afterthought, 'when they do nail the bastard thanks to your hard work, they won't even invite you to the party.'

The silence was so intense he could hear the hiss of burning tobacco as Leon inhaled. Tony got to his feet and shoved his springy black hair back from his forehead. 'You probably think I'm exaggerating. Believe me,

I'm barely scratching the surface of how bad this job will make you feel. If you don't think it's for you, if you're having doubts about your decision, now's the time to walk away. Nobody will reproach you. No blame, no shame. Just have a word with Commander Bishop.' He looked at his watch. 'Coffee break. Ten minutes.'

He picked up his folder and carefully didn't look at them as they pushed back chairs and made a ragged progress to the door and the coffee station in the largest of the three rooms they'd been grudgingly granted by a police service already strapped for accommodation for their own officers. When at last he looked up, Shaz Bowman stood leaning against the wall by the door, waiting.

'Second thoughts, Sharon?' he asked.

'I hate being called Sharon,' she said. 'People who want a response go for Shaz. I just wanted to say it's not only profilers that get treated like shit. There's nothing you said just now that sounds any worse than what women deal with all the time in this job.'

'So I've been told,' Tony said, thinking inevitably of Carol Jordan. 'If it's true, you lot should have a head start in this game.'

Shaz grinned and pushed off from the wall, satisfied. 'Just watch,' she said, swivelling on the balls of her feet and moving through the door on feet as silent and springy as a jungle cat.

Jacko Vance leaned forward across the flimsy table and frowned. He pointed to the open desk diary. 'You see, Bill? I'm already committed to running the half-marathon on the Sunday. And then after that, we're filming Monday and Tuesday, I'm doing a club opening in Lincoln on Tuesday night – you're coming to that, by the way, aren't you?' Bill nodded, and Jacko continued. 'I've got meetings lined up Wednesday back to back and I've got to drive back up to Northumberland for my volunteer shift. I just don't see how we can accommodate them.' He threw himself back against the striped tweed of the production caravan's comfortless sofa bench with a sigh.

'That's the whole point, Jacko,' his producer said calmly, stirring the skimmed milk into the two coffees he was making in the kitchen area. Bill Ritchie had been producing *Vance's Visits* for long enough to know there was little point in trying to change his star's mind once it was made up. But this time, he was under sufficient pressure from his bosses to try. 'This documentary short's *supposed* to make you look busy, to say, "Here's this amazing guy, busy professional life, yet *he* finds time to work for charity, so why aren't you?"' He brought the coffees to the table.

'I'm sorry, Bill, but it's not on.' Jacko picked up his coffee and winced at its scalding heat. Hastily, he put it down again. 'When are we going to get a proper coffee maker in here?'

'If it's anything to do with me, never,' Bill said with a mock-severe scowl. 'The lousy coffee's the one thing guaranteed to divert you from whatever you're going on about.'

Jacko shook his head ruefully, acknowledging he'd been caught out. 'OK. But I'm still not doing it. For one, I don't want a camera crew dogging my heels any more than I already have to put up with. For two, I don't do charity work so I can show off about it on prime-time telethons. For three, the poor sick bastards I spend my nights with are terminally ill people who do not need a hand-held camera shoved down their emaciated throats. I'll happily do something else for the telethon, maybe something with Micky, but I'm not having the people I work with exploited just so we can guilt-trip a few more grand out of the viewers.'

Bill spread his hands in defeat. 'Fine by me. Do you want to tell them or will I?'

'Would you, Bill? Save me the aggravation?' Jacko's smile was bright as a shaft of sunlight from a thunder-cloud, promising as the hour before a first date. It was imprinted on his audience like a race memory. Women made love to their husbands with more gusto because Jacko's sexually inviting eyes and kissable mouth were flickering across the inside of their eyelids. Adolescent girls found their vague erotic longings suddenly focused. Old ladies doted on him, without connecting the sub-sequent feelings of unfulfilled sadness.

Men liked him too, but not because they found him sexy. Men liked Jacko Vance because he was, in spite of everything, one of the lads. A British, Common-wealth, and European gold medallist and holder of the world javelin record, Olympic gold had seemed like an inevitability for the darling of the back pages. Then one night, driving back from an athletics meeting in Gateshead, Jacko drove into a dense bank of fog on the A1. He wasn't the only one.

The morning news bulletins put the figures at between twenty-seven and thirty-five vehicles in the multiple pile-up. The big story wasn't the six dead, however. The big story was the tragic heroism of Jacko Vance, British athletics' golden boy. In spite of suffering multiple lacer-ations and three broken ribs in the initial impact, Jacko had crawled out of his mangled motor and rescued two children from the back of a car seconds before it burst into flames. Depositing them on the hard shoulder, he'd gone back into the tangled metal and attempted to free a lorry driver pinioned between his steering wheel and the buckled door of his cab.

The creaking of stressed metal turned to a shriek as accumulated pressures built up on the lorry and the roof caved in. The driver didn't stand a chance. Neither did Jacko Vance's throwing arm. It took the firemen three agonizing hours to cut him free from the crushing weight of metal that had smashed his flesh to raw meat and his bones to splinters. Worse, he was conscious for most of it. Trained athletes knew all about pushing through the pain barrier.

The news of his George Cross came the day after the medics fitted his first prosthesis. It was small consolation for the loss of the dream that had been the core of his life for a dozen years. But bitterness didn't cloud his natural shrewdness. He knew how fickle the media could be. He still smarted at the memory of the headlines when he'd blown his first attempt at the European title. JACK SPLAT! had been the kindest stab at the heart of the man who only the day before had been JACK OF HEARTS.

He knew he had to capitalize on his glory quickly or he'd soon be another yesterday's hero, early fodder for the 'Where Are They Now?' column. So he called in a few favours, renewed his acquaintance with Bill Ritchie and ended up commentating on the very Olympics where he should have mounted the rostrum. It had been a start. Simultaneously, he'd worked to establish his reputation as a tireless worker for charity, a man who would never allow his fame to stand in the way of helping people less fortunate than himself.

Now, he was bigger than all the fools who'd been so ready to write him off. He'd charmed and chatted his way to the front of the sports presenters' ranks in a slash and burn operation of such devious ruthlessness that some of his victims still didn't realize they'd been calculatedly chopped off at the knees. Once he'd consolidated that role, he'd presented a chat show that had topped the light entertainment ratings for three years. When the fourth year saw it drop to third place, he dumped the format and launched *Vance's Visits*.

The show claimed to be spontaneous. In fact, Jacko's arrival in the midst of what his publicity called 'ordinary people living ordinary lives' was invariably orchestrated with all the advance planning of a royal visit but none of the attendant publicity. Otherwise he'd have attracted bigger crowds than any of the discredited House of Windsor. Especially if he'd turned up with the wife.

And still it wasn't enough.

Carol bought the coffees. It was a privilege of rank. She thought about refusing to shell out for the chocolate biscuits on the basis that nobody needed three KitKats to get through a meeting with their DCI. But she knew it would be misinterpreted, so she grinned and bore the expense. She led the troops she'd chosen with care to a quiet corner cut off from the rest of the canteen by an array of plastic parlour palms. Detective Sergeant Tommy Taylor, Detective Constable Lee Whitbread and Detective Constable Di Earnshaw had all impressed her with their intelligence and determination. She might yet be proved wrong, but these three officers were her private bet for the pick of Seaford Central's CID.

'I'm not going to attempt to pretend this is a social chat so we can get to know each other better,' she announced, sharing the biscuits out among the three of them. Di Earnshaw watched her, eyes like currants in a suet pudding, hating the way her new boss managed to look elegant in a linen suit with more creases than a dosser's when she just looked lumpy in her perfectly pressed chain-store skirt and jacket.

'Thank Christ for that,' Tommy said, a grin slowly spreading. 'I was beginning to worry in case we'd got a guv'nor who didn't understand the importance of Tetley's Bitter to a well-run CID.'

Carol's answering smile was wry. 'It's Bradfield I came from, remember?'

'That's why we were worried, ma'am,' Tommy replied.

Lee snorted with suppressed laughter, turned it into a cough and spluttered, 'Sorry, ma'am.'

'You will be,' Carol said pleasantly. 'I've got a task for you three. I've been taking a good look at the overnights since I got here, and I'm a bit concerned about the high incidence of unexplained fires and query arsons that we've got on our ground. I spotted five query arsons in the last month and when I made some checks with uniform, I found out there have been another half-dozen unexplained outbreaks of fire.'

'You always get that kind of thing round the docks,' Tommy said, casually shrugging big shoulders inside a baggy silk blouson that had gone out of fashion a couple of years previously.

'I appreciate that, but I'm wondering if there's a bit more to it than that. Agreed, a couple of the smaller blazes are obvious routine cock-ups, but I'm wondering if there's something else going on here.' Carol left it dangling to see who would pick it up.

'A firebug, you mean, ma'am?' It was Di Earnshaw, the voice pleasant but the expression bordering on the insolent.

'A serial arsonist, yes.'

There was a momentary silence. Carol reckoned she knew what they were thinking. The East Yorkshire force might be a new entity, but these officers had worked this patch under the old regime. They were in with the bricks, whereas she was the new kid in town, desperate to shine at their expense. And they weren't sure whether to roll with it or try to derail her. Somehow she had to persuade them that she was the star they should be hitching their wagons to. 'There's a pattern,' she said. 'Empty premises, early hours of the morning. Schools, light industrial units, warehouses. Nothing too big, nowhere there might be a night watchman to put the mockers on it. But serious nevertheless. Big fires, all of them. They've caused a lot of damage and the insurance companies must be hurting more than they like.'

'Nobody's said owt about an arsonist on the rampage,' Tommy remarked calmly. 'Usually, the firemen tip us the wink if they think there's something a bit not right on the go.'

'Either that or the local rag gives us a load of earache,' Lee chipped in through a mouthful of his second KitKat. Lean as a whippet in spite of the biscuits and the three sugars in his coffee, Carol noted. One to watch for high-strung hyperactivity.

'Call me picky, but I prefer it when we're setting the agenda, not the local hacks or the fire service,' Carol said coolly. 'Arson isn't a Mickey Mouse crime. Like murder, it has terrible consequences. And like murder, you've got a stack of potential motives. Fraud, the destruction of evidence, the elimination of competition, revenge and cover-up, at the "logical" end of the spectrum. And at the screwed-up end, we have the ones who do it for kicks and sexual gratification. Like serial killers, they nearly always have their own internal logic that they mistake for something that makes sense to the rest of us.

'Fortunately for us, serial murder is a lot less common than serial arson. Insurers reckon a quarter of all the fires in the UK have been set deliberately. Imagine if a quarter of all deaths were murder.'

Taylor looked bored. Lee Whitbread stared blankly at her, his hand halfway to the cigarette packet in front of him. Di Earnshaw was the only one who appeared interested in making a contribution. 'I've heard it said that the incidence of arson is an index of the economic prosperity of a country. The more arson there is, the worse the economy is doing. Well, there's plenty unemployed round here,' she said with the air of someone who expects to be ignored.

'And that's something we should bear in mind,' Carol said, nodding with approval. 'Now, this is what I want. A careful trawl through the overnights for CID and uniform for the last six months to see what we come up with. I want the victims re-interviewed to check if there are any obvious common factors, like the same insurance company. Sort it out among yourselves. I'll be having a chat with the fire chief before the four of us reconvene in . . . shall we say three days? Fine. Any questions?'

'I could do the fire chief, ma'am,' Di Earnshaw said eagerly. 'I've had dealings with him before.'

'Thanks for the offer, Di, but the sooner I make his acquaintance, the happier I'll feel.'

Di Earnshaw's lips seemed to shrink inwards in disapproval, but she merely nodded.

'You want us to drop our other cases?' Tommy asked.

Carol's smile was sharp as an ice pick. She'd never had a soft spot for chancers. 'Oh, please, Sergeant,' she sighed. 'I know what your case-load is. Like I said at the start of this conversation, it's Bradfield I came from. Seaford might not be the big city, but that's no reason for us to operate at village bobby pace.'

She stood up, taking in the shock in their faces. 'I

didn't come here to fall out with people. But I will if I have to. If you think I'm a hard bastard to work for, watch me. However hard you work, you'll see me matching it. I'd like us to be a team. But we have to play my rules.'

Then she was gone. Tommy Taylor scratched his jaw. 'That's us told, then. Still think she's shaggable, Lee?'

Di Earnshaw's thin mouth pursed. 'Not unless you like singing falsetto.'

'I don't think you'd feel a lot like singing,' Lee said. 'Anybody want that last KitKat?'

Shaz rubbed her eyes and turned away from the computer screen. She'd come in early so she could squeeze in a quick revision of the previous day's software familiarization. Finding Tony at work on one of the other terminals had been a bonus. He'd looked astonished to see her walk through the door just after seven. 'I thought I was the only workaholic insomniac around here,' he'd greeted her.

'I'm crap on computers,' she'd said gruffly, trying to cover her satisfaction at having him to herself. 'I've always needed to work twice as hard to keep up.'

Tony's eyebrows had jumped. Cops didn't generally admit weaknesses to an outsider. Either Shaz Bowman was even more unusual than he'd initially appreciated or else he was finally losing his alien status. 'I thought everybody under thirty was a wizard on these,' he said mildly.

'Sorry to disappoint you. I was behind the door when the anoraks were being handed out,' Shaz replied. She settled in front of her screen and pushed up the sleeves of her cotton sweater. 'First remember your password,' she muttered, wondering what he thought of her.

Two forces seethed under Shaz Bowman's calm

surface, taking it in turns to drive her. On the one hand, fear of failure gnawed at her, undermining everything she was and all she achieved. When she looked in the mirror, she never saw her good points, only the thinness of her lips and the lack of definition in her nose. When she reviewed her accomplishments, she saw only the places where she had fallen short, the heights she had failed to scale. The countervailing force was her ambition. Somehow, ever since she'd first begun to formulate the ambitions that drove her, those goals had restored her damaged self-confidence and shored up her vulnerabilities before they could cripple her. When her ambition threatened to tip her over into arrogance, somehow the fear would kick in at the crucial point, keeping her human.

The setting up of the task force had coincided so perfectly with the direction of her dreams, she couldn't help but feel the hand of fate in it. That didn't mean that she could let up, however. Shaz's long-term career plan meant she had to shine brighter than anyone else in this task force. One of her tactics for achieving that was to pick Tony Hill's brains like a master locksmith, extracting every scrap of knowledge she could scavenge there while simultaneously worming her way inside his defences so that when she needed his help, he'd be willing to provide it. As part of her approach, and because she was terrified that otherwise she'd fall behind and make a fool of herself in a group that she was convinced were all better than her, she was covertly taping all the group sessions, listening to them over and over again whenever she could. And now, luck had dropped a bonus opportunity into her lap.

So Shaz frowned and stared at the screen, working her way through the lengthy process of filling out an offence report then setting in motion its comparison against the details of all the previous crimes held in the computer's memory banks. When Tony had slipped out of his seat, she'd vaguely registered the movement, but forced herself to carry on working. The last thing she wanted was for him to think she was trying to ingratiate herself.

The intensity of the concentration she imposed upon herself was sufficient for her not to notice when he came back in through the door behind her desk until her subconscious registered a faint masculine smell which it identified as his. It took all her willpower not to react. Instead, she carried on striking keys until his hand cleared the edge of her peripheral vision and placed a carton of coffee topped with a Danish on the desk beside her. 'Time for a break?'

So she'd rubbed her eyes and abandoned the screen. 'Thanks,' she said.

'You're welcome. Anything you're not clear about? I'll take you through it, if you want.'

Still she held back. Don't snatch at it, she cautioned herself. She didn't want to use up her credit with Tony Hill until she absolutely had to, and preferably not before she'd been able to offer him something helpful in return. 'It's not that I don't understand it,' she said. 'It's just that I don't trust it.'

Tony smiled, enjoying her defensive stubbornness. 'One of those kids who demanded empirical proof that two and two were always going to be four?'

A prick of delight that she'd entertained him, quickly stifled. Shaz moved the Danish and opened the coffee. 'I've always been in love with proof. Why do you think I became a cop?'

Tony's smile was lopsided and knowing. 'I could speculate. It's quite a proving ground you've chosen here.'

'Not really. The ground's already been broken. The Americans have been doing it for so long they've not only got manuals, they've got movies about it. It's just taken us forever to catch on, as per usual. But you're one of the ones who forced the issue, so there's nothing left for us to prove.' Shaz took a huge bite of her Danish, nodding in quiet approval as she tasted the apricot glaze on the flaky pastry.

'Don't you believe it,' Tony said wryly, moving back to his own terminal. 'The backlash has only just started. It's taken long enough to get the police to accept we can provide useful help, but already the media hacks who were treating us profilers like gods a couple of years ago are jumping all over our shortcomings. They oversold us, so now they have to blame us for not living up to a set of expectations they created in the first place.'

'I don't know,' Shaz said. 'The public only remember the big successes. That case you did in Bradfield last year. The profile was right on the button. The police knew exactly where to go looking when it came to the crunch.' Oblivious to the permafrost that had settled over Tony's face, Shaz continued enthusiastically. 'Are you going to do a session on that? We've all heard the grapevine version, but there's next to nothing in the literature, even though it's obvious you did a textbook job on the profile.'

'We won't be covering that case,' he said flatly.

Shaz looked up sharply and realized where her eagerness had beached her. She'd blown it this time, in spades. 'I'm sorry,' she said quietly. 'I get carried away, and tact and diplomacy, they're history. I wasn't thinking.' Thick git, she berated herself silently. If he'd had the therapy he would have needed after that particular nightmare, the last thing he'd want would be to expose the details to avid prurience, even if it was masquerading as legitimate scientific interest.

'You don't have to apologize, Shaz,' Tony said wearily. 'You're right, it is a key case. The reason we won't be covering it is that I can't talk about it without feeling like a freak. You'll all have to forgive me. Maybe one day you'll catch a case that leaves you feeling the same way. For your sake, I sincerely hope not.' He looked down at his Danish as if it were an alien artefact and pushed it to one side, appetite dead as the past was supposed to be.

Shaz wished she could rerun the tape, pick up the conversation at the point where he'd put the coffee down on her desk and there was still the possibility of using the moment to build a bridge. 'I'm really sorry, Dr Hill,' she said inadequately.

He looked up and forced a thin smile. 'Truly, Shaz, there's no need. And can we drop the "Dr Hill" bit? I meant to bring it up during yesterday's session, but it slipped my mind. I don't want you all feeling that I'm the teacher and you're the class. At the moment, I'm the group leader simply because I've been doing this for a while. Before long, we'll all be working side by side, and there's no point in having barriers between us. So it's Tony from now on in, OK?'

'You got it, Tony.' Shaz searched for the message in his eyes and his words and, satisfied it contained genuine forgiveness, wolfed the rest of her Danish and returned to her screen. She couldn't do it while he was here, but next time she was in the computer room alone, she intended to use her Internet access to pull up the newspaper archives and check out all the reports of the Bradfield serial killer case. She'd read most of them at the time, but that had been before she'd met Tony Hill and everything had changed. Now, she had a special interest.

By the time she was finished, she'd know enough about Tony Hill's most public profile to write the book that, for reasons she still couldn't understand, had never been written. After all, she was a detective, wasn't she?

Carol Jordan fiddled with the complicated chrome coffee maker, a housewarming present from her brother Michael when she'd moved to Seaford. She'd been luckier than most people caught in the housing market slump. She hadn't had far to look for a buyer for her half of the warehouse flat she and Michael owned; the barrister he'd recently been sharing his bedroom with had been so eager to buy her out that Carol had begun to wonder if she'd been even more of a gooseberry than she'd imagined.

Now she had this low stone cottage on the side of the hill that rose above the estuary almost directly opposite Seaford; a place of her own. Well, almost, she corrected herself, reminded by the hard skull head-butting her shin. 'OK, Nelson,' she said, stooping to scratch the black cat's ears. 'I hear what you're saying.' While the coffee brewed, she scooped out a bowl of cat food to a rapture of purring followed by the sloppy sound of Nelson inhaling his breakfast. She walked through to the living room to enjoy the panorama of the estuary and the improbably slender arc of the suspension bridge. Gazing out across the misty river where the bridge appeared to float without connection to the land, she planned her coming encounter with the fire chief. Nelson walked in, tail erect, and jumped without pause straight on to the window sill where he stretched out, arching his head back towards Carol and demanding affection. Carol stroked his dense fur and said, 'I only get one chance to convince this guy that I know arse from elbow,

Nelson. I need him on my side. God knows, I need somebody on my side.'

Nelson batted her hand with his paw, as if responding directly to her words. Carol swallowed the rest of her coffee and got to her feet in a movement as smooth as the cat's. One of the advantages she'd soon found with a DCI's office hours was that she actually managed to use her gym membership more than once a month, and she was already feeling the benefit in firmer muscle tone and better aerobic fitness. It would have been a bonus to have someone to share it with, but that wasn't why she did it. She did it for herself, because it made her feel good. She took pride in her body, revelling in its strength and mobility.

An hour later, enduring the tour of the central fire station, she was glad of her fitness as she struggled to keep pace with the long legs of the local chief of operations, Jim Pendlebury. 'You seem to be better organized here than CID ever manages,' Carol said, as they finally made it to his office. 'You'll have to share the secret of your efficiency.'

'We've had so much cost-cutting, we've really had to streamline everything we do,' he told her. 'We used to have all our stations staffed round the clock with a complement of full-time officers, but it really wasn't cost effective. I know a lot of the lads grumbled about it, but a couple of years back we shifted to a mix of part-time and full-time officers. It took a few months to shake down, but it's been a huge advantage to me in management terms.'

Carol pulled a face. 'Not a solution that would work for us.'

Pendlebury shrugged. 'I don't know. You could have a core staff who dealt with the routine stuff and a hit squad that you used as and when you needed them.'

'That's sort of what we have already,' Carol said drily. 'The core staff is called the night shift and the hit squad are the day teams. Unfortunately, it never gets quiet enough to stand any of them down.'

With part of her mind, Carol added to her mental profile of the fire chief as they spoke. In conversation, his straight dark eyebrows crinkled and jutted above his blue-grey eyes. Considering how much time he must spend flying a desk, his skin looked surprisingly weathered, the creases round his eyes showing white when he wasn't smiling or frowning. Probably a part-time sailor or estuary fisherman, she guessed. As he dipped his head to acknowledge something she'd said, she could see a few silver hairs straggling among his dark curls. So, probably a few years the far side of thirty, Carol thought, revising her initial estimate. She had a habit of analysing new acquaintances in terms of how their description would read on a police bulletin. She'd never actually had to produce a photofit of someone she'd encountered, but she was confident her practice would have made her the best possible witness for the police artist to work with.

'Now you've seen the operation, I take it you're a bit more willing to accept that when we say a fire's a query arson, we're not talking absolute rubbish?' Pendlebury's tone was light, but his eyes challenged hers.

'I never doubted what you were telling us,' she said calmly. 'What I doubted was whether we were taking it as seriously as we should.' She snapped open the locks on her briefcase and took out her file. 'I'd like to go through the details on these incidents with you, if you can spare me the time.'

He cocked his head to one side. 'Are you saying what I think you're saying?'

'Now that I've seen the way you run your operation,

I can't believe the idea of a serial arsonist hasn't already crossed your mind.'

He tugged at the lobe of one ear, sizing her up. Finally, he said, 'I was wondering when one of your lot would notice.'

Carol breathed out hard through her nose. 'It might have been helpful if we'd been given a nudge in the right direction. You are the experts, after all.'

'Your predecessor didn't think so,' Pendlebury said. He might as well have been commenting on the price of fish. All of the enthusiasm he'd shown earlier for his job had vanished behind an impassive mask, leaving Carol to draw her own conclusions. They didn't make a pretty picture.

She placed the file on Pendlebury's desk and flipped it open. 'That was then. This is now. Are you telling me you've got query arsons that predate this one?'

He glanced down at the top sheet in the file and snorted. 'How far back would you like to start?'

Tony Hill sat alone at his desk, ostensibly preparing for the following day's seminar with the task force officers. But his thoughts were far away from those details. He was thinking about the psychopathic minds out there, already set in the moulds that would generate pain and misery for people they didn't even know yet.

There had long been a theory among psychologists that discounted the existence of evil, ascribing the worst excesses of the most sociopathic abductors, torturers and killers to a linked series of circumstances and events in their past that culminated in one final stress-laden event that catapulted them over the edge of what civilized society would tolerate. But that had never entirely satisfied Tony. It begged the question of why some people with almost identical backgrounds of abuse and deprivation went on not to become psychopaths but to lead useful, fruitful lives, integrated into society.

Now the scientists were talking about a genetic answer, a fracture in the DNA code that might explain this divergence. Somehow, Tony found that answer too pat. It seemed as much of a cop-out as the old-fashioned notion that some men were simply evil and that was that. It evaded responsibility in a way he found repugnant.

It was an issue that had always held particular resonance for him. He knew the reason he was so good at what he did. It was because for so many of the steps down the road that his prey had taken, he had walked in their footprints. But at some point he could never quite identify there had come a parting of the ways. Where they became hunters at first hand, he became a hunter at second hand, tracking them down once they had crossed the line. Yet his life still held echoes of theirs. The fantasies that drove them were about sex and death; his fantasies about sex and death were called profiling. They were chillingly close.

It sometimes seemed chicken and egg to Tony. Had his impotence started because he was afraid the unfettered expression of his sexuality might lead him to violence and death? Or had his knowledge of how often the sexual urge led to killing worked on his body to make him sexually inadequate? He doubted he would ever know. However the circuit worked, it was undeniable that his work had profoundly affected his life.

For no apparent reason, he recalled the spark of uncomplicated enthusiasm he'd seen in Shaz Bowman's eyes. He could remember feeling that way too, before his fascination had been tempered by exposure to the horrors humans could inflict upon each other. Maybe he could use what he knew to give his team better armour than he'd had. If he achieved nothing else with them, that alone would be worthwhile.

In another part of the city, Shaz clicked her mouse button and closed down her software. On autopilot, she switched off her computer and stared unseeingly as the screen faded to black. When she'd decided to explore the resources of the Internet as her first stop on the road to disinterring Tony Hill's past, she'd expected to come across a handful of references and, if she was lucky, a set of cuttings in one of the newspaper archives.

Instead, when she'd input 'Tony, Hill, Bradfield, killer' as key words in the search engine, she'd stumbled upon a darkside treasure trove of references to the case that had put his face on the front pages a year before. There was a grisly handful of websites entirely devoted to serial killers which incorporated Tony's headline case. Elsewhere, journalists and commentators had posted their articles on that specific case on their personal websites. There was even a perverse rogues' gallery, a montage of photographs of the faces of the world's most notorious serial killers. Tony's target, the so-called Queer Killer, featured in more than one guise in the bizarre exhibit.

Shaz had downloaded everything she could find and had spent the rest of the evening reading it. What had started out as an academic exercise to figure out what made Tony Hill tick had left her sick at heart.

The facts were not in dispute. The naked bodies of four men had been dumped in gay cruising areas of Bradfield. The victims had been tortured before death with a cruelty that was almost beyond comprehension. After death, they had been sexually mutilated, washed clean and abandoned like trash.

As a last resort, Tony had been brought in as a

consultant, working with Detective Inspector Carol Jordan to develop a profile. They were moving close to their target when hunter became hunted. The killer wanted Tony for a human sacrifice. Captured and trussed, he was on the point of becoming victim number five, the torture engine in place, his body screaming in pain. He was saved in the nick of time not by the arrival of the cavalry but by his own verbal skills, honed over years of working with mentally disturbed offenders. But to claim his life, he'd had to kill his captor.

As she'd read, Shaz's heart had filled with horror, her eyes with tears. Cursed with enough imagination to create a picture of the hell Tony had lived through, she found herself sucked into the nightmare of that final showdown where the roles of killer and victim were irrevocably reversed. The scenario made her shudder with fear and trepidation.

How had he begun to live with that? she marvelled. How did he sleep? How could he close his eyes and not be assailed with images beyond most people's imagination or tolerance? Little wonder that he wasn't prepared to use his own past to teach them how to manage their futures. The miracle was that he was still willing to practise a craft that must have pushed him to the edge of madness.

And how would she have coped if she'd been the one in his shoes? Shaz dropped her head into her hands and, for the first time since she'd heard of the task force, asked herself if she hadn't perhaps made a terrible mistake.

Betsy mixed a drink for the journalist. Heavy on the gin, light on the tonic, a quarter of a lemon squeezed so that the tartness of the juice would cut the oily sweetness of the gin and disguise its potency. One of the

48

principal reasons that Micky's image had survived untainted by scandal was Betsy's insistence that they trust no one outside the trio that held their secret close. Suzy Joseph might be all smiles and charm, filling the airy sitting room with the tinkle of her laugh and the smoke from her menthol cigarettes, but she was still a journalist. Even if she represented the most accommodating and sycophantic of the colour magazines, Betsy knew that among her drinking cronies there would be more than one tabloid hack ready to dip a hand in a pocket for the right piece of gossip. So Suzy would be plied generously with drink today. By the time she came to sit down to lunch with Jacko and Micky, her sharp eyes would be blurred round the edges.

Betsy perched on the arm of a sofa whose squashy cushions engulfed the anorectically thin journalist. She could keep an eye on her easily from there, while Suzy would have to make a deliberate and obvious shift of position to get Betsy in her line of sight. That also made it possible for Betsy to signal caution to Micky without being seen. 'This is such a lovely room,' Suzy gushed. 'So light, so cool. You don't often see something so tasteful, so elegant, so – *appropriate*. And believe me, I've been in more of these Holland Park mansions than the local estate agents!' She twisted round awkwardly and said to Betsy in the same tones she'd have used to a waiter, 'You have made sure the caterers have all they need?'

Betsy nodded. 'Everything's under control. They were delighted with the kitchen.'

'I'm sure they were.' Suzy was back with Micky, Betsy dismissed again. 'Did you design the dining room yourself, Micky? So stylish! So very, very *you*! So perfect for *Junket with Joseph*.' She leaned forward to stub out her cigarette, giving Betsy an unwanted view of a creped cleavage that fake tan and expensive body treatments couldn't entirely disguise.

Being commended on her taste by a woman who could without any indication of shame wear a brash scarlet and black Moschino suit designed for someone twenty years younger and an entirely different shape was a double-edged compliment, Micky felt. But she simply smiled again and said, 'Actually, it was mostly Betsy's inspiration. She's the one with the taste round here. I just tell her what I want the ambience to be like, and she sorts it out.'

Suzy's reflexive smile held no warmth. Another wasted opening; nothing quotable there, it seemed to say. Before she could try again, Jacko strode into the room, his broad shoulders in their perfect tailoring thrusting forward so he appeared like a flying wedge. He ignored Suzy's fluttering twitters and made straight for Micky, descending upon her with one enveloping arm, hugging her close, though not actually kissing. 'Sweetheart,' he said, his professional, public voice carrying the thrum of a cello chord. 'I'm sorry I'm late.' He half-turned and leaned back against the sofa, giving Suzy the full benefit of his perfectly groomed smile. 'You must be Suzy,' he said. 'We're thrilled to have you here with us today.'

Suzy lit up like Christmas. 'I'm thrilled to be here,' she gushed, her breathy voice losing its veneer and revealing the unmistakable West Midlands intonation she'd devoted herself to burying. The effect Jacko still had on women never ceased to astonish Betsy. He could turn the sourest bitch Barsac sweet. Even the tired cynicism of Suzy Joseph, a woman who had the same relationship to celebrity as beetles to dung, wasn't sufficient armour against his charm. '*Junket with Joseph* doesn't often give me the chance to spend time with people I genuinely admire,' she added.

'Thank you,' Jacko said, all smiles. 'Betsy, should we be heading through to the dining room?'

She glanced at the clock. 'That would be helpful,' she said. 'The caterer wants to start serving round about now.' Jacko jumped to his feet and waited attentively for Micky to get up and move towards the door. He ushered Suzy ahead of him too, turning back to roll his eyes upwards in an expression of bored horror for Betsy's benefit. Stifling a giggle, she followed them to the dining-room door, saw them seated and left them to it. Sometimes there were distinct benefits in not being the official consort, she reminded herself as she settled down with her bread and cheese and *The World at One*.

There was no such relief for Micky, who had to pretend she didn't even notice Suzy's vapid flirting with her husband. Micky tuned out the boring ritual dance going on next to her and concentrated on freeing the last morsels of lobster from a claw.

A change in Suzy's tone alerted her that the conversation had shifted a gear. Time for work, Micky realized. 'Of course, I've read in the cuttings how you two got together,' Suzy was saying, her hand covering Jacko's real one. She wouldn't have been so quick to pat the other, Micky reflected grimly. 'But I need to hear it from your own lips.'

Here we go, Micky thought. The first part of the recital was always hers. 'We met in hospital,' she began.

By the middle of the second week, the task force office felt like home to the entire team. It was no accident that all six of the junior officers chosen for the squad were single and unattached, according both to their records and the unofficial background checks that Commander

Paul Bishop had pursued in canteens and police clubs up and down the country. Tony had deliberately wanted a group of people who, uprooted from their former lives, would be thrown together and forced to develop team spirit. That at least was something he seemed to have got right, he thought, looking around the seminar room where six heads were bowed over a set of photocopied police files he'd prepared for them.

Already, they had started to form alliances, and so far they'd done well to avoid the personality clashes that could split a group beyond salvaging. Interestingly, the associations were flexible, not fixed in rigid pairs. Although some affinities were stronger than others, there was no attempt to make any of them exclusive.

Shaz was the one exception, as far as Tony could tell. It wasn't that there was a problem between her and the others. It was more that she held herself apart from the easy intimacy that was growing between the rest. She joined in the jokes, took part in the communal brainstorming, but somehow there was always distance between her and her fellows. He sensed in her a passion for success that the rest of the squad lacked. They were ambitious, no denying that, but with Shaz it went deeper. She was driven, her need burning inside her and consuming any trace of frivolity. She was always first there in the mornings and last out at night, eagerly snatching any opportunity to get Tony to expand on whatever he'd been talking about last. But her very need for success made her correspondingly more vulnerable to failure. What he recognized as a desperate desire for approval was a blade that could be used against her with devastating effect. If she didn't learn to drop her defences so she could use her empathy, she'd never achieve her potential as a profiler. It was his job to find a way of making her feel she could relax her vigilance without risking too much damage.

At that moment, Shaz looked up, her eyes direct on his. There was no embarrassment, no awkwardness. She simply stared for a moment then returned to what she was reading. It was as if she had raided his memory banks for a missing piece of information and, having found it, had logged off again. Slightly unnerved, Tony cleared his throat. 'Four separate incidents of sexual assault and rape. Any comments?'

The group had moved beyond awkward silences and polite hanging back to give others a chance. In what was becoming an established pattern, Leon Jackson dived straight in. 'I think the strongest link is in the victims. I read somewhere that serial rapists tend to rape within their own age group, and all these women were in their mid-twenties. Plus they all have short blonde hair and they all took time and trouble to stay fit. You got two joggers, one hockey player, one rower. They all did sports where it wouldn't be hard for a weirdo stalker to watch them without attracting any attention.'

'Thanks, Leon. Any other comments?'

Simon, already the devil's advocate designate of the group, weighed in, his Glasgow accent and habit of staring out from under his heavy dark eyebrows multiplying the aggression factor. 'You could argue that that's because the kind of woman who indulges in these kind of sports is exactly the sort that's confident enough to be out in risky places on her own, convinced it's never going to happen to her. It could easily be two, three or even four attackers. In which case, bringing in a profiler is going to be a total waste of time.'

Shaz shook her head. 'It's not just the victims,' she stated firmly. 'If you read their evidence, in each case their eyes were covered during the attack. In each case, they mention that their assailant verbally abused them continually while he was actually assaulting them. That's more than sheer coincidence.'

Simon wasn't ready to give up. 'Come on, Shaz,' he protested. 'Any bloke who's so powerless he needs to resort to rape to feel good about himself is going to need to talk himself up to it. And as for their eyes being covered – there's nothing in common there except with the first and third where he used their own headbands. Look –' he waved the papers – 'case number two, he pulled her T-shirt over her head and tied a knot in it. Case number four, the rapist had a roll of packing tape that he wound round her head. Way different.' He sat back, a good-natured grin defusing the force of his words.

Tony grinned. 'The perfectly contrived lead into the next subject. Thanks, Simon. Today, I'm going to hand out your first assignment, the preamble to which is the beginner's guide to signature versus MO. Anybody know what I'm talking about?'

Kay Hallam, the other woman on the team, raised her hand half a dozen inches and looked questioningly at Tony. He nodded. She tucked her light brown hair behind her ears in a gesture he'd come to recognize as Kay's keynote mechanism for looking feminine and vulnerable to defuse criticism, particularly when she was about to make a point she was absolutely sure of. 'MO is dynamic, signature is static,' she said.

'That's one way of putting it,' Tony said. 'However, it's probably a bit too technical for the plods among us,' he added with a grin, pointing his finger one by one at the other five. He pushed back his chair and started moving restlessly round the room as he talked. 'MO means *modus operandi*. Latin. The way of doing. When we use it in a criminal context, we mean the series of actions that the perpetrator committed in the process of achieving his goal, the crime. In the early days of profiling, police officers, and to a large degree psychologists, were very literal about their idea of a serial offender. It was somebody who did pretty much the same things every time to achieve pretty much the same results. Except that they usually showed escalation, moving, say, from assaulting a prostitute to beating a woman's brains out with a hammer.

'As we discovered more, though, we realized we weren't the only ones capable of learning from our mistakes. We were dealing with criminals who were intelligent and imaginative enough to do exactly the same. That meant we had to get our heads round the idea that the MO was something that could change quite drastically from one offence to the next because the offender found that a particular course of action wasn't very effective. So he'd adapt. His first murder could be a strangulation, but maybe our killer feels that took too long, was too noisy, frightened him too much, stressed him rather than allowing him to enjoy his fulfilment. Next time out, he smashes her skull in with a crowbar. Too messy. So number three, he stabs. And the investigators write them off as three separate killings because the MO looks so different.

'What doesn't change is what we call, for the sake of giving it a name, the signature. The sig, for short.' Tony stopped pacing and leaned against the window sill. 'The sig doesn't change because it's the *raison d'être* of the offence. It's what gives the perpetrator his sense of satisfaction.

'So what does this signature consist of? Well, it's all the bits of behaviour that exceed what is actually necessary to commit the crime. The ritual of the offence. To satisfy the perpetrator, the signature elements have to be acted out every time he goes out on a mission, and they have to be performed in the same style every time. Examples of signature in a killer might be things like: does he strip the victim? Does he make a neat pile of the victim's clothes? Does he use cosmetics on the victim after death? Is he having sex with the victim postmortem? Is he performing some kind of ritualistic mutilation like cutting off their breasts or penises or ears?'

Simon looked faintly queasy. Tony wondered how many murder victims he'd seen so far. He would have to grow a thicker skin or else be prepared to put up with the jibes of colleagues who would enjoy watching the profiler lose his lunch over another vitiated victim. 'A serial offender must accomplish signature activities to fulfil himself, to make the act meaningful,' Tony continued. 'It's about meeting a variety of needs – to dominate, to inflict pain, to provoke distinct responses, to achieve sexual release. The means can vary, but the end remains constant.'

He took a deep breath and tried to keep his mind off the very particular variations he'd seen at first hand. 'For a killer whose pleasure comes from inflicting pain and hearing victims scream, it's immaterial whether he . . .' his voice faltered as irresistible images climbed into his head. 'Whether he . . .' They were all looking at him now and he desperately struggled to look momentarily distracted rather than shipwrecked. 'Whether he . . . ties them up and cuts them, or whether he . . .'

'Whether he whips them with wire,' Shaz said, her voice casual, her expression reassuring.

'Exactly,' Tony said, recovering fast. 'Nice to see you've got such a tender imagination, Shaz.'

'Typical woman, eh?' Simon said with a grunt of laughter.

Shaz looked faintly embarrassed. Before the joke could escalate, Tony continued. 'So you might have two bodies whose physical conditions are very different. But when you examine the scenario, things have been done that were additional to the act of killing and the ultimate gratification has been the same. That's your signature.'

He paused, his control firmly in place again, and looked around, checking he was taking them all with him. One of the men looked dubious. 'At its most simplistic,' he said, 'think about petty criminals. You've got a burglar who steals videos. That's all he goes for, just videos, because he's got a fence who gives him a good deal. He robs terraced houses, going in through the back yard. But then he reads in the local paper that the police are warning people about the video thief who comes in through the back yard, and they're setting up neighbourhood watch teams to keep a special eye on back alleys. So he abandons his terraced houses and instead he goes for between-the-wars semis and gets in through the side windows in the downstairs hall. He's changed his MO. But he still only nicks the videos. That's his signature.'

The doubter's face cleared. Now he'd grasped it. Gratified, Tony picked up a stack of papers divided into six bundles. 'So we have to learn to be inclusive when we're considering the possibility of a serial offender. Think "linking through similarity", rather than "discounting through difference".'

He stood up again and walked around among their work tables, gearing himself up to the crucial part of the session. 'Some senior police officers and profilers have a hypothesis that's more confidential than the secrets of the Masonic square,' he said, capturing their attention again. 'We believe there could be as many as half a dozen undetected serial killers who have been operating in Britain over the past ten years. Some could have claimed upwards of ten victims. Thanks to the motorway network and the historic reluctance of police forces to exchange information, nobody has sat down and made the crucial connections. Once we're up and running, this will be something we'll be considering as and when we have time and staff available to look at it.' Raised eyebrows and muttering filled his momentary pause.

'So what we're doing here is a dummy run,' Tony explained. 'Thirty missing teenagers. They're all real cases, culled from a dozen forces over the last seven years. You've got a week to examine the cases in your spare time. Then you'll have the chance to present your own theories as to whether any of them have sufficient common factors to give us grounds for suspicion that they might be the work of a serial offender.' He handed them each a bundle of photostats, giving them a few moments to flick through.

'I should emphasize that this is merely an exercise,' he cautioned them, walking back to his seat. 'There's no reason to suppose that any of these girls or lads has been abducted or killed. Some of them may well be dead now, but that's probably got more to do with the attrition of life on the street than foul play. The common factor that links them is that none of these kids were regarded by their families as the kind who would run away. The families all claimed the missing teenagers were happy at home, there had been no serious arguments and there were no significant problems with school. Although one or two of them had some history of involvement with the police or social services, there weren't any current difficulties at the time of the disappearances. However, none of the missing kids subsequently made contact with home. In spite of that, it's likely that most of them made for London and the bright lights.'

He took a deep breath and turned to face them. 'But there could be another scenario lurking in there. If there is, it'll be our job to find it.'

Excitement started like a slow burn in Shaz's gut, powerful enough to dim the memories of what she'd read about Tony's last close encounter with a killer. This was her first chance. If there were undiscovered murder victims out there, she would find them. More than that, she would be their advocate. And their avenger.

Criminals are often caught by accident. He knew that; he'd seen programmes about it on the TV. Dennis Nilsen, killer of fifteen homeless young men, found out because human flesh blocked the drains; Peter Sutcliffe, the Yorkshire Ripper, despatcher of thirteen women, nicked because he'd stolen a set of number plates to disguise his car; Ted Bundy, necrophiliac murderer of as many as forty young women, finally arrested for speeding past a police car at night with no lights. This knowledge didn't frighten him, but it added an extra *frisson* to the adrenaline buzz that inevitably accompanied his fire-setting. His motives might be very different from theirs, but the risk was almost as great. The once soft leather driving gloves were always damp with his nervous sweat.

Somewhere around one in the morning, he parked his car in a carefully chosen spot. He never left it on a residential street, understanding the insomnia of the elderly and the late-night revels of the young. Instead, he chose the car parks of DIY stores, the waste ground beside factories, the forecourts of garages closed for the night. Secondhand car pitches were best; nobody noticed an extra car there for an hour or two in the small hours.

He never carried a holdall either, sensing it to be suspicious at that time of night. A policeman spotting him would have no cause to think he'd been out burgling. And even if a bored night-beat bobby fancied the diversion of getting him to turn out his pockets, there wouldn't be much to arouse suspicion. A length of string, an old-fashioned cigarette lighter with a brass case, a packet of cigarettes with two or three missing, a dog-eared book of matches with a couple remaining, yesterday's newspaper, a Swiss Army knife, a crumpled oil-stained handkerchief, a small but powerful torch. If that was grounds for arrest, the cells would be full every night.

He walked the route he'd memorized, staying close to the walls as he moved silently down empty streets, his blank-soled bowling shoes making no sound. After a few minutes, he came to a narrow alley which led to the blind side of a small industrial estate he'd had his eye on for a while. It had originally been a ropeworks and consisted of a group of four turn-of-the-century brick buildings which had recently been converted to their present uses. An auto electrician's sat next to an upholstery workshop, opposite a plumbing supplier and a bakery that made biscuits from a recipe allegedly as old as the York Mystery plays. He reckoned anyone who got away with charging such ridiculous prices for a poxy packet of gritty biscuits deserved to have their factory razed to the ground, but there wasn't enough flammable material there for his needs.

Tonight, the upholstery workshop was going to go up like a Roman candle.

Later, he'd thrill to the sight of yellow and crimson flames thrusting their long spikes into the plumes of grey and brown smoke billowing up from the blazing cloth and the wooden floors and beams of the elderly building. But for now, he had to get inside.

He'd made his preparations earlier that day, dropping a carrier bag into a rubbish bin by the side door of the workshop. Now he retrieved it and took out the sink plunger and the tube of superglue. He walked round the outside of the building until he was outside the toilet window, where he stuck the plunger to the window. He waited a few minutes to be certain the contact adhesive had hardened, then he gripped the plunger with both hands, braced himself and gave a sharp tug. The glass broke with a tiny tinkle, the fragments falling on the outside of the window, just as they would if it had exploded from the heat. He tapped the plunger smartly against the wall to shatter the circle of glass, leaving only a thin ring still glued to the rubber. That didn't worry him; there would be no reason for any forensic expert to reconstruct the window and reveal a missing circle of glass at the heart of the shards. That done, he was inside within a few minutes. There was, he knew, no burglar alarm.

He took out the torch and flipped it quickly on and off to check his position, then emerged into the corridor that led along the back of the main work space. At the end, he recalled, were a couple of large cardboard boxes of scrap material that local handicraft hobbyists bought for coppers. No reason for fire investigators to doubt it was a place where workers might hang out for a sly fag.

It was a matter of moments to construct his incendiary device. First he opened up the cigarette lighter and rubbed the string with the wadding which he'd previously saturated with lighter fluid. Then he put the string at the centre of a bundle of half a dozen cigarettes held loosely together with an elastic band. He placed his incendiary so that the string fuse lay along the edge of the nearest cardboard box, then laid the oily handkerchief beside it with some crumpled newspaper. Finally, he lit the cigarettes. They would burn halfway down before the string ignited. That in its turn would take a little while to get the boxes of fabric smouldering. But by the time they'd caught hold, there wouldn't be any stopping his fire. It was going to be some blaze.

He'd been saving this one up, knowing it would be a beauty. Rewarding, in more ways than one.

Betsy checked her watch. Ten minutes more, then she would break up Suzy Joseph's junket with a fictitious appointment for Micky. If Jacko wanted to carry on charming, that was up to him. She suspected he'd rather seize the opportunity to escape. He'd have finished filming the latest *Vance's Visit* the night before, so he'd be off on one of his charity stints at one of the specialist hospitals where he worked as a volunteer counsellor and support worker. He'd be gone by mid-afternoon, leaving her and Micky to a peaceful house and a weekend alone.

'Between Jacko and the Princess of Wales, you get no peace these days when you've got a terminal illness,' she said out loud. 'I'm the lucky one,' she went on, moving from bureau to filing cabinet as she cleared her desk in preparation for a guilt-free weekend. 'I don't have to listen to the Authorized Version for the millionth time.' She imitated Jacko's upbeat, dramatic intonation. '"I was lying there, contemplating the wreck of my dreams, convinced I had nothing left to live for. Then, out of the depths of my depression, I saw a vision." ' Betsy made the sweeping gesture she'd seen Jacko deploy so often with his living arm. ' "This very vision of loveliness, in fact. There, by my hospital bed stood the one thing I'd seen since the accident that made me realize life might be worth living."'

It was a tale that bore almost no relationship to the reality Betsy had lived through. She remembered Micky's first encounter with Jacko, but not because it had been the earth-shaking collision of two stars recognizing their counterparts. Betsy's memories were very different and far less romantic.

It was the first time Micky had been the lead outside broadcast reporter on the main evening news bulletin. She'd been bringing millions of eager viewers the first exclusive interview with Jacko Vance, hero of the hottest human story on the networks. Betsy had watched the broadcast at home alone, thrilled to see her lover the cynosure of ten million pairs of eyes, hugging herself in delight.

The exhilaration hadn't lasted long. They'd been celebrating together in the flickering glow of the video replay when the phone had interrupted their pleasure. Betsy had answered, her voice exuberant with happiness. The journalist who greeted her as Micky's girlfriend drained all the joy from her. In spite of Betsy's frostily vehement denials and Micky's scornful ridicule, both women knew their relationship was poised on the edge of the worst kind of tabloid exposure.

The patient campaign Micky had gone on to wage against the sneak tactics of the hacks was as carefully planned and as ruthlessly executed as any career move she'd ever made. Every night, two separate pairs of bedroom curtains would be closed and lights turned on behind them. The lamps would go off at staggered intervals, the one in the spare room controlled by a timer that Betsy adjusted to a different hour each night. Every morning, the curtains would be drawn back at diverse times, each pair by the same hands that had closed them.

The only places the two women embraced were behind closed curtains out of the line of sight of the window, or in the hallway, which was invisible from outside. If both left the house at the same time, they parted at the bottom of the steps with a cheerful wave and no bodily contact.

Giving the presumed watchers nothing to chew on would have been enough to make most people feel secure. But Micky preferred a more proactive approach. If the tabloids wanted a story, she'd make sure they had one. It would simply have to be a more exciting, more credible and more sexy story than the one they thought they had. She cared far too much for Betsy to take chances with her lover's peace of mind or their relationship.

The morning after the ominous phone call, Micky had a spare hour. She drove to the hospital where Jacko was a patient and charmed her way past the nurses. Jacko seemed pleased to see her, and not only because she came armed with the gift of a miniature AM/FM radio complete with earphones. Although he was still taking strong medication for his pain, he was alert and receptive to any distraction from the tedium of life in his side ward. She spent half an hour chatting lightly about everything except the accident and the amputation, then left, leaning over to give him a friendly peck on the forehead. It had been no hardship; to her surprise, she'd found herself warming to Jacko. He wasn't the arrogant macho man she'd expected, based on her past experience with male sporting heroes. Nor, even more surprisingly, was he wallowing in self-pity. Micky's visits might have started out as cynical self-interest, but within a very short space of time she was sucked in, first by her respect for his stoicism, then by an unexpected pleasure in his company. He might be more interested in himself than in her, but at least he managed to be entertaining and witty with it.

Five days and four visits later, Jacko asked the question she'd been waiting for. 'Why do you keep visiting me?'

Micky shrugged. 'I like you?'

Jacko's eyebrows rose and fell, as if to say, 'That's not enough.'

She sighed and made a conscious effort to hold his speculative gaze. 'I have always been cursed with an imagination. And I understand the drive to be successful. I've worked my socks off to get where I am. I've made sacrifices and I've sometimes had to treat people in a way that, in other circumstances, I'd be ashamed of. But getting to where I want to be is the most important thing in my life. I can imagine how I would feel if a chain of circumstances outside my control cost me my goal. I guess what I feel for you is empathy.'

'Meaning what?' he asked, his face giving nothing away.

'Sympathy without pity?'

He nodded, as if satisfied. 'The nurse reckoned it was because you fancied me. I knew she was wrong.'

Micky shrugged. It was all going so much better than she'd anticipated. 'Don't disillusion her. People distrust motives they can't understand.'

'You're so right,' he said, an edge of bitterness in his voice that she hadn't heard there before, in spite of the ample reason. 'But understanding doesn't always make it possible to accept something.'

There was more, much more behind his words. But Micky knew when to leave well alone. There would be plenty of opportunity to broach that subject again. When she left that day, she was careful to make sure the nurse saw her kiss him goodbye. If this story was to be credible, it needed to leak out, not be broadcast. And from her own journalistic experience, gossip spread through a hospital faster than legionnaire's disease. From there to the wider community only took one carrier.

When she arrived a week later, Jacko seemed remote. Micky sensed violent emotions barely held in check, but couldn't be sure what those feelings were. Eventually, tired of conducting a monologue rather than a conversation, she said, 'Are you going to tell me or are you just going to let your blood pressure rise till you have a stroke?'

For the first time that afternoon, he looked directly into her face. Momentarily, she thought he was in the grip of fever, then she realized it was a fury so powerful that she couldn't imagine how he could contain it. He was so angry he could barely speak, she realized as she watched him struggle to find the words. At last, he conquered his rage by sheer effort of will and said, 'My fucking so-called fiancée,' he growled.

'Jillie?' Micky hoped she'd got the name right. They'd met briefly one afternoon as Micky had been leaving. She had the impression of a slender dark-haired beauty who managed sultry rather than tarty by an inch.

'Bitch,' he hissed, the tendons on his neck tensing like cords beneath the tanned skin.

'What's happened, Jacko?'

He closed his eyes and breathed deeply, his wide chest expanding and emphasizing the asymmetry of his once perfect upper body. 'Dumped me,' he managed at last, his voice thick with anger.

'No,' Micky breathed. 'Oh, Jacko.' She reached out and touched the tight fist with her fingers. She could actually feel the pulse beating in his flesh, so tightly was his hand clenched. His rage was phenomenal, Micky thought, yet his control seemed in no real danger of slipping.

'Says she can't cope with it.' He gave a grating bark of cynical laughter. 'She can't cope with it? How the fuck does she think it is for me?'

'I'm sorry,' Micky said inadequately.

'I saw it in her face, the first time she visited after the accident. No, I knew before that. I knew because she didn't come near me that first day. It took her two days to get her arse in here.' His voice was harsh and guttural, the heavy words falling like blocks of stone. 'When she did come, she couldn't stand the sight of me. It was all over her face. I repelled her. All she could see was what I wasn't any more.' He pulled his fist away and pounded it on the bed.

'More fool her.'

His eyes opened and he glared at her. 'Don't you start. All I need is one more silly bitch patronizing me. I've had that fucking nurse with her artificial cheerfulness all over me. Just don't!'

Micky didn't flinch. She'd won too many confrontations with news editors for that. 'You should learn to recognize respect when you see it,' she flared back at him. 'I'm sorry Jillie hasn't got what it takes to see you through, but you're better off finding that out now than further down the road.'

Jacko looked astonished. For years now, the only person who'd spoken to him with anything except nervous deference was his trainer. 'What?' he squawked, his anger displaced by baffled astonishment.

Micky continued regardless of his response. 'What you have to decide now is how you're going to play it.'

'What?'

'It's not going to stay a secret between the two of you, is it? From what you said, the nurse already knows.

So by tea-time, it's going to be, "Hold the front page." If you want, you can settle for being an object of pity – hero dumped by girlfriend because he's not a proper man any more. You'll get the sympathy vote, and a fair chunk of the Great British Public will spit on Jillie in the street. Alternatively, you can get your retaliation in first and come out on top.'

Jacko's mouth was open, but for a moment no words came. At last, he said in a low voice that fellow members of the Olympic squad would have recognized as a signal for flak jackets, 'Go on.'

'It's up to you. It depends whether you want people to see you as a victim or a victor.'

Micky's level stare felt as much of a challenge as anything that had ever faced him on the field of competition. 'What do you think?' he snarled.

'I'm telling you, man, this is the *sticks*,' Leon said, waving a chicken pakora in a sweeping gesture that seemed to include not only the restaurant but most of the West Riding of Yorkshire as well.

'You've obviously never been to Greenock on a Saturday night,' Simon said drily. 'Believe me, Leon, that makes Leeds look positively cosmopolitan.'

'*Nothing* could make this place cosmopolitan,' Leon protested.

'It's not that bad,' Kay said. 'It's very good for shopping.' Even outside the classroom, Shaz noticed, Kay slipped straight into the conciliatory role, smoothing down her hair as she smoothed down the rough edges in the conversations.

Simon groaned theatrically. 'Oh please, Kay, don't feel you need to glide effortlessly into bland womanly stuff. Go on, make my night, tell me how terrific Leeds is for body-piercing.'

Kay poked her tongue out at him.

'If you don't leave Kay alone, us women might well consider piercing some treasured part of your anatomy with this beer bottle,' Shaz said sweetly, brandishing her Kingfisher.

Simon put his hands up. 'OK. I'll behave, just as long as you promise not to beat me with a chapati.'

There was a moment's silence while the four police officers attacked their starters. The Saturday night curry looked like becoming a regular feature for the quartet, the other two preferring to return to their former home turf rather than explore their new base. When Simon had first suggested it, Shaz hadn't been sure if she wanted to bond that closely with her colleagues. But Simon had been persuasive, and besides, Commander Bishop had been earwigging and she wanted to avoid a black mark for being uncooperative. So she'd agreed and, to her surprise, she'd enjoyed herself, even though she had made her excuses and left before the nightclub excursion that had followed. Now, three weeks into the Job, she found she was actually looking forward to their night out, and not just for the food.

Leon was first to clear his plate, as usual. 'What I'm saying is, it's primitive up here.'

'I don't know,' Shaz protested. 'They've got plenty of good curry houses, the property's cheap enough for me to afford something bigger than a rabbit hutch, and if you want to go from one part of the city centre to another, you can walk instead of sitting on the tube for an hour.'

'And the countryside. Don't forget how easy it is to get out into the countryside,' Kay added.

Leon leaned back in his seat, groaning and rolling his eyes extravagantly like a terrible caricature of a Black and White Minstrel. 'Heathcliff,' he warbled in falsetto.

'She's right,' Simon said. 'God, you're such a cliché, Leon. You should get off the city streets, get some fresh air into your lungs. What about coming out tomorrow for a walk? I really fancy seeing if Ilkley Moor lives up to the song.'

Shaz laughed. 'What? You want to walk about without a hat and see if you catch your death of cold?'

The others joined in her laughter. 'See, man, it's primitive, like I said. Nothing to do but walk about on your own two feet. And shit, Simon, I'm not the one that's a cliché. You know I've been stopped driving home three times since I moved here? Even the Met got a bit more racially enlightened than thinking every black man with a decent set of wheels has to be a drug dealer,' Leon said bitterly.

'They're not stopping you because you're black,' Shaz retorted as he paused to light a cigarette.

'No?' Leon exhaled.

'No, they're stopping you for being in possession of an offensive weapon.'

'What do you mean?'

'That suit, babe. Any sharper and you'd cut yourself getting dressed. You're wearing a blade, of course they're going to stop you.' Shaz held out her hand for Leon to give her five and, amid the hoots of laughter from the other two, he made a rueful face and hit her hand.

'Not as sharp as you, Shaz,' Simon said. She wondered if it was only the heat of the spices that was responsible for the scarlet flush across his normally pale cheekbones.

'Speaking of sharp,' Kay chipped in as their main courses arrived, 'you can't get anything past Tony Hill, can you?'

'He's smart, all right,' Simon agreed, sweeping his wavy dark hair back from his sweating forehead. 'I just wish he'd loosen up a bit. It's like there's a wall there that you get right up to but you can't see over.'

'I'll tell you why that is,' Shaz said, suddenly serious. 'Bradfield. The Queer Killer.'

'That's the one he did that went well and truly pear-shaped, yeah?' Leon asked.

'That's right.'

'It was all hushed up, wasn't it?' Kay said, her intent face reminding Shaz of a small furry animal, cute but with hidden teeth. 'The papers hinted at all sorts of stuff, but they never went into much detail.'

'Believe me,' Shaz said, looking at her half-chicken and wishing she'd gone for something vegetarian, 'you wouldn't want to know the details. If you want to know the whole story, check out the Internet. They weren't constrained by technicalities like good taste or requests from the authorities to keep things under wraps. I'm telling you, if you can read what Tony Hill went through without having second thoughts about what we're doing, you're a fuck of a sight braver than I am.'

There was a moment's silence. Then Simon leaned forward and said confidingly, 'You're going to tell us, aren't you, Shaz?'

He always arrived fifteen minutes ahead of the agreed time because he knew she'd be early. It didn't matter which she he'd chosen, she'd turn up ahead of schedule because she was convinced he was Rumpelstiltskin, the man who could spin twenty-four-carat gold out of the dry straw of her life.

Donna Doyle – no longer the next one but rather the latest one – was no different from the others. As her silhouette appeared against the dim light of the car park, he could hear the clumsy childish music crashing in his head. '*Jack and Jill went up the hill, to fetch a pail of water . . .*'

He shook his head to clear his ears, like a snorkeller surfacing from a coral reef. He watched her approach, moving cautiously between the expensive cars, glancing from side to side, a slight frown creasing her forehead, as if she couldn't work out why her antennae weren't pointing her to his precise position. He could see she'd done her best to look good; the school skirt that had obviously been folded over at the waist to show off shapely legs, the school blouse open one button further than parent or teacher would ever have allowed in public, the blazer over one shoulder, hanging thus to obscure the backpack of school supplies. The make-up was heavier than the night before, its excess weight catapulting her straight into middle age. And her hair glinted glossy black, the swing of the short bob catching the dull gleam of the car park lights.

When Donna was almost level, he pushed open the passenger door of the car. The sudden interior light made her jump even as she registered his shockingly handsome profile cutting a dark line through the bright rectangle. He spoke through his already lowered window. 'Come and sit with me while I tell you what all this is about,' he said conversationally.

Donna hesitated fractionally, but she was too familiar with the open candour of his public face to pause properly for reflection. She slid into the seat next to him and he made sure she saw him carefully not looking at the expanse of thigh her moves had revealed. For the time being, chastity was the best policy. Her smile was coquettish yet innocent as she said, 'When I woke up this morning, I wondered if I'd dreamed it all.'

His answering smile was indulgent. 'I feel like that all the time,' he said, building another course of bricks on the false foundation of fake rapport. 'I wondered if you'd have second thoughts. There are so many things you could do with your life that would be a greater contribution to society than being on TV. Believe me, I know.'

'But you do those things too,' she said earnestly. 'All that charity work. It's being famous makes it possible for TV stars to raise so much money. People pay money to see them. They wouldn't be shelling out otherwise. I want to be able to do that. To be like them.'

The impossible dream. Or rather, nightmare. She could never have been like him, though she had no notion of the real reason why. People like him were so rare it was almost an argument for the existence of God. He smiled benevolently, like the Pope from the Vatican balcony. It pushed all the right buttons. 'Well, perhaps I can help you make a start,' he told her. And Donna believed him.

He had her there, alone, co-operative, in his car, in an underground car park. What could have been easier than to whisk her away to his destination?

Only a fool would think like that, he'd realized long ago, and he was no fool. For a start, the car park wasn't exactly empty. Businessmen and women were checking out of the hotel, stowing suit carriers into executive saloons and reversing out of tight spots. They noticed a lot more than anyone would expect. For another thing, it was broad daylight outside, a city centre festooned with traffic lights where people sat with nothing better to do than pick their noses and stare slack-jawed at the inhabitants of the next car. First, they'd register the car. A silver Mercedes, smart enough to catch the eye and the admiration. Or, of course, the envy. Then they'd clock the flowing letters along the front wing that announced, *Cars for Vance's Visits supplied by Morrigan Mercedes of Cheshire*. Alerted to the possible proximity of celebrity, they'd peer through the tinted windows, trying to identify the driver and passenger. They weren't going to forget that in a hurry, especially if they glimpsed an attractive teenager in the passenger seat. When her photograph appeared in the local paper, they'd remember, no question.

And finally, he'd got a busy day ahead. There was no space in his schedule for delivering her to a place where he could exact what was due. No point in drawing attention to himself by failing to keep appointments, not turning up for the public appearances that were so carefully constructed to give *Vance's Visits* maximum exposure for minimal effort. Donna would have to wait. For both of them, it would be the sweeter for the anticipation. Well, for him, at least. For her, it wouldn't be long before reality turned her breathless expectation into a sick joke.

So he whetted her appetite and kept her on the leash. 'I couldn't believe it when I saw you last night. You'd be absolutely perfect as the co-host. With a two-handed show, we need contrast. Dark-haired Donna, fair-haired Jacko. Petite Donna, hulking great brute Jacko.' He grinned, she giggled. 'What we're working on is a new game show involving parent and child teams. But the teams don't know they're in the show until we turn up to whisk them off. A total surprise, like *This is Your Life*. That's part of the reason why we need to be so sure that whoever I end up working with is absolutely trustworthy. Total discretion, that's the key.'

'I can keep my mouth shut,' Donna said earnestly. 'Honest. I never told a living soul about coming here to meet you. My mate that was at the opening last night with me, when she asked what we were talking about for so long, I just said I was asking whether you had any advice for me if I wanted to break into TV.'

'And did I?' he demanded.

She smiled, beguiling and seductive. 'I told her you said I should get some qualifications behind me before I made any decisions about a career. She doesn't know enough about you to realize you'd never come out with all that boring shit that I get off my mum.'

'Good thinking,' he told her appreciatively. 'I can promise you I'll never be boring, that's for sure. Now, the problem I've got is that I'm desperately busy for the next couple of days. But I've got Friday morning free, and I can easily set up some screen tests for you. We've got a rehearsal studio up in the north-east and we can work there.'

Her lips parted, her eyes glowed in the dimness of the car interior. 'You mean it? I can be on telly?'

'No promises, but you look the part and you've got a beautiful voice.' He shifted in his seat so he could fix her with a direct gaze. 'All I need to prove to myself is that you really can keep a secret.'

'I told you,' Donna replied, consternation on her face. 'I've said nothing to anybody.'

'But can you keep that up? Can you stay silent until Thursday night?' He put his hand inside his jacket and produced a rail ticket. 'This is a train ticket for Five Walls Halt in Northumberland. On Thursday, you catch the 3.25 Newcastle train from the station here, then at Newcastle, you change to the 7.50 for Carlisle. When you come out of the station, there's a car park on the left. I'll be waiting there in a Land Rover. I can't get out to meet you on the platform because of commercial confidentiality, but I'll be there in the car park, I promise. We'll put you up for the night, then first thing in the morning, you do the screen test.'

'But my mum'll panic if I stay out all night and she doesn't know where I am,' she protested reluctantly.

'You can phone her as soon as we get to the studio complex,' he told her, his voice rich in reassurance. 'Let's face it, she probably wouldn't let you take the screen test if she knew, would she? I bet she doesn't think working in TV is a proper job, does she?'

As usual, he'd calculated to perfection. Donna knew her ambitious mother wouldn't want her to throw her university prospects away to be a game-show bimbo. Her worried look disappeared and she peered up at him from under her eyebrows. 'I won't say a word,' she promised solemnly.

'Good girl. I hope you mean that. All it takes is one wrong word and a whole project can crash. That costs money, and it costs people's jobs too. You might say something in confidence to your best friend, but she'll tell her sister, and her sister will tell her boyfriend, and the boyfriend will tell his best mate over a frame of snooker, and the best mate's sister-in-law just happens to be a reporter. Or a rival TV company executive. And the show's dead. And your big chance goes with it. Let me tell you something. At the start of your career, you only get one bite of the cherry. You screw up, and no one will ever hire you again. You have to have a lot of success under your belt before the TV bosses forgive a bit of failure.' He leaned forward and rested a hand on her arm as he spoke, invading her space and making her feel the sexual thrill of his dangerous edge.

'I understand,' Donna said with all the intensity of a fourteen-year-old who thought she was really a grown-up and couldn't understand why the adults wouldn't admit her into their conspiracy. The promise of an entrée into that world was what made her so ready to swallow something as preposterous as his set-up.

'I can rely on you?'

She nodded. 'I won't let you down. Not with this or anything else.' The sexual innuendo was unmistakable. She was probably still a virgin, he reckoned. Something about her avidity told him so. She was offering herself up to him, a vestal sacrifice.

He leaned closer and kissed the soft, eager mouth that instantly opened under his primly closed lips. He drew back, smiling to soften her obvious disappointment. He always left them wanting more. It was the oldest show-biz cliché in the world. But it worked every time.

Carol wiped up the remaining traces of chicken jalfrezi with the last chunk of nan bread and savoured the final mouthful. 'That,' she said reverently, 'was to die for.'

'There's more,' Maggie Brandon said, pushing the heavy casserole dish towards her.

'I'd have to wear it,' Carol groaned. 'There's no room inside.'

'You can take some home with you,' Maggie told her. 'I know the kind of daft hours you'll be working. Cooking's the last thing you'll have time for. When John was made up to DCI, I considered asking his Chief Constable if the family could move into the cells at Scargill Street since that seemed to be the only way his kids would ever get to see him.'

John Brandon, Chief Constable of East Yorkshire Police, shook his head and said affectionately, 'She's a terrible liar, my wife. She only says these things to guilt-trip you into working so hard there'll be nothing left for me to worry about in your whole division.'

Maggie snorted. 'As if! How do you think he ended up looking like that, eh?'

Carol gave Brandon a shrewd look. It was a good question. If ever a man had been born with a graveyard face, it was Brandon. His countenance was all verticals, long and narrow; lines in his hollow cheeks, lines between his brows, aquiline nose, iron-grey hair straight as the grid line on a map. Tall and thin, with the beginnings of a stoop, all he needed was a scythe to audition for Death. She considered her options. It might be 'John' tonight, but on Monday morning it would be back to, 'Mr Brandon, *sir*.' Better not push her informal relationship with the boss too far. 'And there was me thinking it was marriage,' she said innocently.

Maggie roared with laughter. 'Diplomatic as well as quick, eh?' she got out at last, reaching across to pat her husband's shoulder. 'You did well to get Carol to abandon the fleshpots of Bradfield for the back of beyond, my love.'

'Speaking of which, how are you settling in?' Carol asked.

'Well, this is a police house,' Maggie told her, waving a hand at the brilliant white walls and paintwork, a depressing contrast to the hand-marbled paintwork Carol remembered from their Bradfield dining room. 'But it'll have to do us. We've rented out the house in Bradfield, you know? John's only got another five years till he has his thirty in, and we want to go back there. It's where our roots are, where our friends are. And the kids will all be out of school by then, so it's not like they'll be uprooted again.'

'What Maggie isn't saying is that she feels a bit like a Victorian missionary among the Hottentots,' Brandon said.

'Well, you've got to admit, East Yorkshire's a bit different from Bradfield. Plenty of scenery, but there's not a decent theatre within half an hour's drive of here. There seems to be only one bookshop on the whole patch that sells more than the bestsellers. And as for opera – you can forget it!' Maggie protested, getting to her feet and gathering the empty plates.

'Don't you feel happier about the kids growing up away from the influence of the inner city? Out of the reaches of the drug lords?' Carol asked.

Maggie shook her head. 'They're so insular round here, Carol. Back in Bradfield, the kids had friends from all kinds of backgrounds – Asian, Chinese, Afro-Caribbean. Even one Vietnamese lad. Out here, you stick to your own. There's nothing to do except hang around on street corners. Frankly, I'd take a chance on them having the sense to stay out of trouble in the inner city as a trade-off for all the opportunities they had in Bradfield. This country living is well over-rated.' She marched through to the kitchen.

'Sorry,' Carol said. 'Didn't realize it was such a sore point.'

Brandon shrugged. 'You know Maggie. She likes to get it off her chest. Give it a few more months, she'll be running the village, happy as a pig. The kids like it well enough. How about you? What's the cottage like?'

'I love it. The couple I bought it from did an immaculate restoration job.'

'I'm surprised they were selling it, then.'

'Divorce,' Carol said succinctly.

'Ah.'

'I think they were both more upset about losing the cottage than the marriage. You and Maggie will have to come over for a meal.'

'If you ever find the time to shop,' Maggie said darkly, walking back in with a large cafetiere.

'Well, worst comes to worst, I'll send Nelson out to bring us a rabbit back.'

'He's enjoying the opportunities for murder that living in the country offers?' Maggie asked drily.

'He thinks he's died and gone to feline heaven. You

might crave the inner city, but he's turned into a country boy overnight.'

Maggie poured coffee for John and Carol, then said, 'I'm going to leave you pair to it, if you don't mind. I know you're dying to talk shop and I promised Karen I'd pick her up after the pictures in Seaford. There's enough coffee there to keep you both awake till dawn, and if you feel peckish in a bit, there's home-made cheesecake in the fridge. But Andy's due back around ten, so you'd better help yourself before then. I swear that lad's got worms. That or hollow legs.' She swooped down on Brandon and gave him an affectionate peck on the cheek. 'Enjoy yourselves.'

Unable to resist the feeling that she'd been set up by professionals, Carol took a sip of her coffee and waited. When it came, Brandon's question was hardly a surprise. 'So how are you settling in on the ground?' His voice was casual, but his eyes were watchful.

'Obviously, they're wary of me. Not only am I a woman, which on the evolutionary scale in East Yorkshire comes somewhere between a ferret and a whippet, but I'm also the Chief Constable's nark. Brought in from the big city to crack the whip,' she said ironically.

'I was afraid you'd get lumbered with that,' Brandon said. 'But you must have known how it would be when you took the job on.'

Carol shrugged. 'It's not come as a surprise. But there's been rather less of it than I anticipated. Maybe they're all still on their best behaviour, but I think the Seaford Central Division CID are not a bad crew. Because they were stuck out in the boondocks before the reorganization and nobody was paying much attention, they've got a bit lazy, a bit sloppy. I suspect one or two might be spending a bit more than they're earning, but

I don't think there's any deep-rooted, systemic corruption.'

Brandon nodded, satisfied. Trusting Carol Jordan's judgement had been a steep learning curve for him, and he'd known instinctively she was the one senior officer he wanted to tempt away from Bradfield. With her setting the tone in Seaford, word would spread through other divisions and the CID culture would adapt accordingly, given time. Time and a certain amount of stick which Brandon wasn't afraid to apply. 'Anything on the books that's causing you a problem?'

Carol finished her coffee and poured herself another cup, offering the pot to Brandon, who refused with a shake of the head. She frowned in thought, gathering her arsenal of information. 'There is something,' she said. 'Since we're talking informally?'

Brandon nodded.

'Well, I noticed going through the overnights that there seemed to be a positive spate of unexplained fires and query arsons. All at night, all in unoccupied premises like schools, factories, cafés, warehouses. None of them very big in itself, but taken together, you're looking at a lot of damage. I put a team together to re-interview the previous victims, see if we could find any connection – financially or insurance-wise. Zilch. But I went myself to talk to the local fire chief, and he produced a series of incidents going back about four months. None of the fires could be absolutely, positively put down as arson, but circumstantially, he reckons there have been something between six and a dozen possible deliberate fires per month on his patch,' Carol said.

'A serial arsonist?' Brandon said softly.

'It's hard to imagine another interpretation,' Carol agreed.

'And you want to do what, exactly?'

'I want to catch him,' she said with a grin.

'Well, what else?' Brandon smiled. 'Did you have something specific in mind?' he continued mildly.

'I want to carry on working with the team I've already got on it, and I want to do a profile.'

Brandon frowned. 'Bring someone in?'

'No,' Carol said sharply. 'There's not really enough evidence to justify the expense. I think I can take a pretty good stab at it myself.'

Brandon looked impassively at Carol. 'You're not a psychologist.'

'No, but I learned a lot last year, working with Tony Hill. And since then, I've read everything about profiling I could find.'

'You should have applied for the National Task Force,' Brandon said, keeping his eyes fixed on her.

Carol felt her skin burn. She hoped the wine and the coffee would account for her heightened colour. 'I don't think they were looking for officers of my rank,' she said. 'Apart from Commander Bishop, there's no one above the rank of sergeant. Besides, I prefer to work a patch, get to know the people and the ground.'

'They're due to be up and running a full case-load in a few weeks,' Brandon continued implacably. 'Maybe they'd welcome something like this to cut their teeth on before then.'

'Maybe they would,' Carol said. 'But it's my case. And I'm not ready to let it go.'

'Fine,' Brandon said, interested that Carol had already developed such fierce possessiveness about the work of the East Yorkshire force. 'But keep me posted, yes?'

'Of course,' Carol said. Her sense of relief, she told herself, was entirely because she would now have the chance to cover herself and her team in glory when they cracked the case. Deep down, though, she knew she was lying.

Sleeping in what the estate agent had referred to as the guest bedroom of Shaz's flat would have been beyond most people, particularly if they were the sort who needed to read a few pages before they could nod off. While the bookcase in the living room contained an innocuous mix of middlebrow middle-of-the-road modern fiction, the shelves in the room Shaz thought of as her study held only hard-core horror, most of it masquerading as textbooks. There were a few novels by pathologists of psychopathy and anatomists of agony like Barbara Vine and Thomas Harris, but most of Shaz's working library was both stranger and more brutal than fiction ever dared to be. If there had been a vocational course for serial killers, her library would have comprised the set books.

The lowest shelves held those items which mildly embarrassed her – pulp true-crime biographies of notorious serial killers with lurid nicknames, sensational accounts of careers that had robbed hundreds of people of their trust and their lives. Arranged above these were the more respectable versions of those same lives, portentous renderings that provided thoughtful revelations and insights sociological, psychological and sometimes illogical.

Next, at eye-level for anyone sitting at the table that held Shaz's notepads and laptop, were the battle stories of the veterans of the war against serial offenders. Since it was the best part of twenty years since the infancy of offender profiling, the pioneers had been trickling into retirement for a few years now, each determined to augment his pension with graphic accounts of his contribution to the latest soft science with the case histories of his notable successes and a passing gloss over his failures. They were, thus far, all men.

Above these autobiographies was the serious stuff; books with titles like *The Psychopathology of Sexual Homicide*, *Crime Scene Analysis* and *Serial Rape: A Clinical Study*. The top shelf gave the only indications that she aspired to be hunter rather than hunted, with its selection of legal texts, including a couple of guides to the Police and Criminal Evidence Act. It was a comprehensive collection and Shaz hadn't amassed it in the mere couple of months since she'd won her place on the task force; it had been years in the building, helping her prepare for the day she'd always been convinced would come, when she'd be called upon to bring her very own notorious killer to book. If textual familiarity alone caught criminals, Shaz would have had the best arrest record in the country.

She had begged off the nightclub run following the curry in spite of the blandishments of the other three. It wasn't just that she had never been a great one for clubbing. Tonight, her spare room was infinitely more tempting than anything a DJ or a barman had to offer. The truth was, she'd been in a ferment all evening, eager to get back to her computer and to finish the comparisons she'd begun to run through her database that afternoon. In the three days since Tony had set their assignment, Shaz had spent every spare moment working her way through the thirty sketchy sets of case notes. At last, the opportunity had come to put into practice all the theories and tricks of the trade she'd picked up in her reading. She'd read the papers from start to finish, not once, but three times. Not until she was fairly sure she had them well differentiated in her head did she approach her computer.

The database Shaz used hadn't represented the leading

edge of software development way back when she'd copied it from a fellow student, and now it was practically a candidate for display in a computing museum. But while it might not have all the latest bells and whistles, it was more than capable of performing what she needed. It displayed the material clearly, it allowed her to create her own categories and criteria for sorting the information, and she found its procedures in tune with her instincts and logic and thus easy to use. She'd been inputting data since early that morning, so focused on her work that she hadn't even left the screen to cook lunch, settling instead for a banana and half a packet of digestive biscuits, upending her laptop afterwards to remove the crumbs from the keyboard.

Now, back in front of her screen, stripped of her glad rags and scrubbed clean of her make-up, Shaz was happy. The mouse pointer flickered as fingers clicked on buttons, summoning up menus that interested her far more than anything on offer at the restaurant. She sorted the so-called runaways by age and printed out the results. She followed the same steps for geographical area, physical type, previous police contact, various permutations on their domestic situation, drink and drugs experience, known sexual contacts and interests. Not that the investigating officers had been much concerned with their hobbies.

Shaz pored over the print-outs, reading them individually then spreading them over the desktop so she could more readily compare notes. As she gazed at the printed lists, the slow burn of excitement began in the pit of her stomach. She scrutinized them one more time, double-checking against the photographs in the files to make sure she wasn't willing something into existence that wasn't there. 'Oh, you beauty,' Shaz exclaimed softly, letting out a long sigh.

She closed her eyes and took a deep breath. When she looked again, it was still there. A cluster of seven girls. First, the positive similarities. They all had bobbed dark hair and blue eyes. They were all fourteen or fifteen years old, between 5'2" and 5'4" tall. They had all lived at home with one or both parents. In each case, their friends and family had told the police they were baffled at the girl's disappearance, convinced that she had no real reason to run away. In every instance, the girls had taken almost nothing with them, though in each case, at least one change of clothes appeared to have gone missing with them, which was the main reason why the police hadn't seriously considered them as possible victims of abduction or murder. Reinforcing that view were the times of the disappearances. In each case, the girl concerned had set off for school as usual but had never arrived. She'd also given a false explanation of where she'd be spending the evening. And, although this couldn't be quantified in a way the computer could digest, they were all of a similar type. There was a flirta-tious sensuality in their looks, a knowing quality in the way they embraced the camera that indicated they had left childhood innocence behind. They were sexy, whether they knew it or not.

Next, the negative similarities. None of the seven had ever been in care. None had ever been in trouble with the police. Friends admitted to a bit of recreational drinking, maybe even the occasional joint or even a dab of speed. But no significant drug usage. In none of the seven cases was there any hint that the girls might have been engaged in prostitution or the victims of sexual abuse.

There were problems with the cluster, of course. Three had current boyfriends, four did not. The geographical locations were unconnected – Sunderland was the furthest north, Exmouth the most southerly point. In between were Swindon, Grantham, Tamworth, Wigan and Halifax. The reports also spanned six years. The intervals between the disappearances were not constant, nor did they seem to diminish as time went by, which Shaz would have expected if she were really dealing with the victims of a serial killer.

On the other hand, there might be girls she didn't know about yet.

When Shaz woke early that Sunday morning, she tried to will herself back to sleep. She knew there was only one thing she could do that would advance her search for connections among her theoretical victim cluster and that single task wasn't one that could be hurried. When she'd gone to bed around midnight, she'd promised herself she would achieve it with a lunchtime phone call. But lying wide awake with a racing brain at quarter to seven, she knew she couldn't hold out that long.

Irritated by her inability to make progress except at someone else's hands, she threw back the covers. Half an hour later, she was accelerating up the long incline where the M1 began.

Showering, dressing and swallowing a coffee with the radio news in the background had kept thought at arm's length. Now that the empty black three-lane strip stretched out before her, she couldn't hide behind distraction. The radio presenter's voice wasn't enough on its own. Not even Tony Hill's words of wisdom could hold her today. Impatiently, Shaz pushed a cassette of operatic arias into the stereo and gave up the pretence of concentration. For the next two and a half hours, she had nothing to do but run memories through her mind like old movies on a rainy Sunday.

It was almost ten when she drove down the ramp to the Barbican complex's underground car park. She was pleased to see the car park attendant clearly remembered her, as she'd hoped, though he looked startled to see her face smiling uncertainly round the door of his office. 'Hello, stranger,' he said cheerfully. 'We've not seen you around for a long time.'

'I've moved up to Leeds,' she said, carefully avoiding any hint of how recent her move had been. It had been more than eighteen months since she'd last been here, but the reasons for that were nobody's business but hers.

'Chris didn't say to expect you,' the car park attendant said, getting up from his seat and walking towards her. Shaz backed out of the booth and down the steps as he followed her.

'It was all a bit last-minute,' she said noncommittally, opening her car door.

That seemed to satisfy the attendant. 'Are you here overnight?' he asked, frowning as he scanned the car park for an appropriate space.

'No, I'm not planning on staying long,' Shaz said firmly, starting her engine and crawling down the aisles of cars, following the attendant and slotting the car into the space he indicated.

'I'll let you into the block,' he said as she joined him. 'What's it like up in the frozen north, then?'

Shaz smiled. 'The football's better,' was all she said as he pulled back the massive glass and metal door and waved her inside. Just as well I'm not a terrorist sleeper, she thought as she waited for the lift.

On the third floor, she stopped halfway along the carpeted corridor. Taking a deep breath, she pressed the doorbell. In the silence that followed, she breathed out through her nostrils in a slow steady stream, trying to contain the nervousness that was turning her stomach into a jacuzzi. When she'd almost given up hope, she heard the faint whisper of footfalls. Then the heavy door inched open.

Tousled chestnut hair, bleary brown eyes with dark smudges under them and frown lines between, a snub nose and a yawn half-stifled behind a square hand with blunt, well-manicured fingers appeared in the gap.

For once, Shaz's narrow smile made it as far as her eyes. The blaze of warmth melted Chris Devine, and not for the first time. The hand dropped away from the mouth, but the lips remained parted. Astonishment came first, then delight, then consternation. 'Any chance of a cup of coffee?' Shaz asked.

Chris stepped back uncertainly, pulling the door wide. 'You'd better come in,' she said.

Nothing worth having had ever come easy. He told himself that at regular intervals through two days of torment, though it was not a lesson he was ever likely to forget. His childhood had been scarred with oppressive discipline, any rebelliousness or frivolity stifled by force. He had learned not to show the currents that moved under the surface, to present a bland and acceptable face to whatever adversity people threw in his teeth. Other men might have revealed some traces of the seething excitement that swirled inside whenever he thought of Donna Doyle, but not him. He was too practised at dissemblement. No one ever noticed his mind was ranging through entirely different territory, detached from his surroundings, entirely elsewhere. It was a trait that in the past had saved him pain; now it kept him safe.

In his head he was with her, wondering if she was keeping her promise, imagining the excitement burning in her veins. He thought of her as a changed being, charged with the secret weapon of knowledge, convinced she had the edge on every tabloid astrologer because she knew for sure what her future held.

Of course, hers could not be the same vision as his, he realized that. It would have been hard to imagine two more disparate fantasies, so far apart on the continuum that there could exist no single uniting factor. Apart from orgasm.

Imagining her imagining a false future had its own *frisson* of delight that cohabited and alternated with the sliver of fear that she would not keep her word, that even as he played computer games with the stricken inhabitants of a children's cancer ward, Donna was huddled in a corner of the school cloakroom revealing her secret to her best friend. That was the gamble he took every time. And every time, he'd judged the roll of the dice perfectly. Not once had anyone come looking for him. Well, not in the investigative sense. There had been one time when the distraught parents of a missing teenage girl asked for a TV appeal because, wherever she'd run off to, their daughter would never miss her weekly fix of *Vance's Visits*. Sweet irony, so delicious he'd grown hard for months afterwards just thinking about it. He could hardly have told them that the only way they were ever going to talk to their daughter again was via a medium, could he?

For two nights running, he went to sleep in the early hours and woke at dawn tangled in damp sheets, his pulse racing and his eyes wide open. Whatever the evaporated dream, it robbed him of further sleep, leaving him to prowl the confined spaces of his hotel room, alternately exulting and fretting.

But nothing lasted forever. Thursday evening found him in his Northumberland retreat. Only fifteen minutes' drive from the centre of the city, it was nevertheless as isolated as a Highland croft. Formerly a tiny Methodist chapel that could never have held more than a couple of dozen, it had been bought when it was reduced to four bulging walls and a sagging roof. A team of local builders happy to have the cash in hand renovated it to very particular specifications, never doubting the reasons they were given for the desired features.

He savoured the preparations for his visitor. The sheets were clean, the clothes laid out. The phone was switched off, the answering machine turned down low, the fax shut away inside a drawer. The fibre optics might sing all night with calls for him, but he wouldn't be hearing them till morning. The table was covered with linen so white it seemed to glow in the dark. On it, crystal, silver and porcelain were arranged in traditional patterns. Red rosebuds in an engraved crystal vase, candles splendid in simple Georgian silver. Donna would be captivated. Of course, she wouldn't realize that it would be the last time she'd ever use cutlery.

He looked around, checking everything was as it should be. The chains and leather straps were all out of sight, the silken gag tucked away, the carpentry bench innocent of tools except for the permanently mounted vice. He had designed the workbench himself, all the tools arrayed on a solid piece of wood like the drop leaf of a table attached to the far end of the bench at ninety degrees to the work surface.

One last glance at his watch. Time to drive the Land Rover across the rutted field track to the empty B-road that would take him to Five Walls Halt with its isolated railway station. He lit the candles and smiled with sheer pleasure, confident now that she would have kept faith and silence alike.

Won't you come into my parlour, said the spider to the fly?

Tim Coughlan had finally had his prayers answered. He'd found the perfect spot. The loading bay was slightly less wide than the factory proper, leaving a recess about seven feet square at one end. At first glance, it looked as if the alcove was blocked off by flattened cardboard cartons stacked on their ends. If anyone had bothered to look more closely, they would have noticed that the cartons weren't tightly packed and that, with a little effort, it wouldn't be too hard to squeeze between them. Anyone inclined to investigate further would have found Tim Coughlan's bedsit, containing a stained and greasy sleeping bag and two carrier bags. The first bag contained one clean T-shirt, one clean pair of socks and one clean pair of underpants. The other held one dirty T-shirt, one dirty pair of socks, one dirty pair of boxer shorts and a pair of shapeless cords that might once have been dark brown but were now the colour of seabirds after the oil slick has trapped them.

Tim slouched in a corner of his space, the sleeping bag scrunched into a cushion beneath his bony buttocks. He was eating chips and curry sauce from a polystyrene container. He had the best part of a litre of cider left to wash it down and send him to sleep. He needed something on the cold nights to carry him forward into oblivion.

It had taken long months living rough on the streets before he'd emerged on the other side of the heroin haze that had robbed him of his life. He'd dropped so low that even drugs were above his reach. That, ironically, was what had saved him. Shivering through cold turkey in a Christmas charity shelter, he'd finally turned the corner. He'd started selling the *Big Issue* on street corners. He'd managed to put together enough cash to buy clothes from charity shops that looked like poverty rather than hopeless homelessness. And he'd managed to find work on the docks. It was casual, poorly paid, cash in hand, the black economy at its gloomiest. But it was a start. And that was when he'd found his spot in the loading bay of an assembly plant too strapped for cash to afford a night watchman.

Since then, he'd managed to save nearly three hundred pounds, stashed in the building society account that was probably his only extant connection to his past. Soon, he'd have enough for the deposit and a month's rent on a proper place to live and enough to spare to feed himself while the dole dragged their feet over his claim.

Tim had hit bottom and nearly drowned. Soon, he was convinced, he'd be ready to swim back up to the daylight. He screwed up the chip container and tossed it into the corner. Then he opened the cider bottle and tipped the contents down his throat in a long series of quick gulps. The notion of savouring it never occurred to him. There was no reason why it should.

Opportunity had seldom knocked at Jacko Vance's door. Mostly, he'd gripped it by the throat and dragged it kicking and screaming to centre stage. He'd realized while he was still a child that the only way he was ever going to come by some luck was if he managed to make it himself. His mother, plagued by a kind of post-natal depression that had made him repugnant to her, had ignored him as far as possible. She hadn't actually been cruel, simply absent in any meaningful sense. His father had been the one who paid attention, most often of a negative sort.

He hadn't long been at school when the handsome child with the floppy blond hair, the hollow cheeks and the huge baffled eyes had realized that there was a point in having dreams, that things could be made to happen. His little-boy-lost appearance worked on some teachers like a blowtorch on an icicle. It didn't take him long to work out that he could manipulate them into playing accessories in his own particular power game. It didn't erase what happened at home, but it gave him an arena where he began to understand the pleasure of power.

Although he traded on his looks, Jacko never relied solely on the power of his charm. It was as if he had a built-in understanding that there would be those who needed different weaponry if they were to succumb. Since he'd had the work ethic instilled into him from the moment he had begun to comprehend the messages of speech, it was never a hardship to him to work for his effect. The sports field was the obvious place for him to focus, since he had a certain natural talent and it offered a wider arena to shine in than the narrow stage of the classroom. It was also an area where effort paid off visibly and spectacularly.

Inevitably, the elements of his behaviour that endeared him to those who had power alienated his contemporaries. Nobody ever loved a teacher's pet. He fought the obligatory fights, winning some and losing a few. When he did lose, he never forgot. Sometimes it took years, but he found ways to exact some sort of satisfactory revenge. Often, the victim of his vengeance

96

never knew Jacko was behind his ultimate humiliation, but sometimes he did.

Everyone on the council estate where he'd grown up remembered how he'd got his own back on Danny Boy Ferguson. Danny Boy had been the bane of Jacko's life between the ages of ten and twelve, picking on him mercilessly. Finally, when Jacko had flown at him in a rage, Danny Boy had smashed him to the ground with one hand held ostentatiously above his head. Jacko's broken nose had healed without trace, but his black rage burned behind the charm that the adults saw.

When Jacko won his first junior British championship, he became an overnight hero on the estate. No one from there had ever had their picture in the national papers before, not even Liam Gascoigne when he dropped that concrete slab on Gladstone Sanders from the tenth floor. It wasn't hard to persuade Danny Boy's girlfriend Kimberley to come up west with him for a night on the town.

He'd wined and dined her for a week, then dumped her. That Sunday night in the local, just as Danny Boy was working up to his fifth pint, Jacko slipped the landlord fifty quid to broadcast over the pub's PA system the tape he'd secretly recorded of Kimberley telling him in graphic detail what a lousy fuck Danny Boy was.

When Micky Morgan had started visiting him in hospital, he'd recognized a kindred spirit. He wasn't sure what she wanted, but he had a strong feeling she wanted something. The day Jillie dumped him and Micky offered to help him out, he became certain.

Five minutes after she walked out of the ward, he hired the private eye. The man was good; the answers came even faster than he'd expected. By the time he read her handiwork in the headlines that screamed across all the tabloids, he understood Micky's motives and knew how best he could use her.

JACK THE LAD LETS LOVE GO! HEARTBREAK HERO! LOVE TORMENT OF TRAGIC JACK! He smiled and read on.

> Britain's bravest man has revealed he's making the greatest sacrifice of all.
>
> Days after he lost his Olympic dream saving the lives of two toddlers, Jacko Vance has broken his engagement to his childhood sweetheart Jillie Woodrow.
>
> Heartbroken Jacko, speaking from the hospital bed where he is recovering from the amputation of his javelin-throwing arm, said, 'I'm setting her free. I'm no longer the man she agreed to marry. It's not fair to expect her to carry on as before. I can't offer her the life we'd expected to have, and the most important thing to me is her happiness.
>
> 'I know she's upset now, but in the long run, she'll come to see I'm doing the right thing.'

Now Jillie could never deny his version of events without making herself look a complete bitch.

Jacko bided his time, playing along with Micky's proffered friendship. Then, when he deemed the moment was right, he struck like a rattler. 'OK, so when's payback day?' he asked, his eyes holding hers.

'Payback day?' she echoed, puzzled.

'The story of my love sacrifice,' he said, larding his words with heavy irony. 'Don't they call tales like that a nine-day wonder?'

'They do,' Micky said, continuing to arrange the flowers she'd brought in the tall vase she'd charmed from the nurse.

'Well, it's ten days now since the media broke the news. Jacko and Jillie are officially no longer headline material. I was wondering when I'd get the account for payment due.' His voice was mild, but looking into his eyes was like staring into a frozen puddle on high moorland.

Micky shook her head and perched on the edge of the bed, her face composed. But he knew her mind was racing, calculating how best to handle him. 'I'm not sure what you mean,' she stalled.

Jacko's smile was laced with condescension. 'Come on, Micky. I wasn't born yesterday. The world you work in, you've got to be a piranha. Favours don't get done in your circles without the full understanding that payback day is lurking somewhere in the background.'

He watched her consider lying and reject it; he waited while she considered the truth and rejected that, too. 'I'll settle for having one in the bank,' she tried.

'That's the way you want to play it, OK,' he said nonchalantly. His left hand suddenly snaked out and seized her wrist. 'But I'd have thought you and your girlfriend were in pretty dire need as of now.'

His large hand encircled her wrist. The sculpted muscles of his forearm stood out in strong relief, a shocking reminder of what he'd lost. The grip wasn't tight against her flesh, but she sensed it was unbreakable as the bracelet of a handcuff. Micky looked up from her wrist to his implacable face and he saw a momentary clutch of fear as she wondered what lay behind his impenetrable eyes. He made his face relax into a ghost of a smile and the instant passed. He saw himself reflected in her eyes, not a trace of sinister showing now. 'What a strange thing to say,' she said.

'It's not just journalists who have contacts,' Jacko said contemptuously. 'When you started taking an interest in me, I returned the compliment. Her name's Betsy Thorne, you've been together more than a year. She acts as your PA but she is also your lover. For Christmas you bought her a Bulova watch from a Bond Street jeweller's. Two weekends ago you shared a twin room overnight at a country house hotel near Oxford. You send her flowers on the twenty-third of each month. I could go on.'

'Circumstantial,' Micky said. Her voice was cool; the skin under his grip felt like a burning ring of flesh. 'And none of your business.'

'It's not the tabloids' business either, is it? But they're digging, Micky. It's only a matter of time. You know that.'

'They can't find what isn't there to be found,' she said, slipping into obstinacy as if it were a tailored blazer.

'They'll find it,' Jacko promised her. 'Which is where I might be able to help.'

'Supposing I did need help . . . what form would your help take?'

He released her wrist. Rather than pull her arm to her and rub it, Micky let it lie where he dropped it. 'Economists say good money drives out bad. It's like that with journalists. You should know. Give them a better story and they'll abandon their sordid little fishing expedition.'

'I won't argue with that. What did you have in mind?'

'What about, "Hospital romance for hero Jacko and TV journo"?' He raised one eyebrow. Micky wondered if he'd practised the gesture before the mirror in adolescence.

'What's in it for you?' she asked, after a moment when they'd each stared appraisingly at the other, as if measuring for romantic congruence.

'Peace and quiet,' Jacko said. 'You have no idea how many women there are out there who want to save me.'

'Maybe one of them would be the right one.'

Jacko laughed, a dry, bitter sound. 'It's the Groucho

Marx principle, isn't it? Not wanting to be a member of any club that would let me in. A woman who's demented enough to think that, a) I need saving and b) that she's the person for the job is by definition the world's worst woman for me. No, Micky, what I need is camouflage. So that when I get out of here – which should be quite soon – I can go about my life without every brain-dead bimbo in Britain thinking I'm her chance at the big time. I don't want someone who feels sorry for me. Until somebody I choose comes along, I could use the erogenous equivalent of a bulletproof vest. Fancy the job?'

Now it was his turn to guess what was really happening behind her eyes. Micky was back in control of herself, maintaining the air of bland interest that would later stand her in good stead as the housebound nation's favourite interviewer. 'I don't do ironing,' was all she said.

'I've always wondered what a PA did,' Jacko said, his smile as wry as his tone.

'You better not let Betsy hear you say that.'

'Deal?'

Jacko covered her hand with his. 'Deal,' she said, turning her hand over and clasping his fingers in hers.

The stench hit Carol as soon as she opened her car door. There was nothing quite as disgusting as barbecued human flesh, and once smelled, it could never be erased from the memory. Trying not to gag too obviously, she walked the short distance to where Jim Pendlebury appeared to be conducting an impromptu press conference under the fire brigade's portable arc lights. She'd spotted the journalists as soon as her driver had turned into the car park, and she'd asked to be dropped nearby, well away from the phalanx of scarlet engines where fire officers were still spraying a smouldering warehouse with water. High above his colleagues, one man on a cherry picker sent a soaring arc of water above their heads on to the flaking remains of the roof. Milling around behind the fire brigade were half a dozen uniformed police officers. One or two watched Carol's arrival with vague interest, but soon turned back to the more absorbing vista of the fag end of the fire.

Carol hung back as Pendlebury gave brief and non-committal answers for the benefit of local radio and press. Once they realized they would get nothing much out of the fire chief at that stage, they dispersed. If any of them paid attention to the blonde in the trench coat, they probably assumed she was another reporter. Only the crime reporters had met Carol so far, and it was too early for this to have graduated from a news headline into a crime story. As soon as the night-shift news reporters called in that the factory fire was not only fatal but also suspected arson, the jackals on the crime beat would have their morning assignments on a plate. One or two of them might even be turfed out of bed as unceremoniously as she had been.

Pendlebury greeted Carol with a grim smile. 'The smell of hell,' he said.

'Unmistakably.'

'Thanks for turning out.'

'Thanks for tipping me off. Otherwise I'd have known nothing about it till I got into the office and read the overnights. And then I'd have missed the joys of a fresh crime scene,' she said wryly.

'Well, after our little chat the other day, I knew this one would be right up your street.'

'You think it's our serial arsonist?'

'I wouldn't have phoned you at home at half past three in the morning if I hadn't been pretty sure,' he said.

'So what have we got?'

'Want to have a look?'

'In a minute. First, I'd appreciate a verbal briefing while I'm in a position to concentrate on what you're saying rather than on what my stomach's doing.'

Pendlebury looked slightly surprised, as if he expected her to take such horrors in her stride. 'Right,' he said, sounding disconcerted. 'We got the call just after two, from one of your patrol cars, actually. They'd been cruising and saw the flames. We had two units here within seven minutes, but the place was well ablaze. Another three tenders were here inside the half-hour, but there was no way we were going to save the building.'

'And the body?'

'As soon as they had the fire damped down at this end of the warehouse – which took about half an hour – the officers became aware of the smell. That was when they called me out. I'm on permanent stand-by for all fatal fires. Your lads called in CID, and I called you.'

'So where is the body?'

Pendlebury pointed to one side of the building. 'As far as we can tell, it was in the corner of the loading bay. There seems to have been a kind of alcove at one end. Looking at the ash, there was probably a load of cardboard stashed at the front of it. We've not been able to get in yet, it's still too hot and too chancy in terms of walls coming down, but from what we can see and what we can smell, I'd say the body's behind or underneath all that wet ash down the back of that recess.'

'There's no doubt in your mind that there's definitely a body in there?' Carol was grasping at straws, and she knew it.

'There's only one thing that smells like roast human, and that's roast human,' Pendlebury said bluntly.

'Besides, I think you can just about see the outline of the body. Come on, I'll show you.'

A couple of minutes later, Carol stood by Pendlebury's side at what he claimed was a safe distance from the smoking ruin. It felt uncomfortably warm to her, but she had learned when to trust the expertise of others during her years in the force. To have hung back would have been insulting. As Pendlebury pointed out the contours of the blackened form the fire and water had left at the end of the loading bay, she found herself irresistibly forming the same conclusion as the fire chief.

'When can the scene-of-crime people start work?' she asked dully.

Pendlebury pulled a face. 'Later this morning?'

She nodded. 'I'll make sure the team's on stand-by.' She turned away. 'This is exactly what I didn't want to happen,' she said, half to herself.

'It was bound to happen sooner or later. Law of averages,' Pendlebury said lightly, falling into step with her as she walked back towards her car.

'We should have been all over this arsonist ages ago,' Carol said, angrily searching through her pockets for a tissue to wipe the wet ash from her trainers. 'It's sloppy policing. He should have been nabbed by now. It's our fault that he's still on the loose to kill people.'

'You're not being fair on yourself,' Pendlebury protested. 'You've only been here five minutes, and you picked up on it right away. You mustn't blame yourself.'

Carol looked up from her attempts at cleaning her shoes and scowled. 'I'm not blaming myself, though maybe we could have put a bit more effort into the case. I'm saying that somewhere along the line the police on this patch have let down the people they're supposed to serve. And maybe you should have been a bit more forceful about making the point to my predecessor that you thought you had a firebug.'

Pendlebury looked shocked. He couldn't remember the last time he'd been criticized to his face by a member of another emergency service. 'I think you're a bit out of order, Chief Inspector,' he said, made pompous by his outrage.

'I'm sorry you feel like that,' Carol said stiffly, standing up and straightening her shoulders. 'But if we're going to have a productive working relationship, there's no room for cosiness at the expense of honesty. I expect you to tell me if we're not keeping our end of the deal. And when I see things I don't like, I'll call them. I don't want to fall out with you about this. I want to catch this guy. But we're not going to make any progress if we all stand around saying it can't be helped that some poor bastard is lying there dead.'

For a moment, they glared at each other, Pendlebury uncertain how to deal with her fiery determination. Then he spread his hands in a conciliatory gesture. 'I'm sorry. You're right. I shouldn't have taken no for an answer.'

Carol smiled and thrust out her hand. 'Let's both try and get it right from now in, OK?'

They shook on it. 'Deal,' he said. 'I'll talk to you later, when the forensics team have been all over it.'

As she drove off, Carol had room for only one thought. She had a serial arsonist who had now become a killer on her patch. Catching him was the only show in town. By the time the forensics team had something positive to tell her, she intended to have a draft profile. By the time the inquest opened, she meant to have a suspect in custody. If John Brandon had thought she was driven when they'd worked together in Bradfield, he was in for a surprise. Carol Jordan was out to prove a lot of points to a lot of people. And if she felt discouraged along the way, the stink that clung to her nostrils would be impetus enough to get her moving again.

Shaz turned over and looked at the clock. Twenty minutes to seven. Only ten minutes since she'd looked at it last. She wasn't going to fall asleep again, not now. If she was honest, she thought as she got out of bed and made for the bathroom, she probably wasn't going to sleep properly until Chris had delivered on her promise.

Asking the favour had been less awkward than she'd expected, Shaz reflected as she sat on the loo and leaned over to turn on the bath taps. Time seemed to have smoothed the rough edges of her relationship with Detective Sergeant Devine until it was back where it had been before misunderstandings and false moves had abraded it to a series of painful snags.

From the start of Shaz's career in the Met, Chris Devine had represented everything Shaz aspired to. There had been only two women in CID at the station where Shaz was based in West London, and Chris was the higher ranking. It was obvious why. She was a good cop with one of the best arrest records in the division. Rock solid in a crisis, hard working, imaginative and incorruptible, she also demonstrably possessed a brain and a sense of humour. Even more importantly, she could be one of the lads without ever letting anyone forget she was a woman.

Shaz had studied her like a specimen under a microscope. Where Chris was, she wanted to be, and she wanted that same respect. Already she'd seen too many women officers dismissed as plonks or slits, and she was determined that would never happen to her. Shaz knew that as a brand new uniformed constable, she was an insignificant dot somewhere in Chris's peripheral vision, but somehow she insinuated herself into the older woman's consciousness until, whenever they were in the station taking refs at the same time, they could invariably be found in a corner of the canteen drinking brutally strong tea and talking shop.

The very day Shaz became eligible for a CID aide posting, she'd submitted her name. Chris's recommendation was enough to swing it and, a few weeks later, Shaz found herself on her first night-shift stakeout with Chris. It took her rather longer to realize that Chris was gay, and had been working on the assumption that Shaz's hot pursuit was sexual rather than professional. The night her sergeant kissed her had been the worst moment of her police career.

For an instant, she'd almost gone along with it, so deep-rooted was her ambition. Then reality had clicked in. Shaz might not have been much good at forming relationships, but she knew enough about herself to be clear that it was very definitely men rather than women that she wasn't connecting with. She'd recoiled from Chris's embrace more vigorously than from a sawn-off shotgun. The aftermath was something neither Shaz nor Chris could recall without an uncomfortable mixture of emotions; humiliation, embarrassment, anger and betrayal. The sensible option would probably have been for one of them to seek a transfer, but Chris wasn't prepared to abandon a patch she knew like her own back garden, and Shaz was too stubborn to give up her first best chance at making it on to a permanent CID appointment.

So they'd established an awkward armistice that allowed them to stay on the same team, though whenever they could avoid working shift together, they did. Six months before Shaz's move to Leeds, Chris had been promoted and transferred to New Scotland Yard. They hadn't spoken from that day until Shaz had fetched up on Chris's doorstep looking for a favour.

Shaz chopped fresh fruit into her muesli and reflected that it had been easier than she'd expected to swallow her pride and ask Chris for help, possibly because Chris had been wrong-footed by the presence in her flat – and, clearly, her bed – of a fingerprint technician Shaz remembered from Notting Hill Gate. When Shaz had explained what she wanted, Chris had agreed immediately, understanding exactly why Shaz was so eager to push far beyond what her course leader expected from his officers. And, again as if fate had taken a hand in Shaz's life, it happened that Chris was off duty the following day, so garnering Shaz's information in the minimal time available would be simple.

As she absently shovelled breakfast into her mouth, she imagined Chris spending her day in the national newspaper archives at Colindale, copying page after page of local papers until she'd covered the period surrounding each of the seven disappearances that had captured Shaz's imagination. Shaz ran her empty cereal bowl under the hot tap with happy anticipation swelling inside. She couldn't say why she was so certain, but she was convinced that the first steps on her journey of proof would be waymarked in the local press.

She'd never been wrong so far. Except, of course, about Chris. But that, she told herself, had been different.

'The kind of cases we'll be working are the ones that leave most police officers feeling edgy. That's because the perpetrators are dancing to a different beat from the rest of us.' Tony looked around, double-checking that they were listening to him rather than shuffling through their papers. Leon looked as if he'd rather be somewhere else, but Tony had grown accustomed to his affectations and no longer took them at face value. Satisfied, he continued. 'Knowing you're dealing with someone who has manufactured their own set of rules is a very unsettling experience for anyone, even trained police officers. Because we come in from the outside to make sense of the bizarre, there's a tendency to lump us as part of the problem rather than the solution, so it's important that the first thing we concentrate on is building a rapport with the investigating officers. You've all come here from CID work – any ideas about the sort of thing that might work?'

Simon jumped straight in. 'Take them out for a pint?' he suggested. The others groaned and catcalled at his predictability.

Tony's smile came nowhere near his eyes. 'Chances are they'll have half a dozen good excuses why they can't come to the pub with you. Any other ideas?'

Shaz raised her pen. 'Work your socks off. If they see you're a grafter, they'll give you some respect.'

'Either that or think you're brown-nosing the bosses,' Leon sneered.

'It's not a bad idea,' Tony said, 'though Leon does have a point. If you're going to go down that road, you also need to demonstrate a complete contempt for everyone over the rank of DCI, which can be wearing, not to say counterproductive.' They laughed. 'What does the trick for me is incredibly simple.' He gave them a last questioning look. 'No? How about flattery?'

A couple nodded sagely. Leon's lip curled and he snorted. 'More brown-nosing.'

'I prefer to think of it as one technique among many in the arsenal of the profiler. I don't use it for personal advancement; I use it for the benefit of the casework,' Tony corrected him mildly. 'I have a mantra that I trot out at every available opportunity.' He shifted his position slightly, but that small change altered his body language from comfortable authority to subordinate. His smile was self-deprecating. 'Of course,' he said ingratiatingly, 'I don't solve murders. It's bobbies that do that.' Then, just as swiftly, he returned to his previous posture. 'It works for me. It might not work for you. But it's never going to do any harm to tell the investigating officers how much you respect their work and how you're just a tiny cog that might make their machine work better.' He paused for a moment. 'You have to tell them this at least five times a day.' They were all grinning now.

'Once you've done that, there's a reasonable chance they'll give you the information you need to draw up your profile. If you can't be bothered making the effort, they're likely to hold as much back as they can get away with because they see you as a rival for the glory of solving a high-profile case. So. You've got the investigating officers on your side, and you've got your evidence. It's time to work on the profile. First you assess probabilities.'

He stood up and began to prowl round the perimeter of the room, like a big cat checking the limits of its domain. 'Probability is the only god of the profiler. To abandon probability for the alternative demands the strongest evidence. The downside of that is that there will be times when you end up with so much egg on your face you'll look like an omelette on legs.'

Already, he could feel his heart rate increasing and still he hadn't said a word about the case. 'I had that experience myself on the last major case I worked. We were dealing with a serial killer of young men. I had all the information that was available to the police, thanks to a brilliant liaison officer. On the basis of the evidence,

I drew up a profile. The liaison officer made a couple of suggestions based on her instincts. One of those suggestions was an interesting idea I hadn't thought of because I didn't know as much about information technology as she did. But equally, because it was something only a small proportion of the population would know about, I assigned it a moderately low probability. Normally, that would mean the investigation team would assign it low priority, but they were stuck for leads, so they pursued it. It turned out she'd been right, but in itself it didn't move the investigation much further forward.'

His hands were clammy with perspiration, but now he was actually confronting the details that still shredded his nights, his stomach had stopped clenching. It was less effort than he'd expected to continue his analysis. 'Her other suggestion I discounted out of hand because it was completely off the wall. It ran counter to everything I knew about serial killers.' Tony met their curious stares. His tension had transmitted itself to the entire squad and they sat silent and motionless, waiting for what would come next.

'My disregard for her suggestion nearly cost me my life,' he said simply, reaching his seat and sitting down again. He looked around the room, surprised he could speak so levelly. 'And you know something? I was right to ignore her. Because, on a scale of one to a hundred, her proposition was so unlikely it wouldn't even register.'

As soon as the formal confirmation of the body in the blaze came through, Carol called a meeting of her team. This time, there were no chocolate biscuits. 'I expect you've all heard this morning's news,' she said flatly as they arranged themselves around her office, Tommy

Taylor straddling the only chair apart from Carol's on the basis that he was the sergeant. He might have been brought up never to sit while women were standing, but he'd long since stopped thinking of Di Earnshaw as a woman.

'Aye,' he said.

'Poor bugger,' Lee Whitbread chimed in.

'Poor bugger nothing,' Tommy protested. 'He shouldn't have been there, should he?'

Repelled but not surprised, Carol said, 'Whether he should or shouldn't have been there, he's dead, and we're supposed to be looking for the person who killed him.' Tommy looked mutinous, folding his arms across the chair back and planting his feet more firmly on the floor, but Carol refused to respond to the challenge. 'Arson's always a time bomb,' she continued. 'And this time it's gone off right in our faces. Today has not been the proudest day of my career to date. So what have you got for me?'

Lee, leaning against the filing cabinet, shifted his shoulders. 'I went through all the back files for the last six months. Leastways, all I could get my hands on,' he corrected himself. 'I found quite a few incidents like you told us to look for, some off night-shift CID reports, some off the uniform lads. I was planning on getting them collated on paper today.'

'Di and me, we've been re-interviewing the victims, like you said. There doesn't seem to be any linking factor that we've come across so far,' Tommy said, his voice distant following Carol's snub.

'A variety of insurance companies, that kind of thing,' Di amplified.

'What about a racial motive?' Carol asked.

'Some Asian victims, but not what you'd call enough to make it look significant,' Di said.

'Have we spoken to the insurers themselves yet?'

Di looked at Tommy and Lee stared out of the window. Tommy cleared his throat. 'It was on Di's list for today. First chance she's had.'

Unimpressed, Carol shook her head. 'Right. Here's what we do next. I've had some experience in offender profiling . . .' She stopped when Tommy muttered something. 'I'm sorry, Sergeant Taylor, did you have a contribution?'

Confidence restored, Tommy grinned insolently back at Carol. 'I said, "We'd heard," ma'am.'

For a moment, Carol said nothing, merely staring him down. It was situations like this that could make the job degenerate into a misery if they weren't handled right. So far, it was only cheeky disrespect. But if she let it go, it would quickly slide into full-scale insubordination. When she spoke, her voice was quiet but chill. 'Sergeant, I can't think why you have this burning ambition to go back into uniform and play at community policing, but I'll be more than happy to oblige you if CID work continues not to be to your taste.'

Lee's mouth twitched in spite of himself; Di Earnshaw's dark eyes narrowed, waiting for the explosion that never came. Tommy pushed his shirtsleeves above his elbows, looked Carol straight in the eye and said, 'Reckon I'd better show you what I'm made of then, Guv.'

Carol nodded. 'You better had, Tommy. Now, I'm going to work on a profile, but to make that anything more than a bit of an academic exercise, I'm going to need a lot of raw data. Since we can't find any evidence of linkage between the victims, I'm going to stick my neck out and say we've got a thrill seeker rather than a torch for hire. Which means we're looking for a young adult male. He's probably unemployed, likely to be single and still living with his parents. I'm not going to go into all the psychobabble about social inadequacy and all that right now. What we need to look for is someone with a record of police contact for petty nuisance offences, vandalism, substance abuse, that sort of thing. Maybe minor sex offences. Peeping Tom, exposing himself. He's not going to be a mugger, a burglar, a thief, a fly boy. He's going to be a sad bastard. In and out of minor bother since he was a pre-teen. He probably doesn't have a car, so we need to look at the geography of the fires; chances are if you drew a line linking the outermost fires, he'll live inside its boundaries. He'll probably have watched all the fires from a vantage point, so have a think about where that might have been and who might have witnessed him there.

'You know the ground. It's your job to bring me suspects that we can match against my profile. Lee, I want you to talk to the collator and see who uniform know that fits those criteria. I'll get going on a fuller profile and Tommy and Di will do the routine work-up on the crime itself, liaising with forensics and organizing a door-to-door in the area. Hell, I don't have to tell you how to run a murder inquiry . . .'

A knock at the door interrupted Carol's flow. 'Come in,' she called.

The door opened on John Brandon. It was, Carol realized, a measure of how far she had to go before she'd be accepted into the East Yorkshire force that no one had stuck a head round the door to warn her the chief was on his way. She jumped to her feet, Tommy nearly toppled in his hurry to get out of his chair and Lee cracked his elbow on the filing cabinet pushing himself upright. Only Di Earnshaw was already in place, standing against the back wall with her arms folded across her chest. 'Sorry to interrupt, DCI Jordan,' Brandon said pleasantly. 'A word?'

'Certainly, sir. We're pretty much finished here. You three know what we're after, I'll leave you to it.' Carol's smile managed to dismiss as well as encourage and the three junior officers edged out of the office with barely a backward glance.

Brandon waved Carol to her seat as he folded his long body into the guest chair. 'This fatal fire at Wardlaw's,' he began without formalities.

Carol nodded. 'I was out there earlier.'

'So I heard. One of your series then, I take it?'

'I think so. It's got all the hallmarks of it. I'm waiting to hear from the fire investigators, but Jim Pendlebury, the fire chief, reckons it's got generic similarities to the earlier incidents we'd identified.'

Brandon chewed one side of his lower lip. It was the first time Carol had ever seen him look anything other than completely composed. He breathed heavily through his nose and said, 'I know we talked about this before and you were convinced that you could handle it. I'm not saying that you can't, because I think you're a bloody good detective, Carol. But I want Tony Hill to take a look at this.'

'There's really no need,' Carol said, feeling heat spreading up her chest and into her neck. 'Certainly not at this stage.'

Brandon's gloomy bloodhound face seemed to grow even longer. 'It's no slur on your competence,' he said.

'I'm bound to say that's what it looks like from here,' Carol said, trying not to sound as mutinous as she felt, forcing herself to remember how angry Tommy Taylor's earlier impertinence had made her feel. 'Sir, we've barely started our own inquiries. It may well be that we'll have this whole thing wrapped up in a matter of days. There can't be that many potential suspects in Seaford who fit the serial arsonist profile.'

Brandon shifted in his chair, as if struggling to find an appropriate arrangement for his long legs. 'I find myself in a slightly awkward position here, Carol. I've never been happy with the "theirs not to reason why" approach to command. I've always thought things run better when my officers understand why I issue the orders I do rather than having to rely on blind obedience. On the other hand, for operational reasons, sometimes things have to be taken on trust. And when other units outside my command are involved, even when I think there's no earthly reason for confidentiality, I have to respect what they ask for. If you follow me?' He raised his eyebrows in an anxious question. If any of his officers could read between so oblique a set of lines, it would be Carol Jordan.

Carol frowned as she digested Brandon's words. 'So, hypothetically,' she eventually said, taking her time to think through what she was saying, 'if a new unit was being set up with a specialist area of responsibility, and they wanted a sympathetic force to let them use one of their cases as a sort of guinea pig, even if you thought the officer in charge had a right to know what the score was, you'd be obliged to go along with their demand for confidentiality as to the real reason why they were being handed the case? That sort of thing, sir?'

Brandon smiled gratefully. 'Speaking purely hypothetically, yes.'

There was no answering smile. 'This wouldn't be an appropriate occasion for such an experiment, in my opinion.' She paused. 'Sir.'

Brandon looked surprised. 'Why not?' he asked.

Carol thought for a moment. Few fast-track graduates climbed the greasy pole as fast as she'd done, particularly women. John Brandon's patronage had given her more than she could ever have expected. And she couldn't even be certain if her real reasons for reluctance were the ones she was about to voice. Nevertheless, she'd stuck her neck out this far and she'd never been a quitter. 'We're a new force,' she said carefully. 'I've only just arrived to work with a group of people who have been a team for a long time. I'm trying to build up a working relationship that will allow us to protect and serve our community. I can't do that if I'm stripped of the first major case that's crossed my desk since I got here.'

'No one's talking about taking the case away from you, Chief Inspector,' Brandon said, reflecting Carol's formality. 'We're talking about using the new task force on a consultancy basis.'

'It'll look like you've no confidence in me,' Carol insisted.

'That's nonsense. If I had no confidence in your abilities, why on earth would I have appointed you to a promoted post?'

Carol shook her head in disbelief. He really didn't get it. 'I'm sure the canteen cowboys won't have any trouble coming up with ideas on that score, sir,' she said bitterly.

Brandon's eyes widened as he grasped her meaning. 'You think they . . . That can't be . . . It's ridiculous! I never heard anything so absurd!'

'If you say so, sir.' Carol managed a twisted smile and ran a hand through her shaggy blonde hair. 'I didn't think I looked that rough.'

Brandon shook his head in disbelief. 'It never occurred to me that people would misinterpret your promotion. You're self-evidently such a good copper.' He sighed and chewed his lip again. 'Now I'm in an even worse position than I was when I walked in.' He looked up at her and made a decision.

'I'm going to speak off the record. Paul Bishop has been having liaison problems with the local brass in Leeds. They've made it clear they don't want his team on their ground and they won't let him near any of their crimes. He needs a real case for his officers to learn their trade, and for obvious reasons, he doesn't want some high-profile serial killer or rapist. He rang me because we're next door to him and he asked me to keep an eye out for something that might do for his squad to cut their teeth on before they're officially available to catch cases from every Tom, Dick and Harry. To be perfectly honest, I was going to offer them your serial arsonist even before it turned fatal.'

Carol tried to keep her anger out of her face. It was always the way. Just when you thought you'd got them house-trained, they reverted to Neanderthal. 'It's a murder now. You don't get much more high profile than that,' she said. 'For my own self-respect, never mind the respect of my team, I need to head the investigation. I do not need to be seen to be hanging on the coat-tails of the National Offender Profiling Task Force,' she continued coldly. 'If I'd thought sending in visiting firemen was the best way to police serious crime, I'd have applied to join them. I can't believe you'd undermine me like this. Sir.' The last word came out like a expletive.

Brandon's method of dealing with threatened insubordination was very different from Carol's. A man in his position had little need of veiled threats; he could afford to be more creative. 'I have no intention of undermining any of my officers, DCI Jordan. That's why you will be the only officer who has direct dealings with the task force. You will go to them in Leeds, they will not come on our ground. I will make it clear to Commander

Bishop that his officers will discuss the case with no other officer of the East Yorkshire force. I trust you will find that satisfactory?'

Carol couldn't help feeling a grudging respect for the speed with which her chief had thought on his feet. 'You've made your orders perfectly clear,' she said, leaning back in resignation.

Relieved that the crisis had been resolved without anything that would have been embarrassing to report back to Maggie, Brandon got to his feet with a relaxed smile. 'Thanks, Carol. I appreciate it. Funny, I could have sworn you'd have jumped at the chance to work with Tony Hill again. The two of you hit it off so well when you worked liaison on the Bradfield murders.'

She coaxed her muscles to conjure up a smile from memory and hoped it would pass for the real thing. 'My reluctance was nothing to do with Dr Hill,' she said, wondering whether Brandon would believe her when she couldn't even convince herself.

'I'll let them know you'll be in touch.' Brandon closed the door on his way out, a courtesy Carol was profoundly grateful for.

'I can hardly wait,' she said grimly to the empty room.

Shaz bounced through the door of the police station where the task force was based and grinned at the uniformed officer behind the desk with cheerful expectation. 'DC Bowman,' she said. 'NOP task force. There should be a package for me?'

The constable looked sceptical. 'Here?'

'That's right.' She glanced at her watch. 'It was supposed to be sent by overnight courier. For delivery by nine a.m. And since my watch says it's ten past . . .'

'Then you owe somebody a bollocking, because there's nowt here for you, love,' the constable said, incapable of keeping the satisfaction out of his voice. It wasn't often he had the chance to score a point against a task force outsider *and* patronize a woman in a single go.

'You sure?' Shaz asked, trying not to show the consternation that she knew would only increase his smugness.

'I've got my reading badge, love. Trust me, I'm a bobby. There's no package here for you.' Bored now, he ostentatiously turned away and pretended to be interested in a pile of paperwork.

Fizzing with frustration, her good mood history, Shaz bypassed the bank of lifts and jogged up the five flights of stairs to the task force operations room. 'Never trust someone else, never trust someone else,' pounded in her head in sync with her feet on the stairs and the blood in her ears. She marched straight into the room that held their computer terminals and threw herself into her chair, barely managing to grunt a greeting to Simon, the only other occupant of the room. Shaz grabbed her phone and punched in Chris's home number. 'Bugger!' she muttered when the answering machine picked up. She yanked her personal organizer out of her bag and keyed in Chris's name. Her index finger stabbed out the direct line at New Scotland Yard. The phone was answered on the second ring. 'Devine.'

'It's Shaz.'

'Whatever it is you're after, the answer's no, doll. I don't think I'm ever going to get the dust and ink out from under my fingernails after yesterday's little exercise. Definitely a non-starter on the "fun things to do with your day off" list.'

'I really appreciate it, you know that. Only . . .'

Chris groaned. 'What, Shaz?'

'The stuff hasn't arrived.'

Chris snorted. 'That all? Listen, by the time I'd got finished – which I have to tell you I only managed by flashing the old warrant card and roping the staff in – it was too late to get an overnight delivery. Best they could do was by noon. So you should get it some time this morning. All right?'

'It'll have to be,' Shaz said, aware she was being ungracious, but unable to care.

'Relax, doll. It's never the end of the world. You're going to give yourself an ulcer,' Chris told her.

'I've got to present my case tomorrow afternoon,' Shaz pointed out.

Chris laughed. 'So what's the problem? 'King hell, Shaz, that Yorkshire air's slowing you up. Time was, you were greased lightning. You got a whole night to turn it around. Don't tell me you're getting soft.'

'I do like the odd bit of sleep between dusk and dawn,' Shaz said.

'Just as well you and me never got it together, then, isn't it? Gimme a call if you haven't got the stuff by the middle of the afternoon, all right, doll? Just hang loose. Nobody's going to die.'

'I flaming hope not,' Shaz said to a dead line.

'Problems?' Simon asked, plonking himself down next to her and pushing a mug of coffee towards her.

Shaz shrugged, reaching for the brew. 'Just some stuff I wanted to check out before we report back on the exercise tomorrow.'

Simon's interest suddenly expanded beyond the erotic possibilities of a fling with Shaz. 'You on to something?' he asked, trying for nonchalant and failing.

Shaz's grin was evil. 'You mean you haven't spotted the cluster?'

'Course I have. Saw it right away, no messing,' he said, clearly blustering.

'Right. So you also found the external link?' Shaz enjoyed the momentary blankness that crossed Simon's milk-pale face before he regained command. She snorted with laughter. 'Good try, Simon.'

He shook his head. 'All right, Shaz, you win. Will you tell me what you've got if I buy you dinner tonight?'

'I'll tell you what I've got tomorrow afternoon, same time as I tell everybody else. But if the offer's genuine and not just a bribe, I'd say yes to a drink before we go for the curry on Saturday night.'

Simon thrust out his hand. 'Deal, DC Bowman.' Shaz took his hand and matched his grip.

The prospect of a pre-dinner drink with Simon, enticing though it was, couldn't distract Shaz from the anticipation of her parcel. At coffee break, she was at the front counter before the others had even brewed up. For the rest of the morning, as Paul Bishop took them through the application of a profile to a suspect list, Shaz, normally the most attentive of students, fidgeted like a four-year-old at the opera. As soon as they broke for lunch, Shaz was off down the stairs like a greyhound out of a trap.

This time, her prayers were answered. A cardboard archive box sealed with what looked like an entire roll of packing tape sat on the front counter. 'Any longer and I'd have phoned the bomb disposal squad to get rid of it,' the desk officer said. 'We're a police station, not a post office.'

'Just as well. You'd never stand the pace.' Shaz swept the box off the counter and marched out to the car park with it. She opened the boot of her car and snatched a quick look at her watch. She reckoned she had about ten minutes to spare before her absence from the communal lunch table would excite comment. Hastily, she ripped at the packing tape with her fingernails, managing to unpick it enough to force the lid open.

Her heart sank. The box was almost brimful of photocopies. For a brief moment, she wondered if she couldn't just ignore her hunch. Then she thought of the seven teenage girls, their faces smiling up at her with all the expectation that, however many disappointments life might hold, at least they'd have a life. This wasn't just an exercise. Somewhere out there was a cold-hearted killer. And the only person who seemed to be aware of it was Shaz Bowman. Even if it did take all night, she owed them that effort at the very least.

Seeing him again face to face, Carol was struck by the realization that it was pain that lurked behind Tony Hill's face. All the time she'd known him, she'd never recognized what underpinned his intensity. She'd always assumed that he was like her, driven only by the desire to capture and understand, fired by a passion to elucidate, haunted by the things he'd seen, heard and done. Now, distance had allowed her to comprehend what she had failed to see before, and she found herself wondering how different her behaviour towards him would have been had she really grasped what was going on behind his dark and troubled eyes.

Of course, he'd arranged it so that they would not be alone when they first encountered each other after the intervening months. Paul Bishop had been despatched to greet her when she'd arrived at the task force base in Leeds, smothering her in the charm that had made him such a media darling. His gallantry didn't extend to offering to carry her two briefcases heavy with case files, and Carol noticed with amusement that he couldn't pass a reflective surface without checking his appearance for imperfection, now smoothing an eyebrow, now straightening broad shoulders in a uniform that had plainly been made to measure. 'I can't tell you how thrilled I am to meet you,' he said. 'John Brandon's best and brightest. Some accolade in itself, never mind your track record. That speaks for itself, of course. Did John mention we'd been at staff college together? What a copper that man is, and what a talent spotter.' His enthusiasm was infectious and Carol found herself responding to his flattery in spite of her best intentions.

'I've always enjoyed working with Mr Brandon,' she said. 'How are things bedding down with the task force?'

'Oh, you'll see all that for yourself,' he said dismissively, ushering her into the lift. 'Of course, Tony's been singing your praises to the heavens. What a joy you are to work with, what a delightful colleague, how bright, how easy to deal with.' He grinned down at her. 'And the rest.'

Now Carol knew he was a bullshitter. She had no doubt as to Tony's professional respect for her, but she knew him well enough to be certain he would never have spoken about her in personal terms. His ingrained reticence would have taken far greater subtlety and skill to penetrate than Paul Bishop clearly possessed. Tony would never talk about Carol because to do so, he'd have to talk about the case that had brought them together. And that would mean revealing far more about both of them than any stranger had a right to know. He'd have had to explain how she'd fallen for him and how his sexual inadequacies forced him to reject her, how any hope of them ever getting together had been the last victim of the murderous psychopath they'd tracked. She felt in her bones that he would never have told another living soul these things, and if there was one thing that raised her above her colleagues, it was her instinct. 'Mmm,' she said noncommittally. 'I've always admired Dr Hill's professionalism.' Bishop brushed against her hip as he pushed the button for the fifth floor. If I'd been a man, Carol thought, he'd just have told me which floor to go for.

'It's a real bonus for us that you've worked with Tony before,' Bishop continued, eyeing his hair in the brushed metal doors. 'Our new trainees will be able to learn a lot from watching how you divide up the process, how you communicate, what you both need from each other.'

'"You know my methods, Watson,"' Carol parodied wryly.

Bishop looked momentarily puzzled, then his face cleared. 'Ah, yes.' The lift opened. 'This way. We're going to have coffee together, just the three of us, then you and Tony can work through the initial contact interview with the students looking on.' He strode down the corridor and held a door open for her, standing back while she entered what looked like a scaled-down scruffy school staff-room.

Across the room, Tony Hill swung round, coffee filter in one hand, spoon in the other. His eyes widened at the sight of Carol and she felt a slow smile spread irresistibly across her face. 'Tony,' she said, managing to keep her voice formal. 'How nice to see you.'

'Carol,' he greeted her, dropping the teaspoon on the table with a clatter. 'You look . . . well. You look well.'

She'd have been lying if she'd said the same to him. He was still pale, though she'd seen him paler. The dark smudges under his eyes were less like bruises than they'd been the last time the two of them had stared at each other, but they were still the badges of someone to whom eight hours' sleep was the impossible dream. His eyes had lost some of the strain she'd grown accustomed to seeing there after their one memorable case had finally been resolved, but he still looked tense. Regardless, she wanted to kiss him.

Instead, she placed her briefcases on the long coffee table and said, 'Any chance of a brew, then?'

'Strong, black, no sugar?' Tony checked with the hint of a smile.

'You must have made an impression,' Bishop said, striding past Carol and dropping into one of the sagging chairs, carefully lifting the knees of his trousers to avoid bagging them. 'He can't remember from one day to the next how I like mine.'

'When we worked together before, it was the kind of situation where every detail is engraved on your brain forever,' Carol said repressively.

Tony flashed her a quick look of gratitude then turned away to brew up. 'Thanks for sending the case files over,' he said against the wheezing of the elderly electric kettle. 'I've had them copied and the team have had them to study overnight.'

'Fine. How do you want to play this?' Carol asked.

'I thought we could go into live role-play,' Tony said, still with his back to them as he made the coffee. 'Sit across a table from each other and run through the case file exactly the way we would do it for real.' He half-turned with a tentative smile and a spasm ran across Carol's stomach.

Get a grip, she told herself angrily. Even if he could, he wouldn't want you. Remember? 'That sounds fine,' she heard herself say. 'How were you planning on involving the trainees?'

Tony juggled the three hot mugs in his broad square hands and managed to get them on to the coffee table without spilling much on the tobacco brown carpet. 'Specially chosen to hide the stains,' he muttered, frowning in concentration.

'There's half a dozen of them,' Bishop said. 'So it's not feasible to let them each have a crack at you, even if you were willing to give up that much of your time. They'll watch you and Tony work through the case files. Then, if they have any questions about that part of the process, they'll ask them. After you've gone, Tony will work with them on the drawing up of a profile, which will be passed back to you in a matter of days. What we're hoping is that when you develop a suspect to the point of arresting and charging, you'll liaise with Tony on interview strategies and allow us access to the taped interviews afterwards.' His smile said he wasn't accustomed to being refused.

'That may not be possible,' Carol said cautiously, not completely sure of her position. 'You may have to wait until after a trial to have access to the interview tapes, and then only if the interviewee agrees. I'll need to take advice on that.'

Tiny movements of muscle beneath the skin stripped Bishop's face of its bonhomie. 'My impression from Mr Brandon was that we weren't being slavish about formalities on this one,' he said briskly.

'I'm the investigating officer here, Commander. This is not a classroom exercise. It's an inquiry into an unlawful death and it's my intention to get a conviction if that's appropriate. I will take absolutely no risk that could cost me a successful prosecution. I don't leave windows open for smart defence counsel.'

'She's right,' Tony said unexpectedly. 'We get carried away with ourselves here. It's heady stuff, you know, Paul. The bottom line is, Carol has to make the case against this arsonist stand up in court, and we can't expect her to go along with anything that might interfere with that.'

'Fine,' Bishop said curtly. Ignoring his coffee, he stood

up and headed for the door. 'I'll leave you to it. I've got some phone calls I need to get out of the way if I'm going to sit in on your session. See you later, DCI Jordan.'

Carol grinned. 'Would five get me ten that he'll be on the phone to John Brandon before his backside hits the chair?'

Tony shook his head, eyes glinting with amusement. 'Probably not, actually. Paul doesn't like being crossed, but he keeps his powder dry for the battles that matter.'

'Not like me, rushing in where angels fear to tread, eh?'

Tony met her gaze and recognized the goodwill there. 'Nobody's quite like you, Carol. I was genuinely sorry that you didn't want to join the team here.'

She twitched one shoulder in a shrug. 'Not my kind of policing, Tony. Sure, I like the big cases, but I don't like living in limbo.'

Her words hung between them, freighted with more meaning than any casual bystander could have read. Tony looked away and cleared his throat. 'All the more reason why I'm pleased to have the chance to work this case with you. If we'd already been up and running, I don't expect you'd have come running to us with what looks on the face of it to be a fairly straightforward serial arson that's turned nasty almost by accident. So it's a bonus for the squad that they're going to get to see someone as good as you at work.'

'You know, all I've had since this task force was mentioned in connection with my case is enough flattery to choke a politician,' Carol said, trying to cover her gratification with a sardonic tone.

'When did I ever offer you flattery?' Tony said simply.

Again, Carol's stomach clenched. 'Maybe it's not such a good idea,' she said. 'Having an officer like me along, I mean. You should have given them a reality check and wheeled in one of the cavemen,' she added, struggling to keep her smile in place.

Tony laughed in delight. 'Can you imagine? Great session that would be.' He dropped his voice and broadened his Yorkshire accent. 'Right bloody load of crap this is. You want me to go round asking me suspects if they pissed the bed when they were kids?'

'I'd forgotten you were from round here,' Carol said.

'I hadn't,' Tony said. 'Back in the West Riding, last place on earth I ever wanted to be. But I wanted the task force, and the Home Office were adamant we had to be based outside London. God forbid we should do anything sensible like billet the profiling squad with the intelligence unit. How are you finding it out in the primeval ooze of Seaford?'

Carol shrugged. 'Life among the dinosaurs? Ask me in six months.' She glanced at her watch. 'What time are we due to kick off?'

'Couple of minutes.'

'Fancy catching up over lunch?' She'd practised the casual tone half a hundred times on the motorway coming over to Leeds.

'I can't.' He looked genuinely sorry. 'We eat together in the squad. But I was going to ask you . . .'

'Yes?' Careful, Carol, not too eager!

'Are you in a hurry to get back?'

'No, no rush.' Her heart singing, yes, yes, he's going to ask me to dinner.

'Only, I wondered if you'd like to sit in on the afternoon session?'

'Right.' Her voice bright, her hopes squashed, the light in her eyes dulled. 'Any particular reason?'

'I set them an exercise last week. They're supposed to produce their conclusions today and I thought it might be helpful to have your response to their analyses.'

'Fine.'

Tony took a shallow breath and said, 'Plus, I thought we could maybe have a drink afterwards?'

Apprehension and anticipation had pitched Shaz on an adrenaline high. Even though she'd only squeezed three hours' sleep out of the night, she was buzzing like a raver on an amphetamine high. She'd attacked the photocopied newspapers the minute she'd got home, laying them out in piles on her living-room carpet and pausing only to phone for a pizza. So engrossed was she that she didn't even notice when they sent her a ten-inch Margarita and charged her for a twelve-inch with everything on.

By one in the morning, she'd eliminated everything except the entertainments ads and the sports pages. Her earlier conviction that the external link that would prove her contention was lurking in the local papers was starting to look less like a solid hunch than a desperate clutching at straws. Stretching her stiff back and rubbing her gritty eyes, Shaz got to her feet and staggered through to the kitchen to brew another Thermos of coffee.

Refuelled, she returned to her task, deciding to go for the sports pages first. Maybe the same visiting football team with its loyal supporters? Or a player who had moved from club to club and then become a manager? Maybe a local golf championship that attracted outsiders, or a series of bridge trophies? Eliminating all the sporting possibilities took another couple of hours, and left Shaz jittery with exhaustion, caffeine and a looming fear of failure.

When the connection finally emerged, her first response was that she was hallucinating. It was so outrageous an idea she couldn't take it seriously. She caught herself giggling nervously, like a child who hasn't yet learned the appropriate response to the pain of others. 'This is crazy,' she said softly, double-checking through all seven sets of newspapers to confirm she wasn't seeing things. She lurched stiffly to her feet, trying to loosen her cramped muscles, and staggered through to the bedroom, stripping her clothes off as she went. It was too much to take in at half past three in the morning. Setting her alarm for half past six, Shaz fell face down on the bed where sleep hit her like a truck colliding with a motorway bridge.

Shaz dreamed about television game shows where the winner got to choose how they'd be killed. When the alarm clock went off, she dreamed it was a buzzer on an electric chair. Still groggy from sleep, her memory of what she'd unearthed in the newspapers felt like an extension of the nightmare. She pushed the duvet back and tiptoed through to the living room as if normal footfalls would scare her discovery away.

There were seven ragged piles of photocopies. On the top of each pile was a page from the entertainment section. Each page contained either an advertisement for a personal appearance or a featured interview with the same man. However she cut it, it looked as if one of the nation's darlings was somehow tied in to the disappearance and presumed murder of at least seven teenage girls.

And now she was going to have to share her revelation.

It wasn't difficult to set tongues wagging, Micky had soon discovered. Whenever she visited the rehabilitation unit where Jacko was learning how to use his artificial arm, they made a point of closing the door of his room and sitting close together so that when they were interrupted by a physio or a nurse, they could spring apart and appear embarrassed.

At work, she would phone him when the surrounding desks were occupied and she was almost certain to be overheard. The conversations would swing between animated hilarity, with his name dropped in at regular intervals, and the low, intimate tones her colleague would unimaginatively associate only with lovers.

Finally, to move things up a gear, it was time for scandal and drama. Micky chose a friend on a middle market tabloid. Three days later, the paper splashed with PERVERT TARGETS JACKO'S NEW LOVE.

> Lifesaving hero Jacko Vance's new girlfriend has become the target of a terrifying campaign of vandalism and hate mail.
>
> Since the start of their whirlwind romance, TV journalist Micky Morgan has had
>
> * paint thrown over her car
> * dead mice and birds posted through her letter box
> * a vicious series of poison pen letters sent to her home.
>
> The couple met when she interviewed the world record-holding javelin star in hospital after the motorway pile-up where Jacko's tragic heroism cost him his lower right arm and his Olympic dream. They had been trying to keep their affair under wraps.
>
> But we can exclusively reveal that their secret has leaked to someone who bears a grudge against attractive blonde Micky, 25, a popular reporter on *Six O'Clock World.*.
>
> Last night, at her West London home, Micky said, 'It's been a nightmare. We've no idea who's behind it. I just wish they'd stop.
>
> 'We've been keeping our relationship to ourselves because we wanted to get to know each other better without the glare of publicity. We're very much in love.

The private man is even more exciting than the person the public sees.

'He's brave and he's beautiful. How could I not be madly in love? All we want now is for this heartless campaign to end.'

A spokesman for Jacko, who is undergoing intensive rehabilitation and physiotherapy at London's exclusive Martingale Clinic, said, 'Jacko is obviously disgusted that anyone should treat Micky like this. She's the most wonderful woman he's ever met. Whoever is behind this better hope the police catch them before he does.'

Jacko, who ended his engagement to (Continued on page 4)

The press coverage was hectic for a couple of weeks, then it slowly died away, resurfacing every now and again whenever something happened to either of the alleged lovers. Jacko's emergence from rehab into his old life; his hiring as a TV sports presenter; Micky's new job as an interviewer on breakfast television; Jacko's voluntary work with the terminally ill; all of these and more refreshed interest in their supposed affair. They soon learned it was necessary for them to be seen together somewhere public and high profile at least once a week to avoid speculation in the gossip columns. Often, knowing they were being followed, Jacko ended up spending the night under the same roof as the two women after he and Micky had been clubbing or charity working. After nearly a year of this, Micky summoned Jacko to a powwow over dinner with Betsy.

Her lover's culinary skills had not deserted her since the years she had spent catering for boardroom lunches. As he swallowed the last morsel, Jacko gave the two women his most wolfish grin. 'It must be bad,' he said, 'if it took something that good to soften me up.'

Betsy smiled demurely. 'You haven't had the sticky toffee pudding with home-made hazelnut ice cream yet.'

Jacko pretended to be shocked. 'If I was a police officer, you could be arrested for an offer like that.'

'We do have a proposition for you,' Micky said.

'Something tells me you're not talking three in a bed,' he said, rocking gently on the back legs of the chair.

'You might try and sound a little disappointed,' Betsy said drily. 'The idea that we're so unappealing is bad for what the Americans so charmingly call our self-esteem.'

Jacko's smile reminded Micky disturbingly of Jack Nicholson. 'Betsy, my dear, if you knew what I like to do with my women, you'd be profoundly grateful for my lack of interest.'

'Actually, our ignorance on that very point is one of the factors that has made us reluctant to put our proposal to you before now,' Betsy said, briskly clearing the plates and carrying them through to the small kitchen.

'I'm intrigued now,' Jacko said, tipping forward with a slight thump and leaning his prosthetic arm on the table. He held Micky's eyes in a glittering stare. 'Spill the beans, Micky.'

Betsy appeared in the kitchen doorway and leaned against the jamb. 'It's awfully time consuming, this silly business of you and Micky having to go out enjoying yourselves. I don't mind in the slightest that she's out with you. It's just that we'd both rather spend what limited time we can spare together.'

'You want to call the whole thing off?' Jacko frowned.

'Quite the opposite,' Betsy said, sitting down at the table again and placing her hand over Micky's. 'We rather thought it might be a good idea if the two of you were to get married.'

He looked astonished. Micky thought she had never seen a more genuine expression cross Jacko Vance's carefully controlled features. 'Married,' he echoed. It wasn't a question.

Shaz looked around the seminar room again, assessing her audience, hoping she wasn't about to make a complete fool of herself. She tried to second-guess where the objections would come from and what they'd be. Simon would pick holes on principle, she knew that. Leon would tilt his chair back and smoke, the ghost of a sneer on his mouth, then find some load-bearing prop in her argument and demolish it. Kay would cavil and quibble over details, never seeing the big picture. Tony, she hoped, would be quietly impressed with her brilliance in spotting the cluster and her diligence in pursuing it to a demonstrable external connection. Her groundwork would be the trigger for a major inquiry and when the dust finally settled, her future would be sealed. The woman who nailed the celebrity serial killer. She'd be a legend in squad rooms up and down the country. She'd be in a position to pick her billet.

Carol Jordan was the wild card. A morning watching her work with Tony hadn't provided nearly enough raw material for accurate conjecture about her response to Shaz's theory. To leave as little to chance as possible, she'd have to hang back and let a couple of her colleagues go first so she could watch Carol carefully while they presented their reports.

Leon went first. Shaz was surprised by the brevity of his report, and she didn't think she was the only one. He said that while there were clearly similarities between certain of the cases, given the number of teenage runaways recorded annually it was hard to argue that there was any statistical significance in that. He had, seemingly grudgingly, chosen four girls from the West Country, including one of Shaz's cluster. The connecting factor he'd identified was that all four were reported to have harboured ambitions to become models. He suggested they might have been abducted by one or more pornographers under the pretext of offering them the opportunity to become photographers' models then suckered into a life of blue movies and sex for sale.

A short silence was followed by a few apathetic comments from the room. Then Carol said coolly, 'And how long did you spend on this analysis, Mr Jackson?'

Leon's eyebrows descended. 'There wasn't a lot to analyse,' he said belligerently. 'I did what it took.'

'If I were the investigating officer who had handed this material to you, I would be rather underwhelmed by something so superficial,' Carol said. 'I'd feel disappointed, short-changed, and I'd have a pretty low opinion of a specialist unit which produced nothing of more significance than one of my own officers could have provided in an afternoon's work.'

Leon's mouth opened in astonishment. Neither Tony nor Bishop had ever been so openly critical of anyone's work. Before he could respond, Tony cut in. 'DCI Jordan's right, Leon. It's not good enough. We're supposed to be an elite squad, and we're not going to make any friends if we don't treat every assignment as something serious and worthy of our attention. It doesn't matter if we think a group of cases are Mickey Mouse. To the investigating officers, they're important. To the victims, they're important.'

'This was just an exercise,' Leon protested. 'There isn't an investigating officer. It's just playtime. You can't get worked up about that!' The whine in his voice said, 'It's not fair!' louder than the actual words.

'As I understand it, every one of these cases is real,' Carol said quietly. 'Every one of those kids is on the missing list. Some of them are almost certainly dead.

The pain of uncertainty can often be more damaging than knowledge of the truth. If we ignore people's pain, we deserve their contempt.'

Shaz watched Tony's impassive face incline in a tiny acknowledgement of Carol's words, then followed his eyes across to Leon, who had compressed his mouth into a thin line, half-turning in his seat so he didn't have to look at Carol. 'Right,' said Tony. 'We've established that DCI Jordan doesn't do polite. Who's next for the high jump?'

Shaz could barely contain her impatience during Kay's report, a pedestrian but painstakingly thorough analysis that forged several possible groups with an assortment of linkages. One was identical to Shaz's own cluster, but it was given no extra weight compared to the others. When the recital drew to a close, Tony looked happier. 'A thorough piece of work,' he said, the unspoken 'but' hanging in the air like a relay baton.

Carol picked up the challenge. 'Yes, but it sounds like you're sitting on the fence. An investigating officer wants information presented in a way that underpins specific initiatives. So you need to prioritize your conclusions. "This is quite likely, this is less likely, this is tenuous, this is frankly improbable." That lets the officers on the ground structure their inquiries in the most productive way.'

'In fairness, it's hard to do that in the vacuum of a classroom exercise,' Tony added. 'But we should always attempt to do it. Any ideas regarding the order of priority we should be looking at here?'

Shaz barely contributed to the vigorous discussion that followed. She was too nervous about what lay ahead to care about the impression she might be making. A couple of times, she caught a stray look of inquiry from Carol Jordan, and responded with some innocuous comment.

Then, suddenly, it was her turn. Shaz cleared her throat and assembled her papers in front of her. 'Although there are several superficial similarities that pull together a variety of potential groupings, closer analysis reveals that there is one strong cluster linked by a nexus of common factors,' she began firmly. 'What I intend to show this afternoon is that this cluster is further linked by a significant common external factor and the irresistible conclusion is that the members of this cluster are the victims of a single serial killer.'

She looked up, hearing a gasp from Kay and a guffaw from Leon. Tony looked startled, but Carol Jordan was leaning forward, chin on her fists, gripped. Shaz allowed a small smile to twitch one corner of her mouth. 'I'm not making this up, I promise you,' she said, distributing stapled pages of photocopies around the table.

'Seven cases,' she said. 'The first page you have in front of you is a table listing the common features in these seven disappearances. One of those key connections, in my view, is that all seven girls took a change of clothes with them. But they didn't go for the kind of things you'd choose if you were planning on running away and living on the streets. In every case, what they went missing with was their "best" gear, the fashion outfits they'd have worn if they were going out on a special date, not trainers for walking the streets and ski jackets for staying warm at night. I know teenagers aren't always sensible when it comes to what they wear, but remember, our sample weren't irresponsible, out of control, wild-child girls.'

She glanced up and was gratified to see that Tony was now as rapt as Carol Jordan. 'In each case, they didn't turn up for school and had lied in advance about what they were doing afterwards to give themselves a clear run of about twelve hours. Only one of them had ever come to the notice of the police or social services and that was for shoplifting when she was twelve. They weren't delinquent, they didn't do drink or drugs to any significant degree.

'Now, if you turn to page two, you'll see I've laid out their photographs scaled down to the same size. Don't you think there's a remarkable physical similarity?' Shaz paused for effect.

'That's eerie,' Simon muttered. 'I can't believe I didn't see that.'

'It's more than physical,' Carol said, sounding faintly bemused. 'There's a look they've all got. Something . . . almost sexual.'

'They're dying to become former virgins,' Leon told the room. 'That's what it is. Unmistakable.'

'Whatever it is,' Shaz interrupted, 'they've all got it. The cases are geographically scattered, the time frame is six years at irregular intervals, but the victims look practically interchangeable. Now, that's strong evidence in itself. But Tony's taught us that we should also be looking for external connectors; factors outside the victim's control or influence that are common. Factors that link to the killer, not the victim.

'I asked myself where I might find the relevant external link that would tie together my cluster of putative victims.' Shaz picked up another pile of stapled photocopies and passed them round. 'Local newspapers. I trawled the local papers for two weeks either side of each disappearance. And in the early hours of this morning, I found what I was looking for. You've got it in front of you. Just before each one of these girls died, the same very public personality was in their home town. And each and every one of them, let's not forget, went off with the one and only outfit they'd have chosen from their wardrobes if they were planning on impressing a man.'

The murmur of disbelief was already rising around her as the enormity of Shaz's suggestion hit them. 'That's right,' she said. 'I couldn't believe it either. I mean, who's going to believe the nation's favourite sporting hero and TV personality is a serial killer? And who's going to authorize an investigation of Jacko Vance?'

The soft whimper seemed to be swallowed by the chill darkness. Donna Doyle had never felt more frightened in her short life. She'd never realized that fear could act like an anaesthetic, apprehension dulling excruciating agony to a throbbing ache. What had already happened had been terrible enough. But not knowing what the future held was almost worse.

It had all started so well. She'd kept the secret, in spite of the way it kept bubbling up inside her, almost seeming to press against her lips and demand release. But she knew he'd meant what he'd said about the importance of confidentiality, and this was too good a chance to miss. Excitement at her new prospects had buoyed her up, allowing her to stifle her awareness that what she was doing would cause uproar at home. She rationalized her failure to inform her mother of her plans by telling herself that when everything worked out as she dreamed, there would be so much joy that the trouble would be forgotten. Deep down, she knew that was a lie, but she couldn't bear to let that knowledge interfere with her elation.

Bunking off school had been easy. She'd set off as usual, then, instead of turning in down the road leading to school, she'd carried on into the town centre where she'd dodged into the public lavatories and changed into the clothes she'd carefully folded into her school backpack instead of books. Her best outfit, she knew, making her look older than she was, making her look like the young women she saw on MTV, cool as fuck. In the dim light of the toilet, she applied her make-up and pouted at the mirror. God, she looked good. But would it be good enough for him?

He'd picked her out when she wasn't even dressed up to the nines, she reminded herself. He'd seen her star quality. Dressed like this, she'd knock him dead. Wouldn't she?

The memory of that nonchalant self-confidence was like a sick joke to Donna now, lying in pain and fear in the dark. But at the time it had been more than enough to get her through the day. She'd caught a bus into Manchester, hanging back until it was about to leave, making sure there wasn't one of the neighbours or her mother's boring friends on board. Then she'd run upstairs, sitting at the back so she could see who got on and off.

Having a few hours in Manchester on a weekday on her own was almost adventure enough in itself. She browsed the department stores, played the fruit machines in the video arcades, bought a couple of lottery scratch cards in a newsagent near the station and told herself that winning ten straight off wasn't just a result, it was an omen. By the time she boarded the train, she was irrepressibly high, more than capable of ignoring the nerves that still fluttered annoyingly in her stomach when she thought of what her mum was going to say.

Changing trains wasn't quite so much fun. It was growing dark, and she couldn't understand a word anyone on Newcastle station tannoy said. They didn't sound like Jimmy Nail or Kevin Whately off the telly. They sounded like aliens. Somehow, she managed to find the right platform for Five Walls Halt and nervously boarded the train, aware that she was among strangers with curious faces who eyed her short skirt and dramatic make-up with predatory eyes. Donna's imagination began to work overtime, translating weary commuters into stalkers and mad axemen.

It had been a relief to get off the train and find him waiting in the car park, just like he'd said. And it had been lovely. He'd said all the right things, reassuring her and convincing her she'd done the right thing. He was lovely, she told herself, not a bit like she expected someone off the telly to be.

As they'd driven down narrow country roads, he'd explained that they wouldn't be able to do the screen test until morning, but that he hoped she'd have dinner with him. He said he had a cottage, that she could stay overnight, there was a spare room, which would save him having to drive after he'd had a glass or two of wine. If she didn't mind, of course. Otherwise, he could take her to a hotel.

The part of her that had been well brought up and drilled to wariness wanted to go instantly to a hotel where she could phone her mother and reveal that she was safe and well. But it wasn't an enticing prospect, a night in a lonely room in a strange place where she knew no one, with no company except the TV and her mum complaining down the phone line. The other voice in her head, the tempting adventurous voice, told her she'd never have a chance like this to make her mark. Having him to herself for a whole evening would be the perfect opportunity to impress him so much that the screen test would be a formality.

The voice she stifled through a mixture of apprehension and anticipation pointed out that there might never be a more propitious time to lose her virginity.

'Staying with you'd be great,' she said.

He smiled, briefly turning his eyes away from the road. 'I promise we'll have fun,' he said.

And he hadn't been lying. Not to begin with, anyway. The food had been wonderful, like the really expensive stuff from Marks and Spencer that her mum always said they couldn't afford. And they'd had wine. Lots of different kinds. Champagne to start with, then white wine with the starters, then red with the main course and a sticky aromatic golden one with the pudding. She'd had no idea there were so many different-tasting ones. He'd been lovely, all through dinner. He'd been funny and flirty and full of stories that made her smile and hug herself inside because she was learning all these secrets about telly people.

And he seemed to find her entertaining, too. He was always asking her what she thought, what she felt, who she liked on TV and who she hated. He was interested, staring deep into her eyes and really paying attention, like men were supposed to when they fancied you, not like the lads she'd gone out with from school who were only interested in football and how far you'd let them go. It was obvious he fancied her. But he wasn't slobbering all over her like some dirty old man. He was considerate, treating her like she was a person. With all the conversation, phoning her mum had been the last thing on her mind.

By the end of the meal, she'd been pleasantly woozy. Not drunk, not like at Emma Lomas's party when she'd had five bottles of extra-strong cider and thrown up for hours. Just a bit blurred round the edges, filled with happiness and desire to feel his warm flesh against hers, to bury her face in the citrus and woody smell of his cologne, to make her fantasies reality.

When he got up to make coffee, she followed, a little

unsteady on her feet, conscious of the giddiness that made the room sway gently but not unpleasantly. She came up behind him and slipped her arms round his waist. 'I think you're gorgeous,' she said. 'Fantastic.'

He'd turned and let her lean into him, burying his face in her hair and nuzzling her ear. 'You're very special,' he murmured. 'Very special.'

She felt his erection hard against her stomach. For a moment, a thrill of fear squirmed through her, then his lips were on hers and she was lost to the sensation of what felt like her first kiss. They kissed for what seemed like a lifetime, a dizzying parade of colours spinning behind her eyes as arousal sent her blood charging through her veins.

Almost without her realizing, he moved her gradually round so that her back was against the workbench and he was facing her, still kissing, his tongue darting in and out of her mouth. Suddenly, without warning, his hand clamped over her wrist and yanked her arm to one side. Donna felt cold metal against her flesh and her eyes jerked open. At the same moment, their mouths parted.

Baffled, she looked at her arm, not understanding why it was pinned between the two faces of a big steel vice. He stepped back and quickly spun the handle so the jaws closed on the flushed flesh of her naked arm. Vainly, she tried to pull away. But there was no escape. She was trapped by the arm, pinioned to the workbench vice. 'What are you doing?' she squealed. All her face revealed was hurt puzzlement. It was too soon for fear.

His face was blank. An impassive mask had replaced the interest and affection she'd seen there all evening. 'You're all the same, aren't you?' he said dispassionately. 'You're all out for what you can get.'

'What are you talking about?' Donna entreated him. 'Let me go, this isn't funny. It hurts.' With her free arm, she reached across her body towards the handle of the vice. He raised his arm and smashed her in the face with a backhanded swipe that sent her reeling.

'You do as you're told, you treacherous bitch,' he said, still sounding calm.

Donna tasted blood. A rending sob broke from her throat. 'I don't understand,' she stuttered. 'What did I do wrong?'

'You throw yourself at me because you think I'll get you what you want. You tell me you love me. But if you woke up tomorrow and I couldn't give you what you wanted, you'd throw yourself at the next meal ticket that walked past.' He leaned against her, pressing his body to hers, his weight preventing her from making another attempt at releasing the vice.

'I don't know what you're on about,' Donna whined. 'I never ... Aagh!' Her voice rose in a yell of pain as he turned the vice tighter. Pain shot up her arm as muscle and bone were compacted, the edges of the vice cutting deep and cruel into the tissue of her arm. As her scream subsided into tearful entreaty, he half-turned so that his weight was still on her free arm and tore her dress from top to bottom with one powerful wrench.

Now she was really afraid. She couldn't understand why he was doing this. All she'd wanted was to love him, to be chosen by him to appear on the telly. It wasn't supposed to be like this. It was supposed to be romantic and tender and beautiful, but this was senseless and stupid and she couldn't believe how much her arm was hurting and all she wanted was for it to stop.

He'd barely begun. Within moments, her knickers were in a torn heap at her feet, deep welts in her side where the fabric had bitten into her skin before the seams had finally yielded to his force. Shaking with sobs, her voice a mumbling of meaningless pleadings, she had no resources left to resist as he unzipped his trousers and thrust his cock into her.

It wasn't the pain of losing her virginity that Donna remembered. It was the agony that coursed through her when he bore down on the vice in rhythm with the thrusting of his hips into hers. The breaking of her hymen went unnoticed among the splintering of the bones of her wrist and forearm and the pulverizing of her flesh between the blank metal plates.

As she lay in the dark, she was glad only that she'd passed out then. She didn't know where she was or how she'd got there. All she knew was that she was blessedly alone. And that was enough. For now, that was enough.

Tony walked down Briggate, hands thrust deep into his jacket pockets against the cold, swerving to avoid the last straggles of shoppers and the weary-footed sales assistants making for the bus stops. He deserved a drink. It had been a difficult afternoon. For a time it had looked as if the group spirit nurtured from day one was about to become a memory as differences of opinion escalated into argument then teetered on the edge of hurling abuse.

The first response to Shaz's dramatic hypothesis had been stunned silence. Then Leon had slapped his leg and rocked to and fro on his chair. 'Shazza, baby,' he yelled. 'You are more full of shit than a sewage farm, but you are the best value in town! All right, baby, way to go!'

'Hang on a minute, Leon,' Simon objected. 'You're quick off the mark to slap the girl down. What if she's right?'

'Oh, yeah,' Leon drawled contemptuously. 'Like Jacko Vance is *obviously* a psychopathic serial killer. You've only got to watch him on the telly. Or read about him in the tabloids. Yeah, Jack the Lad, marriage made in heaven, England's glory, the hero who sacrificed his arm and his Olympic medal so that others might live. Very Jeffrey Dahmer, very Peter Sutcliffe. Not.'

Tony had kept half an eye on Shaz during Leon's

outburst, noticing the apparent darkening of her eyes and the tense line of her mouth. She couldn't handle mockery the way she dealt with straightforward criticism, he realized. As Leon paused for breath, Tony jumped in with a dose of irony. 'I just love the cut and thrust of intellectual debate,' he said. 'So, Leon, how about you stop showing off and provide us with some cogent argument against the case that Shaz is making?'

Leon scowled, unable as usual to disguise his emotions. Hiding behind the lighting of a cigarette, he mumbled something.

'Can you let us have that again?' Carol interjected sweetly.

'I said, I didn't think Jacko Vance's personality fit our general terms of reference for serial offenders,' he repeated.

'How do you know that?' Kay cut in. 'All we ever see of Jacko Vance is the image manufactured by the media. Some serial killers have been superficially charming and manipulative. Like Ted Bundy. If you're going to be a top athlete, you have to develop phenomenal self-control. Maybe that's what we're seeing with Jacko Vance. A totally synthetic front covering up a psychopathic personality.'

'Spot on,' Simon said vigorously.

'But he's been married a dozen years or more. Would his wife have stayed with him if he was a psychopath? I mean, he couldn't maintain the mask permanently,' someone objected.

'Sonia Sutcliffe always asserted she was totally unaware that her husband went out topping prostitutes the way some men go to football matches. And Rosemary West still claims she had no idea Fred was using bodies for foundations under their patio extension,' Carol pointed out.

'Yeah, and think about it,' Simon urged, 'couples with jobs like Micky Morgan and Jacko Vance, they're not like the rest of us. Half the time Jacko's on the road doing *Vance's Visits*. Then there's all his hospital voluntary work. And Micky must be in the studio at the crack of sparrowfart getting prepared for her programme. They probably see less of each other than coppers see of their kids.'

'It's an interesting point,' Tony said, cutting across a couple of loud interjections. 'What do you think, Shaz? It's your theory, after all.'

Shaz's jaw was set mutinously. 'I don't hear anybody arguing against my identification of the cluster as a significant entity,' she started.

'We-ell,' Kay said. 'I'm wondering how significant it really is. I mean, I pulled together several clusters that maybe are just as validly connected. The girls who the police thought might have been sexually abused, for example.'

'No,' Shaz said firmly. 'Not with as many linking factors as this group. It's worth saying again that some of the things that connect them are unusual features, unusual enough for investigating officers to make a particular note of them. Like taking their best clothes with them.' Tony was pleased to see she was undaunted by this latest example of Kay's constant nit-picking.

Her rebuttal didn't win her a reprieve, however. 'Of course you'd note that,' Leon chipped in, never squashed for long. 'It's the single factor that indicates you're looking at a runaway rather than the victim of a serial killer. You didn't make a note of it, you'd be a pretty crap detective.'

'Like the one who didn't even notice the cluster in the first place?' Shaz demanded belligerently.

Leon cast his eyes upwards and stubbed out his cigaette. 'You women, when you get an idea in your heads . . .'

'Christ, you talk shite sometimes,' Simon said. 'If we could just get back to what this is supposed to be about . . I'm wondering how much of a coincidence it is that Vance visited those towns. I mean, we don't know how many public appearances he does in the average week. It may be that he's constantly on the road, in which case it wouldn't mean a lot.'

'Exactly,' Kay backed him up. 'Did you check the local newspapers for the missing kids who aren't in your cluster to see if Vance turned up there as well?'

Shaz's pursed lips gave the answer before she even opened her mouth. 'I didn't have the chance,' she admitted reluctantly. 'Maybe you'd like to take on that little task, Kay?'

'If it was a real operation, you'd have to follow up Kay's suggestion,' Carol pointed out. 'But you would have the bodies and time to do it, which you didn't have here. I must say, I'm impressed with what you have achieved with the limited time and resources available.' Shaz's shoulders squared at Carol's praise, but as the DCI continued, she looked wary. 'However, even if it's a genuine connection, it's too much of a leap in the dark to point the finger straight at Jacko Vance. If these disappearances and presumed murders are connected to his appearances, it's much more likely that the perpetrator is a member of Jacko's entourage or even a member of the public who has an initiating stressor in his past that connects to Vance. At its most obvious, perhaps he was rejected by a woman who was a big fan of Jacko's. These would be my first areas of interest, before I came to the assumption that Jacko himself was involved.'

'It's a point of view,' Shaz said, momentarily mortified

that she'd been so carried away with her headline grabbing theory that she hadn't considered that possibility. It was the nearest Tony had ever seen her come to a concession. 'But you think the cluster is worth pursuing?'

Carol had looked desperately at Tony. 'I . . . uh . . .'

Coming to her rescue, he'd said, 'This was only ever going to be an exercise, Shaz. We've got no authority to take any of these cases any further.'

She looked devastated. 'But there's a cluster here. Seven suspicious disappearances. Those girls, they've got families.'

Leon butted in again, sarcasm back in full working order. 'C'mon, Shazza. Get them synapses working. We're supposed to be clearing things up for the plods on the street, not finding more work for them to do. D'you really think anybody's going to thank us for stirring up a load of aggro over a theory that's dead easy to dismiss out of hand as the product of the fevered minds of a bunch of rookies on a special squad that nobody much wants on the job anyway?'

'Fine,' Shaz said bitterly. 'Let's just forget I spoke, eh? So whose turn is it to be shot down in flames next? Simon? We going to get the benefit of your words of wisdom now?'

Tony had taken Shaz's seeming capitulation as a signal to move on. The other team members' analyses had been considerably less controversial, which had allowed him to demonstrate useful tips and pitfalls in data sifting and the developing of conclusions from raw material. As the afternoon had worn on, he'd noticed Shaz slowly recover from the combative reception her ideas had been given. Gradually, she had ceased to look desolate, moving through crestfallen to an air of stubborn determination that he found slightly worrying. Some time in the next few days, he'd have to make time to have a word with her, to point out the quality of much of her analysis and explain the importance of keeping apparently wild conclusions private until she could back them up with something more solid than a hunch.

He turned off the main street into the narrow alley that housed Whitelocks pub, an old-fashioned relic that had somehow survived the years when the city centre died at half past five. If he was honest, the last thing he felt like was a drink with Carol. The history between them meant theirs could never be entirely easy encounters, and tonight he had something he ought to tell her that she wouldn't want to hear.

At the bar, he ordered a pint of bitter and found a quiet table in the far corner. He'd never been one to shirk his obligations. But Shaz's failure to consider one of Jacko Vance's fans or a member of his entourage as a possibility had reminded him of the importance of waiting for data before exposing theories to the harsh scrutiny of others. Just for once, Tony thought he'd take his own mental advice to Shaz and say nothing of his ideas until he too had more evidence.

It had taken Carol half an hour to escape from the probing questions of the two women task force officers. She had the distinct feeling that if she hadn't taken so very definite a leave, the one with the eyes, Shaz, would have pinned her to the wall until she'd sucked her dry of every piece of pertinent information, and a fair amount of impertinent. By the time she pushed open the etched glass door of the pub, she was convinced he'd have given up on her and left.

She saw his wave of greeting as soon as she approached the bar. He was sitting in a wood-panelled nook at the far end of the room, the remains of a pint of bitter in front of him. 'Same again?' she mouthed, making the universal gesture of a hand tipping a glass.

Tony placed one index finger across the top of the other to form a T. Carol grinned. Moments later, she placed a straight glass of Tetley's in front of Tony and sat down opposite him with her own half-pint. 'Driving,' she said succinctly.

'I took the bus. Cheers,' he added, raising his glass.

'Cheers. It's good to see you.'

'And you.'

Carol's answering smile was wry. 'I wonder if there'll ever come a time when you and I can sit opposite each other and not feel there's a third person at the table?' She couldn't help it. It was like a scab she was impelled to pick, always convinced that this time it wouldn't draw blood.

He looked away. 'Actually,' he said, 'you're about the only person who doesn't make me feel like that. Thanks for coming today. I know it probably wasn't the way you would have chosen to reopen our . . .'

'Acquaintance?' Carol said, unable to avoid a sour note.

'Friendship?'

It was her turn to look away. 'I hope so,' she said. 'I hope friendship.' It was less than the truth and they both knew it, but it served its purpose. Carol found a frail smile. 'An interesting bunch, your baby profilers.'

'They are, aren't they? I suppose you saw what they've all got in common?'

'If ambition was illegal they'd all be doing life. In the next cell to Paul Bishop.'

Tony nearly choked on his mouthful of beer, spraying the table and narrowly missing Carol's cream twill jacket. 'I see you haven't lost your killer instinct,' he spluttered.

'What's to be coy about? You can't miss it. High octane aspiration. It fills the room like testosterone in a nightclub. Doesn't it worry you that they all see the task force as a stepping stone in their brilliant careers?'

Tony shook his head. 'No. Maybe half of them will use it as a springboard to what they perceive as greater things. The other half think that's what they're doing, but actually they're going to fall in love with profiling and they're never going to want to do anything else.'

'Name names.'

'Simon, the lad from Glasgow. He's got that sceptical turn of mind that takes nothing on trust. Dave, the sergeant. He likes the idea that it's methodical and logical yet it still has space for flair. But the real star is going to be Shaz. She doesn't know it yet, but she's been bitten by the bug. Don't you think?'

She nodded. 'She's an obsessive workaholic and she can't wait to get to grips with the screwed-up minds out there on the street.' She cocked her head to one side. 'Know what?'

'What?'

'She reminded me of you.'

Tony looked like he couldn't decide whether to be offended or amused and settled for puzzled. 'How odd,' he said. 'She reminded *me* of you.'

'What!' Carol exclaimed, startled.

'This afternoon's presentation. The basic work was solid. The cluster she'd identified is definitely worth consideration as a phenomenon.' He spread his hands and opened his eyes wide. 'To jump from that to the conclusion that Jacko Vance is a serial killer was a leap of imagination unrivalled since your virtuoso performance in the Bradfield case!'

Carol couldn't help laughing at his histrionics. 'But I was right,' she protested.

'You may have been right in *fact*, but you broke all the laws of logic and probability to get there.'

'Maybe Shaz is right. And maybe we're just better at profiling than the boys,' Carol teased.

Tony grunted. 'I wouldn't deny the possibility that girls are better at this,' he said. 'But I can't believe you think Shaz is right.'

Carol pulled a face. 'Six months down the road, she'll be mortified she even suggested it.'

'Knowing cops, one of that bunch will probably set her up with a face-to-face on *Vance's Visits*.'

Carol shuddered. 'I can see it now. Jacko Vance nailed to the wall by those extraordinary eyes, Shaz saying, "And where were you on the night of 17th January 1993?"' When they'd both stopped laughing, she added, 'I'll be fascinated to see what she comes up with for my serial arsonist.'

'Mmm,' Tony said.

She raised her glass in a toast. 'To the mumbo jumbo squad.'

'May we be a long time in heaven before the devil notices we're gone,' he responded wryly and drained his glass. 'Another?'

Carol looked at her watch consideringly. It wasn't that she had to be anywhere; she wanted a moment to decide whether it was better to leave things on this pleasant footing or stay for another drink with the risk they might end up putting the distance back between each other. Deciding not to chance it, she shook her head regretfully. 'No can do, I'm afraid. I want to catch the night-shift CID team before they all disappear into the twilight zone.' She swallowed the last half-inch of beer and stood up. 'I'm glad we had the chance for a chat.'

'Me too. Come back on Monday, we'll have something for you then.'

'Great.'

'Drive safely,' he said as she turned to go.

She half-turned. 'I will. And you take care.'

Then she was gone. Tony sat for a while staring into his empty glass considering why someone might set fires without the pay-off of a sexual thrill. When the glimmer of an idea crept into his mind, he got up and walked alone through the echoing streets.

It wasn't the laughter of Shaz's colleagues that smarted like shampoo in her eyes. It wasn't even Carol Jordan's metaphorical pat on the head. It was Tony's sympathy. Instead of being bowled over by the quality of her work and the incisiveness of her insights, Tony had been kind. She hadn't wanted to hear that it took courage to stick her neck out, that she'd shown real initiative but that she'd fallen into the trap of getting carried away by coincidence. It would have been easier if he'd been dismissive or even patronizing, but the fellow-feeling in his compassion was too obvious for her to hide her crushing disappointment in anger. He'd even told a couple of stories against himself about mistaken conclusions he'd leapt to in his early efforts at profiling.

It was a generosity of spirit that Shaz had no equipment to deal with. The only, and accidental, child of a couple so devoted to each other that the emotional needs of their daughter barely impinged, she had learned to get by without expectations of tenderness or indulgence. She'd been told off for misbehaving, praised absent-mindedly for success, but mostly, she'd been ignored. Her driven ambition had its roots in a childhood where she'd worked desperately hard to win the recognition from her parents that she craved. Instead, her teachers had offered approval, and their off-handed professional assessments had been the only generosity she'd learned to feel at ease with. Now, genuine personal kindness left her baffled and uncomfortable. She could handle Carol Jordan's businesslike appreciation of her work, but Tony's sympathy unsettled her and fired her to do something that would render it redundant.

The morning after the debacle, she endured the chaffing of her colleagues, even managing to join in their banter rather than fixing them with her chill blue stare and stripping their self-confidence to the bone. Underneath the affable surface, though, her mind was churning, thoughts revolving in an attempt to find a way forward that would show she was right.

Trawling the missing persons records in a bid to find other cases that fit the pattern was out of the question. Shaz knew from her days on the beat that somewhere in the region of a quarter of a million people went missing every year, nearly a hundred thousand of them under eighteen. Many of them simply walked away from the pressures of jobs they hated and families who offered them nothing. Others ran from lives grown intolerable. Some were seduced by promises of streets paved with gold. And a few were snatched unwilling from their familiar worlds and plunged into hell. But it was almost impossible to tell which category individuals fell into by a swift scrutiny of the report summary. Even if she could have persuaded her doubting colleagues to join the search, to unearth other possible victims of Shaz's serial killer would take far more resources than they had available.

When Tony announced that the afternoon would be devoted to private study, Shaz felt the itch of her impatience ease. Now she could at least *do* something. Rejecting Simon's suggestion of a pub lunch, she made straight for the city's biggest bookshop. Minutes later, she was standing by the till with a copy of *Jack on the*

Box: the Unauthorized Version by Tosh Barnes, a Fleet Street columnist known for his vitriolic pen, and *Lionheart: the True Story of a Hero* by Micky Morgan, an updated version of the account she'd first written shortly after their marriage. Tony had suggested that even if Shaz was right about the link, the killer would be more likely to be one of Vance's entourage than the man himself. The books might help either to eliminate him or to provide corroborative support for her theory.

A short bus ride and she was home. Popping the top on a can of Diet Coke, she sat down at her desk and plunged straight into his wife's adoring take on Jacko Vance's brilliant career. Great athlete, selfless hero, indomitable fighter, peerless broadcaster, tireless charity worker and sublime husband. As she forced herself through the hagiography, Shaz started to think it might actually be a pleasure to demolish so revoltingly perfect a figure. If her first assumption was right, he didn't so much have feet of clay as an entirely false facade.

It was a relief to reach the end, even though that meant facing the question she'd been pushing to the back of her mind. It was the classic misgiving of serial killer inquiries: how could the wife not know? Even leading such busy lives independent of each other, how could Micky Morgan share her bed and her existence with an abductor and murderer of adolescent girls and not sense something in his head was twisted out of true? And if she knew, or even suspected, how could she sit in front of the cameras day after day interviewing life's victims and victors without a flicker of anything other than professional compassion and composure?

It was a question that had no answer. Unless Tony had been right and it wasn't Jacko himself but a fan or a team member. Suppressing these misgivings, Shaz turned to *Jack on the Box* which proved to be merely an irreverent version of the same myth. Only the anecdotes were different, revealing nothing more sinister than that when he was wearing his professional hat, Jacko Vance was a perfectionist with a corrosive line in invective that could strip even TV's hardest cases of their protective armour. It was hardly a signpost to a homicidal maniac.

But for someone searching for elements that would fit the identikit notion of a serial killer, there were hints and clues that suggested she might not be completely deluded. There were certainly more factors than the average person would exhibit and, in her book, that kept Jacko Vance in the prime suspect slot thus far. It might well be someone else around him, but so far the research she had done had provided nothing to contradict her original theory.

Shaz had made notes as she worked her way through both books. At the end of her initial research, she booted up the laptop and opened a file she'd developed earlier in the profiling course. Headed *Organized Offender Checklist*, it was exactly what it said: a list of potential indicators to reveal to an investigator whether a suspect was a serious contender. She made a copy of the file; then, using her notes for guidance, occasionally referring back to the books, Shaz worked her way down the inventory. When she'd finished, she almost purred with satisfaction. She wasn't crazy after all. This was something Tony Hill wouldn't be able to ignore when it formed Part One of the new dossier she planned to present him with. She printed it out and smiled in satisfaction as she double-checked it.

Shaz was particularly pleased with the concluding paragraph. Concise, to the point, but telling the readers who knew what to look for all they needed to know, she thought. She wished she could get her hands on the newspaper cuttings about Vance and Micky Morgan, particularly the tabloids and the gossip columns. But to put in a formal request to any of the newspaper libraries would set too many alarm bells ringing. On a story this big, she couldn't even dare trust a personal contact.

She considered whether to present Tony with this fresh analysis. In her heart, she knew there wasn't enough to change his mind. But someone was killing young girls and on the balance of probabilities, given how long it had been going on and how many indicators lurked in his background, she reckoned Jacko Vance was her man. Somewhere, there was something that would expose his weakness, and she was going to find it.

The desk sergeant tipped the second spoonful of sugar into his mug of black tea and stirred it languidly, staring at the sluggish whirlpool it produced as if willing it to do something interesting enough to divert him from the pile of paperwork stacked beside him on the desk. The swirling slowed then stilled. Nothing else happened. With a sigh that started in the pit of his stomach, he picked up the first file and opened it.

The reprieve came two pages into the report. His hand shot out to the phone as if it was attached by elastic suddenly released. 'Glossop Police, Sergeant Stone,' he said cheerfully.

The voice on the phone was staccato with nerves, control barely in place. It was a woman, not young, not old, Peter Stone registered automatically as he pulled a pile of scrap paper towards him. 'It's my daughter,' the woman said. 'Donna. She's not come home. She's only fourteen. She never went to her friend's. I don't know where she is. Help me! You've got to help me!' The pitch rose to a frightened squeak.

'I understand how upsetting this is for you,' Stone said stolidly. Himself a father of daughters, he refused to allow his imagination to run riot over the possible disasters that could befall them. Otherwise he'd never have slept again. 'I'll need a few details so we can set

162

about being of some assistance.' His formality was deliberate, a calculated attempt to slow things down and instil calmness in his frantic caller. 'Your name is . . . ?'

'Doyle. Pauline Doyle. My daughter's Donna. Donna Theresa Doyle. We live up Corunna Street. Number 15 Corunna Street. Just the two of us. Her dad's dead, see? He took a brain haemorrhage three years ago, dropped down dead, just like that. What's happened to my Donna?' Tears shook her voice. Stone could hear sniffs and sobs despite her best efforts to stay coherent.

'What I'm going to do, Mrs Doyle, I'm going to send somebody round to take a statement from you. Meantime, can you just tell me how long Donna's been missing?'

'I don't know,' Pauline Doyle wailed. 'She left the house this morning to go to school and said she was going for her tea to her pal Dawn's house. They had some science project they were working on together. When she wasn't home by ten, I rang Dawn's mum and she told me Donna hadn't been there and Dawn said she wasn't in school all day.'

Stone glanced at the clock. Quarter past eleven. That meant the girl had been somewhere other than where she was supposed to be for the best part of fifteen hours. Not officially time to worry yet, but a dozen years in the Job had given him an instinct for the significant. 'You hadn't had words, had you?' he asked gently.

'No-o-o-o,' Mrs Doyle wept. She hiccupped and Stone could hear her breathe deeply to calm her voice. 'She's all I've got,' she said, her voice soft and piteous.

'There could be a simple explanation. It's not uncommon with young girls, going missing overnight. Now, I want you to put the kettle on and brew a pot of tea, because there'll be a couple of officers with you within ten minutes, OK?'

'Thank you.' Forlorn, Pauline Doyle replaced the phone and stared bleakly at the photograph on top of the television set. Donna smiled back at her, a flirtatious, knowing smile that said she was nudging the borderline between child and woman. Her mother stuffed her hand between her teeth to avoid crying out, then stumbled to her feet and went through to the fluorescent brilliance of the kitchen.

At that point, Donna Doyle had been alive and well and slightly drunk.

Once the decision had been taken, all that remained were details. First, the official proposal, arranged for maximum effect during the annual fund-raising telethon that garnered millions for children's charities. Jacko went down on one knee in front of eight million viewers and asked Micky to marry him. She looked suitably stunned, then moved. With tears in her eyes, she said yes. Like every other aspect of their marriage, there was nothing about the whole process that couldn't be screened before the watershed.

The wedding took place in a register office, of course, but that was no reason not to splurge on a party that would keep the gossip column inches flowing for days. Jacko's agent and Betsy were the witnesses, each acting as a kind of unofficial minder to make sure neither member of the wedding drank champagne to the destruction of discretion. Then, afterwards, the honeymoon. A private island in the Seychelles, Betsy and Micky in one cottage, Jacko in the other. On several occasions they spotted him on the beach, with a different woman each time, but no one apart from Jacko himself ever joined them for a meal and they were never introduced to any of his partners.

On the last night, the three had dinner together under the Indian Ocean moon. 'Your friends gone, then?' Betsy had asked, emboldened by the fifth glass of champagne

'Not friends,' Jacko said carefully. His mouth twiste in a strange smile. 'Not even personal assistants, I'n afraid. I don't sleep with friends. Sex is something I kee in the realm of transactions. After the accident, afte Jillie, I told myself I was never ever going to put mysel in a position where anybody could take anything tha mattered from me again.'

'That's sad,' Micky said. 'You lose a lot by not bein prepared to take risks.'

His eyes seemed to glaze over, like a tinted-glass lime window rising to obscure its inhabitant. It was a look she was certain was never seen by his public, nor even the terminally ill and permanently damaged that he gave his time and energy to reassure so potently. If the powers that be had ever seen that darkness behind his eyes, they'd have made sure he never came within a hundred miles of the sick and dying. All the world got was the charm. Come to that, it was mostly all she ever got. But either he willingly let her see more, or else he wasn't aware that she knew him so well. Even Betsy told her she was exaggerating when she spoke of the darkness battened down inside her husband. Only Micky knew she wasn't.

Jacko looked unsmiling into his wife's eyes and said, 'I take plenty of risks, Micky. I just minimize the possibility of damage. Take this marriage. It's a risk, but I wouldn't have taken it unless I'd been certain it was safer for me because you have a lot more to lose than I do if it's ever exposed as a sham.'

'Maybe so,' Micky acknowledged with a tip of her glass. 'But I think it's sad to cut yourself off from the possibility of love, which is what you've done ever since you split with Jillie and started playing games with me.'

'This isn't a game,' Jacko said, his face closed and

tense. 'But if you're worried about me lacking nourishment, don't be. I take responsibility for my own needs. And I promise my solutions will never embarrass you. I am the king of deniability.' He put his left hand over his heart and smiled solemnly.

The words had always haunted Micky, though he had never given her reason to throw them in his face. But sometimes, when she saw expressions cross his eyes that reminded her of the first time she'd seen his contained fury in that sterile hospital room, she wondered what exactly there might be lurking in Jacko's secret world that would require denial. Murder, however, would never have made it to the list.

The trouble with working alone was that you just couldn't cover the ground, Shaz had realized after a fitful night's sleep. There weren't enough hours in the day, she didn't have the authority to make full background inquiries, she had no access to the information network of the bobbies who worked the patches where Jacko Vance had grown up or lived since. There was no one to gossip with. If she was going to make any progress worth speaking of, there was only one possible route to go.

She'd have to stir things up. And that meant calling in more favours. She picked up the phone and rang Chris Devine's number. The answering machine picked up on the third ring. It was a relief not to have to explain the whole seemingly insane enterprise to Chris. When she heard the beep, she said, 'Chris? It's Shaz. Thanks for your help the other day. It was so useful, I need another favour. Any chance you could get me a home number for Jacko Vance? I'll be at home all evening. You're a star, thanks.'

'Hang on,' Chris's voice cut across hers. Shaz jumped

and almost knocked her coffee cup to the floor. 'Hello,' she said. 'Chris?'

'I was in the shower. What are you up to?' Chris' voice was more affectionate than Shaz reckoned sh deserved.

'I want to set up an interview with Jacko Vance, an I haven't got a number for him.'

'Is there some problem with official channels, doll?'

Shaz cleared her throat. 'It's not exactly an officia inquiry.'

'You're going to have to do better than that. Has thi got something to do with the half-dozen trees I had to murder to do the last favour you asked for?'

'Sort of. The exercise I told you about? Well, it' thrown up what looks like a genuine cluster. I think there's a real serial killer out there doing teenage girls And it's connected to Jacko Vance.'

'Jacko Vance? *The* Jacko Vance? *Vance's Visits* Jacko Vance? What's he got to do with a serial killer?'

'That's what I'm trying to find out. Only we're not supposed to be doing this for real yet, so nobody's prepared to take any action unless I can come up with something more concrete.'

'Hang on a minute, doll. Back up a bit, to where you said it's connected to Jacko. How d'you mean, "connected"?' Chris was starting to sound worried, Shaz thought. Time for a bit of back-pedalling. Time also to adopt the less dramatic suggestion of her colleagues.

'It could be something and nothing. Only, this cluster I spotted: he was doing a personal appearance in each of the girls' home towns a couple of days before they went walkabout. It's an odd coincidence, and I'm thinking maybe it's someone in his entourage or some psycho fan of his who has it in for girls who maybe come on too strong to Jacko or something.'

'So, let me get this right. You want to front up Jacko Vance to see if he's noticed any revolving-eyed maniacs hanging around his gigs? And you want to do this unofficial?' Chris's voice mixed incredulity and concern.

'That's about the size of it, yeah.'

'You're off your head, Bowman.'

'I thought that was part of my charm.'

' 'King hell, doll, charm won't get you out of the shit if you put a foot wrong on this one.'

'Tell me something I don't know. Are you going to help me or not?'

There was a long silence. Shaz let it stretch, even though her nerves were stretching to breaking point with it. Finally, Chris caved in. 'If I don't, you'll just go somewhere else, won't you?'

'I have to, Chris. If I'm right, somebody's killing kids. I can't ignore that.'

'It's if you're wrong I'm worried about, doll. You want me to come with you, give you a bit of back-up, make it look more official?'

It was tempting. 'I don't think so,' Shaz said slowly. 'If I end up going down in flames, I don't want to take you with me. But there is something you could do.'

Chris groaned. 'Not if it involves a library.'

'You could cover my back. I'll probably need to give a ring-back number. People like him, they don't take anything on trust. Only, we can't take phone calls on the course because we're always in lectures or group sessions or whatever. If I could use your office number, at least he's going to be getting a police phone if he calls back to check me out.'

'You got it,' Chris sighed. 'Give me five minutes.'

Shaz endured the wait stoically. There were times when she envied smokers, though not enough to start. She stared at the second hand of her watch, tightening her lips as it swept into the sixth minute. When the phone rang, she grabbed it before the end of the first peal.

'Got a pen?' Chris said.

'Yeah.'

'Here you go, then.' She recited the supposedly secret unlisted number she'd wheedled out of the desk officer at Notting Hill police station. 'You didn't get it from me.'

'Thanks, Chris. I owe you.'

'More than you'll ever pay, unfortunately,' Chris said ruefully. 'Hang loose, doll. Talk to you soon.'

'I'll keep you posted. Bye.' Shaz contemplated the piece of paper with a quiet smile of triumph. Here I come, ready or not, she thought, reaching for the phone again. Half past eight wasn't too early to call.

The number rang out a couple of times, then an automated voice told Shaz, 'Your call is being diverted.' A series of clicks, a hollow sound, then the distinctive warble of a mobile phone ringing. 'Hello?' The answering voice was instantly recognizable. Shaz found it disconcerting to have what normally came from the TV issuing from her phone, especially since it wasn't the voice she expected.

'Ms Morgan?' she asked tentatively.

'Speaking. Who is this?'

'I'm Detective Constable Sharon Bowman of the Metropolitan Police. I'm sorry to trouble you, but I need to speak to your husband.'

'I'm afraid he's not at home just now. Nor am I. You've actually come through on the wrong line. This is my personal line. His is a different number.'

Shaz felt a blush creeping up her neck. 'I'm sorry to have disturbed you.'

'No problem. Is it something I can help you with, officer?'

'I don't think so, Ms Morgan. Unless you could possibly give me a number where I can reach him?'

Micky hesitated. 'I'd rather not, if you don't mind. I could pass a message on, if that would do?'

It would have to, Shaz thought grimly. The rich really did do things differently. Just as well she'd already made the arrangement with Chris. 'I think he might have some background information relating to an inquiry we're pursuing. I realize he's a very busy man, but I can meet him any time tomorrow, wherever and whenever suits him. Now, I'm going to be out of the office for the rest of the day, so if he could ring this number . . .' she dictated Chris's direct line. 'And ask to speak to Sergeant Devine. He can make the arrangements with her.'

Micky read the number back to her. 'That right? Tomorrow? Fine, DC Bowman, I'll pass the message on to him.'

'Sorry to have intruded,' Shaz said gruffly.

The familiar chuckle came down the line. 'Think nothing of it. I'm always delighted to help the police. But you'll know that, if you ever see the programme.'

It was so obviously an opening that Shaz couldn't resist. 'It's a terrific show. I watch you whenever I can.'

'Flattery will always get your messages delivered,' Micky said, her voice as seductive as it always managed to be at noon.

'I look forward to hearing from Mr Vance,' Shaz said. She'd never meant anything more in her life.

Pauline Doyle stared at the empty frame on top of the television. The officers who had visited her the night of Donna's disappearance had taken the photograph to have some copies made. They'd seemed concerned about Donna, asking a lot of questions about her friends and her school, whether she had a boyfriend, what she liked to do on a weekend. When they'd eventually left with the photo and a description of Donna, she felt they'd helped her keep hysteria at bay. All her instincts were to run through the midnight streets crying her daughter's name, but the composed responses of the two uniformed officers who had filled her kitchen had soothed her, made her understand this was not the time to act on irrational impulses. 'Best stop here,' the older man had said. 'If she tries to phone home, you don't want her missing you. Leave it to us to look for her. We're the experts, we know what we're about.'

The woman who'd come the following morning had undermined those reassurances. She'd persuaded Pauline to do a detailed audit of Donna's possessions. When they'd established the absence of Donna's favourite dance outfit – a short black Lycra skirt, a body-hugging black-and-white striped T-shirt with a scoop neck and black patent leather Doc Marten's – the detective had visibly relaxed. Pauline understood why. In the eyes of the police, the missing clothes meant just another teenage runaway. They could relax now, stop worrying about their earlier assumption that they might well be looking for a body.

How could she explain in a way that they'd understand? How could she make them see that Donna had neither need nor reason to run away? She hadn't fallen out with Pauline. Quite the opposite. They were close, closer than most women managed to stay to their teenage daughters. Bernard's death had driven them to each other for comfort and they'd continued to share their confidences. Pauline clenched her eyes shut and sent a fierce supplication to the Virgin she'd lost faith in years before. The police wouldn't listen; what harm could it do to pray?

The dawn came up on her left-hand side to road noise and the sound of her own voice. All the way down the M1, Shaz practised the interview. She'd always envied lawyers the comfort of only asking questions to which they knew the answers. To face a professional without role-playing and exploring every possible response would have been madness, so she drove on automatic pilot, rehearsing her questions and the imagined replies. By the time she arrived in West London, she was as ready as she'd ever be. Either he'd let something slip, which she doubted he'd be amateur enough to do, or else she'd panic him into some subsequent action that would confirm everything she'd worked out for herself. Or she might be wrong and the others right and he might simply point her in the direction of a fanatical devotee that he'd spotted with the putative victims. It would be an anti-climax, but one she could live with if it saved lives and put a killer behind bars.

That she might be putting herself at risk never seriously occurred to her in spite of Chris Devine's warnings. At twenty-four, Shaz had no intimations of mortality. Even three years in the police, with the occasional assaults and regular dangers, hadn't dented her sense of invincibility. Besides, people who lived in Holland Park mansions didn't attack police officers.

Especially not when it was their wife who'd made the appointment.

Early as usual, Shaz ignored the instructions to park on their drive that had been passed on to her. Instead, she found a meter in Notting Hill and walked down into Holland Park, strolling down the street where they lived. Carefully counting the numbers, Shaz identified the house belonging to Jacko and Micky. It was hard to believe that somewhere so huge in the heart of Central London was still dedicated to only one household, but Shaz knew from her background reading that this was no mansion split into flats. It was all for Jacko and Micky, the only live-in staff, Micky's long-standing personal assistant Betsy Thorne. Gobsmacking, Shaz thought as she passed the wedding cake white house with its flawless facade. She couldn't see much of the garden, shielded from the world by tall, clipped variegated laurel hedges, but the section beyond the electronic gates appeared to be as immaculate as an exhibit at the Chelsea Flower Show. Shaz felt a momentary doubt in the pit of her stomach. How could she suspect the tenant of such a jewel of the hideous crimes her imagination had constructed? People like this didn't do things like that, did they?

Biting her lip in anger at her lack of self-belief, Shaz turned on her heel and marched back to her car, determination building with the very rhythm of her stride. He was a criminal and when she'd finished with him, the whole world would know it. It took her less than five minutes to drive back to the house and turn into the gateway. She wound down her window and pressed the speaker box. 'DC Bowman to see Mr Vance,' she said firmly.

The gates swung open with a low electric hum and Shaz advanced into what she couldn't help thinking of as enemy territory. Not sure where to leave her car, she opted to avoid blocking the double garage and followed the drive round to the other side of the house, past a Range Rover parked by the front steps, and stopped alongside a silver Mercedes convertible. She turned off the engine and sat for a moment, gathering her energies and focusing on her objective. 'Just do it,' she finally said, her voice low and tough.

She ran up the steps to the front door and pushed the bell. Almost instantaneously, the door swung open and Micky Morgan's face smiled down at her, familiar as family. 'Detective Constable Bowman,' she said, stepping back and waving Shaz inside. 'Come in. I was just leaving.' Micky extended an arm to one side, indicating a middle-aged woman with grey-streaked hair pulled loosely back in a heavy plait. 'This is Betsy Thorne, my PA. We're off to catch Le Shuttle.'

'An overnight break in Le Touquet,' Betsy amplified.

'Lots of seafood and a flutter in the casino,' Micky added, reaching over to take a leather holdall from Betsy. 'Jacko's expecting you. He's just finishing a phone call. If you take that first door on the left, he'll be with you in a minute.'

Shaz finally managed to get a word in. 'Thanks,' she said. Micky and Betsy hovered on the doorstep, till Shaz realized they weren't going to close the door until they were certain she was in the correct place. With an awkward smile, Shaz nodded and walked through the open door Micky had indicated. Only when she'd disappeared from sight did she hear the front door closing. Moving to the window, she saw the women climb into the Range Rover.

'DC Bowman?'

Shaz whirled around. She hadn't heard anyone enter. Across the room, smaller in life than he appeared on

TV, Jacko Vance smiled. Fuelled by her imagination, Shaz saw the grin of the panther just before its prey becomes a carcass. She wondered if she was face to face with her first serial killer. If so, she hoped he didn't realize he was seeing Nemesis.

Her eyes were extraordinary. From behind, she'd looked so average. Brown hair brushing the collar of a tailored dark navy blazer over blue jeans and tan deck shoes. Nothing you'd glance at twice in a crowded bar. But when he startled her into turning round, the blaze of her blue eyes converted her into an entirely different creature. Vance felt a tingle of apprehension coupled with a strange sense of satisfaction. Whatever she was after, this woman wasn't a nobody. She was an adversary. 'Sorry to keep you waiting,' he said, his voice the familiar TV caress.

'I was early,' she said neutrally.

Vance walked towards her, stopping when there was about six feet between them. 'Have a seat, officer,' he said, indicating the sofa behind her.

'Thanks,' Shaz said, ignoring his instruction and moving instead to the very armchair he'd planned to occupy. He'd chosen it because the seat was higher and the light was behind it. He'd intended to place her at a disadvantage, but she'd turned the tables. Irritation stung him like an insect bite and rather than sitting down himself, he moved over to the fireplace and leaned against the ornately carved overmantel. He stared across at her, his silence demanding that she open the bidding.

'I appreciate you making the time to see me,' she said after a long moment. 'I realize how busy you are.'

'You didn't leave me much option. Besides, I'm always happy to be of assistance to the police. Your Deputy Commissioner could fill you in on the details of the number of times I've helped police charities.' The smile never left his voice but didn't make it to his eyes.

The blue stare didn't blink. 'I'm sure he could, sir.'

'Which reminds me. Your warrant card?' Vance didn't move, forcing Shaz to get up and cross the room once she'd taken out the wallet that contained her police credentials. 'I can't believe we'd be so careless,' Vance said conversationally as she approached. 'Letting a stranger across the door without checking she was who she claimed to be.' He gave her Metropolitan Police warrant card a perfunctory glance. 'There's another one, isn't there?'

'I'm sorry? This is the only card Metropolitan Police officers are issued with. It's our ID,' Shaz said, face giving nothing away of the alarm bells ringing in her head, telling her he knew too much and she should clear out while the going was good.

Vance's lips seemed to shrink as his smile became more vulpine. Time to show her who held the cards, he decided. 'But you're not with the Met any longer, are you, DC Bowman? You see, you're not the only one who's done their homework. You have done your homework?'

'I am still an officer of the Metropolitan Police,' Shaz said firmly. 'Anyone who has told you different is mistaken, sir.'

He pounced. 'But you're not based in the Met's area, are you? You're on attachment to a special unit. Why don't you show me your current ID so that I know you are who you say you are and we can get down to business?' Careful, he told himself, don't get carried away just because you're so much smarter than her. You don't know yet what she's doing here. He shrugged winningly, his eyebrows lifting. 'I don't mean to be difficult, but a man in my position can't be too careful.'

Shaz looked him up and down, her face a mask. 'That's very true,' she said, producing her National Profiling Task Force ID, complete with photograph. He reached out for it, but she moved it out of his grasp.

'I've not seen one of those before,' he said chattily, hiding his frustration at not being able to glimpse more than a logo and the word 'profiling', which had leapt out like a burning brand. 'The profiling task force we've all read so much about, eh? Once you're actually up and running, you should get one of your experienced officers to go on my wife's programme, tell the people what's being done to protect them.' Now she'd know he knew she was an absolute beginner.

'That wouldn't be my decision, sir.' Shaz deliberately turned her back on him and walked back to the chair. 'Now, if we could get down to business?'

'Of course.' He spread his left arm in an expansive gesture without making a move towards a chair. 'I'm at your disposal, DC Bowman. Perhaps we could start with you telling me exactly what this is all about.'

'We've reopened the cases of a group of missing teenage girls,' Shaz said, opening the folder she was carrying. 'Initially, we have identified seven cases with strong similarities. The cases cover a period of six years, and we will be expanding our inquiries to see whether there are other cases with common features that we haven't pinpointed yet.'

'I don't quite see what I . . .' Vance frowned convincingly. 'Teenage girls?'

'Fourteen- and fifteen-year-olds,' Shaz said firmly. 'I can't go into the precise details that have linked these cases, but we have grounds for believing they may be connected.'

'You mean, they're not just run-of-the-mill runaways?' he asked, sounding perplexed.

'We have reason to believe their disappearances were planned by a third party,' Shaz said cautiously, never shifting her eyes from his face. The intensity of her gaze made him uncomfortable. He wanted to edge away from her stare, to fidget his way out of her eyeline. But he forced himself to keep his pose casual.

'Kidnapped, is that what you're saying?'

Her eyebrows and a slight movement of her head indicated a shrug. 'I'm not in a position to release any more information,' she said with a sudden smile.

'Fine, but you're still not making much sense. What has a bunch of missing teenagers got to do with me?' He made his voice sound a little edgy. It wasn't hard to do; there was plenty of nervous tension buzzing in his veins to draw on.

Shaz flipped open her folder and drew out a sheaf of photocopied photographs. 'In every case, a couple of days before the girls disappeared, you'd made a public appearance or taken part in a charity event in the towns where they lived. We have reason to believe that each of the girls attended the occasion.'

He could feel the red tide rising up his neck. He was powerless to stop the flush of anger as it climbed into his face. It was an effort to keep himself calm and his voice level. 'Hundreds of people come to my events,' he said evenly, his voice a fraction husky to his ears. 'Statistically, some of them must go missing. All the time.'

Shaz cocked her head, as if she'd also picked up on a change in his tone. She looked like a hunting dog who's just had the faintest whiff of what might possibly be a rabbit. 'I know. I'm sorry we have to bother you with this. It's just that my boss thinks there's an outside possibility that either someone in your entourage or possibly someone who's got an unhealthy interest in you night conceivably be involved in the disappearance of those girls.'

'You mean, you think I've got a stalker who's capturing my fans?' This time, he found it wasn't hard to sound incredulous. As a cover story, it was ridiculous. An imbecile could see that the person she was really interested in wasn't some crazy, nor a member of his entourage. It was him. He could tell by her eyes, obsessively fixed on him, recording his every move, noticing the faint sheen of sweat he could feel on his forehead. And her talk of a boss was just as evidently a bluff. She was a lone wolf, like him. He could smell it on her.

Shaz nodded. 'It could be. Transference, the psychologists call it. Like John Hinckley. Remember him? The guy who shot Ronald Reagan because he wanted Jodie Foster to take notice of him?' Her voice was pleasant, friendly, carefully pitched so he wouldn't feel threatened. He hated her for thinking so simple a technique would slip past him unnoticed.

'This is bizarre,' he said, pushing off from the mantelpiece and striding to and fro on the hearth rug, a hand-knotted silk Bokhara that he'd chosen himself. Staring down at the grey and cream intricacies under his feet calmed him until he was able to meet the woman's intense eyes again. 'It's absurd. If it wasn't so appalling a suggestion, it would be funny. And I still don't see what it has to do with me.'

'It's simple, sir,' Shaz said soothingly.

Feeling patronized, Vance stopped in his tracks and scowled. 'What?' he demanded, charm disintegrating by the second.

'All I want you to do is to look at some photographs and tell me if you noticed the girls for any reason. Maybe they were particularly pushy with you, and someone wanted to punish them. Maybe you noticed one of your staff chatting them up. Or maybe you never spotted any of them. Just a couple of minutes of your time, then I'm out of here,' Shaz coaxed. She leaned forward and spread the photocopies over a kilim-covered footstool the size of a coffee table.

He moved towards her, transfixed by the photographs that she'd arranged to face him. Only a fraction of his work, that was all she'd captured. But every single smiling stare was one he'd destroyed.

Vance forced a laugh. 'Seven faces out of thousands? Sorry, DC Bowman, you've been wasting your time. I've never seen any of them before.'

'Look again,' she said. 'Are you absolutely certain?' There was an edge in her voice that hadn't been there before, sharp and excited. He dragged his eyes away from the pale reflections of the living flesh he'd punished and met Shaz Bowman's implacable eyes. She knew. She might not have the proof yet, but he knew she knew now. He also knew she wouldn't stop until she had destroyed him. It had come down to dog eat dog, and she had no chance. Not handicapped by the law.

He shook his head, a sorrowful smile on his lips. 'I'm positive. I've never clapped eyes on any of them before.'

Without even looking, Shaz pushed the middle picture closer to him. 'You made an appeal in a national tabloid for Tiffany Thompson to call her parents,' she said without inflexion.

'My God,' he exclaimed, forcing his features into an expression of happy astonishment. 'Do you know, I'd completely forgotten about that? You're right, of course, I see it now.'

Her attention was all on his face as he spoke. In a swift movement, he swung his prosthesis round in a short arc and smashed it violently into the side of her head. Her eyes showed a momentary shock, then panic.

As she fell out of the chair, her forehead smacked into the footstool. By the time she crashed to the floor, she was unconscious.

Vance wasted no time. He raced down to the cellar where he grabbed a reel of hi-fi speaker wire and a pack of latex gloves. Within minutes, Shaz was trussed like a hog-tied steer on the polished parquet. Then he ran up to the top floor and opened his wardrobe, scrabbling around on the floor until he found what he was looking for. Back downstairs, he covered Shaz's head with the soft flannel bag that his new leather briefcase had come in. Then he wrapped a few lengths of wire round her neck, tight enough to be uncomfortable but not so that it would constrict her breathing. He wanted her dead, but not yet. Not here, and not accidentally.

As soon as he was sure that she wasn't going to be able to break free, he picked up her shoulder bag and sat down with it on the sofa, gathering the photocopies and the file they'd come from on the way. Meticulously, he began to go through everything, starting with the file. The abstracts of the police reports he skimmed over, knowing he would have the opportunity to look at them in more detail later. When he came to the analysis Shaz had presented to her colleagues, he took his time, weighing and calculating how dangerous to him it might prove. Not very, he decided. The photocopies of the newspaper clippings about his visits to the places in question were meaningless; for every one connected to a disappearance, he could produce twenty that weren't. Putting that aside, he picked up the organized offender checklist. Reading her conclusion so angered him that he jumped to his feet and gave the unconscious detective a couple of savage kicks in the stomach. 'Fuck do you know, bitch?' he shouted angrily. He wished he could see her eyes now. They wouldn't be judging him, they'd be begging him for mercy.

Furious, he stuffed the papers back in the file along with the photocopies. He'd have to study them more carefully, but there wasn't time now. He'd been right to nip this in the bud before anyone else paid attention to this bitch's allegations. He turned to her roomy shoulder bag and pulled out a spiral-bound notebook. A quick flick through the pages revealed nothing of interest except Micky's phone number and their address. Since he wasn't going to be able to deny she'd been here, that had better stay. But he tore out a handful of pages after the last entry, making it look as if someone had ripped out details pertaining to a subsequent appointment, then replaced it in the bag.

Next out was the microcassette recorder, the tape still turning. He stopped the machine and removed the tape, placing it with the blank sheets of paper on one side. He ignored the Ian Rankin paperback and pulled out a filofax. Under that day's date, the only entry read, 'JV 9.30'. He considered adding another cryptic entry and settled for the single letter 'T' underneath her appointment with him. Let them think about that. Inside the front cover, he found what he was looking for. 'If found, return to S. Bowman, Flat 1, 17 Hyde Park Hill, Headingley, Leeds. REWARD.' His fingers groped around the bottom of the bag. No keys.

Vance stuffed everything back into the shoulder bag, picked up the file and crossed to Shaz. He patted her down until he found a bunch of keys in her trouser pocket. Smiling, he went upstairs to his office and found a padded envelope big enough for the file. He addressed it to his Northumberland retreat, stamped it and sealed Shaz's research inside.

A quick glance at his watch told him it was barely

half past ten. He went through to his bedroom and changed into jeans, one of the few short-sleeved T-shirts he possessed, and a denim jacket. He picked up a holdall from the back of the fitted wardrobes that ran deep under the eaves. He took out a Nike baseball cap that was attached to a professional quality wig of collar-length salt-and-pepper hair and put it on. The effect was remarkable. When he added a pair of aviator glasses with clear lenses and a pair of foam pads to fill out his hollow cheeks, the transformation was complete. The only giveaway was his prosthetic arm. And Jacko had the perfect answer to that.

He let himself out of the house, careful to lock up behind himself, and opened Shaz's car. He took a careful note of the seat position, then climbed in and adjusted it to suit his longer legs. He spent a few minutes familiarizing himself with the controls, making sure he was going to be able to manage the stick shift and steer at the same time. Then he set off, stopping only to drop the padded envelope in a pillar box in Ladbroke Grove. As he hit the approach ramp to the M1 shortly after eleven o'clock, he allowed himself a small, private smile. Shaz Bowman was going to be very sorry she'd ever crossed him. But not for long.

The first pain was a scream of cramp in her left leg, penetrating her muzzy unconsciousness like a serrated knife across a knuckle. The instinctive attempt at stretching and flexing the muscle triggered a slash of agony around her wrists. It made no sense to a disorientated mind that had started to throb like a thumb hit with a hammer. Shaz forced her eyes open, but the blackness didn't go away. Then she registered the damp material against her face. It was some sort of hood, made of thick fabric with a soft nap. It covered her whole head, fastening tightly round her throat, making it hard to swallow.

. Gradually, she made sense of her position. She was lying on her side on a hard surface, her hands fastened behind her back with some sort of ligature that bit cruelly into the flesh of her wrists. Her feet were also fastened at the ankle, and both sets of bonds were linked to allow minimal movement. Anything adventurous like stretching her legs or trying to shift her spot cost too much in pain. She had no idea how small or how large her area of confinement was, nor any desire to explore once she had experienced the torment of attempting to turn over.

She had no idea how long she'd been unconscious. The last thing she could remember was Jacko Vance's laughing face looming over her, as if he didn't have a care in the world, secure in the certainty that no one would ever take this pipsqueak detective seriously. No, that wasn't quite right. Something else tugged at her memory. Shaz tried the deep breathing of relaxation techniques and tried to picture what she'd seen. The memory stirred and took shape. Out on the edge of her peripheral vision, his right arm rising, then swinging down savagely like a club. That was the last thing she could remember.

With the memory came terror, sharper than any of her physical afflictions. Nobody knew where she was except Chris, who wasn't expecting to hear from her anyway. She hadn't told anyone else, not even Simon. She hadn't been able to face their mockery, however friendly. Now the fear of being laughed at was going to cost her her life. Shaz was under no illusion about that. She'd asked Jacko Vance questions that made him realize she knew he was a serial killer and he hadn't panicked as she'd believed he would. Instead, he'd worked out for himself that she was a maverick. That although her deductions were a threat to him, he could win himself a stay of execution by getting rid of her, the renegade cop in hot pursuit of a solo hunch. Removing Shaz would, at worst, buy him time to cover his tracks or even leave the country.

Shaz felt a wave of sweat drench her skin. There was no question about it. She was going to die. The only question was how.

She'd been right. And being right was going to kill her.

Pauline Doyle was desperate. The police refused to regard Donna's disappearance as anything other than a typical teenage runaway. 'She'll have gone to London, probably. There's no point in us looking for her round here,' one of the uniformed officers she'd mithered at the counter of the police station had said in exasperation one night.

Pauline might shout from the rooftops that someone had stolen her daughter, but the evidence of the missing outfit was more than enough to convince overworked cops that Donna Doyle was just another teenager bored with home and convinced the streets somewhere were paved with gold. You only had to look at her photograph, that knowing smile, to understand she was nothing like as innocent as her poor misguided mother wanted to believe.

With the police showing no interest beyond a routine posting of Donna on the missing list, Pauline was stymied. Not for her the passionate television appeals for the missing daughter, not with the absence of official backing. Even the local paper wasn't interested, though the women's editor toyed with the idea of running a feature on teenage runaways. But like the police, when she saw Donna's photograph, she thought again. There was something about Donna that defied any attempt to portray her as an innocent abroad, seduced by chaste dreams. Something about the line of her mouth, the tilt of her chin said that she had crossed the line. The women's editor reckoned Donna Doyle was the sort of Lolita that would make most women want to put blinkers on their husbands.

Her frustration spilling over into nightly storms of tears, Pauline decided the time had come to take matters into her own hands. Her job in the estate agency wasn't particularly well paid. It was enough to feed and clothe her and Donna and to keep a roof over their heads, but not much more than that. There was still a couple of thousand left over from Bernard's insurance. Pauline had been saving that for when Donna went off to university, knowing how tight things would be then.

But if Donna didn't come back, there would be no point in saving it for university, Pauline reasoned. Better then to spend the money to try and get her home and let higher education fend for itself. So Pauline took Donna's photograph to the local print shop and had them make up thousands of flyers with her daughter's image occupying the whole of one side. The text on the reverse read, 'HAVE YOU SEEN THIS GIRL? Donna Doyle went missing on Thursday 11th October. She was last seen at quarter past eight in the morning, on her way to Glossop Girls Grammar. She was wearing school uniform of maroon skirt, maroon cardigan, white open-necked blouse. Her shoes were black Kickers, and she had a black anorak. She was carrying a black Nike backpack. If you saw her at any time after that, please contact her mother, Pauline Doyle.' It gave the address in Corunna Street, and telephone numbers at home and the agency.

Pauline took a week off work and stuffed the leaflets through letterboxes from dawn till dusk. She started in the town centre, thrusting the reproductions of Donna's face at anyone who would take them, and gradually worked her way out into suburban streets, not noticing the steepness of the hills she climbed or the blisters that swelled inside her shoes.

No one phoned.

While Shaz Bowman was lying on his hard floor in London, conscious only of fear and pain, Jacko Vance was exploring her domain. He'd made good time to Leeds, stopping only to fill up with petrol and visit the disabled toilet at the motorway services. He'd wanted to use its sanitary disposal unit to get rid of the tape he'd unravelled from Shaz's microcassette. In the car park, he'd crushed the casing underfoot, leaving the fragments to scatter in the blustery wind that swept across the Midlands.

Finding Shaz's home had been made even easier by her recently purchased *A to Z*, which conveniently had the street circled in blue biro. He parked the car round the corner and forced himself to combat his twitching nerves by strolling slowly down the street, empty except for a couple of small boys playing cricket on the opposite pavement. He turned in at the gate of number 17 and tried one of the two Yale keys in the heavy Victorian front door. That he got it right first time convinced him that the gods really were on his side.

He found himself in a gloomy hallway, lit only by two thin lancet windows on either side of the door. Peering into the murk, he saw a wide and graceful staircase rising ahead of him. There seemed to be one ground-floor flat on either side. He chose the left-hand side, and was proved right again. Breathing more easily now, convinced everything was going his way, Vance let himself into the flat. He wasn't planning on staying long, just enough to scout out the lie of the land, so he moved swiftly through the rooms. As soon as he saw the living room, he realized that Shaz could not possibly have chosen a flat better suited to his purpose. The French windows led out on to a garden surrounded by high walls, shaded by tall fruit trees. At the end, he could discern the outlines of a wooden door in the brick wall.

Only one thing remained to be done. He slipped off his jacket and unfastened his prosthesis. From the hold-all, he took an object he'd persuaded the props department to make for him a couple of years back, supposedly as a practical joke. Using the fittings from one of his previous artificial arms, an earlier model now discarded, they'd built a plaster cast with disturbingly realistic fingertips protruding from the end. Once it was fitted, especially with a jacket over it and a sling holding it in place, it looked exactly like a broken arm. When he was satisfied he'd arranged it correctly, Vance re-packed the holdall, took a deep breath and decided it was time to go.

He let himself out of the French windows, pushing them to behind him, then strode confidently down the gravel path to the gate. He could feel the hair on his neck prickling under the wig, wondering if there were eyes behind any of the windows at his back, eyes that would remember what they'd seen once his handiwork was over and exposed to the public gaze. In a bid for reassurance, he reminded himself that any description they could come up with would sound nothing like Jacko Vance.

He unbolted the back gate, convinced that no one

would fasten it again before he returned. He found himself in a narrow lane that ran between two sets of walled back gardens and led out on to one of the main roads that ran down towards the city centre. Walking to the station took the best part of an hour, but he had barely ten minutes to wait for a London train. He was back in Holland Park and restored to Jacko Vance by half past seven.

Before he made his final preparations, he slammed a twelve-inch pizza into the oven. It wasn't his usual idea of Saturday night dinner, but the carbohydrate should stop his stomach turning somersaults. Tension always hit him in the gut. Whenever the fever of anticipation had him in its grasp, he'd have to endure cramps and clenches, knots and nausea. He'd learned early on in his days as a live sports commentator that the only way to stop the churning and grumbling was to stodge out in advance. What worked for TV worked just as well for murder, he'd soon discovered. Now, he always ate before he picked up his targets. And of course, he always ate with them before the act itself.

While the pizza was cooking, he loaded his Mercedes. Exertion was easier on an empty stomach. Now everything was ready for Shaz Bowman's final performance. All he had to do was get her on stage.

Donna Doyle was also alone. But, deranged by agony, she lacked the luxury of introspection. The first time she'd woken from broken sleep, she'd felt strong enough to explore her prison. Her fear was still overwhelming, but it was no longer paralysing. Wherever she was, it was dark as a grave and had the dank smell of the tiny coal cellar at home. She used her good arm to help her gain a sense of where she was and what was around her. She was, she realized, lying on a plastic-covered mattress. Her fingers explored the edges and felt cold tiles. Not as smooth as the ceramic ones in the bathroom at home, more like the glazed terracotta on Sarah Dyson's mum's conservatory steps.

The wall behind her was rough stone. She struggled to her feet, realizing properly for the first time that her legs were shackled. She bent and let her fingers trace the outline of an iron cuff round each ankle. They were attached to a heavy chain. One-handed, it was impossible to gauge how long it was. Four hesitant steps along one wall brought her to a corner. She turned through ninety degrees and moved on. Two steps and her shin crashed painfully against something solid. It didn't take long both by touch and smell to identify it as a chemical toilet. Pathetically grateful, Donna subsided on to it and emptied her bladder.

That only reminded her of how thirsty she was. Hunger she wasn't too sure about, but thirst was definitely a problem. She stood up and carried on along the wall for another few feet before the chain round her ankles brought her up short. The jerk sent a spasm of pain shooting from her arm into her neck and head, and she gasped. Slowly, bent like an old woman, she retraced her steps and moved past the other end of the mattress, her hand brushing the wall.

Within a few feet, the questions of food and drink were answered. A stiff metal tap produced a surge of icy water which she drank thirstily, falling to her knees to get her head right underneath the flow. As she did, she knocked something over beyond her. Her thirst slaked, she groped blindly for whatever she'd bumped into. Probing fingers found four boxes, all large and light. She shook them and heard the familiar rustle of cornflakes.

An hour of investigation later and she was forced to realize that was it. Four boxes of cornflakes – she'd tested each one – and as much freezing water as she could drink. She'd tried running the water over her shattered arm, but the pain had made her head reel. This was it. The bastard had left her chained up like a dog. Left her to die?

She sat back on her heels and keened like a bereft mother.

But that had been a couple of endless days ago. Now, delirious with pain, she moaned and gibbered, occasionally passing out, occasionally drifting exhausted into tormented sleep. If she'd been able to comprehend the state she was in, Donna wouldn't have wanted to live.

The car stopped. Shaz slid irresistibly forward into the bulwark separating the narrow confines of the boot from the back seat, crushing her wrists and shoulders again. She tried to strain upwards to bang her head on the lid in a desperate bid to attract someone's attention, but all she achieved was a fresh wave of pain. She tried not to sob, afraid that if mucus blocked her nose, she'd suffocate, unable to breathe through the gag that Vance had tied over the hood before he'd rolled her agonizingly across hard floors, over a carpeted area and down a short flight of steps, then hoisted her into the boot of the car. She had been horribly amazed at the strength and dexterity of this one-armed man.

Shaz breathed as deeply as she could; too far and her chest expansion made her stiff shoulder muscles protest. Only sheer willpower kept her from gagging at the stench of her own urine. Let's see you get rid of that from your boot carpet, she thought triumphantly; she couldn't do anything to save her life, but she was still determined to seize every opportunity to prevent Jacko Vance from walking away from his crimes. If SOCO ever got this far, a piss-stained carpet would make their day.

Abruptly the muffled music stopped. Ever since they'd set off, he'd listened to hits of the sixties. Shaz had forced herself to pay attention and had counted the tracks. At an average of three minutes a song, she reckoned they'd been driving for somewhere around three hours of what had felt like motorway after the first twenty minutes or so. That probably meant the north; heading west would have taken them on to the motorway more quickly. Of course, it was possible that he could have confused her by driving a circuit round the M25, orbiting London until he'd laid a completely false trail. Shaz didn't think so; she doubted whether he felt any need to mislead her. She wasn't going to be alive to tell anyone, after all.

It was probably dark by now; she'd lain bound in the house for what felt like several hours before Vance had returned to deal with her. If they were in the depths of the country, there would be no one to see or hear her. Somehow, she thought that was probably Vance's plan. He must have taken his victims somewhere isolated to escape detection. She could think of no reason why he'd treat her differently.

A car door closed with a soft thud and a faint click. Then a metallic sound closer to hand and the soft hydraulic sigh of a boot opening. 'God, you stink,' Vance said contemptuously, dragging her carelessly forward.

'Listen,' he continued, sounding closer. 'I'm going to free your feet. I'm going to cut them free. The knife is very, very sharp. Mostly I use it to joint meat. If you take my meaning.' His voice was almost a whisper, his hot breath penetrating the hood next to her ear. Shaz felt another ripple of nausea. 'If you try to run, I'll gut you like a pig on a butcher's hook. There's nowhere to run to, see? We're in the middle of nowhere.'

Shaz's ears told her different. To her surprise, there was the rumble of traffic not far off, the underlying mutter of city life. If she had half a chance, she'd take it.

She felt the cold blade of the knife briefly against the skin of her ankle, then her feet were miraculously free. For a second, she thought she could kick out then make a run for it. Then her circulation reasserted itself and spasms of excruciating pins and needles squeezed a moan from the dry mouth behind the unyielding gag. Before the cramp could pass, Shaz felt herself hauled over the edge of the boot. She collapsed in an unco-ordinated heap before he slammed the boot shut and yanked her to her feet. He half-dragged, half-carried her through a gap or a gateway where she bashed her shoulder on the wall, then down a path and up a couple of steps. Then he pushed her sharply and she crashed to a carpeted floor, her legs still useless rubbery handicaps.

Even through the haze of disorientation and pain, the closing of the door and the rattle of curtains being drawn sounded strangely familiar to Shaz. A fresh dread seized her and she began to shiver uncontrollably, losing control of her bladder for the second time in the past hour.

'God, you're a disgusting bitch,' Vance sneered. Again she felt herself irresistibly hauled upwards. This time she was dumped unceremoniously in a hard, upright chair. Before she could adjust to the fresh pain in her shoulders and arms, she felt a new restraint being fastened to her leg, attaching it to the chair like a broken limb to a splint. In a desperate bid for freedom, she forced her other leg to kick out, rejoicing in the jarring connection with Vance's body, exulting in his cry of surprised pain.

The blow to her jaw snapped her head back with a crack that sent waves of sick pain down her spine. 'You fucking stupid cow,' was all he said before he grabbed her other leg and forced it against the chair while he bound them tightly together.

She felt his legs between her knees. The warmth of his body was almost the worst suffering she'd had to endure so far. He raised her arms agonizingly and forced them back down over the back of the chair to hold her irresistibly upright. Then the hood was pulled away from her flesh and she heard the whisper of a razor-sharp blade through cloth. Blinking at the sudden appalling brightness, Shaz's stomach was gripped with a cold cramp as she discovered her worst fear was a reality. She was sitting in her own living room, strapped to one of the four dining chairs she'd bought only ten days before in Ikea.

Vance pressed his body against hers as he cut the hood away just above the gag, leaving her able to see and hear properly, but incapable of any noise other than a muffled grunt. He stepped back, giving her breast a cruel tweak with his artificial hand as he went.

He stood staring at her, flicking the blade of the butcher's filleting knife against the table edge. Shaz thought she had never seen a more arrogant human being. His pose, his expression, everything reeked of self-important righteousness. 'You really fucked up my weekend,' he said witheringly. 'Believe me, this is not how I planned to spend Saturday night. Dressing up in fucking surgical greens and latex in some shitty flat in Leeds is not my idea of a good time, bitch.' He shook his head pityingly. 'You're going to pay, Detective Bowman. You're going to pay for being a stupid little fuck.'

He put the knife down and fumbled under his top. Shaz glimpsed a bum bag as he unzipped it and took out a CD-ROM. Without another word he walked out of the room. Shaz heard the familiar hum then clatter as first her computer then her printer were switched on.

Straining her ears, she fancied she heard the clicking of the mouse and the sound of keys being struck. Then, unmistakably, the vibrating thrum of paper loading and printing.

When he returned, he carried a single sheet of paper which he held in front of her face. She recognized the print-out of an illustrated encyclopaedia article. She didn't have to read the words to understand the symbolism of the line drawing at the top of the page. 'You know what this is?' he demanded.

Shaz just stared at him, her eyes bloodshot but still arresting. She was determined not to give in to him on any level.

'It's a teaching aid, student detective Bowman. It's the three wise monkeys. See no evil, hear no evil, speak no evil. You should have taken that as your class motto. You should have stayed away from me. You should have kept your nose out of my business. You won't be doing that again.'

He let the paper flutter to the floor. Suddenly he lunged forward, hands pushing her head back. Then his prosthetic thumb was over her eyeball, pushing down and out, rending muscles, ripping the hollow globe free from its moorings. The scream was only inside Shaz's head. But it was loud enough to carry her over into blessed unconsciousness.

Jacko Vance studied his handiwork and saw that it was good. Because his usual killings were fuelled by a completely different set of needs, he'd never contemplated them in a purely aesthetic light before. But this was a work of art, laden with symbolism. He wondered if anyone would be smart enough to read the message he'd left and, having read it, to heed it. Somehow, he doubted it.

He leaned forward and made a slight adjustment to the angle of the sheet of paper in her lap. Then, satisfied, he allowed himself the luxury of a smile. All he had to do now was to make sure she'd left no messages behind. He began to search the flat methodically, inch by inch, including the waste bins. He was used to the company of corpses, so the presence of Shaz's remains caused him no stress. He was so relaxed as he meticulously searched her kitchen that he actually caught himself singing softly as he worked.

In the room she'd made her office, he found more than he'd bargained for. A box of photocopies of newspapers, a pad of rough notes, files on the hard disk of her laptop and back-ups on floppy disk, print-outs of various drafts of the analysis he'd found earlier in the file she'd brought to his house. What was even worse was that much of the print-out didn't seem to have any matching files on the computer. There were copies on floppy disk, but not on the hard disk. It was a nightmare. When he spotted the modem, he almost panicked. The reason the files weren't on her hard disk was that they were somewhere else, presumably on some National Profiling Task Force computer. And there was no way he could access that. His only hope was that Shaz Bowman had been as paranoid with her computer files as she seemed to have been about sharing her showdown with a colleague. Either way, there was nothing he could do about it now. He'd get rid of every trace there was here and just have to hope that nobody would go looking in her computer files at work. If the Luddite cops he knew were anything to judge by, it would never occur to them that she might have techie tendencies. Besides, she wasn't supposed to be working cases, was she? Not according to the contacts he'd so cautiously and entirely naturally exploited to find out what he had about her before their meeting. There was no reason why anyone should connect so bizarre a death to her profiling training.

But how was he going to deal with all this *stuff*? He couldn't take the material with him in case a chance encounter with a traffic cop led to a search of his car. Equally, he couldn't leave it behind, pointing a giant finger of blame in his direction. He wasn't singing now.

He crouched in one corner of the office, thinking furiously. He couldn't burn it. It would take too long and the smell would be bound to attract the attention of her neighbours. The last thing he needed was the fire brigade. He couldn't flush it down the toilet; it would block the drains in no time at all unless he tore it into tiny fragments, and that would take till dawn and beyond. He couldn't even dig a hole in the garden and bury it, since the discovery of the bitch's body would only be the starting point for a massively thorough investigation, beginning with the immediate environs of the body.

In the end, the only solution he could come up with left no choice but to take all the incriminating evidence with him. It was a scary thought, but he kept telling himself that luck and the gods were with him, that he'd been untouchable up to now because he took every precaution humanly possible and left only a fraction of the risk to a benevolent fate.

Vance loaded a couple of bin liners with the material and staggered out to the car with them, every step an effort. He had been working on ditching Detective Constable Shaz Bowman for something like fifteen or sixteen hours, and he was running out of mental and physical energy. He never used drugs when he was working; the false sense of power and capability they induced were certain steps to fallibility and stupid mistakes. But just this once, he wished he had a neatly folded paper packet of cocaine in his pocket. A couple of lines of charlie and he'd be flying through the tasks that remained instead of dragging his weary body down this bloody gravel path through the arse end of Leeds.

With a small groan of relief, he dropped the second bin liner in the boot. He paused momentarily, wrinkling his nose in disgust. Leaning forward and sniffing, he confirmed his suspicion. The bitch had pissed in his car, soaking the carpet. One more item to dispose of, he thought, glad he had a ready solution to the problem. He stripped off his surgical greens and gloves and pushed them into the spare-tyre well then gently closed the lid with a soft snap of metal. 'Goodbye, DC Bowman,' he muttered as he lowered himself wearily into the driving seat. The clock on the dashboard told him it was nearly half past two. Provided he wasn't stopped by the cops for being in possession of a smart motor in the small hours of the morning, he'd be at his destination by half past four. The only difficulty would be fighting his instinct to hammer the pedal to the metal so he could put as much distance between him and his achievement as possible. With one hand sweating and the other as cool as the night air, he drove out of the city and headed north.

He made it ten minutes ahead of schedule. The maintenance area of the Royal Newcastle Infirmary was deserted, as he knew it would be until the Sunday morning skeleton shift arrived at six. Vance backed his car into a space in the service bay right next to the double doors that led through to the incinerators that dealt with the hospital's surgical waste. Often when he'd finished his voluntary work with the patients, he'd come down here to have a brew and a gossip with the service staff. They were proud to count a celebrity like Jacko Vance as a friend, and they'd been more than honoured to provide him with his own smart card to admit him to the maintenance sectors so he could come and go at will. They'd even known him to come down on his own in the middle of the night when there was no one else around and help them out by getting stuck in to the incineration work himself, stoking the furnace with the sealed bags of waste that came down from clinics, wards and operating theatres.

It never occurred to them that he added his own fuel to the flames.

That was one of the many reasons why Jacko Vance never feared discovery. He was no Fred West with bodies underpinning the foundations of his home. When he'd finished taking his pleasure with his victims, they disappeared forever in the fierce disintegrating heat of the RNI's incinerator. For an appliance that routinely swallowed the waste of an entire city hospital, two bin bags full of Shaz Bowman's research would be a mere *amuse bouche*. He'd be in and out in twenty minutes. Then the end would be in sight. He could fall into his favourite bed, the one at the heart of his killing floor, ignore all the other distractions and sleep the sleep of the just.

PART TWO

'Anybody know where Bowman is?' Paul Bishop asked impatiently, looking at his watch for the fifth time in two minutes. Five blank faces stared back at him.

'Gotta be dead, hasn't she?' Leon grinned. 'Never late, not Shazza baby.'

'Ha ha, Jackson,' Bishop said sarcastically. 'Be a good boy and call down to the front desk, see if they've taken a message from her.'

Leon tipped his chair forward on to all four feet and slouched out of the door, the wide shoulders of his sharply tapering jacket managing to make his six feet of skinniness look challenging. Bishop started drumming his fingers on the edge of the video remote control. If he didn't get this session kicked off soon, he'd be running late. He had a series of scene-of-crime videos to get through then a meeting with a Home Office minister scheduled for lunch. Bloody Bowman. Why did she have to be late today of all days? He'd give her till Jackson got back and then he was forging ahead with the session. Too bad if she missed something crucial.

Simon spoke softly to Kay. 'Have you spoken to Shaz since Friday?'

Kay shook her head, her light brown hair falling like a curtain across one cheek to create the image of a fieldmouse peering through winter grasses. 'I left a message when she didn't turn up for the curry, but she didn't get back to me. I was half-expecting to see her at the women's swim last night, but she wasn't there either. Mind, it wasn't a firm arrangement or anything.'

Before Simon could say anything more, Leon returned. 'Not a dicky bird from her,' he announced. 'She's not rung in sick or anything.'

Bishop tutted. 'Well, we'll just have to manage without her.' He briefed them on the morning's programme, then pressed 'play' on the video.

The aftermath of uncontrolled violence and viciousness that unfolded before them made little impact on Simon. Nor did he have much to contribute to the discussion afterwards. He couldn't get Shaz's absence out of his head. He'd gone round to her flat to pick her up on Saturday night for their pre-curry drink, as they'd agreed. But when he'd rung the bell, there had been no reply. He'd been early, admittedly, so, thinking she might have been deafened by the shower or the hair dryer, he'd walked back to the main road and found a phone box. He'd let her number ring out until the call was automatically disconnected, then he'd tried twice more. Unable to believe she'd stood him up without a word, he'd walked back up the hill to the flat and tried the doorbell again.

He knew which ground-floor flat was Shaz's – he'd given her a lift home after they'd all been out for a drink one evening and, already wistfully hoping he might pluck up the courage to ask her out, he'd lingered long enough to see which set of lights came on. So, just by looking, he could see that the curtains were closed across the deep bay of the master bedroom at the front of the house although it wasn't long dark. As far as he was concerned, that meant she'd been getting ready to go out. Though not, it appeared, with him. He was about to give up and go to the pub alone to drown his humiliation in Tetley's when he noticed the narrow passage running down the side of the house. Not giving himself time to wonder whether he was either justified or wise, he slipped down the ginnel, through the wrought-iron gate and into the gloomy darkness of the back garden.

He rounded the corner of the house and almost tripped over a short flight of steps leading up from the garden to a pair of French windows. 'For fuck's sake,' he muttered angrily, catching himself before he pitched headlong. He peered through the glass, cupping his hand round his eyes against the stray beams of light from the next-door house. He could see dim shapes of furniture against a faint glow that appeared to be coming from another room opening off the hall. But there was no sign of life. Suddenly a light snapped on from the floor above, casting an irregular rectangle of light right next to Simon.

Instantly aware that he must appear more like burglar than policeman to any casual observer, he'd slid back into the darkness against the wall and returned to the street, hoping he'd managed to avoid anyone's attention. The last thing he needed were jibes from the local uniforms about the Peeping Toms of the profiling squad. Baffled by Shaz's apparent rebuff, he'd walked miserably down to the Sheesh Mahal to meet Leon and Kay for the agreed meal. He wasn't in the mood to join in their speculation that Shaz had had a better offer, concentrating instead on getting as much Kingfisher lager down his throat as he could.

Now, on Monday morning, he was seriously worried. It was one thing standing him up. Let's face it, she could probably do a lot better than him without trying too hard. But to miss a training session was completely out of character. Oblivious to Paul Bishop's words of wisdom, Simon sat and fretted, a pair of frown lines dividing his dark brows. As soon as the screech of chairs on floor announced the end of the session, he went in search of Tony Hill.

He found the psychologist in the canteen, sitting at the table the profiling squad had made their own. 'Can you spare a minute, Tony?' he asked, his dark intense expression almost a mirror image of his tutor's.

'Sure. Pull up a coffee and join me.'

Simon looked uncertainly over his shoulder. 'It's just that the others'll be down any minute, and . . . well, it's a bit . . . you know, sort of private.'

Tony picked up his own coffee and the file he'd been reading. 'We'll grab one of the interview rooms for a minute.'

Simon followed him down the corridor to the first witness interview room without a red light showing. The air smelled of sweat, stale cigarettes and, obscurely, burnt sugar. Tony straddled one of the chairs and watched Simon pace for a moment before he leaned into one corner of the room. 'It's Shaz,' Simon said. 'I'm worried about her. She didn't turn up this morning and she didn't phone in or anything.'

Tony knew without being told there was more to it than that. It was his job to find out what. 'I agree, it's not like her. She's very conscientious. But something could have come up unexpectedly. A family problem, perhaps?'

One corner of Simon's mouth twitched downwards. 'I suppose so,' he conceded reluctantly. 'But she would have phoned somebody if that's what it was. She's not just conscientious, she's obsessive. You know that.'

'Maybe she's had an accident.'

Simon pounced. 'Exactly. My point exactly. We should be worried about her, shouldn't we?'

Tony shrugged. 'If she has had an accident, we'll hear about it soon enough. Either she'll call us or else some- one else will.'

Simon clenched his teeth. He was going to have to explain why it was more urgent than that. 'If she's had an accident, I don't think it was this morning. We had a sort of date on Saturday night. Leon and Kay and me and Shaz, we've taken to going out on a Saturday night for a curry and a few bevvies. But I'd arranged to have a drink with Shaz first, just the two of us. I was supposed to meet her at her flat.' Once he'd started, the words poured out of him. 'When I turned up, there was no sign of her. I thought she'd had second thoughts. Bottled out, whatever. But now it's Monday, and she's not turned up. I think something's happened to her, and whatever it is, it's not trivial. She could have had an accident at home. She could have slipped in the shower and hit her head. Or outside. She could be lying in hospital somewhere and nobody knows who she is. Don't you think we should do something about it? We're supposed to be a team, are we not?'

A dreadful premonition shimmered at the edge of Tony's mind. Simon was right. Two days was too long for a woman like Shaz Bowman to drop out of sight when that meant letting down a colleague and missing work. He got to his feet. 'Have you tried ringing her?' he asked.

'Loads of times. Her answering machine's not on, either. That's why I thought maybe she'd had an acci- dent in the house. You know? I thought, she might've switched the machine off when she came in, and then something happened and . . . I don't know,' he added impatiently. 'This is really embarrassing, you know? I feel like a teenager. Making a fuss about nothing.' He shrugged away from the wall and crossed to the door.

Tony put a hand on Simon's arm. 'I think you're right. You've got a policeman's instinct for when something doesn't smell right. It's one of the reasons you're on this squad. Come on, let's go round to Shaz's flat and see what we can see.'

In the car, Simon leaned forward in his seat as if willing them forward. Realizing any attempt at conversation would be futile, Tony concentrated on following the young officer's terse directions. They pulled up outside Shaz's flat and Simon was on the pavement before Tony could even turn off the engine. 'The curtains are still drawn,' Simon said urgently as soon as Tony joined him on the doorstep. 'That's her bedroom on the left. The curtains were drawn on Saturday night when I was here.' He pushed the bell marked 'Flat 1: Bowman'. They could both hear the irritating buzz from within.

'At least we know the bell's working,' Tony said. He stepped back and looked up at the imposing villa, its York stone blackened by a century of the internal combustion engine.

'You can get round the back,' Simon said, finally releasing the bell push. Without waiting for a response, he was off down the ginnel. Tony followed him, but not quickly enough. As he reached the corner, he heard a wail like an agonized cat in the night. He emerged in time to see Simon reel back from a pair of French windows like a man struck in the face. The young policeman sank to his knees and emptied his guts on the grass, groaning incoherently.

Shocked, Tony took a few hesitant steps forward. As he came level with the steps leading up to the windows, the sight that had stripped Simon McNeill of his manhood turned his stomach to ice. Beyond thought, beyond emotion, Tony stared through the glass at something that looked more like a pastiche of a Bacon painting executed by a psychopath than it did a human being. At first, it was more than he could grasp.

When realization came a moment later, he'd have sold his soul for that previous incomprehension.

It was not the first mutilated corpse Tony had ever faced. But it was the first time he'd had any personal connection to a victim. Momentarily, he put a hand over his eyes, massaging his eyebrows with thumb and forefinger. This wasn't the time to mourn. There were things he could do for Shaz Bowman that no one else was capable of, and crawling round on the grass like a wounded puppy wasn't one of them.

Taking a deep breath, he turned to Simon and said, 'Call this in. Then go round the front and secure the scene there.'

Simon looked up at him beseechingly, his baffled pain impossible to ignore. 'That's Shaz?'

Tony nodded. 'That's Shaz. Simon, do as I say. Call this in. Go round the front. It's important. We need to get other officers here, now. Do it.' He waited until Simon stumbled to his feet and reeled towards the ginnel like a drunk. Then he turned back and stared through the glass at the ruination of Shaz Bowman. He longed to be closer, to move round her body and take in the horrific details of what had been done to her. But he knew too much about crime scene contamination even to consider it.

He made do with what he could see. It would have been more than enough for most people, but for Tony it was a tantalizing partial picture. The first thing he had to do was to stop thinking of this shell as Shaz Bowman. He must be detached, analytical and clear-headed if he was to be any use at all to the investigating officers. Looking again at the body in the chair, he found it wasn't so hard to distance himself from memories of

Shaz. The deformed freakish head that faced him bore so little resemblance to anything human.

He could see dark holes where her startling eyes had last looked out at him. Gouged out, he guessed, judging by what looked like threads and strings trailing from the wounds. Blood had flowed and dried round the black orifices, making the hideous mask of her face even more grotesque. Her mouth looked like a mass of plastic in a dozen hues of purple and pink.

There were no ears. Her hair stuck out in spikes above and behind where the ears should have been, held in place by the dried blood that had sprayed and flowed over them.

His eyes moved down to her lap. A sheet of paper was propped up against her chest. Tony was too far away to make out the words, but he could distinguish the line drawing easily. The three wise monkeys. A shiver shook him from head to foot. It was too early to tell, but from what he could see, there was no sign of any sexual assault. Coupled with the deadly calculation of the three wise monkeys, Tony read the scene. This was no sex killing. Shaz hadn't caught the chance attention of some psychopathic stranger. This was an execution.

'You didn't do this for pleasure,' he said softly to himself. 'You wanted to teach her a lesson. You wanted to teach all of us a lesson. You're telling us you're better than us. You're showing off, thumbing your nose at us because you're convinced we'll never find anything to incriminate you. And you're telling us to keep our noses out of your business. You're an arrogant bastard, aren't you?'

The scene before him told Tony things it would never reveal to a police officer trained to look only for the physical clues. To the psychologist, it revealed a mind that was incisive and decisive. This was a cold-blooded killing, not a frenzied, sexually motivated attack. To Tony, that suggested that the killer had identified Shaz Bowman as a threat. Then he'd acted on it. Brutally, coldly and methodically. Even before the SOCOs arrived, Tony could have told them they would find no significant material clues to the identity of this perpetrator. The solution to this crime lay in the mind, not the forensic lab. 'You're good,' Tony murmured. 'But I'm going to be better.'

When the sirens tore the silence into shreds and uniformed feet pounded down the ginnel, Tony was still standing at the windows, memorizing the scene, drinking in every detail so it would be there later when he needed it. Then and only then he walked round to the front of the house to offer what consolation he could to Simon.

'Hardly bloody urgent,' the police surgeon grumbled, opening his bag and pulling out a pair of latex gloves. 'State she's in, an hour's neither here nor there. Not like doctoring the living, is it? Bloody pager, bane of my bloody life.'

Tony resisted the impulse to hit the chubby doctor. 'She was a police officer,' he said sharply.

The doctor flashed him a shrewd look. 'We've not met, have we? You new here?'

'Dr Hill works for the Home Office,' the local DI said. Tony had already forgotten the man's name. 'He runs this new profiling task force you'll have heard about. The lass was one of his trainees.'

'Aye, well, she'll get the same treatment from me as a Yorkshire lass would,' the doctor said drily, turning back to his grim task.

Tony was standing outside the now open French

windows, looking in on the crime scene where a photographer and a team of SOCOs worked their way round the room. He could not take his eyes off the wreckage of Shaz Bowman. No matter how hard he tried, he could not avoid the occasional flashback image of what she had been. It heightened his resolve, but it was a provocation he could well have done without.

Worse for Simon, he thought bitterly. He'd been taken, putty-skinned and trembling, back to police HQ to give a statement about Saturday night. Tony knew enough about the workings of the official mind to realize that the murder squad were probably treating him as their current prime suspect. He was going to have to do something about that sooner rather than later.

The DI whose name he couldn't remember walked down the steps and stood behind him. 'Helluva mess,' he said.

'She was a good officer,' Tony told him.

'We'll get the bastard,' the DI said confidently. 'Don't you worry about that.'

'I want to help.'

The DI raised one eyebrow. 'Not my decision,' he said. 'It's not a serial killer, you know. We've never seen owt like this on our patch.'

Tony fought to suppress his frustration. 'Inspector, this is not a first-time killing. Whoever did this is an expert. He might not have killed on your patch or used this precise method before, but this is not the product of amateur night out.'

Before the inspector could respond, they were interrupted. The police surgeon had finished his grisly work. 'Well, Colin,' he said, walking over to them, 'she's definitely dead.'

With a quick sidelong glance, the policeman said,

'Spare us the gallows humour for once, Doc. Any idea when?'

'Ask your pathologist, Inspector Wharton,' the doctor said huffily.

'I will. But in the meantime, can you give me a ballpark figure?'

The doctor peeled off his gloves with a snap of latex. 'Monday lunchtime . . . let me see . . . Some time between seven o'clock Saturday night and four o'clock Sunday morning, depending on whether the heating was on and how long for.'

DI Colin Wharton sighed. 'That's a bloody big window of opportunity. Can't you get it tighter than that?'

'I'm a doctor, not bloody Mystic Meg,' he said caustically. 'And I'm going back to my game of golf, if you don't mind. You'll have my report in the morning.'

Tony impulsively put a hand on his arm. 'Doctor, I could use some help here. I know it's not really your place to say, but you've obviously developed a lot of expertise in this kind of thing.' When in doubt, flatter. 'The injuries . . . Do you know if she was still alive, or are they postmortem?'

The doctor pursed full red lips and stared back consideringly at Shaz's body. He looked like a small boy puckering up for his maiden aunt, calculating how much of a tip it was going to earn him. 'A mixture of both,' he said finally. 'I reckon the eyes both went while she was still alive. I think she must have been gagged or she'd have screamed the place down. She probably passed out then, a combination of shock and pain. Whatever was poured down her throat was very caustic and that's what killed her. The total disintegration of her respiratory tract, that's what they'll find when they open her up. I'd stake my pension on it. Looking at the amount of blood, I'd reckon the ears came off more or less as she was dying. They're neatly cut off, though. No trial attempts like you usually get with any kind of mutilation. He must have one hell of a sharp knife and a lot of nerve. If he was trying to make sure she'd end up like them three wise monkeys, he went the right way about it.' He nodded to the two men. 'I'll be off, then. Leave you to it. Good luck finding him. You've got a right nutter here.' He waddled off round the side of the house.

'That bastard's got the worst bedside manner in the whole West Riding,' Colin Wharton said in disgust. 'Sorry about that.'

Tony shook his head. 'What's the point in dressing up something as brutal as that in fancy words? Nothing alters the fact that somebody took Shaz Bowman apart and made sure we knew why.'

'What?' Wharton demanded. 'Have I missed something here? What d'you mean, we know why? I don't bloody know why.'

'You saw the drawing, didn't you? The three wise monkeys. See no evil, hear no evil, speak no evil. The killer destroyed her eyes, her ears, her mouth. Doesn't that say something to you?'

Wharton shrugged. 'Either the boyfriend's the killer, in which case he's a certifiable nutter and it doesn't matter what screwed-up shite was going round his head. Or else it was some other nutter who's got it in for coppers because he thinks we stick our noses into things that we'd be better off leaving alone.'

'You don't think it could be a killer who specifically had it in for Shaz because she was sticking her nose in somewhere it didn't belong?' Tony suggested.

'I don't see how it could be,' Wharton said dismissively. 'She's never worked any cases up here, has she?

You lot aren't catching live ones yet, so she's not had the chance to get up some local nutter's nose.'

'Even though we're not catching new cases, we've been working on some genuine old ones. Shaz came up with a theory the other day about a previously unidentified serial killer . . .'

'The Jacko Vance story?' Wharton couldn't stop the snigger. 'We've all had a good laugh about that one.'

Tony's face tightened. 'You shouldn't have heard anything about it. Who let that out of the bag?'

'Nay, Doc, I'm not for dropping anybody else in it. Besides, you know there are no secrets in a nick. That were too good a joke to keep a secret. Jacko Vance, serial killer. It'll be the Queen Mum next!' He spluttered with laughter and clapped Tony indulgently on the shoulder. 'Face it, Doc, chances are you picked a wrong 'un when you co-opted the boyfriend. You don't need me to tell you that nine times out of ten we never end up looking beyond whoever the stiff's been shagging.' He raised a speculative eyebrow. 'Not to mention the person who finds the body.'

Tony snorted derisively. 'You'll be wasting your time if you try pinning it on Simon McNeill. He hasn't done this.'

Wharton turned to face Tony, pulling a Marlboro out of its pack with his teeth. He caught it in his lips and lit it with a throwaway lighter. 'I heard you lecture once, Doc,' he said. 'Over in Manchester. You said the best hunters were the ones who were most like the prey. Two sides of the same coin, you said. I reckon you were right. Only, one of your hunters has gone native on you.'

Jacko flapped a dismissive hand at his PA and hit a button on the remote control. His wife's face filled the king-size TV screen as she handed her audience over to the newsroom for the midday headlines. Still nothing. The longer the better, he couldn't help thinking. The less accurate the pathologist could be about the time of death, the further it could be distanced from the stupid cow's visit to his home. As he killed the TV picture and turned to the script in front of him, he wondered momentarily what it must be like to have the sort of life where no one would notice you'd been lying dead for a couple of days. It was never likely to happen to him, he thought, self-satisfied as ever. It had been a very long time since he'd been that insignificant in anyone's life.

Even his mother would have noticed if he'd disappeared. She might well have been delighted at the prospect, but she'd have at least noticed. He wondered how Donna Doyle's mother was reacting to the disappearance of her daughter. He'd seen nothing on the news, but there was no reason why she should cause more of a stir than any of the others.

He'd made them pay, all of them, for what had been done to him. He knew he couldn't take it out on the one who deserved it; it would be too obvious, the finger pointing straight at him. But he could find surrogate Jillies all over the place, looking just as ripe and delicious as she'd been when he'd first pinned her to the ground and felt her virginity surrender to his power. He could make them understand what he'd been through, feel what he'd felt in ways that the treacherous bitch had never comprehended. His girls could never abandon him; he was the one with power over life and death. And he could make them discharge her debt over and over again.

Once, he had believed that there would come an occasion when these surrogate deaths would have purged him for good. But the catharsis never lasted. Always, the need came creeping back.

Lucky he'd got it off to such a fine art, really. All those years, all those deaths, and only one off-the-wall maverick cop had ever suspected.

Jacko smiled a very private smile, one his fans never saw. The means of payment had had to be different for Shaz Bowman. But they'd been satisfying, nonetheless. It made him wonder if it might not be the time to ring a few changes.

It never did to become a slave to routine.

Frustration drove Tony up the stairs two at a time. No one would let him near Simon. Colin Wharton was stonewalling, claiming he didn't have the authority to allow Tony to collaborate on the investigation. Paul Bishop was out of the building at one of his interminable and ever-convenient meetings, and the Divisional Chief Superintendent was allegedly too busy to see Tony.

He threw open the door of the seminar room, expecting to see the four remaining members of his task force engaged in some meaningful activity. Instead, Carol Jordan looked up from the file of papers in front of her. 'I was beginning to think I'd got the day wrong,' she said.

'Ah, Carol,' Tony sighed, subsiding into the nearest chair. 'I completely forgot you were coming back this afternoon.'

'Looks like you weren't the only one,' she said drily, gesturing at the remaining empty seats. 'Where's the rest of the team? Playing truant?'

'Nobody's told you, have they?' Tony said, looking up at her with angry eyes in a pained face.

'What's happened?' she asked, her chest constricting. What had happened now to drill more anguish into him?

'You remember Shaz Bowman?'

Carol nodded with a rueful smile. 'Ambition on legs.

Blazing blue eyes, uses her ears and mouth in the correct proportion of two to one.'

Tony winced. 'Not any more she doesn't.'

'What's happened to her?' The concern in Carol's voice was still more for Tony than for Shaz.

He swallowed and closed his eyes, summoning the picture of her death and forcing all emotion out of his voice. 'A psychopath happened to her. Somebody who thought it would be entertaining to gouge out those blazing blue eyes and chop off those wide-open ears and pour something so corrosive into that smart mouth that it ended up looking like multicoloured bubble gum. She's dead, Carol. Shaz Bowman is dead.'

Carol's face opened in incredulous horror. 'No,' she breathed. She was silent for a long moment. 'That's terrible,' she finally said. 'So much life in her.'

'She was the best of the bunch. Desperate to be the best. And she wasn't arrogant with it. She could work with the others without making it obvious that she was the racehorse among the donkeys. What he did to her, it went straight to the heart of who she was.'

'Why?' As she had done so often in their previous case, Carol picked the important question.

'He left her with a computer print-out. A drawing and an encyclopaedia entry about the three wise monkeys,' Tony said.

Understanding flashed into Carol's eyes, followed swiftly by a confused frown. 'You don't seriously think ... That theory she came out with the other day? It can't be anything to do with that, can it?'

Tony rubbed his forehead with his fingertips. 'I keep coming back to it. What else is there? The only live case we've had anything to do with is your arsonist, and none of them came up with enough to threaten anyone.'

'But Jacko Vance?' Carol shook her head. 'Surely you

can't believe that? Grannies from Land's End to John O'Groats dote on him. Half the women I know think he's as sexy as Sean Connery.'

'And you? What do you think?' Tony asked. There was no innuendo in the question.

Carol turned the question over in her mind, making sure she had the right words before she spoke. 'I wouldn't trust him,' she eventually said. 'He's too glossy. Non-stick. Nothing leaves a lasting impact. He'll be charming, sympathetic, warm, understanding. But as soon as he moves on to the next interview, it's like the previous encounter never happened. Having said that . . .'

'You'd never have thought of him as a serial killer,' Tony said flatly. 'Me neither. There are some people in public life that you wouldn't feel overly surprised to see on a fistful of murder charges. Jacko Vance isn't one of them.'

They sat in silence facing each other across the room. 'It might not be him,' Carol said at last. 'What about somebody in his entourage? A driver, a minder, a researcher. One of those hangers-on, what do they call them?'

'Go-fers.'

'Yeah, go-fers, right.'

'But that still doesn't answer your question. Why?' Tony pushed himself to his feet and started pacing out the perimeter of the room. 'I don't see how anything she said in here could conceivably have made it into Jacko Vance's circles. So how did our theoretical killer know she was on to him?'

Carol swung round awkwardly in her chair so she could watch him as he crossed behind her. 'She wanted to be a glory girl, Tony. I don't think she was ready to let it drop. I think she decided to follow up her idea. And one way or another, she alerted the killer.'

Tony reached the corner and stopped. 'Do you know . . .' was all he had time for before the door opened on Detective Chief Superintendent Dougal McCormick. His bulky shoulders almost filled the frame.

An Aberdonian, he resembled one of the black Aberdeen Angus cattle from his native territory: black curls tumbling over a broad forehead, liquid dark eyes always on the lookout for the red rag, wide cheekbones seeming to drag his fleshy nose across his face, full lips always moist. The only incongruity was his voice. Where a deep roar should have rumbled in his chest, a melodious light tenor emerged. 'Dr Hill,' he said, closing the door behind him without looking at it. His eyes flickered in Carol's direction then looked a question at Tony.

'DCS McCormick, this is DCI Carol Jordan from the East Yorkshire force. We're helping her with an arson inquiry,' Tony said.

Carol stood up. 'Pleased to meet you, sir.'

McCormick's nod was almost imperceptible. 'If you'd excuse us, I need a moment with Dr Hill,' he said.

Carol knew when she was being dismissed. 'I'll wait down in the canteen.'

'Dr Hill won't be staying on the premises,' McCormick said. 'You'd do better to wait in the car park.'

Carol's eyes widened, but she simply said, 'Very well, sir. I'll see you outside, Tony.'

As soon as Carol had closed the door behind her, Tony rounded on McCormick. 'And what exactly do you mean by that, Mr McCormick?'

'What I said. This is my division and I'm running a murder inquiry. A police officer has been . . . destroyed, and it's my job to find out who's responsible. There's no sign of forcible entry in Sharon Bowman's flat and, by all accounts, she was no fool. So the chances are she knew her killer. And as far as I know at this point in time, the only people Sharon Bowman knew in Leeds were her fellow officers in the task force, and you, Dr Hill.'

'Shaz,' Tony interrupted. 'She hated being called Sharon. Shaz, that's what she was called.'

'Shaz, Sharon, whatever, it makes little difference now.' McCormick brushed the objection aside with all the casual grace of a bull flicking its tail at a fly. 'The point is that you people are the only ones she'd have let in. So I don't want you talking to each other until my murder squad officers have had a chance to interview each and every one of you. Until further notice, this task force is suspended. You will not be authorized to occupy police premises and you are not to communicate with each other. I've already discussed this with Commander Bishop and the Home Office, and we're all agreed that's the appropriate path to go down. Is that clear?'

Tony shook his head. It was all too much. Shaz was dead, horribly dead. And now McCormick wanted to arrest one of the handful of people who might actually be able to provide a way through to her killer. 'You might, by some stretch of the imagination, have authority over the officers in my squad. But I'm not a police officer, McCormick. I don't answer to you. You should be using our talents, not pissing on us. We can help, man, can't you understand that?'

'Help?' McCormick's voice was scornful. 'Help? What were you planning on doing? I've heard some of the daft ideas your lot have come up with. My men are going to be chasing leads, not jokes. Jacko Vance, for heaven's sake. You'll be asking us to arrest Sooty next.'

'We're on the same side,' Tony said, smudges of scarlet rising across his cheekbones.

'Maybe so, but some kinds of help turn out to be more of a hindrance. I want you out of here now, and I don't want you bothering my men. You will report back to this station at ten tomorrow morning so that my officers can interview you formally about Sharon Bowman. Have I made myself clear, Dr Hill?'

'Listen, I can help you here. I understand killers; I know why they do the things they do.'

'It's not hard to work that out. They're sick in the head, that's why.'

'Granted, but they're all sick in the head in their own particular ways,' Tony said. 'This one, for example. I bet he didn't assault her sexually, did he?'

McCormick frowned. 'How did you know about that?'

Tony ran a hand through his hair and spoke passionately. 'I didn't know in the sense of being told. I know because I can read things in a crime scene that your men can't. This wasn't a run-of-the-mill sexual homicide, Superintendent, this was a deliberate message to us that this killer thinks he's so far ahead of us he's never going to be caught. I can help you catch him.'

'Sounds to me like you're more interested in covering up for your own,' McCormick said, shaking his head. 'You've picked up some information at the scene of the crime and turned it into some fancy theory. It'll take more than that to convince me. And I haven't got time to wait till you pick up the next bit of gossip. As far as this station's concerned, you're history. And your bosses at the Home Office agree with me.'

Fury drove Tony's normal tools of flattery and appeasement underground. 'You are making one hell of a mistake, McCormick,' he said, his voice rough with anger.

The big detective gave a snort of laughter, 'I'll take that risk, son.' He gestured with his thumb towards the door. 'Away you go, now.'

Realizing he couldn't win on this battleground, Tony bit down hard on the flesh of his cheek. The flavour of humiliation was the coppery taste of fresh blood. Defiantly, he walked over to his locker and pulled out his briefcase, filling it with the missing person files and the squad's analyses. Snapping the lock shut, he turned on his heel and walked out. On his way through the police station, officers fell silent as he passed. He was thankful that Carol wasn't there to witness his rout. She would never have been able to keep the silence that was his only remaining weapon.

As the front door swung shut behind him, he heard an unidentifiable voice behind him call out, 'Bloody good riddance.'

In a rare moment of lucidity in the ocean of pain, Donna Doyle contemplated her brief life and the foolish trust that had brought her to this place. Regret swelled inside her like a strange tumour, devouring everything it encountered. One mistake, one attempt to follow the rainbow to the pot of gold, one act of faith that was no more preposterous than the one the priest talked about every Sunday, and here she was. Once upon a time, she'd have said she'd do anything for a chance at stardom. Now she knew it wasn't true.

It wasn't fair. It wasn't as if she'd just wanted to be famous for herself. With the fame would have come money, so her mum wouldn't have had to scrimp and save and worry about every penny like she'd had to all the time since Dad had died. Donna had wanted it to be a surprise, a wonderful, wicked, exciting surprise. Now it would never happen. Even if she got out of here, she knew she wasn't going to be a star, not ever. She might be famous for fifteen minutes, like the song said, but not for being a one-armed TV star like Jacko Vance. Even if they found her, she was finished.

They could still find her, she told herself. She wasn't just whistling in the dark, she thought defiantly. They'd be looking for her by now, surely. Her mum would have gone to the police, her picture would be in the papers, maybe even on the telly. People all over the country would see her and search their memory. Somebody would remember her. There had been loads of people on the trains. Half a dozen other passengers had got off with her at Five Walls Halt. At least one of them *must* have noticed her. All dolled up in her best outfit, she knew she looked tasty. Surely the police would be asking questions, working out whose Land Rover she'd got into? Wouldn't they?

She groaned. In her heart, she knew this would be the last place she would lie. Alone in her tomb, Donna Doyle wept.

Tony sat hunched forward in the armchair, staring into the flickering gas flames of the fake hearth. He was still nursing the same glass of Theakston's he'd had since they'd arrived back at Carol's cottage. She'd refused to take no for an answer. He'd had a shock, he needed someone to discuss the case with, and she needed his input on her arsonist. She had a cat to feed, he had none, so logically their destination should be an hour down the motorway to the outskirts of Seaford.

Since they'd arrived, he'd said barely a word. He'd sat with his eyes on the fire and his mind projecting the film of Shaz Bowman's death. Carol had left him alone, taking the chance to throw together a packet of chicken breasts from the freezer, a couple of chopped onions and a jar of ready-made cider and apple sauce. She'd put the result into the oven with a couple of baking potatoes and left it on a low heat while she made up the guest bedroom. She knew there was little point in expecting anything more or less from Tony.

She poured herself a large gin and tonic, adding a couple of chunks of frozen lemon, and returned to the living room. Without saying anything, she tucked her legs under her and let the armchair opposite his swallow her up. Between them, Nelson lay stretched out like a long black hearth rug.

Tony looked up at Carol and managed a faint smile. 'Thanks for the peace and quiet,' he said. 'It has a very welcoming ambience, your cottage.'

'That's one of the reasons why I bought it. That and the view. I'm glad you like it.'

'I . . . I keep imagining it,' he said. 'The process. Tying her up, gagging her. Torturing her with the knowledge that she wasn't going to get out of it alive, not knowing what she knew.'

'Whatever that was.'

He nodded. 'Whatever that was.'

'I suppose it brings it all back to you?' Carol said softly.

He let out a long breath. 'Inevitably,' he said through tight lips. He looked up at her, his keen eyes shining under the jut of his frowning eyebrows. When he spoke again, his voice was a brisk contrast, indicating he wanted to escape the memories that were sometimes almost as bad as the experience itself. 'Carol, you're a detective. You heard Shaz's presentation, you were one of the ones who passed judgement on it. Imagine you'd been on the other end of our criticisms. Imagine you're back at the start of your career, with it all to prove. Don't think too hard about this. Give me your gut reaction. What would you do?'

'I'd want to prove you were wrong and I was right.'

'Yes, yes,' Tony acknowledged impatiently. 'That's a given. But what would you *do*? How would you go about it?'

Carol sipped her drink and considered. 'I know what I'd do now. I'd put a small team together – just a sergeant and a couple of DCs – and blitz every one of those cases. I'd go back and talk to friends, family. Check out whether the missing girls were Jacko Vance fans, whether they'd gone to the event he was appearing at.

If they did, who they went with. What their companions noticed.'

'Shaz didn't have either the time or the team for that kind of operation. Think back to what it was like when you were young and hungry,' Tony urged.

'As to what I'd have done then . . . Given no resources, you have to fall back on your own assets.'

Tony gave her an encouraging nod. 'Meaning?'

'Smart mouth, fancy footwork. You know you're right, that's the bottom line. You know the truth is out there waiting for the proof to go round it. Me? I'd shake the tree and see what falls out.'

'So you'd do what, specifically?'

'These days, I'd probably drop some poison in the ear of a friendly journalist and plant a story that would mean something more to our killer than it would to the casual reader. But I haven't seen any signs that Shaz had those kind of contacts or, if she did, that she used them. What I'd probably have done in her shoes, if I'd had the bottle, would have been to set up a meeting with the man himself.'

Tony sat back in his chair and took a long swallow of beer. 'I'm glad you said that. It's the sort of idea I'm always reluctant to bring out into the open in case you lot starts laughing because no self-respecting police officer would dream of doing something so risky either to life or career.'

'You think she made contact with Jacko Vance?'

He nodded.

'And you think that whatever she said to him . . .'

'Or to someone around him,' Tony interrupted. 'It might not be Vance. It might be his manager or his minder or even his wife. But yes, I think she said something to someone in that group of people and she made a killer afraid.'

'Whoever it was didn't waste much time.'

'He didn't waste time and he's clearly got a lot of nerve to kill her in her own living room. To risk a cry, a scream, the noise of furniture being knocked over, anything untoward in a house split into flats.'

Carol sipped her drink, savouring the growing edge of lemon as the frozen fruit thawed completely. 'And he had to get her there in the first place.'

Tony looked puzzled. 'What makes you say that?'

'She'd never have agreed to meet someone she suspected was a serial killer in her own home. Not even with the hubris of youth. That would be like inviting a fox into the henhouse. And if he turned up there later, after the official interview, she'd hit the panic button, not let him in. No, Tony, she was already his prisoner by the time she got home.'

It was such flashes of insight backed with impeccable logic that had made Carol Jordan such a joy to work with before, Tony remembered. 'You're right, of course. Thank you.' He toasted her mutely with his glass. Now he knew where to start. He finished his beer and said, 'Any chance of another one? Then I think we need to talk about your little problem.'

Carol uncurled herself from the chair and stretched like Nelson. 'You sure you don't want to talk some more about Shaz?' Tony's expression of distaste told her all she needed to know. She went through to the kitchen for another beer.

'I'll save it for your West Yorkshire colleagues tomorrow morning. If you haven't heard from me by teatime, you'd better make sure I've got a decent brief,' he called after her.

When she was settled again in the armchair, he dragged his brooding eyes away from the fire and pulled a couple of sheets of lined paper from his briefcase. 'At the tail end of the week, I got the squad to work on their idea of a profile for you. They had a day to work up an individual profile, then on Friday, they collaborated on a joint effort. I've got a copy of it with me, I'll show you later.'

'Terrific. I didn't want to say anything before, but I've been working on a profile of my own. It'll be interesting to see how they compare.' She tried to keep her voice light, but Tony heard the desire for his praise, nevertheless. It made what he had to say all the more awkward. Sometimes he wished he smoked. It would give him something to do with his hands and mouth at times like this.

Instead, he ran a hand over his face. 'Carol, I have to tell you that I suspect you've all been wasting your time.'

Unconsciously, her chin jutted forward. 'Meaning what?' The words were more aggressive than the tone.

'Meaning that I don't think your fires fit into any known category.'

'You mean they're not arson?'

Before he could answer, a heavy knock reverberated through the cottage. Startled, Carol spilled a few drops of her drink. 'Are you expecting visitors?' Tony asked, turning to the dark window behind him to see if anything penetrated the darkness outside.

'No,' she said, jumping to her feet and moving across the room to the heavy wooden door that opened into the small stone porch. As she unlatched the door, a chill gust of wind filled the room with a cold waft of estuary silt. Carol looked surprised. Beyond her, Tony glimpsed the outline of a large male shape. 'Jim,' she exclaimed. 'I wasn't expecting you.'

'I tried to ring you this afternoon and I kept getting the runaround from Sergeant Taylor. So I thought I might as well head on up here and see if I could run you to earth.' As Carol stepped back, Pendlebury followed her in. 'Oh, I'm sorry – you've got company.'

'No, your timing couldn't be better,' she said, waving him towards the fire. 'This is Dr Tony Hill from the Home Office. We're just talking about the arson case. Tony, this is Jim Pendlebury, the fire chief in Seaford.'

Tony ceded his hand into the bone-grinding grip of a competitive handshake. 'Pleased to meet you,' he said mildly, refusing the invitation to joust.

'Tony is in charge of the new National Offender Profiling Task Force in Leeds,' Carol said.

'Tough job.' Pendlebury thrust his hands into the deep pockets of the fashionably oversized mac he was wearing. They emerged with a bottle of Australian Shiraz on the end of each. 'Housewarming present. Now we can all discuss our firebug with a bit of lubrication.'

Carol fetched glasses and corkscrew and poured wine for herself and Pendlebury, Tony waving his glass to indicate he'd stick with the beer. 'So, Tony, what have your baby boffins got to tell us?' Pendlebury asked, stretching his long legs out in front of him, forcing Nelson to move to one side. The cat gave him a malevolent glare and curled into a ball beside Carol's chair.

'Nothing Carol couldn't work out for herself, I imagine. The problem is that I suspect what they've done is irrelevant.'

Pendlebury's laugh sounded too loud in the confines of the cottage. 'Am I hearing things?' he said. 'A profiler admitting it's all a load of bollocks? Carol, have you got the tape running?'

Wondering how many more times he would have to smile politely while his life's work was denigrated, Tony let Pendlebury wind down before he spoke. 'Would you use a screwdriver to drive a fence post into the ground?'

Pendlebury cocked his head to one side. 'You're saying profiling is the wrong tool for the job?'

'That's exactly what I'm saying. Profiling works on certain crimes where the motivation is psychopathic to some degree.'

'Meaning?' Pendlebury asked, drawing his legs up and leaning forward, his interest wholly engaged, his face sceptical.

'Do you want the thirty-second version or the full lecture?'

'You'd better give me the idiot's guide, me being a mere fireman.'

Tony ran a hand through his thick dark hair, a reflex that always left him looking like a cartoon mad scientist. 'OK. Most crimes in this country are committed either for gain or in the heat of the moment, or under the influence of drink or drugs. Or a combination of all of the above. The crime is a means to an end – acquiring cash or drugs, gaining revenge, putting a halt to unacceptable behaviour.

'A handful of crimes have their roots in stranger soil. They grow from an inner psychological compulsion on the part of the criminal. Something drives him – and it's almost always a him – to perform certain acts that are an end in themselves. The criminal act can be as petty as stealing women's underwear from washing lines. It can be as serious as serial murder. Serial arson is one such crime.

'And if what we were dealing with here was serial arson, I'd be the first to defend the value of a psychological profile. But as I was saying to Carol just before you arrived, I don't think you've got your common or garden thrill-seeking firebug in Seaford. It's not a torch for hire either. What you've got here is a beast of a different colour altogether. More of a hybrid.'

Pendlebury looked unconvinced. 'Want to tell us what you mean by that?'

'I'd be happy to,' Tony said, leaning back and cradling his glass in his linked fingers. 'Let's eliminate the hired arsonist for a start. While it's true that a handful of the fires have probably been an answer to the building owner's prayers, in the vast majority of cases, there seems to be no financial gain. Mostly, we're looking at massive inconvenience and, in a few cases, positive damage to the businesses or sections of the community affected. They're not grudge fires either – different insurance companies, no reason why anyone would have it in for such a wide spectrum of buildings. There's no common link at all, except that the fires were all set at night and up until the last one, they took place in deserted premises. So, no reason to think there is a professional torch for hire behind the blazes. Agreed?'

Carol bent over to pick up the wine and refill her glass. 'You'll get no argument from me.'

'What if there was a mixture of motives behind the hiring? What if he was hired sometimes for gain, sometimes for grudge?' Pendlebury stubbornly asked.

'Still leaves too many unaccounted for,' Carol said. 'My team ruled out a torch for hire almost from the start. So, Tony, why isn't it some emotional retard doing it for kicks?'

'I could be wrong,' he said.

'Oh, yeah. Your track record is littered with mistakes,' Carol said ironically.

'Thank you. Here's why I don't think it's some nutter. All these fires have been carefully set. In most cases, there have been almost no forensic traces, just the identification of the seat of the fire and some indication of lighter fuel and ignition trails. Mostly there's no sign of forced entry either. If there hadn't been such a spate of these fires over a relatively short period of time, chances are most of them would have been written off as accidents or carelessness. That would point to a professional torch, except that we've already written that off for other reasons.' He picked up the papers he'd dropped by his chair earlier and gave his notes a quick glance.

'So we've got someone who's controlled and organized, which firebugs almost never are. He brings stuff with him and also uses available materials. He knows what he's doing, yet there's no sign of him having graduated to this from small-scale fires in rubbish tips, garden sheds, building sites.

'Then you've got to consider that most firebugs are sexually motivated. When they set fires, they often masturbate or urinate or defecate at the sites. There have been no traces of that, nor of any pornographic materials. If he doesn't wank at the fire site, he probably does it at the vantage point where he watches the fire from. Again, there are no reports from outraged members of the public of anyone exposing themselves in the vicinities of the fires. So, another negative.'

'What about timing?' Carol interrupted. 'He's doing it more often than he was when he started out. Isn't that typical of a serial offender?'

'Yeah, it's in all the books about serial killers,' Pendlebury added.

'It's less true of firebugs,' Tony said. 'Especially the ones who go in for the more serious arson attacks like this. The gaps are unpredictable. They can go weeks, months or even years without a big blaze. But within the series, you do get sprees, so yes, the timing of these fires might support the idea that you're looking at a serial offender. But I'm not trying to suggest that these fires are the work of several individuals. I think it's one person. I just don't believe he's a thrill seeker.'

'So what are you saying?' Carol said.

'Whoever is setting these fires is not a psychopath. I believe he has a conventional criminal motive for what he's doing.'

'So what is this so-called motive?' Pendlebury asked suspiciously.

'That's what we don't know yet.'

Pendlebury snorted. 'Minor detail.'

'Actually, in a sense it is, Jim,' Carol chipped in. 'Because once we've established that it's not a psychopath operating on unique and personal logic, we should be able to apply reasoning to uncover what's behind the fires. And once we've done that . . . well, it's just a matter of solid coppering.'

A look of disgruntled annoyance had settled over Jim Pendlebury's face like an occluded cold front on the weather map. 'Well, I can't think of any reason for setting these fires unless you get a kick out of them.'

'Oh, I don't know,' Tony said casually, starting almost to enjoy himself.

'Share it then, Sherlock,' Carol urged him.

'Could be a security firm coming round in the wake of the fires offering cut-rate night watchmen. Could be a fire-alarm or sprinkler-system company facing hard times. Or . . .' his voice tailed off and he cast a look of speculation at the fire chief.

'What?'

'Jim, do you employ any part-time firemen?'

Pendlebury looked horrified. Then he took in the half-smile twitching the corner of Tony's mouth and misread it completely. The fire chief visibly relaxed and grinned. 'You're at the wind-up,' he said, wagging a finger at Tony.

'If you say so,' Tony said. 'But do you? Just as a matter of curiosity?'

The fireman's eyes showed uncertainty and suspicion. 'We do, yes.'

'Maybe tomorrow you could let me have their names?' Carol asked.

Pendlebury's head thrust forward and he stared intently into Carol's closed face. His broad shoulders seemed to expand as he clenched his fists. 'My God,' he said wonderingly. 'You really mean it, don't you, Carol?'

'We can't afford to ignore any possibilities,' she said calmly. 'This is not personal, Jim. But Tony has opened up a valid line of inquiry. I'd be derelict in my duty if I didn't follow it through.'

'Derelict in your duty?' Pendlebury got to his feet. 'If my fire crews were derelict in their duty, there wouldn't be a building in this city left standing. My people put their lives on the line every time this nutter has a night on the town. And you sit there and suggest one of them might be behind it?'

Carol stood up and faced him. 'I'd feel just the same if it was a question of a bent copper. No one's accusing anyone at this stage. I've worked with Tony before, and I'd stake my career that he doesn't make mischievous or ill-considered suggestions. Why don't you sit down and have another glass of wine?' She put a hand on his arm and smiled. 'Come on, there's no need for us to fall out.'

Slowly Pendlebury relaxed and gingerly lowered himself back into his chair. He allowed Carol to top up his glass and even managed a half-smile at Tony. 'I'm very protective of my officers,' he said.

Tony, impressed at Carol's smooth handling of a potentially explosive situation, had shrugged. 'They're lucky to have you,' was all he said.

Somehow, the three of them managed to shift the

conversation on to the more neutral territory of how Carol was settling in at East Yorkshire. The fire chief slipped into professional Yorkshireman mode, keeping everyone happy with a series of anecdotes. For Tony, it was a blessed rescue from thoughts of Shaz Bowman's last hours.

Later, in the small hours and the loneliness of Carol's spare room, there was no distraction to damp down the flames of imagination. As he pushed away the nightmare vision of her distorted and devastated face, he promised Shaz Bowman that he would expose the man who had done this to her. No matter what the price.

And Tony Hill was a man who knew all about paying the ferryman.

Jacko Vance sat in his soundproofed and electronically shielded projection room at the top of the house, behind locked doors. Obsessively, he replayed the tape he'd spliced together from his recordings of the late evening news bulletins on a variety of channels, terrestrial and satellite. What they all had in common was the news of Shaz Bowman's death. Her blue eyes blazed at him again from the screen time after time, an exciting contrast to his last memory of her.

They wouldn't be showing pictures of her like that. Not even after the watershed. Not even with an X-certificate.

He wondered how Donna Doyle was feeling. There had been nothing on TV about her. They all thought they had star quality, but the truth was none of them raised the faintest flicker of interest in anyone except him. For him, they were perfect, the ultimate representation of his ideal woman. He loved their pliancy, their willingness to believe exactly what he wanted them to believe. And the perfection of the moment when they realized this encounter was not about sex and fame but pain and death. He loved that look in their eyes.

When he saw that translation from adoration to alarm, their faces seemed to lose all individuality. They no longer merely resembled Jillie, they became her. It made the punishment so easy and so perfectly right.

What also made it appropriate was the unfairness. Almost all of his girls spoke about their families with affection. It might be shrouded behind a veil of adolescent frustration and exasperation, but it was obvious as he listened to them that their mothers or fathers or siblings cared about them even though their sluttish readiness to do whatever he wanted demonstrated they didn't merit that concern. He'd deserved their lives, and what had he got?

Anger surged through him, but like a thermostat, self-control cut in and tamped the fires down. This was not an appropriate time or place for that energy, he reminded himself. His anger could be channelled in a variety of useful directions; ranting pointlessly about what he had been deprived of wasn't one of them.

He took a series of deep breaths and forced his emotions into another mould. Satisfaction. That's what he ought to be feeling. Satisfaction at a job well done, a danger neutralized.

> Little Jack Horner
> Sat in the corner
> Eating his pudding and pie.
> He put in his thumb
> And pulled out a plum
> And said, "What a good boy am I!"

Vance giggled softly. He'd put in his thumbs and pulled out the glistening plum of Shaz Bowman's eyes and felt the silent scream vibrating in his very core. It

242

had been easier than he'd expected. It took surprisingly little force to pop an eye free from its roots.

The only pity of it was that you couldn't then see her expression when you poured the acid in or sliced the ears off. He didn't anticipate any need for there to be a next time, but if there were, he'd have to think carefully about the order of the ceremony.

Sighing with satisfaction, he rewound the tape.

If Micky hadn't been such a purist about her morning routine, they might have heard about Shaz's death on the radio news or seen it on satellite TV. But Micky insisted on no exposure to the day's news until she was behind the closed door of her office at the studios. So they breakfasted to Mozart and drove in to Wagner. No one from the programme was ever foolish enough to thrust a tabloid at Micky as she strode from car parking slot to her desk. Not twice, anyway.

So, because their early morning start forced them to bed before the late bulletins that had alerted Jacko, it was Betsy who had the first shock of recognition at Shaz's picture. Even dulled by newsprint, her blue eyes were still the first thing that demanded notice. 'My God,' Betsy breathed, moving round behind Micky's desk the better to examine the front pages.

'What is it?' Micky said without pausing in the habitual process of removing her jacket, placing it on a hanger and checking it critically for creases.

'Look, Micky.' Betsy thrust the *Daily Mail* towards her. 'Isn't that the policewoman who came to the house on Saturday? Just as we were leaving?'

Micky registered the thick black type before she took in the photograph. SLAUGHTERED, it read. Her eyes moved to Shaz Bowman's smiling face underneath the peak of a Metropolitan Police cap. 'There can't be two

243

of them,' she said. She sat down heavily on one of the visitors' armchairs that faced her desk and read the melodramatic copy that provided Shaz's epitaph. Words like 'nightmare', 'gory', 'blood-soaked', 'agony' and 'gruesome' leapt out to ambush her. She felt strangely queasy.

In a television career that had spanned war zones, massacres and individual tragedy, no one in Micky's life had ever been touched personally by any of the catastrophes she had reported. Even a connection as tangential as hers to Shaz Bowman was all the more shocking because it had no precedent. 'Jesus,' she said, stretching the syllables. She looked up at Betsy, who read the shock in her face. 'She was in our house on Saturday morning. According to this, they think she was murdered late Saturday or early Sunday. We spoke to her. And within hours, she was dead. What are we going to do, Bets?'

Betsy moved round the desk and crouched beside Micky, hands flat on her thighs, staring up into her face. 'We're going to do nothing,' she said. 'It's not up to us to do anything. She came to see Jacko, not us. She's nothing to do with us.'

Micky looked appalled. 'We can't do *nothing*,' she protested. 'Whoever killed her, they must have hooked up with her after she left our house. At the very least, it lets the police know she was alive and well and walking around of her own free will in London on Saturday morning. We can't ignore it, Bets.'

'Sweetheart, take a deep breath and think about what you're saying. This isn't any old murder victim. She was a police officer. That means her colleagues are not going to be satisfied with a one-page statement saying she came to the house and we left. They're going to be stripping our lives down to the bone, on the off chance that there's something there they should know about. You know and I know that we just won't stand up to that kind of scrutiny. I say, leave it to Jacko. I'll give him a call and tell him to say we'd gone before she arrived. It's simplest that way.'

Micky pushed herself back violently. The chair slid along the carpet and Betsy almost toppled forward. Micky jumped to her feet and started pacing agitatedly. 'And what happens if they start questioning the neighbours and there's some nosy old biddy who remembers DC Bowman arriving and then us leaving? Anyway, I was the one who spoke to her in the first place. I made the appointment. What if she jotted that down in her notebook? What if she even taped the call, for God's sake? I can't believe you think we should just shut up about it.'

Betsy struggled to her feet, her chin tipped back to reveal a stubborn set to her firm jaw. 'If you'd stop being such a bloody drama queen, you'd see I'm talking sense,' she said in a low, angry voice. She'd spent too long providing the advice that Micky routinely acted upon to abandon the role now it had become so crucial. 'No good will come of it,' she added ominously.

Micky stopped by the desk and picked up the phone. 'I'm ringing Jacko,' she said, glancing at her watch. 'He won't be up yet. At least I can break the news more gently than the tabloids.'

'Good. Maybe he'll talk some sense into you,' Betsy said caustically.

'I'm not calling for permission, Betsy. I'm calling to tell him I'm about to phone the police.' As she punched in her husband's private number, Micky looked sadly at her lover. 'God, I can't believe you're running so scared that you'd kid yourself you can walk away from doing the right thing.'

'It's called love,' Betsy said bitterly, turning away to hide the tears of anger and humiliation that had sprung without warning.

'No, Betsy. It's called fear . . . Hello, Jacko? It's me. Listen, I've got some terrible news for you . . .'

Betsy turned her head and watched Micky's mobile face with its frame of silky blonde hair. It was a sight that had given her pleasure beyond dreams of avarice over the years. All she felt now was an unreasonable, unfathomable sense of impending disaster.

Jacko leaned back on his pillows and considered what he'd just heard. He'd been in two minds whether to call the police himself. On the one hand, it argued for his innocence, since, for all he knew, nobody outside his household knew DC Bowman had been anywhere near him. On the other hand, it made him look a little too eager to be involved in a high-profile murder inquiry. And one of the things everyone who had read a book on psychopathic killers knew was that the murderer often tried to insert himself into the investigation.

Leaving it to Micky was somehow much safer. It demonstrated his innocence at second hand; she was his devoted wife, crammed with public probity and therefore to be trusted in her account of events. He knew it was safe to assume she'd go straight to the police as soon as she saw Shaz's picture, which would be well before his normal rising time, so there would be no question of him having known and said nothing. Because, of course, officer, he'd been too busy to watch the evening news the previous day. Why, sometimes he barely had time to watch his own show, never mind his wife's!

What he had to do now was to work out his strategy. There would be no question of him having to schlepp up to Leeds to talk to the investigating plods; the police would come to him, he felt sure. If he was proved wrong, he wouldn't call in any favours just yet. He'd play along, the magnanimous man with nothing to hide. Of course you can have an autograph for your wife, officer.

The important thing now was to plan. Imagine every contingency and work out in advance how best to deal with it. Planning was the secret of his success. It was a lesson he'd almost had to learn the hard way. The first time, he'd not really worked out the eventualities ahead of time. He'd been intoxicated by the possibilities he saw opening in front of him, and he'd not realized how necessary it was to project all the conceivable outcomes and work out how to deal with them. He'd not had the Northumberland cottage then, relying foolishly on a tumbledown walkers' hut that he remembered from hill-walking expeditions in his youth.

He'd thought no one would be using the place in the dead of winter and knew he could drive right up to it on an old drovers' track. Because he dared not leave her alive, he'd had to finish her off the night he'd taken her there. But it had been almost dawn by the time she'd taken her last breath. Shaken and exhausted by the effort of confining her, carrying the heavy vice that would crush her arm to a bloody pulp, then killing her with a wicked ligature made from a guitar string (symbolic, if he'd but considered it, of another of the accomplishments he'd lost), the planned burial had been beyond him. He decided to leave her where she was and come back the following night to deal with the carcass.

Jacko sucked his breath in at the memory. He'd been on the main road, only a couple of miles from the turn-off to the track, when the local news bulletin announced that the body of a young woman had been discovered by a group of ramblers within the past hour. The shock had nearly sent the Land Rover off the road.

Somehow, he'd controlled himself and driven home in a lather of clammy sweat. Amazingly, he hadn't left sufficient forensic traces for there to be any trail leading back to him. He was never questioned. As far as he knew, he was never even considered. The previous connection was so minimal as to be insignificant.

He'd learned three crucial things from that experience. Firstly, he needed to find a way to make it last so he could savour her suffering as she went through what he'd endured.

Secondly, he didn't actually enjoy the act of killing. He liked what led up to it, the agony and the terror, and he loved the sense of control that having been responsible for taking a life gave him, but despatching a strong, healthy young woman was no fun. Far too much like hard work, he had decided. He didn't much mind whether they died of septicaemia or despair, he preferred it when he didn't have to do it himself.

And thirdly, he needed a place of safety, both metaphorically and literally. Micky, Northumberland and the voluntary work with the terminally ill had been the tripartite answer. For the six months it had taken to put that answer together, he'd simply had to be patient. It hadn't been easy, but it had made the next one all the more sweet.

He wasn't about to give up on that sweet and secret pleasure just because Shaz Bowman had thought she was smarter than him. All it would take was a little bit of planning.

Jacko closed his eyes and considered.

Carol took a deep breath and knocked on the door. A familiar voice told her to come in and she walked into

Jim Pendlebury's office as if there had never been a moment's tension between them. 'Morning, Jim,' she said briskly.

'Carol,' he said. 'Come with some news for me?'

She sat down opposite him, shaking her head. 'I've come for the list of part-time firemen we spoke about last night.'

His eyes widened. 'You're not still entertaining that daft idea in the cold light of morning?' he said scornfully. 'I thought you must just be humouring your guest.'

'When it comes to criminal investigation, I'd back Tony Hill's ideas over yours any time.'

'You expect me to sit back and help you turn my men into scapegoats?' he said, his voice low. 'When they're the ones who stand at risk every time we get a call-out?'

Carol sighed in vexation. 'I'm trying to put an end to that risk. Not just for your firefighters, but for the poor sods like Tim Coughlan who don't even know they're taking a chance. Don't you understand that? This isn't a witch-hunt. I'm not out to frame the innocent. If you think that's what I'm about, then you certainly don't know enough about me to have the right to turn up at my home unannounced and uninvited and expect to cross the threshold ever again.'

Long seconds dragged past while they stared each other down. Finally, Pendlebury shook his head in resignation, his mouth a thin line. 'I'll give you the list,' he said, loathing every word. 'But you won't find your arsonist on it.'

'I hope not,' she said calmly. 'I know you don't believe me, but I don't want this to be one of yours, any more than I enjoy the prospect of uncovering police corruption. It undermines all of us. But I can't ignore the possibility now it's been pointed out to me so convincingly.'

He turned away and walked his chair over to a filing

cabinet. He pulled out the bottom drawer and took out a sheet of paper. With a flick of the wrist, he floated it across the desk to her. All it contained were the names, addresses and telephone numbers of Seaford's twelve part-time fire officers.

'Thank you,' Carol said. 'I appreciate this.' She half-turned to go, then looked back as if struck by an after-thought. 'One thing, Jim. These fires. Do they all come under one division or are they more spread out?'

He pursed his lips. 'They're all on Seaford Central's patch. If they hadn't been, you wouldn't be walking out the door with that bit of paper.'

It confirmed what she'd already thought. 'I figured it might be something like that,' she said, her voice offering armistice. 'Believe me, Jim, there'd be nobody happier than me if all your lads check out.'

He looked away. 'They will do. I know those lads. I've trusted my life to them. Your psychologist – he knows nothing about it.'

Carol walked to the door. As she opened it, she looked back. He was staring intensely at her. 'We'll see, Jim.'

The steel-capped heels of her brown boots clattered on the stairs as she ran down to the anonymous security of her car. The pain of Jim Pendlebury's conviction that she would scapegoat a fellow member of the emergency services cut deep. 'Damn it,' Carol said, slamming the door closed behind her and jabbing the key angrily at the ignition. 'Damn it all to hell.'

Working on the principle that any psychologist worth his salt would see straight through any attempts at manipulation, they'd clearly decided to dispense with finesse. They had, however, paid Tony the compliment of rank. Detective Chief Superintendent McCormick and Detective Inspector Colin Wharton rubbed shoulders at the narrow table in the interview room. The tape was running. They hadn't even bothered with the spurious reassurance that it was for his benefit.

They'd run through the discovery of the body first, their questions clearly directed at tripping him up in his assertion that he'd never been to Shaz's flat before and had no idea which windows were hers. Now they were moving into areas for which there was less obvious justification. Tony was not unprepared. He'd fully expected to be given a hard time. For one thing, he wasn't actually a cop, so if they were looking for a scapegoat, he'd be a preferable choice to one of his team. Add to that the local force's resentment at having to hand over space and resources to a bunch of outsiders led by a Home Office boffin they regarded as one step away from a leader of Satanic rituals, and he was inevitably on a hiding to nothing. With this in mind, he'd been running alternative scenarios on the projection screen inside his head almost before his eyes had opened. Concern about the interview had preoccupied him through breakfast, in spite of Carol's best efforts to reassure him that it would be no more than routine.

On the train back to Leeds he had stared out of the window without registering anything except that he had to find a way to convince his interrogators that they should be looking outside Shaz's circle of friends and colleagues for whoever had done this to her. Now he was faced with the reality, he wished he'd caught a train to London instead. Already the muscles in his shoulders were cramped into tight knots. He could actually feel the creeping rigidity climbing up the back of his neck and into his scalp. He was going to have one hell of a headache.

'Take us right back to the beginning,' McCormick said brusquely.

'When did you first meet DC Bowman?' Wharton demanded. At least they weren't playing 'nice cop, nasty cop'. They were both comfortably displaying their true colours as oppressive aggressors.

'Commander Bishop and I interviewed her in London about eight weeks ago. The exact date is in our office diary.' His voice was blank and even, kept so by willpower alone. Only a Voice Stress Analyser could have detected the micro-tremors skittering beneath the surface. Luckily for Tony, the technology hadn't penetrated that far.

'You interviewed her together?' McCormick with the question this time.

'Yes. Following the interview, Commander Bishop withdrew and I administered some psychological tests. Then DC Bowman left and I did not see her again until the start of the task force's training period.'

'How long were you alone with Bowman?' McCormick again. Wharton was leaning back in his seat, fixing Tony with a professional blend of speculation, contempt and suspicion.

'It takes about an hour to carry out the tests.'

'Long enough to get to know somebody, then.'

Tony shook his head. 'There's no time for casual conversation. In fact, that would be counter-productive. We were aiming to keep the selection process as objective as possible.'

'And the decision to take Bowman on the squad was unanimous?'

Tony hesitated for a moment. If they hadn't already talked to Paul Bishop, they would. There was no point in any diversion from the truth. 'Paul had some reservations. He thought she was too intense. I argued that we needed some diversity on the team. So he agreed to

Shaz and I conceded on one of his choices that I was less enthusiastic about.'

'Which one was that?' McCormick asked.

Tony was too smart to walk into that one. 'You'd better ask Paul about that.'

Wharton suddenly leaned forward, thrusting his heavy blunt features towards Tony. 'Find her attractive, did you?'

'What kind of question is that?'

'About as straightforward as you can get. Yes or no. Did you find the lass attractive? Did you fancy her?'

Tony paused momentarily, assembling his careful response. 'I registered that her looks would have made her appealing to a lot of men, yes. I was not myself sexually attracted to her.'

Wharton sneered. 'How could you tell? From what I've heard, you don't respond like most red-blooded blokes, do you?'

Tony flinched as if he'd been struck. A tremor ran through his taut muscles and his stomach grew turbulent. The inquiry that had inevitably followed the case he'd worked with Carol Jordan the year before had had to be told of his sexual problems. He had been promised absolute confidentiality, and if the reactions of the police officers he had encountered since were anything to go by, he had been granted that. Now, overnight, Shaz Bowman's death seemed to have stripped him of that right. He wondered momentarily where they'd gained their information, hoping this didn't mean his impotence would now be common gossip. 'My relationship with Shaz Bowman was purely professional,' he said, forcing his voice to stay calm. 'My personal life has nothing to do with this inquiry whatsoever.'

'That's for us to decide,' McCormick stated baldly.

Without pausing, Wharton continued. 'You say your

relationship was purely professional. But we have statements that indicate you spent more time with Bowman than you did with other members of the squad. Officers would arrive of a morning to find the two of you deep in conversation. She would stay behind at the end of group sessions for a word in private. A very close relationship seems to have sprung up between you.'

'There was nothing untoward between Shaz and me. I've always been an early starter in the morning. Check it out with anyone who's ever worked with me. Shaz was having some problems mastering the computer software we're using so she came in beforehand to put in some extra time. And yes, she did stay behind after group sessions with questions, but that was because she was fascinated with the work, not for any seedy ulterior motive. If your murder inquiry had taught you anything at all about Shaz Bowman, you'd know the only thing she was in love with was the Job.' He took a deep breath.

There was a long moment's silence. Then McCormick said, 'Where were you on Saturday?'

Tony shook his head, mystified. 'You're wasting your time with this. You should be using us to catch the killer, not trying to make it look like one of us is guilty. We should be talking about the meaning of what this killer did to Shaz, why he left the picture of the three wise monkeys on the body, why there was no sexual interference with the body nor any forensic traces.'

McCormick's eyes narrowed. 'I'm interested that you're so definite about the absence of forensic traces. Now how would you happen to know that?'

Tony groaned. 'I don't *know* it. But I did see the body and the scene of crime. From my experience of psychopathic killers, I reckoned it was the most likely scenario.'

'A police officer or someone who works closely with

the police would recognize the significance of forensic evidence,' McCormick said cannily.

'Everybody who has a TV set or who can read recognizes the significance of forensic evidence,' Tony countered.

'But they don't all know how to erase all traces of their presence like people who are accustomed to watching SOCOs avoiding the contamination of evidence at a crime scene, do they?'

'So you're saying there was no forensic evidence?' Tony challenged, latching on to the one piece of information that seemed significant.

'I didn't say that, no,' McCormick retorted triumphantly. 'Whoever killed Sharon Bowman probably thinks they didn't leave a trace. But they'd be wrong.'

Tony's mind raced. It couldn't be finger or shoe prints; that would be completely at odds with the organized precision of this killer. It might be hairs or fibres. Hair would only be useful if they had a serious suspect to match it against. Fibres, on the other hand, could be tracked down by a forensic expert. He hoped West Yorkshire used the best. 'Good,' was all he said. McCormick scowled.

Wharton opened a folder and placed a sheet of paper in front of Tony. 'For the tape, I am showing Dr Hill a photostat of DC Bowman's diary for the week of her death. There are two entries for the day she was murdered. JV, nine thirty. And the letter T. I put it to you, Dr Hill, that you had arranged to meet Shaz Bowman on Saturday. That you did in fact meet her on Saturday.'

Tony ran a hand through his hair. The confirmation of Carol's idea that Shaz would have confronted Vance with what she knew gave him no satisfaction. 'Inspector, I made no such arrangement. The last time I saw Shaz alive was at the end of the working day on Friday. What

I was doing on Saturday could not be less relevant to this inquiry.'

McCormick leaned forward and spoke softly. 'I'm not so sure about that. T for Tony. She could have been meeting you. She could have met you out of office hours away from the squad room, and the boyfriend could have found out about it and let it wind him up. Maybe he confronted her with it and she admitted she fancied you more than she fancied him?'

Tony's lip twitched in contempt. 'Is that the best you can come up with? That's pathetic, McCormick. I've had patients who came up with more credible fantasies. Surely you must recognize that the crucial thing here is the diary entry that says JV, nine thirty? Shaz may have *intended* talking to me after that interview, but she never made it. If you're interested in what the killer was doing on Saturday, you really should be checking out Jacko Vance and his entourage.' As soon as the name was out of his mouth, Tony knew he'd blown it. McCormick shook his head pityingly and Wharton jumped to his feet, his chair shrieking on the cheap vinyl flooring.

'Jacko Vance tries to *save* lives, not take them. You're the one with the track record here,' Wharton shouted. 'You've already killed somebody, haven't you, Dr Hill? And as you psychologists are always telling us, once the taboo's breached, it's gone for good. Once a killer . . . Fill in the blanks, Doctor. Fill in the fucking blanks.'

Tony closed his eyes. His chest hurt, as if a punch to the diaphragm had robbed him of air. All the progress he'd made over the past year was stripped away and again he smelled sweat and blood, felt them slick on his hands, heard the screams ripped from his own throat, tasted the Judas kiss. His eyes snapped open and he looked at Wharton and McCormick with a hatred he'd forgotten he was capable of. 'That's it,' he said, standing up. 'Next time you want to talk to me, you'll have to arrest me. And you'd better make sure my lawyer's on the premises when you do.'

Only his desire not to give them the satisfaction held him together as he marched out of the interview room, through the police station and out into the fresh air. No one made any move to stop him. He set off across the car park, desperate to make it to the street before his stomach lost its battle with breakfast. Just as he reached the kerb, a car pulled up beside him and the passenger window descended. Simon McNeill's dark head loomed towards him. 'Want a lift?'

Tony recoiled as if from a blow. 'No . . . I . . . No thanks.'

'Come on,' Simon urged. 'I've been waiting for you. They kept me in half the night. They'll try and pin this on me given half a chance. We need to find out who killed Shaz before they decide it's time to make an arrest.'

Tony leaned into the car. 'Simon, listen very carefully to me. You're right that they want it to be one of us. I'm not sure they'd go so far as to manufacture evidence against anybody. But I don't intend to sit back and wait and see if that happens. I intend to find out who's behind this, and I can't have you along. It's dangerous enough going up against a man who's capable of what this guy did to Shaz. It'll be hard enough for me to watch my own back without having to watch yours as well. You might be a great detective, but when it comes to going head to head with psychopaths like this, you're an absolute beginner. So do us both a favour. Please. Go home. Deal with your loss. Don't try to be a hero, Simon. I don't want to bury another one of you.'

Simon looked as if he wanted to burst into tears and thump Tony. 'I'm not a child. I'm a trained detective.

I've worked on murder squads. I cared about her. You can't shut me out. You can't stop me nailing this bastard.'

A long sigh. 'No, I can't. But Shaz was a trained detective. She'd worked on murders. She knew she was rattling a killer's cage. And she still got demolished. Not just killed, but annihilated. It's not conventional police methods that are going to sort this out, Simon. I've done this once before. Believe me, I know what it's like and I wouldn't wish it on another living soul. Go home, Simon.'

With a screech of rubber on asphalt, Simon's car streaked away from the kerb. Tony watched it take the next left far too fast, the rear spoiler fishtailing out of sight. He hoped it would be the biggest risk Simon had to take until Shaz's killer was dealt with. He knew a traffic accident would be the least of his own worries.

There was something to be said for delirium. When feverish sweat ran down her face and added another layer to the sour staleness that covered her sticky skin, it meant she could escape into hallucinations that were infinitely preferable to reality.

Donna Doyle lay huddled against the wall, holding on to the chimeras of childhood memory as if they could somehow save her. One year, her mum and dad had taken her to the Valentine Fair at Leeds. Candyfloss, hot dogs and onions, the blurry kaleidoscope of lights on the waltzer, the sparkling jeweller's window of the city spread beneath her from the top of the Ferris wheel as they swung gently in the cold night air, the neon glow of the fair like a carpet at their feet.

Her dad had won her a big teddy bear, electric pink fun fur with a goofy grin stitched across its white face. It had been the last present he'd given her before he died. It was all his fault, Donna thought, snivelling. If he hadn't gone and died, none of this would have happened. They wouldn't have been poor and she wouldn't have had to think about being a telly star, she could have listened to her mum and stuck in at school and gone to university.

Tears crept out of the corners of her eyes and she beat her left fist against the wall. 'I hate you,' she cried, screaming at the wavering image of a thin-faced man who had adored his daughter. 'I hate you, you bastard!'

At least the incoherent sobs tired her out, letting her consciousness slide mercifully from her again.

The brashness that characterized Leon's performance among his peers was gone. Instead, he was locked behind the blank insolent face he'd seen on too many young blacks, both in custody and on the street. His street. He might have the warrant card that said he was one of them, but he had enough smarts to know that the two Yorkshiremen sitting across the interview room table were still The Man.

'So, Leon,' Wharton was saying in seemingly expansive mode, 'what you're telling us squares with what we've already heard from DC Hallam. The pair of you met at four o'clock and went tenpin bowling. Then you went for a drink in the Cardigan Arms, after which you met Simon McNeill for a curry.' He smiled encouragingly.

'So neither of you two killed Shaz Bowman,' McCormick said. Leon had him figured for a racist, his pink slab of a face showing no rapport, his eyes hard and cold, his wet mouth permanently a mere twitch away from a sneer.

'None of us killed Shaz, man,' Leon said, deliberately drawing out the last word. 'She was one of us. Maybe we've not been a team for long, but we know how to stick together. You're wasting your time on us.'

'We've got to go through the motions, lad, you know

that,' Wharton said. 'You're going to be a profiler, you know that over ninety per cent of murders are committed by families or lovers. Now, when Simon turned up, how did he seem?'

'I don't know what you mean.'

'OK. Did he seem agitated, wound up, in a state?'

Leon shook his head. 'None of that, no. He was a bit quiet, but I put that down to Shaz not being there. I reckoned he fancied her, and he was disappointed when she didn't show.'

'What made you think he fancied her?'

Leon spread his hands. 'Stuff. You know? The way he tried to impress her. The way he was always checking her out. The way he'd always be bringing her into the conversation. The way a man does when he's interested, know what I mean?'

'Did you think she was interested in him?'

'I don't reckon Shaz was too interested in anybody. Not in the shagging sense. She was too obsessed with the Job to be bothered with it, if you ask me. I don't think Simon was going to drop lucky and get his leg over. Not unless he had something she wanted bad, like the inside track on a serial killer.'

'Did he say he'd been round her house?' McCormick interjected.

'He never mentioned it, no. But you wouldn't, would you? I mean, if you thought a woman had just stood you up, you wouldn't be telling people about it. Not saying anything isn't strange behaviour. Saying something, setting yourself up for having the piss taken out of you all round the squad room, now that would be strange.' Leon lit a cigarette and gave McCormick the blank-eyed stare again.

'What was he wearing?' Wharton asked.

Leon frowned with the effort of recollection. 'Leather

jacket, bottle green polo shirt, black jeans, black Docs.'

'Not a flannel shirt?'

Leon shook his head. 'Not when we met him. Why? You found some flannel fibres on her clothes?'

'Not her clothes,' Wharton said. 'We think she was –'

'I don't think we'll be going into details about the forensic evidence just now,' McCormick interrupted firmly. 'Weren't you worried when DC Bowman didn't show up for this big night out?'

Leon shrugged and blew out a stream of smoke. 'Not worried, no. Kay figured she'd got a better offer. Me, I thought she probably had her head in her computer, doing her homework.'

'Bit of a teacher's pet, was she?' Wharton asked, sympathy to the fore again.

'Nah. She was just a grafter, that's all. Look, shouldn't you be out there catching the bastard who did this, instead of wasting your time with us? You're not going to find her killer in the task force. We signed up to solve shit like this, not commit it, man.'

Wharton nodded. 'So the sooner we get this over, the better. We need your help here, Leon. You're a trained detective, but you've also got trained instincts, or else you wouldn't be on this task force. Give us the benefit of your insights. What do you make of Tony Hill? I mean, you do know that he didn't want you on the task force, don't you?'

Tony stared at the dark blue screen. McCormick and Wharton might have barred him from the task squad offices, but either they didn't know about the group's networked computer system or they had no idea how to exclude him from it. The set-up was straightforward. It had to be; the people using it were less computer literate than the average seven-year-old. All the PCs in the office were linked via a central processing and storage unit. A modem connection made it possible for any of the team who was working off site to plug straight into their personal data store as well as any of the general material that was available to everyone. For security reasons, they each had personal logins as well as individual passwords. The trainees had all been instructed to change their passwords weekly to avoid possible leaks. Whether any of them bothered was a moot point.

What none of the squad knew was that Tony had a list of every individual login. In effect, he could dial up the office computer and pretend to be any of them, with the machine none the wiser. Of course, without the password, he wouldn't get very far with the private material, but he'd be in the system.

As soon as he'd returned home from his interview, he'd switched on his home computer. First, he'd called up Shaz's application form and test responses, all scanned in as soon as she'd been accepted for the squad. He printed them out, along with the progress reports that both he and Paul Bishop had compiled.

Then he signed off as himself and signed in as Shaz. Now, the best part of two hours and a pot of coffee later, he was no further forward. He'd tried everything he could think of. SHAZ, SHARON, BOWMAN, ROBIN, HOOD, WILLIAM, TELL, ARCHER, AMBRIDGE . . . He'd run through every character he could think of from the eponymous radio soap opera. He'd tried her parents' names, every town, city, institution and street name mentioned in her CV. He'd even attempted the obvious JACKO, VANCE and the less obvious MICKY, MORGAN. And still he was staring at a screen that said, 'Welcome to the National Offender Profiling Task Force. Please type in your password now: –'. The cursor had been flashing so long the only thing he could say with total certainty was that he had no epileptic tendencies.

He stood up and prowled round the room. He didn't have an idea to bless himself with. 'Enough,' he muttered in exasperation. He lifted his jacket from the chair where he'd thrown it and shrugged it on. A walk down to the shop for the evening paper, that might clear his head. 'Don't fool yourself,' he muttered as he opened his front door. 'You just want to see what those pillocks have told the latest press conference.'

He walked down the path bisecting two flower beds where grimy rose bushes fought a rearguard action against urban enemies both human and industrial. As he turned into the street, he noticed a couple of men in a nondescript saloon car opposite. One was scrambling out of the passenger seat to the accompaniment of the engine being over-enthusiastically started. Shocked, Tony recognized all the hallmarks of an amateurish stakeout. Surely they couldn't be wasting their human resources keeping tabs on him?

At the corner, he stopped to look in the window of Bric'n'Brac, a junk shop with sad pretensions. Its proud owner kept the glass clean, which allowed Tony to take a look over his shoulder and across the street. The man who'd jumped out of the car was over there, loitering by the bus stop, pretending to read the timetable. It was an activity that marked him out as a stranger more than almost anything else could have done; the locals knew the anarchic practices of the rival bus companies too well to regard the timetable as anything other than a bad joke.

Tony walked on to the corner. Under the cloak of crossing the road, he threw a look over his shoulder. The car had turned round and was creeping down his street about fifty yards behind him. There was no doubt about it. If these were the best the local force had to offer, Shaz Bowman's killer didn't have much to worry about.

Despairing of his supposed colleagues, Tony bought an evening paper from the local newsagent and walked slowly home, reading as he went. At least the police weren't publicly saying anything to attract ridicule. In fact, they weren't saying anything much at all. Either they were playing things very close to their chest, or they had nothing to play with. He knew which he believed was the case.

Once inside, under the guise of drawing a curtain across to protect his computer screen from the bright sun, he checked for his watchers. They were both back in the car, parked in the same spot as before. What were they waiting for? What did they expect him to do?

If it wasn't so appalling in its potential consequences, it would be funny, he thought as he grabbed the phone and dialled Paul Bishop's mobile. When Bishop answered, Tony dived straight in. 'Paul? You're not going to believe this. McCormick and Wharton have got it into their heads that someone connected to the task force killed Shaz, since we're the only people up here she knew.'

'I know,' Bishop said, sounding depressed. 'But what can I do? It's their inquiry. If it makes you feel any better, I do know they've been in touch with her old division, asking them to check out if there were any villains down there who might have had enough of a grudge against her to follow her up here. So far, no joy. But her old CID sergeant has apparently been in touch to say she acted as intermediary to set up a meeting between Jacko Vance and Bowman on Saturday morning. It looks as if she was determined to pursue that wild idea of hers about the teenage girls.'

Tony let out a sigh of relief. 'Well, thank God for that. Now maybe they'll begin to take us seriously. I mean, they have to be asking at the very least why Vance hasn't come forward and revealed this himself, given that Shaz's picture has been all over the papers.'

'It's not quite that simple,' Bishop said. 'Vance's wife actually rang in within minutes of the other call to say Bowman had come to the house on Saturday morning. She said her husband hadn't seen the papers yet. So no one's actually hiding anything.'

'But they are at least going to talk to him?'

'I'm sure they will.'

'So they'll have to treat him as a suspect.'

Tony heard Bishop exhale. 'Who knows? The trouble is, Tony, I can make gentle suggestions, but I've no authority to stop them running this their own sweet way.'

'I was told that you'd agreed with them that the squad should effectively be suspended,' Tony pointed out. 'You didn't have to go along with that, surely.'

'Come on, Tony, you know how difficult the politics of the task force are. The Home Office is adamant that we don't cause problems on the ground. It was a small concession. The squad hasn't been disbanded. Nobody's being reassigned to their old units. We're just out of the operational loop until this case is either resolved or out of the headlines. Try and treat it like a sabbatical.'

Exasperated, Tony got to the initial point of his call. 'It's a pretty strange sabbatical that includes a stakeout straight out of the Keystone Cops on my doorstep.'

'You're joking?'

'I wish I was. I walked out of my interview with them this morning after they accused me of being their best bet because I'm already a killer. And now I've got Beavis and Butthead on my tail. This is intolerable, Paul.'

He could hear Bishop take a deep breath. 'I agree, but we're just going to have to roll with the punches until they get bored with us and start running a proper investigation.'

'I don't think so, Paul,' Tony said, his voice clipped and authoritative. 'One of my team is dead and they won't let us help find out who killed her. They're quick enough to remind me that I'm not one of them, I'm an outsider. Well, that cuts both ways. If you can't persuade them to get out of my face, I will be holding a press conference of my own tomorrow. And I promise, you won't like it any more than Wharton and McCormick will. It's time to pull some strings, Paul.'

'I hear you, Tony,' Bishop sighed. 'Leave it with me.'

Tony dropped the phone back into its cradle and pulled the curtain back. He switched on his desk lamp and stood in front of the window staring mutinously out at his watchers. He reviewed the information Paul Bishop had given him and related it to what he had learned at the crime scene. This killer was angry because Shaz had stuck her nose into his business. That indicated that she had been right in her supposition that there was at large a serial killer of teenage girls. Something she had done had panicked the murderer into making her his next target. The only thing she had apparently done that was connected to her theory was to visit Jacko Vance within hours of her death.

He knew now that Shaz Bowman's killer could not be some crazed fan of Vance's. There was no way for even the most dedicated stalker to find out in the short interval before her murder who Shaz was or the reason for her visit to Vance's house.

He had to find out more about the encounter between Shaz and Vance. If the killer was one of his entourage, it was possible he'd been present. But if Vance had been alone when Shaz confronted him, the finger pointed only at him. Even if he'd picked up the phone the minute she'd left and reported her suspicions to someone else, there was no way such a third party could have picked up Shaz's trail, discovered where she lived, or persuaded her to open her door to him in the time available.

As he reached this conclusion, his watchers departed. Tony threw his jacket down and dropped like a stone into the chair facing the screen. It was a small victory, but it renewed his appetite for the struggle. Now he had to find the proof to demonstrate that Shaz had been right and it had killed her. What would Shaz Bowman have used as a password? A fictional hero? Warshawski and Scarpetta were too long. KINSEY, MILLHONE, MORSE, WEXFORD, DALZIEL, HOLMES, MARPLE, POIROT all failed. A fictional villain? MORIARTY, HANNIBAL, LECTER. Still nothing.

Normally, the sound of a car pulling up outside wouldn't have penetrated his concentration. But after the day he'd had, the stilling of the engine sounded louder than an alarm buzzer. He looked out and his heart sank again. The last three people he wanted to see piled out of a familiar scarlet Ford. Mob-handed, Leon Jackson, Kay Hallam and Simon McNeill crowded up the path, sheepishly acknowledging his scowl through the window. With a groan, he got up and unlocked the door, turning straight on his heel and walking back down the hall to his study.

They followed him, crowding into the small room and, without waiting to be asked, finding places to settle; Simon on the window sill, Leon leaning elegantly against a filing cupboard, Kay in the armchair in the opposite corner. Tony swivelled round in his chair and glared, trying not to acknowledge the resignation he felt. 'Now I understand why people confess to crimes they haven't committed,' he said, only half-joking. They were impressive in spite of their youth and their uncertainty.

'You wouldn't take me seriously, so I brought in reinforcements,' Simon said. He looked too pale to be conscious, Tony registered, noticing for the first time a dusting of freckles across the bridge of his nose.

'That McCormick and Wharton, they've got it in for us,' Leon burst out. 'I've been in there all afternoon, with them doing kissy faces, "Come on, Leon, you can tell us what you really think about Tony Hill and Simon McNeill." Man, they are two sick fuckers, let me tell you. "McNeill fancied Bowman, but she was in love with Hill, so he killed her out of jealousy, what do you reckon? Or Hill wanted to get into Bowman's knickers but she was more interested in a date with McNeill and he killed her in a fit of jealous rage." More bullshit than a farmyard, made me sick.' He pulled his cigarettes out, then paused. 'Is this OK?'

Tony nodded, pointing to a lopsided Christmas cactus on a shelf. 'Just use the saucer.'

Kay leaned forward in her chair, elbows on knees. 'It's like they can't see past the end of their noses. And while they're trying to find evidence against you, they're not looking anywhere else. Least of all at what Shaz was digging into. They think her theory about a serial killer preying on teenagers is the sort of stupid thing us girls come up with because we've got our hormones in a twist. Well, we figured that if they won't do what needs to be done, we better had.'

'Do I get a word in edgeways?' Tony said.

'Be our guest,' Leon said, with an expansive gesture.

'I appreciate how you feel. And it does you credit. But this isn't a classroom exercise. It's not, "Five Go Hunting a Psychopath." This is the most dangerous game, in both senses of the word. The last time I got involved with a serial killer, it nearly cost me my own life. And, with great respect to your talents as police officers, I knew a hell of a lot more than all three of you rolled into one. I'm not prepared to take the responsibility of having you working with me off the books.' He ran a hand through his hair.

'We know it's the real thing, Tony,' Kay protested. 'And we know you're the best. That's why we've come to you. But we can do stuff you can't. We've got warrant cards. You don't. Strange cops only trust other cops. They won't trust you.'

'So if you won't help us, we'll just have to do the best we can without you,' Simon said, his mouth set in a stubborn line.

The shrill insistence of the phone came as a relief. Tony's hand closed over the receiver. 'Hello?' he said cautiously, eyeing the other three as if they were an unexploded bomb.

'It's me,' Carol said. 'I just called to see how you'd got on.'

'I'd rather tell you face to face,' he said briskly.

'You can't talk just now?'

'I'm in the middle of something. Can we meet later?'

'My cottage? Half past six?'

'Better make it seven,' he said. 'I've got a lot to do here before I can get away.'

'I'll be there. Safe journey.'

'Thanks.' He gently replaced the phone. He closed his eyes momentarily. He hadn't realized how isolated he'd been feeling. It was the existence of police officers like Carol, and the stubborn belief that one day they'd be in the majority, that made his job bearable. He opened his eyes again to find the three junior members of his squad staring avidly at him. The ghost of an idea was taking shape at the back of his mind. 'What about the other two?' he stalled. 'Saw sense, did they?'

Leon breathed smoke. 'Got no bottle. They're frightened to rock the boat in case their promotion prospects get drowned.'

'Who gives a shit about promotion when someone like Shaz gets killed and nobody cares enough to catch the killer? Who'd want to be a copper on that kind of force?' Simon spat.

'I'm sorry,' Tony said. 'The answer's still no.'

'Fine,' Kay said. Her smile could have cut steak. 'In that case, we'll move on to Plan B. The sit-in. We're staying on your case till you come on board. Where you go, we go. Twenty-four hours a day. Three of us, one of you.'

'Not good odds.' Leon lit a fresh cigarette while the embers of the previous stub still glowed.

Tony sighed. 'OK. You won't listen to me. Maybe you'll listen to somebody who really knows the score.'

The dashboard clock said it was just after seven; the radio played the theme from *The Archers*, revealing the clock was three minutes slow. Tony's car jounced up the rough track from the road, his suspension giving its age away. He rounded the last bend and saw with satisfaction that the lights were on in Carol's cottage.

She was framed in the doorway as he closed the car door behind himself. He couldn't remember the last time he'd felt so glad to be walking into someone else's company, someone else's territory. The only sign that his companions were completely unexpected was the slight lift of her eyebrows.

'Kettle's on, beer's cold,' she greeted them, offering Tony a gentle squeeze of the arm. 'Is this your bodyguard?'

'Not as such. I am currently being held hostage,' he said drily, following her indoors. His squad didn't wait for an invitation. They were right there on his heels. 'You remember Kay, Leon and Simon? They're going to hang round my neck like millstones until I agree to work with them on uncovering who killed Shaz.' In the living room, he gestured with his thumb towards the sofa and chairs. The threesome sat. 'I was hoping you would help me talk them out of it.'

Carol shook her head, acting bemused. 'They *want* to work with you on a live case? God, the rumour mill must have deteriorated one hell of a lot recently.'

'Coffee first,' Tony said, lifting a hand and placing it lightly on her shoulder, steering her towards the kitchen.

'Coming up.'

He closed the door behind them. 'I'm sorry for landing you with this. But they wouldn't listen to me. The problem is that West Yorkshire are acting like Simon's the prime suspect and I'm a close second. And this lot are not going to lie down and take that. But you know what it's like when you're working a serial killer case and it gets personal. They don't have the experience to handle this. Vance or someone close to him has already killed the best and brightest of them. I don't want any more deaths on my conscience.'

Carol spooned coffee into the filter and switched it on as he spoke. 'You're absolutely right,' she said. 'However . . . unless I misjudge them completely, they're going to pursue this anyway. The best way to make sure you don't lose another one is to take control. And the way to do that is to work with them. Set them all the drudge jobs, the runaround background inquiries that baby detectives cut their teeth on. Anything dodgy, anything we think is dangerous or needs expert interrogation techniques, we'll sort out.'

' "We?" '

Carol clapped the palm of her hand to her forehead and grimaced. 'Why do I feel like I've just been suckered?' She punched his arm. 'Put some sugar and milk and mugs on a tray and take it through before I get seriously cross.'

He did as he was told, feeling strangely gratified that he had moved from the Lone Ranger to team captain in the space of a few hours. By the time Carol brought the coffee through, he'd shared the new deal with a self-satisfied team.

He opened his laptop on the stripped pine dining table, jacked the modem into the phone line, and plugged the transformer into the nearest power point. As the others arranged themselves so they could see the screen, Carol asked Tony, 'How bad was the interview?'

'I walked out in the end,' he said succinctly as he watched the machine boot up. 'It was what you might call hostile. When it comes to, "Hey, lads, hey," they don't really think I'm on the same side, you see. But they're saving the prime suspect slot for Simon. He had the bad luck to get Shaz to agree to a date on the very night she was killed. But I'm probably second favourite in the book that some smart-arse on the murder team will be running.' He looked up and Carol could see the hurt behind the assumed self-possession.

'Stupid bastards,' Carol said, putting his mug of coffee next to the computer. 'But then, they are Yorkshiremen. I can't believe they're not using you lot.'

Leon gave a bark of mirthless laughter. 'Tell us about it. You let people smoke in here?'

Carol glanced at him, taking in the fingers beating a silent tattoo on his thigh. Better that the tobacco combusted than he did. 'You'll find a saucer in the cupboard above the kettle,' she said. 'Only in this room, please.'

As he left, she took over his chair and settled down next to Tony, watching the screen change as his fingers hit the keys.

Tony worked his way into the task force computer system with Shaz's login. He pointed to the flashing cursor. 'This is what I've been racking my brains over all afternoon. I can get on to the system as Shaz, but I can't figure out her password.' He ran through the attempts he'd made, ticking the categories off on his fingers. Leon, Kay and Simon started throwing out their own suggestions based on what they knew of their late colleague.

Carol listened carefully, left hand teasing the tendrils of blonde hair on the back of her neck. When Tony and the other three had run out of steam and ideas, she said, 'Missed the obvious, didn't you? Who did Shaz look up to? What did she want to be?'

'Running Scotland Yard? You think I should try famous Met Commissioners?'

Carol reached over and pulled the laptop within touch-typing range. 'Famous profilers.' She typed in RESSLER, DOUGLAS, LEYTON. Nothing happened. A rueful quirk of the lips, then she typed TONYHILL. The screen went momentarily blank, then a menu appeared. 'Fuck, I wish I'd taken a bet on it,' she said wryly. Around her, the trainee profilers applauded, Leon wolf-whistling and whooping.

Tony shook his head, astonished. 'What do I have to do to get you on the national squad?' he asked. 'You're wasted in ordinary CID work at your rank. All that admin when you should be harnessing that inspiration to catch pychopaths.'

'Right,' Carol said sarcastically, pushing the laptop back towards him. 'If I'm so good, how come I didn't work out that my arsonist was a crook, not a crazy?'

'Because you were working alone. That's never the best way to operate when you're dealing with psychological analysis. I think profilers should work in pairs, detective and psychologist, complementary skills.' He took the cursor down to the 'File directory' option and hit ENTER.

The quality of their meeting of minds was not a conversation Carol wanted to have, especially not in company as sharp as the present one. Deftly, she moved the subject forward, bringing Leon, Kay and Simon up to speed with Tony's theory that the arsonist was a part-time fireman with a conventional criminal motive.

'But what *is* the motive?' Kay asked. 'That's the important bit, isn't it?'

'If it's criminal, you always want to know who benefits,' Leon pointed out. 'And since there's no common ownership or insurance, maybe it's somebody high up in the fire service who doesn't want any more cutbacks.'

Tony looked up from the file names he was scrolling through. 'Nice idea,' he said. 'Devious, though. And as a proponent of Occam's Razor, I'm going to go for the most straightforward theory. Debt,' he said and turned his eyes back to the screen.

'Debt?' Carol's voice was full of doubt.

'That's right.' He swung round to face her. 'Somebody who owes money all over the place, somebody with a credit rating that's fallen through the floor. His house has been repossessed or it's on the point of it, he's got a stack of county court judgements against him and he's robbing Peter to pay Paul.'

'But a night callout is, what? Fifty, a hundred quid max, depending on how long they're out there? You surely don't think somebody would put his liberty, his mates' lives, at risk for that sort of cash!' Simon protested.

Tony shrugged. 'If you're up against the wall, perpetually juggling creditors, an extra hundred quid a week can make all the difference to staying in one piece and having your legs broken, your car snatched, your electricity cut off, the bank putting you into bankruptcy. You pay twenty quid off one debt, fifty off another, a tenner here, a fiver there. You show willing. It keeps everybody off your back. The courts are reluctant to take drastic steps if you can show you're really trying. Any sensible person knows that it's only postponing the evil hour, but when you're in debt up to your eyeballs, you stop thinking straight. You get into this self-deluding fantasy that if you can just get over this hump, you'll be heading towards getting straight again. Nobody cons themselves better than a bad debtor. I've seen pathetic idiots who owe the best part of twenty grand to a loan shark still employing a cleaning lady and a gardener because getting rid of them would be an admission that their lives were totally out of control. Look for somebody who's teetering on the brink of insolvency, Carol.'

Already back in communion with the computer screen, he muttered, 'Let me see ... MISPER.OOI. That'll be the report she did for the squad, wouldn't you think?'

'Seems likely. And MISPERJV.OOI could be her Jacko Vance inquiries.'

'Let's take a look.' Tony opened the file. Shaz's words spilled down the screen, giving him a strange sense of communing with the dead. It was as if those extraordinary blue eyes were hovering behind his head, fixing him with their inexorable stare. 'My God,' he whispered. 'She wasn't playing games.'

Leon peered over his shoulder. 'Fuck,' he breathed. 'You fucking witch, Shazza.' It summed up everyone's feelings perfectly as they stared at Shaz's briefing from beyond the grave.

ORGANIZED OFFENDER CHECKLIST

Jacko Vance
Re: MISPER cluster

High birth order
Only child.

Father's work stable
Civil engineer – often away from home for prolonged periods on long-term contracts.

Absent father
See above.

Parental discipline perceived as inconsistent
See above; also, mother appears to have suffered postnatal depression, rejected JV and later treated v. strictly.

Higher than average IQ
Regarded as bright by teachers but never did as well as expected academically; poor exam performer.

Skilled occupation, work history uneven
First as a champion javelin thrower then as TV presenter; perfectionist, prone to temper tantrums and firing junior members of team; if not for medal-winning prowess/popularity with TV audience, would have lost several contracts over the years because of arrogant and overbearing behaviour.

Socially adept; may be gregarious and good talker, but can't connect emotionally

See above; relates very well to members of the public on superficial level; however, one of reasons why his marriage is perceived as so successful is that he appears to have no intimate relationships with either gender outside that relationship.

Living with partner

Wife, Micky, been together for twelve years. A very public marriage, the golden couple of UK TV. However, often away from home both on business and on extensive charity work.

Controlled mood during commission of crime

Unknown: but Vance is known in the business for coolness under pressure.

Use of alcohol or drugs during commission of crime

Unknown. No history of drink problem, some hint that there may have been a problem with painkiller addiction following accident in which Vance lost his arm.

Mobile; car in good condition

Vance has a silver Mercedes convertible and a Land Rover. Both are automatics and have been adapted for his disability.

Follows crimes in the media

He's perfectly placed to do this – he has direct access to all areas of the media. He numbers many journalists among his circle of acquaintance.

Victims share common characteristics
   Yes – see appendix A on original cluster of
   seven victims.

Unsuspicious demeanour
   Millions of people would trust him with their
   lives or their daughters. In a poll four years
   ago, he was voted the third most trustworthy
   person in Britain after the Queen and the
   Bishop of Liverpool.

Looks average
   Impossible to comment objectively. The gloss
   of celebrity, grooming and an expensive
   wardrobe makes it hard to judge beyond the
   facade.

Mental illness in immediate family
   Nothing known; mother died eight years ago,
   cancer.

Alcohol or drugs problem in immediate family
   Nothing known.

Parents with criminal records
   Nothing known.

Emotional abuse
   Mother reportedly told him he was ugly and
   clumsy, 'just like your father'. Mother appeared
   to blame him for his father's absences.

*Sexually dysfunctional – incapable of mature,
consensual relationship with another adult*
   Nothing to support this: marriage very public.
   No indications that MM unhappy with
   marriage or has lover. ??? Check newspaper
   gossip columns ??? Check with uniforms on
   local patrol – any signs ???

Cool, distant mother; very little touching or emotional warmth as child
Implied in both books.

Egocentric world view
All the evidence – even from MM's adoring account – supports this.

Beaten as child
MM recalls him speaking of his father coming home from trip and thrashing him for failing eleven-plus; otherwise, nothing known.

Witnessed sexually stressful situation as child, e.g. marital rape, mother engaged in prostitution
Nothing known

Parents separated in childhood or early adolescence
Parents divorced when he was twelve. According to MM book, his obsession with athletics was bid to gain father's attention.

Autoerotic adolescence
Nothing known.

Rape fantasies
Nothing known.

Obsession with pornography
Nothing known.

Voyeuristic tendencies
Nothing specific known; but cf. *Vance's Visits*, the ultimate poke-your-nose-in television.

Aware his sexual/emotional relationships are abnormal and resents it
Nothing known.

Obsessive
   Attested to by work colleagues and rivals
   alike.

Irrational phobias
   Nothing known.

Chronic liar
   Several instances of him 'remaking' past
   incidents; compare two books.

Initiating stressor?
   Jacko Vance's first girlfriend was Jillie
   Woodrow. He was unsuccessful with girls
   before her, and by the time they got together,
   he was almost sixteen and she was just
   fourteen. Apart from his obsessive sports
   training, she was his only interest. They had a
   relationship that was exclusive, compulsive
   and consuming. He appears to have been a
   dominating influence upon her. They were
   engaged as soon as she turned sixteen,
   opposed by her parents and his mother; he
   was no longer in touch with his father by this
   time. After the accident when he lost his arm,
   MM's account claims he set Jillie free since he
   was no longer the man she'd contracted to
   marry; TB's version is that she had been
   looking for a way out of the claustrophobic
   relationship for some time and fixed on his
   accident as a way out, claiming she was
   repelled by his injury and the prospect of
   living with a man with a prosthesis. MM and
   Vance got together shortly afterwards. Just
   before they married, Jillie did a 'kiss and tell'
   with the *News of the World* revealing that
   Vance had forced her to indulge in

sadomasochistic rituals, tying her up to have sex in spite of her protests that it frightened her. Vance tried to prevent the story's publication, denying it vigorously. He failed to get an injunction, but never sued for libel, claiming that he couldn't afford the legal process. (Probably true at that stage in career.) Either the end of the relationship with Jillie in such stressful circumstances or her subsequent revelations could have been a powerful enough stressor to trigger off the first in Vance's series of crimes.

'Oh, shit,' Carol said as she reached the end of Shaz's analysis. 'You really have to wonder, don't you?'

'You think Jacko Vance could be a serial killer?' Kay asked.

'Shaz thought so. And I think she might have been right,' Tony said grimly.

'There's something bothering me about this,' Simon said. Encouraged by a questioning look from Tony he continued. 'If Vance is a sociopath, how come he saved those kids and tried to rescue that lorry driver in the accident where he lost his arm? Why did he not just leave them to it?'

'Good point,' Tony said. 'You know I hate to theorize ahead of the data, but looking at what we know so far, I'd say Jacko spent most of his formative years desperate for attention and approval. When the accident happened, he automatically went down the road that would make him look good in other people's eyes. It's not uncommon for what looks like heroism to be a desperate craving for glory. I think that's what happened there. If you still think we're barking up the wrong tree, let me tell you about a conversation I had with Commander

Bishop this afternoon.' He told them about Shaz's appointment with Vance and the conclusions he'd drawn from that.

'You're going to have to let McCormick and Wharton know about this file,' Carol said.

'I don't feel much like it, the way they treated me.'

'You want them to put Shaz's killer away, don't you?'

'I want Shaz's killer put away,' Tony said firmly. 'I just don't think those two have the imagination to deal with the information. Think about it, Carol. If I tell them what we've found here, first off, they won't want to believe it. They'll think we've tinkered with her files. I can just imagine the interview with Vance. He slipped effortlessly into the broad Yorkshire of his childhood. 'A'right, Mr Vance, we're sorry to trouble tha, but we think the lass here last Saturday thought tha were a serial killer. Daft, tha knows, but seeing as 'ow she got herself murdered that night, we thought we'd better come and 'ave a word. 'Appen tha might've seen summat, some weirdo following her, like.'

'They're not that bad, surely,' Carol protested, spluttering with laughter in spite of herself.

'You ask me, he's being generous,' Leon muttered.

'They're not going to go in and *interrogate* Jacko Vance,' Simon said. 'They're going to be overawed, they're going to be on his side. All they'll do is mark his card.'

'And Jack the Lad is a clever bastard,' Tony continued. 'Now he knows they know about Shaz's visit, he'll be the biggest Goody Two Shoes on legs. So there's part of me that thinks, no, don't tell them.'

There was a long silence. Then Simon said, 'So what now?'

Tony had taken a notepad from the laptop bag and started scribbling. 'If we're going to do this, we've got

284

to do it right. Which means I act as controller and co-ordinator. Carol, is there a local takeaway that delivers?'

She snorted with derision. 'Out here? Do me a favour. There's bread, cheese, salami, tuna, salad stuff. Give me a hand, team. we'll throw some butties together while our leader cogitates.'

When they returned fifteen minutes later with mounds of sandwiches and a mixing bowl filled with crisps, Tony was ready for them. Sprawled round the room with bottles of beer and plates of food, they listened while he explained what he wanted them to do.

'I think we're all agreed that on the balance of prob-abilities, Shaz was killed because of the work she'd done since she came to Leeds. There's no indication that she had any kind of personally threatening experiences up to that point. So we take as our starting point the assumption that Shaz Bowman correctly identified the existence of an as yet unknown serial killer of teenage girls.' He raised his eyebrows in a question and noted four nods.

'The external connector in these cases concerned Jacko Vance. Shaz assumed him to be the killer, though we shouldn't fail to consider that our target could con-ceivably be someone in his entourage. Me, I'm inclined to go for Vance.'

'Good old Occam,' Simon muttered wryly.

'Not just on the least complicated principle,' Tony said. 'My view is coloured by the length of time these killings apparently cover. I don't know if there's anyone who has been professionally close to Vance for that long. Even if they had, I'm not convinced that they would have the charisma to lure young women into what looks superficially like a runaway bid.

'So, we've got Shaz's profile of Vance. It's inevitably superficial. She only had access to what was in the public

285

domain that she could get her hands on readily. That seems to have consisted mainly of two biographies, one written by his wife, the other by a showbiz hack. We need to dig a lot deeper than that before we can check whether this man is a serious possible for the series of killings we're postulating. This is an unusual job for us profilers. Usually we're making deductions from crime to offender. This time, we're going from putative offender to hypothetical murders. I don't feel entirely confident about it, if I'm honest. It's fresh territory for me. So we need to be very careful before we put our heads anywhere near the parapet.' More nods. Leon stood up and moved across to the doorway so he could smoke without polluting everyone else's food.

'We get the message,' Leon drawled. 'Our missions, should we choose to accept them, are . . . ?'

'We need to track down his fiancée, Jillie Woodrow. The person responsible for interviewing Jillie should also carry out a general investigation into his early life – family, neighbours, school friends, teachers, any local bobbies still on the payroll or recently retired. Simon, are you up for that?'

Simon looked apprehensive. 'What exactly do I do?'

Tony signalled to Carol with his eyes. 'Find out everything you possibly can about Jacko,' she said. 'Deep background. If you want a cover story for everyone except Jillie, say we're investigating threats against him and we think the reason may lie deep in his past. People love a bit of melodrama. With Jillie, that won't work. It might be worth hinting that you're investigating allegations made against Jacko by a prostitute, perhaps imply that you suspect they're malicious lies?'

'OK. Any ideas how I find her, given that I haven't got access to the PNC?'

'I'll get to that in a minute,' Tony said. 'Leon, I want

you to start digging into what was going on in his life around the time of the accident where he lost his arm. That and his early TV career. See if you can find his old trainer, the first people he worked with when he was starting out in sports' broadcasting. Athletes on the British team with him, that sort of thing. OK?'

'Just watch me,' Leon said, cold and serious for once. 'You won't be sorry you asked me, man.'

'Kay, your job is to go round the parents of the girls Shaz identified in her cluster and re-interview them. All the usual misper stuff, plus anything and everything you can pull out about Jacko Vance.'

'The local lads should be more than happy to hand off their case files to you,' Carol put in. 'They'll be so delighted that somebody else is prepared to take responsibility for such a no-hoper, they'll probably give you the freedom of the nick.'

'All of which DCI Jordan here will set up for you in advance,' Tony continued. 'She will be your facilitator, the one who speaks to ranking officers in other police stations around the country and gets you the information that will kick-start your inquiries. Stuff like where Jillie Woodrow is now, what happened to Vance's coach, which victim's parents have moved to Scunthorpe.'

Carol stared open-mouthed for a long moment. Leon, Simon and Kay looked on with the delight of adolescents watching grown-ups on the verge of behaving badly. 'Fine,' she eventually said, her voice loaded with sarcasm. 'I have so little to do at work, it'll be a pleasure fitting it in. So, Tony, what are you going to be up to while the rest of the squad are doing all the hard graft?'

He reached for a sandwich, checked the filling, then looked up with a smile that appeared entirely free from guile. 'I'm going to shake the tree,' he said.

*

Detective Inspector Colin Wharton looked like a refugee from one of those dreadfully predictable gritty northern cops-and-robbers dramas that the networks churned out to fill the gap between the late news and bedtime, Micky thought. Once handsome in a craggy way, too much drink and junk food had blurred his features and shrouded his blue eyes in heavy pouches. She imagined him on a second marriage which would be in trouble; the kids from his first marriage would be the teenagers from hell; and he'd have a vague but worrying recurring pain somewhere in his internal organs. She crossed her legs demurely and gave him the smile that had reassured a thousand studio guests. She just knew he'd be a complete sucker for it. Him and Detective Constable Sidekick, who looked one step away from asking for her autograph.

She glanced at her watch. 'Jacko should be back any minute. It'll be the traffic. Same with Betsy. My personal assistant.'

'You mentioned that,' Wharton said. 'If it's all the same to you, we might as well get started. We can talk to Ms Thorne and Mr Vance when they get here.' He consulted a folder spread across his tightly trousered lap. 'I'm told you spoke to DC Bowman the day before she died. How did that come about?'

'We've got two phone lines – one for me and one for Jacko. They're ex-directory, very private. Only a handful of people have the numbers. I switch mine over to the mobile when I'm out and DC Bowman came through on that. It must have been about half past eight on Friday morning – I was with one of my researchers at the time, she could probably confirm that.' Realizing she was wallowing in inconsequentiality, too obvious a marker for nervousness, Micky paused for a moment.

'But it wasn't your researcher?' Wharton prompted her.

'No. It was a voice I didn't recognize. She said she was Detective Constable Sharon Bowman from the Metropolitan Police and she wanted to arrange an appointment with Jacko. My husband.'

Wharton nodded encouragingly. 'And you said?'

'I told her she'd come through on my line and she apologized and said she'd been told this was his private number. She asked if he was there, and when I said he was away she said could she leave a message. I don't normally act as Jacko's secretary, but since she was with the police and I didn't know what it was about, I thought it would be best just to make a note of what she wanted and pass it on to him.' She smiled, aiming for the self-deprecating air of a woman unsure of herself faced with authority. It was a blatant performance, but Wharton didn't seem to notice.

'Sensible approach, Ms Morgan,' he said. 'What was the message?'

'She said it was merely a formality, a routine matter, but she'd like to interview him in connection with a case she was working on. Because of her other commitments, she said it would have to be Saturday, but she'd happily fit in with his arrangements. The time and place would be up to him. And she left a number where he could get back to her.'

'Do you still have that number?' Wharton asked, just another standard question.

Micky picked up a notepad and held it out to him. 'As you see, we start a fresh page for each day. It's a catch-all – phone messages, programme ideas, domestic bits and pieces.' She handed it over, pointing to a few lines near the top of the page.

Wharton read, 'Det. Con. Sharon Bowman. Jacko. i/

v ???Saturday??? you name time + place. 307 4676 Sgt. Devine.' That confirmed the telephone statement Chris Devine had already given them, but Wharton wanted to double-check. 'This number . . . is it London?'

Micky nodded. 'Yes. 0171. Same code as ours, that's why I didn't bother writing it down. Well, it would be, wouldn't it? She was with the Met.'

'She was on secondment to a unit in Leeds,' he said heavily. 'That's why she was living there, Ms Morgan.'

'Oh God, of course,' she said hollowly. 'Do you know, for some reason that just hadn't registered. How odd.'

'Indeed,' Wharton said. 'So, you passed the message on to your husband and that was that?' he said.

'I left the message on his voice mail. He mentioned later that he'd arranged for her to come to the house on Saturday morning. He knew I wouldn't mind since Betsy and I were going off on Le Shuttle on a freebie. Perks of the job.' She gave him the full-beam smile again. Wharton wondered sourly why the women in his life never managed to look so gratified when they spoke to him.

Before he could ask the next question, he heard footfalls on the parquet floor of the hall. He half-turned as the door opened behind him. His first impression of Jacko Vance was a sense of tremendous energy contained within expensive tailoring. There was something irresistibly watchable about him, even doing something as banal as crossing the room and extending his left hand in a gesture of welcome. 'Inspector Wharton, I presume,' Vance said warmly, affecting not to notice the policeman's fluster as he half-rose, reached out with the wrong hand then clumsily shifted his papers and grabbed at the proffered hand in an awkward shake. 'I'm Jacko Vance,' he said, pretending a humility Micky recognized as false as her own. 'Desperate business, this.'

Vance turned away from the detective, nodding a friendly greeting at the hovering constable and dropped on to the sofa next to his wife. He patted her thigh. 'All right, Micky?' His voice dripped the same concern he always showed the terminally ill.

'We've just been going over DC Bowman's phone call,' she said.

'Right. Sorry I'm late. Got held up in traffic in the West End,' he said, his mouth curling upwards in a familiar self-deprecating smile. 'So, what can I tell you, officer?'

'Ms Morgan passed a message on to you from DC Bowman, is that right?'

'Absolutely,' Vance said confidently. 'I called the number she'd left and spoke to a detective sergeant whose name I have completely forgotten. I said that if DC Bowman came to the house on Saturday morning between half past nine and noon, I would see her then.'

'Very generous, a busy man like yourself,' Wharton said.

Vance raised his eyebrows. 'I always try to help the authorities when I can. It didn't inconvenience me in any way. All I had planned for the day was to catch up on some personal paperwork then drive up to my cottage in Northumberland in time for an early night. I was running a charity half-marathon at Sunderland on Sunday, you see.' He leaned back negligently, fully expecting his throwaway line to be noted, believed and filed away in support of his innocence.

'What time did DC Bowman arrive?' Wharton asked.

Vance pulled a face and turned to Micky. 'What time was it? You were just leaving, weren't you?'

'That's right,' she confirmed. 'Must have been around half past nine. Betsy could probably tell you more exactly. She's the only one in the house with any sense of time.' She smiled wryly, amazed at how ready this policeman was to accept that two major TV personalities who anchored key programmes couldn't measure time instinctively to the last half-minute. 'We more or less passed on the doorstep. Jacko was on the phone upstairs, so I pointed her in here, and we were off.'

'I didn't keep her waiting more than a couple of minutes,' Vance continued seamlessly. 'She apologized for interrupting my weekend, but I explained that in this job, we don't really have weekends. We take time for ourselves when we can, don't we, darling?' He gazed adoringly at her, slipping his arm round her shoulders.

'Not often enough,' Micky sighed.

Wharton cleared his throat and said, 'Can you tell me what it was DC Bowman wanted to talk to you about?'

'You mean, you don't know?' Micky demanded, the dormant news reporter inside her springing into action. 'A police officer comes all the way from Yorkshire to London to interview someone with as high a profile as Jacko, and you don't know what it was in aid of?' She looked astonished, leaning forward, forearms on thighs, hands spread open.

Wharton shifted in his seat and stared fixedly at a point on the wall between the two long windows. 'DC Bowman was attached to a new unit. Strictly speaking, she should not have been on operational duties at present. We think we know what she was working on, but as yet we have no independent corroboration of that. It'd help us a lot if Mr Vance could just tell us what transpired between the two of them on Saturday morning.' He breathed out heavily through his nose and shot them a quick look that mingled embarrassment and pleading.

'No problem,' Vance said easily. 'DC Bowman was

very apologetic about invading my privacy with her questions, but she said she was working on a series of missing teenage girls. She thought they had been lured away from home by the same individual. It appeared that some of these girls had been at one of my public appearances shortly before they dropped out of sight and she wondered if some nutter was targeting my fans. She said she wanted to show me pictures of the girls, just in case I'd noticed them talking to a particular person.'

'One of your entourage, you mean?' Wharton prompted, proud of knowing the right word.

Vance laughed, a rich baritone laugh. 'I'm sorry to disappoint you, Inspector, but I don't exactly have an entourage. When I'm doing the programme, I have a team who work very closely with me. Sometimes when I'm doing PAs – public appearances, that is – my producer or my researcher will come along to keep me company and provide a bit of back-up. But that apart, anything I spend on minders or whatever comes out of my pocket. And since most of the work I do involves earning cash for charities as well, it seems crazy to spend any more than is absolutely necessary. So, as I explained to DC Bowman, there are no loyal retainers. What there is, however, is a hard core of devotees. There are, I suppose, a couple of dozen fans who turn up regularly at virtually every event I do. Strange people, but I'd always considered them harmless.'

'It's a mark of celebrity,' Micky said matter-of-factly. 'If you don't have your retinue of attendant weirdos, you're nobody. Badly dressed men in anoraks and women in polyester slacks and acrylic cardies. All of them with dreadful haircuts. Not the sort your average teenage girl would run off with, take it from me.'

'Which is pretty much what I told DC Bowman,' Vance continued. They were so smooth, so natural, he thought. Maybe it was about time they made some programmes together. He made a mental note to explore the idea with his producer. 'She showed me a few photographs of the girls she was concerned about, but none of them rang any bells.' His shrug was disarming. 'Not surprising. I can sign upwards of three hundred autographs at a PA. Well, I say sign ... scrawl would be more like it.' He looked ruefully at his prosthetic hand. 'Writing's one of the many things I can't do properly any more.'

There was a moment's silence. To Wharton it felt as long as Remembrance Sunday. He searched around for a meaningful question. 'How did DC Bowman respond, sir? To your lack of recognition, I mean.'

'She seemed disappointed,' Vance said. 'But she admitted it had always been a long shot. I said I was sorry not to have been more help, and she left. That must have been around ... oh, half past ten, thereabouts?'

'So she was here for about an hour? That seems quite a long time for a few questions,' Wharton said, punctilious rather than suspicious.

'It does, doesn't it?' Vance agreed. 'But I did keep her waiting a few minutes, then I made us both some coffee, we did the usual small talk. People always want to know behind-the-scenes gossip about *Vance's Visits*. Then I had to go through all the photographs. I took my time. Missing girls is too serious a subject to take lightly. I mean, no contact with their families after all this time – years, in some cases, according to DC Bowman – chances are they could have been murdered. It merited my attention.'

'Quite so, sir,' Wharton said heavily, wishing he hadn't bothered asking. 'I don't suppose she mentioned any plans she might have for the rest of the day?'

Vance shook his head. 'Sorry, Inspector. I had the

impression she had another appointment, but she didn't say where or with whom.'

'What gave you that impression, sir?' Wharton looked up, for the first time feeling he might be doing more than going through the motions.

Vance frowned for a moment, as if thinking. 'After I'd finished with the photographs, I offered to make fresh coffee. But she looked at her watch and seemed startled. As if she hadn't realized the time. She said she had to be going, she'd no idea we'd been talking for so long. She was out the door within minutes.'

Wharton closed his notebook. 'As I think I should be too, sir. I very much appreciate both of you taking the time to talk to me. If there's anything else, which I very much doubt, I'll be in touch.' He rose and gave his junior officer a 'let's go' jerk of the head.

'You don't need to speak to Betsy?' Micky asked. 'She shouldn't be long.'

'I don't think that'll be necessary,' Wharton said. 'Frankly, I think DC Bowman's visit here was almost certainly nothing to do with her death. We just have to tie up the loose ends.'

Vance crossed to the door and opened it to usher them out. 'A shame you have to be dragged down here when the real work's waiting for you in Yorkshire,' he said, his sympathetic smile adding weight to the commiseration in his voice.

Micky said goodbye and watched from the window as Vance saw the police officers off the premises. She wasn't sure what her husband was hiding. But she knew him well enough to know that what she had just heard was only a distant relative of the truth, the whole truth and nothing but the truth.

When he walked back into the room, she was leaning against the fireplace. 'Are you going to tell me what you didn't tell them?' she asked, her eyes giving him the shrewd appraisal that could always penetrate his glossy surface.

Vance grinned. 'You're a witch, Micky. Yes, I'll tell you what I didn't tell them. I did recognize one of the girls whose picture Bowman showed me.'

Micky's eyes widened. 'You did? How come? Where from?'

'No need to panic,' he said scornfully. 'It's perfectly innocent. When she went missing, her parents contacted us. Said she was my biggest fan, blah, blah, blah, never missed a show, blah, blah, blah. Wanted us to put out an appeal for her to contact them.'

'And did you?'

'Course not. It wouldn't fit the format of the programme at all. Somebody from the office sent them a sympathetic letter and we got one of the tabloids to run a story saying, "Jacko begs runaway to phone home".'

'So why didn't you tell Wharton? If you did something for the press, there'll be cuttings somewhere! They could dig them out and then you'll be in deep shit.'

'How? They don't even know what Bowman was doing, which doesn't sound like they've got her files, does it? Look, Mick, I never met the girl. I never spoke to her. But if I tell DI Plod I recognized her ... shit Mick, you know the police are the leakiest sieve in town. Next thing you know, it'll be "Jacko in murder quiz" splashed all over the front pages. No thanks. I can do without it. They can't connect me to a single one of Bowman's runaways. The king of deniability remember?'

Micky shook her head, admiring his chutzpah in spite of herself. 'More like Teflon Man,' she said. 'I've got to hand it to you, Jacko. When it comes to playing the audience like a fiddle, even I can't hold a candle to you.

He crossed to her and kissed her cheek. 'Never try to bullshit a bullshitter.'

Carol walked next morning into her office to find her crew had wrong-footed her by being there ahead of her. Tommy Taylor sprawled in the chair opposite hers, legs wide apart to emphasize his masculinity. Lee had the window cracked open, blowing his smoke out to join the traffic fumes. Di was in her usual position leaning against the wall, arms folded over her badly fitting suit. Carol itched to drag her kicking and screaming to the January sales to kit the woman out in clothes that would both fit and flatter her instead of the expensive and nasty stuff she chose now.

Carol made straight for her bastion behind the desk, flipping open her briefcase as she sat. 'Right,' she said. 'Our serial arsonist.'

'Crunchy nut cornflake,' Lee said.

'Actually, not,' Carol said. 'Apparently, our firebug is as sane as you or me. Well, me, anyway, since I can't speak for you three. According to a psychologist whose judgement I trust implicitly, we're not dealing with a psychopath. The man who's setting these fires has a straightforward criminal motive. And that points to Jim Pendlebury's part-timers.' The three stared at her as if she'd suddenly slipped into Swedish.

'You what?' Lee managed to speak first.

Carol distributed copies of the list the fire chief had given her. 'I want deep background checks into these men. Particular attention to financial details. And I don't want them to get so much as a sniff that we're interested.'

Tommy Taylor found his voice. 'You're accusing *firemen*?'

'I think you'll find we're supposed to call them firefighters these days,' Carol said mildly. 'I'm not accusing anybody yet, Sergeant. I'm trying to gather enough information on which we can base a decision.'

'Firemen *die* in fires,' Di Earnshaw sniped mutinously. 'They get injured, they inhale smoke. Why would a fireman set fires? He'd have to be a real sicko, and you just said this bloke isn't. Surely that's a contradiction in terms?'

'He's not sick,' Carol said firmly. 'Desperate, maybe, but he's not suffering from a mental illness. We're looking for someone who's so deep in debt he's lost sight of anything except how to get out of it. It's not that he wants to put his mates at risk; he's just not allowing himself to include them in the equation.'

Taylor shook his head sceptically. 'It's a helluva slur on the fire service,' he protested.

'No more so than outside inquiries into allegations of police corruption. And we all know that happens.' Carol's voice was dry. She shuffled the case papers back into her briefcase then looked up at them. 'You lot still here?'

Lee tossed his cigarette into the street below in an eloquent gesture and pushed himself into a slouching walk to the door. 'I'm on it,' he said.

Taylor stood up and ostentatiously rearranged the outward evidence of his gender. 'Aye,' he said, following Lee and indicating to Di Earnshaw that she should follow.

'Softly, softly,' Carol said to the retreating backs.

If spines could speak, Di Earnshaw's would have uttered a fluent 'Fuck off.' The door closed behind them and Carol leaned back in her chair, one hand massaging the tight knots at the base of her skull. It was going to be a very long day.

*

Tony reached for the phone automatically, mumbling, 'Tony Hill here, can you hang on a minute,' before finishing the sentence he was typing into his computer. He looked at the receiver in his hand as if not quite certain how it had arrived there. 'Yes, sorry, Tony Hill speaking.'

'This is DI Wharton.' His voice was neutral.

'Why?' Tony asked.

'What?' Wharton stumbled, wrong-footed.

'I asked why you were calling. What's so strange about that?'

'Aye, right. Well, I'm calling out of courtesy,' Wharton said with a brusqueness that contradicted his words.

'That's novel.'

'There's no need to get clever. My boss would have no problem with bringing you in for another visit.'

'He'd have to take that up with my lawyer. You've had your one free shot. So what was this courtesy you wanted to extend me?'

'We had a telephone call from Micky Morgan, the TV presenter who, as you may or may not know, is Mrs Jacko Vance. She volunteered the information that Bowman visited their house in London on Saturday morning to interview her husband. So we took a trip down there and spoke to Mr Vance ourselves. And he's in the clear. Bowman might have made a fool of herself in front of your little clique, but she wasn't daft enough to repeat her nonsense to the man himself. Turns out all she wanted to ask was if he'd seen anybody at his events stalking these missing girls. And he hadn't. Not surprising, when you consider how many faces pass his in a week. So you see, Dr Hill, he's clean. They came to us, we didn't go to them.'

'And that's it? Jacko Vance told you he'd waved goodbye to Shaz Bowman on the doorstep and that's good enough for you?'

'We've no reason to think otherwise,' Wharton said stiffly.

'The last person to see her alive? Aren't they usually worth a look?'

'Not when they have no known connection to the victim, a reputation for probity that's never been challenged and they said goodbye twelve hours before the crime was committed,' Wharton said, his voice laced with acid. 'Especially when they're a registered disabled, one-armed person who's supposed to have overwhelmed a highly trained, able-bodied police officer.'

'Can I ask one question?'

'You can ask.'

'Was there a witness to this interview or did Vance see Shaz alone?'

'His wife let her into the house, but she left them to it. Bowman saw him alone. But that doesn't automatically mean he's lying, you know. I've been in this game a long time. I can tell when folk are telling me lies. Face it, Doctor, you're well off target. I can't say I blame you for trying to divert us, but we're sticking with the people that she knew.'

'Thanks for letting me know.' Not trusting himself to say more, Tony dropped the phone back into its cradle. The blindness of the human animal never ceased to amaze him. It wasn't that Wharton was a stupid man; he was simply, in spite of years in the police service, conditioned to the belief that men like Jacko Vance could not be violent criminals.

In a way, Wharton's call was what he had been waiting for. The police could not avenge Shaz Bowman and vindicate his own work. It was up to him now, and there was a mordant satisfaction in that. Besides, Wharton's answer to his question had confirmed Vance as prime suspect in Tony's eyes. It had to be him. Tony had already eliminated a psychotic fan; now he could eliminate the members of Vance's entourage. If no one else had witnessed the interview, no one else could have picked up Shaz's trail after she left the house.

Picking up the phone again, Tony called the number he'd obtained earlier from Directory Enquiries, anticipating this moment. When the switchboard answered, he said, 'Can you put me through to the *Midday with Morgan* production office?' Then he leaned back to wait, a grim little smile curving his lips.

John Brandon fiddled with the handle of his coffee cup. 'I don't like it, Carol,' he admitted. She opened her mouth to respond and he lifted a finger to silence her. 'Oh, I know you're no more fond of the idea than I am. It's still a big step, pointing the finger at the fire service. I only hope we're not making a terrible mistake here.'

'Tony Hill's been right before,' she reminded him. 'And when you look at his analysis, it makes sense the way nothing else does.'

Brandon shook his head despairingly, looking more like a world-weary undertaker than ever. 'I know. It's such a depressing thought, though. To put so many lives at risk for so little. At least when coppers go bent, people don't usually end up dead.' He sipped his coffee. The aroma wafted across the desk to Carol, making her mouth water. Normally he offered her a cup; it was a measure of how shocked he was by her report that she wasn't sharing the fragrant brew. 'Ah well,' he said. 'Keep me informed of what your team comes up with. I'd appreciate advance notice of an arrest.'

'No problem. There was one other thing, sir?'

'Was that the bad news or the good news?'

'I think it was the bad news. Depending on what you think of the other matter, sir.' Carol's smile held no cheer.

The Chief Constable sighed and half-turned in his swivel chair to stare out across the estuary. As usual, the boss had the best view, Carol thought irrelevantly as an ocean-going trawler slid from one window to the next. 'Let's hear it, then,' he said.

'It also concerns Tony Hill,' she said. 'You know about the murder on his squad?'

'Hellish business,' Brandon said accurately. 'The worst thing that can happen in this job is losing an officer. But losing one like that ... It's your biggest nightmare.'

'Especially if you've got memories like Tony Hill's to draw on.'

'You're not wrong.' He looked shrewdly across at her. 'Apart from our natural compassion, how does this engage us?'

'Officially, not at all.'

'But unofficially?'

'Tony's having some problems with West Yorkshire. They appear to be treating him and his profiling trainees as their principal suspects instead of an effective resource. Tony feels they've dismissed other avenues for arbitrary reasons, and he's determined that Shaz Bowman's killer shouldn't escape simply because the investigating officers are taking a blinkered approach.'

A smile escaped and spread across Brandon's face. 'Those his words?'

Carol's answering smile was complicit. 'Not verbatim, sir. I didn't take a contemporaneous note.'

'I can see why he feels the need to take action,' Brandon said cautiously. 'Any investigator would have the same reaction. But we have rules in the police service that prevent officers investigating crimes where they have a personal interest. Those rules exist for the very good reason that crimes close to home distort an officer's judgement. Are you sure it wouldn't be best to let West Yorkshire get on with this in their own way?'

'Not if it means leaving a psychopath on the streets,' Carol said firmly. 'There's nothing wrong that I can see with the way Tony's mind's working.'

'You still haven't explained what this has to do with us.'

'He needs help. He's working with some of his task force officers, but they're all currently on suspension, so they don't have access to any official channels. Plus he needs input from an experienced police officer to counterbalance his viewpoint. He can't get that from West Yorkshire. All they want to do is find a reason to stick him or one of his team behind bars.'

'They never wanted to host that unit in the first place,' Brandon said. 'It's not surprising they see this as an excuse to shoot it down in flames. Nevertheless, it is their case and they're not looking to us for assistance.'

'No, but Tony is. And I feel I owe him, sir. All I'd be doing is a little background digging to provide his team with raw materials like names and addresses. I intend to give him what help I can. I'd prefer to do it with your blessing.'

'When you say help . . . ?'

'I won't be treading on West Yorkshire's heels. The angle Tony's interested in is miles away from their inquiries. They won't know I'm there. I'm not going to drop you in a jurisdictional wrangle.'

Brandon swallowed the last of his coffee and pushed the cup away from him. 'Damn right, you're not. Carol, do what you've got to do. But you're doing it off the books. This conversation never happened, and if it all comes on top, I never met you before.'

She grinned and got to her feet. 'Thank you, sir.'

'Stay out of trouble, Chief Inspector,' he said gruffly, dismissing her with a flutter of his fingers. As she opened the door to leave, he added, 'If you need my help, you have my number.'

It was a promise Carol hoped she'd never have to collect on.

Sunderland was the furthest north, Exmouth the most southerly point. In between were Swindon, Grantham, Tamworth, Wigan and Halifax. In each place, a teenage girl's disappearance had snagged Shaz Bowman's attention. Kay Hallam knew that somehow she had to squeeze fresh juice from those investigations that would shore up the edifice of circumstantial evidence Tony was building against Jacko Vance. It wasn't an easy assignment. Years had passed and with them the sharpness of memory. Doing it single-handed wasn't the best option either. In an ideal world, there would be two of them, taking a couple of weeks to complete the task, conducting interviews with brains that weren't exhausted from driving the length and breadth of the country.

No such luxury. Not that she wanted to hang around. Whoever had killed Shaz didn't deserve a minute longer at liberty than they'd already had. It was tough enough sitting on her hands while she waited for the results of DCI Jordan hammering the phones. Now there was a role model, Kay thought as she prowled from room to room of her terraced Victorian artisan's cottage. Whatever Carol Jordan had done, she'd obviously done it right. 'If you want to be successful, hang around with successful people and copy what they do,' Kay recited, a familiar mantra from one of her American self-improvement tapes.

The call came at lunchtime. Carol had spoken to all of the CID divisions who had dealt with the missing girls. In three cases, she'd even managed to contact the investigating officer, though investigation was probably too exalted a word for the cursory inquiries into missing teenage girls who didn't appear to want to be found. She had arranged for Kay to survey the slender files, and she'd contrived to elicit addresses and phone numbers for the distraught parents.

Kay put the phone down and studied a road atlas. She reckoned she could do Halifax in the afternoon and Wigan that evening. Then down the motorway to the Midlands and an overnight motel. Breakfast at Tamworth then hammer down to Exmouth for late afternoon. Back up the motorway to overnight at Swindon, then cross-country to Grantham. A stop the following day in Leeds to report to Tony, then she could finish off in Sunderland. It sounded like the road movie from hell. Even Thelma and Louise got it more glamorous than this, she thought.

But then, unlike some of her colleagues, she'd never expected it to be glamorous. Hard graft, job security and a decent pay cheque were all Kay had ever supposed she'd get from the police. The gratification of detective work had come as a surprise. And she was good at it, thanks to an eye for detail that her less appreciative colleagues called anal. Profiling seemed like the ideal area for using her observational skills to the full. She hadn't imagined her first case would be so close to home, or how personal it would feel. Nobody deserved what Shaz Bowman had endured, and nobody deserved to get away with it.

That was the thought Kay held on to as she hacked her

way round the network of motorways that crisscrossed England. She noticed that all of her destinations were either close by one of those motorways or to one of the other major arterial roads peppered with fast-food joints tacked on to petrol stations. She wondered if there were any significance in that. Did Vance arrange to meet his victims at service areas they could easily scrounge a lift to? It was almost the only fresh thing to come out of two days' work, she thought grimly. That and the faintest ghostly glimmering of a pattern. But the stories of the parents were depressingly similar, and distressingly short on significant detail, certainly where Vance was concerned. She'd managed to talk to a couple of friends of missing girls, and they'd been scarcely more helpful. It wasn't that they didn't want to help; Kay was the sort of interviewer people always talked to. Her mousey insignificance belied her intelligence; she was no threat to women and made men feel protective. No, it wasn't that they were holding back, it was simply that there wasn't much to be said. Yes, the missing girls were daft on Jacko, yes, they'd been to events where he was present and yes, they were really excited about it. But nothing more than that flimsy gleaning.

By Grantham, she was operating on automatic pilot. Two nights in motels with the beds too soft and the constant high zip, zing and zoom of all-night traffic diluted but not deleted by double glazing was no recipe for a productive interview, but it was better than no sleep at all, she scolded herself as she yawned expansively before ringing the doorbell.

Kenny and Denise Burton didn't seem to notice her exhaustion. It had been two years, seven months and three days since Stacey had walked out of the front door and never returned and the shadows under their eyes indicated neither had had a decent night's sleep since.

They were like twins; both short, burly with pale, indoor skin and puffy fingers. Looking at the wall of photographs of their slim, bright-eyed daughter, it was hard to believe in genetics as a science. They sat in a living room that was a monument to the expression 'a place for everything and everything in its place'. There were a lot of places in the cramped room; corner display cabinets, alcoves shelved to accommodate knickknacks without number, a feature fireplace with built-in niches. It was a claustrophobic, timidly conventional room. With the two bars of the electric fire throwing out dusty heat, Kay could hardly breathe. It was no wonder Stacey hadn't been reluctant to leave.

'She was a lovely girl,' Denise said wistfully. It was a refrain Kay had come to hate, hiding as it did every useful element of an adolescent girl's personality. It also reminded her discouragingly of her own mother, forever obliterating the reality of Kay's identity behind the anodyne phrase.

'Not like some,' Kenny said darkly, smoothing his greying hair back over the bald patch threatening to burst through like a cartoon bump on the head. 'She was told to be in by ten, by ten she'd be in.'

'She'd never have gone off of her own free will,' Denise said, the next line in the litany perfectly timed, perfectly placed. 'She had no reason to. She must have been abducted. There's no other explanation.'

Kay avoided the painfully obvious one. 'I'd like to ask some questions about the days before Stacey disappeared,' she said. 'Apart from going to school, did she go out at all that week?'

Kenny and Denise didn't pause for thought. In counterpoint, they said, 'She went to the pictures.'

'With Kerry.'

'The weekend before she was taken.'

'Tom Cruise.'

'She loves Tom Cruise.' The defiant present tense.

'She went out on the Monday as well.'

'We wouldn't normally allow her out on a school night.'

'But this was special.'

'Jacko Vance.'

'Her hero, he is.'

'Opening a fun pub in town, he was.'

'We wouldn't normally have allowed her into a pub.'

'What with her only being fourteen.'

'But Kerry's mum was taking them, so we thought it would be all right.'

'And it was.'

'She was home right on time, right when Kerry's mum said they'd be.'

'Full of it, our Stacey was. She got a signed photo.'

'Personally signed. To her personally.'

'She had that with her. When she went.' There was a pause while Kenny and Denise swallowed their grief.

Kay took advantage. 'How did she seem after their night out?'

'She was very excited, wasn't she, Kenny? It was like a dream come true to her, talking to Jacko Vance.'

'She actually got to talk to him?' Kay forced herself to sound nonchalant. The faint pattern she'd discerned was growing stronger with each interview.

'Like a moonstruck calf she was, after,' Stacey's father confirmed.

'She'd always wanted to go on the television.' The counterpoint was back.

'Your people reckoned she'd run off to London to try and break into showbiz,' Kenny said contemptuously. 'No way. Not Stacey. She was far too sensible. She agreed with us. Stay at school, get her A-levels, then we'd see.'

'She could have been on the television,' Denise wistful now.

'She had the looks.'

Kay cut in before they could get off and running again. 'Did she say what she'd talked about with Jacko Vance?'

'Just that he was really friendly,' Denise said. 'I don't think he said anything in particular to her, did he, Kenny?'

'He hasn't got time to take a personal interest. A busy man. Dozens of people, no, hundreds of people want him to sign an autograph, exchange a few words, pose for a picture.'

The words hung in the air like the afterimage of sparklers. 'Pose for a picture?' Kay said faintly. 'Did Stacey have her picture taken with him?'

They nodded in sync. 'Kerry's mum took it.'

'Could I see it?' Kay's heart was suddenly thudding like a drum, her palms sweating in the stuffy room.

Kenny pulled an embossed album from under a coffee table stained a colour unknown in nature. With practised hand, he turned swiftly to the last page. There, blown up to ten by eight was a fuzzy snapshot of a cluster of people surrounding Jacko Vance. The angle was skewed, the faces blurred, as if seen through a heat haze. But the girl standing next to Jacko Vance, the one he was unquestionably talking to, his hand on her shoulder, his head inclined towards her, the girl looking up with the adoring look of a new puppy was without a shadow of a doubt Stacey Burton.

It had been harder than Wharton had expected to talk to Detective Sergeant Chris Devine. When he'd rung her office, he'd discovered she'd signed up for a couple of days' compassionate leave following her initial telephone statement to the murder inquiry. It was the first time Wharton had encountered anyone who seemed to be genuinely grieving for Shaz Bowman; he'd not been the officer charged with breaking the news to her devastated parents.

By the time Chris had returned the message on her answering machine, Wharton was already in London interviewing Vance and his wife. It had been easy to arrange to meet at her flat afterwards.

The hard-nosed copper in him had warmed to Chris Devine immediately she'd opened her door and greeted them with, 'I sincerely hope you're going to nail the bastard who did this.' He wasn't bothered by the array of artistic photographs of beautiful women that covered the walls of her flat. He'd worked with dykes before and on balance he thought they were a damn sight less disruptive than most of the straight women on the force. His sidekick was less sanguine, carefully choosing to sit facing the wall of glass that looked out from the modern block of flats to the ancient church left incongruously standing at the heart of the Barbican complex.

'I hope so, too,' he'd said, perching on the lumpy futon sofa and wondering fleetingly how people ever slept on the things.

'You've been to see Jacko Vance?' Chris said almost before she was settled in the big wing chair opposite him.

'We interviewed him and his wife yesterday. He confirmed what you'd already told us about the appointment DC Bowman kept with him on the day she died.'

She nodded, pushing her thick chestnut hair away from her face. 'I had Vance down as the type that would keep a note of everything.'

'So what was all that about?' Wharton asked. 'Why

were you helping DC Bowman maintain the illusion that she was a Met officer?'

The frown line between her eyes deepened. 'I'm sorry?'

'Your direct line in the CID office was left as a contact number for DC Bowman. The impression it gave was that she was still a Met officer.'

'She *was* still a Met officer,' Chris pointed out. 'But there was nothing sinister in giving my number as a contact. During their training period, the profiling squad officers can't take phone calls in working hours. Shaz asked if I'd sort it, that's all.'

'Why you, Sergeant? Why not the desk officer where she was stationed? Why not leave her home number and ask him to call in the evening?' There was nothing hostile in Wharton's manner; he was genuinely interested in the answer.

'I suppose because we were already in contact over the case,' Chris said, feeling irritation rise inside her but giving no outward sign. Her years in the police had left her with the tendency to see innuendo in everything and the ability not to show her reaction.

'You were? In what respect?'

Chris turned her head and her dark eyes looked over Wharton's shoulder to the sky beyond. 'She'd already asked for my help. She needed some newspapers photocopied and I went out to Colindale to do it for her.'

'You were responsible for that parcel?'

'I was, yes.'

'I've heard about that. Must have been hundreds of pages, box that size and weight. That's a lot of work for an officer as busy as you must be,' Wharton said, starting to lean a little now he suspected there might be more going on here than met the eye.

'I did it in my own time. OK, Inspector?'

'That's a lot of time to give up for a junior officer,' Wharton suggested.

Chris's mouth tightened momentarily. With her snub nose, she had more than a passing resemblance to Grumpy from the Seven Dwarves. 'Shaz and I were partners on the night shift for a long time. We were friends as well as colleagues. She was probably the most talented young officer I've ever worked with and frankly, Mr Wharton, I don't see how questioning why I was happy to give up my day off to help her is going to help you put her killer away.'

Wharton shrugged. 'Background. You never know.'

'I know, believe me. You should be asking about Jacko Vance.'

In spite of himself, Wharton couldn't help an ironic grin. 'Don't tell me you fell for that as well?'

'If you mean, do I go along with Shaz's theory that Jacko Vance was killing teenage girls, the answer is, I don't know. I've not had the chance to review her evidence. But what I do know is that Vance arranged with me that she should come to his house early on Saturday and she was dead by the next morning. Now, the way we work things down here is we get very interested in the last known person to see a murder victim alive, and according to Shaz's mum, you don't seem to have any record of anyone seeing her after she left Vance's house. That would make me very interested in Jacko Vance. What are the profiling squad saying about it?'

'I'm sure you'll appreciate that until we can conclusively rule out her immediate colleagues from our inquiries, we can't use them to investigate the case.'

Chris's mouth fell open. 'You're not using Tony Hill?'

'We think she may have known her killer, and the only people she knew in Leeds were the ones she was working with. You're an experienced detective. You

312

must see that we can't risk contaminating the inquiry by taking any of them into our confidence.'

'You've got the most talented profiler in the country in the palm of your hand, a man who actually knew the victim and knew what she was working on, and you're ignoring him? Is there some reason you don't want to catch Shaz's killer? I bet Tony Hill doesn't think you should be letting Jacko Vance off the hook.'

Wharton smiled indulgently. 'I can understand you getting a bit emotional about this case.' Chris seethed inside but said nothing as he continued. 'But I can assure you, I've spoken to Mr Vance and there's nothing to suggest that he had anything to do with the murder. According to him, all DC Bowman was interested in was whether he'd spotted any of her so-called cluster of missing girls in the company of any regular attenders at his events. He said he hadn't and that was that.'

'And you take his word for it? Just like that?'

Wharton shrugged. 'Like I said, why wouldn't we? Where's the evidence to suggest anything suspicious?'

Chris stood up abruptly and picked up a packet of cigarettes from a corner table. She lit up and turned back to face Wharton. 'He is the last person that we know who saw her,' she said, her voice harsh.

Wharton's smile was meant to placate but only enraged. 'We don't know that, with respect. She'd written the letter "T" in her diary beneath the appointment with Vance. As if she was going on somewhere else. You wouldn't know who "T" is, would you, Sergeant?'

A deep inhalation of smoke, a long exhalation, then Chris said, 'I can't think of anyone. Sorry.'

'You don't think it might refer to Tony Hill?'

She shrugged. 'It could, I suppose. It could mean almost anything. She could have been going to the

Trocadero to play laser games, for all I know. She never said anything about any other plans to me.'

'She didn't come here?'

Chris frowned. 'Why would she?'

'You said you were friends. She was in London. I'd have thought she'd have popped in, especially with you being so helpful and all.' There was a tougher element in Wharton's voice and his jaw thrust outward.

'She didn't come here.' Chris's mouth clamped shut.

Sensing a weak spot, Wharton pushed harder. 'Why was that, Sergeant? Did she prefer to keep a bit of distance between you? Especially now she'd got herself a boyfriend?'

Chris walked briskly to the door and opened it. 'Goodbye, Inspector Wharton.'

'That's a very interesting response, Sergeant Devine,' Wharton said, taking his time getting to his feet and checking that his junior officer was still taking notes.

'If you want to insult Shaz's memory and my intelligence, you're not doing it in my home. Next time, make it formal. Sir.' She leaned against the door, watching them walk down the hall to the lifts. 'Arsehole,' she muttered under her breath. Then she let the heavy door swing shut and crossed to the phone where she rang an old flame in the Home Office. 'Dee? It's Chris. Hey, doll, I need a favour. You've got a psychologist on the payroll, geezer called Tony Hill. I need a personal number . . .'

Jimmy Linden had noticed the young black man even before he'd reached his seat in the sixth row of the empty stand. Years of working with promising young athletes had developed his instinct for spotting strangers. It wasn't only sex perverts you had to be on the lookout for. The drug pushers were just as dangerous with their promises of steroid magic. And Jimmy's youngsters were the very ones most prone to falling for their promises. Anyone who wanted to be the best at javelin, hammer, shot or discus needed the kind of muscle that anabolic steroids could provide a lot more easily than training.

No, it never hurt to keep a weather eye out for strangers, especially here at Meadowbank Stadium where he coached the Scottish junior squad, the pick of the bunch, all of them desperate for that edge that would make them a champion. Jimmy looked up again at the stranger. He looked in pretty good shape, though if he'd ever had dreams of being a contender, he should have knocked those fags on the head a long time ago.

As the session drew to a close and the young athletes climbed into their tracksuits, Jimmy spotted the stranger getting up and disappearing down the stairway. When he emerged trackside moments later, demonstrating he had some official reason for being there, Jimmy felt the muscles in the back of his neck relax slightly, the first sign he'd had that they'd been tense. Old age was creeping up at a gallop, he thought wryly. Used to be he was that close to his body that not a nerve fluttered without him knowing about it.

Before he could follow the sweating bodies into the changing rooms, the stranger stepped in front of him and flashed a warrant card. It was too fast for Jimmy to suss which force he belonged to, but he knew what the card was. 'Detective Constable Jackson,' the man said. 'I'm sorry to bother you at work, but I could use half an hour of your time.'

Jimmy tutted, his whippet face narrowing in displeasure. 'You'll not find any drugs with this lot,' he said. 'I run a clean team, and they all know it.'

Leon shook his head and smiled. 'It's nothing to do with your squad. I just need to pick your brains about some ancient history, that's all.' There was no trace of the smart-mouthed jive talk he used on his fellow profilers.

'What kind of ancient history?'

Leon noticed Jimmy's eyes flickering after his disciples and realized the trainer still had things he wanted to say to them. Hastily, he said, 'It's nothing to worry about, honestly. Look, I noticed a half-decent café just down the road. Why don't you meet me there when you're done here and we can have a chat?'

'Aye, OK,' Jimmy said grudgingly. Half an hour later he was facing Leon over a mug of tea and a plate piled with the sort of bakery products that earned Scotland its nickname of the Land O'Cakes. He must be one hell of a coach, Leon thought as the little man wolfed down a coconut-covered snowball. All the successful throwing jocks Leon had ever known were big blokes, broad in the shoulder and heavy through the thighs. But Jimmy Linden resembled a medieval ascetic, the classic long-distance runner, one of those creatures of bone and sinew who stride easily across the finishing line at marathons, eyes on the middle distance, looking as if the only thing they could want was the next twenty-six miles.

'So what's this all about?' Jimmy said, wiping his mouth with surprising daintiness on a proper mono-grammed cotton handkerchief pulled from the sleeve of his sweatshirt.

'For reasons that will become obvious, I can't go into too much detail. We're investigating a case that may have its roots deep in the past. I thought you might be able to give me some pointers.'

'About what? All I know anything about is athletics, son.'

Leon nodded and watched a meringue disappear. 'I'm going back now a dozen or more years ago.'

'When I was based down south? Before I came back up here?'

'That's right. You coached Jacko Vance,' Leon said.

A shadow passed across Jimmy's face. Then he cocked his head to one side and said, 'You're not telling me somebody's putting the black on Jacko and thinking they'll get away with it?' Amusement lit up his watery blue eyes.

Leon winked. 'You didn't hear that from me, Mr Linden.'

'It's Jimmy, son, everybody calls me Jimmy. So, Jacko Vance, eh? What can I tell you about the boy wonder?'

'Anything you can remember.'

'How long have you got?'

Leon's smile was tinged with grimness. He hadn't forgotten why he was in Edinburgh. 'As long as it takes, Jimmy.'

'Let me see. He won the British under-fifteen title when he was only thirteen. I was coaching the national squad at the time and I said as soon as I saw him throw that he was the best chance of an Olympic gold that we'd had in a generation.' He shook his head. 'I wasn't wrong. Poor bugger. Nobody deserves to watch the event they should be winning when they're trying to learn how to use an artificial limb.' Leon understood the implied but unspoken, 'not even Jacko Vance'.

'He never considered doing the disabled games?' Leon asked.

Jimmy snorted derisively. 'Jacko? That would have meant admitting he was disabled.'

'So you became his coach when he was thirteen?'

'That's right. He was a worker, I'll say that for him. He was lucky, living in London, because he had good access to me and to the facilities, and by Christ, he made the most of it. I used to ask him, did he not have a home to go to?'

'And what did he say to that?'

'Ach, he'd just shrug. I got the impression that his mother wasn't bothered what he was doing as long as he was out from under her feet. She was away from his father by then, of course. Separated, divorced, whatever.'

'Did his parents not come along, then?'

Jimmy shook his head. 'Never saw the mother. Not a once. His dad came to one meeting. I think it was the time he was going for the British junior record, but he blew it. I mind his dad took the piss out of him good style. I took him to one side and told him if he couldn't back his boy up, he wasn't welcome.'

'How did he take that?'

Jimmy took a gulp of tea and said, 'Ach, stupid bastard called me a bum boy. I just told him to fuck right off, and that was the last we saw of him.'

Leon made a mental note. He knew Tony would be interested in this. As he saw it, the young Jacko had been desperate for attention. His mother was indifferent, his father absent and his whole being was focused on his sporting achievement in the hope that somehow that would win him approval. 'So, was he lonely, Jacko?' He lit a cigarette, ignoring the disapproving look on the coach's narrow face.

Jimmy considered the question. 'He could mess about with the best of them, but he wasn't really one of the lads, know what I mean? He was too dedicated. He couldn't loosen up enough. Not that he was a loner. No, he always had Jillie in tow, hanging around him, telling him he was wonderful.'

'So they were devoted to each other?'

'She was devoted to him. He was devoted to himself,

but he liked the adoration. Unconditional, like you get from a collie dog. Mind you, even Jillie got the hump sometimes. I moved heaven and earth to keep that pair together. Whenever she got fed up with taking the back seat to his training or competitions, I used to bolster her up with how great she'd feel when he stood there on the Olympic rostrum picking up the gold. I'd say, most girls, the only gold they ever got was a poxy wedding ring, but she was going to get a gold medal.'

'And that was enough, was it?'

Jimmy shrugged, wafting Leon's smoke away with one hand. 'To be honest, it got so that was the only thing that kept her going. When he started competing on the senior circuit, and Jillie was that wee bit older, she started taking notice of the way the other lads treated their girls. And Jacko didn't stand up too well to the comparison. If he hadn't have lost his arm, she might just have put up with it for the acclaim and the cash that went with it, because athletes were just about starting to make megabucks around then and the writing was on the wall for more to come. But as soon as she decided he wasn't going to be a cash machine or a household name, she got shot of him.'

Leon was on full alert. 'I thought he dumped her? Didn't I read at the time that he broke off the engagement because he wasn't the man she'd signed up for and it wasn't fair to tie her down? Something like that?'

Jimmy's mouth curled into a contemptuous smile. 'So you fell for that load of toffee? That was just the story Jacko leaked to the press, to make him look like the big man instead of the sad bastard who'd been dumped.'

So Shaz might well have been right, Leon thought. Circumstance had piled two traumatic stressors right on top of each other. First Vance had lost his arm and his future. Then he had lost the one person who had believed in him as a human being rather than as a throwing machine. It would take a strong man to survive that unscathed; a warped one would need to take revenge against a world that had done this to him. Leon stubbed out his cigarette and said, 'Did he tell you the truth?'

'No. Jillie did. I was the one drove her to the hospital that day. And I saw Jacko after she told him.'

'How did he take it?'

Jimmy's eyes dripped contempt. 'Oh, just like a man. He told me she was a heartless bitch who was only after one thing. I told him he didn't have to give in to his injuries, that he could train for the disabled games and that it was just as well he found out the truth about Jillie now. He told me to fuck off and never come near him again. And that was the last time I saw him.'

'You didn't go back to the hospital?'

The trainer's face was bleak. 'I went every day for a week. He wouldn't see me. Refused point-blank. He didn't seem to realize I had lost my dreams, too. Anyway, I got the chance of this job back in Scotland round about then, so I came back here and started all over again.'

'Were you surprised when he popped up as a television celebrity?'

'I can't say I was, no. He needs somebody telling him he's wonderful, that one. I've often wondered if all those millions of viewers are ever enough, if he's still as desperate to be adored as he was back then. He could never see any value in himself that wasn't reflected in other folks' eyes.' Jimmy shook his head and signalled for another cup of tea. 'I suppose you want to know if he had any enemies and what his deep dark secrets were?'

An hour later, Leon knew that what Jimmy Linden had told them at the start of their conversation was the stuff that had mattered. Just as well, he realized as he sat in the car afterwards. For some reason, his miniature tape recorder had failed to turn over automatically and had only recorded the first half of their chat. Feeling well pleased with himself nevertheless, Leon set out on the long journey south, wondering who'd done best so far. He knew it wasn't a competition. He'd liked Shaz enough to do it for her sake. But he was sufficiently human to realize that if he performed well out on the street, it would do him no harm. Especially since he now understood that as far as Tony Hill was concerned, he had more than a little to prove.

It wasn't difficult to spot the sports stadium and leisure-centre complex. Spotlit against the dark Malvern Hills, it was visible for miles from the motorway. Once he'd turned off on to minor roads and a rash of mini-roundabouts, however, Tony was glad he'd called in advance for directions. The centre was too recently built for most locals to know where it was, so the anonymous voice that had given explicit guidance over the phone was clearly used to the process.

As it turned out, he'd have arrived safely if he'd simply followed any other car heading in the same direction. The car park was already crowded when he reached it, and he had to park a few hundred yards away from the main entrance with its banner proclaiming, 'Grand Opening Gala – with Special Guests Jacko Vance and Stars from the England Squad'. Footballers for the lads, Jacko for the women, he thought as he walked briskly across the Tarmac, grateful for the bulk of the stadium acting as a buffer against the chill night wind.

He joined the throng of eager people thrusting through the turnstiles, casting a practised eye along the staff checking tickets. He chose a middle-aged woman who looked competent and motherly, and squeezed through the press of bodies to present himself at her window. He slipped his Home Office credentials out of his pocket and showed them to her, arranging his face into a rueful, harried expression. 'Dr Hill, Home Office, sports research group. I was supposed to have a VIP pass, but it didn't arrive. I don't suppose . . . ?'

The woman frowned momentarily. She gave him a swift appraisal, reckoning whether he was up to something, realizing the queue behind him was building up, finally deciding it was someone else's problem if he was, she pressed the release button to let him through. 'You want the directors' suite. Round to the right, second floor.'

Tony let the natural movement of the crowd carry him forward into the vast echoing area under the grandstand, then edged to one side to study the giant map of the stadium cunningly laid out on the underside of the tiered seating. Whoever had designed it had been aware of the three-dimensional surface it would be reproduced on, and it somehow managed to be clear from whatever angle it was viewed. According to the programme he'd just bought, there would be live music in the main arena, followed by a demonstration five-a-side football match featuring England squad players, then an Irish dance spectacular. For those who had shelled out an extra fifty pounds or won one of the contests run by the local TV, radio and newspapers, there would be a chance to meet the celebrities. And that was where he needed to be.

He slid through the crowd, calculating his moves so he upset no one on his route to the executive lift. The lobby was cordoned off with heavy crimson ropes. A security guard wearing a belt loaded with enough equipment to stock a hardware store stared balefully out from under a cap worn low like a guardsman. Tony knew it was nothing more than bravado. He flashed his credentials at the guard, moving purposefully as if the last thing he expected was to be challenged. The man took a step backwards and said, 'Wait a minute.'

Tony was already at the lift, pressing the call button. 'It's OK,' he said. 'Home Office. We like to turn up when they least expect us. Got to keep an eye on things, you know.' He winked and stepped into the car. 'Don't want another Hillsborough, do we?' The doors slid closed on the bemused face of the guard.

After that, it was easy. Out of the lifts, down the hall, in through the open double doors, a glass of something straw-coloured and fizzy from the nearest waistcoated flunkey and he was established. Tony took in the long windows that ran the length of the opposite wall, looking down on the all-weather pitch. He could just see a team of majorettes strutting their stuff down below. A thin crowd bunched around the edges of the room. At the far end, over by the window, Jacko Vance stood at the centre of a cluster of middle-aged women and a few men. His hair gleamed in the refracted light from the spotlights over the pitch, his eyes shone in the soft lighting of the executive suite. Even though he'd already glad-handed his way through two charity appearances that day, his body language was still warm, welcoming, his smile treating everyone as a welcome equal. He looked like a god dealing with his worshippers without condescension. Tony gave a thin smile. The third event since he'd gone out on the prowl for Jacko, and every time he'd struck gold. It was almost as if there were a connection, an invisible fibre optic linking the hunter and the prey. This time, though, he'd make certain those roles were never reversed. Once had been enough for that.

Tony moved to one side and made his way up the room, using the legitimate guests as cover. After a few minutes, he had travelled the length of the room, occupying a corner opposite Vance but slightly behind him. His eyes moved regularly from side to side, scanning the area immediately around the TV star, never lingering for long, but never leaving Vance unattended for more than a moment.

He didn't have long to wait. A young woman with slicked back blonde hair, John Lennon glasses and a scarlet cupid's bow bounced into the room clutching a bag emblazoned with SHOUT! FM, checking over her shoulder to see that her charges were still firmly in tow. Following in a ragged line came three adolescent girls overdressed and overpainted, a couple of youths with more spots than charm and an elderly woman whose hair was so rigidly set it appeared the rollers were still bound into it. Three paces behind slouched a nerd in a gilet with a dozen bulging pockets, a pair of battered SLR cameras hanging negligently round his neck. The winners of some moronic phone-in competition, Tony guessed. He could think of one question they wouldn't have been asked: How many teenagers has Jacko Vance murdered? It would take a year or two after he'd finished his work for that to filter down into the trivia quiz books.

The bouncy blonde approached where Vance was holding court. Tony could see Vance look up at her then dismissively abandon her for the middle-aged woman in the turquoise sari he'd been charming previously. The blonde lunged through the inner circle round Jacko, only to be headed off by the woman Tony had noticed running interference for Jacko the first time he'd staked him out. Their heads huddled together, then the PA nodded and touched Vance on the elbow. As he turned, his professional gaze slid round the room and caught Tony. The sweep of his eyes paused momentarily, then continued, nothing else in his expression changing.

The blonde's competition winners were ushered into the presence of their idol. He smiled down on them, charm personified. He chatted, signed autographs, shook hands, pecked cheeks and posed for photographs. Every thirty seconds, his eyes lost their focus and glanced unerringly at where Tony stood leaning against the wall, sipping fake champagne, his pose and his expression reeking assurance and confidence.

As the competition winners reached the end of their audience, Tony moved away from his vantage point and headed for the little group, still standing near Vance, their expressions ranging from ecstasy to an affected nonchalance, depending on how cool they felt the need to be. All bonhomie, Tony insinuated himself into their group, his expression a model of openness and geniality. 'I'm sorry to butt in on you,' he said. 'But I think you might be able to help me. My name's Tony Hill and I'm a psychological profiler. You know how stars like Jacko are always being plagued by stalkers? Well, I'm working with a team of crack police officers on ways to find out who those stalkers are before they start causing real problems. What we're trying to do is to come up with a psychological profile of the perfect fan, the good supporter. Someone like you, the sort of fan any celebrity would be glad to have on their side. We need to do this so we can get what's called a control profile. All we need is a short interview with you. Half an hour, tops. We come to your place or you come to us, we pay you £25, and you get the comfort of knowing you might have stopped the next Mark Chapman.' He loved the way their faces always changed when he mentioned the money.

Tony took out the pre-printed name and address slips from his inside pocket. 'How about it? Painless anonymous questionnaire, you help us save a life and you earn yourself £25. Just fill in your name and address on one of these and one of my researchers will be in touch.' Out came the handsome embossed National Offender Profiling Task Force business cards. 'This is who I am.' He handed them out. By now, all except one of the youths had their hands out for a form. 'There we go,' he said, providing them with pens.

He looked across at Vance. His face was still smiling, his mouth forming words, his hands patting an elbow here, a shoulder there. But his eyes were on Tony; dark, questioning, hostile.

The house was nothing special, Simon thought as he parked the car. A three-bedroomed dormer bungalow on a thirty-year-old development that was well on course to disprove the adage that life begins at forty. She'd have done a lot better if she and Jacko had stayed together. She certainly wouldn't have ended up in a town like Wellingborough where a night out at the DIY superstore was most people's idea of a good time.

He was amazed at the speed with which Carol Jordan had come up with Jillie Woodrow's whereabouts, particularly since she was three years into her second marriage. 'Don't ask,' Carol had said when he'd complimented her, admitting it would have taken him days to make that much progress. He remembered Tony Hill mentioning something to Carol about her brother in the computer industry and wondered if their shoestring task force had just added data burglary to its irregularities.

He sat in the car and looked across the narrow street at the house belonging to Jillie and Jeff Lewis. It looked spick and span and relentlessly suburban with its perfectly trimmed lawn and borders filled with neatly equidistant hebes and heathers. There was a year-old Metro on the drive and net curtains across the picture window. If Jillie Lewis's attention had been caught by the sound of his engine, she could be watching him and he'd have no idea at all.

This was almost certainly going to be the most crucial interview of his career to date, Simon thought, gearing himself up for the task. He had no clear idea of what he was going to ask, but if Jillie Lewis had information that would nail Jacko Vance for the murder of Shaz Bowman, he was determined to prise it out of her, one way or another. He hadn't had the chance to find out whether he would ever have been allowed to owe Shaz more than a colleague would. But even that was more than debt enough for him. Simon got out of the car and pulled on the jacket of his Marks and Spencer suit. Straightening his tie and his shoulders, he took a deep breath and walked up the path.

The door opened seconds after his ring, stopped short by a flimsy chain that he could have been past in seconds if he'd had a mind to. For a brief, mad moment, he wondered whether this was the cleaner or the nanny. The woman who faced him across the doorstep bore no superficial resemblance to the old newspaper photographs of Jillie Woodrow, nor to the teenage girls on the missing list. Her hair was a streaked blonde urchin cut rather than the dark bob he'd expected, and she'd lost every vestige of puppy fat, being skinny to the point where, if he were her husband, Simon would be surreptitiously reading up on anorexia. He was about to make his apologies when he recognized the eyes. The expression had hardened, there were lines starting to show at the edges, but these were Jillie Woodrow's dark blue soulful eyes. 'Mrs Lewis?' he asked.

327

The woman nodded. 'Who are you?' Simon presented his warrant card and she gasped, 'Jeff?'

Quickly Simon reassured her. 'It's nothing to do with your husband. I'm currently attached to a special investigations unit in Leeds, but my home force is Strathclyde. I don't have any local connection.'

'Leeds? I've never been to Leeds.' When she frowned, discontent was written across her face like an advertising hoarding.

Simon smiled. 'Lucky you. There have been times lately when I've wished I could say the same thing. Mrs Lewis, this is a very awkward situation and it would be a lot easier for me to explain it inside with a cup of coffee than it is on the doorstep. Can I come in?'

She looked uncertain, making a show of checking her watch. 'I'm supposed to be at work,' she said, carefully not saying when.

'I wouldn't be here if it wasn't important,' Simon said, his apologetic smile displaying the charm that had been one of the assets that had taken him this far in his career.

'I suppose you'd better come in, then,' she said, slipping the chain off and stepping back. He walked into a hall that looked as if it belonged to a show house. Spotless, tasteless and immaculate, it led into a kitchen that no one appeared ever to have cooked in. Jillie led the way and gestured to the circular table crammed into one corner. 'You better have a seat,' she muttered as she picked up a kettle, dark green to match the tiles along the splashback of the sink. 'Coffee, then?'

'Please,' Simon said, wedging himself behind the table. 'Milk, no sugar.'

'I suppose you think you're sweet enough,' Jillie said sourly, taking a jar of cheap instant from the cupboard and spooning it into two china mugs. 'I suppose this is something to do with Jacko Vance, is it?'

Simon tried not to reveal how taken aback he was. 'What makes you say that?'

Jillie turned and leaned against the worktop, crossing her jean-clad legs and folding her arms protectively over her chest. 'What else would it be? Jeff's an honest hardworking salesman, I'm a part-time data processor. We don't know any criminals. The only thing I've ever done that anybody outside these four walls would be interested in was being Jacko Vance's girlfriend. The only person I've ever had anything to do with who would interest some special investigation unit is Jacko bloody Vance, come back to flaming haunt me again.' It was a defiant outburst and she concluded it by turning her back on him and managing to make vicious the act of pouring two coffees.

Not quite sure where to go next, Simon said, 'I'm sorry. It's clearly a sensitive subject.'

Jillie dumped the coffee in front of him. Given the pristine kitchen, he was surprised she didn't run for a cloth when it slopped on the pine tabletop. Instead, she retreated back against the worktop, clutching her coffee like a child with a hot-water bottle. 'I've got nothing to say about Jacko Vance. You've had a wasted journey from Leeds. Still, I suppose you get good mileage since it's the taxpayers that foot the bill and not some skinflint company.'

Her bitterness seemed to have infected the coffee, Simon thought ruefully, sipping the brew to give himself time to think of a reply. 'It's a serious inquiry,' he said. 'We could use your help.'

She banged her mug down on the worktop. 'Look. I don't care what he says. It's not me that's pestering him. I had this up to the back teeth just after I first married Jeff. I had cops round half a dozen times. Was I sending Jacko anonymous letters? Was I making abusive phone calls to his wife? Did I parcel up dog turds and post them to his office? Well, the answer's the same now as it was then. If you think I'm the only person Jacko Vance has upset in his selfish journey to the top of the greasy pole, you have got a serious imagination deficiency.' She stopped short and glared at him. 'I don't do blackmail, either. You can check. Every penny in and out of this house is accounted for. I've had that accusation to contend with, and that's a load of flaming rubbish as well.' She shook her head. 'I can't believe that *pig*,' she fumed.

Simon held his hands up in a placatory gesture. 'Whoa, wait a minute. I think you've got hold of the wrong end of the stick here. I didn't come to see you because Jacko made a complaint. Sure, I want to talk to you about Jacko, but I'm only interested in what he's done, not what he says you've done. Honest!'

She gave him a sharp look. 'What?'

Uneasy that he might have gone too far, Simon said, 'As I said, this is all very sensitive. Jacko Vance's name has come up in an inquiry and my job is to make some background checks. Without alerting Mr Vance to our interest, if you take my point.' He hoped he didn't look as nervous as he felt. Whatever he'd expected, it hadn't been this.

'You're investigating Jacko?' Jillie sounded incredulous but had started to look almost cheerful.

Simon shifted in his chair. 'Like I said, his name has come up in connection with a serious matter . . .'

Jillie punched her thigh. 'Yes! And not before bloody time. Don't tell me, let me guess. He hurt some poor bloody woman too much and didn't terrify her enough to make her keep her mouth shut, is that it?'

Simon sensed the interview spiralling out of his control. All he could do was cling on with his fingernails and hope he wouldn't get shaken off somewhere along the way. 'What makes you say that?' he asked.

'It was bound to happen some day,' she said, all but gleeful. 'So, what do you want to know?'

By the time he got home, Tony's eyes were gritty with staring at too many night motorway miles. He hadn't intended to check his answering machine, but the flashing light caught his eye as he passed the door of his study. Wearily, he hit the playback button. 'Hi. My name's Chris Devine. Detective Sergeant Chris Devine. I was Shaz Bowman's CID partner in London for a while. She used me to set up her appointment with Jacko Vance. Give me a call whenever you get in. Doesn't matter how late it is.'

He grabbed a pen and scribbled the number, reaching for the phone as soon as the message clicked off. The phone rang half a dozen times, then was picked up. 'Is that Chris Devine?' he said to the silence.

'Is that Tony Hill?' The voice was pure South London.

'You left a message on my machine. About Shaz?'

'Yeah. Listen, I've had them turnips from West Yorkshire down here, and they told me they're not working with you. Is that right?'

He liked a person who didn't waste time. 'They feel it would compromise the integrity of their investigation to involve me or any of Shaz's other immediate colleagues,' he said caustically.

'Bollocks,' she said in disgust. 'They haven't got a fucking clue, pardon my French. So are you running your own investigation, or what?'

It was like being pinned to the wall by a very large weight, Tony thought. 'I'm obviously very keen to see Shaz's killer caught,' he tried.

'So what are you doing about it?'

'Why do you ask?' he parried.

'To see if you need an extra pair of hands, of course,' she said, exasperated. 'Shaz was a great kid, and she was gonna be a great cop. Now, either Jacko Vance topped her for reasons we don't entirely know yet, or somebody else did. Either way, the trail starts at his front door, no?'

'You're right,' Tony said. Now he knew what cement felt like under a steamroller.

'And you're working the case?'

'In a manner of speaking.'

Her sigh sounded like something from the Shipping Forecast. 'Well, in a manner of speaking, I could help. What do you need from me?'

Tony's mind raced. 'I'm a bit stalled on leverage where Vance and his wife are concerned. Something that might help me put a bit of a wedge between them might help.'

'Like, Micky Morgan's really a dyke?'

'That sort of thing, yes.'

'You mean that's not enough?' Chris demanded.

'That's for real?'

She snorted. 'Course it's for real. They're so far in the closet you'd take them for a pair of winter coats, but they're coke.'

'Coke?'

'The real thing. She's been with Betsy for donkey's years. Way before she even met Jacko.'

'Betsy Thorne? Her PA?'

'PA, bollocks. Lover, more like. Betsy had a good little catering business with her ex, then she met Micky Morgan and it was wham, bam, thank you, ma'am. They used to go to a couple of very discreet places in the early days. Then they disappeared off the scene and, next thing you know, she pops up as Jacko Vance's tottie. But Betsy's still right there in the picture. See,

Micky was on the up and up, and there were rumours that the tabloids were going to nail her for being a dyke.'

'How do you know all this?' Tony said faintly.

'How do you think? Christ, twelve, fifteen years ago, you didn't stay in this job if you were out. We used to go to the same places. Places where everybody was in the same boat so nobody ever shopped anybody else. Take it from me, whoever Jacko Vance is shagging, it's not his wife. Tell you the truth, that's what made me think Shaz was maybe on to something.'

'Did you tell Shaz about this?'

'I hadn't thought about Micky Morgan from one year's end to the next. It only came to me after I set up the interview. I was gonna let Shaz know when she belled me to tell me how she'd got on with Jacko. So no, I never got round to telling her. Is this any use to you?'

'Chris, it's fabulous. You're fabulous.'

'That's what they all say, babe. So, you want me to help, or what?'

'I think you already have.'

When Carol walked into her domain, the threesome were already there in their accustomed places, a trickle of smoke curling out of the corner of her window from Lee's cigarette. She sensed the smoking was meant as a challenge. But although she'd never smoked – or perhaps for that very reason – the faint tang of cigarettes was something that seldom troubled her. Carol found the energy for a smile and tried not to slump when her backside hit the chair. 'So, what have we got?'

Tommy Taylor rested his left ankle on his right knee and squirmed lower in the chair. Carol didn't envy him the lower back pain he was storing up for later years. He tossed a file negligently on to her desk. As it slithered towards her, the edges of the papers inside spilled out. 'We know more about this lot's finances than their wives do.'

'From what I hear about Yorkshire, that's not saying much,' Carol said. Tommy and Lee Whitbread grinned. Di Earnshaw's dour expression didn't crack.

'By heck, ma'am, I think that might just be a sexist remark,' Lee said.

'So sue me. What have we got?'

'It's all in the file,' Tommy said, jerking a thumb towards her.

'Summarize.'

'Di?' Tommy said. 'You're the wizard with words.'

Di unfolded her arms and thrust her hands into the pockets of an olive green jacket that made her look ripe for throwing up. 'Mr Pendlebury wasn't very keen, but he did authorize us to gain access to payroll information which provided us with bank details, addresses and dates of birth for our suspects. With that information we were able to check county court judgements . . .'

'And a little bird helped us with some commercial credit checking,' Lee chipped in.

'But we don't talk about that,' Tommy said repressively.

Carol said, 'Can we edit out the stand-up and cut to the chase?'

Di's lips pursed in their now familiar disapproval. 'Two candidates stand out. Alan Brinkley and Raymond Watson. They're both heavily in debt, as you'll see. Both local men. Watson's single, Brinkley's wed about a year since. They're both on the edge of having their houses repossessed, both got CCJs against them, both juggling Peter to pay Paul. These fires have been a bit of a blessing for the pair of them.'

'It's an ill wind,' Taylor added.

Carol opened the file and took out the sheets relating to the two men. 'Good work. You did well to get this much detail.'

Lee shrugged. 'When you get down to it, Seaford's a big village. Favours owed, favours paid.'

'As long as we don't cross the line when it comes to wages day,' Carol said.

'Don't you trust us, ma'am?' Tommy drawled.

'Give me five good reasons why I should.'

'So, d'you want us to pull them in for questioning?' Lee asked.

Carol considered for a moment. What she actually wanted was to consult with Tony, but she didn't want them to know their guv'nor wasn't able to make her own decisions. 'I'll get back to you when I've had a chance to go through these in more detail. There might be more fruitful options than trying to sweat it out of them.'

'We could try for a search warrant.' Lee again, the eager beaver of the team.

'We'll discuss it again in the morning,' Carol promised. She watched them leave, then shoved the file into her bulging briefcase. Time for a quick tour of the squad room, making sure the rest of the CID were doing what they were supposed to be doing with the cases dominating the stacks of paper on their desks. She hoped no one expected inspiration. Perspiration was about all she had left to offer.

She was about to walk through the door when the phone rang. 'DCI Jordan,' she said.

'Brandon here.'

'Sir?'

'I've just been speaking to a colleague over in West Yorkshire. In the course of our chat, we got round to talking about their officer murder. He mentioned that their prime suspect seems to have done a runner. Some chap called Simon McNeill. He said they'd probably be putting out an internal bulletin tomorrow morning asking other forces to keep a lookout for McNeill and detain him if they find him.'

'Ah.'

'I thought you might be interested,' Brandon said airily. 'With our patch being next door to theirs.'

'Absolutely, sir. As soon as I get the official notice, I'll be sure to mention it to the squad.'

'Not that I expect he'll turn up here.'

'Mmm. Thank you, sir.' Carol gingerly replaced the receiver. 'Oh, shit,' she said softly.

Tony licked his finger and smoothed down a couple of unruly hairs in his left eyebrow. He studied himself critically in the mirror that was, apart from a pair of orange polypropylene bucket chairs, the only furnishing in a room little bigger than a cupboard where he had been asked to wait. He thought he looked appropriately serious in his one decent suit even if Carol had told him it made him look like a time-warped professional footballer. But not even she could fault his dove grey shirt and dark magenta tie, he decided.

The door opened to reveal the calm-faced woman who had introduced herself as Micky's PA but whom he'd identified, thanks to Chris, as Micky's lover Betsy. 'Everything all right?' she asked.

'I'm fine.'

'Good.' Her voice was warm and encouraging, like the best type of primary school teacher. Her smile, however, was perfunctory, Tony realized, her mind clearly elsewhere. 'Now, this is quite unusual for us, because normally Micky likes to come completely fresh to her guests. But because . . . well, because she feels *involved*, however tangentially, with your tragic loss, she wants to have a few words with you ahead of time. I take it you have no objection?'

There was something about that steely upper class voice that left no possible room for demurral. Lucky Micky, he thought, to have such a lioness at the gates. 'I'd be delighted,' he said, quite truthfully.

'Good. She'll be along in a few minutes. Is there anything you need? Some coffee? Mineral water?'

'Does the coffee come from a machine?' he asked.

The smile this time was genuine. 'I'm afraid so. Indistinguishable from the tea, the hot chocolate and the chicken soup.'

'I'll pass, then.'

The head disappeared and the door snicked shut. His stomach fluttered apprehensively. Public displays always stressed him. But today there was the additional tension of his campaign to unsettle Jacko Vance to the point where he would make a mistake. Staking out Vance's personal appearances was only the opening shot across the bows. Insinuating himself into the heart of Vance's wife's TV programme was an incremental upping of the stakes. There was no point in trying to kid himself otherwise.

He cleared his throat nervously and compulsively rechecked his appearance in the mirror. The door opened without warning and suddenly Micky Morgan was in the room. Tony forced himself to turn slowly to face her. 'Hello, Ms Morgan,' he said, extending a hand.

'Dr Hill,' Micky said. Her handshake was swift, cool and firm. 'Thanks for coming on the programme.'

'My pleasure. There's so much misunderstanding about what we do, I always welcome the chance to set the record straight. Especially since we're in the news again for all the wrong reasons.' He deliberately dropped his eyes momentarily.

'Quite. I was genuinely sorry to hear about Detective Constable Bowman. I only met her very briefly, but she struck me as being very sharp, very focused. As well as being very beautiful, of course.'

Tony nodded. 'She'll be missed. She was one of the best young officers I've ever had the privilege of working with.'

'I can imagine that. It's a terrible thing for police officers to lose one of their own.'

'There's always a lot of anger flying around, covering up for the fact that they tend to feel a death in the family is a reflection of their competence, that somehow they should have been able to prevent it if they'd only been doing their jobs properly. And in this instance, I share that guilt.'

'I'm sure there was nothing you could have done to prevent it,' Micky said, impulsively putting a hand on his arm. 'When I told my husband you were coming on the programme, he said the same thing, and he's got even less reason to feel responsible.'

'No reason at all,' Tony said, surprised he could sound so sincere. 'Even though we're now coming round to thinking that her killer may have made contact with her in London rather than in Leeds. In fact, I was hoping you might give me the chance to put out an appeal for witnesses?'

Micky's hand flew to her throat in a curiously vulnerable gesture. 'You don't think she was stalked from our house, do you?'

'There's no reason to think that,' he said hastily.

'No?'

'No.'

'Thanks for the reassurance.' She took a deep breath

and pushed her blonde hair back from her face. 'Now, the interview. I'm going to ask about why the unit was set up, how it's constituted, what sort of offences you'll be covering and when the task force will go into action. Then I'll move on to Sharon . . .'

'Shaz,' Tony interrupted. 'Call her Shaz. She hated being called Sharon.'

Micky nodded. 'Shaz. I'll move on to Shaz, which will give you the chance to ask for any help you want to solicit. Is that OK? Is there anything else you particularly want the opportunity to say?'

'I'm sure I'll be able to get the message across,' he said.

She reached for the door handle. 'Betsy, my PA – you spoke to her earlier – she'll come and fetch you shortly before we go on air. You'll be the last item before we break for the news bulletin.'

'Thanks,' he said, wanting to say something to build a bridge between them but not knowing what that might be. She would be his best way under Jacko Vance's defences if he could only find a way to manipulate her into unconsciously helping him.

'You're welcome,' Micky said. Then she was gone, leaving nothing behind her but the faint scent of cosmetics. He'd only have one more chance to get her on his side. He hoped he'd make a better job of it.

It had better be worth it, Vance thought. He'd cancelled lunch cooked personally by Marco Pierre White for this, and the notoriously temperamental chef would make him suffer for it. He locked his office door and closed the blinds. His secretary knew better than to put any calls through, and neither his producer nor his PA knew he was still in the building. Whatever *Midday with*

Morgan revealed, there would be no one to see his reaction.

He threw himself on to the long leather sofa that dominated one side of the room and put his feet up. His face a mask of petulance, he turned on the giant TV screen with the remote control just as the familiar titles started to roll. He had nothing to fear, he knew that. Whatever Shaz Bowman had thought she'd known, she hadn't been able to convince her colleagues. He'd already dealt with the police. They'd eaten out of his hand, and rightly so. Some academic psychologist doling out half-baked theories could hardly threaten him without the backing of the plod. Nevertheless, being careful had kept him safe until now, and he wasn't about to give in to the temptation towards arrogance that such a successful career might breed.

He'd been able to glean some information about Tony Hill from his sources, though not as much as he would have liked. Again, he had been careful to keep the questions casual, taking pains not to have his inquiries arouse curiosity. What he'd learned had pricked his interest. He'd been behind the controversial Home Office study that had led to the setting up of the profiling task force that Shaz Bowman had aspired to. He'd been involved in a serial killer hunt in Bradfield where he'd ended up with blood on his hands because he hadn't been smart enough. And there were murmurings that there was something borderline perverse about his sexuality. That had really got Vance's adrenaline pumping, but it was the one angle he simply had to leave alone or risk his source wondering exactly what his concern was with the psychologist.

Fascinated though Vance was with his speculations about Tony, his thoughts were no competition for the TV screen. His attraction to the glamour of television had never waned in all his years on the performing end of the camera. He loved the medium, but most of all, he loved live TV with all its high-wire risks. Even though he ought to have been wondering how to neutralize Tony Hill if that became necessary, he couldn't resist Micky. Familiarity had bred respect rather than contempt for her professional skills and her talent. She really was one of the best. He'd spotted that right from the word go, recognized that she was one to have on his side. That he'd been able to keep her there so effectively had been a huge bonus.

She'd been good back then, but she'd improved, no doubt about that. Confidence had been part of that, Betsy another part. Her lover had shown her how to submerge the rougher edges of aggression beneath a surface of unruffled, gently probing interest. Most of Micky Morgan's victims didn't even realize how effectively they'd been filleted till someone played the tape back to them afterwards. If there was any ruffling of Tony Hill's surface to be done, a live interview with Micky would do it. He'd hinted to her that there might be darkness lurking behind her guest's facade. Now it was up to her.

He watched the first fifty minutes of the programme with a connoisseur's eye, assessing and appraising the performance of his wife and her colleagues. That Midlands reporter was going to have to go, he decided. He'd have to tell Micky. Vance hated journalists who brought the same breathless urgency to stories of distant wars, cabinet reshuffles and soap opera plots. It revealed a lack of empathy most successful hacks learned to hide early on.

It was strange, he thought, how he'd never felt the slightest twinge of sexual desire for his wife. True, she wasn't his type, but even so, he'd periodically found women attractive who didn't conform to his blueprint of desire. Never Micky, however. Not even on those rare occasions when he'd glimpsed her naked. It was probably as well, given the basis of their relationship. One glimmer of what he really wanted from the female of the species and Micky would be history. And he definitely didn't want that. Particularly not now.

'And after the break,' Micky said with that intimate warmth he suspected of causing erections among unemployed youths throughout the land, 'I'll be talking to a man who spends his days inside the heads of serial offenders. Psychological profiler Dr Tony Hill reveals the inside secrets of the new national police task force. And we pay tribute to the officer who has already tragically lost her life in that battle. All that, and the news on the hour, after the break.'

As the adverts took over, Vance pressed the record button on the video remote. He swung his feet to the floor and leaned forward, intent on the screen. The last commercial faded to the logo of *Midday with Morgan* and his wife was smiling out at him as if he were the only light of her life. 'Welcome back,' Micky said. 'My guest now is the distinguished clinical psychologist Dr Tony Hill. Nice to have you with us, Tony.'

The director switched to a two-shot, giving Vance his first sight of Shaz Bowman's boss. The colour drained from his cheeks then raced back in a dark flush. He'd thought Tony Hill was going to be a stranger. But he knew the man on the screen. He'd spotted him first three gigs ago at the sponsored sequence dancing competition. Lurking on the fringes, talking to some of the regulars. He'd initially written him off as the latest addition to the sad squad of his camp followers. But the night before, at the sports centre, when he'd spotted him handing business cards out to the others, he'd wondered. He'd planned to send someone over to check him out, but it had slipped his mind. Now, here was the stranger, sitting on a sofa talking to Vance's wife in front of millions of viewers.

This was no routine nutter. This was no dumbshit plod. This was Shaz Bowman's boss. This might just also be an adversary.

'How has the tragic death of one of your trainees affected the squad?' Micky asked solicitously, her eyes glistening perfectly to convey heartfelt sympathy as she leaned forward.

Tony's eyes slid away from hers, the pain obvious. 'It's been a shocking blow,' he said. 'Shaz Bowman was one of the brightest officers it's ever been my privilege to work with. She had a real flair for offender profiling work, and she'll be impossible to replace. But we're determined that her killer will be caught.'

'Are you working closely with the investigating officers on the case?' Micky asked. His response to what she'd thought was a routine question was interesting. His eyebrows flashed up and his eyes widened momentarily.

'Everyone on the profiling task force is doing all they can to help,' he said quickly. 'And it's possible that your viewers could also help us.'

She was impressed with the speed of his recovery. She doubted if one in a thousand of her viewers had even noticed the blip. 'How is that, Tony?'

'As you know, Shaz Bowman was murdered in her flat in Leeds. However, we have reason to believe this wasn't a random killing. Indeed, her murderer may not even be a local man. Shaz was in London on Saturday morning, about twelve hours before she was murdered. We don't know where she went or who she saw after about ten thirty on Saturday morning. It's possible that her killer made contact with her that early in the day.'

'You mean it could have been a stalker?'

'I think it's possible that she was followed back to Leeds from London.'

That wasn't quite the same thing, but Micky knew she didn't have time to quibble. 'And you hope someone witnessed this?'

Tony nodded and stared directly into the camera with the red light showing. She could see his sincerity on the monitor in front of her. God, he was a natural, all nervousness gone as he made his impassioned appeal. 'We're looking for anyone who saw Shaz Bowman after half past ten on Saturday morning. She was very distinctive-looking. She had particularly bright blue eyes, very noticeable. You may have seen her alone or with her killer, perhaps filling her car with petrol – she drove a black Volkswagen Golf. Or possibly in one of the motorway service areas between London and Leeds. You may have noticed someone taking an unusual amount of interest in her. If so, we need to hear from you.'

'We have the number of the Leeds incident room,' Micky cut in as it appeared on a ribbon across the foot of the monitor screen. She and Tony disappeared to be replaced by a head and shoulders shot of Shaz grinning at the camera. 'If you saw Shaz Bowman on Saturday, no matter how briefly, call the police and let them know.'

'We want to catch him before he kills again,' Tony added.

'So don't be afraid to call West Yorkshire Police or even your local police station if you can help. Tony, thanks for coming in and talking to us.' Her smile shifted to the camera because her director was bellowing from the control room. 'And now, over to the newsroom for the lunchtime bulletin.'

Micky leaned back and let out her breath in an explosive sigh. 'Thanks, Tony,' she said, unclipping her mike and leaning forward so their knees touched in the angle of the sofa.

'It's me that should be thanking you,' he said in a rush as Betsy strode efficiently towards them. She reached over his shoulder to unfasten his mike.

'I'll see you out,' Betsy said.

Micky jumped to her feet. 'It's been fascinating,' she said. 'I wish we could have had longer.'

Grabbing the chance, Tony said, 'We could have dinner.'

'Yes, I'd like that,' Micky said, sounding surprised at herself. 'Are you free this evening?'

'Yes. Yes, I am.'

'Let's make it this evening, then. Is six thirty OK? I need to eat early, working this show.'

'I'll book a table.'

'No need. Betsy'll see to it, won't you, Bets?'

There was a flicker of indulgent amusement in the woman's face, Tony thought. Almost immediately, the professional mask was back. 'No problem. But I need to get Dr Hill off set, Micky,' she said, with an apologetic smile at him.

'OK. See you later, Tony.' She watched Betsy hustle him away, savouring the anticipation of picking the brains of someone really interesting for a change. The demented bleating in her earpiece brought her back to the cold reality of getting the rest of the programme out of the way. 'We go straight to the classroom anarchy piece, yeah?' she said peering up at the control booth, her mind back on her job, Shaz Bowman already a memory.

*

Carol stared out of her office window at the port below. It was cold enough to get rid of the casual strollers. Everyone out there was brisk, even the dog walkers. She hoped her detectives were following their example. She dialled the hotel number Tony had left her. She was as eager to hear about his TV appearance as she was to pass on her own news. She didn't have to listen to the 'Cuckoo Waltz' for long. 'Hello?' she heard him say.

'*Midday with Morgan* was great, Tony. What did you think? Did you see Jack the Lad?'

'No, I didn't see him, but I liked her more than I expected to. She's a good interviewer. Lulls you into a false sense of security then sticks in a couple of awkward questions. I managed to make the points I wanted to make, though.'

'So Vance wasn't around?'

'Not at the studios, no. But she said she'd told him I was going to be on, so I wouldn't take any bets on Jack the Lad having missed today's programme.'

'Do you think she has any idea?'

'That we suspect her husband?' He sounded surprised at the question.

'That her husband's a serial killer.' He was a little slow tonight, Carol thought. Normally he read any conversation as if he'd seen the script in advance.

'I don't think she has the faintest notion. I doubt she'd be with him if she did.' He sounded unusually positive. It wasn't like Tony to categorize things as black or white.

'He really is a smooth operator.'

'As silk. Now we have to sit back and see how much more it takes to unsettle him. Starting with tonight. I'm taking his wife out to dinner.'

Carol couldn't help the pang of jealousy, but she kept

her voice even. She'd had plenty of practice with Tony. 'Really? How did you manage that?'

'I think she's genuinely interested in the profiling,' he said. 'Let's hope I can dig some information out of her that we can use.'

'If anyone can, you can. Tony, I think we've got a problem. With Simon.' Briefly, she relayed her conversation with John Brandon. 'What do you think? Should we persuade him to turn himself in?'

'I think we leave it up to him. If you're comfortable with that? Given that he might well be sitting in your living room again before all of this is over.'

'I don't expect it to be a problem,' Carol said slowly. 'It's only an internal bulletin we're talking about here. It's not as if there's going to be a nationwide manhunt with his picture splashed across the papers. Well, not for a couple of days yet, anyway. If it runs into next week and he's not been home or in contact with his friends and family, it might get more serious, in which case we'd have to persuade him to come in from the cold.'

'You're assuming he won't meekly walk into police HQ in Leeds?'

Carol snorted derisively. 'What do you think?'

'I think he's got too much invested in what we're doing. And speaking of which, how have the team been doing?'

She filled him in on Kay's grand tour of the grieving. When she came to the photograph she'd pried from the unwilling hands of Kenny and Denise Burton, Carol heard a sharp intake of breath.

'The zealots,' he said.

'I'm sorry?'

'Zealots. Fanatics. Jacko Vance's disciples. I've been to three of his public appearances so far, and there's a

347

few obsessives who show up every time. Just three or four of them. I noticed them right away.'

'You ever end up on the dole, you could get a job as a spotter for Neighbourhood Watch,' she said. 'You could call it Nutter Watch.'

He laughed. 'The point is, two of them were taking photos.'

'Gotcha?'

'Could be. Could very well be. This is very, very good. This might just give us the edge. He's clever, Carol. He's the best I've ever seen, ever heard about, ever read about. Somehow, we've got to be better.' His voice was soft but keen, charged with determination.

'We are. There are five of us. He only ever sees things from one angle.'

'You're so right. I'll talk to you tomorrow, OK?'

She could sense his eagerness to be active, to be gone. She couldn't blame him. Micky Morgan would be a real challenge to his skills and Tony was a man who adored a challenge. Whether he obtained fresh information from her or merely used their dinner date to set the cat among Jacko Vance's pigeons, he would be more effective than anyone else she could think of. But she couldn't let him go just yet. 'There's one more thing . . . the arsonist?'

'Oh God, yes, of course, I'm sorry. Any progress?'

She outlined the discoveries of her team, giving a thumbnail sketch of the two suspects. 'I'm not sure at this stage whether to bring them both in for questioning and try for a search warrant for their homes, or set up surveillance. I thought I'd run it past you.'

'How do they spend their money?'

'Brinkley and his wife go in for conspicuous consumption. New cars, household goods, store credit cards.

Watson looks like a gambler. He raises cash any way he can and passes it on to the bookies.'

Tony said nothing for a moment. She pictured him frowning, a hand running through his thick black hair, his deep-set eyes dark and distant as his mind moved over the question. 'If I was Watson, I'd bet on Brinkley,' he said eventually.

'How so?'

'If Watson is truly a compulsive gambler, he's convinced it's the next bet, the next lottery ticket that will solve all his problems. He's a believer. Brinkley hasn't got that conviction. He thinks if he can just keep ahead of the game, cut down on spending, find some extra cash, he can get out of this mess by some conventional route. That's my reading of it. But whether I'm right or wrong, bringing them in for questioning isn't going to get you a result. It might stop the fires, but nobody will ever be charged with them. A search warrant won't help either, from what you've told me about how the fires are started. I know it's not the answer you want to hear, but surveillance is your best chance of a conviction. And you need to cover both of them in case I've got it wrong.'

Carol groaned. 'I knew you were going to say that,' she complained. 'Surveillance. A copper's favourite job. A budgetary nightmare.'

'At least you only have to cover the hours of darkness. And he's operating frequently, so it's not going to last for long.'

'That's supposed to make me feel better?'

'It's the best I can manage.'

'OK. Not your fault. Thanks for your help, Tony. Off you go and enjoy dinner. I'm going home to a frozen pizza and, hopefully, updates from Simon and Leon. And, please God, an early night. Sleep . . .' The last word sounded like a caress.

Tony laughed. 'Enjoy it.'

'Oh, I will,' she promised fervently. 'And Tony – good luck.'

'In the absence of miracles, I'll settle for that.'

The click of his receiver going down sliced off any chance of her telling him the other thing she'd initiated that day. She couldn't work out exactly why she'd felt impelled to do it, but her instinct told her it was important. And past experience had taught her painfully that her instinct was sometimes far more reliable than logic. Something had niggled at the back of her mind until, in the midst of all the other tasks for the day, she'd found time to send a query out to all the other police forces in the country. Detective Chief Inspector Carol Jordan of East Yorkshire Police wanted to hear about any recent reports of teenage girls inexplicably missing from home.

'Mike McGowan? That's him, over in the corner booth, duck,' the barmaid said, gesturing with her thumb.

'What does he drink?' Leon asked. But the barmaid had already moved on to another customer. The pub was moderately busy, occupied almost completely by men. In a small East Midlands town like this, there were clear distinctions between pubs where men went to spend their time with women and ones where they went to avoid that necessity. The giveaway here was the large board outside advertising 'All day satellite sport, giant screens'.

Leon sipped his lager shandy and took a moment to watch Mike McGowan. Jimmy Linden had offered his name as the media expert on Jacko Vance. 'Like me, Mike spotted him early on and he wrote a lot about him over the years,' he'd said. When Leon had contacted McGowan's old paper in London, he'd discovered that the journalist had been made redundant three years before. Divorced, his children grown and scattered round the country, there had been nothing to keep McGowan in the expensive capital, so he'd returned to the Nottinghamshire town where he'd grown up.

The ex-reporter looked more like a caricature of an Oxbridge don than any national newspaperman Leon had ever seen. Even sitting down, he was clearly tall. A mop of grey-blond hair cut in a heavy fringe that flopped over his eyes, big tortoiseshell glasses and pink and white skin gave him the same boyish looks that Alan Bennett and David Hockney turned into trademarks. His jacket was the sort of ancient tweed that takes fifteen years to look wearable then lasts another twenty without any sign of attrition. Beneath it he wore a grey flannel shirt and a striped tie with a narrow tight knot. He sat alone in the narrow corner booth, staring up studiously at a 56-inch TV screen where two teams were playing basketball. As Leon watched, McGowan tapped the bowl of a pipe against the ashtray, automatically cleaning and filling it without taking his eyes from the screen.

When Leon loomed up next to him, he still didn't take his eyes off the basketball. 'Mike McGowan?'

'That's me. And who are you?' he said, local vowels as distinctive as the barmaid's shattering the illusion of lofty academe.

'Leon Jackson.'

McGowan threw him a quick look of assessment. 'Any relation to Billy Boy Jackson?'

Astounded, Leon almost crossed himself. 'He was my uncle,' he blurted out.

'You've got the same shaped head. I should know. I was ringside the night Marty Pyeman fractured your uncle's skull. That's not what you've come to see me about, though, is it?' The quick glance this time was shrewd.

'Can I get you a drink, Mr McGowan?'

The journalist shook his head. 'I don't come here for the drink. I come for the sport. My pension's crap. I can't afford a satellite subscription or a screen like this. I was at school with the landlord's dad, so he doesn't bother that I make a single pint last the best part of the day. Sit down and tell me what you're after.'

Leon obeyed, taking out his warrant card. He tried to snap it shut and away, but McGowan was faster. 'Metropolitan Police,' he mused. 'Now what would a London bobby with a Liverpool accent be doing with a retired hack in darkest Nottinghamshire?'

'Jimmy Linden said you might be able to help me,' Leon said.

'Jimmy Linden? Now there's a name from the past.' He closed the warrant card and slid it across to Leon. 'So what's your interest in Jacko Vance?'

Leon shook his head admiringly. 'I never said I had an interest in the man. But if that's who you want to talk about, be my guest.'

'My, they're teaching them subtlety these days,' McGowan said acidly, striking a match and applying it to his pipe. He sucked and expelled a cloud of blue smoke that swallowed whole the feeble spiral from Leon's cigarette. 'What's Jacko supposed to have done? Whatever it is, I bet you never manage to nick him for it.'

Leon remained silent. It nearly killed him, but he managed it. This clever old bastard wasn't going to put one over on him, he thought, almost convincing himself.

'I haven't seen Jacko in years,' McGowan finally said. 'He's not that keen on faces who remember what he was like when he had all his limbs. He hates being reminded of what he lost.'

'You'd think what he's got now would be compensation,' Leon said. 'Great job, more money than any reasonable geezer could spend, gorgeous wife, house the size of a stately home. I mean, how many Olympic gold medallists got a better deal than that?'

McGowan slowly shook his head. 'Nothing can compensate a man who thinks he's a god for the discovery of his vulnerability. That lass of his was lucky she got out from under. She'd have been the obvious choice when it came to making somebody pay for what the gods had done to Jacko Vance.'

'Jimmy said you knew more about Jacko than anybody else.'

'Only superficially. I followed his career, I interviewed him. I probably caught a few glimpses behind the mask, but I wouldn't say I knew him. I can't think of anybody that did. Really, there's nothing I want to say about Jacko Vance that I haven't already put in writing.'

McGowan breathed out another plume of smoke. Leon thought it smelled like Black Forest gateau, all cherries and chocolate. He couldn't imagine wanting to smoke a pudding. 'Jimmy also said that you kept cuttings files on the athletes that really interested you.'

'My, you did get a lot out of old Jimmy. He must have taken to you in a big way. Mind you, he's always had a lot of respect for black athletes. He reckoned they had to work twice as hard as anybody else to get their start. I suppose he reckoned it was probably much the same in the police.'

'Or maybe I'm just a good interviewer,' Leon said drily. 'Any chance of you letting me take a look at your cuttings?'

'Any in particular, Detective?' McGowan teased.

'I'd be guided by you as to what was interesting, sir.'

McGowan, his eyes firmly on the basketball, said, 'A

career as long as mine, it'd be hard to pick out particular highlights.'

'I'm sure you could manage it.'

'This finishes in ten minutes. Perhaps you'd care to come back and look at my files?'

Half an hour later, Leon was sitting in a room in McGowan's two-bedroomed terrace that managed to be both spartan and cluttered. The only furniture was a battered leather swivel chair that looked as if it had seen service in the Spanish Civil War, and a scarred and scratched gun-metal grey desk. All four walls were covered with industrial metal shelving and packed with shoeboxes, each with a label stuck to the outer edge. 'This is incredible,' he said.

'I always promised myself that when I retired, I'd write a book,' McGowan said. 'Amazing how we delude ourselves. I used to travel the world covering the top sporting events. Now my world's shrunk to the satellite screens in the Dog and Gun. You'd think I'd be depressed. But the funny thing is, I'm not. I've never been so bloody contented all my born days. It's reminded me that what I always liked best about sport was watching it. Freedom without responsibility, that's what I've got now.'

'A dangerous mixture,' Leon said.

'A liberating mixture. Three years ago, you turning up would have had me sniffing a story. I'd not have rested until I'd found out what was going on. Now, it's hard to imagine how I could care less. I'm more excited about the Vegas fight on Saturday than I could ever be about anything Jacko Vance has said or done.' He pointed to a shelf. 'Jacko Vance. Fifteen shoeboxes full. Enjoy yourself, lad. I've got an appointment with a tennis match at the Dog and Gun. If you're gone before I get back, just pull the front door closed behind you.'

When Mike McGowan returned just before midnight, Leon was still working his way systematically through the cuttings. The journalist brought him a mug of instant coffee and said, 'I hope they're paying you overtime, lad.'

'More of a labour of love, you might say,' Leon said wryly.

'Yours or your boss's?'

Leon thought for a moment. 'One of my mates. Call it a debt of honour.'

'The only kind worth paying. I'll leave you to it. Try not to slam the door behind you when you go.'

Leon was half aware of the sounds of someone getting ready for bed: floorboards creaking, plumbing grumbling, a toilet flushing. Then silence apart from the whisper of yellowed newsprint.

It was almost two when he found what he thought he might just be looking for. There was only one cutting, a fleeting mention. But it was a start. When he let himself out into the dark and empty street, Leon Jackson was whistling.

Her eyes were as candid as any he could remember. She pushed the last morsel of the smoked duck on to her fork, speared a final mange tout and said, 'But surely it has an effect on you, spending so much time and energy getting inside such twisted logic?'

Tony took longer than he needed to finish his mouthful of polenta. 'You learn to build Chinese walls,' he said at last. 'You know but you don't know. You feel but you don't feel. I imagine it's similar to being a news journalist. How do you sleep at night after you've been out reporting on something like the Dunblane massacre or the Lockerbie bombing?'

'Yes, but we're always outside the event. You have to get inside or you fail, surely?'

'You're not always outside the event, though, are you? When you met Jacko, the story invaded your life. You must have had to build walls between what you knew of the man personally and what you reported to the world. When his ex-girlfriend was doing her kiss-and-tell revelations with the tabloids, you can't have looked at that as just another story. Didn't it affect the way you viewed your world?' he said, seizing the first chance he'd had to get her talking about her husband.

Micky pushed her hair back from her face. Twelve years on, he could see the contempt for Jillie Woodrow hadn't grown less. 'What a bitch,' she muttered. 'But Jacko said it was mostly fiction, and I believe him. So it didn't really get under my defences.'

The arrival of the waiter let her off the hook and he cleared their plates in silence. Then, alone again, Tony repeated the question.

'You're the psychologist,' she parried, reaching into her bag and producing a pack of Marlboro. 'Do you mind if I . . . ?'

He shook his head. 'I didn't realize you did.'

'Only after dinner. A maximum of five a day,' she said, a droll twist to her mouth. 'The control freak's control freak, that's me.'

The expression gave him a jolt. The one and only time he'd used the expression, he'd been talking about a compulsive killer who had almost robbed him of his own life. To hear it from her lips was dislocating and strange.

'You look like you've seen a ghost,' she said, inhaling her first mouthful of smoke with an air of sensuous pleasure.

'Just a stray memory,' he said. 'There are a lot of very

bizarre resonances kicking around inside my head.'

'I bet. Something I've always wondered is how you *know* when you're getting it right in a profile.' She inhaled deeply and blew pale filtered smoke down her nostrils, an expression of interest on her face.

He gave her an appraising look. It was now or never. 'The same way any of us work out anything about people. A mixture of knowledge and experience. Plus knowing the right question to ask.'

'Such as?'

The interest was so genuine he almost felt guilty for what he was about to do to their pleasant evening. 'Doesn't Jacko mind that Betsy's in love with you?'

Her face froze and her pupils dilated in a panic reflex. After a long moment she swallowed and managed a faint laugh. 'If you were trying to wrong-foot me, you certainly succeeded.' It was one of the best recoveries he'd ever seen, but he hadn't imagined the confession in her eyes.

'I'm no danger to you,' he said softly. 'Confidentiality is second nature to me. But I'm not a fool either. You and Jacko, it's as fake as a nine-bob note. Betsy was there first. Oh, there were rumours. But you and Jacko had the most public courtship since Charles and Diana. It killed the gossip.'

'Why are you bringing this up?' she asked.

'We're both here because we're curious. I've answered all the questions you asked me. You can return the compliment, or not.' His smile was, he hoped, warm.

'God,' she said wonderingly. 'You have got a nerve.'

'How do you think I got to be the best?'

Micky looked speculatively at him, waving away the waiter who was approaching with the dessert menus. 'Bring us another bottle of the Zinfandel,' she said as an afterthought. She leaned forward and spoke softly. 'What do you want to ask?'

'What's in it for Jacko? Surely he's not gay?'

Micky shook her head emphatically. 'Jillie dumped Jacko after his accident because she didn't want to be with a man who wasn't perfect. He swore he would never enter into another sexual relationship where his emotions were engaged. He needed a decoy to keep the women away from him, I needed a man to hide Betsy behind.'

'Mutual benefit.'

'Oh, yes, mutual benefit. And to be fair to Jacko, he's never tried to renege on the deal. I don't know what he does for sex, though I suspect well-paid call girls come into it. Frankly, I don't care as long as he never embarrasses me.' She stubbed out her cigarette and gave him the accomplished frank gaze she normally directed at the camera.

'I'm amazed that someone who's paid to be curious about other people is so lacking in curiosity about her own husband.'

Her smile was ironic. 'If there's one thing that eleven years of marriage to Jacko has taught me, it's that nobody gets to know Jacko. It's not that I think he tells lies,' she said consideringly, 'just that I don't think he tells very much of the truth. Different people get little bits of Jacko's truth, but I don't think anybody gets it all.'

'How do you mean?' Tony picked up the discreetly delivered bottle of wine, refilling Micky's glass and topping up his almost full one.

'I get to see Jacko behaving in public like the perfect, solicitous husband, but I know that's an act. When there's only the three of us around, he's so distant it's hard to believe we've all lived under the same roof for the last dozen years. When he's working he acts like people expect a TV celeb to behave – perfectionist, a bit OTT, yelling at the crew and his PA when things don't get done just so. But with the public, he's Mr Charm. Then, when it comes to raising money, he's a hard-headed businessman. Do you know that for every pound he makes for charity, he earns two for himself?'

Tony shook his head. 'I suppose he'd argue that he's generating funds for the charity they wouldn't get otherwise.'

'And why should he work for free? Right. Me, when I do charity events, I don't even take my expenses. But then there's the other side, the volunteer work he does with people who are terminally ill or severely damaged after accidents. He spends hours by their bedsides, listening, talking, and nobody knows what goes on between them. One time a journalist tried to sneak in a tape recorder to reveal "the secret heart of Jacko Vance". Jacko found out about it and he smashed the tape recorder. He literally stamped it to pieces. They thought he was going to do the same to the journalist, but the guy had the good sense to make his legs do the walking.'

'A man who likes his privacy,' Tony said.

'Oh, he gets plenty of that. He's got a house in North-umberland, out in the middle of nowhere. I've seen it once in twelve years and that was only because Bets and I were driving up to Scotland and we decided to drop in on him. I practically had to force him to make us a cup of tea. I've never felt less welcome in my whole life.' Micky smiled indulgently. 'Yes, you could say that Jacko likes his privacy. But that's OK with me. Better that than hanging around in my face all the time.'

'He can't have been very pleased to have the police

poking their noses in, then,' Tony said. 'After Shaz Bowman's visit, I mean.'

'You're not kidding. It was actually me who called the police, you know. The way Betsy and Jacko reacted, you'd think I'd shopped them on a murder rap. It was a nightmare, trying to make the pair of them see that we couldn't ignore the fact that this poor woman had been at the house not long before she was murdered.'

'Just as well one of you has a sense of duty,' Tony said drily.

'Well, yes. Besides, at least one other person knew she was coming to the house – that other police officer that Jacko spoke to. It wasn't as if we could hope to keep it to ourselves.'

'I feel so guilty about Shaz,' Tony said, half-turning away. 'I knew she was worrying away at some theory of her own, but I didn't think she'd take action on it without clearing it with me.'

'You mean you don't know what she was working on either?' Micky said incredulously. 'The cops who came to the house didn't seem to have much of a clue, but I thought you'd be sure to know.'

Tony shrugged. 'Not really. I know she had some idea that there was a serial killer preying on teenage girls and that he might be a celebrity stalker as well. But I didn't have the details. It was only supposed to be a training exercise, not the real thing.'

Micky shivered and emptied her glass. 'Can we change the subject? It's bad for the digestion, talking about murder.'

For once, he wasn't about to argue. The gamble had paid off handsomely. And he'd never been greedy. 'OK. Tell me how you got the Agriculture Minister to admit his involvement with that biotechnology company.'

*

Carol stared down the three mutinous faces opposite her. 'I know nobody likes stakeout work. But that's the way we're going to catch our man. At least the intervals between his outings are pretty short, so the chances are we're going to get lucky within a few days. Now, this is the way I want it to work. We're going to do it single-handed. I realize that makes it tougher, but you know what budgets are like. I've spoken to uniform and they've agreed to let us have some bodies to cover during daylight hours. Each night at ten, two of you will pick up the surveillance. You'll each work two nights on and one off. You will each use the other as back-up if it looks like we've got something going off. We start today. The first watchers are out there now. Any questions?'

'What if we get clocked?' Lee asked.

'We don't get clocked,' Carol said. 'But if the unthinkable happens, you pull off, call your oppo and swap targets at the first opportune moment. I appreciate this is a tough operation with such a low body count. But I have every confidence that you can pull this off. Don't disappoint me, please.'

'Ma'am?' Di said.

'Yes?'

'If we're really that tight on staffing levels, why don't we prioritize our two suspects and focus on the most likely with all our resources?'

It was an awkward question, and an intelligent one. It was one Carol herself had debated with Nelson over breakfast that morning. It had taken her mind off a growing fear that was coming to obsess her. 'Good question,' she said now. 'I considered it myself. Then I thought, what if we go for the wrong candidate and we only find that out after another fatal fire?' She let the question hang in the air. 'So I decided it was probably better in terms of public policy to opt for thin cover over both suspects.'

Di nodded. 'Fair enough. I just wondered.'

'Right. Sort out the rota among yourselves, and knock off now until ten. Keep me posted. Anything happens, I'm only a phone call away. Don't keep me in the dark.'

'When you say only a phone call away, ma'am . . .' Tommy drawled suggestively.

'I want to be there when you make an arrest.'

'Aye, that's what I thought you meant.'

His feigned disappointment was aimed at annoying her, she knew. Determined not to show he'd succeeded, Carol smiled sweetly. 'Believe me, Tommy, you should be grateful for that. Now get out of here and let me get some work done.' Her hand was on the phone before she'd finished speaking. She hit the first number on a list in front of her, tapping her pad with a pencil as Seaford's finest trooped out with all the brio of a snail on Valium. 'Close the door behind you, please,' she called. 'Hello? Force control? This is DCI Jordan from East Yorkshire. I need to talk to someone about Mispers . . . I sent out an information request about teenage girls . . .'

Tony eased the car on to the slip road, wondering whether he'd enjoy driving more if he had one of those ultimate driving machines he saw in all the glossy adverts instead of a clapped out old Vauxhall. Somehow, he doubted it. But that wasn't what he was supposed to be thinking about as his windscreen wipers slapped the slanting Yorkshire rain away to reveal a distant prospect of Bradford. At the ring road, he followed the achingly precise instructions he'd been given and eventually pulled up outside a terraced house whose obsessive neatness was matched only by the military precision of its single flower bed. Even the curtains appeared to have been drawn back so that exactly the same amount of lining showed at each side of the window.

The doorbell was a nasty insistent buzz. It opened to reveal a man Tony had spotted at every Jacko Vance event he'd attended. He'd persuaded him and a couple of other camera-toting enthusiasts to part with names and addresses on the pretext that he was doing a study of the phenomenon of fame as seen through the eyes of the fans rather than the famous. It was meaningless drivel, but it made them feel important enough to be co-operative.

Philip Hawsley was first, for no better reason than living nearest. As he followed him into a preternaturally tidy front room that smelled of furniture polish and air freshener, and looked like a heritage museum recreation of lower middle class life in 1962, Tony registered all the signs of the obsessive compulsive. Hawsley, who could have been any age between thirty and fifty, constantly ran his fingers over the buttons of his beige cardigan to check they were all in place. He studied his fingernails at least once a minute to ensure they hadn't grown dirty since he last looked. His greying hair was cropped in a short, military style and his shoes were polished to mirror radiance. He invited Tony to sit, pointing out the chair he wanted him to occupy, and offered no refreshment, sitting down very precisely opposite the psychologist, ankles and knees pressed firmly together.

'Quite a collection,' Tony said, glancing round the room. An entire wall was given over to shelves of video tapes, each labelled with a date and name of a programme. Even from where he was sitting, he could see the vast majority were *Vance's Visits*. A laminated wall unit held a series of albums and scrapbooks. Half a dozen books sat on a shelf above the unit. Pride of place went to a large framed colour photograph sitting on the wall-mounted gas fire. It showed Hawsley shaking hands with Jacko Vance.

'A small tribute, but mine own,' Hawsley said in a prissily camp voice. Tony could imagine all too vividly how he would have been teased as an adolescent. 'We're the same age, you know. To the very day. I feel our fates are inextricably linked. We're like two sides of the same coin. Jacko is the public face and I am the private.'

'It must have taken years to amass all this material,' Tony said.

'I've dedicated myself to maintaining the archive,' Hawsley said primly. 'I like to think I have a better overview of Jacko's life than he does himself. When you're so busy living it, you don't have time to sit and reflect on it the way I do. His bravery, his common touch, his warmth, his compassion. He's the complete man of our time. It's one of life's little paradoxes that he had to lose part of himself to gain that pre-eminence.'

'I couldn't agree more,' Tony said, naturally falling back into the conversational techniques that years of working with the mentally ill had delivered into his repertoire. 'He's an inspiration, is Jacko.' He sat back and let Hawsley's adulation flow over him, pretending to fascination when what he felt was disgust for this killer who disguised himself so well that the innocent and ill fell for his every pretence. Eventually, after Hawsley had relaxed enough to inch back from the edge of his chair into an approximation of comfort, Tony said, 'I'd love to see your photograph albums.'

The crucial dates were carved on his memory. 'For the purposes of our study, we're going to be looking at precise points in people's careers,' Tony said as Hawsley opened the cabinet and started taking down albums. Every time Tony mentioned a month and year, Hawsley chose a particular volume and laid it on the coffee table in front of Tony, open at the appropriate pages. Jacko Vance was clearly a busy man, doing between five and twenty appearances a month, many of them related to charity fund-raising, often for the hospital in Newcastle where he did volunteer work.

Hawsley's memory for detail when it related to his idol was phenomenal, a mixed blessing for Tony. On the plus side, it gave him plenty of time to scrutinize the images before him; the minus side of the equation was that his droning voice came close to sending Tony into a hypnotic trance. Soon, however, Tony felt a quiver of excitement that snapped him back to full attentiveness. There, just two days before the first of Shaz Bowman's cluster of teenage girls had disappeared for good, was Jacko Vance opening a hospice in Swindon. In the second of Hawsley's four photographs of the event, Tony saw a face he'd memorized, right next to Jacko Vance's gleaming head. Debra Cressey. Fourteen when she vanished. Two days earlier, gazing up adoringly at Jacko Vance as he signed an autograph, she'd looked like a girl in paradise.

Two hours later, Tony had identified another missing girl next to Vance, this time apparently in conversation with her. A third possibility was straining upwards on tiptoe to steal a kiss from a laughing Vance. But her head was half-turned from the camera, making it hard to be certain. Now all he had to do was to extract the photographs from Hawsley. 'I wonder if I could borrow some of these photographs?' he asked.

Hawsley shook his head vigorously, looking deeply shocked. 'Of course not,' he said. 'It's vital that the integrity of the archive is maintained. What if I were called on and there were missing items from the inventory? No, Dr Hill, I'm afraid that's completely out of the question.'

'What about negatives? Do you still have them?'

Clearly offended, Hawsley said, 'Of course I do. What kind of sloppy operation do you think I'm running here?' He rose and opened the cupboard in the wall unit. Negative storage boxes were stacked on the shelves, each as obsessively labelled as the videos. Tony shuddered inwardly, imagining the painstaking listing of every negative in the box. Not so much anal retentive as banal retentive.

'Well, could I borrow the negatives so I can have them copied?' he asked, determinedly keeping the edge of exasperation out of his voice.

'I can't let them out of my possession,' Hawsley said stubbornly. 'They're significant.'

It took another fifteen minutes to find the acceptable compromise. He drove Philip Hawsley and his precious negatives to the local photographic shop where Tony paid an extortionate sum to have prints made of the relevant photographs while they waited. Then he drove Philip Hawsley home so he could replace the negatives in their proper place before their companions noticed they'd gone.

Driving down the motorway to the next name on his list, he allowed himself a short moment of triumphalism. 'We're going to get you, Jack the Lad,' he said. 'We are going to get you.'

All Simon McNeill really knew about Tottenham was that they had a second-rate football team and they killed a copper during a riot some time in the eighties when he'd still been at school. He didn't expect the natives to be friendly, so it was no surprise when his appearance at the local electoral roll office was greeted with less than rapture. When he explained what he wanted, the stick insect in a suit behind the counter cast his eyes heavenwards and sighed. 'You'll have to do it yourself,' he said grudgingly. 'I haven't the staff to spare, especially with no notice at all.' He showed Simon into the dusty archives, gave him a ten second run-down on the filing system and left him to it.

The results of his search were not encouraging. The street where Jacko Vance had grown up had consisted of about forty houses back in the sixties. By 1975, twenty-two of the houses had disappeared, replaced, presumably, by a block of flats called Shirley Williams House. The eighteen remaining houses revealed a steady turnover of registered electors, few people seeming to remain for more than a couple of years, particularly during the grim poll tax years of the mid-eighties. Only one name remained constant throughout. Simon pinched the bridge of his nose to ease the beginning headache. He hoped Tony Hill was right, that all this would bring them closer to nailing Shaz's killer. The image of her face rose painfully before him, her startling blue eyes bright with laughter. It was almost more than he could bear. No time to brood, he told himself as he shrugged back into his leather jacket and set off to find Harold Adams.

Number 9 Jimson Street was a tiny terraced house in dirty yellow London brick. The little oblong of garden that separated it from the street was choked with empty beer cans, crisp packets and takeaway food containers. A scrawny black cat stared up malevolently as he opened the gate, then sprang for freedom with a chicken bone in its teeth. The street smelled of decay. The desiccated shell who opened the door after much rattling of bolts and turning of locks looked as if he must have already been an old man when Jacko Vance was a boy. Simon's heart sank. 'Mr Adams?' he asked, without much hope of intelligent response.

The old man cocked his head in an effort to defeat his stoop and look Simon in the eye. 'You from the council? I told that woman already, I don't need a home help and I don't want meals on wheels.' His voice sounded like a hinge in desperate need of oil.

'I'm from the police.'

'I never saw anything,' Adams said swiftly, moving to close the door.

'No, wait. It's nothing like that. I want to talk about somebody who lived here years ago: Jacko Vance. I want to talk about Jacko Vance.'

Adams paused. 'You're one of them journalists, aren't you? You're trying to con an old man. I'm going to call the police.'

'I *am* the police,' Simon said, waving his open warrant card in front of faded grey eyes. 'Look.'

'All right, all right, I'm not blind. You lot are always telling us, you can't be too careful. What d'you want to talk about Jacko Vance for? He hasn't lived here for . . . let me see, must be seventeen, eighteen years now.'

'Could I come in and have a chat, maybe?' Simon said, half-hoping Adams would send him off with a flea in his ear.

'I suppose so.' Adams pulled the door wide and stood back to let Simon enter. He caught a whiff of the old man smell of spilled urine and stale biscuits before he turned into the living room. To his surprise, the place was spotless. There wasn't a speck of dust on the screen of the huge TV set, not a mark on the lace-edged arm protectors on the easy chairs, not a smear on the glass of the framed photographs that lined the mantelpiece. Harold Adams was right; he didn't need a home help.

Simon waited for the old man to settle in his own chair before he sat down.

'I'm the last one left,' Adams said proudly. 'When we came here in 1947, it was like a big family, this street. Everybody knew everybody's business and, just like a family, they was always falling out. Now, nobody knows anybody, but they still fall out just the same.' When he grinned, Simon thought, his face looked like the skull of a predatory bird whose eyes had somehow survived.

'I bet they do. So you knew the Vance family pretty well?'

Adams sniggered. 'Not much of a family, you ask me. His dad, called himself an engineer, but as far as I could see, all that meant was he had an excuse for disappearing at the drop of a hat for weeks on end. Mind you, it wouldn't surprise me if he earned a bob or two. He was always dressed better than the street, if you get my meaning. Never spent a shilling on the house or the wife and kid that he didn't have to, though.'

'What was she like?'

'Off her head. She had no time for that lad, not even when he was a babe in arms. She'd stick him out the front in his pram and just leave him there for hours. Sometimes she even forgot to take him in when it started raining and my Joan or one of the other women would have to go and knock on her door and tell her. My Joan used to say that some days she was still in her dressing gown at dinner time.'

'Did she drink, then?'

'I never heard that, no. She just didn't like the kid. Cramped her style, I suppose. When he got older, she just let him run wild, then when people went to complain, she'd come down on him like a ton of bricks. I don't know what went on behind closed doors, but sometimes you'd hear that kid sobbing his heart out. Never did no good, mind.'

'How do you mean?'

'He was a nasty piece of work, that Jacko Vance. I don't care what they say about him being a hero and sportsman, he had a nasty streak a mile wide. Oh, he could be all charm when he thought it would get him somewhere. He had all the wives in this street wrapped round his little finger. They were always giving him little treats, letting him watch telly round their house when his mum locked him out.' Adams was enjoying himself. Simon suspected it wasn't often these days that his malice was allowed free rein. He was determined to make the most of it.

'But you knew different?'

Adams sniggered again. 'I knew everything that went on in this street. I caught that little bugger Vance once round the back of the lock-up garages off Boulmer Street. He had a cat by the scruff, you know, so it couldn't fight him off. He was dipping its tail in a jar of petrol when I came round the corner. And there was a box of matches on the ground beside him.' The momentary silence was eloquent. 'I made him let the cat go, then I kicked his arse for him, good and proper. I shouldn't think I stopped him, though. Cats were always going missing round here. People used to comment on it. Me, I had my own ideas.'

'Like you said, a nasty piece of work.' It was almost too good to be true. Simon had spent too much time preparing for his assignment in Leeds not to recognize the accepted markers for psychopathy in a background history. Torturing animals was textbook stuff. And this man had seen it first hand. He couldn't have found a better source if he'd searched for weeks.

'He was a bully, an' all. Always picking on the little

kids, daring them to do dangerous things, getting them hurt, but he never laid a finger on them himself. It was like he set it up to happen and then stood back and watched. Me and Joan, we were glad our two were grown and gone by then. And by the time the grandkids came along, Vance had discovered he could throw a silly spear further than anybody else. We hardly saw him after that, and good riddance to bad rubbish, if you ask me.'

'You'll not find many people with a bad word to say about that man,' Simon said mildly. 'He saved some lives, you can't argue with that. He does a lot of work for charity. And he gives up his time to work with the terminally ill.'

Adams screwed up his face in a sneer. 'I told you, he likes watching. He probably gets a kick out of knowing they'll be dead soon and he'll still be strutting around like Lord Muck on the telly. I'm telling you, sonny, Jacko Vance is a nasty piece of work. So, what are you after him for?'

Simon smiled. 'I never said I was after him.'

'So what d'you want to go around talking about him for, then?'

Simon winked. 'Now, you know I can't reveal the details of a police investigation, sir. You've been extremely helpful, I will say that much. If I was you, I'd keep an eye on the television for the next few days. With a bit of luck, you'll find out exactly why I came here.' He got to his feet. 'And now, I think I'd better be on my way. My senior officer will be very interested in what you have to say, Mr Adams.'

'I've been waiting years to say it, sonny. Years, I've been waiting.'

*

Barbara Fenwick had been killed six days before her fifteenth birthday. If she'd lived, she'd have been almost twenty-seven. Her mutilated body had been found in a walker's hut on the moors above the city, strangled. There were signs that she had had sexual intercourse against her will, though there had been no trace of sperm either inside or outside her body. What made the crime unusual was the nature of her injuries. Where most psychopathic killers disfigured the sexual organs of their victims, this killer had crushed the girl's right arm to a bloody pulp, shattering bones and tearing muscle till it was difficult to reconstruct which fragment went where. Even more interestingly, the pathologist had been insistent that the injuries were consistent with the application of increasing pressure rather than a single, terrible impact.

It had made no sense to the investigating officers.

The finders of Barbara's body were in the clear, having been camping and hiking together for the previous six days. Her parents, who had been distraught since her disappearance five days previously, were also under no suspicion. The girl had been alive and well for a couple of days after they had reported her missing and her stepfather had been in the company of his wife and at least one police officer ever since. The parents had said all along that their daughter was happy at home, that she would never have run away, that she must have been abducted. The police had been sceptical, pointing out that Barbara's best clothes were missing and that she had told her parents a lie about her movements following school the day she disappeared. Added to that, she'd bunked off school, and not for the first time.

It had made no sense to the investigating officers.

Barbara Fenwick hadn't been a wild, troublesome teenager. She wasn't known to the police, her friends denied she drank more than the occasional can of sweet cider and no one thought she'd ever experimented with drugs or sex. Her last boyfriend, who had chucked her a month before to go out with someone else, said they'd never gone all the way and he thought in spite of her sexy looks she was probably, like him, a virgin. She'd been doing reasonably well at school and had ambitions to train as a nursery nurse. The last reliable sighting of her had been on the local bus to Manchester on the morning of her disappearance. She'd told the neighbour who had spotted her that she was going to the Dental Hospital for an appointment to do with her wisdom teeth. Her mother said Barbara didn't have any sign of wisdom teeth, a fact borne out by the pathologist.

It had made no sense to the investigating officers.

There had been nothing in her behaviour to suggest a girl about to go off the rails. She'd been out to a disco with a bunch of friends on the Saturday night before her disappearance. Jacko Vance had been there, making a celebrity appearance, signing autographs for charity. Her friends said she'd had a great night.

None of this had made any sense to the investigating officers.

But it made a lot of sense to Leon Jackson.

The stone slab was so well engineered that it didn't even make the sinister grating sound of a horror film. When a small electrical current applied pressure to a particular, precise point, it simply pivoted silently through 180 degrees to reveal the steps that led to the small crypt that no one would any longer suspect existed beneath the converted chapel. Jacko Vance flipped the switch that flooded the crypt with harsh fluorescent light and descended.

The first thing he noticed was the smell, hitting him before his head was far enough underground to be able to see the creature that had once been Donna Doyle. The putrefaction of pulverized flesh mingled with the stale smell of unwashed fevered skin and the acrid reek of the chemical toilet. He felt his stomach turn, but told himself he'd smelled worse in the terminal ward as gangrene devoured the bodies of people who had already had as much amputated as could reasonably be excised. It was a lie, but one that stiffened his sinews.

At the bottom of the steps, he stood and stared at the pathetic creature pressing herself against the cold stone wall as if she expected to be able to push her way through it and so escape him. 'God, you're disgusting,' he said contemptuously, taking in her matted hair, foul wounds and the dirt she'd gathered bumping into things in the dark.

He'd left her boxes of breakfast cereal and she had water from the tap on the rising main. There was no excuse for her to be in this state; she could have made an effort to clean herself up instead of sitting on the mattress in her own filth, he thought. The leg irons allowed her enough freedom of movement for that, and the pain from her arm hadn't been enough to stop her from eating, judging by the open packets lying around her. He was glad he'd opted for a plastic-covered mattress so he could hose off her disgusting presence when he'd finished with her.

'Look at yourself,' he sneered, swaggering across the room towards her, unbuttoning his jacket and tossing it over a chair that was well out of her reach. 'Why should I want anything to do with a mess like you?'

The whimpering noise that came from Donna's bruised lips was wordless. With her undamaged hand, she grabbed at the blanket in a poignant attempt to cover her nakedness. In one swift step, Jacko was towering over her, yanking the rough woollen cover away from her. With his prosthetic arm, he smashed her across the face and she fell back on the mattress, tears spilling and mingling with the blood and mucus from her nose.

Vance stepped back and spat at her. Coolly, he stripped himself, folding his clothes and placing them neatly on the chair. He was hot and hard, ready for what he'd come there for. He'd had to wait longer than usual, longer than he'd wanted because of that inconvenient bitch Bowman. After the discovery of her body he hadn't dared come near the place until he'd seen off the police, wary of attracting their notice. And even if Tony Hill thought he had something on him, there was no proof and no one to pay him any attention. It was safe to come back for another dose of what made life worth living, the sweet allotment of vengeance, the savour of suffering.

He dropped to his knees on the mattress, forcing the teenager's legs apart with a rough hand, relishing her protests, her futile attempts at prevention, her sad little cries of repudiation. As he thrust into her, he let his full weight fall on her injured arm.

Donna Doyle finally produced a coherent sound. The scream that echoed round the grim little crypt was, unequivocally, 'No!'

Carol yanked open the door and practically dragged Tony into the cottage. 'We were beginning to wonder if you'd got lost,' she said, marching ahead of him to the dining table where a wide-mouthed Thermos of soup sat next to a couple of loaves of olive bread and a selection of cheeses.

'Accident on the motorway,' he said, dropping a folder on to the table and sinking into a chair. He looked disoriented and sounded preoccupied.

Carol poured two mugs of soup and passed one to Tony. 'I need to talk to you before the others get here. Tony, this isn't just an academic exercise any more. I think he took another one a few days before he killed Shaz.'

Suddenly she had all his attention. Whatever had been on his mind when he'd walked through the door was thrust aside and his dark blue eyes burned into hers. 'Evidence?' he demanded.

'I had a hunch, so I put out a Misper request nationwide. I got a call this afternoon from Derbyshire. Donna Doyle. Aged fourteen. From Glossop. About five miles from the end of the M57.' Carol gave him a copy of the fax the local CID had sent her. 'The mother put this flyer together because the police weren't terribly worried. The usual pattern, you see. She left the house to go to school in the morning, with an excuse for not being home until late. Her best clothes were missing. Premeditated runaway, case not so much closed as discreetly ignored. But I had a chat with the WPC who interviewed the mother before they lost interest. I didn't lead her; she volunteered that a couple of nights before she went missing, Donna had been out with one of her friends at a charity do where Jacko Vance was the guest of honour.'

'Shit,' Tony exhaled. 'Carol, depending on what he does with them, she could still be alive.'

'I didn't even want to think it.'

'It's possible. If he keeps them before he kills them – and we know a lot of serial offenders do that for the power charge it gives them – chances are he won't have risked going near her since he murdered Shaz. Christ, we've got to find a way to locate his killing ground. And soon.' They looked at each other with the constricting realization that another life could depend on how well they did their jobs. 'He's got a cottage in Northumberland,' Tony said.

'He's not going to be doing it on his own doorstep,' Carol objected.

'Probably not, but I wouldn't mind betting that his killing ground is a short drive from there. What have the team got?' he said grimly.

Carol glanced up at the clock. 'I don't know. They're due here any minute. They were meeting in Leeds and coming on together. They've all checked in, and it sounds like we've hit a lot of pay dirt.'

'Good.' Before he could say more, they both heard the sound of an engine labouring up the hill to the cottage. 'Here comes the cavalry, by the sounds of it.'

Carol opened the door and the trio trooped in, all looking remarkably pleased with themselves. They piled into chairs round the table, pulling off jackets and coats and dumping them on the floor, eager to begin. Tony ran a hand through his hair and said, 'We think he took a girl just before he killed Shaz. She could still be alive.' It gave him no pleasure to watch the light bleed out of their eyes, to see their faces change from the glow of satisfaction to the pinched pale of anxiety. 'Carol?'

Carol relayed the information she'd already given Tony, while he went to the kitchen and poured out the coffee he'd smelled brewing. When he returned, he said, 'We're not going to have the luxury of time to draw out a detailed profile and brainstorm all the elements of it. We're going to have to go hell for leather to get evidence and do what we can to save another life. So. Let's hear how we've all been doing. Kay, why don't you kick off?'

Succinctly, Kay reported on her interviews with the bereft parents. 'The bottom line is that they're all telling the same story. There are no significant discrepancies, either with what they originally told the police, or with each other's version of events. I managed to pick up a photograph of one of the girls with Jacko Vance, and I have established that they all went to events in their local area within a few days of their disappearance. But no stronger connection than that. Sorry.'

'You've nothing to apologize for,' Tony said. 'You did a great job. It can't have been easy, getting this much out of people who are still suffering because their child is on the missing list. The picture is helpful, too, because we can tie that down very specifically. Good job, Kay. Simon?'

'Thanks to Carol, I was able to track down the fiancée who chucked Jacko after his accident. If you remember, Shaz put forward the theory it was that emotional event, coupled with the shock of his accident, that tipped him over the edge into killing. Well, from what I heard, he maybe didn't have that far to fall.

'According to Jillie Woodrow, there was nothing normal about Jacko's bedroom habits. Right from the start of their sex life, he had to be in control. She was supposed to be passive and adoring. He hated her touching him sexually and, on occasion, he actually slapped her for laying hands on him. He became more interested in S&M pornography and wanted her to act out fantasies from magazines and books and from his own imagination. She didn't mind being tied up, she says, and she didn't much mind the spanking or the whipping, but when he started on the hot candle wax and the nipple clamps and the outsize vibrators, she drew the line.' He glanced down at the brief notes he'd made to ensure he got through his report without missing out anything crucial.

'She reckons that somewhere around the time his athletics career took off and he started banking big money, he began going to prostitutes. Nothing seedy, nothing low rent or street corner. From what he let slip, she thinks he had a couple of expensive call girls that he used, women who would either go along with the more extreme stuff that he wanted, or else they'd lay on the kind of lassies that it didn't matter if he messed up. Junkies, that sort of thing. According to Jillie, she was desperate to get out, but she was terrified of how he'd react. Outside the bedroom, he was the perfect partner. Solicitous, kind, generous, but incredibly possessive. So, after the accident, she grabbed the chance with both hands. She figured if she told him while he was in the hospital, he wouldn't be able to react. And he'd be stuck in there long enough to cool down and get over her.' Simon looked up and was surprised by how grim Tony looked.

'And we all know what happened next, don't we?' Tony said. 'Micky Morgan. The marriage of convenience.'

The faces around the table went from incomprehension to shocked amazement as he filled them in on what he'd heard first from Chris Devine and then from Micky herself. 'So we're seeing some fascinatingly aberrant behaviour here,' he said. 'Still hard to stand anything up that a senior officer would stake his arrest record on, but we know now, don't we?' They didn't have to say anything. The answer was in their eyes.

'There's more,' Simon said, launching into Harold Adams's tale.

'Man, the more we find out, the more incredible it is that Jack the Lad is still walking the streets,' Leon sighed, lighting his third cigarette since he'd walked in. 'Wait till you hear what I've dug up.' He passed on the meagre information he'd obtained from Jimmy Linden in a matter of minutes. 'Then he told me about this retired journo, Mike McGowan. This guy has forgotten more about sport than we'll ever know. He's got archives the British Library would kill for. I tell you, it took me half the night to get through the stuff he's got on Jack the Lad. And then I found this.'

With a flourish, Leon produced a brittle clipping and five photocopies of the article. It came from the *Manchester Evening News* and dealt with the murder of Barbara Fenwick. Emphasized in yellow highlighter, one paragraph stood out. '"Barbara was no party girl, according to her friends. Her last Saturday night out was typical. She was one of a group who went to a disco where sports hero Jacko Vance was making a charity appearance." This was just fourteen weeks after the accident,' Leon pointed out.

'He didn't hang about, did he? Got stuck right into the charity work,' Simon said.

'Well, we never doubted that he was driven,' Tony commented. 'So, is there any evidence that Vance actually met this girl?'

'The high point of her night out was getting his autograph.' Leon passed round copies of the summary he'd prepared from the police evidence store. 'They wouldn't let me photocopy the files, so I had to do this. I reckon she was his first victim,' he said confidently.

'And I reckon you're right,' Tony breathed. 'Oh, this is good, Leon, this is really good. He got better after this. My God, those hillwalkers must practically have stumbled over him. Look, it says they saw what they thought was a Land Rover heading off down the track just after they came over the ridge. Jack the Lad got a fright. He realized he needed a proper killing ground, a place where he wasn't going to be disturbed. We think that might be in Northumberland, by the way. Near his cottage. But without more information . . .' He rubbed his hands over his face. 'A twelve-year-old case, though. Where's the evidence?'

Leon looked slightly downcast. 'They don't know. They moved all the unsolved stuff to a new location about five years ago, and all the forensics on this case have either got lost or misfiled. Not that there was much, according to the abstract. No prints, no body fluids. Some tyre tracks, but that's no use a dozen years on.'

'The investigating officers. That's who we need to talk to. But before we discuss what comes next, I'd better tell you what I've come up with. It's pretty meagre compared to the huge strides you three have taken, but it does give us a handy chunk of circumstantial evidence.' Tony opened his folder and fanned out an array of photographs. 'I've done the rounds of the zealots. I have to say it was very like being back working in a secure mental hospital. At the risk of baffling you with professional jargon, they're all a few bricks short of a wall. However, after enduring the histories of their assorted obsessions with Jacko Vance, what we've got is a selection of photographs of Jacko taken at events where we know our putative victims were also present. Four of the pics put him next or near to one of our missing girls. In another five or six, it's possible that the girl in the picture is one of ours, but by no means certain without computer enhancement.' He leaned over and began carving himself a chunk of bread.

'With Kay's pick-ups, that makes five. We've got an overlap,' Carol said.

'I don't suppose it's enough to start an official investigation?' Tony asked without hope. He started to slice some cheese.

Carol pulled a face. 'The trouble is, there's no connection to my patch. If one of these girls had disappeared from East Yorkshire, I'd be willing to have a go at getting something moving, but I can't find one. Even so, I don't know where we could take any investigation. All we've got is highly circumstantial; it's nowhere near enough to bring him in for questioning, never mind a search warrant.'

'So you don't reckon we could convince West Yorkshire to take another look at Vance, even with this much?' Kay asked.

Simon snorted. 'Are you kidding? Given what they think about me? Every time I see a cop car on the road, I start sweating. Anything we come up with is tainted because they're convinced I'm the killer and you're protecting me. I don't think they're going to believe a word we say.'

'Point taken,' Kay said.

'What we need is a witness who saw him with Shaz after she's supposed to have left his house. Ideally, someone who saw them in Leeds,' Leon suggested.

'Ideally, a bishop of the Church of England,' Carol said cynically. 'Don't forget, it has to be somebody whose word would stand up against the people's champion.'

The hand that was cutting the cheese slipped and Tony sliced the edge off his index finger. He jumped to his feet, blood dripping from the wound. 'Shit, fuck and God damn it,' he exploded. He thrust his finger into his mouth and sucked.

Carol grabbed the paper napkin wrapped round the Thermos to catch drips and bandaged it round his finger, gripping it tightly. 'Klutz,' she said briskly.

'It was your fault,' he said, subsiding into the chair.

'My fault?'

'What you said. About unimpeachable witnesses.'

'Yes?'

'The camera doesn't lie, right?'

'Depends if it's digital or not,' Carol said ironically.

'Don't be difficult. I'm talking cameras that are already used to convict criminals.'

'What?'

'Motorway cameras, Carol. Motorway cameras.'

Leon snorted in derision. 'Don't tell us you've fallen for that one?'

'What?' Tony said, puzzled.

'Great myths of our time number forty-seven. Motorway cameras catch villains. Not.' Leon leaned back in his chair, his cynical swagger full on.

'What do you mean? I've seen those programmes on TV, police videos of car chases. And what about all those speeding convictions on the back of still photographs from the motorway cameras?' Tony demanded indignantly.

Carol sighed. 'The cameras operate perfectly. But only in certain situations. That's what Leon's getting at. The still cameras only snap vehicles travelling well in excess of the speed limit. They're not going to flicker a shutter at much under ninety. And the videos are only actually turned on if there's an incident in progress or a traffic-flow problem. The rest of the time, they're just not running. And even when they are, you'd need state-of-the-art enhancement software to get anything convincing from them.'

'Wouldn't your brother know somebody?' Simon asked. 'I thought he was some sort of computer whizz kid.'

'Well, yes, but we haven't got anything to show him yet, and we're not likely to have,' Carol objected.

'But I thought when Manchester city centre got blown to bits by the IRA, the police backtracked the route the bombers' van took using the motorway cameras?' Tony said persistent to the last.

Kay shook her head. 'They thought they might have been able to pick it up on the photos of the speeders, but there wasn't enough detail . . .' Her voice tailed off and her face lit up.

'What is it?' Carol asked.

'Private CCTV videos,' she breathed. 'Remember? Greater Manchester Police put out an appeal for any garages or food outlets with CCTV surveillance on possible routes to submit their recordings. We won't get Vance or Shaz on motorway surveillance, but we'll get them wherever they stopped for petrol. Logically, Shaz would have filled up before she left Leeds. She'd have got all the way to London, but she'd not have made it all the way back on a single tank. And the chances are, she would have used a motorway service area rather than come off the motorway just for petrol.'

'And you lot can get access to these tapes?'

Carol groaned. 'It won't be access that's the problem. Most companies are happy to co-operate. Usually they don't even bother asking what it's all in aid of. It's the prospect of all those hours of jerky video. I'm getting a migraine just at the thought of it.'

Tony cleared his throat. 'Actually, Carol, I was going to suggest that you come with me to talk to the police officers who investigated Barbara Fenwick's murder.' He gave an apologetic smile to the other three. Simon and Kay looked merely disappointed, but Leon looked mutinous. 'I'm sorry, but this needs a senior officer to look good. And it needs to be small scale. We don't want to give these guys the hump. We want to avoid giving the impression that they did a lousy job and we're the crack troops coming in to clear up the mess. This is one for me and Carol. What I'd like you to do is divide up the motorway and check out all these service station cameras.' Now all three looked deeply fed up. 'I'd do it myself if I could,' Tony said sympathetically. 'But this is one for the warrant card.'

Inarticulate grumbling came from round the table. 'We know,' Simon said scathingly.

'And Donna Doyle might still be alive,' Carol pointed out.

The trio of detective constables stared at each other, eyes dark and serious. Leon nodded slowly. 'And even if she isn't, the next one is.'

One of the first lessons Tony Hill had learned as a profiler was that preparation was never wasted. It was hard for him and Carol to work up enthusiasm in the stacks of a dusty police document store, but they both knew how important it was to stay alert as they combed the files. The drudgery of poring over every available piece of information was as vital to painting an accurate picture of a killer as the flair that some people seemed naturally to bring to the job. Plodding alone never made a good profiler, but neither did flashy charisma. He'd been happy to be proved wrong about Leon. His superficial approach to the training exercise had confirmed all Tony's prejudices about his peacock display. But either he'd learned from the humiliation of being shown up in front of the rest of the team or else he was one of the ones who could only ever do it for real. Either way, Tony thought as he and Carol ploughed the identical furrow a day later, he couldn't fault the job he'd done.

At the end of a couple of hours, they leaned back in their seats almost simultaneously. 'Looks like Leon didn't miss a thing,' Tony said.

'Looks that way. But if we're going to talk to the man who ran the case, we needed to know that for ourselves.'

'I really appreciate your help in this, Carol,' he said quietly, knocking the papers into a neat pile. 'You didn't have to stick your neck out.'

One corner of her mouth twisted in what might have been a smile or a trace of pain. 'I did, you know,' was all she said. What she didn't say was that they both knew she would never be able to turn her back on his need, personal or professional. And that she also knew the feeling was mutual, provided they both stayed within the limits they seemed to have evolved to keep themselves whole.

'You're sure you can spare the time away from your arson investigation?' he asked, understanding what lay unspoken.

She stacked papers in a file box. 'If anything's going

to happen, it'll happen at night. That may be the price you have to pay for crashing in my spare room.'

'I think I can just about afford that,' he said wryly. He followed her back to the counter where they returned the files to a uniformed PC who looked like his thirty was approaching but not fast enough for him.

Carol gave him her best smile. 'The officer in charge of this inquiry – Detective Superintendent Scott? I take it he's retired now?'

'Finished up ten years ago,' the man said, hefting the heavy boxes and heading for the distant shelves where they had come from.

'I don't suppose you know where I could find him?' Carol called to his retreating back.

His voice floated back, muffled by the shelves. 'He lives out Buxton way. Place called Countess Sterndale. There's only three houses.'

It took a few minutes to obtain directions to Countess Sterndale, which didn't appear on their map, and another thirty-five to drive there. 'He wasn't lying, then,' Tony said at the end of the single-track road that concluded in a tree-lined loop round a circle of grass. A battered Queen Anne manor house faced them and over to their left was a pair of long, low cottages with heavy slate roofs and thick limestone walls. 'Which one, d'you reckon?'

Carol shrugged. 'Not the manor, unless he was on the take. Eeny meeny, miny mo . . .' She pointed to the right-hand cottage.

As they walked across the grass, Tony said, 'You take the lead. He'll open up more easily to a copper than a mumbo jumbo man.'

'Even though I'm a woman?' Carol asked ironically.

'You have a point. Play it as it lays.' He opened a smartly painted gate which swung back silently. The path was herringbone brick, not a single weed in the interstices. Tony raised the black iron knocker and let it fall. The sound echoed behind the door. As it died away, heavy footsteps approached and the door opened to reveal a broad man with iron grey hair brilliantined in a side parting and a toothbrush moustache. He looked like a forties matinee idol put out to grass, Carol thought, stifling a smile. 'I'm sorry to trouble you, but we're looking for ex-Detective Superintendent Scott,' she said.

'I'm Gordon Scott,' he said. 'And you are?'

This was where it got difficult. 'DCI Carol Jordan, sir. East Yorkshire Police. And this is Dr Tony Hill from the National Profiling Task Force.' To her surprise, Scott's face lit up with delight.

'Is this to do with Barbara Fenwick?' he said eagerly.

Dismayed, Carol looked helplessly at Tony. 'What makes you say that?' he asked.

A laugh rumbled in his chest. 'I might have been out of the game for ten years, but when three people in two days turn up to look at the files of my only unsolved murder, somebody picks up the phone. Come in, come in.' He ushered them into a comfortable sitting room, ducking to avoid cracking his head on the door frame. The room felt lived in, with magazines and books in unruly piles by the pair of armchairs that faced each other across the beamed fireplace. Scott waved them into the chairs. 'How about a drink? My wife's off doing the shopping in Buxton, but I can just about manage tea. Or a beer?'

'A beer would be great,' Tony said, reluctant to wait while Scott brewed tea. Carol nodded agreement and moments later he returned with three cans of Boddington's.

Scott moved a large ginger cat and settled his bulky

frame in the window seat, reducing the light in the room by at least half. He popped the top of his beer, but before he drank, he launched into speech. 'I was that glad when I heard you were looking at Barbara Fenwick's murder. I worried at that case for the best part of two years. It kept me awake nights. I'll never forget the look on her mother's face when I arrived with the news we'd found the body. It still haunts me. I always thought the answer was out there, we just didn't have what it took to get it. So when I got the call and I heard it was the profiling task force . . . well, I have to say, my hopes have been raised. What's drawn you to Barbara?'

Tony decided to take advantage of Scott's enthusiasm and offer him frankness. 'This is a somewhat unorthodox investigation,' he began. 'You may have read about the murder of one of my squad.'

Scott nodded his big head sadly. 'Aye, I saw. You have my sympathies.'

'What you won't have read is that she was working on a theory that there is an unsuspected serial killer of teenage girls on the loose and that he's been doing it for a long time. It started off as a classroom exercise, but Shaz couldn't sit on it. My team and I think that's why she was killed. Unfortunately, West Yorkshire Police don't agree. The main reason for that is the person Shaz put in the frame.' He glanced at Carol, ready for some seemingly official back-up.

'There is a significant amount of circumstantial evidence that points to Jacko Vance,' she said baldly.

Scott's eyebrows climbed. 'The telly man?' He let out a soft whistle and his hand went automatically to the cat, stroking its head rhythmically. 'I'm not surprised they didn't want to know. So how does this connect to Barbara Fenwick?'

Carol outlined how Leon's researches had turned up

the clipping that had brought them to Gordon Scott's case files. When she had finished, Tony said, 'What we hoped was that there was stuff that never made it on to paper. I know from working with Carol what it's like on a murder squad. You have a feeling in your water, hunches that you never confide to anybody except your partner, never mind put in a memo. We wondered what the gut feelings were among the officers who actually worked the case.'

Scott took a long draught of beer. 'Of course you did. And quite right, too. The trouble is, there's bugger all I can tell you. A couple of times, we got the wrong smell off some of the nonces we had in for questioning, but it was always something else that they were wound up about. To be honest, the gut feeling on our team was total frustration. We just could not get a handle on the bugger. He seemed to have come out of nowhere and vanished the same way. We ended up convinced it was someone from off our patch who'd stumbled across the girl when she was doing a routine bunk off school. And that would sort of fit in with your idea, wouldn't it?'

'Broadly, except that we think he sets it up a lot more carefully than that,' Tony said. 'Oh well, it was worth a try.'

'Sir, there didn't seem to be a lot of forensic evidence,' Carol prompted.

'No. That set us back a bit. Truth to tell, I'd no experience of a sex offender who took that kind of forensic care. Mostly they're hot-headed, spur of the moment, leave all sorts of traces, go home covered in mud and blood. But there was almost nothing to work off. The only distinctive thing was the crushed arm, according to the pathologist. She wouldn't stick her neck out on paper, but she had this notion that the girl's arm had been crushed in a vice.'

The thought of such cold-blooded torture sent a shiver of unwelcome echoes through Tony's stomach. 'Ah,' he said.

Scott struck his forehead with the heel of his hand. 'Of course! Vance lost his arm, didn't he? He was going for the Olympics and he lost his arm. Perfect sense, why didn't we think of something like that at the time? God, what an idiot I am!'

'There's no reason why you should have considered it,' Tony said, wishing he meant it, wondering how many lives might have been saved if a psychologist had been brought in all those years ago.

'Is the pathologist still working?' Carol asked, as ever straight to the point.

'She's a professor now at one of the London teaching hospitals. I've got her card somewhere,' Scott said, getting to his feet and lumbering out of the room. 'God, why didn't I think more about the arm?'

'It's not his fault, Tony,' Carol said.

'I know. I sometimes wonder how many more people have to die before everybody recognizes psychologists aren't just witch doctors,' he said. 'Listen, Carol, in the interests of speed, I think we should get Chris Devine to follow up on this pathologist. She's desperate to help, and she's got the experience to know the kind of things she should be looking for. What do you say?'

'I think that's a good idea. To tell you the truth, I was dreading telling you that I couldn't go to London now. I need to be around tonight in case the arsonist decides to have a go.'

He smiled. 'I remembered.' It was probably the first time in his career as a profiler that something outside the case obsessing him had impinged. That was the trouble with working with Carol Jordan. She affected him in ways no one else ever had. When he didn't see her, he could conveniently forget that. Working this closely, it was impossible to ignore. He gave her a grave smile. 'I'm too scared of upsetting John Brandon to let you chance blowing the arson collar,' he lied.

'I know.' She detected the lie, but did not show it. It was neither the time nor the place for some kinds of truth.

Kay had lost count. She couldn't remember if this was the seventh or the eighth set of videos she'd inspected. Having drawn the short straw in the division of the sites, she'd set off on the M1 from Leeds before dawn and driven all the way to London. Then she turned the car round and retraced her journey, stopping at every service area she came to. Now it was late afternoon and she was sitting in yet another scruffy office, stuffy with stale sweat and smoke, watching jerky images dancing in front of her as she fast-forwarded through the tapes. She was awash with bad coffee, her mouth still slimy and fat-flavoured from the long ago breakfast at Scratchwood Services. Her eyes were gritty and tired, and she wished she was anywhere else.

At least they'd managed to narrow the time frame down. They reckoned the earliest Shaz or Vance could possibly have hit the first northbound services on the motorway was eleven in the morning, the latest seven at night. Adjusting the times forward for each service area wasn't difficult.

The tapes took much less running time than real time, since, rather than taping continuously, the cameras only took a certain number of still frames per second. Even so, she'd spent hours working her way through the recordings, fast-forwarding until she saw either a black Volkswagen Golf or one of the cars registered to Jacko Vance – a silver Mercedes convertible or a Land Rover.

The Golf was common enough to cause frequent pauses, the other cars turning up less often.

She thought she was faster now than when she'd started. Her eyes were in tune with what she was searching for, though she feared she was beginning to flag and worried that might make her miss something crucial. Forcing herself to concentrate, Kay flicked forward until the familiar black pram-like shape of another Golf appeared. She slowed to normal speed, then almost at once she registered that the driver was a male with grey hair sticking out from under a baseball cap rather than either of her expected targets so her finger moved towards the fast-forward button. Then, suddenly, it swerved to the pause button as she noticed that there was something odd about the man.

But the first thing that struck her on closer scrutiny had nothing to do with the person who'd climbed out of the driver's seat and headed for the petrol pump. What Kay spotted was quite different. Although the car was sitting at an awkward angle to the pumps, she could make out the last two letters of the number plate. They were identical to the final digits of Shaz's registration.

'Ah, shit,' she breathed softly. She rewound the tape and watched it again. This time she identified what had caught her eye about the driver. He was awkwardly left-handed, to the point where he hardly used his right arm at all. Just as Jacko Vance would inevitably be if he were using equipment that wasn't specially designed to accommodate his disability.

Kay studied the tape a few more times. It wasn't easy to make out the man's features, but she wouldn't mind betting that Carol Jordan would know someone who could help them over that particular hurdle. Before the night was over, they'd have something on Jacko Vance that even a team of highly paid defence lawyers wouldn't be able to get him out of. And it would be down to her, the best tribute she could pay to a woman who had been on the way to becoming a friend.

She flipped open her mobile phone and called Carol. 'Carol? It's Kay. I think I might have something your brother would like to see . . .'

It wasn't that Chris Devine objected to pathologists having a day off. What pissed her off royally was that this particular pathologist spent her free time sitting in the pouring rain in the middle of nowhere waiting for a glimpse of some bloody stupid bird that was supposed to be in Norway but had managed to get lost. There was nothing clever about getting lost, Chris muttered as she felt more rain slide between her neck and her collar. Bloody Essex, she thought bitterly.

She sheltered from the gusting easterly so she could take another look at the rough map the bird warden had sketched out for her. She couldn't be far away now. Why did these bloody hides have to be so inconspicuous? Why didn't they just make them look like her nan's house? She had more bloody birds in her back garden than Chris had seen all afternoon on the marshes. The birds were too flaming sensible to come out on a day like this, she grumbled as she stuffed the map back in her pocket and set off round the edge of the copse.

She almost missed the hide, so well was it camouflaged. Chris pulled back the wooden door and forced the scowl from her face. 'Sorry to butt in,' she said to the three people cramped inside, grateful that her head at least was out of the wind. 'Is one of you Professor Stewart?' She hoped she was in the right place; it was impossible to tell even genders inside waxed jackets, woolly scarves and thermal hats.

A gloved hand rose. 'I'm Liz Stewart,' one of the figures said. 'What's going on?'

Chris sighed with relief. 'Detective Sergeant Devine, Metropolitan Police. I wonder if I could have a word?'

The woman shook her head. 'I'm not on call,' she said, her Scottish accent growing stronger in indignation.

'I appreciate that. But it is rather urgent.' Chris unobtrusively edged the door wider so the wind could whip inside the rickety structure.

'Oh, for God's sake, Liz, go and see what the woman wants,' an irritated male voice said from under one of the other hats. 'We're not going to see anything worthwhile at all if you two stand there screaming like fishwives.'

The grudging professor squeezed past the other two and followed Chris outside. 'There's some shelter under the trees,' Professor Stewart said, pushing past her and scrambling through the undergrowth until they were out of reach of most of the weather. In the clearing, Chris could see she was a sharp-featured forty-something with clear amber eyes like a hawk. 'Now, what is all this about?' she demanded.

'You worked a case twelve years ago. An unsolved murder of a teenage girl in Manchester, Barbara Fenwick. Do you remember it?'

'The girl with the crushed arm?'

'That's the one. The case has cropped up in connection with another investigation. We think we're looking at a serial killer, and it's possible that Barbara Fenwick is the only one of his victims where the body's turned up. Which makes your postmortem pretty significant.'

'Which it will still be on Monday morning,' the professor said briskly.

'Yeah, but the girl we think he's holding might not make it that long,' Chris said.

'Ah. You'd better fire away then, Sergeant.'

'Retired Superintendent Scott told my colleagues that you had thought, but didn't put in your report, that the arm looked like it might have been crushed deliberately in something like a vice rather than accidentally, is that right?'

'That was my opinion, but it was only speculation. Not the sort of fanciful thing I'd put in a formal post-mortem report unless I had considerably stronger grounds for my belief,' she said repressively.

'But if you were pressed, you'd say that?'

'If I were asked directly if it were possible, yes, I'd have to agree.'

'Was there anything else you didn't write down because it was "fanciful"?' Chris asked.

'Not that I can think of.'

'I know you said you didn't put it in your formal report, but would you have put something in your notes to that effect?'

'Oh yes,' the professor said, as if it were the most natural thing in the world. 'That way, if it became important later, the prosecution could introduce it more readily.'

Chris closed her eyes momentarily in a short prayer. 'And have you still got your notes?'

'Of course. In fact, I've got something even better than that.'

The cafe of the motorway services at Hartshead Moor on the M62 had never been anyone's idea of a good Saturday night out, which made it perfect for their purposes. The ad hoc investigative team was now augmented by Chris Devine, who had slotted in as if she'd always been there. Already, it seemed she and Carol were about to sign up as blood sisters, both because of their common experiences in the Job and because they were the nearest thing the team had to senior officers.

The group had colonized a distant corner with no prospect of being overheard or disturbed since it was right on the border of the smoking area. Leon, dispirited at drawing a blank, was buoyed up by Kay's results. But Simon's face was showing signs of strain inevitable in a man whose name was on the wanted list, turned on by the very group who had given him a sense of community. Tony wondered how long the younger man could stand it without his judgement slipping dangerously.

Carol cut into his thoughts. 'I've arranged for Kay to meet a friend of my brother who can enhance these pictures for us, to cut the margin of doubt to the bone.'

'You're not coming along?' Kay asked, looking slightly worried.

'Carol has responsibilities in East Yorkshire tonight,' Tony said. 'Is that a problem, Kay?'

She looked embarrassed. 'Not a problem, not as such. It's just . . . well, I don't know this bloke, and he's doing this as a favour, right?'

'That's right,' Carol said. 'Michael says he owes him.'

'It's just that . . . well, if I want to push a bit harder, you know, if I don't think he's going to the max because he can't be bothered, or it's going to cost too much, I can't actually lean on him the way Carol could.'

'She's got a point,' Chris affirmed from the smoking table she was occupying with Leon. 'She's not even the one who's asked for the favour. And it's Saturday night. Even computer nerds must have something better to do than a favour for somebody who can't be bothered to turn up in person. That'll be how it looks. I think Carol should be there.'

Carol stirred her sludgy coffee. 'You're right. I can't fault your logic. But I can't afford to be off my patch tonight.' She glanced at her watch and made rapid calculations.

'No, Carol,' Tony said hopelessly, knowing already he was wasting his breath.

'If we left now ... we could be there by nine ... I could be back in Seaford by one at the latest. And nothing ever happens before then ...' Coming to a decision, Carol grabbed her coat and bag. 'All right. Come on, Kay, we're off.' As they walked towards the door with Kay scrambling to catch up, Carol turned. 'Chris – good hunting.'

'So what do we do now?' Leon demanded aggressively, lighting another cigarette from the butt of the one he'd been smoking. 'I feel like I've wasted a whole day fucking about with motorway cameras. I want to be doing something worthwhile, you know?'

Tony was glad Chris Devine had come to join them; he had a feeling he was going to have to rely on her experience now the others were starting to fray round the edges. 'Nobody's been wasting their time, Leon. We've come a long way today,' he said calmly. 'We need to build on that. The information Chris has got from the pathologist is a big step forward. But on its own, it's still not worth a whole lot. He profiles right. Everything we learn about him puts another tick in the box. But we're still in the realms of supposition.'

'Even with a victim with a crushed right arm?' Simon asked incredulously. 'Come on, that's got to be a clincher. What more do we need, for God's sake?'

'Given the kind of lawyers Jack the Lad is going to be able to afford, we'd be laughed out of court – always supposing we got that far,' Tony said. 'I'm sorry, but that's the way it is.'

'The crushed arm is good stuff,' Chris said. 'But it's not a lot of use as an isolated case. What we need is something to compare it with. Only so far there haven't been any bodies, right?' The others nodded. 'But you reckon he'd got another one just before Shaz fronted him up? Well then, chances are he'd started on her but he hadn't finished. So we find her, we tie her to him, and we've got him. Anything wrong with that?'

'No, except we don't know where he keeps them before he kills them,' Tony said.

'Course we don't. Or do we?'

If they'd been dogs, their ears would have pricked up. 'Go on,' Tony encouraged her.

'The great thing about being a dyke my age is that when I was getting into the scene, everyone who had a job was in the closet. Now, half the women I used to drink with are bosses all over the shop. One of them just happens be a partner in the agency that handles Jacko's publicity.' She pulled out a sheaf of fax paper from inside her jacket. 'Jacko's schedule for the last six weeks. Now, unless he's Superman or his wife is in on this, there's only one area of the country he could possibly be keeping this kid.' She leaned back and watched them cotton on to what had leapt out at her.

Tony ran his hand through his hair. 'I know he's got a cottage up there. But it's a huge area. How can we narrow it down?'

'He could be using his own place,' Leon said.

'Yeah,' Simon butted in eagerly. 'Let's get up there, take a look at this hideaway.'

'I don't know,' Chris said. 'He's been so careful about everything else, I can't believe he'd do something so risky.'

'Where's the risk?' Tony demanded. 'He brings the girls there under cover of darkness, they're never seen or heard from again. There's never a trace of the bodies. But Jack the Lad does volunteer work at the hospital in Newcastle. They must have an incinerator. He's always pushing the image of himself as being a man with the common touch. I'd guess he regularly pops down to the boiler room, having a natter with the lads. And if he helps them load the incinerator from time to time, well, who's going to notice the extra bag of body parts?'

A chilled silence fell over the group. Tony scratched the stubble on his chin. 'I should have worked this out before now. He's a control freak. The only killing ground he'd trust would be one he had total control over.'

'So let's go.' Simon said, pushing his cup away and reaching for his jacket.

'No,' Tony said firmly. 'Simon, this is not the time for Action Man tactics. We need to plan carefully here. We can't just go charging in mob-handed and hope what we find justifies the action. His lawyers would make mincemeat of us. We need to have a strategy.'

'That's easy for you to say, man,' Leon said. 'You're not the one the cops are looking to arrest. You can sleep in your own bed at night. Simon needs this to be sorted.'

'All right, all right,' Chris said mildly. 'It wouldn't hurt to do a trawl locally with pictures of Donna Doyle. Looking at his timetable, she must have got there under her own steam. I bet he sends them up on the train or the coach. We need to blitz the bus terminal and the train station, talk to the staff. And the locals. If there's a small local station near to Jack the Lad's hideaway, somebody might have seen her getting off the train.'

Simon stood up, dark eyes burning. 'So what are we waiting for?'

'No point in hitting it before morning,' Chris said.

'It's a two and a half hour drive from here. We're not doing anything better, are we? Let's go now, find a cheap hotel and get cracking first thing in the morning. You up for it, Leon?'

Leon stubbed out his cigarette. 'Long as I don't have to go in your car. What're you driving, Chris?'

'You wouldn't like my music. We'll take all the cars. OK, Tony?'

'OK. Provided you stay well away from his house. I have your word on that, Chris?'

'You got my word, Tony.'

'That go for you two? Bearing in mind Chris is technically your senior officer?'

Leon scowled but gave a grudging nod. Simon, too, conceded. 'OK. I probably shouldn't be making the decisions anyway.'

'What've you got planned, Tony?' Chris asked.

'I'm going home to draw up a full profile based on all we know now. I can't say I blame you for wanting to hare off up the A1, but if Carol and Kay come back with the goods, I'm proposing we go to West Yorkshire first thing in the morning and persuade them to make this official. So, nothing except local inquiries until we've spoken. OK?'

Chris nodded sombrely. 'Trust me, Tony. Shaz meant too much to me to risk fucking this up.'

If she'd been trying to take the gung-ho madness out of the two male officers' eyes, she succeeded. Even Leon stopped bouncing on the balls of his feet. 'I hadn't forgotten that,' Tony said. 'Or how much she wanted to catch Jack the Lad.'

'I know,' Chris said. 'Fucking mad bitch, she'd have loved this.'

*

Once upon a time she'd understood most of what there was to know about computers, Carol thought wistfully. Back around 1989, she was almost as much of a whizz with CP/M and DOS as her brother. But she'd gone into the police force and it had eaten up her life. While she'd been getting to grips with the Police and Criminal Evidence Act, Michael had been assimilating software and hardware that often moved forward on a daily basis. Now she was the one-eyed woman in the kingdom of 20/20 vision. She knew enough to crunch numbers and process words, to retrieve lost files from limbo and to rewrite boot files so that a reluctant machine could be persuaded to talk to its user. But ten minutes with her brother and his mate Donny and she knew that, these days, this was the culinary equivalent of being able to boil a kettle. From the look on Kay's face, it wasn't any better for her. It was just as well she'd come along, Carol thought. At least she had enough knowledge to know when the boys were spinning off into a world of their own and the authority to drag them back to the job in hand.

The two men sitting in front of a computer screen the size of a pub TV muttered to each other incomprehensibly about video drivers, local buses and smart caches. Carol knew what the words meant, but she couldn't connect them to anything they were doing with keyboard and mouse. Donny, Michael had told her, was the best man in the north when it came to computer-enhancing photographs or video stills. And he just happened to work in the same building where Michael's software company had its suite of offices. And, in spite of Chris's convictions, he was so devoid of a life that he was thrilled to be dragged away from *The X Files* and a microwave dinner to show off his toys.

Carol and Kay looked over their shoulders at the

screen. Donny had already done everything he could with the number plate, yielding confirmation of the last two letters and a strong probability of a match with the third. Now he was working on the driver. He'd already tweaked and twiddled with some full-length shots of the man, pronouncing himself finally satisfied with one and printing out a couple of colour copies for the two women to pore over. The more Carol looked, the more convinced she was that under the Nike baseball cap and behind the aviator glasses, Jacko Vance was peeking out at her. 'What do you think?' she asked Kay.

'I don't know if you'd pick him out of a line-up, but if you know who you're looking for, I think you can tell it's him.'

Now, without any prompting from them, Donny was working on a head and shoulders of the man who'd filled the Golf with petrol at lunchtime on the Saturday Shaz Bowman died. It was hard to find a good shot to work with because the peak of the cap shaded his face most of the time when he wasn't actually bending over the fuel tank. Only by advancing one frame at a time did Donny finally come up with a single shot where the man in the cap glanced swiftly up at the pump to check how much petrol he'd taken.

Watching Donny painstakingly improve the quality of the picture was agonizing. Carol couldn't keep her eyes off her watch, gripped with the knowledge that she should be elsewhere and if anything happened in Seaford she'd be in deep shit. The minutes crawled by while the powerful processor drove a search through the computer's massive memory for the next best alternative to the pixels on the screen. Although it was making more calculations per second than the human brain could comfortably comprehend, the computer seemed to Carol to take forever. At last, Donny turned away from the screen and pushed his own baseball cap back on his head. 'Best you're going to get,' he said. 'Funny, he looks familiar. Is he supposed to?'

'Can you print me off half a dozen copies?' Carol said. She felt mean ignoring his good-natured question, but it wasn't the time or place to tell Donny that, apart from cheeks that were undeniably too chubby, the face he'd recreated was that of the nation's favourite TV personality.

Michael was either quicker on the uptake or more familiar with the medium. 'He looks like Jacko Vance, that's what's got you confused, Donny,' he said innocently.

'Yeah, right, that dickhead,' Donny said, swinging round in his chair and blinking at the women. 'Fucking hell, shame it's not him you're going to arrest. You'd be doing the world a favour, getting that shit he does off the box. Sorry I couldn't get a better head shot, but there wasn't a lot to go on. Where did you say you got the tape from?'

'M1 services. Watford Gap,' Kay said.

'Yeah, right. Pity you weren't looking for your man in Leeds.'

'Leeds?' Carol leapt on the word. 'Why Leeds?'

''Cos that's where the state-of-the-art CCTV development company is. Seesee Visions. They are the total business. They think civil liberties is that posh but polite department store in London.' He laughed at his own bad joke. 'Double wicked fuckers, they are. You can't miss them. That sodding great smoked glass monolith just after the end of the motorway. You want somebody coming off the M1 at Leeds, they've got it taped.'

'What do you mean, somebody coming off at Leeds?' Carol's fingers were twitching with the desire to grab Donny by the shirt and make him get to the point.

Donny cast his eyes upwards as if he were tired of dealing with mental defectives. 'Right. History lesson. Nineteenth-century Britain. Little pockets of mains water supply, gas providers, railway companies. Gradually, they all linked up to make national utilities. With me so far?'

'And there's me thinking nerds knew nothing about the Victorian era apart from Charles Babbage,' Carol snapped. 'OK, Donny, we did the Industrial Revolution at school. Can we get to CCTV?'

'OK, OK, be chill. CCTV is kind of like the baby utilities were then. But soon it won't be. Soon we're going to have all these inner-city systems linking up with private security systems and motorway cameras and we're going to have a national network of CCTV. And these systems will be so finely tuned that they can recognize you or your wheels and if you're not supposed to be some place, then the big fuck-off security guards are gonna remove you. Like if you're a convicted shoplifter and Marks and Sparks don't want you hanging out in their food hall, or you're a known perv and your local launderette doesn't want you in there ogling the knickers –' He made a throat-cutting gesture.

'So what exactly has all this got to do with the M1?'

'Seesee Vision are the masters of the universe when it comes to leading-edge techno. And they test all their new gear on the traffic flow off the M1. Their stuff is so well developed they can give you a high-res picture of the drivers and the front-seat passengers, never mind baby stuff like number plates.' Donny shook his head in wonder. 'I went for a job there, but I didn't like it. You could tell it was seagull city.'

'Seagull city?' Carol asked faintly.

'The bosses fly in, do a lot of screaming, grab everything worth having, crap over everybody and fly out again. Not my scene.'

'Do you think they'd co-operate with me?'

'They'd wet their pants. They're desperate to make a big impression on your lot. When this national network finally creaks into being, they want to be in the driving seat. The company of choice.'

Carol looked at her watch. It was after ten. She should be heading back to Seaford, on the spot if her team had to swing into action. Besides, no one in authority would be at Seesee Vision at this time of night.

Donny spotted her glance and read her mind. 'There'll be somebody there this time of night, if that's what you're wondering. Give them a bell. You got nothing to lose.'

But Donna Doyle might, Carol thought, catching Kay's pleading look. And besides, Leeds was halfway between Manchester and Seaford. Her team were grown-ups. It wouldn't be the first time they'd had to think for themselves.

First, the victims. It was always the place to start. The problem here was to convince anyone that there were victims. It was always possible that they were wrong, Tony realized. They so badly wanted Shaz to have been right, they so desperately needed to be instrumental in putting a stop to the person who had killed her that they might all be deluding themselves about the value of the material they had uncovered. It was almost conceivable that the circumstantial evidence piling up against Jacko Vance was just that and no more.

But that way madness lay. Madness and the prospect of poor Simon being arrested as soon as he crossed the threshold of his own home. 'The victims,' Tony said. He stared at the laptop screen and started to type.

The first known victim in this putative cluster is Barbara Fenwick whose murder took place twelve years ago (see attached summary prepared by DC Leon Jackson for crime details). We can say with some degree of certainty that this was the first killing by this perpetrator since there is no previous record of this signature behaviour, namely the pulverizing of the lower right arm. This is clearly signature behaviour; there is no need to inflict such an injury in order to commit sexual assault and murder. It is extraneous, it is ritualistic and therefore it is safe to assume that it has particular significance for this offender. Given the ceremonial nature of this signature behaviour, it is likely that he has used the same implement to produce these injuries in all his killings; other victims could therefore be expected to display very similar disfigurement.

There is at least one other indication that this was a first murder. The killer had chosen what he thought was a sufficiently isolated and safe place to carry out his crime undisturbed, but he was in fact almost caught in the act. This will have frightened him considerably and he will have taken immediate steps to secure his future killing grounds. That he was successful in this is shown by the fact that no bodies have been recovered from his subsequent victims.

In the absence of bodies, what possible grounds can there be for assuming a serial offender?

He paused and referred back to the list of common features that Shaz had presented to the profiling team what felt like an age ago. The least he could do was make sure the work she'd left wasn't wasted. With a few changes and additions, he typed in the list then continued.

While two or three common features are to be expected with any such grouping, the number and congruence we can identify here is of far too high a level to be coincidental. Of particular importance is the degree of physical similarity between the victims. They could be sisters.

Perhaps more significantly, they could also be sisters of a woman called Jillie Woodrow as she looked fifteen or sixteen years ago, when she first became the earliest known lover of Jacko Vance, our prime suspect. It is not coincidence, in my opinion, that Vance was robbed of a brilliant athletic career when he lost his lower right arm in an accident that crushed it beyond hope of restoration.

Further, the date of the killing of Barbara Fenwick was a mere fourteen weeks after Jacko Vance's accident. For much of that time, he was in hospital recovering from his injuries and subsequently undergoing extensive physiotherapy. It was during this hospitalization that Jillie Woodrow took the opportunity to terminate what had become an increasingly oppressive and unwelcome relationship (see appended notes of interview with JW, conducted by DC Simon McNeill). The combined stress of these two events would be sufficient to trigger a sexual homicide in one who was predisposed to realize his sociopathic responses in violent behaviour.

He has never released his sexual impulses in a normal fashion since. His extremely high-profile marriage is a sham, his wife being a lesbian whose 'personal assistant' is in fact her lover and has been since before the wedding took place. Vance and his wife have never had sexual intercourse and his wife assumes he uses 'high-class call girls' to provide him with a sexual outlet. There is no suggestion that she has any suspicion of his homicidal activities.

When Vance's early life is set against the criteria that experience has demonstrated are common features among homicidally active sociopaths, a remarkable degree of commonality is obvious. We have witness interviews that attest to a difficult relationship with a rejecting mother, an often absent father whom the subject was desperate to impress, bullying of younger children, cruelty to animals and sadistic, controlling sexual behaviour, and evidence of powerful and perverse sexual fantasies. His sporting prowess can be identified as a massive overcompensation for the worthlessness he felt in every other area of his life, and the loss of that prowess as a devastating blow to his extremely fragile self-esteem.

In those circumstances, women would be the obvious victim gender. He would perceive his mother and subsequently his fiancée as having emasculated him. But he is far too intelligent to vent his rage on the obvious targets, and so he has assumed a series of surrogates. These are girls who bear a strong resemblance to Jillie Woodrow at the age when he first seduced her.

It should be borne in mind that captured serial killers have in the main been above average intelligence, in some cases well above. We should not therefore be surprised that uncaught and unsuspected serial offenders exist who are using their greater intelligence more effectively. Jacko Vance is, in my opinion, an example of this principle in action.

He leaned back in his chair. So much for the psychology. He'd have to draw up a more detailed table of corresponding preconditions, but that wouldn't take long. Added to the hard evidence he hoped Carol and

Kay would produce that night, he felt sure that there was enough material to make certain that within twelve hours, West Yorkshire would have started to take Jacko Vance seriously.

Detective Sergeant Tommy Taylor knew a pile of crap when he saw it. And surveilling part-time firemen was the biggest pile of crap he'd seen in a very long time. He'd spent the night before watching Raymond Watson, which in effect meant watching Raymond Watson's house. It wasn't as if it was packed with architectural detail to keep the mind active. A bog-standard terraced house with a pocket handkerchief front garden that boasted a tired rose bush contorted by the north-east winds into a shape some modern sculptors would have given their eye teeth to achieve. Flaked paintwork, scabby varnish on the front door.

Watson had come home at eleven the night before, after the last race at the dog track. There was no meeting tonight, so he'd arrived home just after seven, according to the seconded uniforms who'd been keeping an eye out in their mufti. Since then, nothing. Unless you counted putting out the milk bottles as a major event.

The lights had gone off about ten minutes after that. An hour later, there was no sign of life anywhere. The back streets of Seaford weren't noted for their liveliness after midnight. The only thing that was going to get Raymond Watson out of his kip now was a major fire, Taylor reckoned. He grunted and shifted in the car seat, scratching his balls and sniffing his fingers afterwards. Bored shitless, he flicked the switch on his personal radio and called Di Earnshaw. 'Owt happening your end?' he asked.

'Negative,' came the reply.

'If Control come through to you with news of a fire

411

that our lads are getting called out on, give me a shout on the PR, OK?'

'Why? Are you leaving the car on foot pursuit?' She sounded eager. Probably as bored as him, excited by the thought of some action even at second hand.

'Negative,' Taylor said. 'I need to stretch my legs. These fucking sardine tins weren't built for the likes of me. Like I said, anything doing, give me a shout. Over and out.'

He turned the key in the ignition. The engine coughed to life, sounding freakishly noisy in the quiet side street. Bollocks to Carol Jordan's daft ideas. Less than a mile away there was a club that kept late doors, catering mainly for the sailors off the foreign ships. There was a pint there with Tommy Taylor's name on it, unless he was very much mistaken. It was time he checked out the possibility.

Carol and Kay followed the security guard down blindingly white corridors. He opened a door and stood back, waving them into a large, dimly lit room. Computer monitors occupied almost every horizontal surface. A young woman in jeans and a polo shirt, hair dyed platinum blonde and cut flat to her head, glanced over her shoulder, registered the new arrivals and turned back to the screen she'd been engrossed in. Fingers tapped keys and the display changed. Carol caught movement in her peripheral vision and turned her head. A tall man in a suit that screamed money was perched on the edge of a computer desk over to one side. What she'd caught was him unfolding his arms and dropping his hands in preparation for rising to greet them.

He took a step towards them, pushing a persistent cowlick of mid-brown hair out of his eyes. If he was going for boyish, Carol thought, he'd missed it by about a generation. 'Detective Chief Inspector Jordan,' he said, clearly relishing the bass resonance of his voice. 'And Detective Constable Hallam. Welcome to the future.'

God help me, Carol thought. 'You must be Philip Jarvis,' she said, forcing a smile. 'I'm impressed and grateful that you were prepared to help me out at this time of night.'

'Time waits for no man,' he said, as proudly as if he'd coined the phrase. 'Or woman, come to that. We recognize the importance of your work and, like you, we operate twenty-four hours a day. We are, after all, in the same business, the business of crime prevention and, when that fails us, catching those responsible.'

'Mmm,' Carol murmured noncommittally. It was clearly a prepared speech that placed no reliance on a response.

Jarvis smiled benevolently, revealing the sort of brilliant white dental work more common in New York than Yorkshire. 'This is the viewing room,' he said with a sweep of his arm, undaunted by the obviousness of his statement. 'It's fed either from our fully automated library or by live feeds from the many cameras we have being road-tested on the site. The operator chooses the source and summons the images he or she wants to look at.'

He ushered Carol and Kay forward until they were standing behind the woman. Close up, Carol could see her skin was older than her face, faded to unhealthy by the lack of natural light and the radiation from the monitors. 'This is Gina,' Jarvis announced. He made her sound like royalty. 'When you told me the date and time period you were interested in and the vehicle index numbers that you wanted to know about, I got Gina on to it right away.'

'As I said, I really appreciate this. Have you had any luck?'

'Luck doesn't enter into it, Chief Inspector,' Jarvis said with throwaway arrogance. 'Not with a leading-edge system like ours. Gina?'

Gina tore her eyes from the screen and pushed off with her feet, spinning round to face them, grabbing a sheet of paper from the desk. 'Seventeen minutes past two on the afternoon in question.' Her voice was clipped and efficient. 'The black Volkswagen Golf left the M1 heading for the city centre. Then, at eleven thirty-two p.m., the silver Mercedes convertible did exactly the same thing. We can supply timed and dated tapes and still photographs of both events.'

'Is it possible to identify the drivers of either vehicle?' Kay asked, trying to keep the excitement out of her voice and failing. Gina flicked an interested eyebrow upwards and stared.

'Obviously, the daytime shots pose fewer problems in that respect,' Jarvis butted in. 'But we're using very high-end experimental media with the night filming at present, and with our computer enhancement technology, it would be possible to come up with surprisingly good images.'

'If you knew who it was you were looking at, you would be able to recognize them. If you were planning on doing a "does anyone know this man" on *Crimewatch UK*, you might have one or two problems,' Gina qualified.

'You say this system's experimental. How well do you think this evidence would stand up in court?' Carol asked.

'One hundred per cent on the vehicles. More like a seventy-five per cent chance on the drivers,' Gina said.

'Come on now, Gina, let's not be so pessimistic. It depends, like so much evidence, on how it's presented to the jury,' Jarvis protested. 'I'd happily testify that I'd stake my reputation on the reliability of the system.'

'And you're a qualified expert witness, are you, sir?' Carol asked. She wasn't trying to put him on the spot, but time was short and she needed to know how firm was her ground.

'I'm not, no, but some of my colleagues are.'

'Like me,' Gina said. 'Look, Ms Jordan, why don't you look at what we've got and see if that isn't enough to help you get the corroborative evidence so it won't depend on what a jury thinks about our technology?'

When she left half an hour later, Kay was clutching a bundle of video tape and laser-printed stills that both women knew in their bones would corner Jacko Vance. If Donna Doyle remained alive, they were her last best hope. Carol could hardly wait to tell Tony. She looked at her watch when she got back to the car. Half past midnight. She knew he'd want to see what she had, but she needed to get back to Seaford. And Kay could always take the material over to him now. Carol stood by her car, undecided.

To hell with it, she thought. She really wanted to talk over the evidence with Tony. He'd only get one shot at McCormick and Wharton and she needed to make sure he'd prepared a case that would speak directly to a copper's idea of evidence.

She had her mobile if they really needed her, after all.

Detective Constable Di Earnshaw pushed her shoulders hard back against the car seat, thrusting her pelvis forward in a vain attempt to loosen her stiff spine and find a comfortable position in the unmarked CID car. She wished she'd been able to bring her own little Citroën whose seat seemed moulded to her contours. Whoever had designed the police Vauxhall had obviously been a hell of a lot narrower in the hips and longer in the leg than she had any hope of ever achieving.

At least the discomfort kept her awake. There was a kind of spiteful pride in Di's determination to stay on the job. She was as convinced as Tommy Taylor that these stakeouts were a total waste of time and money, but she reckoned there were more subtle and effective ways of demonstrating that to the powers that be than skiving off. She knew her sergeant well enough by now to have a pretty shrewd idea of how he was passing the weary hours as night crawled relentlessly toward dawn. If Carol Jordan found out, he'd be back in uniform so fast he wouldn't know what had hit him. CID was such a gossip factory, she was bound to find out sooner or later. If not on this job, then on another, perhaps one that actually counted.

Di wouldn't dream of doing anything so obvious to undermine Jordan's authority. More in sorrow than in anger, that would be her line. The pitying smiles behind Jordan's back, the back-stabbing, 'I shouldn't really say this, but . . .' at every opportunity. Make it look like every cock-up emanated from Jordan's orders, every success from the troops' initiatives. There was almost nothing as destructive as constant undermining. She should know. She'd experienced plenty of it in her years with the East Yorkshire Police.

She yawned. Nothing was going to happen. Alan Brinkley was tucked up in bed with his wife inside their pretentious modern box on a so-called executive development with ideas above its station. Never mind that it would be easier to keep clean and maintained, Di preferred her little trawlerman's terraced cottage down by the old docks, even though they were now a tourist trap heritage centre. She loved the cobbled streets and the salt on the air, the sense that generations of Yorkshirewomen had stood on those doorsteps and scanned the horizon for their men. She should be so lucky, she thought with a moment's self-hatred.

She checked her watch against the clock on the dashboard. In the ten minutes that had passed since she'd last done it, the two had managed to remain precisely five seconds out of sync. Yawning, she switched on her small portable radio. Hopefully the phone-in she personally called prole-speak would be over and the DJ would be playing some decent sounds. Just as Gloria Gaynor stridently revealed that as long as she knew how to love, she knew she'd stay alive, soft light abruptly appeared behind the four frosted glass panels of the mock-Georgian fanlight in the Brinkleys' front door. Di grabbed the steering wheel tightly and sat up hurriedly. Was this it? Or was it insomnia pushing someone towards a cup of tea?

Just as suddenly as it had appeared, the light vanished. Di slumped back with a sigh, then from under the garage door, a thin rope of brightness stretched across the driveway. Startled, she punched the off button on the radio and wound down the car window, letting the raw night air flood her airways and sharpen her senses. Yes, there it was. The unmistakable cough of a car engine.

Within moments, the garage door shuddered upwards and the car rolled forward on to the drive. It was Brinkley's car, no mistake. Or rather, it was the car on which Brinkley had only ever paid three hire-purchase instalments and which would be snatched back just as soon as the repo men figured out how to grab it without actually breaking into Brinkley's garage. As she watched, Brinkley himself got out of the car and walked back to the garage, reaching inside presumably to hit the button that closed the door behind him.

'Oh boy,' Di Earnshaw said, winding up her window.

She pressed the record button on her personal microcassette recorder and said excitedly, 'Alan Brinkley is now leaving his home by car at one twenty-seven a.m.' Dropping the tape machine on the seat beside her, she grabbed the personal radio that was meant to keep her in close touch with Tommy Taylor. 'This is Tango Charlie. Tango Alpha, do you read me? Over.' She started her engine, careful to avoid the reflex of turning on her lights. Brinkley had pulled off the drive now and was driving out of the cul-de-sac, signalling a right turn. She eased her foot off the clutch, still driving without lights, and picked him up on the winding avenue that ran through the housing development and out to the main road.

She clicked the radio as she drove, repeating her message to her sergeant. 'Tango Charlie to Tango Alpha. Subject on the move, do you read me? Tango Alpha, do you read me? Over.' At the main road, Brinkley turned left. She counted to five, then switched on her lights and turned after him. He was heading for the city centre three miles away, keeping his speed steady, just above the limit. Not so careful he'd be pulled on suspicion of over-cautious drunk driving, not so fast he'd attract a tug for speeding. 'Tango Charlie to Tango Alpha.' She swore silently at her errant boss. She needed back-up and he wasn't there. She thought about calling in to control, but they'd only send a troop of patrol cars that would scare off any arsonist for three counties.

'Oh, shit,' she complained as Brinkley turned off the main road into the dimly lit streets of a small industrial estate. It looked very much as if this was it. Turning off her lights again, she followed cautiously. As the high walls of the units closed around her, she decided she had to call for uniformed back-up. She turned up the volume on her police radio and picked up the mike. 'Delta Three to control, over?'

There was a crackle of static, then nothing. Her heart sank as she realized she was in one of a handful of radio shadows that peppered the city centre. She might as well have been in a black hole for all the chance she had of raising back-up. There was nothing else for it. She was on her own.

Donna Doyle no longer felt any pain. She was swimming through a warm soup of delirium, revisiting memories through a distorting lens. Her dad was still alive, alive and throwing her up into the air in the park where the trees waved at her. Their branches turned into arms and Donna was in the centre of a ring of friends playing party games. Everything was bigger than usual, because she was only six and things always loomed larger when you were little. The colours bled into each other and it was Well Dressing week, the carnival floats melting over the streets like jellies left out in the sun.

And there she was at the heart of the parade, on a dais in a pick-up truck covered in crepe-paper flowers that swelled big as cabbage roses in her fevered derangement. She was the Rose Princess, radiant in layers of stiff petticoat, the glory of the occasion cancelling out the discomfort of the itchy fabric on the warm summer afternoon and the plastic tiara cutting into the soft flesh behind her ears. Through the misty dislocation between dream and reality Donna wondered why the sun was burning with such tropical fervour that it made her sweat and then shiver.

Outside her consciousness, the swollen, discoloured meat that hung uselessly down by her side continued to decay, sending more poisons into her body, continually shifting the balance between toxicity and survival. The rotting stink and the corrupt flesh were only the outward signs of a deeper putrefaction.

Her eager body couldn't wait for death to begin the business of decomposition.

Getting out of the car to close the garage door, Alan Brinkley had noticed his breath puff white on the night air. It was a bitter one, all right. Winter was gripping tight. Just as well he'd got one earmarked that didn't involve a long walk. The last thing he needed was fingers numbed with cold fumbling about their work. But there was nothing like a good fire to warm a man to the bone, he'd thought with an ironic smile as he revved the car engine to encourage the heater to deliver its scarlet promise of warmth.

His target was a specialist paint factory at the far end of a small industrial estate on the edge of town. For once, he could avoid the walk from his chosen parking spot because the unit next to his goal was a body shop. There were always half a dozen cars parked outside in varying stages of being resprayed or restored after an accident. One more wouldn't be noticeable. Not that there was anyone to notice. He happened to know for a fact that the guard employed to patrol the estate was never there between two and three thirty. Brinkley had watched him often enough to know that the guy was a victim of greedy bosses. He had too many premises to protect and not enough time to keep an eye on them properly.

He turned into the narrow canyon between tall warehouses that led into the estate and nosed slowly down the access road that led to the body shop. He killed the engine and lights then double-checked that none of the items in his kit had slipped out of his pocket. They were all there: the string, the brass cigarette lighter smelling of petrol, the packet of seventeen cigarettes, the dog-eared book of matches, last night's evening paper, his seven-bladed Swiss Army knife and a crumpled oil-stained handkerchief. He leaned across and took the small but powerful torch out of the glovebox. Three deep breaths with eyes closed and he was ready.

He got out of the car and glanced quickly around. His gaze swept over the cars surrounding the body shop. He saw without seeing the nose of a Vauxhall sitting in the shadow of a warehouse just on the curve of the access road. He failed to register that he hadn't passed it moments before since there was no thrum of an engine or blur of lights to alert him. Certain there was nothing else moving in the landscape, he cut across the Tarmac apron to the paint factory. God, this was going to be one hell of a display, he thought with satisfaction. He wouldn't mind betting that when this went, it would take one or two other buildings with it. Another couple of conflagrations like this and Jim Pendlebury was going to have to say, 'Bugger the budget,' and take him on full-time. It wouldn't be enough even to pay off the interest on the debts he and Maureen seemed to have accumulated like fleas on a cat, but it would keep the creditors at bay while he could work out a way to get their heads above water once and for all.

Brinkley shook his head to clear away the clutter of worry and dread that engulfed him whenever he allowed their mountain of debt to cast its shadow over him. He couldn't do this unless his mind was focused, and whenever he thought about the amount he owed, his head swam and he couldn't imagine ever making it out the other side in one piece. He kept telling himself that what he was doing was the only way he had to survive. The dosser who had died had already given up on that struggle long before Brinkley had come on the scene. He would be different. He would survive. So now he had to stifle distractions and concentrate on achieving the right result without getting caught.

Getting caught would defeat the whole purpose. He'd never get the debts paid off then. Maureen would never forgive him getting caught.

Brinkley thrust his hand between the industrial-sized rubbish skip and the wall of the factory, his fingers closing on the bag he'd stowed there earlier. This time, the office window was his best bet for entry. The fact that it was wide open to the eyes of anyone who happened to walk or drive down the access road didn't worry him. None of the units worked a night shift, the security guard wasn't due for another hour and the paint factory was the last building before the dead end of a seven-foot security fence. Nobody would be taking a short cut down here.

It took less than five minutes to get inside, and only another seven for his practised hands to set his standard fuse. The cigarette smoke billowed upwards, to his nostrils the most fragrant aroma around, its sweetness mingling with the chemical smells of the paint that permeated the air of the factory. The paint would go up like a pillar of flame in the desert, Brinkley thought with satisfaction as he backed down the dark corridor, his eyes never leaving the smouldering fuse.

He felt behind him for the open doorway of the office where he'd come in. Instead of empty space, his fingers brushed against warm fabric. Startled, he whirled in his tracks and the glare of a torch hit his eyes like a thrown glass of wine. Blinded, he tried to blink the light away. He struggled to back through the doorway, but, disorientated, stumbled sideways into the wall. The light moved and he heard the door snick shut.

'You're fucking nicked,' a woman's voice said. 'Alan Brinkley, I am arresting you on suspicion of arson . . .'

'No!' he roared like a cornered animal, throwing himself forward at the light. They collided and crashed to the ground in a tangle of limbs and a crash of office furniture. The woman beneath him struggled and wriggled like a furious kitten, but he was heavier and stronger, his upper body developed through years of fire officer's training.

She tried to hit him with the torch, but he easily fended off the blow with his shoulder, sending the light rolling across the floor where it came to rest against a filing cabinet, rocking slightly and throwing a seasick light on the struggle. He could see her face now, her mouth screwed open in a rictus of determination as she tried to break free. If he could see her, she could see him, his panicking mind screamed.

Getting caught would defeat the whole purpose. He'd never get the debts paid off then. Maureen would never forgive him getting caught.

He brought one knee up over her abdomen and leaned on it to crush the air from her lungs. He pushed his forearm against her throat, pinning her to the floor. As her tongue thrust out in a desperate fight for air, he grabbed her hair with his free hand and yanked her head forward against the brace of his forearm. He felt rather than heard something snap. Suddenly she was limp. The fight was over.

He fell away from her, curling on the floor in a foetal crouch. A sob rose in his throat. What had he done? He knew the answer well enough, but he had to repeat the question continually inside his head. He rolled on to his knees, head hanging like a disgraced dog. He couldn't leave her there. They'd find her too soon. She needed to be somewhere else.

A groan dragged from his lips. He forced himself to touch flesh that already felt dead and cold in his imagination. Somehow he hauled the woman's body over his shoulders in the traditional fireman's lift. Staggering to his feet, he lurched through the doorway and back towards the seat of the fire. He carried on beyond the fuse that now smelled harsh, on to where cases of paint tins stood on pallets waiting to be loaded on lorries. The fire would burn hot here, leaving the forensic people little to go on. There would certainly be nothing left to connect him to her. He let the body fall loose-limbed to the floor.

Wiping tears from his eyes, Brinkley turned and ran into the welcoming cold of the night. How had it come to this? How had a few good times, a taste for the good life, brought him to this place? He wanted to fall to the ground and howl like a wolf. But he had to get to his feet, get to the car, answer his pager when it summoned him to the fire station. He had to get through this. Not for his sake but for Maureen's.

Because getting caught would defeat the whole purpose. He'd never get the debts paid off then. Maureen would never forgive him getting caught.

'Shouldn't you be in Seaford?' he'd asked.

'I've got my phone with me. It'll only take me half an hour longer on the motorway than it does from the cottage. And we need to sort out what we've got and what comes next.'

'You'd better come in, then.'

It took Carol longer to read Tony's report than he

needed to scan the photographs and watch the videos she'd brought, but he didn't mind that. He kept replaying the tape and shuffling the date-stamped photographs, a tight smile on his lips, fire in his eyes. Eventually, Carol reached the end. The look of complicity they shared told them both that they had been right, and now they could demonstrate a case that could no longer be ignored. 'Good work, Doctor,' Carol said.

'Good work, Detective Chief Inspector,' he echoed.

'Vengeance is mine, saith the profiler.'

He bowed his head in acknowledgement. 'I wish I'd paid more attention when Shaz first raised it. Maybe we could have achieved this without such a high price then.'

Carol reached out impulsively and covered his hand with hers. 'That's ridiculous, Tony. No one would have mounted an investigation on the basis of what she came up with at that classroom session.'

'I didn't mean that, exactly.' He ran his fingers through his hair. 'I meant that I'm supposed to be a psychologist. I should have seen that she wasn't going to let it go. I should have discussed it with her, made her feel that she wasn't being discounted, explored ways we could have taken the matter further without putting her at risk.'

'You might as well say it's Chris Devine's fault,' Carol said briskly. 'She knew Shaz was going to interview him and she let her go alone.'

'And why do you think Chris is spending her valuable time off tearing round Northumberland with Leon and Simon? It's not out of a sense of duty. It's out of a sense of guilt.'

'You can't take responsibility for them all. Shaz was a copper. She should have considered the risk. There was no need for her to go in like she did, so even if you had tried to stop her, she probably wouldn't have paid any attention. Let it go, Tony.'

He lifted his head and read the compassion in her eyes. He gave a rueful nod. 'We need to go official on this now, if we're going to avoid accusations that we're as out of control as Shaz was.'

Carol slipped her hand away from his. 'I'm glad you said that, because I'm starting to feel really edgy about uncovering hard evidence like this without any formal relationship to the investigation and no chain of custody on any of the physical evidence apart from "It was in my handbag, Guv." I keep thinking about the defence counsel making mincemeat out of me on the witness stand. "And so, DCI Jordan, you expect the jury to believe that on this maverick quest for justice – that only you, as opposed to the entire West Yorkshire force, could conduct – you just happened upon the one piece of evidence that links my client to the murder of DC Bowman, a woman he met once for less than an hour? And what is it your brother does again, Ms Jordan? Computer wizard, would that be a fair description? The sort of whizz kid who can make a digital image say anything he wants it to say?" We need to get this under West Yorkshire's umbrella so they can construct the case properly.'

'I know. There comes a point where you have to stop playing at being the Lone Ranger and we're there now. We need to cover your back as well. In the morning, I'll go straight over to the murder room. How does that sound?'

'It's not that I want to wash my hands of this, Tony,' she said plaintively. 'It's just that we're going to lose it if we don't bring it in.'

He felt a rush of warmth towards her. 'I couldn't have

achieved any of this alone. When Jacko Vance faces a jury, it'll be thanks to you coming on board.'

Before she could reply, her phone rang, splitting the closeness between them like an axe in wood. 'Oh, shit,' she said, grabbing the handset and hitting the button. 'DCI Jordan.'

The familiar voice of Jim Pendlebury came down the line. 'We've got what looks like another one, Carol. Paint factory. It's gone up like a torch.'

'I'll be there as soon as I can, Jim. Can you give me a locus?' Without being asked, Tony shoved pencil and paper across to her and she scribbled down directions. 'Thanks,' she said. She ended the call and closed her eyes momentarily. Then she hit the memory buttons and was connected to her communications room. 'This is DCI Jordan. Has there been anything from DS Taylor or DC Earnshaw?'

'Negative, ma'am,' came the anonymous voice. 'They were supposed to be maintaining radio silence unless they had something specific to their stakeouts.'

'Will you see if you can raise them and get them to meet me at the site of the paint factory fire on the Holt Industrial Estate. Thanks. Good night.' She looked at Tony, perplexed. 'It seems we were wrong,' she said.

'The arsonist?'

'He's struck again. But neither Tommy Taylor nor Di Earnshaw radioed in, so it looks as if it was neither of our suspects.' She shook her head. 'Back to square one, I guess. I'd better get over there and see what's going on.'

'Good luck,' Tony said as she pulled on her mac.

'It's you that'll need the luck, talking round Wharton and McCormick,' she said as he followed her down the hall. On the doorstep, she turned and impulsively put a hand on his arm. 'Don't beat yourself up about Shaz.'

She leaned into him and kissed his cheek. 'Concentrate on beating up Jack the Lad.'

Then she was gone, leaving nothing behind but a shiver of her scent in the night air.

Above the blur of sodium and neon, it was a clear, starry night. From his eyrie on top of the Holland Park house, Jacko Vance stared out across the London night and imagined the Northumberland stars. There was a loose end, the only possible strand that could unravel and leave him stripped of his protective colouring. It was time for Donna Doyle to die.

He hadn't actually had to kill one for a long time now. It wasn't the killing he enjoyed. It was the process. The disintegration of a human being through the degradation of pain and infection. One had been defiant. She had refused to eat or drink or to use the chemical toilet. She'd been a challenge, but she hadn't lasted long. She had failed to consider the infective possibilities of piss and shit all over the floor. All she'd been thinking about was making herself too disgusting for him to touch, and she'd failed in that, too.

But he'd have to get rid of this particular Jillie soon. Her existence had been worrying him, a constant itch like a fleabite under a waistband. But while the police had been sniffing around after Shaz Bowman's death, he hadn't wanted to make an untoward move. An unscheduled dash for Northumberland would have been suspicious. The swift visit he had made hadn't been long enough to deal with the bitch properly. Then there had been Tony Hill's involvement to consider. Did the man have anything or was he just trying to rattle him into doing precisely the one thing that would expose him?

Either way, she had to go. That she might still be alive was a possibility that put him in mortal danger.

He should have disposed of her on the night he killed Bowman, but he'd been afraid that his movements might come under too close scrutiny for comfort. Besides, he'd been too exhausted to have been certain of making a proper job of it.

He'd just have to rely on the invisibility of her hiding place, entombed beneath the stone flags. The only people who knew about the old crypt were the two builders he'd hired to install the perfectly engineered opening. Twelve years before, people had still believed in the nuclear threat. His talk of wanting to create a bomb shelter had gone down as merely eccentric among the locals. It would, he felt certain, be long forgotten.

Nevertheless, she had to go. Not tonight. He was filming early in the morning and he needed what sleep his apprehensions would allow him. But in a day or two, he could slip away overnight and see to the girl.

He'd have to make the most of it. It would have to be a little while before he could indulge himself again. A thought flickered into his mind. If he was ever going to feel safe again, perhaps Tony Hill needed to be taught a lesson more personal than Shaz Bowman. Jacko Vance gazed across the city and wondered if there was a woman in his life. He'd remember to ask his wife in the morning if Hill had said anything over dinner about a partner.

It had been no hardship killing Shaz Bowman. A repetition with Tony Hill's girlfriend could only be easier.

Hands thrust deep into the pockets of her mac, collar turned up against the harsh estuary wind, Carol Jordan stared stonily at the still smoking ruin of the paint factory. Her vigil was already three hours old, but she wasn't ready to leave yet. Fire officers, their distinctive yellow helmets smudged with greasy residue, moved in and out of the fringes of the building. Somewhere inside that creaking shell, some of them were trying to penetrate to the seat of the fire. Carol was beginning to accept that she didn't need the evidence of their eyes to know why Di Earnshaw hadn't responded to the control room's radio messages telling her to come to the fire site.

Di Earnshaw had been there already.

Carol heard a car draw to a halt behind her, but she didn't turn her head. A rustle of the crime scene tapes, then Lee Whitbread moved into her line of sight, proffering a carton of burger joint coffee. 'I thought you could probably do with this,' he said.

She nodded and took the brew wordlessly. 'No news, then?' he asked, his normally eager expression apprehensive.

'Nothing,' she said. She flipped off the polystyrene lid and raised the cup to her lips. The coffee was strong and hot, surprisingly good.

'There's been nothing at the station, neither,' Lee said, cupping his hands round his mouth to light a cigarette. 'I bobbed round her house, just to check, like, that she hadn't knocked off and gone home, but there's no sign. Bedroom curtains are still shut, so maybe she's got her head down and earplugs in?' Like every cop, his occupational pessimism was always tempered with hope when it appeared that a colleague was in line for a police funeral.

Carol couldn't bring herself to share even the fragile hope of earplugs. And if she knew Di Earnshaw wasn't the sort to go on the missing list, Lee must be doubly sure that his fellow DC was out of action for good. 'Have you seen DS Taylor?' she asked.

Lee hid his expression behind his hand as he smoked

furiously. 'He says she never called in. He's back at the station, seeing if anything comes up there.'

'I hope he's coming up with something a little more imaginative than that,' Carol said grimly.

Three figures emerged from the dark hulk of the factory and pulled the breathing apparatus from their mouths. One detached himself from the other two and walked towards them. A few feet away from her, Jim Pendlebury came to a halt and pulled off his helmet. 'I can't tell you how sorry I am, Carol.'

Carol's head tilted back, then dropped in a tired nod. 'No doubt, I suppose?'

'There's always room for doubt until they've done the business down the path. lab. But we reckon it's a female, and there's what looks like a melted down radio next to the body.' His voice was soft with sympathy.

She looked up at his compassionate expression. He knew what it was like to lose people he was nominally responsible for. She wished he could tell her how long it would take before she could look herself in the mirror again. 'Can I see her?'

He shook his head. 'It's still too hot in there.'

Carol exhaled, a short, sharp sigh. 'I'll be in my office if anyone wants me.' She dropped the carton of coffee, turned away and ducked under the tapes, hurrying blindly in the direction of her car. Behind her, the coffee pooled on the Tarmac. Lee Whitbread flicked his cigarette butt into it, watching it fizz depressingly before dying. He looked up at Jim Pendlebury. 'Me too. We've got a fucking cop killer to nail now.'

Colin Wharton shuffled the pile of video stills together then leaned across and ejected the tape from the video recorder in the training suite that Tony's team had abandoned what felt like half a lifetime ago. Avoiding Tony's eye, he said, 'It proves nothing. OK, somebody else was driving Shaz Bowman's car back from London. It could be anybody behind that disguise. You hardly see anything of the guy's face, and these computer enhancements ... *I* don't trust them, and juries are worse. By the time fucking Rumpole the defence brief's finished, they assume anything that's come from a computer's been doctored to make it show what we want it to show.'

'What about the arm? You can't doctor that. Jacko Vance has a prosthesis on his right arm. The man putting the petrol in never uses that arm at all. It's really noticeable,' Tony pressed.

Wharton shrugged. 'There could be all sorts of reasons for that. Could be that the man in question is left-handed. It could be that he'd hurt his arm in a struggle to overpower Bowman. It could even be that he knew about that daft bee Bowman had in her bonnet about Jacko Vance, and he decided to play on that. *Punters* know about video cameras now, Dr Hill. Vance *works* in the business – do you really think he's not going to have thought about cameras?'

Tony ran a hand through his hair, gripping the ends as if he were holding on to his temper. 'You've got Vance coming off the motorway at Leeds in his own wheels at the crucial time. Surely that's too much of a coincidence?'

Wharton shook his head. 'I don't think so. The man has a cottage in Northumberland. He does all that volunteer work up there. OK, the A1 might be the more direct route, but the M1's a faster road, and it's easy enough to pick up the A1 north of the city. He might even have decided he wanted fish and chips at Bryan's on the road,' he added with a pale attempt to lighten the atmosphere.

434

Tony folded his arms as if this would hold his dark anger inside. 'Why won't you take this seriously?' he asked.

'If Simon McNeill wasn't on the run, we might not assume everything you produce is tainted,' Wharton said angrily.

'Simon has nothing to do with this. He did not murder Shaz Bowman. Jacko Vance did. He is a cold-blooded killer. Everything I know about psychology tells me he killed Shaz Bowman because she threatened to bring his playhouse down about his ears. We've got pictures of him driving her car, she's nowhere in sight. Then in his car, covering the same ground. You've seen the psychological profile I prepared. What more do we have to do to persuade you to at least take a serious look at the man?'

The door behind him opened. DCS Dougal McCormick thrust his massive torso into the room. His face was the dark red of a man who'd had too much drink at lunchtime, a sheen of sweat gleaming on his fleshy cheeks. His light voice had dropped half an octave with the alcohol. 'I thought you were barred from here unless we came for you?' he added, stabbing a finger at Tony.

'I brought you the evidence to make a case against Shaz Bowman's killer,' Tony said, his voice weary now. 'Only Mr Wharton doesn't seem to be able to grasp its significance.'

McCormick shouldered his way into the room. 'Is that right? What have you got to say to that, Colin?'

'There's some very interesting motorway petrol station footage that's been computer-enhanced to show someone else driving Shaz Bowman's motor the afternoon she was killed.' Silently, he spread the pictures out for McCormick to check. The Chief Superintendent screwed up his dark eyes and studied them closely.

'It's Jacko Vance,' Tony insisted. 'He took her car back to Leeds, then made his way back to London before driving north again, presumably with Shaz in the boot.'

'Never mind Jacko Vance,' McCormick said dismissively. 'We've got a witness.'

'A witness?'

'Aye, a witness.'

'A witness to what, exactly?'

'A neighbour who saw your blue-eyed boy Simon McNeill going round the back of Sharon Bowman's flat the night she was killed and didn't see him come back out front again. I've got a team taking his place apart even as we speak. We were looking for him already, but now there'll be a public announcement. Maybe you'd know where we could find him, eh, Dr Hill?'

'You're the ones who disbanded my squad. How would I know where Simon is now?' Tony said, his voice a cold disguise for the frustration boiling inside.

'Ach, well, never mind. We'll be able to put our hand on him sooner or later. I've no doubt my boys will end up with something better to show a court than some videos your girlfriend's brother's tarted up.' Seeing Tony's startled expression, he nodded grimly. 'That's right, we know all about you and DCI Jordan. Do you really think we don't talk to each other in this job?'

'You keep telling me you're interested in evidence, not supposition,' Tony said, hanging on to his self-possession by sheer force of will. 'For the record, DCI Jordan is not now nor has she ever been my girlfriend. And my contention that Vance is the killer does not rely solely on the video evidence. I'm really not trying to teach you how to suck eggs, but at least look at the report I've drawn up. There's solid evidence there.'

McCormick picked the folder up from the table and flicked through it. 'A psychological profile is not what

I'd call evidence. Rumour, innuendo, jealous people getting their own back. That's what you're relying on here.'

'His own wife says he's never slept with her. You're not telling me that's regarded as normal behaviour in West Yorkshire?'

'She might have all sorts of reasons for lying to you,' McCormick said dismissively, dropping the report with a soft rustle.

'He met Barbara Fenwick a couple of days before she was abducted and murdered. It's there, in Greater Manchester Police's murder file. One of his first ever charity events after the accident that destroyed his dream. We have photographs of him at later events with other girls who have disappeared and never been heard from again.' Tony's voice was discouraged now. He'd failed to establish a rapport that would have allowed the two policemen to back down and consider what he had to say. Worse than that, he seemed to have alienated McCormick to the point where if he said 'black', McCormick would retort, 'white'.

'A man like that meets hundreds of lassies a week and nothing ever happens to them,' McCormick said, sinking into a chair. 'Look, Dr Hill, I know it's hard to accept that you've had the wool pulled over your eyes, with you being a senior Home Office psychologist. But look at your man McNeill. He was in love with the lassie, and she doesn't seem to have felt the same about him. We've only got his word for it that she was supposed to be meeting him for a drink in advance of their night out with the other two. He was seen going round the back of the house at about the time she could have died. We've got his fingerprints on the glass of the French windows. And now he's done a disappearing act. You've got to admit, it's a hell of a lot more persuasive than a stack of circumstantial evidence against a man who's a national hero. What you're trying to do, Dr Hill, it's understandable. I'd probably feel the same as you if it was one of my officers in the frame. But face it, you made a mistake. You picked a bad apple.'

Tony stood up. 'I'm sorry we can't see eye to eye on this. I'm particularly sorry because I think Jacko Vance is holding another teenage girl prisoner, and she might still be alive. Gentlemen, there are none so blind as those who will not see. I sincerely hope your blindness doesn't cost Donna Doyle her life. Now, if you'll excuse me, I have work to do.'

Wharton and McCormick made no attempt to prevent him leaving. As he reached the door, Wharton said, 'It would better for McNeill if he didn't wait to be arrested.'

'I don't think so, somehow,' Tony said. Out in the car park, he leaned against the car door, head on folded arms. What the hell was left to do? The only senior police officer who believed his flimsy evidence was Carol, and she had no clout with West Yorkshire Police now, that much was clear. The evidence they still needed was the sort that came from TV reconstructions and nationwide press appeals; not resources available to a discredited psychologist, a pair of maverick cops from opposite ends of the country and a ragbag of junior detectives.

Conventional means had failed them. Now it was time to throw away the rule book. He'd done it before and it had saved his life. This time, it might just save someone else's.

Carol stood in the doorway of the squad room, fists on hips, glaring down the room. The news had travelled ahead of her and the only two detectives on the premises were clearly downcast by it. One was typing up notes, the other working bleakly through a wad of paperwork. Neither moved more than their eyes, a quick sidelong glance to register her arrival.

'Where is he?' Carol demanded.

The two detectives flicked their eyes towards each other, mutual understanding and decisions passing instantly between them. The one at the keyboard spoke, keeping his eyes on his work. 'DS Taylor, ma'am?'

'Who else? Where is he? I know he was here earlier, but I want to know where he is now.'

'He went out just after the news came through about Di,' the other man said.

'And where will he be?' Carol wasn't giving an inch. She couldn't afford to. Not for the sake of her future authority, but for her own self-respect. The buck stopped with her, and she had no wish to evade that responsibility. But she needed to understand how her operation had gone so disastrously wrong. Only one man might be able to tell her, and she was determined to find him. 'Come on,' she urged. 'Where?'

The two detectives exchanged another look. This time resignation was the key component. 'Harbourmaster's Club,' the typist said.

'He's in a drinking den at this time of the morning?' she demanded angrily.

'It's not just a bar, it's a club, ma'am. Originally for officers on merchant ships. You can get meals there, or just go in and read the papers and have a cup of coffee.' Carol turned to leave, but the typist continued. 'Ma'am, you can't go there,' he said, his voice urgent.

The look she gave him had induced rapists to confess. 'It's men only,' the young detective stammered. 'They won't let you in.'

'Jesus Christ!' Carol exploded. 'God forbid we should disturb the native customs. All right, Beckham, stop

439

what you're doing and get down the Harbourmaster's Club. I want you and DS Taylor back here within half an hour, or I'll have your warrant card as well as his. Do I make myself clear?'

The file folder closed and Beckham jumped to his feet, brushing past her with an apology as he hurried out. 'I'll be in my office,' Carol growled at the remaining detective. She tried to slam the door behind her, but the hinges were too stiff.

Carol flopped into her chair, not even taking off her mac. Bleak self-reproach settled oppressively, immobilizing her. She stared emptily at the back wall where Di Earnshaw had stood during their briefing, remembering the dead fish stare, the badly fitting suit, the pug-nosed face. They'd never have been friends, Carol knew that instinctively, and in a way that made what had happened worse. Coupled with the guilt of Di Earnshaw's death in her own botched operation, Carol had the guilt of knowing she hadn't liked the woman very much, that if she'd been forced under duress to choose a victim from her command, Di wouldn't have been last on the list.

Carol ran through the case history again, wondering what she could have, should have done differently. Which was the decision that got Di Earnshaw killed? However she cut it, she came back to the same thing every time. She'd not kept a tight enough grip on the investigation, or a close enough eye on junior officers who weren't worried about discrediting her with their sloppy policing. She'd been too busy playing knight-in-shining-armour games with Tony Hill. Not for the first time, she'd let her emotional response to him interfere with her judgement. This time, the consequences had been fatal.

The peal of her phone cut across her self-flagellation

and she grabbed it in the middle of the second ring. Not even a major guilt-trip could stifle her instincts to the point where she could ignore a ringing phone on her office desk. 'DCI Jordan,' she said, her voice dull.

'Guv, it's Lee.' His voice sounded brighter than it had any right to be. Even as negative a personality as Di Earnshaw had the right to a little more sorrow from her immediate colleagues.

'What have you got?' Carol asked brusquely, swivelling round in her chair to stare out of the window at the deserted windswept quay.

'I found her car. Tucked away down the side of one of the other warehouses, well out of sight. Guv, she had this little tape recorder. It was lying on the passenger seat, so I got one of the traffic lads to get me into the car. It's all there, name, time, route, destination, the lot. There's more than enough there to nail Brinkley!'

'Good work,' she said dully. Better than nothing, it still wasn't enough to assuage the guilt. Somehow, she knew that when she told Tony that, after all, he'd been right, he wouldn't consider it an acceptable trade-off either. 'Bring it in, Lee.'

She turned to replace the handset to find John Brandon standing in the doorway. Wearily, she started to get up, but he motioned her to stay seated, folding his long limbs into one of the comfortless visitor's chairs. 'A bad business,' he said.

'No one to blame but me,' Carol said. 'I took my eye off the ball. I left my officers to their own devices on an operation they all thought was a waste of time. They weren't taking it seriously, and now Di Earnshaw's dead. I should have stayed on their tails.'

'I'm surprised she was out there without back-up,' Brandon said. The words were censure enough without the look of reproach on his face.

'That wasn't the intention,' Carol said flatly.

'For both our sakes, I hope you can substantiate that.' It wasn't a threat, Carol realized, seeing the warmth of regret in his eyes.

Carol stared unseeing at the scarred wood of her desk top. 'Somehow, I can't get worked up about that now, sir.'

Brandon's voice hardened. 'Well, I suggest you do, Chief Inspector. Di Earnshaw doesn't have the luxury of feeling sorry for herself. All we can do for her now is take her killer off the streets. When can I expect an arrest?'

Stung, Carol jerked her head up and glared at Brandon. 'Just as soon as DC Whitbread gets back here with the evidence, sir.'

'Good.' Brandon got to his feet. 'Once you have a clearer idea what happened out there last night, we'll talk.' The ghost of a smile crossed his eyes. 'You're not to blame, Carol. You can't be on duty twenty-four hours a day.'

Carol stared at the empty doorway after he'd gone, wondering how many years it had taken John Brandon to learn how to let go. Then, weighing up what she knew of the man, she wondered if he ever had, or if he'd simply learned to hide it better.

Leon looked around, bemused. 'I thought Newcastle was supposed to be the last place on earth where men were men and sheep ran scared?'

'You got a problem with a vegetarian pub?' Chris Devine asked mildly.

Simon grinned. 'He only pretends he likes his meat raw.' He sipped his pint experimentally. 'Nothing wrong with the bevvy, though. How did you find out about this place?'

442

'Don't ask and you won't be embarrassed, babe. Just trust your senior officer, especially when she's a woman. So, how are we doing?' Chris asked. 'I got nowhere showing her picture round the station. Nobody in the buffet or the ticket office or the bookstall remembered seeing her.'

'The bus station was the same,' Simon reported. 'Not a sausage. Except that one of the drivers said, was it not that lass that went missing in Sunderland a couple of years back?' They contemplated the irony glumly.

'I got a sniff,' Leon said. 'I talked to one of the train guards, and he put me on to a cafe where all the drivers and guards go for a brew and a bacon butty on their breaks. I sat down with the guys and flashed the photos. One of them reckoned he was pretty sure he'd seen her on the Carlisle train. He remembered because she double-checked with him what time the train got into Five Walls Halt and that they were running on time.'

'When was this?' Chris asked, offering him an encouraging cigarette.

'He couldn't be sure. But he reckoned it was the week before last.' Leon didn't have to remind them that timetable would fit perfectly with Donna Doyle's disappearance.

'Where's Five Walls Halt?' Simon asked.

'It's somewhere in the middle of nowhere this side of Hexham,' Chris informed him. 'Near Hadrian's Wall. And presumably another four. And don't ask how I know that either, right?'

'So what's at Five Walls Halt that she'd want to get off there?'

Leon looked at Chris. She shrugged. 'I'm only guessing, but I'd say it might be somewhere near Jacko Vance's place in the country. Which, I don't have to tell you, we're not supposed to be going anywhere near.'

'We could go to Five Walls Halt, though,' Leon said.

'Not until you finish that pint, we can't,' Simon prompted.

'Leave the pint,' Chris instructed him. 'She can't have been the only one who got off the train there. If we're going knocking on doors, we don't want to smell like a brewery.' She got to her feet. 'Let's go and discover the beauties of the Northumberland countryside. Did you bring your wellies?'

Leon and Simon exchanged a look of panic. 'Thanks, Chris,' Leon muttered sarcastically as they trailed after her into the soft rain.

Alan Brinkley stood under the shower, the cascade of water almost scalding. The man who made the decisions had finally decreed that the officers who had fought the fierce fire at the paint factory could be stood down and replaced by a smaller crew who would damp down the hot spots and keep their fresh eyes peeled for anything significant among the wreckage. No one in authority was taking any chances now the body had been found.

At the thought of the body, a shudder convulsed Brinkley from head to foot. In spite of the steaming heat, his teeth chattered involuntarily. He wasn't going to think about the body. Normal, he had to be normal. But what was normal? How did he usually behave when there had been a fatal fire? What did he say to Maureen? How many beers did he drink the night after? What did his mates see in his face?

He slumped against the streaming tiles of the shower cubicle, tears falling invisibly from his eyes. Thank God for the privacy of the new fire station, not like the old communal showers they'd had when he'd learned his trade. In the shower now, no one could see him weep.

He couldn't get the smell out of his nostrils, the taste

444

out of his mouth. He knew it was imagination; the chemicals in the paint factory overlaid any hint of incinerated flesh. But it was as real as it had ever been. He didn't even know her name, but he knew what she smelled like, what she tasted like now.

His mouth opened in a silent scream and he pounded with the sides of his fists against the solid wall, making no sound. Behind him, the shower curtain rattled back on its metal hoops. He turned slowly, pressing himself into the corner of the cubicle. He'd seen the man and the woman before, inside the scene-of-crime tapes at the fires. He watched the woman's lips move, heard her voice, but could not process what she was saying.

It didn't matter. He suddenly knew this was the only relief. He slid down the wall into a foetal crouch. He found his voice and started to sob like a damaged child.

Chris Devine was only a few miles out of Newcastle when her mobile rang. 'It's me, Tony. Any joy?'

She filled him in on the limited success of their morning, and in turn he told her about his failure to convince Wharton and McCormick to take him seriously. 'It's a nightmare,' he said. 'We can't afford to hang around indefinitely on this. If Donna Doyle is still alive, every hour could count. Chris, I think the only thing to do is for me to confront him with the evidence and hope we can panic him into a confession or an incriminating move.'

'That's what killed Shaz,' Chris said. Mentioning her name brought the grief back like a physical blow. If she could ignore the bright presence Shaz had been in her life and the darkness of her absence, she could get through this in a fair simulacrum of the normal breezy Chris Devine. But every time Shaz was mentioned by name, it knocked the breath from her. She suspected she wasn't the only one who suffered a reaction; it would explain why Shaz was seldom spoken of directly.

'I wasn't planning on going it alone. I need back-up.'

'What about Carol?'

There was a long silence. 'Carol lost an officer in the night.'

'Ah, shit. Her arsonist?'

'Her arsonist. She's beating herself up because she thinks her involvement in this made her derelict in her duty. She's wrong, as it happens, but there's no way she can walk away from her responsibilities in Seaford today.'

'Sounds like she's got more shit on her plate right now than anyone should ever have to eat. Yeah, forget Carol.'

'I'm going to need you down there, Chris. Can you bear to pull out and go back to London? Now?'

She didn't have to hesitate for a moment. When it came to catching the man who brutalized Shaz Bowman's beautiful face before destroying her soul, there wasn't much Chris would have refused. 'No problem. I'll flag the lads down and tell them.'

'You can tell them Kay's on her way, too. She was waiting for me when I got back from Leeds HQ this morning. I'll call her and tell her to head for Five Walls Halt station. She can meet Simon and Leon there.'

'Thank God there'll be one person there with a bit of common sense,' she said ironically. 'She can keep the lid on Die Hard one and two.'

'Getting a bit gung-ho, are they?'

'There's nothing they'd love more than kicking Jacko Vance's head in. Failing that, they'd settle for his front door.' She spotted a lay-by on the fast dual carriageway and indicated she was going to pull over, checking in her mirror that Simon and Leon were following.

'I was thinking of reserving that pleasure for myself.'

Chris gave a grunt of sardonic laughter. 'Join the queue, babe. I'll call you when I hit the M25.'

The officers in the canteen broke into a ragged round of applause as Carol and Lee Whitbread walked in. Carol nodded a distant acknowledgement, Lee doing better with a wan smile. Two coffees, two doughnuts, her treat, then they were out of there and heading back to the CID room. It would be at least an hour before Alan Brinkley's solicitor could get there, and till then, he was off limits.

Halfway up the stairs, she turned and blocked Lee's way. 'Where was he?'

Lee looked shifty. 'I don't know,' he mumbled. 'Must have been in a radio black spot.'

'Bollocks,' Carol said. 'Come on, Lee. This isn't the time for false loyalty. Di Earnshaw would probably still be alive if Taylor had been watching her back like he was supposed to. It could have been you. Next time it could be. So where was he? Over the side?'

Lee scratched his eyebrow. 'The nights we were on together, he stuck with it till gone midnight. Then he called in and said he were going for a bevvy to Corcoran's.'

'If he'd done that with Di, why would she have been shouting for back-up over the radio?' Carol demanded.

Lee squirmed, his mouth twisting awkwardly. 'He wouldn't have told Di. Not one of the lads, was she?'

Carol closed her eyes momentarily. 'You're telling me I've lost one of my officers because of traditional Yorkshire male chauvinism?' she said incredulously.

Lee dropped his eyes and studied the step he stood on. 'None of us thought owt would happen.'

Carol turned on her heel and marched upstairs,

leaving Lee to trail in her wake. This time when she shouldered open the squad-room door, Tommy Taylor jumped to his feet. 'Guv,' he began.

'Chief Inspector to you. My office. Now.' She waited for him to move ahead of her. 'You know something, Taylor? I'm ashamed to work in the same squad as you.' The other detectives in the room suddenly developed total fascination with their routine tasks.

Carol kicked the door shut behind her. 'Don't bother sitting down,' she said, moving behind her desk and dropping into her chair. For this interview, she didn't need artificial aids like standing while her junior officer sat. 'DC Earnshaw is lying in the morgue incinerated because you went on the piss while you were supposed to be working.'

'I never . . .' he began.

Carol simply raised her voice and continued. 'There will be an official inquiry where you can bullshit all you like about radio black spots. By that time, I'll have statements from every drunk in Corcoran's. I am going to bury you, Taylor. Until you're officially drummed out of this force, you're on suspension. Now get out of my squad room and stay away from my officers.'

'I never thought she were at risk,' he said pathetically.

'The reason we get our wages is that we're always at risk,' Carol snapped. 'Now get out of my sight and pray you don't get reinstated because there isn't a cop in East Yorkshire who would piss on you if you were on fire.'

Taylor backed out, carefully closing the door behind him. 'Feel better now?' Carol said under her breath. 'And you're the woman who said she'd never pass the buck.' Her head dropped into her hands. She knew any inquiry would lay little blame at her door. It didn't stop her feeling that Di Earnshaw's blood stained her hands as much as Taylor's. And once the identification was official, she was the one who'd have to break the news to her parents.

At least she wouldn't have to worry about Jacko Vance and Donna Doyle any more. That, thank God, must be someone else's problem by now.

When Chris Devine had talked about knocking on doors, Simon and Leon had pictured a neat little village with two or three streets. Neither of them had considered the area served by a small station halfway between Carlisle and Hexham. Apart from the straggle of houses that made up Five Walls Halt itself, there were farms, smallholdings, outlying pockets of agricultural cottages now colonized by city commuters, holiday homes and cramped council estates snagged improbably in the distant corners of narrow valleys. They'd ended up in a tourist information office buying Ordnance Survey maps.

Once Kay arrived, they split the area among themselves, agreeing to meet back at the station at the end of the afternoon. It was a thankless task, but one that Kay was more successful with than the others. People always talked more to a woman on their doorstep than they ever would to a man. By late afternoon, she'd got two possible sightings of Donna Doyle. Both put her on their regular evening train home, but neither could be certain of the day.

She'd also discovered the location of Jacko Vance's hideaway. One of the doors she'd knocked on had belonged to the roofer who'd replaced the black slate roof of the former chapel only five years before. Her oblique raising of the subject and her gossipy questioning about Vance had left him unsuspicious. He would merely mention down the pub that night that women coppers were just like any other women when it came to being pushovers for a famous name with a nice smile and a big bank balance.

By the time the three reconvened, she had added a few more bits and pieces to her store of knowledge. Vance had bought the place a dozen years before, maybe six months or so after his accident. It hadn't been much more than four walls and a roof, and he'd spent a fair whack of cash on doing it up. When he'd married Micky, the locals had expected them to use it as a weekend cottage, but instead he'd used it more as a retreat; a useful base for the voluntary work he did at the hospital in Newcastle. No one knew why he'd chosen the area. He had no roots or connections to it as far as anyone knew.

Leon and Simon were excited by her information. They had little to offer themselves apart from a couple of dubious sightings of Donna. One put her in the station car park, getting into a vehicle. But the witness couldn't remember the day, the time or the make of the wheels. 'It's no coincidence that witness sounds very like witless,' Leon said. 'We're not getting anywhere with this shit. Let's go over Vance's place.'

'Tony said to stay away,' Simon objected.

'I'm not sure it's a good idea,' Kay agreed.

'What harm can it do? Listen, if he picked up the kid here and took her back to his gaff, chances are somebody local might have seen him. We can't just go back to Leeds now, not knowing this much.'

'We should call Tony first,' Simon said stubbornly.

Leon cast his eyes heavenwards. 'OK,' he sighed. He made great play of getting his phone out and tapping in a number. Neither of the others thought to check it was Tony's number. As the ringing tone continued without interruption, Leon said triumphantly, 'He's not answering, right? So what harm can it do if we go and check it out? Shit, that kid could still be alive, and we're talking about sitting on our butts till Christmas? Come on, we got to *do* something.'

Kay and Simon exchanged a look. Neither wanted to contradict Tony's orders. But equally, they were too infected with the glory of the chase to bear sitting around doing nothing while a young woman's life might be on the line. 'All right,' Kay said. 'But all we do is take a look around. Right?'

'Right,' said Leon enthusiastically.

'I hope so,' Simon said wearily. 'I really hope so.'

Chris Devine sipped a double espresso and drew deeply on another cigarette in an attempt to keep her tiredness at bay. At tea-time on a Sunday, the Shepherd's Bush diner was less lively than a funeral parlour. 'Run it past me again,' she commanded Tony.

'I go to the house. According to your contact's schedule for him, Vance was supposed to be compering a charity fashion show in Kensington this afternoon, so he's not going to be in Northumberland.'

'Are you sure we shouldn't be hitting his place up there first?' Chris interrupted. 'If Donna Doyle's still alive . . .'

'And if she's not there? We couldn't start poking around without the locals noticing and probably getting straight on the phone to Vance. And then we're completely blown. At the moment, he doesn't know for sure that anybody's close to him. All he knows is that I've been sticking my nose in. That's the only advantage we've got. We have to go straight for the direct confrontation.'

'What if his wife's there? He's not going to risk her hearing anything you might have to say to him about Shaz.'

'If Micky and Betsy are there, he'll make damn sure he gets me out of their way before I get the chance to say a word. In a way, it's safer for me if they are around, since I'm more likely to get out in one piece.'

'I suppose so. You better take me through it, then,' she said, exhaling a cloud of smoke.

'I tell Jacko I've been working independently of the police and I've uncovered important video evidence relating to Shaz Bowman's death that I think he might be able to help us with. He'll let me in because I'm alone and he'll figure he can dispose of me the same way he got rid of Shaz if it emerges that I really am a lone maverick. I show him the enhanced video and the stills and accuse him. You are sitting outside in your car with a radio receiver and a tape recorder picking up everything that's transmitted from the mike in this natty little pen I bought in Tottenham Court Road on the way here.' Tony wiggled the pen in front of Chris's nose.

'You don't seriously think he's going to roll over?'

Tony shook his head. 'I think if he's alone, he'll try to kill me. And that's where you come in like the cavalry, leaping tall buildings with one mighty bound.' His words were light, but his tone was sombre. They looked bleakly at each other.

'So let's do it,' Chris said. 'Let's nail the fucker to a tree.'

It had taken them less than ten minutes to discover it was impossible to stake out Jacko Vance's converted chapel without being as obvious as a wolfhound in a flock of sheep. 'Fuck,' Leon said.

'I don't think he picked somewhere like this by chance,' Simon said, looking around at the bleak hillside opposite the hideaway. On either side of the gravel circle in front of the tall narrow building were fields of sheep

452

held at bay by wire fences. Even in the thickening dusk, it was obvious there was neither human being nor habitation within sight.

'It's funny,' Kay mused. 'Normally, celebs like a bit of privacy. Gates, walls, high hedges. But you must be able to see this place for miles if you walked over the moors.'

'Cuts both ways, man,' Leon said. 'They can see you, but you get plenty of warning when anybody approaches you. Look at that road. Them fucking Romans didn't mess about, did they? Any Picts came looking for trouble, you'd see them soon as they hit the horizon.'

'He likes the kind of privacy where you can't be spied on,' Simon said. 'I reckon that means he's got a lot more to hide than some starlet sucking his toes.'

'And I reckon we ought to check out what it is,' Leon said.

They looked at each other for a long moment. Kay shook her head. Simon said, 'There is no way I'm going to be party to kicking Jacko Vance's door in.'

'Who said anything about kicking his door in?' Leon said. 'Kay, you talked to the guy that put the roof on this place. He say anything about locals that work here? Gardener, cleaner, cook? Anything like that?'

'Oh, yeah, like he's going to have a cleaner in premises where he's stashing murder victims,' Simon scoffed scornfully.

'This guy loves the double bluff,' Leon said. 'He loves putting one over on the stupid old plod. There's nothing would appeal to him more than having some old dear polishing the secret panel when he's got some kid chained up behind it. What did the guy say, Kay?'

'He didn't say anything,' she said. 'But if anybody knows that, chances are it's the nearest neighbour.'

'So who does the best Geordie accent?' Leon demanded, pointing directly at Simon.

'This is not a good idea,' he protested. Ten minutes later, he was knocking at the door of the first dwelling they came to, a large square farmhouse that faced out over the moorland towards Hadrian's Wall less than a mile away. He shifted from one foot to the other.

'Calm down,' Kay said. 'Just flash the warrant card dead fast. They'll never examine it closely.'

'We're going to lose our careers over this,' Simon muttered through clenched teeth.

'I'd rather chance that than let Shaz's killer walk.' Kay's frown changed to a radiant smile as the door opened on a small dark scowling man. It wasn't hard to imagine his Pictish ancestors making Roman lives a misery.

'Aye? What is it?'

They flipped their warrant cards open and closed in unison. The man looked momentarily confused, then resumed his glower. 'DC McNeill from Northumbria Police,' Simon gabbled. 'We've had a report of intruders at Mr Vance's place down the road. We can't obtain entry to the property, and we wondered whether you knew if there was a local keyholder?'

'Did the local man not tell you?' he demanded in an accent Kay found almost incomprehensible.

'Why no,' Simon said, laying on the Newcastle accent. 'We cannot get hold of him, with it being Sunday, like.'

'You want Doreen Elliott. Back down the road past Vance's place, gan down the first turning on the left and her cottage is down the dip. She keeps an eye on the place for him.' The door began to close.

'Thanks,' Simon said weakly.

'Aye,' the man said, shutting the door firmly in their faces.

454

Half an hour later, they had the keys to Jacko Vance's pied-à-terre in their possession. Unfortunately for them, they also had Mrs Doreen Elliott in the passenger seat of Kay's car, determined to make sure Jacko's precious property didn't come to harm in the clumsy hands of the police. Kay could only hope for the older woman's sake that they didn't find what she feared behind Jacko Vance's heavy wooden front door.

The gate had been released at the mention of his name and Tony walked up the drive, with each step becoming more immersed in the persona he had chosen for the encounter. He wanted Vance to think he was uncertain and capable of being outwitted. He would take control by appearing to be the weaker of the two. It was a risky strategy, but one he felt confident he could handle.

Vance had opened the door wreathed in smiles, greeting him by his first name. Tony could only allow himself to be swept inside, assuming a faintly confused look. 'I'm so sorry, you've missed Micky,' Vance said. 'She's spending the weekend with some friends in the country. But I didn't want you to go off without taking the opportunity to meet you face to face,' he continued as he ushered Tony in. 'Of course, I saw you on my wife's programme the other day, but I've been noticing you at all my events lately. You should have come over and introduced yourself, we could have had a chat before now, saved you coming all the way to London.' He was the model of charm and suavity, his words flowing calm and mollifying.

'Actually, it wasn't Micky I came to see. I wanted to talk to you about Shaz Bowman,' Tony said, trying to appear stiff and awkward.

A momentary look of puzzlement. Then Vance said, 'Ah, yes, the detective who was killed so tragically.

Right. I had it in mind that it was something altogether other that you wanted to . . . Are you actually working with the police on the case, then?'

'As you'll recall from the interview I did with your wife, I was in charge of the unit Shaz was on attachment to. So, naturally, I have taken a role in the investigation,' Tony said. Hiding behind formality would make Vance feel he was uncomfortable.

Vance's eyebrows rose, his dancing blue eyes teasing as they always seemed to on TV. 'I heard your role in the investigation was on the opposite side of the fence,' he said mildly. 'That you were answering questions rather than asking.'

Vance's inside information, however gleaned, could be turned to his own advantage, Tony realized. In a way, it actually played into the strategy he'd outlined to Chris. 'You have good sources,' he said, trying to sound grudging. 'But I can assure you that although I'm working independently of the police, the evidence I have uncovered will be placed in their hands at the appropriate time.' That planted the idea he was working solo.

'And what has all of this to do with me?' Vance leaned casually against the newel post of the staircase that curved upwards.

'I have some video footage that I think you might be able to cast some light on,' Tony said, patting his jacket pocket.

For the first time since his greeting, Vance looked slightly disconcerted. His face cleared momentarily and the golden boy smile was back. 'Then I suggest you come upstairs with me. I have a room on the top floor that I use for screenings for small and select audiences.' He stepped to one side and with a graceful sweep of his real arm indicated that Tony should climb ahead of him.

Tony mounted the stairs. He told himself it didn't

matter which room they were in; Chris could still hear him, and if things turned dangerous, she'd have time enough to mount a rescue. He hoped.

He paused at the landing, but Vance silently directed him up the next flight. 'First door on the right,' he said as they emerged on the top landing, an astonishingly bright area lit by a four-sided pyramid skylight.

The room Tony entered was long and narrow. The far wall was mostly occupied by a video screen. To his left, bolted to the floor, was a tall trolley holding a video recorder and a film projector. Behind it, shelves built round an editing desk were crammed with video tapes and film canisters. A cluster of comfy-looking leather slings on wooden frames completed the furnishings.

The window was what should have made Tony's heart sink. Although it was transparent, it had clearly had some sort of coating applied to it. Had he paid the same attention to his surroundings as he did to their occupants, he'd have noticed the precaution previously in government buildings where things went on that officials didn't want to become common knowledge. The coating made the windows impervious to radio signals, preventing electronic eavesdropping. This, added to the baffles that covered the walls, ensured that the room was to all intents and purposes sealed to the outside world. He could scream all he liked. Chris Devine would no longer be able to hear him.

Chris stared at the Holland Park mansion, wondering what the hell to do. Tony and Vance's voices had been coming through loud and clear then suddenly, nothing. The last thing she'd heard had been Vance saying, 'First door on the right.' It wasn't even enough information to work out which room they were in, since she had no idea which way the staircase turned.

At first, she'd thought there was something wrong with the equipment – a loose wire, a dislodged battery. Terrible seconds raced past as Chris quickly checked what she could. But the reels of tape were still turning, although nothing was coming through on the receiver. She clutched her forehead, trying to figure out what was happening. Certainly there had been no sound of a struggle, no indication that the transmitter had been spotted. It could even be that Tony had turned it off. If, for example, he'd found himself in the kind of environment where electronic feedback might betray him. Vance had spoken of a special viewing room, the kind of place that might just house that sort of sensitive electronic gear.

She could feel herself dithering and hated herself for it. Anything could be happening to Tony. He was in a house with a killer, a man he fully expected to try to murder him.

She could, she supposed, try his mobile. They had agreed she would only use the phone as a last resort. Well, there was nothing else she could attempt in the face of radio silence. She hit the memory button that summoned his number and hit 'send'. Moments of nothing then the familiar three tones followed by the infuriatingly calm female voice intoning, 'I'm sorry. The Vodaphone you are calling has not responded. Please try later.'

'Shit, shit, shit,' Chris hissed. There was nothing else for it. She might blow Tony out of the water, but better that than cost him his life by wavering like this. Chris jumped out of her car and ran up the road towards the Vance mansion.

Oblivious to the danger he had walked into, Tony turned to face Vance. 'Smart set-up,' he said.

Vance couldn't help preening. 'The best money can buy. So, what was it you wanted me to look at?'

Tony handed him the video cassette and watched him slot it into the machine, noticing that here on his home ground Vance's handicap was almost unnoticeable. A jury might find it hard to believe that he could be as awkward as he appeared when filling Shaz Bowman's car with petrol. Tony made a mental note to suggest a restaging of the event for the court's benefit.

'Grab a seat,' Vance said.

Tony chose a chair where he could just see Vance in his peripheral vision. As the tape started to play, Vance used a remote control to dim the lights. Tony readied himself for the next stage of the confrontation. The first section showed the unenhanced sequence of the disguised Vance at the motorway filling station. Barely thirty seconds into the film, Vance made a low sound in the bottom of his throat, almost a growl. As it continued to play, the sound grew in volume and rose in pitch. Tony realized the man was laughing. 'Is that meant to be me?' he eventually squeezed out between laughter, turning his grinning face to Tony.

'It is you. You know it, I know it. And soon the rest of the world will know it,' Tony hoped he'd struck the right note, somewhere between bravado and whingeing. As long as Vance was confident he was in control, there was the chance he might make a mistake.

Vance's eyes flicked past him to the screen. In slo-mo, the enhanced video was playing. To anyone who knew who they were looking for, it was hard to resist the resemblance between the man on the video and the one with the remote control. 'Dear, oh dear,' he said sardonically. 'You think anyone's going to build a case on something as obviously doctored as that?'

'There's not just that,' Tony said mildly. 'Keep

watching. I like the footage of you arriving back in Leeds to finish the job off.'

Ignoring him, Vance hit the button that stopped the tape. He flipped it out of the player and tossed it back to Tony, all with single-handed smoothness. 'I don't move like that,' he said contemptuously. 'I'd be ashamed of myself if I'd adapted that poorly to my disability.'

'It was an unfamiliar car, a strange situation.'

'You'll have to do better than that.'

Tony threw a copy of his report at Vance. His left hand shot out in a trained reflex and caught it. He opened it at the first page and glanced at it. For a moment, the skin round his mouth and eyes tightened. Tony could sense the sheer force of will that stopped him from a more powerful reaction. 'It's all there,' Tony said. 'A selection of your victims. Photographs of you with them. Their astonishing resemblance to Jillie. The mutilation of Barbara Fenwick. It's all tied in to you.'

Vance lifted his handsome face and shook his head pityingly. 'You haven't got a hope,' he said contemptuously. 'Circumstantial trash. A load of doctored photographs. Have you any idea how many people have their photographs taken with me in a year? The only surprising thing in statistical terms is that more of them don't end up murdered. You're wasting your time, Dr Hill. Just like DC Bowman before you.'

'You can't talk your way out of this, Vance,' Tony said. 'This goes way beyond coincidence. There isn't a jury in the land will fall for that.'

'There isn't a jury in the land that won't contain half a dozen of my fans. If they're told this is a witch-hunt, they'll believe me. If I hear another word of this, I will not only set my lawyers on you but I will also go to the press and tell them about this sad little man who works for the Home Office and is obsessed with my wife. He's deluded, of course, just like all the sad little men who fall in love with an image on the TV screen. He thinks just because she had dinner with him that she'd fall into his arms if I was out of the picture. So he's trying to frame me for a bunch of non-existent serial killings. Let's see who ends up looking like a fool then, Dr Hill.' Gripping the folder under his right upper arm, Vance ripped it across.

'You killed Shaz Bowman,' Tony said. 'You've killed a lot of other girls, but you killed Shaz Bowman and you are not going to walk away from that. You can tear up my report as many times as you like, but we are going to get you.'

'I don't think so. If there was anything like evidence in this folder, there would be a team of senior police officers here. This is fantasy, Dr Hill. You need help.'

Before Tony could respond, a green light started flashing on the wall near the door. Vance strode over and picked up a handset. 'Who is it?' He listened for a moment. 'There's no need for you to come in, Detective. Dr Hill is just leaving.' He replaced the receiver and gave Tony a measured look. 'Well, Dr Hill? Are you? Or do I have to call police officers who will be rather more rational on the subject of DC Bowman than Sergeant Devine?'

Tony got to his feet. 'I'm not giving up on this,' he said.

Vance gave a shout of laughter. 'And my friends at the Home Office thought you had such a promising career. Take my advice, Dr Hill. Go on holiday. Forget about Bowman. Get a life. You've obviously been working too hard.' But his eyes were not laughing. In spite of his experience at presenting a facade for the world, even Jacko Vance could not prevent apprehension leaking out from behind his genial expression.

Tony resisted the impulse to show the jubilation he felt and began to descend the stairs with the air of a man drowned in defeat. He'd achieved almost exactly what he'd expected. It wasn't quite the same goal as he'd revealed to Chris Devine, since he hadn't been sure he could carry it off. Well satisfied, Tony plodded down the hall and through Jacko Vance's front door.

The chapel had been built for a small but passionately devout congregation. It was simple but genuinely beautiful in its proportions, Kay thought as she stood in the doorway. The conversion to living space had been done tastefully, retaining the sense of airiness. Vance had chosen furnishings with simple, uncluttered lines, the only ornamentation a series of bright gabbeh rugs scattered over the stone flags of the floor. The single room had a galley kitchen, a small dining area and a sitting space with a couple of sofas angled round a big low slate table. At the far end, a raised sleeping gallery had been built. Underneath was what looked like a workbench fitted out with tools. Kay felt the clench of excitement in her stomach as she watched Simon and Leon range through the room, ostensibly looking for signs of the fictitious intruder.

By her side, Doreen Elliott stood foursquare and firm, a squat blunt obelisk of a woman in her fifties with a face as impassive as the massive stones of Hadrian's Wall itself. 'Who did you say reported the intruder?' she demanded, jealously guarding her rights as custodian of Jacko Vance's privacy.

'I don't know exactly,' Kay said. 'I think the call came from a car phone. Someone driving past saw a flickering light inside, like a torch.'

'Must be a quiet night for three of you to come out on something like this.' Her acerbic tone indicated that the local police generally failed to meet her exacting standards.

'We were in the area,' Kay said. 'It was easier to divert us than to send out other officers. Besides,' she added with a confiding smile, 'when it's someone like Jacko Vance involved, well, I suppose we try a bit harder.'

'Hmmph. What do they think they're looking for, that pair?'

Kay looked down the room where Simon seemed to be scanning the floor, lifting the corners of rugs with his toe and peering underneath. Leon was methodically opening kitchen cupboards and drawers, looking, she knew, for any indication that Donna Doyle might have been here.

'Just checking nothing obvious is missing, and there's nowhere for anyone to hide,' she said. Simon had given up on the rugs and moved on to the workbench. She saw his back stiffen as he got closer. His steps changed almost to a prowl and he angled his head all the better to study whatever had caught his attention. He turned to face them, and Kay saw the brightness of discovery in his eyes.

'Looks like Mr Vance is quite into woodwork,' Simon said, gesturing with his head to Leon.

'He makes wooden toys for the bairns in the hospital,' Mrs Elliott said, as proudly as if he were her own son. 'He cannot do enough for them. Never mind the George Cross, they should give him a medal for the hours he puts in with people at death's door. You cannot measure the comfort he gives folk.'

Leon had joined Simon at the workbench. 'Some serious kit here,' he said. 'Man, these chisels are sharp as razors.' His face was sombre and grim. 'And you want to see this vice, Kay. I've never seen anything like it.'

'He needs that to hold the wood,' Mrs Elliott said

firmly. 'With his arm the way it is, he cannot manage without it. He calls it his extra pair of hands.'

Tony trudged down Vance's drive, head down, the sound of the slamming door still ringing in his ears. He raised his eyes and caught Chris's anxious look. Giving her a broad wink, he maintained his dejected body language until he was through the electronic gates and back on the street, hidden from the house by the high hedge.

'What the fuck happened in there?' Chris demanded.

'What do you mean? I was just getting into my stride when you butted in,' Tony protested.

'You went off the air. I didn't know what the hell was going on.'

'What do you mean, I went off the air?'

'It just went dead. He said, "First on the right," then total silence. For all I knew, he'd topped you.'

Tony frowned, trying to work out what had happened. 'He must have that room electronically shielded,' he eventually said. 'Of course. The last thing he'd want is anyone doing any snooping round him that he didn't know about. It never crossed my mind.'

Chris cupped her hands against the wind and lit a cigarette. 'Jesus,' she exploded softly in a long stream of smoke. 'Don't ever give me a fright like that again. So what happened? Did he cough? Don't tell me he coughed and we didn't get it on tape?'

Tony shook his head, walking her across the street to where he'd parked his car in full view of Vance's house. He glanced back and was pleased to see his target standing at a window on the top floor looking down at them. 'Get in my car for now, I'll explain,' he said.

He started the engine and drove round the corner. 'He poured scorn on the evidence,' Tony said as he turned into another street, doubling back to get behind where Chris was parked a couple of hundred yards from Vance's gate, out of the line of sight from the house. 'He made it plain that he thought we had nothing on him and that if we didn't call off the dogs he'd come after me.'

'He threatened to kill you?'

'No, he threatened to go to the papers and make an idiot of me.'

'You sound pretty pleased with yourself for somebody that just blew their big showdown,' Chris said. 'I thought he was supposed to either roll over and spill his guts or else try to top you?'

Tony shrugged. 'I didn't really expect him to confess. And if he was going to kill me, I don't think he'd have done it on the spot. He might have convinced Wharton and McCormick that there was nothing sinister about Shaz visiting him before she died, but I think even they would have to pay attention if I was killed after I'd just been to Vance's house. No, what I wanted to do was unsettle him to the point where he starts to worry how well he's covered his tracks.'

'And what good does that do?' She wound the window down an inch to flick her ash clear.

'With a bit of luck, it sets him off like a clockwork mouse, straight for his killing ground. He needs to make sure there's nothing that can incriminate him in the unlikely event that I could ever persuade the police to apply for a search warrant.'

'You think he'll go now?'

'I'm banking on it. According to his schedule, he's got nothing on tomorrow until a meeting at three. After that, the week starts looking horrendous. He's got to go for it now.'

Chris groaned. 'Not the M1 *again*.'

'You up for it?'

465

'I'm up for it,' she said wearily. 'What's the plan?'

'I go now. He's seen me drive off with you, so he should think the coast's clear. I'll head on up to Northumberland and you try to stay with him when he emerges. We can keep in touch by phone.'

'At least it's dark,' she said. 'Hopefully he won't notice the same headlights in his rear-view mirror.' She opened the door and got out, leaning back in to speak. 'I can't believe I'm doing this. All the bloody way down from Northumberland to London just to turn round and go back there again. We must be demented.'

'No. Just determined.'

He was that, all right, Chris thought as she walked to her car and watched Tony do a three-point turn and return the way he'd come. God, she thought. It was already seven. Five, six hours back to Northumberland. She hoped there wasn't going to be too much action at the other end of the trip because she would be dead on her feet.

She tuned the radio to a golden oldies station and settled down to sing along with the sixties. She didn't have long to harmonize before the gates of Vance's house slid back and the long silver nose of his Mercedes appeared. 'You fucking beauty,' she said, turning on her ignition and rolling forward to keep him in her sights. Holland Park Avenue, then up to join the A40. As they headed out through Acton and Ealing, Chris felt a vague sense of uneasiness. This wasn't just the pretty way to Northumberland. It was perverse. She couldn't believe he was going to drive all the way out west to the orbital M25 just to circle round to the northbound M1.

She stayed close enough not to lose him at the lights, always managing to keep a single car between them. It was hard driving, but at least the streetlights helped. Eventually, the signs for the M25 appeared and Chris prepared to take the slip road even though Vance showed no signs of leaving the carriageway. Probably do a last-minute lane change, she thought, if he thinks he might have a tail.

But he didn't move and it was she who had to do the last-minute rescue, stamping on the accelerator to keep in touch with his tail lights. She only made it because he was driving a scant handful of miles above the limit, like a man who absolutely doesn't want to be stopped for speeding. She grabbed her phone and hit the recall button for Tony's number.

'Tony? It's Chris. Listen, I'm on the M40 heading west tight on Jack the Lad's tail. Wherever he's going, it's not Northumberland.'

The discovery of the vice injected a new urgency into the search. Acutely aware of how bizarre this must seem to Doreen Elliott, Kay desperately tried to distract her with conversation. 'They made a lovely job of converting this place,' she said brightly.

It was clearly the right thing. Mrs Elliott turned to the kitchen and ran a hand along the polished smoothness of the solid wood. 'Our Derek did the kitchen. He wanted no expense spared, like. Everything you could possibly want, all the latest stuff.' She pointed to the cupboard fronts. 'Washer-dryer, dishwasher, fridge, freezer, all tucked away.'

'I'd have thought he'd have brought his wife up with him more often,' Kay tried.

It was clearly the wrong thing. Mrs Elliott frowned. 'Well, he told us they'd be using it as a weekend place. But in the end, she never came. He said she was too much of a city girl. She doesn't like the country, you see. Well, you only have to look at her on that TV programme to see she'd not fit in with the likes of us. Not like Mr Vance.'

'What, she's never been here at all?' Kay tried to sound as if this was news to her. She had half her attention on Simon and Leon, but she was still keeping watch on Mrs Elliott's reactions. 'We're just trying to work out who else might have a key. For security reasons,' she added hastily as the older woman's face grew more slab-like.

'Never seen hide nor hair of her.' Then a smirk. 'That's not to say there's never been a woman's hand on the place. Well, a man's entitled to his compensations if his wife cannot bring herself to share his interests.'

'You've seen him here with other women, then?' Kay asked, aiming for casual.

'Not actually seen him, no, but I come in once a fortnight to give the place a clean, and there's been a couple of times I've unloaded the dishwasher and there's been glasses with lipstick traces. It doesn't always come off in the machine, you see. So putting two and two together, I suppose he's got a girlfriend. But he knows he can rely on us to keep our mouths shut.'

Only because no one's ever asked you, Kay thought cynically. 'As you say, if his wife won't come to a place like this . . .'

'It's a palace,' Mrs Elliott said, doubtless comparing it to the dark kitchen of her own cottage. 'I tell you something: I bet it's the only house in Northumberland with its own private nuclear shelter.'

The words fell into the conversation like a bomb.

'A nuclear shelter?' Kay asked faintly. Simon and Leon froze where they stood like gun dogs on point.

She mistook the stillness of their surprise for doubt. 'Right under our feet,' Mrs Elliott said. 'I'm not making this up, pet.'

*

Chris had barely finished the call to Tony when she saw the tail lights ahead of her wink to indicate that Vance was about to take the next slip road. Chris followed, leaving her move to the last possible moment. They turned north then, a couple of miles from the motorway, Vance signalled a left turn. At the junction, Chris slowed down and saw something that made her swear like a football supporter.

She switched off her main lights and drove cautiously down the narrow lane on sidelights only. She rounded a bend and there on her left was Jacko Vance's destination.

The private airfield was floodlit. Parked on a strip of Tarmac, Chris saw a dozen small planes standing in front of four hangars. She watched Vance's headlamps cut twin cones through the darkness round the perimeter then be swallowed up in the greater brightness as he drew up behind one of the planes. A man jumped out of the cockpit and waved. Vance got out of his car and walked to the plane, greeting the pilot with a clap on the shoulder.

'Oh, fuck,' Chris said. For the second time in the space of an hour, she had no idea what to do. Vance could have chartered the plane to get him to Northumberland ahead of any possible pursuit. Or he could have chartered it to get him out of the country. A quick flight across the Channel into the open borders of Europe and he could be anywhere by morning. Should she opt for dramatic intervention or leave him to take off?

It was a gamble, and one she didn't want to take responsibility for. Her eyes scanned the airfield, settling on the small control tower that jutted out beyond the furthest hangar. Then she saw Vance and the pilot disappear aboard. Seconds later, the propellers stuttered into life. 'Fuck it,' Chris said and put the car in gear. She raced round the airport perimeter fence and reached the control tower just as the small plane taxied out on to the runway.

She raced inside, startling the man who sat at a plotting desk beside a computer. Chris thrust her warrant card in his face. 'That plane on the runway. Has it filed a flight plan?'

'Yeah, yeah, he has,' the man stammered. 'He's going to Newcastle. Is there some sort of a problem? I mean, I can tell him to abort his take-off if there's a problem. We're always keen to help the police . . .'

'No problem,' Chris said grimly. 'Just forget you ever saw me, OK? No little radio messages saying anybody was interested, OK?'

'No, I mean yes, whatever you say, officer. No messages.'

'And just to make sure,' Chris said, pulling up a chair and giving him the predatory smile that sucked confessions from hard men, 'I'm staying right here.' She pulled out her phone and called Tony. 'Sergeant Devine,' she said. 'Subject is aboard private plane, destination Newcastle. You're going to have to deal with it from here on in. Suggest you organize a reception committee with the troops on the ground at his ultimate destination. OK?'

A bemused Tony stared at the shifting lights ahead of him on the motorway and said, 'Oh, shit, a plane? I take it you can't speak freely?'

'Correct. I'm staying here to make sure subject isn't given a warning by the control tower.'

'Ask him how long it'll take to Newcastle.'

There was a muffled conversation, then Chris came back on the line. 'He says they're flying an Aztec, which should do it in about two and a half to three hours. No chance you can beat the clock.'

'I'll do what I can. And Chris – thanks.' He ended the call and carried on driving on automatic pilot. So, somewhere between two and a half and three hours? Then he'd have to find his way to Five Walls Halt, either by taxi or by hiring a car, which wouldn't be easy at ten o'clock on a Sunday night. Even so, Tony realized Chris was right. There was no way he could possibly arrive at Vance's bolt hole ahead of him.

'Which is why he did it, of course,' he said aloud. Vance was no fool. He would expect Tony to know about his other home and to make for there once he'd stirred things up. What Vance hadn't known was that Tony already had three police profilers in Northumberland. At least, he presumed they were still making inquiries up there, since he'd heard nothing to the contrary. Come to that, he'd heard nothing since mid-afternoon, when he'd checked in with Simon to discover that they were going door-to-door in a bid to trace any sightings of Donna Doyle.

It wasn't enough, though. Three junior CID officers, none from the local force, none with any experience of command. They'd be uncertain, not knowing when or whether to challenge Vance. They wouldn't know when to hang back and when to move. It needed more than any of them had to give. There was only one person who could get there in time and keep Leon, Simon and Kay in check.

She answered on the second ring. 'DCI Jordan.'

'Carol? It's me. How are you doing?'

'Not good. To be honest, I'm grateful for the human contact. I've been feeling like a leper. I'm an outcast from the infantry because they think I'm partly responsible for Di Earnshaw's death. I'm isolated from John Brandon because there will have to be an inquiry which he can't be seen to influence. And I'm out of the loop when it comes to questioning Alan Brinkley in case I compromise the interrogation for personal reasons. And I have to tell you that breaking the news to her parents left me feeling that the Ancient Greeks' method of dealing with bad news must sometimes have been a relief to the messenger.'

'I'm sorry. You must wish now I hadn't dragged you into this Vance business,' he said.

'I don't,' she said firmly. 'Somebody's got to put a stop to Vance, and nobody else would listen to you. I don't blame you for what went wrong in Seaford. That's my responsibility. I shouldn't have tried to do surveillance on a shoestring. I knew you were right and I should have carried that conviction through and demanded the bodies to do the job properly instead of settling for a skeleton crew. If I had, Di Earnshaw would still be alive.'

'You can't know that for sure,' Tony protested. 'Anything could have happened. Her partner could have gone for a piss at the crucial moment, they could have separated to circle the building. If anyone's to blame, it's the sergeant. Not only were they supposed to look out for each other, he was her immediate boss. He owed her a duty of care and he failed her.'

'And what about my duty of care?'

Tony shook his head. 'Oh, Carol, ease up on yourself.'

'I can't. But enough of that. Where are you? And what's happening with Vance?'

'I'm on the M1. It's been a complicated day.' As he hammered on in the outside lane oblivious to anything but the traffic and the woman on the end of the phone, he brought Carol up to speed.

'So now he's somewhere between London and Newcastle?' Carol asked.

'That's right.'

'You're not going to make it in time, are you?'

'No.'

'But I could?'

'Possibly. Probably, if you stuck the blue light on. I can't ask you to, but I . . .'

'There's nothing for me to do here. I'm off duty, and nobody's going to call out the CID leper tonight. I'm better off doing this than sitting here feeling sorry for myself. Get me some directions. I'll call you when I get near Newcastle.' Her voice was stronger and firmer than it had been at the start of the call. Even if he'd wanted to argue, he realized it would have been pointless. She was the woman he'd taken her for, and she wouldn't walk away from a challenge.

'Thanks,' he said simply.

'We're wasting time talking.' Abruptly, the line went dead.

The price of Tony's skill was the empathy he brought to situations like this. He understood precisely what Carol was going through. Very few people ever experienced a justified sense of responsibility for the death of another human being. Everything Carol had been certain of had suddenly shifted on to shaky ground and no one who had not shared a similar experience could help her back to terra firma. But he understood and he cared enough to try. He suspected that his phone call had, serendipitously, been the first step in the right direction. Hoping he was correct, Tony stared into the narrowing tunnel of red lights and carried on driving north.

On the exact location of the entrance to the basement shelter, Mrs Elliott was rather more vague. 'It's under the flags somewhere. He had a couple of lads from

Newcastle over to install it so that you cannot see it just by looking.'

The three police officers glared in frustration at the metre-square stone slabs that made up the floor. Then Simon said, 'If you can't see it, how do you get down there?'

'Our Derek said they'd installed an electric motor,' Mrs Elliott said.

'Well, if there's a motor, there's gotta be a switch,' Leon muttered. 'Si, you start on the right-hand side of the door. Kay, you start on the left. I'll go up to the sleeping gallery.' The two men moved away and started flicking switches, but Kay was held back by Mrs Elliott's hand on her sleeve.

'What do you need to find the shelter for?' she asked. 'I thought you said there was supposed to be a prowler? They're not going to be down there.'

Kay dug out her most reassuring smile. 'When we're dealing with a celebrity like Mr Vance, we have to be especially careful. A prowler in his house could be a lot more serious than a straightforward burglar. If someone was stalking him, for example, they could be hiding in waiting for him. So we have to take this extremely seriously.' She covered the woman's hand with her own. 'Why don't we wait outside?'

'What for?'

'If there is someone down there, it could be very dangerous.' Kay's smile felt strained. If Donna Doyle was trapped in the cellar, discovering her would be a revelation that would give even the stolid Doreen Elliott nightmares for the rest of her life, Kay knew. 'It's our job to protect members of the public, you know. How do you think my boss would react if I let you be taken hostage by some nutter with a knife?'

Mrs Elliott let herself be led into the tiny porch with

only a single backward glance at Simon and Leon moving round the room snapping switches on and off. 'You think it's a stalker, then?' she asked avidly. 'Up here?'

'It wouldn't necessarily be someone from around here,' Kay said. 'These people are obsessive. They'll follow a celebrity for weeks, months, learning every detail of their life and routine. Have you seen any strangers hanging around?'

'Well, we get the tourists and the hikers, but mostly they're only here for the wall. They don't hang about.'

Before Kay could say more, her phone rang. 'Will you excuse me? I'll only be a minute,' she said, slipping back inside to take the call. 'Hello?'

'Kay? It's Tony. Where are you?'

Oh, shit, she thought. Why me? Why couldn't he have phoned Leon? 'Er . . . we're inside Jacko Vance's house in Northumberland,' she said. Simon glanced across at her, but she waved to him to continue his search.

'What?' Tony exclaimed, outraged.

'I know you said to wait, but we kept thinking about Donna Doyle . . .'

'You broke in?'

'No. We're perfectly entitled to be here. A local woman has a key. We informed her there had been reports of a prowler and she let us in.'

'Well, you'd better get out asap.'

'Tony, she could be here. This place has got a sealed basement. Vance told the builders he wanted a nuclear shelter.'

'A nuclear shelter?' His incredulity was palpable.

'It was a dozen years ago. People still believed Russia was going to nuke us,' Kay reminded him plaintively. 'The point is, she could be down there and we wouldn't hear her, not even standing right above her. We've got to find the door.'

'No. You've got to leave it. He's on his way there. He's chartered a plane, Kay. He's probably coming up there to make sure he's not left any loose ends. Kay, we need to catch him in the act. We need to stake the place out and watch him go down there to an untouched crime scene.'

As he spoke, Kay looked on in amazement as the ground moved only feet away from her. Silently, a single slab tilted and swung open in response to a switch flicked by Simon. As the fetid air escaped, Kay gagged. Recovering herself, she said, 'It's too late for that. We've found the door.'

Simon was already at the opening in the floor, peering down a set of stone steps. His groping hands found a switch and flooded the area with light. A long moment passed then he turned to Kay, his face the colour of putty. 'If that's Tony, you better tell him we've found Donna Doyle, as well.'

He drummed his fingers gently against the arm rest, the only movement in a body still as a lion preparing for the pounce. He didn't even brace himself against the jolts of the pockets of turbulence the small twin-engined plane hit occasionally, but let his body shift with the movement. Once upon a time, he used to bite the nails of his right hand when he was nervous. Losing his arm had been an extreme cure for a bad habit, he was fond of saying wryly in public. Now, he had cultivated stillness, understanding that nervous tics made nothing happen faster or easier. Besides, stillness was much more unsettling for everyone else.

The engine note changed as the pilot prepared to land. Jacko peered out of the window, staring down at the smudge of suburban streetlights through the fine rain. He'd left Tony Hill standing. There was no way he could have beaten the aircraft. And he had no back-up, Jacko knew from his own discreet inquiries, confirmed by what both Micky and Tony himself had admitted.

The wheels hit the runway and jolted him against his seatbelt. A slight swerve, a correction, then they were heading for the flying club hangars at a gentle taxi. They had barely come to a standstill when Jacko had the door open. He jumped to the Tarmac and looked around, his eyes searching for the familiar shape of his Land Rover. Sam Foxwell and his brother were always glad to earn the twenty quid he paid them whenever he needed the Land Rover brought to the airport and when he'd spoken to them from the car phone, they'd promised to have it there for him.

When he couldn't spot it, he felt a shiver of panic. They couldn't have let him down, not tonight of all nights. The pilot interrupted his thoughts, pointing to the side of the hangar in deep shadow. 'If you're looking for your Land Rover, I think it's tucked round there. I noticed it when I was taxi-ing.'

'Cheers.' Jacko dug into his pocket and took a twenty-pound note from his money clip. 'Have a beer on me. See you soon, Keith.'

As he thundered along the narrow Northumberland side roads that were the quickest route to the place he considered his real home, he reviewed what he had to do in the couple of hours' grace he had before Tony Hill could possibly arrive. First, check if the bitch was still alive and if she was, see she didn't stay that way. Then, take the chain saw to her, get her bagged and into the Land Rover. Clean the basement with the high-pressure hose and set off for the hospital. Would he have time? Or should he simply disable the motor that opened the door on its swivel? After all, Hill had no way of knowing about the basement shelter and the local police were not going to mount a search on his say-so, not when it would offend an upstanding local taxpayer like Jacko Vance. And there was no guarantee that Tony Hill would even show up.

Maybe he should just settle for making sure she was dead and leave the clearing up for later. There would be a certain delight in entertaining Tony Hill only feet away from his latest victim. His mouth twisted in an ugly snarl. Donna Doyle would have to be his last victim for a while. Damn the man. Tony Hill should have let sleeping bitches lie. Jacko had plans for Tony Hill, though. One day, when it had all gone quiet and Tony Hill had resigned himself to the fact that he'd failed, that plan would go into action and he'd wish he'd never stuck his nose into someone else's business.

The headlights sliced through the deep darkness of the countryside, breasting the hill that rolled down to his sanctuary. Where there should have been nothing but blackness, light spilled out over the cropped moorland grass and the grey gravel of his drive. Jacko stamped on the brakes and the Land Rover screamed to a jittering halt. What the fuck?

As he sat there, mind racing, adrenaline pumping, a pair of headlights on full beam crept up behind him, angling across the narrow road so there was no possibility of going backwards. Slowly, Vance took his foot off the brake and let the Land Rover cruise down the hill towards his home. The lights shifted and fell into convoy behind him. As he grew closer, he saw a second car parked diagonally just beyond his gateway, effectively blocking the road beyond.

Vance drove on to his property, the cold grip of fear in his stomach focusing his mind. When he rolled to a halt he jumped out of his vehicle, every inch the outraged householder, and confronted the young black man standing in his doorway. 'What the hell's going on?' he demanded.

'I'm afraid I'm going to have to ask you to wait outside, sir,' Leon said deferentially.

'What do you mean? This is my house. Has there been a burglary or what? What's going on? And who the hell are you?'

'I'm Detective Constable Leon Jackson of the Metropolitan Police.' He held out his warrant card for inspection.

Vance switched the charm on. 'You're a long way from home.'

'Pursuing an investigation, sir. It's amazing where a line of inquiry can take us in these days of electronic communications and efficient travel networks.' Leon's voice was impassive, but his eyes never left Vance.

'Look, you know who I am, obviously. You know this is my place. Can't you at least tell me what the hell is going on?'

A horn beeped and Vance turned to see the car that had followed him down the hill stop just outside the gate, blocking the road in the opposite direction. He was hemmed in completely. Jesus, he hoped the bitch was dead. Another young man got out of the car and walked across the gravel. 'Are you from the Metropolitan Police as well?' Vance asked, forcing himself to maintain his professionally beguiling mode.

'No,' Simon said. 'I'm from Strathclyde.'

'*Strathclyde?*' Vance was momentarily confused. He'd taken someone from London few years ago, but he'd never brought anyone down from Scotland. He hated the accent. It reminded him of Jimmy Linden and all that meant to him. So if there was a cop here from

Scotland, they couldn't be tracking the girls. It was going to be fine, he told himself. He could walk away from this.

'That's right, sir. DC Jackson and myself have been working on different aspects of the same case. We were in the area and we had a report from a passing motorist of a prowler here. So we thought we'd better check it out.'

'That's very commendable, officers. Perhaps I could go inside and check to see if anything's missing or broken?' He moved to edge around Leon, but the policeman was too fast for him. He extended his arm, blocking Vance, and shook his head.

'I'm afraid not, sir. It's a crime scene, you see. We need to make sure nothing interferes with it.'

'A crime scene? What on earth has happened?' Concerned, try to sound concerned, he warned himself. This is your house, you're an innocent man and you want to know what's happened on your property.

'I'm afraid there's been a suspicious death,' Simon said coldly.

Jacko made himself take what looked like an involuntary step backwards, covering his face with his hands to make sure no sign of the relief that flooded him was visible to the police. She was dead, hallelujah. A dead woman could never testify. He pasted an expression of worried anxiety on his face and looked up. 'But that's terrible. A death? Here? But who ... How? This is my home. Nobody comes here except me. How can there be someone dead here?'

'That's what we're trying to establish, sir,' Leon said.

'But who is it? A burglar? What?'

'We don't think it was a burglar,' Simon said, trying to keep the lid on the rage he felt face to face with the man who had killed Shaz and who was trying to pretend

480

he had nothing to do with the putrefying mess in his cellar.

'But . . . the only person who has keys is Mrs Elliott. Doreen Elliott at Dene Cottage. It's not . . . It's not her?'

'No, sir. Mrs Elliott is in excellent health. It was Mrs Elliott who let us in to the property and gave us permission to search. One of our colleagues has taken her home.' There was something in the way the black cop held his stare when he said this that sent a tremor of fear skittering round Vance's nerves. The message coming through loud and clear between the spoken words was the unspoken warning that his first line of defence had crumbled. This was not an illegal entry and search.

'Thank God for that. So who is it?'

'We can't speculate at this point, sir.'

'But you must be able to tell me if it's a man or a woman, surely?'

Simon's lip curled. He could hold back no longer. 'As if you didn't know,' he said, his voice thick with angry contempt. 'You think our heads button up the back?' He turned away, his hands balling into fists.

'What is he talking about?' Vance demanded, moving into the angry mode of the innocent bystander who senses they're about to become snagged up in someone else's trouble.

Leon shrugged and lit a cigarette. 'You tell me,' he said negligently. 'Oh good,' he said, looking over Vance's shoulder. 'Looks like the cavalry.'

The woman emerging from the car that had drawn up behind Simon's didn't look much like the cavalry to Vance. She couldn't have been more than thirty. Even shrugged into an oversized mac, she was clearly slim and pretty, with short blonde hair cut thick and shaggy. 'Good evening, gentlemen,' she said briskly. 'Mr Vance, I'm Detective Chief Inspector Carol Jordan. Would you excuse me for a moment, while I confer with one of my colleagues. Leon, can you keep Mr Vance company for a minute? I want to take a look inside. Simon, a word, please?'

Before he had the chance to say anything, she'd swept Simon inside, managing to open the door so narrowly that Vance had no chance to see within. 'I don't understand what's going on,' Vance said. 'Shouldn't there be scene-of-crimes people here? And uniformed officers?'

Again, Leon shrugged. 'It's not very like the telly, life.' He continued smoking down to the tip then threw his cigarette on the porch step and ground it out.

'Do you mind?' Vance said, pointing. 'This is my house. My doorstep. Just because somebody got themselves killed inside doesn't mean the police can vandalize the place, too.'

Leon raised an eyebrow. 'Frankly, sir, I think that's the least of your worries right now.'

'This is outrageous,' Vance said.

'Me, I find suspicious death enough outrage for one night.'

The door inched open and Simon and Carol reemerged. The woman looked sombre, the man faintly sick, Vance thought. Good. She didn't deserve to die pretty, the bitch. 'Chief Inspector, when is someone going to tell me what is going on here?'

He'd been so busy watching her, he hadn't noticed the two men had moved to either side of him in a flanking movement. Carol locked eyes with him, her cold blue stare a match for his. 'Jacko Vance, I am arresting you on suspicion of murder. You do not need to say anything, but I must warn you that it may harm your defence if you do not mention when questioned something which you later rely upon in court. Anything you do say may be given in evidence.'

Disbelief blazed across his face as Simon and Leon closed in on him. Before it had really sunk in that not only was this woman arresting him but these idiots were laying hands on him, a cuff of steel clamped hard over his left wrist. He recovered himself as they tried to man-handle him back towards the Land Rover, convulsing beneath their hands in a desperate attempt to free him-self by sheer superiority of strength. But he was off balance, and his feet went from under him on the gravel.

'Don't let him fall,' Carol yelled, and somehow, Leon managed to get under Vance as he hit the ground. Simon hung on grimly to the other end of the handcuffs, yank-ing Vance's arm back, making him squeal.

'Make my day, shithead,' Simon shouted. 'Give me a reason to give you a taste of what you gave Shaz.' He hauled upwards on Vance's arm, forcing him to struggle to his feet.

Leon scrambled back upright and pushed Vance in the chest. 'You know what would really make me happy? You trying to leg it, that would make me fucking delirious, because then I'd have an excuse for kicking seven colours of shit out of your scumbag body.' He pushed him in the chest again. 'Go on, go for it. Go on, do one.'

Vance stumbled back, as much to escape the venom in Leon's voice as to ease the pain on his arm. He hit the Land Rover with a thud. Simon yanked his arm down and fastened the other end of the handcuffs to the bull bar. He took a deep breath then spat in Vance's face. When he turned to face Carol, there were tears in his eyes. 'He'll not be going anywhere in a hurry,' he croaked.

'You are going to regret this night,' Vance said, his voice low and dangerous.

Carol stepped forward and put a hand on Simon's

arm. 'You did well, Simon. Now, unless anybody's got any better ideas, I think it's about time we called the police.'

There was something generic about police stations, Tony thought. The canteens never served salad, the waiting areas always smelled of stale cigarettes in spite of smoking having been banned for years, and the decor never varied. Looking round the interview room in Hexham police station at three in the morning, he realized he could be anywhere from Penzance to Perth. On that gloomy thought, the door opened and Carol came in with two mugs of coffee. 'Strong, black and brewed some time in the last week,' she said, dropping into the chair opposite him.

'What's happening?'

She snorted. 'He's still screaming about wrongful arrest and false imprisonment. I've just given a statement of explanation.'

He stirred his coffee and took in the signs of strain round her eyes. 'Which was?'

'In the area on inquiries, the lads got a report of a possible prowler. They thought it would be quicker to check it out themselves – being into inter-force co-operation – so they found a keyholder who was happy to let them in and gave permission to search,' Carol recited, leaning back and staring sightlessly at the ceiling. 'Concerned about the possibility of a hidden stalker, they opened the basement where they found the dead body of a young white female who answered the description of Donna Doyle, whom they knew to be on the missing list. Since Mr Vance is the only person known to frequent the house, it was clear he must be a suspect in what was obviously a suspicious death. I considered he was a fugitive risk. He was at the scene with a vehicle capable of leaving the road and avoiding pursuit.

'Although my authority does not extend into the force area of Northumbria Police, I am empowered to effect a citizen's arrest. Placing Mr Vance in restraints which caused him minimal discomfort seemed a better alternative than leaving him at large where any movement towards his vehicle might have led to an over-reaction on the part of the officers I was working with. Cuffing him to the Land Rover was, in effect, for his own protection.'

By the time she ended her recital, they were both grinning. 'Anyway, the local lads did me the favour of re-arresting him when they got there.'

'What about charging him?'

Carol looked depressed. 'They're waiting for Vance's brief to arrive. But they're running very scared. They've seen your dossier and they've interviewed Kay and Simon and Leon, but they're still wary. It's not over, Tony. Not by a long way. The fat lady hasn't even arrived yet.'

'I just wish that they hadn't opened that cellar. That they'd staked the place out and witnessed him opening it and going down there with Donna's body.'

Carol sighed. 'She hadn't been dead long, did you know?'

'No.'

'The police surgeon thought less than twenty-four hours.' They sat in silence, each wondering what they could have done better or faster, whether more or less orthodoxy could have won them a faster response. Carol broke the uneasy stillness. 'If we can't put Vance away, I don't think I want to be a copper any more.'

'You feel like that because of what happened to Di Earnshaw,' Tony said, laying his hand on her arm.

'I feel like that because Vance is a lethal weapon and

if we can't neutralize the likes of him, we're nothing more than glorified traffic wardens,' she said bitterly.

'And if we can?'

She shrugged. 'Then maybe we redeem ourselves for the ones we lose.'

They sat in silence, sipping coffee. Then Tony ran a hand through his hair and said, 'Have they got a good pathologist?'

'I've no idea. Why?'

Before he could answer, the door opened on the worried face of Phil Marshall, the superintendent in charge of the division. 'Dr Hill? Could I have a word?'

'Come in, it's a shop,' Carol muttered.

Marshall closed the door behind him. 'Vance wants to talk to you. Alone. He's happy for the conversation to be taped, but he wants it to be just you and him.'

'What about his brief?' Carol asked.

'He says he just wants Dr Hill and himself. What do you say, Doc? Will you talk to him?'

'We've got nothing to lose, have we?'

Marshall winced. 'From where I'm standing, we've got quite a lot to lose, actually. Frankly, I want evidence to charge Vance with or else I want him out of here within the day. I'm going to no magistrate to ask if I can keep Jacko Vance under lock and key on the basis of what you've given me so far.'

Tony took out his notebook and tore out a sheet of paper, scribbling down a name and number. He handed it to Carol. 'This is who we need to get up here. Can you explain to them while I'm in with Jack the Lad?'

Carol read what he'd written and comprehension lit up her tired eyes. 'Of course.' She reached out and squeezed his hand. 'Good luck.'

Tony nodded, then followed Marshall down the corridor. 'We'll be taping it, of course,' Marshall said. 'We've got to be squeaky clean on this one. He's already talking about suing DCI Jordan.' He stopped outside an interview room and opened the door. He nodded to the uniformed officer in the corner and the man left.

Tony stepped into the room and stared at his adversary. He couldn't believe that there was still no dent in that arrogant exterior, no crack in the charming facade. 'Dr Hill,' Vance said, not a tremor in the professionally smooth voice. 'I wish I could say it was a pleasure, but that would be too much of a lie for anyone to swallow. A bit like your insane accusations.'

'Dr Hill has agreed to talk to you,' Marshall interrupted. 'We will be taping the conversation. I'll leave you now.'

He backed out and Vance waved Tony to a chair. The psychologist shook his head and leaned against the wall, arms folded. 'What did you want me for?' Tony asked. 'A confession?'

'If I wanted confession, I'd have asked for a priest. I wanted to see you face to face to tell you that as soon as I get out of here I will be suing you and DCI Jordan for slander.'

Tony laughed. 'Go ahead. We're neither of us worth a fraction of your annual earnings. You'll be the one who ends up shelling out a fortune in legal costs. Me, I'd relish the opportunity to get you on a witness stand under oath.'

'That's something you'll never achieve.' Vance leaned back in his chair. His eyes were cold, his smile reptilian. 'These trumped-up accusations won't stand up in the cold light of day. What have you got? This dossier of yours with its doctored photographs and circumstantial coincidences. "Here's Jacko Vance on the M1 at Leeds the night Shaz Bowman died." Well, yes, that's because my second home is in Northumberland and that's the best way to get there.' His sonorous voice dripped sarcasm.

'What about, "Here's Jacko Vance with a body in the cellar?" Or, "Here's a photo of Jacko Vance with the dead girl from his cellar when she was still living, breathing and laughing?" ' Tony asked, keeping his voice level and mild. Let Vance get worked up, let him be the one to strain at the leash of his self-control.

Vance's response was a sardonic smile. 'It was your officers who provided the answer to that,' he said. 'They were the ones who raised the possibility of a stalker. It's not so unlikely. Stalkers become obsessed with their targets. I don't find it too hard to imagine a stalker tracking me back to Northumberland. Everybody locally knows Doreen Elliott keeps a set of my keys and, like most of the people round here, she never locks her door if she's only popping next door for a cup of tea, or down to her vegetable garden to dig some potatoes. Child's play to borrow the keys and have a set made.'

As he warmed to his theme, his smile broadened and his body language grew more relaxed. 'It's also common knowledge that I had a nuclear shelter built in the chapel crypt. Slightly embarrassing in these days of détente, but I can live with that,' Vance continued, leaning forward now, his prosthesis resting on the table, his other arm hooked over the back of the chair. 'And let's not forget the very public vendetta with my ex-fiancée who, as you rightly pointed out, bears a strong resemblance to these poor missing girls. I mean, wouldn't you think you were doing me a favour by killing her image if you were obsessed with me?' His grin was positively triumphal.

'And you are, aren't you, Dr Hill? Or rather, as I will take great pleasure in explaining to the world's press, you're obsessed with my wife, I believe. Shaz Bowman's tragic death gave you the opportunity to force your way into our lives and when dear, sweet Micky agreed to have dinner with you, you formed the view that without me, she'd fall into your arms. And your sad delusion has brought us to this point.' He shook his confident head pityingly.

Tony lifted his head and stared into a pair of eyes that could have come from Mars for all the humanity they contained. 'You killed Shaz Bowman. You killed Donna Doyle.'

'You'll never prove that. Since it's a complete fabrication, you'll never prove it,' Vance said with an air of nonchalance. Then he raised one arm and covered first his eyes, then his mouth and finally, stroked his ear. To a casual observer, it was merely the gesture of a tired man. Tony read it instantly as the taunt it was.

He pushed off from the wall and took two long steps across the room. Leaning on his fists, he thrust his face into Vance's personal space. In spite of himself, the TV star craned his head back like a tortoise retreating into its shell. 'You may be right,' Tony said. 'It is entirely possible that we will never nail you for Shaz Bowman or Donna Doyle. But I'll tell you something, Jacko. You weren't always this good. We'll get you for Barbara Fenwick.'

'I have no idea what you're talking about,' Vance said contemptuously.

Tony stood up and slowly began to stroll around the confined space as leisurely as if it were the local park. 'Twelve years ago when you killed Barbara Fenwick there were a lot of things forensic science couldn't do. Take toolmarks, for example. Pretty crude, the comparisons they made back then. But these days, they've got scanning electron microscopes and back-scatter electron microscopes. Don't ask me how they work, but they can compare an injury to an implement and say whether the two match up. Within the next few days, they'll be matching the bones in Donna Doyle's damaged arm to the vice in your house.' He glanced at his watch. 'With a bit of luck, the pathologist will be on her way now. Professor Elizabeth Stewart. I don't know if you've heard of her, but she has a terrific reputation in forensic anthropology as well as pathology. If anyone can find the match between your vice and Donna's injuries, it's Liz Stewart. Now, I realize that doesn't implicate you if we accept the fantasy you've been spinning here.'

He turned slowly to face Vance. 'But it would if the vice matched Barbara Fenwick's bone injuries, wouldn't it? Serial killers often like to use the same weapon for all their murders. But it's hard to imagine a stalker who's followed you around on a killing spree for twelve years and never put a foot wrong, don't you think?'

This time, he saw a flicker of uncertainty in Vance's confident mask. 'What utter rubbish. Just for the sake of argument, even if you got an exhumation order, no Crown Prosecutor is going to push a case that depends on a mark on a piece of bone that's been in the ground for twelve years.'

'I couldn't agree more,' Tony said. 'But you see, the pathologist who did the postmortem on Barbara Fenwick had never seen injuries quite like that. They intrigued her. And she is a university professor. Professor Elizabeth Stewart, actually. She applied to the Home Office to retain Barbara Fenwick's arm so she could use it as a teaching aid. To illustrate the effect on bone and flesh of blunt trauma from compression. Funnily enough, she noticed that there was a slight imperfection on the bottom edge of the implement that inflicted the injuries. A tiny projection of metal that made a mark in bone as distinctive as a fingerprint.' He let the words hang in the air. Vance's eyes never left his face.

'When Professor Stewart moved to London, she left the arm behind. For the last twelve years, Barbara Fenwick's arm has been perfectly preserved in the anatomy department of Manchester University.' Tony smiled gently. 'One solid piece of irrefutable evidence tying you to a weapon used on a murder victim, and suddenly the circumstantial looks very different, don't you think?'

He walked to the door and opened it. 'And by the way – I don't fancy your wife in the slightest. *I've* never been so inadequate that I had to hide behind a lesbian.'

In the corridor, Tony signalled to the uniformed officer by the door that he should go back into the interview room. Then, exhausted by the effort of confronting Vance, he leaned against the wall, sliding down into a squat, elbows on knees and hands over his face.

He was still there ten minutes later when Carol Jordan emerged from the viewing room where she and Marshall had watched the encounter between the hunter and the killer. She crouched in front of him and took his head between her hands. He looked into her face. 'What do you think?' he said anxiously.

'You convinced Phil Marshall,' she said. 'He's spoken to Professor Stewart. She wasn't too thrilled at being woken in the middle of the night, but when Marshall explained what was what, she got really excited. There's a train gets in from London around nine. She'll be on it, with her famous slides of the injury. Marshall's organized someone to go over and collect Barbara Fenwick's arm from Manchester University first thing. If it looks like a match, they'll charge him.'

Tony closed his eyes. 'I just hope he's still using the same vice.'

'Oh, I think you'll find he is,' Carol said eagerly. 'We

were watching. You couldn't see from where you were, but when you hit him with Professor Stewart and her preserved arm, his right leg started jittering up and down. He couldn't control it. He's still got the same vice. I'd stake my life on it.'

Tony felt a smile gather the corners of his mouth. 'I think the fat lady just landed.' He put his arms round Carol and stood up, bringing her with him. He held her at arm's length and grinned down at her.

'You did a great job in there. I'm really proud to be on your team.' Her face was solemn, her eyes grave.

Tony dropped his arms and took a deep breath. 'Carol, I've been running away from you for a long time,' he said.

Carol nodded. 'I think I understand why.' She looked down, reluctant to meet his eyes now they were finally having this conversation.

'Oh?'

The muscles along her jaw tightened, then she looked up at him. 'I didn't have blood on my hands. So I could never understand what it feels like to be you. Di Earnshaw's death changed that. And the fact that neither of us could save Donna . . .'

Tony nodded bleakly. 'It's not a comfortable thing to have in common.'

Carol had often visualized a moment like this between them. She had thought she knew what she wanted to happen. Now, she was taken aback to find her responses so different from what she had imagined. She put a hand on his forearm and said, 'It's easier for friends to share than lovers, Tony.'

He gazed at her for a long moment, frowning. He thought of the bodies Jacko Vance had incinerated in the hospital where he gave his time to sit with the dying. He thought of the loss of what Shaz Bowman could have achieved. He thought of all the other deaths that still lay ahead of them both. And he thought of redemption, not through work, but through friendship. His face cleared and he smiled. 'You know, I think you could be right.'

EPILOGUE

Murder was like magic, he thought. The quickness of his hand had always deceived the eye, and that was how it was going to stay. They thought they had him trapped, sewn into a bag and wrapped with chains of guilt. They thought they were lowering him into a tank of proof that would drown him. But he was Houdini. He would burst free when they least expected it.

Jacko Vance lay on the narrow police cell bed, the real arm tucked behind his head. He stared at the ceiling, remembering how he had felt in hospital, the only other place where he'd had no choice about staying put. There had been pockets of despair and impotent anger and he knew those would probably afflict him again before he was free of this place and others like it. But when he'd been in hospital, he'd known he would be free of it all one day and he'd focused all his powerful intelligence on shaping that moment.

True, he'd had Micky's help then. He wondered if he could still rely on her. He thought that as long as he could cast credible doubt, she would stand by him. As soon as it looked like he was going under, she'd be gone. Since he had no intention of letting that happen, he thought he could probably be sure of her.

The evidence was flimsy. But he couldn't deny that Tony Hill was impressive in his command of it. He would be hard to discredit in a courtroom, even if Vance succeeded in planting advance press stories accusing the psychologist of being obsessed with Micky. And there was a risk there. Hill had somehow discovered that Micky was a lesbian. If he leaked that in response to an accusation against him, it would do serious damage both to Micky's credibility and his own image as a man who needed no other woman but his adorable wife.

No, if it came to a court battle, even with a jury of telly addicts, Vance would be at risk. He had to make certain it never went past a preliminary hearing. He had to destroy the evidence against him, to demonstrate there was no case to answer.

The greatest threat came from the pathologist and her reading of the toolmarks. If he could discredit that, there were only circumstantial details. Together, they weighed heavy, but individually, they could be undermined. The vice was too solid a piece of substantiation to submit to that.

The first step was to cast doubt on whether the arm from the university really belonged to Barbara Fenwick. In a university pathology department, it could not be held under the sort of security of a police evidence room. Anyone could have had access to it over the years. It could even have been replaced with another arm deliberately crushed in his vice by, say, a police officer determined to frame him. Or students could have swapped it in some macabre prank. Yes, a little work there could force a few cracks into the reliability of the preserved arm.

The second step was to prove the vice had not belonged to him when Barbara Fenwick had died. He lay on the hard mattress and racked his brains to find an answer. 'Phyllis,' he eventually murmured, a sly smile creeping across his face. 'Phyllis Gates.'

She'd had terminal cancer. It had started in her left breast then worked its way through her lymphatic system and finally, agonizingly, into her spine. He'd spent several nights by her bedside, sometimes talking, sometimes simply holding her hand in silence. He loved the sense of power that working with the virtual dead gave him. They'd be gone, and he would still be here, on top of the world. Phyllis Gates was long gone, but her twin brother Terry was alive and well. Presumably he was still running his market stall.

Terry sold tools. New and second-hand. Terry credited Vance with the only happiness his sister had known in the last weeks of her life. Terry would walk on hot coals for Vance. Terry would think telling a jury he'd sold the vice to Vance only a couple of years previously was the least he could do to repay the debt.

Vance sat upright, stretching out his arms like a hero accepting the adulation of the crowd. He'd worked it out. He was as good as a free man. Murder was indeed like magic. And one day soon, Tony Hill would find that out for himself. Vance could hardly wait.